HARBOR HOPES

THREE-IN-ONE COLLECTION

LYNN A. COLEMAN

BARBOUR
PUBLISHING

Cover design: Kirk DouPonce, DogEared Design

Published by Barbour Publishing, Inc., P.O. Box 719, Uhrichsville, Ohio 44683, www.barbourbooks.com

Our mission is to publish and distribute inspirational products offering exceptional value and biblical encouragement to the masses.

Member of the
Evangelical Christian
Publishers Association

Printed in the United States of America.

Dear Reader,

  Harbor Hopes is a collection of three of my novels set in the fictional town of Squabbin Bay, Maine. I developed the series after a visit to Maine for a family gathering. Paul and I traveled around some of the rustic coastal towns that are often referred to as "down east." This series had a profound effect on me while I was researching and writing these novels. I developed my love for digital photography from *Photo Op* research. And I finally was able to find the right mix in a romance regarding a person's need for salvation and still meet the requirements for a romance novel with *Suited for Love*. As I've reread these stories for this publication, all the memories of being in Maine, researching the novels, and reliving the joy of God inspiring my words came back.

  Issues of trust and faith abound today in all areas of our lives. As each of my characters deal with those issues in their lives throughout the three novels, I hope you'll see God's provision for them. When we're going through a trial in our own lives, it is hard to see God working, but we know from experience that He is. The trick is to recognize it sooner rather than later in your own life and let God help you through. My goal as an author is to write an enjoyable story that I pray will also challenge each reader to think about their own walk with God.

  I want to thank you for taking the time to read these stories, and I pray they will bless you as much as they've blessed me.

In His grip,
Lynn

PHOTO OP

Dedication

I'd like to dedicate this book to my loving husband, Paul, who is my constant encourager, lover, and friend. Thank you for all the hard work you put in on my behalf to help each project be the best it can be.

Chapter 1

Dena glanced into the rearview mirror and touched up her lipstick. Grabbing her fully loaded cameras and backpack from the passenger seat, she ran into the church.

"Hey, Mom, didn't think you were going to make it." Jason wiped his hands on a semi-white apron. "Get in late last night?" He kissed her cheek.

Dena returned the affection and stepped back. "Yeah, I was busy developing some pictures and lost track of time." She glanced at her wristwatch. "I'm not that late."

"No problem. Your booth is outside. The teens set up a few lobster pots and buoys. I think they did a real good job. But you'll probably want to rearrange things."

"Probably." Dena chuckled.

Jason knew her all too well. She had been a professional photographer since he was a teen, and he had seen her work many photo shoots. Asking her to donate a full day of work wasn't too unusual. She'd do anything for her son. Plus, the money raised would help support the youth ministries at Jason's newest pastorate.

Billy and Susie ran into the church kitchen. "Grandma!"

Dena's joy spread from her heart to her open arms. She knelt to meet them. Billy, eight, thrust his arms around her. Five-year-old Susie followed with equal enthusiasm, and Dena reached down to catch herself from landing on her backside. "How are Grandma's little ones this morning?"

"Okay." Billy kissed her on the cheek. "There's so many booths, Grandma. And lots of food." *Any more enthusiasm and I'd need to wear earplugs.*

Dena stood up, straddling Susie on her hip. "And what about you, pumpkin?"

"I so 'cited. Daddy got a cotton candy machine." Susie's toothless grin widened. A natural blond with curly hair, the child reminded her of Jason when he was little. But thankfully, Susie had more feminine features, too—like her mother's nose and chin.

Susie wiggled down and ran off with her brother.

"Don't eat too much and get a tummy ache," Dena warned.

"We won't," the children said in unison.

"You're going to have your hands full tonight." She winked at Jason.

"Loaded up on the antacids yesterday. The kids don't know it, but there are corn dogs and french fries, along with the traditional Maine lobster and clam dinner this evening."

"I think I brought enough film." Dena tapped her large camera case. "Plus, I have my digital."

"Great. If you don't mind, could you get some candid digital shots just for the church? Maybe the Web page? How's the new digital SLR camera you bought yourself for Christmas?"

Dena grinned. "The learning curve has taken a bit longer than I'd hoped, but I'm getting the hang of it. I'll use the F2 for the professional shots." She pulled her old Nikon F2 SLR 35 mm camera out of the camera bag and placed it around her neck. In another month she hoped to be comfortable with digital. There were definite advantages to film. When out in the wilds, she didn't have to charge batteries or bring a laptop computer. What her son didn't know was that she now had two digital SLRs and a half dozen automatic lenses to go with them. She held up Old Faithful. "I can control the shots more with this one."

"Whatever, Mom. You're the pro."

Dena noticed the pies lined on the counter. "Need a hand bringing these out?"

"Sure." Jason balanced six pies on a large tray.

Dena scooped up two, one in each hand. "Lead on."

He pushed through the swinging doors with his back and stepped into the fellowship hall. Dena caught the door with her foot and kicked it open again, wiggling through the doorway, deftly holding the cream-covered pies.

They crossed the fellowship hall, weaving past tables, workers, and a few children running around. It smelled of wood, floor wax, and a slight musty odor. The pie table stood in close proximity to the front door. "Ah," Dena said, "getting them as they're leaving after tempting them when they walk in, huh?"

Jason's crooked grin hiked up his face. "Something like that." He placed his tray on the corner of an already full table and began making room for his six pies. Dena examined the area and decided to put the pies on the other end.

"I think we brought too many out," Jason offered.

"Do you have any crates we could stick under the table to place these pies on?"

"Jason, what are you doing?" Marie, Jason's wife, placed her hands on her hips. "Those are the pies for the pie-eating contest, not to sell. Didn't you notice the extra whipped cream on them?"

"Ahh, no. Sorry." He began placing the pies he'd put on the table back on his tray. "Guess you might as well bring those back to the kitchen, Mom."

"Sure." She chuckled. Some things never changed. Jason had been in the ministry for six years, and this was his second church. He was great at preaching, teaching, and caring for the members of his congregation. But little things, like where this went or that, always seemed to elude him. Thankfully, the Lord had blessed him with a wife who was gifted in the areas where he was lacking.

Dena turned sideways and pushed the door open with her shoulder, swinging her body forward as the doors opened. A little one ran under her arms. Dena lifted the pies, keeping them safe. "Kids," she muttered.

She turned toward the child. "Better slow down, sport."

The door banged into her arm and knocked it backward.

Shocked, she stood paralyzed as whipped cream and chocolate pudding slowly oozed down her face.

"I'm so sorry." A handsome man with rugged shoulders and sandy blond hair stood in front of her holding a wire bushel basket full of lobsters. "Can I help you?"

"No," she stammered.

"Mom, are you all right?" Marie came running up to her side.

"Grab the camera. Unhook the strap. Get it off me before the cream and pudding can work their way down on top of it."

"Sure." Marie fumbled with the strap and removed the camera.

"I'm sorry," the stranger apologized again.

Dena wiped the cream from her eyes. The one-man demolition crew placed his basket of lobsters on the floor. "Let me give you a hand."

"No, thanks, I'll just go to the parsonage and wash up." She turned and faced her daughter-in-law. "Marie, can you lend me a blouse?"

"Sure, Mom. Let's get some of the mess off you first." Dena followed Marie the rest of the way into the kitchen.

The stranger stood there, aghast. *He might be a klutz, but he sure is a handsome one.* Dena stopped in midstride. Since when did she notice the opposite sex? Having been a widow for the past twenty years, dating was something she'd given up on long ago. At first she'd been emotionally raw from losing Bill. After that, she was too busy providing for herself and the children. She hadn't had time.

"Here, use this." Marie offered a handful of paper towels.

"Now I'm really running late."

"Don't worry about it, Mom. The photo booth is only open when you're there."

Dena scooped mounds of whipped cream and chocolate off her white cotton blouse. "Do you have any spot remover at home? I'd like to get some on this blouse before the chocolate sets."

"Of course. With Billy and Susie, I'd be crazy not to have some on hand."

"Or with me." Dena chuckled. "I can't believe I didn't look."

"Well, there aren't any windows in those doors, so even if you had, you wouldn't have seen Wayne coming."

She never pictured a "Wayne" as being a rugged, outdoors type, but the name agreed with him. Of course, John Wayne fit that bill, but that was his last name. Actually, she recalled it wasn't even his real name. "I take it he was bringing in the lobsters for tonight's dinner."

"Yeah." Marie led the way to the back alley that would bring them to the rear door of the parsonage. The church and parsonage sat kitty-corner to each other, with a parking lot in the rear of the two buildings.

The parsonage was an old Victorian-style home with a large front porch. Inside, the hardwood floors showed years of use, but, with a little tender loving care, Dena was certain they could be restored. Many things needed fixing in the old place, and slowly Jason and Marie were getting them done. The congregation could afford it, but the previous pastor hadn't expressed concern about the condition of the house. The church members had remodeled the kitchen with all new appliances before Jason and his family arrived.

They stepped into the master bedroom. Marie pointed to the bathroom and then walked over to the closet.

"What about this one?" Marie pulled out a drop-collar white blouse with tiny teardrop roses in a pale pink.

"That'll be fine, thanks. Do you mind if I take a shower first? I feel kinda sticky."

"No problem." Marie pulled some clean towels from the closet and handed them to Dena. "Here ya go. Unless you need something else, I'm going to go back. There's no telling what that son of yours will mix up next."

"Sorry, he's your husband now." Dena waved off her daughter-in-law. "His shortcomings aren't my responsibility anymore."

"Thanks a bunch." Marie chuckled and exited.

❦

"I'm so sorry, Reverend. I didn't mean to bang into your mother. That was your mother, right?"

A low rumble escaped Pastor Russell's lips. "Yeah, that was my mom."

"It was kinda hard to tell. Not that I've ever seen her before. But I heard she was coming to town, and Mrs. Russell called her 'Mom,' so I just kinda put two and two together." He was rambling. He felt like a fool. The poor woman was literally creamed by those pies. Wayne fought to keep a smirk from surfacing as he pictured the cream sliding down her face and hanging from her chin.

"She'll be fine, Wayne." The pastor leaned over the basket of lobsters. "They all safe?"

Wayne looked down at the thick blue elastics used to keep the lobsters' powerful claws shut. "Yup. Wouldn't want someone losing a finger while putting them on the grill or in the pot."

Jason pulled his hand out of the basket.

Wayne snickered. "Landlubber."

"Hey, I'm learning. At least I don't expect live ones to be red anymore."

Wayne rolled his eyes. "Good. Look, Pastor Russell, I can't stay. I'm glad to lend a hand in any way I can, but I'm afraid I have a job I must complete today."

"That's fine, Wayne. Donating the lobsters is a tremendous gift."

"Wish I could have gotten more, but that's all I was able to pull out of my pots this week."

"It's a fine catch, thank you." Wayne took the pastor's extended hand. For a landlubber, he was all right. Pastor Jason's first year with the church had gone very well. People were excited about their church and enjoyed challenging themselves in their walk with the Lord. The small community of Squabbin Bay seemed just the right fit for Pastor Russell and his family. Wayne noticed he'd become more careful to give God His due in prayer, praises, money, and just plain old acknowledgment of who God is.

"I'll try and come back as soon as possible," Wayne offered.

"If you can't make it, I'll understand. Lord's blessings on your day, Wayne."

"Thanks, Pastor. Same to you."

He thought of mentioning that Jess was coming in today so they could have their picture taken, but now didn't seem like the right time to bring it up. Leaving the church, he slipped into the cab of his old pickup truck. He turned the key and the engine purred to life. The truck didn't look like much, but it ran well. A man didn't need a whole lot more.

As he pulled out of the parking lot, the image of the cream-covered woman replayed, and he finally surrendered. Wayne laughed so hard, tears edged his eyelids. The killer was when she wiped the cream off her eyes. He knew she was fighting giving him a piece of her mind. Her hands showed she was older than the rest of her appeared. Of course, she had to be older than he was to be the mother of Pastor Russell. He tried to imagine her with Jason's face. Wayne shuddered. *Nope, won't go there.* He pulled up to the house where he was building some new cabinets, grabbed his toolbox from the bed of the truck, and proceeded inside.

Henry Drake was in his eighties and liked work done well. He'd watch over Wayne's shoulder constantly. At first Wayne found it quite annoying. But when he learned that Henry was a combination of lonely and curious, he soon appreciated him hanging around.

"Morning, Henry. Sorry I'm late."

"Heard you creamed the pastor's mother."

Wayne groaned.

Chapter 2

Wayne hoisted his toolbox into the back end of the pickup, then rolled his shoulders and stretched. His cell phone rang as he slipped into the cab, requiring awkward contortions to retrieve it. "Hello."

"Hey, Dad, I'm at the church fair. Where are you?"

"Just finished up Henry Drake's job. I've got to run home for a shower. And I'll meet you there."

"No problem. Remember, you promised to take a picture with me."

"How could I forget?" Wayne turned the key and headed toward his place. "So, did you bring the mystery man with you?"

"Daaaad!" Jess dragged his name out long enough that he could hear the laughter in her voice.

"Well, did ya?" he sang back.

"Trev promised he'll visit next time."

Third time. The kid doesn't want to meet me. I don't like it, Lord. "Well, I'm looking forward to meeting him."

"You will like him, Dad, I promise."

"I'm sorry for you that he couldn't make it this weekend, honey."

"I love him, Daddy. He's a good man. He works hard, just like you."

Wayne felt a slight grin rise on his right cheek. He'd worked hard for the past twenty-two years. Jess was in her senior year of college and seriously considering marriage. Life was changing, and perhaps a bit too fast. He wasn't sure.

"I love ya, Jess, and I trust you." He let out a slow breath. It wasn't easy trusting your daughter to the dangers of the world. Especially knowing she came into this world because of a mistake he'd made with her mother when he was seventeen years old.

"Thanks, Daddy. I love you, too. Don't forget to dress for the picture. I've seen some of the photographs the pastor's mother has done; they're awesome. She ought to be a professional."

"She is. Pastor Jason says she travels the world."

"Wow. Maybe I should switch majors."

"If you do, you'll pay for it. I've paid for one college education. I won't be paying for a second."

Jess laughed. "Gotcha."

"I'll be there in half an hour, forty minutes tops."

"Okay, later."

The phone went dead before he could respond. Four years, and it still bothered him that she was growing up and would one day be totally on her own. She'd been his life. He'd worked overtime to bring in the monies needed. Jessica's mother had quickly agreed to his raising her. It had been an easy arrangement. Terry didn't want a child, and at sixteen she'd had a lot of growing up yet to do. The first year they'd flirted with the idea of getting married and becoming a real family after she got out of high school. They soon realized they had nothing more than a physical attraction between them. Terry had signed full custody over to Wayne, and for a while she visited Jess. After a couple years, college, a new city, and eventually her own family, Terry did little more than write an occasional letter.

Lord, please don't let the sins of the father be passed down to the daughter. His silent prayer for twenty years now, since he'd accepted Jesus as his personal Lord and Savior, remained as fervent as ever. If ever anyone understood the grace of God taking mistakes and turning them into blessings, he certainly did. Jessica was his pride and joy. He just wasn't ready to see her completely out of his life.

❧

The churchyard bustled with people. "Hey, Wayne." John Dixon waved. "How's it goin'?"

Wayne shook John's beefy hand. "Fine, fine. How 'bout yourself?"

"Couldn't be better. The wife's fixing to have quite a vegetable garden this year."

"Zucchini?" Wayne couldn't help but wonder how they would get rid of all the zucchini this year. Last year they'd brought it in bushel baskets to the church. Most folks had enough of the vegetable from their own gardens. A couple boys took a basket full and used it for target practice.

John's grin slipped as he looped his thumbs behind his red suspenders. John and Rita were in their sixties, and the garden grew each year as John put out fewer lobster pots. "I've got her planting half as many of those. This year I expect to have a bumper crop of pumpkins. Now a man can make a profit from those."

"Rita sure has a green thumb." Wayne scanned the crowd, looking for his daughter.

"Jessica?" John asked.

"Yeah, have you seen her?"

"Saw her over by the dunk tank. Pastor Jason was taking quite a drenching."

Wayne was glad he'd dressed in his fisherman's sweater. He wouldn't be taking a dip in the tank today. "Did you have a hand in dunking him?"

"Well, maybe once." John looked from side to side. "I adjusted the sensitivity so high, you can practically blow on it and it will dunk the man."

"John, is that any way to treat the pastor?"

John winked. "Why not? It's for charity."

"I might just go and rescue the man by readjusting your adjustment."

"Don't bother. Dennis Cowen already figured it out and fixed it."

"Wise man."

"Spoilsport is what I say." John chuckled at his own humor.

"I take it it's your turn next in the dunking pool?" Wayne suggested.

"Now what would be the fun in seeing an old man getting dunked?"

"Plenty, especially if the pastor is the first to take a shot at ya."

John roared. "I'll fess up later, after dinner."

"You do that." Wayne winked. "Well, I've got to find Jess. I promised her we'd have our picture taken."

"Heard you creamed the pastor's mother earlier."

Wayne felt the back of his neck get as red as a boiled lobster. "It was an accident."

"Seems a handyman like yourself might find the time to put some windows in those doors so others won't run into the same fate," John suggested.

"Already thought of it. Finding the time will be the problem."

"I hear ya." John looked past Wayne's shoulder. "I've got to find Rita. I'm looking forward to dinner and want to get our seats."

"Later." Wayne waved and walked toward the events area before John came up with something else to chat about. He was a nice guy and all, but John knew how to bend a man's ear.

Wayne waved at Billy Hawkins, who was leading his old paint horse around the church's perimeter, giving pony rides. It carried a young girl in blond hair and pigtails whose smile showed a mixture of joy and fear. He moved farther back toward the dunking pool where a gang of people had gathered around one shriveled-up pastor. His blue lips proved he'd been dunked one too many times. "Better dry off, Pastor." When Wayne was the youth director, he'd seen the inside of the tank quite often.

Pastor Jason smiled. "I see you aren't risking it."

"No, sir. I promised Jessica a picture."

He shivered. "Ah, good plan."

His wife, Marie, came up beside him with an oversized towel and wrapped him up. They were an interesting couple. They appeared very content with their relationship, and that's what mattered most, Wayne reckoned.

"Daddy!"

He turned in the direction of his daughter's voice. She held up a cream pie and pointed at him. Across the table was Jess's best friend since kindergarten, Randi. "Don't you dare. You said you wanted this picture."

She placed the pie back on the bake sale table and scooted up beside him. "Had to tease you. Everyone's talking about how you creamed the pastor's mother. Nearly ruined her favorite camera, too." She leaned back and called out to Randi, "Call me?"

PHOTO OP

"All right." Randi waved and headed in the opposite direction.

Wayne cupped his hand over the one Jess placed in the crook of his elbow. "Perhaps we better not bother Mrs. Russell."

"Afraid she has a pie waiting for you?"

"Since when did you become a wicked woman?" he teased. Playful banter had been a part of his and Jess's relationship ever since she was five.

"Learned it from a master." She kissed his cheek.

They strolled toward the photo booth. "It's good to see you. How are your final papers coming?"

"I've got a serious case of senioritis."

"How so?"

"I can't concentrate. Thank the Lord I'm managing somehow. But Dr. Wilson is probably longing for this class of seniors to graduate. Soon."

Wayne wrapped her in his arms. "Like you said, it's senioritis. And while I didn't go to college, I do recall my senior year in high school."

"Me, too. This is worse. Big time."

He kissed the top of her head. "You'll get through it. I love you, princess."

She leaned up and kissed him again. "I love you, too."

They stopped at the small table to register for their photo. Misty Williams, a gal who was in the junior high youth group he'd led a few years ago, smiled and blew a pink bubble that nearly covered her face. "Hey ya, Mr. Kearns, want your picture taken?"

❧

Dena spotted Wayne Kearns through her digital camera's 300mm zoom lens long before he saw her. He was wrapped in the arms of a girl half his age. *He could be her father!* she wanted to scream. Observing them a bit longer than necessary, Dena saw they truly loved each other. *Forgive me, Lord. Who am I to say who should and shouldn't be together? Jason spoke highly of Wayne and cherished his ministry with the church.* After taking a few pictures of the couple, she lowered the camera. It was the only way to get some candid shots in between the portrait pictures.

"Mommy, I don't want my picture taken."

She knelt down to the five- possibly six-year-old girl with reddish brown hair. Dena rolled her shoulders and fired off a prayer. At fifty-two, there were many reasons she no longer did studio work—and dealing with testy children was one of them. But for Jason and the Lord, she could endure anything. "What's a pretty little girl like you doing here?"

The young child scrunched up her face.

Dena mimicked the girl. "You don't have to have your picture taken, but it would be a shame if the church directory didn't have a picture of such a pretty seven-year-old."

"I'm five," she corrected, and a smile lifted the corners of her lips.

"My, my. You definitely look mature. A fine young lady if ever I saw one."

"Really?"

"Really." Dena extended her hand to shake the child's. "Sorry I can't take your picture, but it was a pleasure meeting you."

Hesitantly, the freckled girl extended her hand. "You can take my picture, if you'd like."

"Why, thank you, Miss. . . . What is your name?"

"Clarissa."

"Clarissa. A pretty name to go with a pretty face. Come, sit right here and I'll take your picture. Then you can go back to the church fair and play the games. What's your favorite game, Clarissa?" Dena adjusted the camera on the tripod and changed the f-stop for the now-glowing child. In her hand Dena held the remote attached to the camera. She smiled. In the eighties, when she'd purchased the cable release, it was state-of-the-art. Today it seemed old-fashioned—a simple cable with a piston and a push button on the end.

"I like the ring toss. I got a teddy bear."

Click. Dena fired off a fast round of several frames. "Wow, you must be really good. I've never managed to get a ring on one of those posts. How did you do it?"

Clarissa's features changed to a thoughtful pose. *Click.* Dena took another picture.

"Daddy says it's in the wrist. He taught me." She beamed.

Click. "Well, your daddy must be pretty special. Smile for the camera."

Clarissa glowed. Dena clicked off two more shots. "All done."

"Really?"

"Really."

"Can I see the picture now?"

"No, sweetheart. This camera only takes pictures with film."

"Daddy's camera shows you the picture right away."

Dena chuckled and lifted the camera she was wearing around her neck for that occasional digital shot. "This camera works like your daddy's."

"Oh." Clarissa narrowed the distance between her eyebrows.

Clarissa's mother called out, "Come now, Clarissa, others are waiting."

Dena turned to Wayne Kearns and his. . .girlfriend? Wife? "What can I do for you this evening? The standard picture for the church or something more?"

"Jess and I would like to have a family portrait done."

Family portrait. He married the girl? Well, I suppose that's the proper thing to do. Forgive me, Lord. I'm doing it again. What is it about this man that unnerves me so? Possibly the fear of another pie attack, she reasoned. "Fine. Sit back here. I'll take the one for the church directory first. Did Misty show you the possible backgrounds?"

"Yes." He motioned for Jess to sit down, then stood behind her.

Dena looked through the lens of the camera as he placed his hands lovingly on the beautiful young woman's shoulders. "I'm sorry," Dena said. "Would you mind sitting, Wayne? You're too tall for Jess's height in the chair. The picture would be unbalanced."

"No problem," he answered.

Jess popped up from the chair. "See, I told you for years you were too tall. It has nothing to do with me being short."

Years? Just how young was she when he married her? Dena blinked away the thoughts and arranged the couple. "Place your hands on his shoulders like so," she instructed.

Jess obeyed.

"Relax a bit, Mr. Kearns."

"He hates having his picture taken," Jess supplied.

"Oh, do I need to tell you how pretty you are?"

Wayne's eyebrows shot up in shocked surprise.

Not funny! Dena chastised herself as she went behind her camera to refocus. *I can't believe I said that.* She wished she had an old Cirkut camera so she could drape its dark cloth over her head and hide.

Wayne crossed his arms.

Great. Real professional, Dena. "Okay, where are those smiles I saw earlier?" Dena coaxed.

Jess massaged Wayne's shoulders.

He reached up and patted Jess's hands, splashing a grin across his face that could charm any woman. "I'm doing this for you, honey."

Lord, help me, I'm attracted to a married man. She glanced down at his ring finger. Nothing. She glanced up at Jess's. A small silver band encircled it. *He didn't buy her gold? Who is this guy?*

"Thanks, Dad." Jess kissed the top of his head.

"Dad?" The word tumbled from Dena's lips before she could stop it. Heat warm enough to be a hot flash rose across her cheeks. But this had nothing to do with hormones.

Or did it?

Chapter 3

Dena moved through the last of her customers as quickly as possible. As much as she would like a lobster dinner, she'd decided not to step foot in the church. She'd made a perfect fool of herself today. Tromping through the Florida Everglades fighting off alligators seemed more desirable than being here on the rocky coast of Maine.

Jason and Marie had been encouraging her to move up here. She'd even started to pack up her condo in Boston. But today proved she belonged in the city. *Lots of people, no one knows who you are, and you can live out your embarrassing moments in private.* She'd been offered more pieces of cream pie today than there were stars in the sky.

She put the last of her equipment in her backpack, collapsed the tripod, and headed for the car. Dena slammed the trunk closed and leaned against the back end, inhaling the cool night air. The stars played off a deep sea of midnight blue.

"Mrs. Russell."

Dena closed her eyes. She knew Wayne's voice. It rolled down her spine like the water rushing over her shoulders in the hot springs of North Carolina.

"I'm sorry about earlier today."

She didn't turn to greet him. "It was an accident, Mr. Kearns. Don't think a thing of it."

"Oh, I'll be hearing about how I creamed the pastor's mother for the rest of the year, I reckon."

Dena held back a giggle.

"I also apologize for the confusion in the photo booth."

She turned and faced him now. There he stood, six feet tall, with rugged shoulders and a face so handsome even the darkness couldn't cloak it. "I'm sorry. I don't know why I would assume she was anything but your daughter."

He took a step forward, his hands behind his back. His teeth flashed in a bright smile that set her insides quivering. *Stop these foolish thoughts,* she reprimanded herself, fighting for some semblance of control.

"It's flattering that you'd think someone as beautiful as Jess would be attracted to me."

"Actually, I was more concerned with something Jason had said about you working with the youth—"

Wayne let out a guffaw, then stopped the laughter. "I'm sorry. You're not from around here, so you wouldn't know she's my daughter. Jess is a senior at Gordon College."

"Congrats."

"I'm proud of her, as you probably could tell. Look, I figured you're feeling embarrassed enough, so I brought you something." He handed her a Styrofoam box. "I hope you like lobster."

"Thank you." She accepted the container. "I love it."

He glanced at the church, then back at her. "Great. Well, I hope you come and visit Squabbin Bay again sometime. Perhaps at a time when you can relax and not spend the day working."

"Actually, I'm staying for a few days." *Now why did I tell him that?*

"Wonderful. Enjoy your visit." He headed back to the church. "Oh, just for the record, you did a great job raising that boy of yours."

"Thank you." Jason had grown to be a fine man, and it was nice hearing it from the people the Lord had placed under his shepherding care. Perhaps she could move here after all.

She drove to the small cottage she'd been renting for the past couple of months. At the time it seemed like the logical thing to do. Admittedly, she'd only been able to visit twice. Her cell phone rang. "Hello?"

"Hey, Mom, I heard you were up at Jason's this weekend."

"Chad, where are you?" As a commercial pilot, her youngest son kept a schedule that always had him on the move.

"Fifty miles away. I'm coming up with someone I'd like you to meet."

Her grin broadened. Chad had been talking about Brianne for two years, but they'd only started dating a year ago. With him flying all over the country, it was hard for them to spend any real time together. "I have a spare room at the cottage, but you'll be bunking on the couch."

"Not too lumpy, I hope."

"Don't know. Never slept on it."

"Just came off a five-day trip. I could sleep on a rock. I was hoping to get up in time for Jason's church fair. How's it going? Is it over?"

"Fine. I had no idea *that* many people lived in Squabbin Bay. I left before it finished. I'm on my way to the cottage."

"Run out of film?"

Dena turned down the dirt road that led to her cottage. "Me? Never. Do you know how to get here?"

"More or less. I'll call you when I'm in town, and you can give me directions."

"Sure. I'll make up the bed for Brianne."

"Thanks, Mom. She's looking forward to meeting you."

She could hear the joy in her son's voice. Dena's confidence in the Lord that this was the right gal for Chad rose another notch. "I'm looking forward to meeting her, too. See you soon, son."

Dena pulled up to the remote, weathered, shingled cottage overlooking a small inlet. The moonlight danced on the water, and a whiff of salty air brushed past her nose. The powerful pull of the ocean renewed her as the surf crashed on the shore below.

Taking in a deep breath, she sighed and went into the quaint cottage. It had two small bedrooms, a bath, and a simple kitchen that opened into the living room. A modest table divided the two rooms. The cottage also sported a porch, which, at first, Dena had wished wasn't screened in, until she met her match in mosquitoes, black flies, and the numerous other flying insects. This seemed particularly ironic when she considered all the wilds she'd photographed. She set the camera backpack on the counter, made the bed in the guest room, and laid out some bedding for Chad near the couch. Thankfully, the house came fully furnished.

Moments later she set some water in the teakettle to boil and opened the dinner Wayne Kearns had packed for her. Lobster salad set on a bed of romaine lettuce. A fresh bun of Portuguese sweet bread and some green grapes rounded out her meal. "Perfect." She dove her fork in.

Her cell phone rang.

"Hello?"

"Hey, Mom, we just passed the church and are heading east on Main Street."

Dena gave directions between mouthfuls. When she finished eating, her stomach gurgled. She had polished off the church meal and began scavenging through the refrigerator looking for something more. A black and furry container sat in the back of the fridge, something from her last visit. With the tips of her fingers, she grabbed the furry creature and tossed it, container and all.

"Mom, I see a fork in the road."

"Back up; you missed the drive. There's no marker, and it's really tough to find." She tapped the refrigerator door shut. "Did you guys bring any food?"

"Just some junk food for the road. Why, are you hungry?" Chad asked.

"Starving!"

Chad laughed. "Worked hard, didn't you?"

Admittedly, she was famished after any full day of shooting. Her appetite always increased when she worked hard. Thankfully, weight had never been an issue. Her own sister, Carrie, had a very different metabolism, forcing her to constantly watch her weight. "Kinda."

"Hey, I think I found it."

"Hang on, I'll turn the outside lights off and on." She stepped to the side door and flicked the switch up and down a couple of times.

"I see you. We'll be there in a minute."

"Great." Dena clicked her phone shut and went outside to greet them.

Chad's idea of junk food—almonds, dried fruit, and some bottled fruit juice—abated her hunger.

"Mom, Brianne and I have something to tell you."

❧

"Good morning, Dad. How many did you pull in this morning?" Jess sat at the breakfast table with a cup of tea and a bagel loaded with cream cheese.

"Ten. It's an off season, I guess."

"Bummer. I guess I can't hit you up for a fancy red sports car like Mrs. Russell's for a graduation present, huh?"

Wayne pulled out a chair at the table. "Never even considered it. In fact, I was starting to plan what kind of a gift you'd be getting me for your graduation."

"Huh?" The bagel in Jess's hand plopped back on the plate.

"You know, pay me back, thank me—those kinds of things. Personally, I'd like a '68 Mustang convertible in pristine condition."

"Dream on, Dad." Jess retrieved the fallen bagel and bit into it.

Wayne reached over and grabbed the other one off her plate.

"Hey, get your own." She swatted his hand.

"Why? You can make another for the both of us."

Jess rolled her eyes heavenward, picked up her plate, and headed for the kitchen. "Thanks for taking the picture with me."

"Not a problem, princess. So, tell me, besides senioritis, what's happening at school?" Wayne leaned against the counter and sampled the bagel. He couldn't help but be curious about one Mr. Trevor Endicott. *Having a historical New England name didn't necessarily mean he was a good man, and*—he continued to fret—*and, I don't like it that he's declined to meet with me three times throughout the past semester.*

Jess folded her arms across her middle. "What you're really asking about is Trev, isn't it?"

She had him there. "Yes. And everything else. You know me, Mr. Nosy Dad from way back." He tried not to be too nosy, and he tried to keep a balance between her need for privacy and his own responsibility to watch and protect her.

Jess's laughter eased the slight tension in the room. "You'll never change."

"Not likely." Wayne poured a cup of coffee. "Want one?" he asked, lifting the pot.

"No, thanks. I'm heading back to school right after church. I'll grab a cup there at the fellowship hall. Trev is taking me out to dinner tonight."

"Jess, I don't want to sound like a broken record—"

"Then don't. You need to trust me, Dad."

"It's not that I don't trust you. But it is odd that this young man has managed to avoid seeing me on three separate occasions. Doesn't that bother you?"

"Yes, but there've been very good reasons each and every time."

"I see. And what happened this time?" Wayne sipped his coffee and prayed for the Lord's leading. *Guide me, Lord.*

Jess plopped down at the kitchen table. "He was called into work to cover for someone."

"He couldn't say he had other plans?"

Jess nibbled her lower lip. Wayne took in a deep breath. *She's concerned, too.*

"Tell you what. I'll plan a trip down there next weekend and take the two of you out to dinner."

"Really?" She jumped up from her seat.

"Sure. I understand what it is to work for a living."

"Thanks, Daddy. I'll tell Trev. He'll be so excited."

I hope so, Wayne prayed. The one thing that really got under his skin was anyone hurting his daughter.

"What did you think of Mrs. Russell, the pastor's mother?" Jess asked.

Where'd that come from? She sat there staring at him with a foolish grin on her face.

"She seemed like a nice person," he finally commented—not that he wanted his daughter to know he found the woman attractive.

"Hard to tell with all that cream on her face, huh?"

Wayne grabbed a hand towel and twisted it into a rat's tail. "You'd think I'd get a little respect from my own daughter." He snapped the towel.

Jess picked up another, and their mock battle ensued. He took aim and snapped the end of the towel at her knee. She countered with a snap at his elbow. They stopped after they were unable to stand up straight from their own laughter.

"Seriously, Dad. What did you think of Dena Russell? I saw you give her that plate of food."

※

Dena stretched her stiff body as she got up from bed. She glanced at the alarm clock. The red digital glow of the numbers read ten o'clock. Dena moaned.

"Chad, Brianne, we overslept. Get up!" she called out before exiting the bedroom door. In the kitchen, she found the young couple snuggled up beside each other, sipping their coffee.

"You overslept, Mom." Chad's grin filled his face. His features were softer than Jason's, but she still saw Bill in both of her sons. "I was about to wake you. I tried an hour ago, but it was no use."

"Sorry." She'd been doing that more and more lately after a hard day of work. Getting older definitely had a downside. She headed back to the bedroom. "I'll be ready in seven minutes, then we'll leave for church."

Chad and Brianne giggled. Dena tossed her head from side to side. *Young love.*

Showered and dressed, the small group went to church. Dena sat back in the old oak pew. Jason had told her that they'd been made from local lumber nearly three hundred years ago. Dena scanned the congregation. She'd photographed just about everyone.

"Grandma, Uncle Chad!" Billy yelped out, leaving the pew where he'd been with his mom.

"Shh," Dena warned.

Chad scooped the boy up in a bear hug. "Hey, buddy, how you doing?"

"Good. You should have been here yesterday. Dad got dunked over and over again."

The entire congregation started to chuckle.

"Oh, man, I wish I'd been here to see that. I wouldn't have minded dunking your daddy myself."

Billy leaned toward his uncle's ear. "Mr. John made it easy to dunk him," he said in a rather loud whisper.

Dena glanced over to John Dixon. *I wonder how Jason will get back at him.* She winked. John's wife buried her head deeper into her church bulletin.

Jason called the service to order. "Good morning, everyone. I trust all of you had a good time yesterday. We raised three thousand dollars for the youth ministries, thank the Lord."

A round of applause erupted.

Jason raised his hands to abate the praise. "Hang on, there's more good news to thank the Lord on." The room hushed. "Jessica Kearns informed me this morning that she will be graduating with honors from Gordon College in two weeks."

Dena scanned the congregation, looking for Wayne and his daughter, Jessica. The broad smile on her father's face showed just how proud he was.

"I'd say the college scholarship fund and investing in our youth has seen a long and good history in this church. With God's help, I pray we continue to be sensitive to the Lord's leading for our youth." Jason drew the congregation back to the purpose of their meeting, of fellowship with one another and fellowship with God.

Dena closed her eyes and silently prayed. It had been hard being a single mother, raising three kids through their teen years, supporting them, and still trying to be there when they came home from school. But her career choice had paid off. Purchasing the storefront with an upstairs apartment allowed her to have the studio at home and be near her children. And when they had grown and left for college, taking photo opportunities around the world for national magazines and other media groups had helped pay for their college educations. A tear edged her eye. *Thank You, Lord. Without Your help, I couldn't have done it. Now I'm blessed with two grown sons and a grown daughter, each of them making their own families.* Chad and Brianne's engagement and desire to marry quickly had startled her, but she was happy for them. After a long discussion, they'd decided to get married next weekend in Maine and honeymoon for a week in the Caribbean.

Church. She opened her eyes and focused on Jason. Out of the corner of her eye, she caught a glimpse of Wayne Kearns. Her heart fluttered. Her palms began to sweat. She closed her eyes and reopened them, staring straight ahead. She was a grown woman and had no time for romance.

She snuck another glance at the very handsome Wayne Kearns. *He's too young.* He looked over at her and smiled. Her cheeks flamed.

She closed her eyes and bowed her head. *Dear God in heaven, what's come over me?*

Chapter 4

Wayne Kearns couldn't help but be amused by Dena Russell. She was a beautiful woman, even with whipped cream hanging off her nose. On the other hand, he felt guilty for having been the cause of her embarrassment. Jess had informed him that everyone brought or offered her a piece of pie throughout the entire fair. If Squabbin Bay was noted for anything apart from the lobster industry, it had to be that it was a town of practical jokers. And while he understood that, he wasn't too sure that the beautiful Mrs. Russell would. Pastor Russell had told him on more than one occasion how his mother had virtually raised him and his siblings alone.

Of course, Pastor Russell knew of Wayne's past, and being a single parent since the age of eighteen had been very difficult in the beginning.

He thought back on the service, to the brief moment when his gaze caught Dena's. Wayne shook off the memory and paced the deck overlooking his backyard. Once again the image of Dena's cream-covered face came into view.

Wayne stomped off the deck, over to his truck, and headed back to church. He'd planned to spend the afternoon with Jess, but she'd gone back to see her boyfriend. *Boyfriend!* Did he even like the sound of that word?

Wayne turned off the engine in the church parking lot. He pulled out his toolbox and marched into the fellowship hall. Within minutes he had the doors off their hinges and laid out on a couple of sawhorses. John Dixon was right; these doors needed windows.

"Hello!" Wayne heard someone call as he clicked off his jigsaw. He turned to greet the pastor. A slight heat rose on the back of his neck.

"Hi. I decided to fix these doors."

Pastor Russell placed his hands on his hips. "Need a hand?"

"Not really. I can frame out the windows, but I don't have the glass to fill in the holes today."

Pastor Russell leaned over the door. "I see. Wouldn't it have been better to wait until you had the glass?" He chuckled.

"Probably. But my guilt got the best of me. I feel so badly about your mom. I heard that just about everyone brought her a piece of pie yesterday."

Jason Russell smiled. "Just about." He leaned back against the other sawhorse. "She can handle it."

Wayne sanded the edges of the pine frame he would place around the hole he'd cut for the window.

"Wayne, can I ask you something?"

"Sure, what's up?"

"Well, old Ben Costa said it's been a bad year for lobstering. Have you noticed?"

"Yeah, it happens every now and again. Why, is Ben hurting?"

"Some. The church has been able to help."

"I'll keep an eye out for him."

"Thanks. It isn't like he hadn't planned ahead for retirement."

Wayne left the sandpaper on the door and brushed off his hands. "Yeah, Maggie getting cancer really knocked out their savings. One thing about this community, people help one another."

"Very true. But if everyone's feeling the crunch with the low hauls this year. . ." Pastor Jason looked up at the ceiling and let his words hang for a moment. "We could be in for an interesting year."

Wayne nodded. He lobstered, but he also worked as a carpenter. With a daughter to raise, he couldn't afford the lean seasons of fishing only.

"Jason," Dena Russell called while entering the room.

"I'm coming, Mom." Pastor Russell turned back. "Sorry, I told the family I'd only be a minute. My brother, Chad, is getting married next weekend."

"Congratulations."

"Thanks, now to figure out how to do premarital counseling in a week." Pastor Russell slapped Wayne on the back. "Thanks for the windows."

"You're welcome."

Dena stood in the doorway.

"Hi," he said.

"Hi."

Wayne looked down at the door lying in front of him.

"Peace offering?" she asked.

"Kinda. I had the afternoon free, and, well, while I might have innocently creamed you with a pie, what would have happened if it were a small child?"

"Ah, I see your point." She glanced back at Pastor Russell exiting the building. "Could you use a hand?"

Her smile sent a kicker of a punch deep in his gut. "Sure," he managed to speak. Wayne found himself in unfamiliar territory. For years, he'd been too busy to consider a relationship. Now, in less than twenty-four hours, he found himself unable to think of anything but getting to know this woman.

"What can I do?"

"Could you sand the rough edges off this framing?"

"Sure." She took the sandpaper and began to work.

Wayne paused for a moment and caught himself staring. He walked over to the other door and cut open the hole for the window.

A few minutes later, Dena asked, "Are we staining or painting?"

"I'll stain to go with the original."

"Okay, where's the stain?"

"Didn't bring any. I'll take care of that later in the week after I can get to the store and purchase the stain and glass."

She nodded and sat down on a chair.

"Pastor Russell said he was trying to convince you to move up here."

Dena chuckled. "Yes, he is."

"What's keeping you in the city?"

"Convenience, mostly. I travel a lot for my work, and Logan, in spite of the traffic, is a good airport for foreign travel."

"From what your son says, you're on the road a lot."

"Yeah, he's trying to get me to slow down a bit. Personally, I wouldn't mind, but each new trip is exciting, a new world to explore and photograph. I love it."

Wayne lined up the angled cut for the corners of the frame for the second door. "I haven't been any farther than Boston. I've lived Down East in Squabbin Bay all my life. I've seen many photographs of places I would love to see someday. But more than likely, I won't get much farther than various spots in New England."

The small board slipped.

Dena stood before him. "Can I hold the board for you?"

"Thanks." He could smell the light lavender scent of her perfume. *Perhaps she should stay in Boston.*

⁊

"Why did I offer to help him, Lord?" Dena spoke out loud in the security of her automobile. With Chad and Brianne now getting married in Squabbin Bay, she'd have to stay for the week. "A wedding in a week. Lord, is the end of the world at hand and I don't know about it?"

On the other hand, the kids made sense. Their schedules conflicted so often, it was impossible for the two of them to have much time off together.

Dena went over the list of things she needed to do. She placed the phone's hands-free headset to her ear and started her calls while driving to the market to purchase some food. She'd have to travel to Boston for appropriate wedding clothing. She drummed her fingernails on the steering wheel. *What to wear?*

"Hello?"

"Hi, Jamie. It's Dena Russell."

"Hey, Dena, what's happening?"

"A ton. I'm wondering if you'd like to cover an assignment for me." Dena filled in the eager photographer about the assignment in Australia.

"Thanks so much. I owe you."

"Just do me proud and come back with some excellent shots."

"I promise. Thanks. Thanks again."

"You're welcome."

"Bye." Jamie hung up the phone.

The rest of the day, Dena found herself busy making wedding plans, rearranging her schedule, and trying to figure out when to develop the pictures she'd taken the day before at the church fund-raiser.

By nightfall she found herself with a cup of black coffee, sitting on the deck, looking out over the bay. Crickets chirped and the stars shone their brilliance.

Wayne's handsome green eyes floated back in her memory. They seemed to appear overhead in the night sky. "Lord, what's wrong with me? Why am I attracted to a man I don't even know?"

The phone rang.

Dena jumped up and answered it. "Hello?"

"Hi, Mom." Amber's voice sounded cheery but tired.

"Hi, honey. What's up?"

"You mean besides Chad's rush wedding? He's so Chad. It's a good thing he flies jets; nothing else would be fast enough for him."

Dena laughed. "Agreed. So, to what do I owe the pleasure of hearing your sweet voice tonight?"

"David and I have a slight problem."

"Money?"

"Yeah, sorry, but can you help us out again?"

"Sure, I'll pay for the trip. You don't have to pay me back. Also, I'll rent another cottage for the weekend for your whole family."

"No, Mom, we can make do at your place."

"Maybe you can, but I can't. I love you, but this place is too small for five extra people. Not to mention Chad will be staying here, too."

"Ah, well, I hate for you to pay so much."

"Amber, it'll be my pleasure. My present to Chad. After all, he doesn't need a lot of wedding gifts. He's had his own place for years and has made good money."

"True." Amber's voice lowered. "David's overcoming the layoff, but he's so worried and depressed about our finances."

Dena spent a few minutes trying to encourage Amber about her and David's financial situation. There were many days, shortly after Bill died, when she didn't think she would be able to survive and keep the family intact. But the Lord had provided, and, after many years, He provided above and beyond what she ever expected.

"Jason says you had a run-in with a cream pie."

"Yeah, and this town is a bunch of pranksters. Just about every one of them came up to me with a slice of pie afterward. The poor man who hit me felt so guilty he was at the church this afternoon putting windows in the doors where it happened."

Amber's laughter reminded Dena of when Amber was a teen still living at home.

"I heard he nearly ruined Old Faithful."

"Don't remind me. The only thing that probably helped me keep my cool was that my camera didn't get damaged. Wayne's handsome green eyes wouldn't have been sparkling then."

"Handsome..." Amber paused. "Green eyes."

Horror rushed over Dena. Why had she ever expressed her inner thoughts to her daughter?

"Tell me more, Mom."

"Nothing to tell," she fumbled through her words.

"Uh-huh. You're attracted to the pie man."

"Amber, please. I merely said he had handsome eyes, and you know how I've always loved green eyes. I've photographed hundreds, but I've never fallen in love with any."

"Love." Amber sobered. "Mom, are you all right?"

"I'm fine, sweetheart. No problem about the money; it's a gift for Chad. Let David know that is how I'm looking at it."

"Thanks again, Mom." Amber giggled. "And I'll be praying about your handsome, green-eyed pie man. Maybe there will be another wedding in the family."

"Huh. Nope, all of you will be hitched after Chad ties the knot with Brianne. That's it; no one else to marry off."

"Mom." Amber paused. "Isn't it possible the Lord might want you to have another helpmate? I mean, Daddy's been gone for nearly twenty years. Wouldn't it be nice to have someone to talk to and be with now that we're all grown and married?"

Dena leaned her head against the wall in the kitchen. "I don't know, Amber. I've been single most of my life. And I'm rather set in my ways. I'm not sure I want someone interrupting my routine."

"Fair enough. Love ya, Mom, and thanks."

"You're welcome." Dena listened to the dial tone on the phone for a moment before she hung up the receiver. *Love. Marriage. Companionship. Do I want those, Lord?*

Wayne's handsome image replayed in her mind for the umpteenth time tonight.

Dena took in a deep breath. *Stop being a foolish old woman,* she admonished. The roll of the surf echoed through the night air. *A stroll on the beach will help me clear my mind. I hope.*

⁂

Wednesday morning met Wayne with continued frustrations. The lobstering was more than bad this year—it was downright ridiculous. He pulled in only five keepers. He scanned the gray ocean as fog drifted over the sea. A call to the local game and fisheries warden was in order. It didn't seem possible they'd overfished the lobsters in Squabbin Bay, but. . . Wayne removed his cap and rubbed the back of his neck.

He scanned the coast and saw a figure walking along the beach. *I wonder if it's Dena Russell.* He turned the wheel and headed his boat toward shore. Ever since he met one Dena Russell, his mind had been tossing around the idea of dating like a loose buoy floating on the waves.

He put the engine to idle and leaned over to pick up another one of his buoys. Again, he found the pot empty. He filled the bait bag and tossed the pot overboard.

Another skiff peeked out of the fog. *Who's that?* he wondered. He watched for a moment to see if he recognized the vessel. But the fog was too thick, and the boat slipped farther into the gray mist. *That's odd.* He set the boat in gear and debated about going closer to shore. The cottage she had rented was on top of the cliff. And who else would have such a huge camera lens, except for a professional?

He eased the boat closer toward shore and squeezed the air horn.

Dena turned and focused on him. He brought the boat a bit closer. She walked toward him.

"Hi," he called out.

"Hi. You're lobstering?" she asked.

"Trying—not too many today."

"Which buoys are yours?"

He pointed out. "The red with a silver stripe." Each fisherman had his own color design on his buoys so they were easily identified one from another.

"Perhaps you should not pull the same pots as your partner." She grinned. "You might catch more."

"Partner?" Wayne aimed the boat toward shore and cut the engine. "What partner?"

Chapter 5

Dena watched Wayne toss an anchor and secure the line. "What do you mean, a partner?" he asked. "I don't have a partner; haven't for years." But hadn't she seen someone. . . ? "I thought I saw someone pulling a pot earlier with those markings."

"How? Is that a telephoto lens?" He stood on the boat as if he were a part of it. His body shifted with the waves as the boat bounced up and down in the mild surf.

"Yes. And yes, I did notice him through the lens."

"Did you snap a picture?"

"No, I'm afraid not, why?"

Wayne rubbed the back of his neck. "Because if you did see someone pulling up my pots, they were stealing."

"Oh, sorry, no." Now why hadn't she taken a snapshot of the man? *Because it was gray and not a very picturesque photograph,* she reminded herself.

"Guess that would have been too easy." Wayne hiked up his hip boots and slipped over the stern of the boat.

"I'm sorry. I didn't have any reason to believe the person was doing anything illegal." Dena felt foolish. She'd witnessed a crime but knew little. She hadn't even paid that much attention to the details of the boat or the man's clothing, nothing. She'd been too busy thinking about another lobsterman, the one before her right now.

"I and a few other lobstermen have been having a bad year. If we have a poacher, that could explain it. Besides me, only Ben Costa has pots in this area."

"I'll be happy to watch, and if I see anything, I'll photograph it."

He let out a deep breath. "Thanks. I doubt whoever it is will be back this week. But you never know. How early were you out here?"

Dena looked down at the small patch of sand on this relatively rocky coastline. "I was up at four. I thought I'd get some sunrise shots in."

"Sun doesn't rise 'til close to six. What woke you up so early?"

Of course, a fisherman would know when the sun rises. Dena cleared her throat. "Unable to sleep."

"Dena, I—" He coughed. "I was wondering if you'd like to go to dinner one night this week."

Dena wrapped her waist with her arms and braved looking straight into

31

Wayne's handsome green eyes. "I—" What did she want to say? That she was a widow and didn't date? What kind of an excuse was that? "I don't date," she stammered.

"Oh, well, I haven't been on one since the last time my sister set me up on a blind date fourteen years ago. So, I guess I'm really asking for you to join me for dinner. More of an opportunity to get to know one another at a time when a pie isn't involved."

Dena chuckled. "No pie is a good plan." She wanted to get to know this man. More than that, her prayer time had been filled with prayers for him and Jess. For her upcoming graduation and the changes that would happen to their small family after she graduated.

Dena remembered all too well what it was like when Jason graduated college and Amber left home to live on campus. But the final blow had been when Chad enlisted in the armed services. Through the air force, he had gained his college education and his flying experience.

She locked her gaze back on Wayne. "All right, I'd love to."

A smile creased his ruggedly handsome face. "Great. How's tonight?"

"Jason has a midweek prayer meeting."

"Right. I forgot it was Wednesday. I could pick you up before the meeting, and we could go together."

Heat washed over her body. "This is a small town, right?"

He knitted his eyebrows, then they rose slightly. "Oh, yeah. I forgot. Okay, we could go to the restaurant in separate cars. . . . Wait, that won't matter. Half the town will see us at the restaurant anyway."

Dena chuckled. "True. All right, let's light up those phone lines tonight and arrive at the church together. If I'm going to make a fool of myself. . ." She couldn't believe she let that much of her inner thoughts slip out.

Wayne reached over and grasped her hand. "Dena, I've got to be honest. I'm attracted to you, but I'm scared. I'm an old man set in my ways."

"Old? You? Do you have any idea how old I am? Far too old for dating or even. . ." She cut herself off.

"You can't be a day over thirty-nine." He winked.

"Hmm, that would put me at the ripe old age of six when I had Jason."

Wayne let out a low chuckle; then his gaze met hers. "We're both old enough not to mince words. Let's see if this is something the Lord is doing in our lives."

"Agreed." Yes, the Lord needed to be central in this relationship, if there was even going to be a relationship. Perhaps she was just jumping the gun. Perhaps the Lord had intended for them simply friendship, nothing more. "When should I be ready?"

"Five forty-five."

"That's precise."

"It's the Yank in me." He grinned.

They said their good-byes, and Dena watched him pilot his boat out of the inlet. The fog had lifted, and a bright blue sky emerged. "Okay, Lord." She looked toward heaven and held out her hands. "It's Your move."

Fear knotted in her stomach. She let out a long sigh. "Give me peace, Lord."

&

After returning his boat to the harbor, Wayne spent the rest of the morning finishing the Gallager job. His mind focused more on the upcoming evening than on the job at hand. He nailed and renailed the railing five times. If he kept that up, he'd be paying the customer.

He stopped by old Ben Costa's house and talked with him about this year's fishing. Wayne noted that his hauls were similar to Ben's, small and decreasing weekly. Then he stopped by his parents' house and turned over their garden in time for their summer visit. By four o'clock he needed a shower and some serious time to get ready for his date.

Date. The word nearly lodged in his throat. After all these years, he finally asked someone on a—he coughed. "Date." He took the stairs two at a time and sealed himself off in his bathroom.

He pulled out a pair of jeans and an off-white cable-knit sweater, one his mother had knitted for him years ago. A pair of leather Top-Siders, and he had his outfit. He glanced in the mirror. "Show the real you, Wayne. Or it's not even worth her time or yours," he challenged himself.

At five o'clock he made his normal midweek call to Jess. "Hi, honey. How you doing?" he asked.

"Fine, Dad. I'm cramming for my archaeology exam."

"I'll say a prayer for you tonight."

"Thanks. Trev said he's looking forward to seeing you on Saturday."

"Great, I'm looking forward to meeting this man."

They talked for another ten minutes about her week, finals, and how full her schedule was. Graduation ceremonies were days away. Wayne planned on attending everything a parent could.

"Well, I've got to go, sweetheart."

"Okay. Short call tonight, what's up? Everyone's okay, aren't they?" she inquired.

"Everyone's fine. I—" Did he dare tell her that he had a dinner date? "I made plans to join someone for dinner."

"Great—give Bob and Wendy my love."

Was he that predictable that his daughter knew everything about him? Or at least she thought she did. "Actually, I'll be going out with Mrs. Russell—"

He pulled the phone from his ear as Jess shrilled out, "All right, Dad!"

After they said good-bye, he hung up the phone and grabbed his keys from the kitchen table. His old truck with faded blue paint didn't look like a vehicle one would use to escort a woman on a date. On the other hand, he was going to be himself. And part of who he was rolled on four wheels and served a function. It wasn't his top priority. That was his daughter, his blessing from God, a true miracle. The message of grace played out day after day in his life, seeing the way the Lord took his mistakes and washed them and turned them into blessings. "You're awesome, Lord. Keep me from worrying about my appearance tonight. Help me focus on just being myself."

❧

"Hello?" Dena answered the phone.

"Hi, Mom. Marie said she forgot to invite you for dinner tonight. If you haven't made anything yet, you're welcome to come on over."

"Thanks, Jason, but I'm busy." Dena curled the phone cord around her first finger. *How does a woman tell her grown son she's going out on a date?*

"Okay, I'll see you later."

"Later." Dena hung up the phone and glanced at the clock. She had five minutes, if her clock was set the same as his. Tires crunched the oyster-shelled driveway. *Guess not,* she mused.

Years of travel made her aware of how flexible time could be for some cultures. But Wayne said he was a Yank, and New Englanders typically arrived five to ten minutes before they were expected, in order to be on time. She walked over to the kitchen door that met the driveway and opened it.

He stepped out of his truck wearing blue jeans and an off-white fisherman's sweater. She laughed. She was wearing the same outfit.

"What's so funny?" Wayne examined himself, twisting around, looking for something that might be hanging off his backside.

"Nothing. We just have similar tastes in clothing."

His gaze landed back on her. His lips thinned and turned up at the corners of his mouth. "Who made your sweater? My mom knitted this one years ago."

"I purchased it in Scotland."

"You have seen the world, haven't you?"

"Not completely, but, yes, I've traveled quite a bit." He stood there a step below her. The top of his head was covered with a myriad of curls. She stepped back into the kitchen. "Come in. I'm just about ready."

Wayne entered the house with a confident stride. *Why am I so nervous? Wayne doesn't seem to be,* she pondered. "Make yourself comfortable. I'll be back in a sec."

"No problem. I forgot to ask, where would you like to go?"

"You name it." She headed to the bedroom. "It's your town; wherever you recommend will be fine with me." *Get ahold of yourself, girl. You're fifty-two years old and butterflies flew out a long time ago.* At least she thought they had. *Okay, face it. You're attracted to him. Now get a grip,* she scolded herself.

Facing the mirror, she slipped on the only pair of earrings she'd brought up for this trip—pearls. They blended well with the sweater, but normally she would have put in something darker that would offset her jeans. *Oh well, it's not a beauty pageant. Just a casual dinner.* "Ha," she quipped out loud. A final brush of her hair, and she had primped as much as she could. After all, he was in the other room and waiting.

"Okay, Lord, guide us." She opened the door and saw him staring out the sliding glass door, looking out over the ocean. "It's a beautiful view, isn't it?"

"Yes." He turned and faced her. "Both of them."

They stood for a moment in an awkward pause. He cleared his throat. "We better get going so we're not late for church."

"Good idea." She scooped up her Bible and followed him to the door. He held it open for her.

A gentleman. "Thanks. Would you like to take my car or yours?"

His smile faded. She watched his eyes go back and forth from her car to his truck. It took a moment, but then it hit her. Her red Mercedes convertible to his old truck shouted volumes. "I don't mind going in your truck."

His shoulders straightened. "I'm fine with either; you pick."

She stepped toward his truck. "Then yours; we won't have to shuffle vehicles." She hoped she didn't sound like a snob. The Mercedes had been the one vice she'd allowed herself. She'd been making good money for the past few years, and it had always been her dream car. She loved driving it up to Maine from Boston. So often it stayed parked in the garage.

"It's not much, but it runs well," he weakly offered.

"Wayne, don't misread my offer about the car. I'm as comfortable in a truck as I am in my car."

He nodded.

She didn't have a lot of money, but she made a comfortable living. The price of the Mercedes had been a real bargain, and she figured that if she treated it right, she'd have the car for twenty years, maybe more. It felt like a frugal investment at the time, but right at this moment, she wondered.

"I suppose I'm a little sensitive about my truck." He chuckled. He opened the passenger door for her. "It just seemed wiser to keep this one, do the work myself, and have a few more dollars to help Jess pay for her college education."

"Makes sense to me." She stepped up and sat down on the bench seat. He scooted around the truck and entered the driver's side. "I didn't even have a car seven years ago. I was still helping the kids with their schooling."

"How many children do you have?" he asked as he turned on the engine.

"Three. Jason is my oldest; he's thirty-three. Amber lives in Nashua with her husband and three children. Chad, who you might have met on Sunday, is my baby."

"Jess is my only. I'm not sure I could have handled more than one," he stated.

"They can be a handful. Bill died when Jason was only thirteen. Raising three kids through their teen years on my own was tough at times."

"I can imagine."

The tension between them dissipated quickly. Dena relaxed, and she sensed Wayne was relaxing, too. "I bought the Mercedes five years ago. It was my dream car. I hardly get to drive it, which is why I don't mind driving up to Squabbin Bay every once in a while to see the kids."

"My dream car is a classic Mustang convertible."

Dena laughed. "That was my second choice. But unlike you, I don't work on cars, and I figured that I'd have a pretty hefty maintenance bill on a car like that."

"True, if you can't do the work yourself."

He pulled into a small parking lot. The restaurant sat on a bluff overlooking the ocean. "Squabbin's has the best seafood in town. But it also has a healthy turf menu."

"Sounds great. I'm starving."

He cupped her elbow and led her into the restaurant. *Yes*, she thought, *we definitely could become close friends.*

Chapter 6

Dena sat stiffly beside him in his truck.

"That wasn't too bad, was it?" he asked.

Dinner had been wonderful. They found they were similar in their life views and personal tastes. Arriving together at church raised more than a few eyebrows. Wayne thought Pastor Russell almost fell over. One stern look from Dena, and Pastor Russell cleared his throat and continued the prayer meeting. She must have been quite a disciplinarian, he mused.

She let out a deep sigh. "Not too. I probably should have told Jason my dinner plans. It might have lessened the shock."

"I thought I saw the teenager in him ready to protect his mother."

Dena chuckled. "You did. Jason took on a lot of responsibility. I purchased a studio with an apartment in the upstairs with the insurance money I received after Bill died. So, while I was close at hand, Jason had the responsibility of watching the kids while I worked."

"Ah, so he became the man of the house."

"Yeah. I tried to avoid it as much as possible by encouraging him to go out for some sports. But it still happens, as much as you try to prevent it. Older children are just naturally protective of the one parent who's survived."

"Jess tried to mother me for a while. I think all kids go through a phase. But in my case, her mother married when Jess was eight, and by the time she was ten, she'd only receive an occasional card from her. It's sad, really, but Terry wasn't ready to be a mother."

"The divorce must have been hard. I'm sorry."

"Terry and I never married. All part of my unsaved past, I'm afraid. We were in high school. I was a senior and she was a sophomore. And, well, one thing led to another and she was pregnant. I told her I'd raise the baby if she didn't abort it, and she agreed. At first Terry tried to be a part of Jess's life, but she still had to finish high school. Her parents strongly encouraged her to go to college, and, well. . .she started slipping away from Jess then.

"Jess and I have talked about it many times. She's a good kid. She understands it wasn't anything she'd done, but that her mother was just a kid herself."

"I'm sorry, I didn't know."

Wayne let out a nervous chuckle. "No reason you should have. I'll tell you one thing, becoming a single father at eighteen made it real clear that premarital sex was not only wrong, it had consequences. I don't think I could have

37

raised her without my parents' support. I was twenty by the time I let the Lord into my life."

He eased the truck down the dirt road that led to Dena's cottage. "What about you? When did you get saved?"

"I was thirteen, but I didn't get really serious until college. I've found my faith deepens with each new season in my life. When Bill died and I was alone to raise three kids, I struggled. Why did God take him? Why didn't we buy more life insurance? All those kinds of questions, and more. But looking back, I see that God was always with me, always leading me in the right direction. Of course, I didn't always listen and had to learn a few lessons the hard way." The lilt of her laughter warmed him.

He set the transmission in park.

"Would you like to come in for a glass of iced tea?" she offered.

He was exhausted, but he didn't want the evening to end. He enjoyed her company. "I'd love to."

Dena's cell phone rang. Wayne stayed seated in the truck.

"Hello?" she answered then stiffened. "I just got home; I'll call you later." She listened. "Right. Okay, talk to you tomorrow."

Wayne shifted his torso and turned toward her. "Pastor Russell?"

Dena nodded.

"I don't have to come in for the iced tea," he offered.

"No, don't be silly. He's just curious and he can wait."

Wayne smiled. "I left my cell phone at home. Jess knows I had dinner plans with you, so I'm certain I have a message waiting for me."

"Do you think they'll want to chaperone?"

"Probably, but they wouldn't dare say it. They'd want to, but—"

Laughter filled the cab. Dena laughed so hard, tears edged her eyes.

"Come on, let's get that iced tea and sit on the porch." Dena pulled the door handle before he had a chance to open it for her.

"Sounds wonderful." Wayne slipped out of the cab and stretched. "There's a little chill in the air tonight."

They reached the kitchen door and found a note attached. "What's this?" Dena pulled it down and scanned the contents.

"Anything the matter?" he asked.

"No, not really. The owner has decided to sell the place, so he's giving me fair warning."

"Ah, I knew Troy was thinking of moving down to South Carolina. Guess he decided. Can't blame him—his daughter's there, and the weather up here is hard on older folks."

Dena placed the note on the kitchen counter and retrieved two tall glasses. "You know, hot cocoa might be nicer with the temperature dropping."

"I'd love some."

"Great." She moved through the kitchen with an elegant grace. She fascinated him on so many levels. Each time he discovered something new about her, it just made him want to know more.

"Dena?"

"Huh?" She filled the teakettle with some water and placed it on the stove.

"I've had a wonderful evening tonight."

"Me, too." He watched as she bent slightly and turned on the gas flame, adjusting it to the size of the kettle.

"I think. . ." He paused.

What did he think? That he loved her? No, it's too soon—he couldn't fall in love after one date.

"I'd like to go out with you again." There. He said it.

She leaned back against the counter and crossed her legs at her ankles. "Truthfully, I'd like that, too."

His countenance brightened.

"But." She held up a finger. "I'm far too busy the rest of the week, and after the wedding I desperately need to go to Boston and take care of business. I was supposed to be in Australia this week."

"Oh, so when will you be back again?"

"I don't know; maybe three weeks."

He took a step closer and reached for her hand. "Can we plan on getting together when you return?"

A gentle smile curled her lips. "I'd like that."

The kettle whistled, stopping him from raising her hand to his lips.

☙

That Thursday morning Dena had awakened feeling more centered than she had in years. She liked Wayne and had really enjoyed their time together. They'd surprised themselves by talking till after midnight. A part of her wished she could have spent more time with him the rest of the week, but Chad's wedding had taken up every bit of her free time. Chad had picked up the various pieces of camera equipment from her Boston apartment she needed to photograph the wedding, as well as a suitable dress for the mother of the groom.

After the wedding she'd returned to Boston. By the end of the following week, Dena found herself longing for another date with Wayne. She called her landlord in Maine and asked him what he wanted for the property. Finding it a more-than-fair asking price, she agreed to purchase it. Jason was right; she needed to slow down.

Dena tapped out Wayne's home phone number.

"Hello." Hearing his voice helped soothe her nerves.

"Hi, it's Dena."

"Dena, I'm so glad you called. How are you?"

"Fine, busy. I'm sorry, but I won't be able to get up there for a month."

"Oh."

She could hear his disappointment. "I was wondering if you could do me a favor."

"Sure, what do you need?"

"Well, as you know, Jason wants me to move up there." She curled the phone cord around her finger. "I'm afraid I can't do that just yet, and I'm not sure I'll ever completely be able to move up there, but I did take a positive step. At least, I think it's a positive step."

"You're rambling," he chortled. The lilt of his laughter sent a shiver from behind her ear to the back of her neck.

"Right. Well, I purchased the cottage from Troy."

"I heard."

"Oh, right, small town. Anyway, what I'm thinking is, if I'm going to stay there for any length of time, I'll need a darkroom added to the cottage."

"Sounds reasonable."

"That's where you come in. Can you draw up some plans and give me an estimate?"

"Sure."

"I'm not looking for anything fancy but something functional, and possibly something that would not detract from the charm of the cottage. Is that possible?"

"I can work on it. But I've never put in a darkroom. Don't you need sinks and stuff like that?"

"Yes. I can send you some plans from my darkroom here. That should give you a good idea of the space and things I need."

"Sounds good. Dena, let's be careful we don't develop just a business relationship."

"I know it sounds like I might be trying to create distance between us, but I looked over my summer commitments, and I really can't get out of them without putting several companies in a jam."

"I understand. But—"

"Let's not just talk business," she finished for him.

"Right."

She could picture his handsome smile in her mind. "Oh, I have a gift for you and Jess."

"What?"

"It's a surprise. You'll just have to wait."

Wayne laughed. "Just don't make me wait too long."

"Not too long, I promise. As soon as I can get up there, I'll be there. It's a six-hour drive, so just driving up for one night seems a bit foolish, don't you think?"

"Depends on what you're driving up for."

"Touché." Dena uncurled the cord from her forefinger. "Wayne, is it silly to say I've missed you?"

"No more than for me to admit the same."

Dena thought for the hundredth time, how could their schedules blend? He lived in Maine, she in Boston. Traveling abroad would put a definite strain on any relationship they could develop. "Wayne, how's this going to work?"

"I don't know, Dena. One step at a time, I guess. What if we call one another once or twice a week and just talk?" he suggested.

"I'd like that."

"Dena, I hate to bring this call to a close, but I've got to run. The sheriff just pulled up."

"Sheriff?"

"Yeah, we're trying to figure out who's poaching our lobsters."

"Okay. As soon as I figure out when I can get back, I'll let you know."

"Great. Thanks for calling. Bye."

"Bye." Dena let the phone fall from her fingertips back into its cradle. *I wish I had taken photos of that lobsterman when I saw him. But I didn't know anything was wrong.*

Wayne's brief meeting with the sheriff produced little. If only Dena had photographed the poachers. But "if only" washed out with the tide and meant nothing—merely empty thoughts that produced little except more frustration.

The desire to call Dena and continue their conversation caused him to hesitate by the phone for a moment. Then he remembered her request for an addition on the cottage.

It still boggled his mind that she could just purchase a place at the drop of a hat. Then again, land in the area didn't bring a premium asking price. In some ways, he wanted to ask Pastor Russell about his mother, to learn who she was and how often she traveled. Obviously a photographer made more money than he thought.

Money. He'd have to guard his heart about that. He had struggled for years when Jess was first born. And even today, while he lived comfortably enough, he still supported himself with two jobs. Of course, there was the cost of private college tuition.

Lord, the danger I see is that I could be jealous of Dena's money and her ability to just go anywhere at a moment's notice. Or purchase a house just for an occasional getaway. He continued to pray and worked his way out to his truck.

He picked up a spare key from Troy and went to the cottage to get a closer look. It was a typical summer cottage with little insulation. *If Dena is going to stay here in the winter, she might want something warmer.* He tapped the figures on the yellow legal-size pad of paper with his pencil.

For a few thousand more than the cost of the darkroom addition, he could raise the roof and add a loft for a master bedroom suite with a wonderful view of the ocean. Probably more than a few thousand—more like another ten. It was something he would do if he owned the place. But who knew how long she'd want to keep the property?

Wayne called Pastor Russell. With greetings aside, he asked, "Could you give me your mother's home phone number? I'm at her cottage, and she asked me to do some remodeling."

"Sure, just a minute." Wayne heard some papers rustling. "Area code 617..." As he continued, Wayne scribbled it down on the legal pad.

"Thanks."

"Not a problem. Tell Mom I'll be calling later about Amber."

"Sure." Wayne wondered what was going on with Dena's daughter but figured it wasn't his place to ask.

A few moments later, he tapped out Dena's number and put it in the phone's directory. When her machine answered, Wayne left a message and his cell phone number.

"Lord, I wish she didn't have to work so much." He glanced back up to the rafters. And here he was thinking of suggesting she increase her renovation budget. *Better stick to basics, or I'll never see the woman.*

After a few final measurements, he went back home to an empty house. Jess would be home for a few weeks after graduation, then she was off to begin her career. Working out of Boston. Perhaps he should consider visiting Boston more often.

His cell phone rang. Dena's name appeared on the display. His heart skipped a beat. "Hi," he answered.

"Hi, sorry I missed your call. What's up?"

"I went to your place and have some basic ideas I'd like to bounce off you regarding the location of the darkroom."

"Sure, go ahead."

Wayne outlined three different options.

"Hmm, I kinda like the idea of an additional bedroom. The place is so small. Of course, I didn't buy it for the cottage as much as for the view."

"Yeah, it's a phenomenal view. In fact, I was dreaming and thinking it would be nice to add a second floor and build a master bedroom suite over the darkroom."

"That sounds wonderful. How much would it cost?"

"Off the top of my head, I'd say another ten."

"Hmm. That's sounds really nice. Let's go with it."

Why didn't I keep my mouth shut? She'll be on another trip to pay for this. "It's your dollar."

"Right." She sighed. "I suppose if I took that month-long photo shoot in

Africa, I could afford it."

That was exactly what I wanted to avoid. "Dena, I . . ." He paused.

"Yeah, I know."

"What?"

"That it would be longer between times when we could see one another."

"Exactly. It's strange how easily we can finish each other's sentences, and we barely know one another."

"Strange is an understatement. It's downright scary. Why, after all these years, am I even interested in spending time with a man?"

Wayne chuckled. "My charming personality, of course."

"And humbleness," she quipped.

"Seriously, I should mention that Jess is taking a job in Boston. So I'll probably be traveling down there every now and again."

"Where is she going to live?"

"I don't know. She's hoping she and a group of her friends can find a place together. Personally, I think they should have started looking a few months before graduation, but you know kids."

"Right—they have all the answers."

"And for some odd reason, things work out for them at a moment's notice. I never understood that. Of course, when I was their age, I never did anything foolish."

"Of course not." They laughed in unison. "Seriously, Wayne, if she needs a place to stay for a bit, she's welcome to spend some time in the spare room at my condo."

"That's awfully generous of you. I'll let her know."

"Generous? Don't be too sure. I might be hoping for her to be paid a visit by her handsome father."

"You think I'm handsome?"

Wayne chuckled under his breath as he heard Dena groan. *She hadn't planned on letting that slip out, either,* he mused.

Chapter 7

Four days later, Dena still couldn't believe the words she'd allowed to slip out. Since that call, she'd been arguing with herself—and the Lord—about the wisdom of building a relationship with Wayne.

"But he's a stranger, Lord," she argued once again. Dena tapped the computer keys and pulled up her schedule for the next week. "Where can I steal the time?"

She'd planned a trip to Savannah, Georgia, for a magazine layout that was due by the end of next week. Then the idea hit her. She dialed Wayne's cell phone number.

Dena glanced back at her schedule. "Wayne, are you busy tomorrow morning?"

"Not too; what are you thinking?"

"I'll drive up tonight and we can have breakfast together. I'll have to leave tomorrow afternoon in order to catch an early flight out of Boston."

"That seems like a lot of driving for a breakfast date."

"Ah, but you haven't tasted my lobster omelet."

Wayne chuckled. "Tell you what, I'll bring the lobster."

"I was counting on that." Dena smiled.

"When do you think you'll get here tonight?" he asked.

"Close to ten, I think; sooner if possible."

"Drive safely. I'll put the lobsters and some fresh food in the refrigerator for you."

"Thanks, not too much or it will spoil."

"Gotcha." He paused. "Call me if you get sleepy on the road."

"Thanks. Bye."

"Until tomorrow, bye."

Dena's phone rang as soon as she hung up. "Hello?"

"Dena, hi, it's Jamie."

"Hi, Jamie. How was Australia?"

"Awesome. I can't thank you enough for the opportunity. But I feel I owe you a portion of the contract. That was a pretty healthy paycheck."

Dena knew exactly how much she'd given up, but she had to be there for Chad's wedding. "No problem. Your bailing me out on short notice is payment enough."

"If you're sure."

"I'm sure." Dena scanned down the row of photos on the light box.

"Well, thanks again, and if you need some help again, don't hesitate to call."

Dena thought for a moment. Perhaps she could use Jamie as a subcontractor. "Jamie, maybe we could work out a deal. I've recently purchased property up north, and I want to oversee some renovations."

"Uh-huh."

Dena continued. "What I'm thinking is perhaps you could do some subcontracting for me."

"I'm all ears. What do you have in mind?"

"At this point, I'm just brainstorming. Why don't we schedule a meeting after I return from Savannah?"

"Sounds great. Call me; I'm flexible."

Dena ended her conversation with Jamie and began to dream. *I wonder if I could operate out of Squabbin Bay if I hired several freelancers.*

On the other hand, if I went down to one overseas assignment a month, I could still work my own business without having to balance other people's schedules. Or I could increase my workload in order to make certain my subs have enough work. Of course the danger there is if someone couldn't make it, I'd have to fill in. And do I really want all those headaches?

Dena stretched the kinks out of her neck. She had a six-hour drive ahead of her to think and pray on this. Right now she needed to finish her office work in order to get on the road at a decent hour.

❧

Dena turned the key off. The engine quit. Her body continued to vibrate. She opened the door and took in a refreshing breath of salt air. Grabbing her overnight bag from the front passenger seat, she headed to the kitchen door. Inside, she found Wayne had put a fresh bouquet of brightly colored wildflowers. A note lay on the table.

Hope you had a good trip. There's some fresh fruit in the fridge, and I cooked and cleaned the lobster for you. I'm looking forward to your special omelet and, most importantly, your company.

Your friend,
Wayne

The note glided back down to the table. She went to the refrigerator and checked out the supplies. Fresh strawberries and whipped cream were arranged on a small plate and a simple one-word note lay across the top. *Enjoy.*

Dena pulled out the small platter, reached for a strawberry, and dipped it into the bowl of whipped cream. "Yum," she moaned. "I like your style, Wayne."

❧

The sun rose over the horizon as Wayne left the harbor and headed for the inlet where he kept his pots. The salt air invigorated him. He glanced up at Dena's cottage. The house stood dark, but her car was in the driveway. A smile rose on his face; then he set his mind back on his work. The sooner he got it done, the sooner he'd be able to spend some time with Dena. It still boggled his mind that she was willing to drive six hours one way just to spend a few moments with him.

He pulled up the trap and discovered another empty pot. Oddly, he'd gotten excited when his catch increased the last haul. But today he found the same old pattern, a lobster here and a lobster there. Half were too small, and he had to throw them back.

He dumped the last pot over the side and caught a glimpse of Dena's cottage from the corner of his eye. A warm glow emanated from a single light in the kitchen window. Wayne checked his wristwatch. Seven o'clock. *At least she got some sleep.*

Popping the throttle into gear, he sped back to the harbor. The boat sliced through the waves and made headway through the gentle surf. *Lord, I don't understand this lobstering problem. Why is someone stealing from us small-time guys? The large companies aren't noticing a drop at all. Did Dena actually see the poacher? I'm okay financially, but old Ben Costa and others will be hurting this winter if they don't have a good season. Of course, You know all about that, Lord. But I suspect it doesn't hurt to remind You every now and again.*

Wayne continued his prayers as he docked his boat. Then his prayers shifted toward Dena. *Lord, only You know what's happening between the two of us. Father, I admit I'm attracted to her; it's just that I'd given up on finding someone special in my life years ago. Why now?*

Wayne clapped the mud from his shoes on the exterior of the truck's door frame and climbed into the cab. He headed home to clean up.

Showered and dressed, he smelled like a new man. He grabbed the small gift bag sitting on his counter. Its fancy bow evidenced that he hadn't wrapped the item himself, but he hoped she'd appreciate the small gesture. He hesitated with the bag in midair. *Have I gone overboard, Lord? The fruit, the groceries, the prepared lobster? No, I was simply taking advantage of going to the grocery store for her and picking up some perishable items. It's not my fault that the strawberries were in season.* He paled. *What if she's allergic to strawberries?*

Knock it off, Kearns. If she is, she is. You didn't know, and you simply struck out.

His truck bounced down the various roads as he wove his way toward Dena's cottage. He swerved to avoid a large pothole and turned down the long driveway to Dena's. The ocean came into view as it melded with the rich blue sky. *Lord, I do love this view.*

He shifted his gaze to the back door of the cottage. *On the other hand, I enjoy that one just as much.* He cut the engine and jumped out the driver's door. "Hi."

❧

Dena couldn't believe she'd opened the door before Wayne had even parked the truck. "Hi," she returned his greeting. Her palms began to sweat. She rubbed them on her jeans. "Thanks for the food."

"You're welcome."

He ambled up to her with his left hand behind his back and a great smile on his face. *Lord, he's handsome. Help me keep my feet on the ground.* "Come in." She stepped back and gave him room to pass. She caught a glimpse of something purple, she thought.

He glanced at the small table. She'd arranged it with two simple place settings and crystal stemmed glasses. The cottage didn't offer much in the way of fancy dishes. "I haven't started the omelets yet. I didn't want them to dry out."

"No problem."

"Thanks for the strawberries; they were delicious."

His grin broadened. *It doesn't take much to please this man,* she mused. On the other hand, he'd gone out of his way to create a fine feast. "There's a few left if you'd like some," she offered.

"I'd love them."

Dena went to the refrigerator and pulled out the small tray. Instantly, he reached for one.

"You're not used to waiting so long to eat, are you?"

"Guilty as charged, I'm afraid. I've been up for three hours already."

"I'm so sorry. Let me cook those omelets."

"Dena." He reached for her wrist. The heat of his hand around her wrist radiated up her arm. "I'm fine. I can survive for a while longer."

A rush of longing to be wrapped in his arms coursed through her. *Where'd that come from, Lord?* She stepped back. He released his hold. "I don't mind, and to tell you the truth, I've nibbled on a piece or two of the lobster. There are fresh muffins in the basket under the linen napkin."

"I thought I smelled something good when I walked in—blueberry?"

"Yes, good nose." She turned her back to him and faced the small stove. "So, how was the lobstering this morning?" A pleasant conversation flowed between them as she made their breakfast.

When the omelets were done, she spun around with the hot frying pan. On the table at one of the place settings sat a shimmery purple gift bag with white and lavender tissue paper neatly sticking out. "What's this?"

"Oh, just a little something for you." He winked.

Who is this man? And how does he know the little things that say "special" to me? "I'm not sure what to say."

"Absolutely nothing. It's just something to remind you of Maine while you travel to Savannah. At least I hope you'll take him to Savannah."

She slid the omelets out of the pan and onto their respective plates. "Can I open it now?" She placed the warm pan on the counter.

Wayne grabbed a pot holder and stuck it under the pan. "Sure."

Feeling like a giddy schoolgirl, she reached into the tissue paper and felt something soft, furry. "A stuffed animal."

"You must be horrible at Christmastime."

"Oh, hush." She pulled out the small stuffed animal. "A puffin. He's adorable." The bird was native to Maine; its brightly colored beak made it quite recognizable. Years ago, she'd done a photo shoot on the aquatic bird for a national magazine.

Wayne pulled out his chair and sat down beside her. "I'm glad you like it."

She looked down at her plate. "We'd better eat while it's warm."

Wayne reached for her hand. "Let's pray."

Dena felt a rush of embarrassment warm her cheeks and bowed her head.

"Father," Wayne led, "we thank You for this meal, and we ask Your guidance in our conversation and Your direction for our growing friendship. In Jesus' name, amen."

"Amen." Dena glanced up at Wayne. With each passing moment, she found more and more she liked about this man. The fact that he wanted the Lord to guide their budding relationship was a major plus in her book.

He cut his omelet with his fork and took a large bite. "Mmm," he moaned.

Dena smiled. She knew her own abilities to cook, and cook well, but it brought a certain satisfaction to hear Wayne appreciate it.

"This is wonderful. I've never had an omelet with this kind of sauce before. What is it?"

"Basically, it's a hollandaise sauce like you'd use with eggs Benedict. But I always felt it went well with lobster omelets."

"Well, I've never had it this way, and it's great." Wayne forked another morsel of his omelet.

"Thank you." Dena sampled her own cooking and cherished the wonderful New England flavor of this dish. "Do you have any questions regarding the darkroom plans?"

"Nope," he mumbled with his mouth full. He finished swallowing, wiped his mouth with his napkin, and continued. "I didn't see anything there that didn't make sense. I'm thinking you might want to section off that plumbing from the house, so if you're going to be gone for long periods of time in the winter or won't be using the darkroom, we could drain it so the pipes won't freeze. It will save on the heating bill not to have to heat that area of the house."

"Interesting. Let me mull that over."

"Okay. Oh, I spoke with Jess, and she loves the idea of staying with you while she searches for an apartment in the city."

"Great. It will give us a chance to get to know one another."

Wayne placed his fork on his plate and wiped his mouth once again. "Dena, I love the fact that you've gone out of your way so we can spend some time together but. . ." He paused.

Her heart raced. Had she done the right thing coming up, or had it been a mistake? It felt right at the time. How were they going to develop a relationship if they didn't spend time together?

"What I mean is, I'm flattered. I don't understand what's happening between us, but I don't want it to stop. I don't understand how we can have much of a relationship with you living in Boston and me in Maine but—"

"I know," Dena interrupted. "It doesn't make sense. It's driving me crazy, too. That's why I wanted to come up—to spend some time with you in person. Not on the phone, not about business—just some one-on-one time to get to know each other. Do you have e-mail?"

"Yes."

"Good. We can write while I'm away. Wayne, as you know, I'm going to be on the road most of the summer. My schedule is very full. It's normal, I guess. I'm committed. I can't get out of the various photo shoots. But my schedule isn't nearly so full in the fall."

"Are you always this busy?"

"I guess. I haven't really thought about it. Since the kids have been grown, I've kept busy taking assignments I didn't feel free to take when they were younger."

"I think I understand. I'm pretty busy with the two jobs, but a man has to do what a man has to do. Jess went to college and I needed to pay for it."

"I helped all three of mine get through college. They're all married now. It's amazing how fast children grow."

"Yup. I remember the first day Jess went off to kindergarten. I couldn't concentrate on anything that day. Now she's graduated from college and has a serious boyfriend, who I finally got to meet for all of thirty seconds at her graduation. I don't trust the guy, but Jess keeps saying I need to trust her and her decisions."

"Of course you do. But that doesn't stop you from getting down on your knees and praying for the Lord to remove those blinders on you, or both of you, whatever is the case. Don't tell anyone, but I've been known to make a wrong assumption on my children's behalf every now and again."

Wayne chuckled. "Who hasn't?"

"True."

"Dena, I like you, but can a relationship between us really work?"

Chapter 8

Over the next four weeks, Wayne found himself asking that same question over and over again. Dena had traveled to Savannah and was now across the ocean in Africa somewhere. Each night they exchanged e-mails. Jess had moved into Dena's condo, and he found himself visiting Boston twice in a month. He booted up his computer and set a tall glass of iced tea beside the keyboard. The air was thick with humidity. An evening breeze from the east helped cool the house. Upstairs in his bedroom, he had one small air conditioner that fit inside the window frame. The rest of the house was outfitted with ceiling fans.

The Fourth of July was days away, and the summer heat seemed awfully warm for this time of year. Wayne took a swig of his iced tea, wiped his brow, and clicked on his e-mail. Disappointment filled him as he looked at an empty e-mail box. *Where's Dena's e-mail?*

He rolled his chair back and walked over to the front window that looked out on the small fishing harbor below. He glanced at his watch. Eight thirty, which would put it at one thirty in the morning where Dena was. Either the e-mail got lost in cyberspace, held up in a cyber highway traffic jam, or she hadn't been able to send him one. She did say there would be times when she'd be out of contact.

Turning back to the computer, he marched over to it and sat back down. His fingers froze for a moment over the keyboard. He tapped out a brief message.

> *Hi, I'm assuming you were unable to connect. I trust all is well. I missed not seeing a letter from you tonight. Know that I'm thinking and praying for you.*
> *Love,*
> *Wayne*

He reread what he wrote. He'd never signed an e-mail to her with "love" in it before. His right forefinger stood poised over the DELETE key. Did he love her? Well, in one sense he did. But would she interpret that as romantic love?

He deleted the comma and paused. Gnawing his lower lip, he positioned his finger over another key and retyped his salutation.

> *In Christian Love,*
> *Wayne*

Letting out a slow breath, he thought about that statement. It was true. It was honest. He could send this. *But...* He hesitated.

Somehow, it seemed too formal, too distant. They were becoming good friends. They found they could talk with one another on a variety of subjects.

Wayne hit the DELETE key and removed the salutation. Then he typed another.

> *Love,*
> *Your friend, Wayne*

He rolled his chair back and stared at the computer screen. *Yes, that one fits.* Grabbing the mouse with his right hand, he clicked the SEND icon.

Was he really ready to take this relationship to the next level? In some ways, it had seemed so natural to type "love." He did love her, but there were so many obstacles in their relationship. Her life's work took her around the world. His left him stuck within a thirty-mile radius.

He got up and strode over to the front window and looked at the lights surrounding the harbor. She would be here for a week around the Fourth of July. They could discuss whether to go further with this relationship or stop it before either one of them went too far. He had to be pragmatic about this. He loved Maine. He loved his life. He loved lobstering. How could Dena Russell ever fit into such a small world?

She couldn't, he reasoned.

"Lord, how can we compromise here?"

A stray thought hit him. *Aren't you getting ahead of yourself, old man?*

The phone rang. Wayne shook off his foolish thoughts and answered. "Hello?"

⁂

Dena stretched her stiff body, trying not to disturb her traveling companion on the airplane seat beside her. The plane was making its final approach into Logan airport. The trip to Côte-d'Ivoire had been truncated due to internal uprisings in the government there.

Strangely, she'd been pleased to learn she was going home sooner than anticipated. *The first order of business is a bath.* She'd left the bush in a hurry and had taken the first morning flight out of the country, from Abidjan, finally arriving in Paris. Normally, she would have taken a room there and unwound before returning home. But instead of her normal layover, she took the next flight back to Boston.

Dena swallowed and eased the pressure building up in her ears. She'd learned to bring cough drops to help with the process. They seemed to work better than chewing gum. The plane banked and headed for the one runway at Logan that made those who had never before flown into that airport feel certain the plane was going to crash into Boston Harbor.

She rolled her shoulders. Seven hours from Paris was a long flight, but not as long as some she'd taken over the years. "Home," she muttered. *My own shower and bed in less than an hour.*

The plane's wheels skidded on the tarmac, and the engines roared as they reversed to slow the large jet. Once they were stopped at the gate, a single chime sounded, and the cabin burst into activity. Dena grabbed her two carry-ons, which contained her photography equipment and a change of underwear, should her baggage get lost. She would not allow her cameras, film, and equipment out of her possession. And with all the new scanning equipment since 9/11, no film was safe—which made going digital a huge advantage. However, being in the bush with no electricity for two weeks made digital impractical at the same time.

The convenience of being able to take the T from the airport to her condo had been one of the deciding features when she first purchased the place eight years ago. Although lugging her suitcases through public transit wasn't something she enjoyed doing every day, it was more tolerable than paying the outrageous overnight parking fees at Logan, or any airport for that matter. Being single, living in the city, and having a job that took her out of town more days than not required certain adjustments, she reminded herself as she pulled her overburdened bag up through the doors to the subway car.

The air locks of the sliding doors exhaled, and the transit authority train pulled forward. Living in Maine year-round would present another set of obstacles, she pondered. Dena glanced out at the row of tenement houses that lined the tracks. An image of an early morning sunrise refracting off the water of the Atlantic skimmed through her mind. Maine had its advantages, too.

Dena sighed. *Should I spend more time up there, Lord? I know Jason thinks I ought to slow down, and it would be nice to enjoy the grandchildren more. . . .* Wayne's rugged face and cheerful smile came to mind. *And there's him.*

The train stopped at State Street, where Dena switched from the blue line to the orange line. A few short minutes on the train and she'd be home. *Home. . .my own bed. It sounds so heavenly, Lord.* Dena leaned against a post and closed her eyes.

Thankfully, her apartment was less than half a block from the train station. Dena hiked up the slight hill and pressed the button for the lobby elevator in her building.

Loud music filled the hallway as she exited the elevator. "Great," she mumbled. School was out, and some teens decided it was time to play their music as loud as possible until their parents came home.

Dena fumbled for her keys and walked down the hallway to her apartment. The music grew louder the closer she came to her own place. Slipping her key in the lock, she flung the door open. "What's going on in here?"

"Wayne."

"Dena?" Wayne couldn't believe his ears. "Where are you?"

"Home, in Boston."

"When did you arrive?" He sat down in his overstuffed chair by the bay window and toed off his shoes.

"Thirty minutes ago and, well, I. . ." Her voice wavered.

"What's the matter?"

"I think I blew it with Jess."

"Jess? What's going on?"

Dena went on to explain about her arrival and not being too happy to find the music blaring in her apartment. But that wasn't the worst of it. She'd found Jess and Trev wrapped in each other's arms on the sofa. She'd made it clear when Jess moved in that no men were allowed in the house if there was no one else around. "Needless to say, I blew my stack. Trevor pulled Jess by the hand and stormed out of the apartment. I'm sorry, Wayne. I'm short on sleep and—"

"It's not your fault. Jess knew your requirements. I knew this boy wasn't to be trusted."

"Wayne, they were only kissing. But I'm glad I came in when I did."

"Me, too." *Lord, help me get through to Jess before she makes a mistake she'll regret.* "Thanks for calling. I'll call her cell phone and see if I can reach her. Does she still have a place to stay with you, or do you want her to find a new place?"

"She and I will have to have a heart-to-heart before I can decide that."

"I understand. And, Dena—I'm sorry."

"They're young and in love. Sometimes that combination isn't very conducive to making the right choices."

"Jess knows better."

"I'm sure she does. But what concerns me is, she didn't know I was coming home early."

"Yeah." Wayne closed his eyes and prayed Jess and Trev hadn't allowed their emotions to rule over their brains. Wayne wanted to trust Jess. She insisted on it. But she had to stop making such foolish decisions if he were to completely trust her. "Let me call her."

"Okay. I'll talk with you later."

"Bye, and thanks for calling."

"You're welcome."

He tapped in his daughter's cell phone number and prayed she'd pick up.

"Hi, Dad. Did Mrs. Russell call you?"

Caller ID on cell phones was a blessing, sometimes. "Yes. What's going on, Jess?"

"I'm sorry, Dad. Trev just stopped by for a minute and well. . ."

"And your word no longer means anything?"

"No, I mean, I'm sorry. I'm so sorry, Dad. Trev and I weren't thinking." He could hear the tears in her voice.

"No, you weren't. Is he there with you right now?"

"Yes."

"Put him on, please."

A male voice cleared his throat. "Hello, sir."

Wayne pinched the bridge of his nose. He didn't think of himself as a "sir" at the moment. He just wanted to shake some sense into this kid. "Trevor, I'm not pleased with your actions or Jess's this evening."

"I know, sir. I'm sorry. It won't happen again. I pulled Jess out of the place before that woman kicked her out."

Wayne held back a chuckle. At least the kid was trying to protect his daughter, albeit with a stupid move. "Trev, Jess was wrong to let you into the apartment. She'd given her word. You were wrong for showing up there in the first place. You knew the rules."

"Yes, sir. I'm sorry. It won't happen again."

"Well then, I think you'd better march yourself back to Dena's and apologize to her for abusing her trust. She just returned from twelve hours of travel to come home to—"

Trev coughed. "You're right. We'll go over there. But if she—"

"If she has anything to say, you'll stand there and take it like a man. Do you understand?"

"Yes, sir."

"Good. Let me speak with Jess."

A momentary pause lapsed before Wayne heard his daughter's voice. "Daddy, we didn't—"

"Jess," he interrupted, "you're an adult now. You are responsible for your own actions. I'm trying to trust you, but you've been making some foolish decisions lately when it comes to Trev. If you two are going to develop a mature relationship with the Lord in the middle of it, you're going to need to start making some better decisions."

"You're right. It's just so hard to. . ."

"I know, sweetheart. You need to make this right with Dena. I don't know if she'll let you continue living there, though. That's something you'll have to work out with her."

Jess sniffled. "I understand."

"I told Trevor to take you back to Dena's and face her like a man. My suggestion is for you to do the same. Face the consequences of your actions, Jess. I know it's hard, but in the end it will help you make better choices in the future. Trust me on this one."

"Okay." Jess paused. "Daddy, where do I go if she says I can't stay there?"

Wayne wanted to say, *Come home where you belong*, but knew he couldn't do that. Jess was growing up. She needed to face her problems head-on. "You'll have to deal with that when the time comes."

"All right." She quickly said good-bye and hung up the phone.

Wayne got up from the chair and paced back and forth to the kitchen. Why was it so much easier when she was five? At five he could be her rescuer. Now he had to sit on the sidelines and pray she'd make the right decisions. "Lord, give her strength. Help her make the right choices and not fall into the same mistakes I made with her mother all those years ago. Please don't allow that scripture to be played out in her life that the sins of the father are passed down."

How was it that life moments could bring back life sins? God had forgiven him years ago, and most of the time he forgave himself. But when times like this popped up, he'd reflexively take his past back and worry about his daughter's future. "Why is that, Lord?"

He glanced up at the ceramic lobster clock that hung on his kitchen wall. Jess had made it for him while in the eighth grade. It was painted in blues, greens, and browns—not the typical red everyone associates with lobsters. Instead, she'd chosen to paint an uncooked lobster.

It was nine o'clock. He should be in bed if he was going to get up at four to lobster in the morning. But who could sleep? Would Jess call him back? Would Dena?

Wayne paced some more and fetched another tall glass of iced tea. He took it outside and sat on the front steps. "Lord," he prayed, "how is it that the two women I care most about are so many miles away?"

Chapter 9

The last thing Dena had wanted to deal with last night was a two-hour sit-down with Jess and Trev. Jess was a good kid. Wayne had done a marvelous job raising her, but like most young adults, she and Trevor didn't always think before acting.

Jess wouldn't be making the same mistake again, of that Dena was certain. The evening had almost been a replay of one ten years prior when she found her own daughter, Amber, locked in an embrace with her boyfriend—now husband.

After a relaxing time in the Jacuzzi, Dena managed to fall into peaceful sleep. The next morning she woke and scanned her room before getting out of bed. It doubled as an office. Her room was hardly what a woman would call a retreat, but it was functional.

Wasn't functional what she needed? Her mind drifted back to the rustic cottage in Maine. That was most definitely not functional. The small bedroom barely fit the bed, and the white Cape Cod curtains, fluffy comforter, ruffled pillow shams, and bed skirt added a distinctly feminine touch. The hand-forged iron candleholders she'd purchased from a local blacksmith added to the quaint atmosphere.

Dena scanned her Boston bedroom again. On her dresser were piles of receipts that needed to be filed. Rolls of film cluttered the room. The small desk bulged with paper, film, and prints. *No wonder I like it so much in Maine.* The humor of the situation didn't escape her.

Stretching, she rose from her bed and dressed in a casual pair of jeans and a simple white blouse. She needed some order in her life, and the only way to get it was to spend a massive amount of time organizing her room and separating her business section from her personal section. *A small, folding room divider would do nicely,* she decided.

The first order of the day was breakfast. She hadn't eaten since Paris and she was starved. "Morning," Dena said as she passed Jess in the hallway.

"Dena, I'm sorry again about last night."

"Shh, we've already gone over it. It's forgiven and in the past."

"Thanks." The young girl's face brightened with the electric smile she'd seen at the church fair.

"You're welcome. Now what's for breakfast?"

Jess's eyes widened. "Breakfast?"

"You know, the meal you start the day with."

"Ah, you haven't looked at a clock, have you?"

"No, why?"

Jess chuckled. "It's two o'clock in the afternoon."

"Oh. Well, maybe a brunch would be in order." *No wonder I'm starved.* Dena scoured the cabinets looking for something quick and easy. Somehow, premade soups and meals that just required adding water wouldn't cut it. She reached for her favorite Chinese food menu and called in an order, then went into her room to check her business phone messages.

❧

The doorbell rang for the third time. The first had been her brunch. The second was Trevor looking for Jess. *It's probably Jess*, she figured. *She forgot her key or something.* Dena marched to the door and opened it. "Wayne?"

"Hi. Is Jess here?"

"No, I don't think so. I've been in my room working. What's the matter?"

Wayne handed her a crumpled piece of paper. She opened it and examined it carefully. "A credit card bill?"

"Yup, for a new stereo. Jess didn't need a new stereo, and she certainly didn't have my permission to charge one on my account."

"Oh boy."

"Oh boy, is right. What do you make of this Trevor character?"

Dena opened the door wider and stepped back. "Come in. Make yourself comfortable."

"Jess has always been a levelheaded kid. I don't understand these changes in her behavior. I never would have thought she would disregard your wishes and allow a man in the apartment while you were away. And now this. I don't know what to make of it."

"Love." Dena sat down on the couch beside Wayne.

"What?"

"She's in love and making foolish choices. They both are. Tell me, did she have permission to use your credit card in the past?"

"Of course. I gave her a card for emergencies. Personally, I don't see the purchase of a stereo as an emergency, do you?"

"Of course not, but I'm no longer twenty-two."

Wayne leaned the back of his head against the wall. He let out an exasperated huff. "I thought this parenting stuff got easier once they were grown and out of the house."

Dena chuckled. "One would hope. Actually, a year or two after college, it does ease up some. I still worry about all three of mine. Once you add the grandchildren to the mix—well, it's a never-ending cycle."

"I'm beginning to see that. Somehow, I did expect it to be easier by this point."

Dena patted his shoulder. "It will be."

"So, do you really think those two are in love?"

"Oh yeah. All the classic signs are there. They're so caught up with themselves, they forget what used to be normal for them. I once caught Amber and David in a similar position when I came home from an afternoon at the studio."

"Obviously, you didn't strangle them." Wayne winked.

"Obviously, or I wouldn't have those adorable grandchildren now. Seriously, I was much harder on Amber than I was on Jess. She's a guest in my home. I'm hardly her parent and—"

Wayne held up his hand. "I already gave last night over to the Lord and to whatever decisions you made during your conversation with them."

"We reached an agreement. I think I helped her understand how to not give in to those impulsive responses, but only time will tell." Dena picked up the credit card bill. "This is another matter, though."

"Yeah. It's not that I can't afford the item; it's the principle of not asking and just assuming I'd pay for it."

"Why should you?"

Wayne knitted his eyebrows. His handsome green eyes held her captive for a moment.

Dena cleared her throat and tried to recall her own advice given to Jess last night. *Count to ten, pause, and slowly exhale.* "Don't pay the bill. Well, I mean you should pay it so that your credit isn't messed up, but you should make her pay you back."

"Trust me, she's going to pay for this purchase and any others."

Dena got up and walked across the room to the slider that opened to a very small terrace overlooking the Charles River. She heard his footfalls on the carpet following behind her.

"Dena," Wayne whispered, placing his hands on her shoulders, "I've missed you."

She turned and faced him. She reached up and glided a lock of his hair back into place. "I've missed you, too."

His fingers caressed the back of her neck. He lowered his head slowly. Dena closed her eyes. She wanted his kiss. She needed his kiss.

Somewhere in the back of her mind she heard something. She should pay attention to it—

"Daddy! What are you doing here?"

❧

Accepting a dinner invitation from Dena seemed the logical way to calm down after Jess admitted to having spent the money and didn't see what the big deal was about. Trevor needed a stereo, so she bought it. It was that simple. Well, not in his book. Since when did women start buying expensive gifts for their boyfriends? Weren't men supposed to do that? Had he been out of the dating game so long that the rules had changed?

"Earth to Wayne." Dena's voice broke through his muddled thoughts.

"I don't get it. I don't see what she sees in that boy."

Dena lifted the fork to her mouth and paused. "He's not that bad of a kid. He didn't ask for the stereo. It was just something Jess wanted to give him."

"I suppose. But still."

An edge of a smile rose. "You've got to face it; Jess made the mistake all on her own. Last night it was the two of them."

"True. But I don't like it any better. In fact, I think it bothers me more. At least if I thought she was being manipulated by the kid, it would make some sense."

"Perhaps, but you'd have another set of worries on your hand."

"True." He reached across the table and took her silky hand into his. "I'm sorry she barged in on us."

"She's a good kid, Wayne. She'll get through this period of adjustment."

He caressed the top of her hand with his thumb. "You avoided my comment."

"Which one?"

Most of the evening, she had skirted around the subject of their near kiss. "I want to kiss you."

"Not here," her voice squealed in a whisper.

"No, not here, but soon. I'm just putting you on notice." He winked.

She squirmed in her chair. "Excuse me." She placed the linen napkin down on the table beside her half-eaten dinner. "I need to visit the ladies' room."

That was smart, Kearns. What are you going to do for an encore? You know the lady is cautious.

Wayne drummed the table with his fingers. When she returned, he started to stand. She motioned for him to sit down and sat in the chair beside him.

"Wayne, I have to be totally honest with you." Her voice was so low he could barely make out the words. "I want to kiss you, too, but I'm terrified. Our relationship, as limited as it is, has awakened emotions in me that I thought were long dead. And they've come back with a vengeance. I need time to control these desires before we engage in anything more than holding hands. I know this sounds foolish but—"

"Shh." He started to place his finger upon her lips but then thought better of it. "I understand, and I can be patient. Please keep being honest with me, and I'll be praying for you. You can pray along the same lines for me, as well."

"It's a deal." She grinned and slipped back into her original seat.

"So, now that we've decided what we can't do in our relationship, why don't we discuss your next trip to Maine? When will you be able to come up?"

"Obviously, I have a week I hadn't planned on. But what's the shape of my cottage? Can I stay there while the remodeling is going on?"

Wayne eased back in his chair. "The progress is good, but you'll need to vacuum and dust real well before you stay there. I hooked up a plastic wall that has kept most of the sawdust from invading your living area. Although, come to think of it, you'll have to change your clothes in the kitchen. The plastic wall is clear, and with the bathroom and master bedroom walls removed, you—"

She held up her hand and crimson stained her cheeks. "I'll figure something out. I can shower at Jason's."

"I could find some black polyethylene. It would give you some privacy, but the black would absorb the heat and could make the house unbearable during the midday hours."

"No, don't bother, I'll work something out. Actually, I realized this morning that I have a lot of organizing I need to catch up on. My room is in organized chaos, if you can imagine."

"Actually, I can't. Your cottage is so neat, and from what I can see in your Boston condo, it's the same way."

Dena chuckled. "You haven't seen my bedroom." Again her cheeks broke out into the shade of a dark pink rose.

"I'll take your word for it, but I find it hard to believe."

She laid her fork down on the table. "What I'm realizing is that I didn't make space for me. My bedroom doubles as my office. Since I gave up the studio and have been doing strictly freelance, my condo is also my workplace. I think that's what Jason has been trying to say—that my life revolved more around my work than around me, my family, and my relationship with the Lord. In Maine, my place has some nice feminine touches. Here, it's an office with a bed in it."

"Hmm." Wayne sat back. "I guess my dining room is my office. But my bedroom is simply a place to sleep. I've never thought of it in terms of a place to retreat."

"The rest of the house is always open for guests. But the bedroom, well, that's private, a place of solace. When Bill was alive, he and I often would retreat to the bedroom as our private place to just talk and unwind. After he died, the bedroom was my place to cry out to God in private. The kids were always welcome to come in, but, I don't know, it was where I did my devotionals, prayed my heart out, and tried to maintain some sort of sanity while raising three kids without a husband. Now my bedroom is, like I said before, an office with a bed in it. Nothing special."

Wayne nodded. He hadn't thought of his room as his private prayer closet to the Lord. It had been, but he hadn't thought of it in those terms before. "Interesting point."

Wayne's mind drifted back to more pressing matters. "What am I going to do with Jess?"

Dena reached over and squeezed his hand. He knew she understood. "Pray like crazy and trust God."

Dena hadn't planned on another late night with Jess. But Jess needed an older woman to talk to.

Dena needed more time to grapple with her reemerging desires. Her body was waking up to things she'd once known and had long put to sleep with God's grace. Now she needed God's grace to get her through these early temptations and desires.

She walked over to her desk and sat down. Picking up a file folder, she began to sort and place items in their proper locations. If she couldn't sleep, at least she could get some work done.

"Ugh." She plopped the folder back down on her desk. This was exactly the problem—having her office in her bedroom. She went back to her bed, snuggled under the covers, and opened her Bible. Perhaps she'd find some relief in its words.

The next morning she found herself packing up the car and half of her paperwork. She was going to Maine, walls or no walls. She needed to spend time with Wayne and the building plans anyway, she reasoned.

Seven hours later, she drove up to her cottage and found Wayne loading his truck. "Hi. I thought you weren't going to come up."

"I thought so, too." Dena shut the car door.

"What's up?"

"You, me, these silly desires."

"They aren't silly."

"Okay, I'll give you that. But something has to be done about them. I can't live like this. And I figure the only way is to spend time with you and get over these initial—whatever these emotions are called. I can't have them. They're destroying my concentration."

Wayne smiled and walked up to her. He locked her in an embrace that kept their bodies from touching completely, but close enough that she felt comfort in his arms. "I'm all for us spending more time together, but I'm not sure that's the answer."

"Are you imply—"

He cut her off. "They could get worse, more intense. On the other hand, we're two very mature adults and should be able to deal with them."

Dena took in a long, slow breath. "I hope so. My only other option is to never see you again."

He tenderly kissed the top of her head. "We can't have that. Come here." He led her by the hand to the tailgate of his truck and sat down beside her. He grasped her hands and started to pray. "Lord, You know our desires. You created them. Please give us the grace and strength to deal with them and rest peacefully in You. Amen."

"Amen. And thanks. We need to pray together more often."

"My pleasure. So, should I come back in a little while and bring some takeout?"

Dena smiled. "That would be wonderful. But how'd you like to strain those muscles of yours for a bit longer and help me lug this stuff in?" She popped the trunk open.

"Is this your entire office?"

"Nope, just half of what needs to be filed." She rummaged through the files and took out a large envelope. "I've been meaning to give these to you for a long time."

"What are they?"

"Open the envelope and see."

Wayne unfastened the metal clip then pulled out three large prints. "Oh, man. Dena, these are beautiful."

"I'm glad you like them. I figured with your recent concerns for Jess, they might give you a little comfort." She loved the pictures of Wayne and Jess together. Their love for one another was electric. Could her love for Wayne be just as powerful, if not more?

Chapter 10

Wayne wiped the sweat from his brow. The supports and frame of the addition were up. Today he was trying to box in with plywood the areas he could in order to give Dena some privacy.

He turned at the sound of a car driving up to the cottage. Pastor Russell and family were in tow. In a matter of seconds, the two children bounced out of the car and ran to the house calling out, "Grandma!"

Pastor Russell, dressed in jeans and a T-shirt, came over to him. "Hi, Wayne. Need a hand?"

Normally he wouldn't take a pastor up on such an offer, but for the sake of the pastor's mother's privacy, it made sense. "Sure, I'm trying to—"

The pastor held up his hand and cut him off. "I know; Mom called. I'll be right back." Wayne watched as the pastor lifted a cooler from his trunk and handed it to his wife. Then he pulled a hammer out of the trunk and came right over.

"Tell me where to begin."

Wayne decided the best way to go was to set the boards in place with a couple tack nails and let Pastor Russell follow behind and secure each board. The men worked until lunch, and Wayne was pleased with what they'd accomplished.

"So this is where her darkroom will be?" Pastor Russell asked.

"Yup, and on the other side of this wall"—he pointed to an empty area—"she'll have her Jacuzzi."

Pastor Russell smiled. "I won't mind coming over to use that from time to time."

"Only if you promise to look after the place," Dena teased.

"Slave driver," the pastor teased right back.

"Leech," she said and winked.

"Why do you think I wanted you to move up here?"

Marie, Pastor Russell's wife, slapped him on the arm. "You're horrible."

Pastor Russell rubbed his arm. "She started it."

Marie rolled her eyes and Dena laughed. Wayne held back his own smirk. Then Dena's gaze fell upon his. "You should see us when all three of my children are here."

"Brace yourself," Marie warned.

"It is interesting seeing the pastor in a different light."

"Call me Jason, please."

Wayne nodded. He didn't think he could call his pastor by his first name. It seemed disrespectful, somehow.

Dena wrapped her arm around his, and her love filled him. It was a bold move for Dena to make in front of her son. It meant she was serious about developing their relationship. This warmed his heart even more.

"Come on, let's go eat before the kids polish off all the food." Dena tugged on his arm, encouraging him to follow her back inside the main part of the cottage.

Wayne washed up at the kitchen sink while the pastor washed up in the bathroom. Pastor Russell came out drying off his hands. "No wonder you wanted Wayne to have some help, Mom."

Dena blushed.

Marie cleared off the kids' dishes, and Billy eased over to his grandmother's side. "Grandma, Susie and I wanna have a sleepover. We wanna see the stars through the wall."

Dena chuckled. "Hmm, I might be able to arrange that. You'd have to ask your mom and dad, though."

"Please," the two children pleaded.

Pastor Russell cleared his throat. The children immediately silenced. "Seems to me your mother asked you to clean your rooms this morning before we left," he said in a stern voice.

Billy and Susie looked at each other. "We did."

"Did you have dinner plans with Wayne, Mom?"

The two children spun their heads back and forth between Wayne and Dena. Dena glanced over to him. As much as he would like another evening alone with Dena, grandchildren were a part of her life, also. "We could take them out for pizza."

"Pizza? All right!" yelped Billy.

Dena winked and mouthed a thank-you. "Sounds like I have some house-guests for the night."

"Yippee!"

Marie chuckled. "Go outside and play for a while," she encouraged the children. When they were gone, she turned to Dena. "Are you sure, Mom?"

"Of course. I don't get to spend much time with them."

"Well, I'll take them home for a couple of hours this afternoon and have them pack their stuff. That should give you a little break."

"Thanks, Mom. The kids will have a blast." Jason winked.

Dena laughed. "I'm sure they will. I'll be exhausted, but they'll do just fine."

The rest of the lunch was spent with some light banter and discussion about the renovations Wayne was making to the house. Then it was back to work. Pastor Russell stayed for another couple of hours and left with his family.

Shortly after they left, Dena came to see Wayne in the new addition. "How's it going?"

"Fine. Your son helped a lot. You should have some real privacy."

"Thanks." She stepped closer. "Thanks also about the children."

"Not a problem. They're good kids."

Dena chuckled. "Sometimes."

She reached up and brushed some sawdust from his cheek. "You're quite handsome."

Shocked for a moment, he faltered with his response. "I think you're rather beautiful yourself. But if we keep talking along these lines, I'm going to kiss you."

Dena's eyes widened and she stepped back. "You're right. I'm sorry."

Wayne reached out and grasped her hand. "It's all right. Remember, we agreed we need to be honest with each other."

Dena looked down at the floor and nodded.

He curled his forefinger and lifted her chin. With every ounce of his being, he wanted to kiss her pale pink lips. But with everything that he stood for, he would not yield to that temptation. "Honey," he whispered. Her eyes sparkled with unshed tears. "Come here." He pulled her into himself and embraced her. "What's the matter?"

❧

Dena closed her eyes and relished his embrace. She felt secure in his arms. Oh, how she ached to be in this special place. For years she'd had no one to hold her except the Lord. And He had gotten her through some difficult moments. But, physically, she couldn't deny the desire to have this closeness with a man once again. How was it possible after all these years that she could find herself in this place? She wiped her eyes. "I'm sorry. I saw you standing there, with— well, we won't go there. Let's just say out of instinct, I wanted to kiss you, too. I don't mean to be cruel."

"Dena, I didn't find it cruel. I found it flattering, and, if I remember correctly, we mutually agreed not to go into a physical relationship at this point in time. That means I'm counting on you to hold me accountable, as I hope you'll allow me to remind you."

"You're right. Why is this so hard for me?"

Wayne leaned back against a sawhorse and crossed his feet at the ankles. "Because we've been there before, and, unlike most people today, we've kept ourselves from others for a long time."

Dena walked over to the hole that would one day be a window in her new bedroom and scanned the ocean. "You're right. And I want to kiss you. I'm just afraid."

"Like we agreed the other night, it's too soon. We can wait. And, Dena, you're worth the wait."

She turned to him and smiled. "You're a special man, Wayne. I love that about you."

"And you're a special woman, and I definitely love that about you. But we have even bigger problems than our attraction."

"What?"

"Our careers. Where we make our homes doesn't mesh very well."

"True. But the length of time between visits might help us."

"Perhaps. Sometimes I wonder if it isn't part of the problem. We don't see each other for a month and then—bam—we're together, and, well, the attraction is intense."

Dena took in a deep breath and eased it out slowly, then faced the ocean again. "You might be right, there. You know I'm leaving for another two weeks. Then I return for a day and fly right out again for another two weeks."

"Yeah, I know." He stood up straight and dusted off his backside from the sawhorse. "I guess I'd rather see you more often. But let's just say we get married one day. I don't mind telling you, I wouldn't want a wife who was only home one day a month."

"Ouch."

"Therein lies our real problem. Goodness knows, I'm attracted to you and even love many of the things about you, but I'm not sure where this relationship will end up. I keep questioning myself and God as to whether it's even wise to get this involved with each other."

"Double ouch."

"Sorry."

Dena gave him a halfhearted smile. "I've had some similar discussions with the Lord. As I said, I'm fighting my head, my heart, and my body when it comes to our relationship. I'm as clueless as you."

"Where's that leave us?" Wayne walked up beside her and leaned out the window frame.

"Adrift on the ocean of love," she chimed.

"Oh, that's bad, really bad." Wayne laughed. "Seriously, should we stop this now?"

"Do you want to stop?"

"Not really. I'm hoping for a miracle, that maybe the Lord has something in mind that neither one of us is aware of at the moment. It seems odd that He'd put us together just to be friends, doesn't it?"

"Yeah, I don't feel this way toward my other male friends."

"Well, that's a relief." Wayne chuckled. "So, where are you going on these next two trips?"

"The Everglades, and then I'll be rafting down the Colorado River for a travel brochure. I get to feel the real adventure and travel with a team."

"Wow, I'd love to do something like that someday."

"Then, why don't you?"

"Work kinda keeps me busy."

"Year-round?"

"Well, yes and no. The income potential isn't all that high in this area, so one has to be frugal, and some of those adventure vacations can be pretty pricey. I have, however, gone white-water rafting here in Maine."

"Really?"

"Yup. But I generally go on a day run. Something I can drive up to and have someone drop my truck at the ending point."

"Do you use a canoe or kayak?"

"Canoe. I've thought about taking a longer trip and camping along the river, but I've worked hard for Jess to have a good college education. That doesn't leave much in the way of extra cash to play around with."

"Wayne." Dena placed her hand on his forearm. "You've given her that and so much more. You're a good father."

He placed his hand on hers. "Thanks, that means a lot."

Their gazes locked. Dena wanted to kiss him, wrap her arms around him, and pull him close. She blinked and stepped back. "Well, I better go prepare the house for the invasion of the grandchildren."

Wayne gave a halfhearted chuckle. "You're on your own after pizza."

"Chicken."

"Bock, ba-ba-bock," he crowed.

❧

Dena kissed Billy and Susie good night.

"Grandma?"

"Yes, Susie." Dena trailed her hands over the soft cotton comforter.

"Do you like Mr. Wayne?"

Oh boy. "Yes, honey. I think he's a nice man."

"I like him, too."

"Mommy said you might marry him," Billy chimed in.

Oh dear. "Well, I don't know if that's going to happen or not. We'll just have to wait and see, okay?"

"Okay." Billy nodded his head.

Dena straightened and stepped away from Susie's bed. "Grandma?"

"Yes, Susie."

"Would we call him Grandpa if you got married?"

Good grief. How do little ones come up with these things? "Honey, it's too soon to talk about such things. I like Mr. Wayne and—" *Goodness, how do you explain this to a five-year-old?* "We'll just have to see." She rubbed Susie's headful of blond curls.

"Okay."

That was easy, Dena mused.

She exited her bedroom, which the kids insisted on sleeping in because of there being no wall. She walked out to the deck and sat down, watching the starlight shimmer over the dark ocean.

Was it wrong to pursue a relationship in which you didn't know the outcome before you entered into it? Of course, who knows when they are going to fall in love with someone? Was she in love with Wayne? Was it worth possibly confusing the children, if she and Wayne couldn't work out their problems with career and locations? Perhaps it was best to end things with him now before she loved him too much.

Too much. . . That means I already love him. Dena groaned.

❧

Wayne delayed his arrival at Dena's, doing odd jobs that could have waited. He needed more time. He hadn't slept a wink last night. Instead, all he could think about was the impossibility of their relationship. He wanted to do more than kiss her. He wanted to make her his wife. He knew it was foolish to desire something so much, so quickly, while getting to know one another. After all, love at first sight was for teens, not two grown adults with mileage. But he had found love, and he'd fallen hard. He knew he loved her, but he also knew his family and life were in this community. He'd never survive in a city. Being on the ocean every morning brought life to his veins. Oh, he knew how silly and trite that sounded, but it was a part of who he was, of that he was certain.

He'd seen her on the beach with her grandchildren while he pulled his pots. *Empty pots*, he amended. She waved. He waved back, but instead of feeling the joy that had been there a month before, his mind swam with confusion.

"Hi," she offered when he arrived at her back door.

"You're making this difficult." He placed his hands in his pockets.

She handed him a mug of hot coffee. "You didn't sleep either, huh?"

"Nope. It isn't working, is it?"

"Not really. There's attraction, and I like you, but you're right. There are more difficulties to our relationship than either one of us is ready to deal with at the moment. I can't give up my career, and you can't give up yours."

"Exactly. So why does it feel like I've been hit in the gut with a four-by-four?"

"Because we do care about each other."

"Dena, I wish I could just close up shop and be with you, but that's not who I am. I live off the sea. I'm a part of a community. There are people who depend on me. I know that others can fill that void but—"

"But you're not ready to give that up, and that's what it would take if you were to be a part of my world. I know, I know. I played the scenario over and over in my mind tons of times last night, too."

"This stinks."

"Yeah," she agreed.

"So where does that leave us?" Wayne asked. He watched her move silently to the coffeepot and refill her mug.

"As friends?"

"Okay." Wayne extended his hand to shake on the matter.

She turned away. "I can't. I'm sorry."

Wayne placed the mug on her table. With every ounce of willpower, he opened the back door. "I understand."

❧

As he worked through the day, he watched her pack her car. He didn't blame her. He'd probably do the same in her shoes. Besides, she had to get ready for her next trip.

"Wayne, e-mail me any questions you have about the addition. I'll be out of contact for a couple of days, but I should be able to connect every now and again. The first week out on the river, I'll be out of contact completely. The Rockies greatly interfere with cell phone service."

"No problem. I think I have everything under control."

"I'm sure you do. I'm sorry, Wayne. I would have liked to work this out."

"Me, too. But I think it's better now before we're in too deep."

"Agreed. Good-bye, and thanks for all the work you're doing on the place."

Wayne waved her off and attempted to swallow the huge lump in his throat.

❧

The next month Wayne found himself miserable. The night before she left, they had been ready to trust the Lord; the next morning, they broke it off because they couldn't see it working. *Quite a man of faith,* he chastised himself.

He even stopped going to church for the month. He couldn't face Dena's son. And seeing him pull into his driveway right now made him want to pretend not to be home. "May I come in?" Pastor Russell asked.

"Sure, come on in."

"Wayne, Mom told me what the two of you decided. Personally, I can't argue with the logic but—"

Wayne gave him a halfhearted grin. "But I should still be in church, I know."

Pastor Russell sat down on the stool by the breakfast nook. "Actually, that isn't what I was going to say, but you're right, you should be in church. I understand your hesitation in light of my connection with my mother, but your spiritual home is in that church."

"What did you want to say, then?"

Chapter 11

Dena stubbed her toe on the corner of a suitcase as she lugged them from the train station. The past two shoots had been the worst of her entire life. And the last thing she wanted to do was face Wayne's daughter in her apartment. She hoped Jess was out on a date with Trevor, a movie—anywhere but in her apartment.

She knew she'd been trying to live her own life and not listen to the many urges from the Lord to call Wayne and just talk with him. But if they were to only be friends, she didn't need to call him. After all, she barely called her other friends when she was on a shoot, she reasoned for the millionth time since leaving Maine. So why did she ache to see him? To be held in his arms? Why hadn't those feelings disappeared by now? It had been a month. No one pines that long for a man they haven't even kissed.

Dena pushed the elevator button for her floor. When the doors opened, she paused for a moment to hear if music was again blaring from her apartment. A slight smile rose on her cheeks when she heard nothing, absolutely nothing. Just the way she liked it. Maybe she just needed to stay home for a few more days and unwind. Maybe rafting down the Colorado wasn't the ideal place to relax. Right—and elephants are purple with pink polka dots. *Face it, Dena, you love him, you miss him, and life is miserable without him.*

She unlocked the door to her apartment. The air smelled stale.

She dumped her luggage on the living room floor and found a note from Jess with her keys.

> *Dear Dena,*
>
> *Thanks for the use of the place. I didn't get the job I wanted in Boston, so I moved back home. Dad says to call him when you return. Something about the addition. Thanks again for everything, especially our talks. They really helped.*
>
> *Love,*
> *Jessica*

Dena picked up the phone and punched in the speed dial code for Wayne. She hadn't bothered to undo that feature. His answering machine picked up.

"Hi, Wayne. I got Jess's note. I'm home. Give me a call when you can. Bye."

She hung up the phone, and within seconds it rang. "Hello."

"Hey, Mom, just get in?"

Dena never thought she'd be so disappointed to hear Chad's voice. "Hey back. Yes, I literally just got in. Where are you?"

"Hawaii."

"Rough life." Dena leaned against the counter.

"Yeah. But I can't complain. Weren't you on the Colorado River yesterday?"

"Touché. What's up?"

"Brianne's pregnant and not doing so well. I was wondering if you could take her over some chicken soup."

"Hold it. Brianne's pregnant?"

"Yeah, we would have told you sooner, but you've been hard to get ahold of the past couple weeks."

"True. So when's the baby due?"

"Mid-March."

"Congratulations, son." Dena toed off her shoes.

"Thanks. Seriously, Mom, she's really sick. I'm concerned."

"I'll run over after I take a shower. I'll pick up some of Mr. Wong's chicken soup. I don't have time to make my own. But I doubt she'll want to eat it, if she's as sick as you say."

"I know it's normal to be sick but—"

"It's your first; you'll get used to it." Dena paused. "Kinda."

"Thanks, Mom. I really appreciate it. I'm glad you're home."

"You're welcome."

"Well, I've got to go. I need to prepare my flight for departure to Japan."

"Bye; thanks for calling." Dena hung up the phone and stripped on her way to the shower. Another grandchild. She grinned. Her quiver was getting fuller.

The phone rang again as she stepped out of the shower. Wrapping herself in a towel, she answered.

"Hi, Mom."

"Amber, what's up?"

"Did you hear Chad's news?"

"Yes, and you're horrible to even mention it, if I hadn't. I'm going to Brianne's now and take her some chicken soup." Dena fished out some clean clothes from her dresser drawers.

"I doubt she'll get it down. She's really sick, Mom." This was a strong statement, coming from Amber, a doctor's assistant.

"Hmm, coming from you, I'd say it's more than the norm."

"Definitely. The poor girl can barely get up without getting nauseous."

"Eww. Did her doctor prescribe anything?"

"Not yet, but she called him this morning."

"Good. How are the kids?"

"Fine, anxious to see Grandma. Will you be able to come up?"

"I don't know, sweetheart. I'll try. I'm off again in three days."

"Mommm." Amber dragged out her name. "You can't keep working like this. It's crazy."

"I know. I'm cutting back, honest."

"Yeah, right."

She couldn't blame Amber for not believing her. For years the kids had been trying to get her to slow down, yet it seemed she was busier than ever. More assignments were coming in. She was regularly booked months in advance. Thankfully, she still had one month blocked out. "I have September off."

"Really? Can we come to your house in Maine for a visit? I'm assuming you'll be up there."

"Some of the time. The rest of the time I'll be in Boston."

"Great, well I won't keep you on the phone. I know you've got a ton to do. Not to mention that Brianne needs some TLC."

"Okay, I'll call you sometime tomorrow and touch base with you."

"Looking forward to it. Bye, Mom."

Dena hung up the phone. "They must smell that I'm home." She glanced over to her answering machine and saw there were fifteen messages. They could wait until she returned from Brianne's. Amber had been really sick during her pregnancies, and for her to say Brianne was really sick meant the poor girl was suffering.

Dena was dressed and in her car within twenty minutes. She placed an order for a quart of Mr. Wong's chicken noodle soup and picked it up on her way over to Brianne and Chad's apartment. Finding Brianne pale and weak, lying in her bed, tugged at her heartstrings. *Have I made myself too inaccessible?*

She spent the night at Brianne's and took her to the doctor the next morning. It was the least she could do.

Driving home after settling Brianne back into her own place, she again prayed for guidance. Her cell phone rang just as she entered the car garage at home. "Hello."

"Hi, Dena, it's Wayne. I tried to get you last evening at your home and finally decided to try your cell phone today."

"I'm sorry, Wayne. Brianne's pregnant and very ill. I was playing nursemaid for the evening. I got your message to call. What's up?"

"Zoning."

"Zoning?" Dena closed the car door with her hip.

"Yeah, they're afraid you'll be dumping dangerous chemicals too close to the ocean, so they've halted the addition until you can prove the chemicals you use in film developing aren't a hazard to the community—most importantly, to the lobster industry."

"Ah, well, I don't have that information handy. Let me talk with a few friends and get back to you on it."

"No problem. Sorry for the delay."

There was a pregnant pause between them. Leaning up against the garage wall, afraid to break the connection of the cell phone by entering the elevator, Dena asked, "How's Jess?"

"She's fine, but a little depressed that things didn't come together in Boston. But even more depressed that Trevor hasn't moved to Maine."

I can imagine. She held back the words of her heart. "Are there any other opportunities for her down here? She's more than welcome to stay at my place and continue her search."

"I'll let her know. Truthfully, I'm a wee bit concerned. A month ago she was making foolish decisions because of her overconfidence. Now she's not making any decisions."

"You got your baby back, but it's not the same, is it?"

"Nope, and I don't know why."

"Because she's changed. You've changed. You need to keep encouraging her to go out and face the world."

"Yeah, but it's. . ." He cut himself off.

"It's nice to watch over her once again. I know. Been there, done that. Hardest thing is to push them back out of the nest. Even if you don't have her leave the house, you at least have to get her out there in Squabbin Bay and working for a living."

"I know you're right. And she and I had that very same talk a couple of days ago. I still don't like it."

Dena chuckled. "Who does?"

❧

It had felt good talking with Dena about Jess once again. But as he hauled another empty pot out of the ocean this morning, his frustration grew. He'd never known a season as bad as this. And he couldn't understand why the poachers hadn't been caught yet.

He threw off his work gloves and grabbed his cell phone from the little cubby on the dash that kept it dry while he was on the ocean and looked at the reception. *Two bars; not too bad.* He dialed Dena's number.

"Hi, Dena, it's me, Wayne. I was wondering. . .could I hire you?"

"Wayne?" She yawned. "What?"

He went on to explain his idea of hiring her to stake out the bank by her cottage and photograph any and all fishermen pulling pots, specifically his pots.

"I'm willing to try."

"At least I'll have the evidence to prove my point to the Coast Guard. It's hard to believe the sheriff hasn't caught anyone yet. Everyone knows it has to be thieves. I've tried altering my times, and still I'm not catching much of anything." He placed one glove back on his left hand. "When can you come up?"

He heard some tapping as if a pen was being spun back and forth in her hand. "I guess I could come up late tonight. Chad will be home, so Brianne won't be alone."

"Brianne?" he asked.

"She's pregnant and very sick."

"Oh right, you mentioned that. Look, I hate to cut this short, but I'm on my cell. Leave a message and let me know when you can come and do the stakeout."

"You make it sound so cops-and-robberish."

"Well, it is. I need your help, Dena. You're the only person I know who has the telephoto equipment and wouldn't look conspicuous using it, especially from your own property."

"True. Okay, I'll get back with you. I just want to make certain Brianne's okay."

"No problem. I understand, and thanks. I really appreciate this. By the way, how much do you charge?"

Dena laughed. "We'll barter on it. I have some new ideas I'd like to explore with the addition."

"Hmm. I'd better end this conversation quickly before it costs me even more. Bye, Dena, and thanks."

"You're welcome. Bye."

He closed his cell phone and glanced up at her cottage. The addition stood out like a sore thumb, but in the end it would blend well with the original structure, especially after they stained and painted the exterior.

He scanned the ocean for any traces of the poachers. A distant roar of an engine caught his senses. *Should I?* He set the boat in motion and headed in the general direction of the remote sound. He knew most of the lobstermen in the area. Surely he'd be able to recognize someone out of place. On the other hand, what would he do if he caught someone?

Wayne eased the throttle lever back. *This is foolishness.* He turned back toward the harbor and prayed once again that justice would be found for those who were victims of these thieves and that the thieves would be caught. *Soon,* he emphasized.

❧

Later on that evening, he fought the desire to purchase some perishable items for Dena's refrigerator. She had family in the area, and they could help or she could purchase her own. They had to learn to be just friends. *Isn't that what Pastor Russell had been preaching when he came calling?* Wayne tried to remember details of their conversation. He'd been right that Wayne had been skipping church because Dena's son was the pastor. And as much as he enjoyed Pastor Russell, he couldn't help but be reminded of Dena and what they could have had together if their schedules and lives would have allowed it.

He straightened up and locked the addition. The cabinets and sinks had been placed in the darkroom. All the fixtures were now in place in the master bath, which included her Jacuzzi. Brushing off the sawdust from his trousers, he opened the truck's door. His cell phone rang.

"Hi, Dad, it's me."

"Hi, Jess. What's up?"

"I just got a call from Dena. She said she's on her way and will be able to help you out tomorrow morning."

"Great, thanks."

There was a long pause. "Dad?"

"Hmm?"

"What are you two doing tomorrow?"

The fewer who knew the better. He didn't want Dena to feel any pressure in case these thieves were better organized than he suspected. "There're some things on her addition we need to go over." This was true, but hardly the reason she was coming to town.

"Daaaad!" Jess whined. "Are you two getting back together? You should, you know. You've been pretty near unbearable. What's the big deal? She has a career and so do you. Don't tons of couples work those things out?"

"Jessica Elizabeth, this is not your concern. Besides, we aren't getting back together, as you put it. We're simply working together on business matters."

"Whatever. Look, Dad, smell the coffee. You like her. You're miserable without her. So figure something out."

Wayne squeezed his eyes shut. His relationship with Dena was far more complicated than Jess understood, and he wasn't about to be lectured on the intricacies of love by his daughter. "Jess," he said, in that tone only she would understand the true meaning of.

"Oh, all right. But please stop moping around like you've lost your best friend."

She is my best friend, isn't she, Lord? "Fine." Changing the subject, he asked, "So, did you find a job?"

"No, but Trev is coming up this weekend."

"Did you look?"

"Yes, but I'm being particular. I don't want to just waitress after four years of college."

He couldn't blame her. "Okay, but soon you'll need some income to hold you over until the right job comes along."

"I know, Daddy, and I plan on working any job if I have to."

"Great. Well, hopefully you won't have to. I'll see you later."

"Actually, I'm going out with Marsha and Randi. We're traveling up to Bangor tonight. I'm going to look through some business directories for possible jobs to apply for."

"That's my girl. Okay, have fun. Talk with you later."

"Bye, Dad. Oh, I forgot. Can I borrow forty bucks for dinner and the search?"

"Sure, you know where I keep the cash."

"Thanks. Bye, Daddy." He could hear the skipping up and down for joy in her voice.

Wayne wagged his head. He was so easy.

*

Dena slapped the alarm. Four a.m. She pushed herself up off the bed and groaned as her body protested this early morning wake-up call. But she'd promised Wayne she'd be on the lookout. Dressing quickly, she grabbed her digital camera with the largest zoom lens she had from the kitchen table where she had set it up last night and walked in darkness to the edge of the cliff. Her pulse raced in anticipation as she walked stealthily through the brush. Not that anyone on the ocean could hear her up here.

She lay down on the ground and scanned the predawn horizon. It was August, and the air was a cool sixty-five degrees, not the stifling temperature it would be in Boston. It was dark enough that she couldn't see the water and could barely make out some of the small rock islands in the harbor. Dena rested her head on her left arm and listened for sounds of boat engines. The waves gently crashing on the rocky shoreline was all she could hear.

Dena yawned. Her eyelids closed then opened again. A seagull squawked. "Night goggles might help," she quipped. In Africa she had waited in the bush for just the right moment when the animals would stir. But for some reason, waiting on the bluff for possible poachers didn't carry the same excitement.

Maybe it had to do with the fact that she wasn't really certain she could help. She had a vague idea where Wayne's pots were. With the night option on the digital camera, she hoped she could be of some use to Wayne.

The roar of an engine cut the silence. Dena aimed her camera toward the ocean. She eased her stance. "That's not a boat engine, that's a car." She turned to see what she could only assume was Wayne's truck pulling into her driveway with his parking lights on.

She didn't know whether to be upset or happy for the company.

"Dena, are you out here?"

"Over here."

He cautiously walked in the dark toward her. His silhouette seemed larger as it cast a dark shadow in the dim light of the stars. "Hi. I brought some coffee." He handed her a warm paper cup.

"Thanks."

"It's too early to see anything yet, isn't it?"

"Yup, but I wanted to be in place just in case something happens."

"Good plan. Normally I'm arriving at the harbor about now, getting the boat ready."

"Do all lobstermen fish this early?"

"No, but because I also do carpentry work, I like to get the lobstering out of the way first."

Wayne lay down on the ground beside her and placed a pair of binoculars in front of him.

આ

Four mornings later, nothing had happened yet. During the daytime hours, they finalized some of the finishing touches for the addition and dealt with the EPA regulations for the disposal of the chemical fixer and silver recovery. At night, Dena stayed alone in the cottage. She ached to be with Wayne, but she didn't feel right barging in on Jason and his family every night, either. So there she sat night after night, alone. All alone.

"Wayne?"

"Hmm," he mumbled.

"I've been thinking. We might have given up too soon."

He rolled on his side and faced her.

Taking in a deep breath, she continued. "I know my schedule is ridiculous but—"

He reached out to her. "Dena, I want you in my life. You've become my best friend, even though we've barely spent any time talking with each other this past month. I know last month we were saying we'd trust the Lord, and then an hour or so later we decided it wouldn't work. Where's our faith?"

"We both see lots of potential for a relationship, but neither one of us wants to get hurt."

"Yeah, so what's the answer? I can't stop thinking about you. I pray for you daily—actually many times during the day."

Dena giggled. "And I've been miserable. Just ask anyone who was on those shoots with me."

"Jess hasn't stopped complaining about my mood. So, like I said, where does that leave us?"

"Between a rock and a high place?" She pointed toward the ocean.

"Bad pun." He gently stroked the top of her hand with the ball of his thumb.

She moved her camera and inched toward him. Reaching out for his rugged face, she caressed him with her fingertips. "I've missed you."

He captured her fingers and kissed them ever so lightly. "I've missed you, too."

She wanted to kiss him. She knew he wanted to kiss her. After weeks of desire, she leaned forward and captured his lips with her own.

The putter of a boat engine rang in her ears.

Chapter 12

Wayne savored their kiss for days. While Dena and he hadn't caught a glimpse of the thieves, they had finally walked through their first barrier—themselves. She was now in Phoenix and working on another project. But they talked every night.

He tapped out a brief e-mail to Dena, letting her know that he missed her and looked forward to her return. He also mentioned he was thinking of pulling his pots for the season and sitting it out. In some ways, lobstering just seemed more frustrating than profitable. The few lobsters he was bringing in didn't even cover gas and bait. He finished the e-mail, clicked SEND, and went to the living room to enjoy a quiet evening at home. Jess was out with Trevor, and he was free to read the latest Alton Gansky novel.

Settling in his chair, he cracked open the new spine. He opened to the first page and had read the first line when a loud horn blast thundered through the evening air. Tossing his book down on the coffee table, he listened carefully to the town fire alarm. Two long, then two short blasts, and the pattern repeated three times. He was in his truck by the third series. Twenty-two meant Tarpon Cove Road.

As a volunteer fireman, he always went out. Thankfully, the sleepy little town of Squabbin Bay rarely had any fires. Wayne and the fire truck arrived at Tarpon Cove Road from opposite directions. Letting the fire truck pass, he followed down the street. Only a few houses dotted the out-of-the-way road. "Lord, keep everyone safe."

His heart caught in his chest when he saw Ben Costa's roof in flames. He pulled onto the sidewalk and jumped out of his truck. Ben sat on his front lawn, coughing. Another neighbor sat beside him, wrapping his arm around the old man. "Are you okay, Ben?"

Ben nodded yes. Wayne ran on toward the house. They needed to save as much of the home as possible.

Wayne worked with the other men for a couple of hours as they tried to save what they could of Ben's house. Pastor Russell came to the fire and added his hands to the work. Thirty men in all and two fire trucks came to fight the fire. The smell of wet, smoldering wood filled the air. Ben still sat on his front lawn as Wayne glanced back at the ruined structure. The house was an old wooden Victorian. Precious little could be saved.

With a bottled water in his hand, Wayne sat down beside Ben. "What happened?"

"I fell asleep in my chair while waiting for my dinner to cook."

"I'm sorry, Ben. Is there any way I can help you?"

"My kids been after me to sell the place and move in with them. Guess I'll be doing that now."

Wayne glanced back at the ruins. It had been a grand house in its day, but Ben's advanced years and the lean lobstering seasons of late had probably added to the building's tinderbox condition.

"I didn't know boiling water could burn a man's house down," he mumbled.

The hairs on the back of Wayne's neck rose. *First question, did he have a gas stove? Second question, what kind of pan did he use? Third question, how could a pan of boiling water ignite this large of a blaze?* "Let me talk with the chief, Ben." He gave him a comforting slap on the back. "I'll be right back."

Wayne walked over to Chief Emerson. "Hey, Buck. Any idea what started the fire?"

Buck removed his helmet and wiped his brow with a soiled handkerchief. "It's a strange one. Come here." The chief led him to the back of the house.

"See this?" He pointed to the scorched stones of the foundation.

Wayne nodded.

"And take a look at this." He led him toward the remaining walls of the kitchen. Wayne could see a pan still sat on the stove. Buck pointed in the opposite direction. "See that line? There was accelerant on these walls. Someone set the place on fire."

"Who?"

"That I don't know. But I'd say Squabbin Bay has a problem if someone's targeting old men in their homes."

Who would want to hurt Ben Costa? Did the person who set the fire even know it was Ben's house? "I'm going to take Ben home to my place tonight. He can call his daughter from there."

"Good idea. What did he tell you?"

Wayne filled Buck in on Ben's thoughts about how the fire started.

"So, whoever set the fire knew Ben was in there, unless I can find evidence of a timer. I'd guess they were in the house covering the kitchen wall with the accelerant while he was sleeping." Buck stepped back. "I need to talk with the sheriff. Excuse me."

Who would want to kill Ben?

Wayne called Jess from his cell.

"Hello," Jess answered.

"Jess, it's Dad. There's been a fire. I'm bringing Ben Costa home. Would you make up my bed with fresh sheets?"

"Sure. Is he okay?"

"Fine. He's going to be just fine." For tonight, he felt it best not to go into the details of the fire. "Thanks, sweetheart."

"You're welcome. By the way, Dena called."

"Thanks. Would you call her back and let her know what's happened? It's going to be awhile before I can come home."

"No problem. Talk to you later."

"Bye." He hung up his cell phone and rejoined Ben on the front lawn. The police were cordoning off the house with bright yellow plastic tape. The fire chief and sheriff were sitting with Ben, gently plying him with questions.

"Nope, don't have a problem with nobody, 'cept for them buggers stealing my lobsters."

"Have you caught someone taking your lobsters?" Sheriff McKean asked.

"Not yet, but I'm getting close. I can feel it in my bones. Their engine has a certain skip in the pistons. It's a very distinct sound. I've been listening. I know my hearin' ain't what it used to be, but I'm as certain as the nose on my face I'd know the sound of that engine if I heard it again."

So had the poachers targeted Ben? Were they responsible for this?

෧

Dena rose long after the sun and headed for the bluff overlooking the ocean. There had been no evidence of the poachers coming before dawn on the mornings she and Wayne had been staked out between her assignments. Besides, she needed the couple extra hours of sleep after coming in late from her last photo shoot in Phoenix.

Her September vacation couldn't come soon enough. *I'll decide then what to do about future shoots and how busy I want my schedule to be.* With her mind decided, she scanned the horizon once again. Two days had gone by since she'd learned from Wayne that the fire at Ben Costa's was definitely arson, and that added a whole new level of seriousness to catching these poachers.

A boat nosed out beyond the peninsula that stuck out on the southern point. Dena aimed her camera and tried to zoom in on the bow and any markings on the vessel. It appeared to be similar to the other lobster boats in the area. Dena shot a few pictures, but the boat held its course out to sea.

A few more lobster boats and a couple of sailboats headed out to sea from the north and the south of her position. But no one came to pull Wayne's pots, not even Wayne.

Okay, something's not adding up, Lord. If the harvest is so poor in the summer, why would someone steal now? Wouldn't they wait until winter? She decided she'd have to ask Wayne about that.

A small sailboat sailed into the bay. Its hull was wide, and the mast seemed to be more toward the bow than toward the center of the craft. Dena clicked off some more pictures. A couple of young people dove from the boat and swam in the bay. She watched them for a few moments, vicariously sharing the pleasure these young people enjoyed in a summer morning swim.

Deciding today would not prove productive in catching the poachers, she headed back to her cottage. The darkroom was finished, though the final touches on the exterior of the house and the bedroom carpeting had yet to be completed. Dena was very pleased with Wayne's work.

Her mind drifted back to the time she'd found him with his shirt off and working on the roof, his body well bronzed by the sun, his rugged features a feast for her eyes. As she stood looking at the spot where she had found him weeks ago, she caught herself drifting into unsafe territory. She shook her head and continued into the house.

In the bathroom, she freshened up for the day and discovered her roots were showing. She reached for her touch-up dye and applied it to the roots. Weeks on remote shoots were lousy for keeping up her blond hair. She had no idea what her real color was anymore. As she approached thirty, her hair started darkening, and as time passed, she started to rely more and more on a bottle.

With a towel around her neck and tinfoil wrapped around her roots, she glanced at her wristwatch and proceeded to the kitchen to make herself some breakfast.

She rounded the corner and screamed, then ran back into the bathroom.

"Dena, it's me, Wayne," he called from behind the closed door.

Wayne standing in the kitchen had not been what she expected to see. "I know it's you. What are you doing here?"

"I came to work. I didn't mean to scare you. Come out, please."

"No." *Okay, call it vanity, Lord, but I don't want him to see me with my hair like this.*

"No? What's the matter?"

"Nothing."

"Dena, for pity's sake, please come out."

"Later. I'm washing my hair."

"Honey, I saw your hair. I know that you're dyeing it. Come on out."

Heat blazed across her cheeks. "Wayne," she whined, "give a gal some dignity."

His laughter only flustered her more, but she wasn't certain why. Was she upset with herself for being so silly? Was she frustrated with him because he knew she dyed her hair? Or was she upset simply because she had been caught dyeing—with tinfoil in her hair, no less? In any case, she would not face him at this point in time.

"All right, I'll be in the master bedroom installing the light fixtures and ceiling fan. Come and get me when you're ready."

She didn't bother to answer him. She leaned against the bathroom door and slid to the floor. *He knows I dye my hair?* She groaned.

❧

Wayne whistled to stop himself from laughing at Dena's attempt to hide the fact that she colored her hair.

Standing on the stepladder, he pulled down the white, black, and red wires from the ceiling. He unscrewed the black plastic caps he'd placed on the wires earlier. Using his shoulder and head to brace the fan, he connected the proper wires to each screw and tightened them. Tucking the wires up into the hole, he attached the base of the fan to the ceiling. Once it was in place, he moved over to the other light fixtures in the master bathroom.

"Hi," Dena said. Her hair was still damp, but the renewed color shouted, "Hey there, notice me!"

"Hi." He stepped down from the ladder and met her halfway. "Sorry, I didn't mean to embarrass you."

A light rose blush swept across her cheeks. "No problem. So, what did you want to speak with me about?"

"Nothing. I just came in to say hello." He reached for her hands and marveled at their softness once again. "You're beautiful, Dena."

She released her hands from his and wrapped him in an embrace. "I've missed you, too."

He briefly captured her lips with his own then pulled back slightly. "You are beautiful, honey."

"Thanks. You're not so bad yourself." She tapped the end of his nose with her finger. "I have a question for you, totally off subject."

"What?"

"Something occurred to me as I was waiting to photograph potential thieves. It seems odd for people to steal in the summer if the lobsters bring less money at this time of year."

"Hmm." Wayne leaned against the stepladder. "That is an interesting point."

"It just doesn't seem to make much sense. I know there is some money in it, since the commercial lobstermen still fish. But if it's only the smaller operators like yourself and Ben Costa who are being hit this summer, why would they bother? I mean, wouldn't it make more sense to hit the larger companies, those with more pots, to earn more?"

"Again, you raise a good point." Wayne pondered this new information. She was right; it didn't make much sense, other than the fact that the thief still made off with a hundred or so lobster pots' worth of income. "I pulled my pots in for the season."

"I wondered, when I didn't see you out there this morning."

"It was simply too costly to keep it going."

"How long ago? Perhaps, if it's been enough days, the thieves won't be back."

"Hmm, hadn't thought of that. You're probably right. Ben has a few pots in this inlet still."

"I'll try again to get a shot of them if they should come by, but I'm thinking it's more and more likely that you've seen the last of them."

"Until I put my pots out again in November," he quipped, then shifted his weight and stood. "So, how long are you here for?" Something inside him longed for her to say forever, but he knew that wouldn't be happening.

"Five days."

"Wow, what happened to give you this big of a break?"

"I gave an assignment away."

He walked back over to her. "Dena, can you afford it?"

"I don't believe I have an option. I'm tired, Wayne, really tired. This commuting is hard on me."

He embraced her and encouraged her to lay her head on his shoulder. "Honey, maybe I can schedule time off the next break you have and drive down to Boston. What do you think?"

She lifted her head. "Are you serious?"

"Yes. It hardly seems fair for you to do all the traveling. If I'm not lobstering, I can rearrange the jobs a bit. So when is your next turnaround time?"

They made their plans for the next visit then went back to their individual tasks for the day. Dena paid a visit to her son and grandchildren while Wayne finished up, getting the room ready for the next day's carpet delivery, then he returned home to prepare for their date.

Showered and shaved, he escorted Dena to dinner at a seafront shanty. It had plenty of texture for her photographer's eye, he hoped. But it also had some of the best seafood in the entire area. "What do you think?" He held her hand as they entered the small restaurant.

"It's charming, in a rustic kind of way."

"I thought you might enjoy it." He led her through the door. His fingers touched the small of her back, and a wash of comfort filled him. How was it that with so little time together, he felt so at peace with Dena?

"I'm glad you're here for five days," he whispered into her ear.

"Me, too."

The waiter, who doubled as the host, led them to a table that sat in front of a large picture window overlooking the harbor. The tables and chairs were of heavy pine with a thick, clear varnish. Candles that doubled as mosquito repellent sat on each of the tables. Ice and water splashed into the Mason jar glasses as the waiter filled them.

"Trust me, the food is great," he reassured her.

"Wayne, this is nothing, trust me. I've been to places where you swat flies faster than you can breathe. I don't enjoy those places much, but I've been there."

Wayne chuckled then sobered. "You've been to so many places I've only dreamed about or watched on National Geographic television specials. I can't imagine."

She propped her elbows on the table and locked her fingers together. "You know, I was serious about you joining me sometime. I'd love to have you come along on a shoot."

"What would I do? We're not married, and it just wouldn't seem right for me to traipse around the country, or the world for that matter, just to be with you. Not that I'd mind being with you; it actually sounds quite wonderful, but—"

"You're rambling," she interrupted.

"Sorry." Wayne closed his eyes and reclined in the chair.

"Do you know how cute you are when you get flustered?"

He opened his eyes and smiled. "No, but I don't mind you telling me."

He enjoyed her laugh. "I know it's not a masculine thing to do, following a woman around on her job, but I'd love for you to experience some of the magnificent creation God has made out there. Not that this area in Maine isn't a great wonder."

"You don't have to explain. I understand what you mean, and I'd like to travel some. But—"

The waiter approached. "Are you ready to order now?"

He hadn't even glanced at the menu. "What's tonight's special?"

"Lobster bisque and swordfish," the waiter replied.

"Hmm. Dena, what would you like?"

"I'm open to anything. You decide."

Wayne scanned the menu. "Let's start with some oyster chowder, the local fresh vegetable medley, wild rice, and swordfish."

The young waiter stepped away.

"Oysters?"

"Do you not like them?"

Dena waved off his defense. "I like oyster chowder."

Chapter 13

Dena stood at the rail of her back porch and looked over the star-covered heavens. Tonight's dinner with Wayne had been wonderful. They were stepping toward a more lasting relationship. When he was beside her, it had seemed perfectly natural to ask him to join her on a shoot. Now, thinking back on the evening, she wondered why she even made the suggestion. After all, they barely knew each other. Well, perhaps that wasn't quite true. They talked and talked every chance they got and sent e-mails whenever a phone call didn't work out. She probably knew him better than she knew Bill when they married.

Lord, it seems like ages since Bill and I were together, and yet he's still a part of me. When I think of the times we spent together, of raising the kids, the memories are so clear and vibrant. I'm fairly sure I love Wayne. But how's an old woman like me, who's been a widow for more years than she was married, going to be comfortable with a man around the house? And what do we do about our careers? Each of us has a strong desire to work. I know I gave some thought to opening a studio up here. My kids would love it. And I know I've given some thought to organizing a team of photographers to go out on shoots, allowing me to take a more managerial approach. But would I really be content to do that? There's been so much adventure in exploring the world.

Dena paused for a moment and listened to the gentle surf rolling up on shore.

You know, Lord, if You're responsible for bringing the two of us together, don't You think it would have been better if we had more compatible careers?

Dena crossed her arms and sat down on the lounge chair.

"Nice sky tonight," Wayne said, bringing out two tall glasses of iced tea.

"Yeah."

"What's the matter?"

Dena took in a deep breath and exhaled slowly. "I was just thinking about our careers. I could lessen my load. My kids would love it."

Wayne sat down on the lounge chair beside her. "Dena, honey, are you happy traveling so much?"

"Honestly?" *Am I?* she wondered. "I don't know. I guess it's why I took the next five days off. I needed a break."

"Look, I know the world is an exciting place to see, and I truly would love to see it. But is that what's most important to you?"

What is most important? "My family is naturally the most important part of my life. But I'll be the first to admit, I've hardly seen them over the past four or five years. It's hard to see how fast Jason and Amber's kids are growing up. And sometimes I feel guilty for not being around more."

Wayne wrapped his arms around her shoulders. "Why don't you tell me how you think you could lessen your workload?"

"Actually, I don't know that it would lessen all that much, but the traveling part I could reduce." Dena went on to explain how she could run a studio, even from here. How she could sell prints of her photographs and circulate some of her older prints for possible publication. Then she told him about subcontracting to other photographers. "Basically, my name would be on the line. I'd earn a percentage of what the photographer would be paid from the clients who hired them to come out for a shoot. But I'd also be helping them get established as well as helping them organize and hopefully keep steady work."

He leaned back on the lounge chair. "I think we should pray about it. It sounds like both possibilities have merit, plus you'd have more time for your family."

"Yes, but it's not just my family I want more time with." She wiggled her eyebrows.

"Woman, you're good for a man's ego. I haven't had anyone wanting to spend time with me since Jess was a young teen."

She turned to face him and grasped his calloused hand. "I'm terrified," she admitted as much to herself as to him.

"You're not the only one. I'm excited about the prospect of possibly finding someone to spend the rest of my life with. But I'm nearly forty-two years old and rather set in my ways."

Dena laughed. "Honey, you aren't set until you've hit fifty, and even then there seem to be changes that keep coming."

"Hmm, you might have a point there. Must be 'cause you're older and wiser."

Dena hauled off and smacked him in the shoulder. "Hey, I don't look a day over thirty-nine."

"True, but I know better. I know your son, and he's in his early thirties," he teased.

"Ahh, guess I didn't need to dye those roots, huh?"

Wayne roared. "You were quite a sight. How often do you have to do that? I mean, tinfoil on your head kinda made you look like you belonged in a sci-fi movie."

She went to swat him again, but he was quicker this time. He captured her hands and pulled her close. Millimeters before their lips touched, he said, "I love you, Dena."

Her heart leapt in her chest. *I love you, too,* she admitted to herself, not allowing the words to form. Instead, she kissed him with an honest fervor that caused them both to pause.

Wayne got up and walked to the railing. "It's getting late. I better get going."

Dena wrapped her arms across her middle. "Yeah, you're probably right."

"Honey, I—"

"Shh. Your instincts are right, Wayne. Go home. I think we both have a lot of thinking to do."

"All right. I'll call you tomorrow night."

Dena remembered he'd told her earlier this evening he had a job a short distance away and that he probably wouldn't get home until nine tomorrow night. She didn't want to let him go but knew it was best. They both needed to get a handle on this after their confessions of love.

They said their good-byes and shared a chaste kiss when he exited the house. She leaned up against the closed door. "Dear Lord, have I missed hearing those words from a man that much?"

≥∙

Dena hadn't professed her love, but her kiss drove the truth home. He tossed and turned all night. The possibilities of Dena's career changing excited him. For the first time since he met her, he saw a genuine prospect of how they might manage to live together as husband and wife. His heart even beat double time thinking about traveling abroad with Dena. If he were to see the world, he'd love to have her at his side.

But as dawn approached, he had to ask himself one very important question. Was he excited because this was the right thing for her to do, or was he excited because this would allow him to stay in Squabbin Bay? Why did he want to stay in this small town so much? Shouldn't he be willing to uproot and move to a place more conducive to Dena's career? After all, wasn't it the twenty-first century? Weren't women's careers just as important as men's? And Dena was certainly old enough that she wouldn't be taking off years to raise children. She'd already done that. *And done it well*, he added.

He headed to the job with that driving question on his mind: Was he willing to give up his career for hers?

All day and during his entire drive home, he continued to turn over every thought that had kept him awake the night before. When he arrived home, he immediately called Dena. No answer.

The little red light on his answering machine blinked. He pressed the PLAY button.

"Hello, you have three messages," the automated message intoned. One was a hang up. One was a sales call for refinancing his mortgage, something he had no interest in doing since he only had a year left on his present payments. And the third was from Dena.

"Hi, Wayne. I'm sorry, but I had to leave town. Brianne is alone and feeling poorly. Her doctor is thinking of putting her in the hospital for a few days and keeping her on an IV. Please pray for her. I'll call you as soon as I'm able. Or you can call my cell. I'm sorry. I really intended to spend this week with you."

He immediately tapped in her cell phone number.

"Hey, Dad." The screen door slammed behind Jess.

He cupped the phone with his hand and said, "Hi."

"What's for supper?" she asked.

"Don't know. Fix something, please."

"Sure." She shrugged and ambled into the kitchen.

Dena's voice mail came on. "Hi, Dena, I'm sorry to hear about Brianne. Jess and I will be praying. Call me when you can. Love ya, bye."

"Brianne's sick again?" Jess leaned against the doorjamb.

"Yeah, it sounds serious. Dena said they were talking about putting her in the hospital."

"I'm sorry. Let Dena know Trev and I'll be praying."

Wayne nodded. "I'm going to shower. What are you making us for dinner?"

"I'll order pizza."

He chuckled, tossing his head from side to side. "You're going to make a great wife one day."

"Yup, I'll have all the take-out numbers memorized."

He waved her off and headed for his room. In the shower, he lathered up, getting rid of the sawdust and grit. The warm water sluiced down his back, relaxing his tired muscles.

You should go to her, a small voice nagged.

He stopped mid-lather and looked from side to side. Should he go to Boston? Would she want him there? What had he been fussing about with himself all day but sacrifice? Couldn't he give Dena a couple days of moral support?

He scrubbed his hair, working up a rich crown of lather, and rinsed it off. Finishing his shower quickly, he dried off and packed an overnight bag.

"Jess," he hollered from his bedroom.

"Yeah, Dad?"

"I'm driving to Boston; make me a pot of coffee—please."

"Okay," she replied.

His cell phone rang. Seeing it was Dena's cell, he answered. "Hi, honey. How is she?"

"She's stabilizing. She's lost a lot of fluid."

"I'm so sorry. Where are you?"

"Brigham and Women's Hospital. It's not too far from my apartment."

"When did you get there?" he asked, stuffing some toiletries into his bag.

"Just before dinner. I'm sorry I can't spend more time with you."

"Shh, Brianne needs you. I'm packing right now. I'm coming down there, unless you don't want me to."

"You're more than welcome—but you don't have to," she whispered.

"Honey, I want to. I'll get a room in a hotel near the hospital."

"No way. You can stay at my place."

"No, Dena. I'd love to, but I don't think that's wise at this point in our relationship."

"Ah, you're probably right. Okay, you can stay at the kids' apartment. Chad's flying in tonight. I finally reached him through his airline."

"Okay. I'll be leaving in an hour or so, so I won't be getting there until dawn."

"Honey, drive down in the morning. Get some sleep."

"Tell you what, I'll pray about it. I'm so awake right now, I don't think the drive would be that bad. But I might get a few hours down the highway and be ready to zonk out."

Dena giggled. "I know you. It's already past your bedtime. You will zonk out, as you put it."

"You're probably right. I'll have my supper and see how awake I'm feeling. If I decide to leave tonight, I promise to pull over and find a room if I get sleepy."

"All right. Call me once you decide. I have to leave the cell phone off while I'm in the hospital, but I'm checking every hour for messages from the kids."

"Does Pastor Russell know?"

"Yes, I called him before I left town."

"Good, he's probably got the church prayer chain going for Brianne."

"I hope so." Dena paused. "Wayne, I'm really concerned. There's a chance she might lose the baby."

"I'll be praying. Hang in there, honey. I'll be there as soon as I possibly can."

"Thanks. And, Wayne—I love you, too. I'm sorry I didn't tell you that last night."

A smile creased his face from ear to ear. "You did, just not with words."

☙

Dena worked the kinks out of the back of her neck as the smell of bacon on the food trays passed in the hallway. It had been a long night. While Chad visited with Brianne, she stayed in the waiting room to give them some privacy.

"Dena," Wayne called, barely above a whisper.

She ran to him and held on, grateful for the presence of the man she loved. For so long she'd had no one to hold on to but the Lord. Wayne's strong body gave her renewed strength. "Thanks for coming."

"You're welcome. How is she?"

"Fair. They want to do an ultrasound to check on the baby." She turned and walked back to the window overlooking the parking lot. "I hate hospitals."

"Huh?"

"They remind me of the night Bill died. I can't help thinking about it when I'm in a hospital. The smells, the sounds—everything reminds me of that night. I've been trying to put it out of my mind so I can concentrate on Brianne."

"What happened, if you don't mind me asking?"

She turned and faced him with a sigh. "He lost control of the car, and we flipped over a couple of times, so they tell me. I don't remember the accident itself. The police said it was a combination of wet roads, tires with a little less tread than they should have had, and driving too fast for the weather. It was one of those roads you know real well if you live in the area—so much so that you have a false sense of security about just how fast you can travel. Bill wasn't speeding, just not going slow enough for the weather conditions."

"I'm sorry."

Dena clung to him one more time. "Thanks. I really don't think too much about it, except for when I'm in a hospital."

"I understand. Would you like to get something to eat?"

"Sure. I don't recall when I ate last."

"Not good. Lead me to the cafeteria. I've never had hospital food."

Dena looped her arm in his and led him down the hallway. "You know, you're adorable."

"Naturally, makes me more kissable."

"Hmm, speaking of which. . ." She leaned closer and kissed him on the cheek.

He stopped. "Not good enough. I've driven six hours. I want the full treatment. On the lips, dear." He winked.

"With pleasure," she obliged.

"Mom?"

Chapter 14

Amber? I didn't see you." Dena's cheeks sported a nice hue of pink.

Reluctantly, Wayne took a step back.

"Obviously," Amber chided.

Wayne had never met Dena's daughter. He'd seen pictures but never had the pleasure. Did she know about Dena and him dating?

"Amber, this is Wayne. Wayne, this is my daughter, Amber."

"Hi, it's a pleasure to finally meet you." Wayne extended his hand.

Amber narrowed her gaze on him and slowly shook his hand. "You're Jess's father?"

"Yup. Have you met Jess?"

"Nope, only talked on the phone with her when she was staying with Mom." Amber turned toward her mother. "Mom, I think we need to talk."

Dena looped her arm around his and patted his upper arm. "Wayne and I were going to the cafeteria for something to eat. Would you like to join us? We could talk there."

"Uh," Amber stammered, "sure."

Okay, she didn't know about Dena and me. Lord, give me a calm spirit after driving six and a half hours on little sleep, he prayed.

Wayne offered to go through the cafeteria line for all of them. Dena hesitated but took him up on his offer. She and her daughter were in a deep discussion as he approached. He set the tray down on the table. "I'll be right back with our drinks." At the beverage counter, he poured their coffees, adding enough cream and sugar for Amber's taste. She seemed to enjoy it very sweet— more like coffee-flavored cream than a regular cup of coffee. Of course, he'd been drinking the stuff black for years. It was another thing he and Dena had in common.

He watched the two women carefully as he made his way back. Dena caught his glance and smiled. His steps surer, he sauntered up to the table. Whatever Amber's concerns, Dena had obviously dealt with them, at least to her satisfaction. "Here ya go, Amber. That was two heaping sugars and a quarter cup of cream, right?"

"Right, thanks."

"You're welcome."

He set Dena's cup in front of her and sat down beside her. "It's a fairly fresh pot," he offered, trying to make conversation. "At least, I think it is. It was nearly full and didn't smell bitter."

Dena reached over and placed her hand on his forearm. "Amber's going to use the cottage in Maine next week, unless it's a problem with the construction."

"Not a problem at all. I should have it finished this weekend."

"Mom's told me so much about the addition. I can't wait to see it."

"Squabbin Bay is a great place, if you like the slower pace." He reached over to the tray of assorted food and passed Dena her salad. "Some folks can't handle it."

Amber's gaze followed every movement he made. "I'd be happy to take your family out fishing one day."

Amber and Dena chuckled. "David gets green just thinking of the ocean."

"Oh, well perhaps a fishing trip wouldn't be a good idea."

"Thanks for the offer." Amber finished her coffee and stood, straightening her white uniform. "Well, I'm going to say hello to Brianne; then I've got to get home. It was nice meeting you, Wayne."

After Amber left, he asked, "Does she work here?"

"No, she took the T straight from work."

"Ah, so, how shook up was she?"

Dena looked down at her lap. "Not too. She reminded me of something I said to her the first night I met you."

"Oh?" He paused. "Are you going to tell me?"

Dena lifted her gaze and locked with his own. "I made a comment about your eyes."

"Oh?"

Dena shifted in her chair.

"Well, I have always had a fascination with green eyes."

Wayne stifled a chuckle with a cough. "And how is it I never knew about this?"

"I've told you that I like your eyes."

"True, but you never specified that it was because they were green."

She straightened in her chair. "Well, you never asked."

"What other secrets do you have in that pretty little head of yours?"

"You'll find out." She paused and winked. "Eventually."

"So, did I pass the Amber test?"

"She's curious, but she's more curious because she found us kissing in a hospital hallway. Seems that isn't something her mother would do."

"In Amber's defense, I'd probably have to agree with her. After all, you did tell me you haven't dated since your husband passed away, so your kids as teens never saw you relating in an intimate way with someone of the opposite sex."

"You have a point there. But come on, I am human," Dena defended.

"No, you're not. You're Mom." Wayne snuggled up beside her. "To your kids, that is. To me, you're the most fascinating woman I've ever been with.

I love you, Dena."

She set her fork down, her salad barely touched. "I love you, too."

"Why don't you visit Brianne one more time this morning, and then I'll take you home so you can get some rest."

She closed her eyes and sighed. "I guess you're right. It's been a long couple of days."

"I'll take care of this," he said, pointing to her salad, "and meet you in the lobby."

"No, I want you to come with me. Chad and Brianne need to meet you, and it would be better for them to have a proper introduction as opposed to the way Amber met you."

"Ah, I see your point. Let me get a container for your salad."

She nodded, and he left her alone at the table. He knew she was terribly concerned for Brianne and the baby. *Lord, how can I help here? I mean, I know I can be of some moral support, but apart from that, I don't have a clue as to what to say, do, or anything.*

"May I have a container to bring home a salad?" he asked the older woman in the gray and white uniform sitting by the register.

"Coming right up." She reached under the counter and pulled up a foam dinner container.

"Thanks." As he made his way back to the table, he noticed how vulnerable Dena appeared. A smile creased her sad face as he came into her view. *Maybe I just need to be here, nothing more, nothing less.*

❧

Hours later, Dena lay in bed, thinking over the day. Chad and Brianne hadn't been surprised to see Wayne. Obviously, Amber had forewarned them. Her cheeks warmed again at the thought of Amber's catching her kissing Wayne. Of course, it was Amber who had encouraged her to think about having a relationship again. What had bothered Amber wasn't that Dena was dating but that Dena had failed to mention that her "friendship" with Wayne had progressed to that point.

No doubt she'd already called Jason and informed him, as well. Dena pulled the covers up to her neck.

She woke up late the next morning. Throwing the covers off, she dressed and glanced at the mirror to straighten her hair, applied a light coat of foundation, and highlighted her eyelashes. Wayne spent the night in Chad and Brianne's apartment. He should be returning any minute now to take her back to the hospital.

The doorbell rang. She quickly turned and the room spun. She reached for the dresser to brace herself.

The chime of the doorbell rang again. She walked slowly toward the front door. "Hi," she said, opening the door for Wayne.

"Are you all right?"

"Fine," she lied, without meaning to. It was just the automatic response to give when someone asked. "Actually, I feel a little lightheaded."

"Did you eat?"

"No." *When was the last time I ate?* she asked herself.

"Dena, honey, sit down. Let me make you something to eat. You can't go nonstop and not refuel."

"I know. I've just been too busy or too nervous."

"I understand, but it's time to think of what's best for you and your family. They don't need someone else in the hospital suffering from dehydration and exhaustion." Wayne marched into the kitchen nook. She watched him through the half wall that served as a breakfast counter on the living room side. Inside the kitchen area, Wayne stopped at the sink.

"How'd you sleep?" she asked.

"All right. It's hard to get used to a strange bed. At least it is for me. You must be used to it with all the traveling you do."

Dena reclined on the sofa. There was something soothing about having Wayne working in her kitchen. "Sometimes I didn't have a bed. A sleeping bag on a cot served me most of the time. Once in a while, it was just the sleeping bag, but I'm at a point where I can insist on a cot as part of my expenses for remote locations. Of course, the natives who have to lug the supplies along would probably prefer not to have the added weight. But I figure if they want me alert and ready to take quality photographs, a good night's sleep is essential."

Wayne chuckled. "I'm having a hard time seeing you roughing it in a sleeping bag. Jess and I go camping and canoeing every year. I think I mentioned that before."

"Yes, when I was heading out on that white-water adventure."

"Right." Wayne's words came back muffled. "Where's your omelet pan?" He closed another cabinet door.

"I don't have one."

"Sure you do. I made an omelet here for Jess—"

"Jess's," they said in unison.

"In that case, you'll just have some fancy scrambled eggs."

"Sounds fine." She watched him go to work on his breakfast creation. "Wayne?" He shifted his weight onto his left leg and turned to face her. "Thanks for coming down. It means a lot."

"No problem. I can't stay too long, but I'll do what I can to help while I'm here."

"Let's just pray that Brianne and the baby are stable today."

"Amen." He whipped the eggs with a whisk.

Dena leaned her head back against the wall and closed her eyes. The next thing she was aware of was Wayne's tender words waking her senses. "Hey, sleepyhead. Breakfast is ready."

She stretched and made her way stiffly over to the breakfast counter. He set a plate full of eggs in front of her. "Ketchup?" he asked.

"Salsa, if you don't mind."

"Salsa? Is that Southwestern?"

Dena shrugged her shoulders. She couldn't remember where or when she'd first had salsa on her eggs. "Could be, but I've been served it in Colorado."

He retrieved a jar of the medium spicy salsa from her refrigerator. "I've seen some put Tabasco sauce on their eggs up here, but I never heard of salsa. I suppose it isn't much different."

"Wanna try some?"

"No, thanks. I never got used to having ketchup on my eggs, never mind something spicier."

"Chicken," she teased.

"Quite possibly. I'm not a fan of spicy hot foods. I can handle a little salsa, mild of course. Actually, my preference with eggs is no sauce at all. Just call me boring." He winked.

Dena chuckled. "You're anything but boring. I find you quite intriguing."

"Hmm, am I a man of mystery?" He scooted around the half wall and sat on a tall stool beside her.

"Hmm, I won't go that far."

He raised a hand to his chest. "Ah, my life is an open book."

"Groan."

"Yeah, that is a bad cliché. Let's pray." He clasped her hand with his and closed his eyes.

She watched for a moment. Beyond his handsome features, she noticed peacefulness in his countenance.

After breakfast they joined the rest of the family at the hospital, discovering that even Jason and his family had come down. They were all pleased to hear that Brianne had gone through the worst part, and she and the baby would be fine. Jason and the children would stay for a couple of days. Marie would stay for a week and oversee Brianne's home recovery time. Chad would be flying out in the morning, at Brianne's insistence. Amber would take over after Marie left if Brianne still needed some help.

And then it hit her. All the family plans did not include her because of her busy schedule. "Lord, I guess it's time for a major life change."

&

Wayne stretched getting out of his truck. A six-hour drive made a man stiff, but thankfully he was finally home. Dena's mood had changed shortly after the family had made their plans regarding Brianne's care. He loved how this family pulled together and supported each other. Dena had done a fine job raising her kids. But what had been bothering her? They never could grab a moment alone for him to ask the question. And pondering it for six hours made him all the more curious. Something was bothering her, and he wanted to know what it was.

He glanced up at the starlit sky. It was probably close to midnight. He'd left Boston at dinnertime. Dena had packed him some sandwiches and a couple of cold drinks.

The smell of cigar smoke hung in the air. Wayne turned and looked around. A small red glow lit up the area near his hedges. "Who's there?"

"It's me—Ben. I been here waitin' for you. Jess said you'd be getting home kinda late." The silhouette of Ben's thin frame came into view.

"Come in and I'll fix you a cup of coffee or something."

"Can't stay. I need to get back to my boat. But I've been hearing some interesting things on the waterfront." Ben walked toward Wayne.

"Such as?"

"Seems you started a trend. Most of the small-time guys are pulling their pots, like you."

Wayne couldn't blame them. He'd crunched the numbers, and it was costing more to go out and bait the traps than he was earning.

"How about yourself?"

"Nah, I ain't never pulled them before, except when the water was too warm and we got hit with a bad case of worms. 'Course those were the days of wood traps. These metal traps last forever, unless they don't have enough weights in 'em when a storm hits."

True, but that's not why he came so late in the night to speak to me. "What's really on your mind, Ben?"

He stepped closer and handed him a large, overstuffed envelope. "It ain't much, but if something happens to me, would you be sure to give these to my daughter?"

He couldn't fault the man for being nervous after his house had been torched, but if he really thought his life was in danger. . . "Ben, what else is going on?"

"Nothin' for certain, yet. But if I'm right, people are going to be mighty surprised when I catch 'em."

Wayne reached out and grabbed Ben's shoulder. "What are you not telling me, Ben?"

"I don't think my house was burned down because of the poaching."

"Okay, what have you heard?"

"Nothing, not a blasted thing. But something's fishy, and I've got a nose for fish. I've been snooping around and, well, there's. . ."

An explosion ripped through the air. Wayne dropped down to the ground. Ben fell beside him and clutched his chest.

"Daddy!" Jess cried.

"Call 911! And stay down," Wayne ordered.

Chapter 15

Dena had never felt so torn in all her life. Being in Long Island and working wasn't helping to take her mind off of Maine and her family. Brianne was recovering, and the kids were lending a hand. Wayne was fine, but Ben's boat exploding made her nervous. Who was out to get the old man? He seemed such a likable guy. Wayne was convinced it had something to do with the poachers. What bothered her was that he wasn't leaving the investigation to the authorities. He had taken a far too personal interest in finding Ben's would-be attackers. Ben had suffered a heart attack when the explosion woke up the tiny village of Squabbin Bay. Fortunately, it was minor, and his daughter came and got him from the hospital. Not taking no for an answer, she had wheeled him, fussin' and fumin', all the way to her car. Now Wayne had taken up where Ben left off in his investigation.

Fortunately or unfortunately—Dena wasn't sure—Ben hadn't shared everything he knew with Wayne. Her prayer was that he wouldn't learn anything further until after the police and Coast Guard had discovered the true nature of the crimes.

Dena zoomed in on a bluff and a young seagull edging his way out of the tall sea grass behind the photo shoot. Holding the camera perfectly still, she ignored the bead of sweat rolling down her forehead. *Click.*

"Dena? Dena?" Kenny called for her.

"Over here," she answered and stood from her squatting position. She wiped the sweat from her brow with a no-longer-white handkerchief. "What's up?"

"I need you to shoot some more publicity photos. The client insists we didn't have the lighting correct."

Dena rolled her eyes heavenward. There were advantages to photographing wildlife as opposed to actors and models who insisted they knew more about the light and angles of a shoot than the photographer. "I'll be right there." She gritted her teeth and reminded herself that she could do this. Tomorrow couldn't come soon enough. Nothing seemed to go right on this trip. From the moment she'd arrived, one problem after another developed. *Is it the shoot or just me?* she wondered.

Putting on her professional smile, she greeted the customer once again, listened to her suggestions, and did as instructed—all the while knowing these photographs would not be used.

An hour later she finished the new round of photographs and said her good-byes. She'd driven from Boston in her own car for this remote shoot on Long Island. She opened her car door to let out the hot air then dropped her camera cases and equipment in the rear seat and put down the top.

A whistle pierced the air. "Nice set of wheels, Dena. Photography must pay more than I thought," remarked a young man as he walked around the car. She recognized him as one of the gofers who'd worked on the set all day.

"After many years and saving all my pennies, I was able to purchase the car."

"No way. How long did it take?"

"Well, if you don't count the eleven years of raising my children, it took four years. I've had the car for five."

"No way," he repeated. "It looks in mint condition." He examined the rear of the car. "Guess you're right; it is an older model."

Dena chuckled. "Yeah. So are you thinking of becoming a photographer?"

"Nah, I'm going into motion pictures. That's where the real money is. Plus, I have connections."

"Well, I wish you much success. Just don't forget to give time to the Lord."

"Oh, man. You're one of those born-againers, aren't you?"

"Guilty. I was a preacher's wife and my oldest son is a pastor."

The young man, with orange-tinged hair, stuffed his hands in his pockets and looked down at the pavement.

"Are you all right?"

"Fine, just heard enough of that God stuff."

Okay, Lord, this is the last thing I want to do right now. But if You want me to witness to this boy, give me the words, Dena prayed. "I'm not sure what you've heard, but there are Christians in Hollywood making movies today."

"Yeah, but I want to make the box office success films. I want to rake in the big bucks."

"Well, then you don't want to be the photographer. You want to be the director or producer. But even those who earn the big bucks have to learn their craft and learn it well. I'm afraid your goal is just making money, not the joy of learning to do a job well and liking it. I can't imagine working all these years and not liking my job."

"You didn't look too happy today."

Guilty again. "I'll admit, it wasn't the most joyous of days for me, but I still enjoy the craft. Did you see me slip away and take some shots when no one was looking?"

"You did?"

"Yup. I came across a beautiful butterfly opening its wings while perched on a flower. I held the camera still until the light shifted slightly and got some good shots before it flew away. Then there was the baby seagull."

"Who you selling those pictures to?"

"No one, most likely. But I have a granddaughter who loves butterflies, and

I'll put a picture or two in a book for her. Or I'll simply give her the photograph to play with."

"But?"

The obvious questions played across his forehead.

"What's your name?"

"Michael."

"Nice to meet you, Michael." Dena extended her hand. Others walked past and headed for their cars. "I take thousands of photographs in a year. Only a small fraction of those are marketable. Could this butterfly be a marketable product? Possibly, but that isn't why I took the picture. I took it because I enjoy taking pictures. I enjoy being able to capture a tiny fraction of what God's created and saving it for others to enjoy." Dena leaned against her car. "Money isn't the answer to all of life's problems. Don't get me wrong, I don't mind earning a comfortable living, but it isn't the only reason to work. You need to find out what is special to you. Success is doing what you love, doing it well, and keeping your head on straight as much as possible. God equips everyone with special gifts. Talk to Him and find out which ones He's given you.

"I've been blessed, no question about it. But there were times when the kids were teens when I didn't know from one day to the next if I'd earn enough to put food on the table. What I did know was that I was doing something I loved and, with God's help, providing for my family."

"What about your husband?"

"Bill died when Jason was thirteen."

"Sorry." He glanced back at her again. "Why was it not an enjoyable day for you today?"

"Several reasons. But I guess the main one is Brianne, my daughter-in-law, was in the hospital last week because she nearly lost her unborn child. If I hadn't agreed to this job weeks before, I would be home helping her."

"Man, your life isn't like this Mercedes, is it?"

Dena chuckled. "Depends on how you look at it. If you're looking at the fancy paint, leather interior, and the Mercedes logo suggesting wealth, you're right, it isn't my life. Now, if you look under the hood and look at all the years of hard work and engineering that went into making this fine machine then, yes, my life is like this car. God's investing years of research and development in me, and He's still working on me. When I'm done, I'll have this fine exterior and a wonderfully crafted engine and I'll be fit for heaven and driving on the streets of gold."

Michael laughed. "You had to be a preacher's wife."

Dena smiled. "True, but Bill died nearly twenty years ago. I've learned a few things since then. Do you go to church?"

"Not really. I have some friends who do. They're like you, really into this God stuff. They've been trying to tell me for a long time that money isn't everything.

But you know, when you live in a place like this and you see the superstars of sports and movies all the time, it's kinda hard not to want it."

"I'm sure. But watch them closely and find out what makes them truly happy. Most of the time, it's the love from their family, not the things they own. A rich man is a man who has a house full of love, even if it's a simple cottage." Dena's mind flashed back to Wayne. He truly was a rich man.

"God bless you, Michael. I hope you decide to find your true gifts and work within those."

"Uh, thanks. I think."

Dena placed her hand on the boy's shoulder. "Keep talking with your friends. Take care, Michael."

"Bye," he said with a wave.

She slipped behind the steering wheel and turned the key. Her cell phone rang.

∂∙

"Hey, honey, how was your day?"

"Strange."

Wayne paced the front porch of the bed-and-breakfast where Dena had rented a room. According to her schedule, she should have been back from the shoot two hours ago. He was beginning to wonder if his surprise visit would be a surprise to him and not her.

"What happened? Are you still on the shoot?" He heard the wind in the background, so he was fairly certain she was in her car. He prayed she wasn't on the highway heading back home.

"Long day. Suffice it to say, I hope I don't have one like that again. I did have a rather interesting encounter with a young man after the shoot."

The little hairs on the back of Wayne's neck rose.

"He noticed my car." She went on to explain her encounter with Michael.

"Did you decide to come home early?"

"No, I'm too exhausted. I'm going to enjoy the night off and possibly spend the morning at the beach before heading home."

"Hmm, sounds wonderful."

"Wayne, I think I need some solitude time. I think the kids might be right about my work schedule. I am losing my joy for the constant travel. But it means a lot of decisions will need to be made. Like how I'm going to support myself, for one."

Wayne sat down on an old wooden sliding rocker. "Are you saying we can't see each other while you're sorting this out?"

"Oh goodness, no. That's not what I meant."

Relief washed over him.

"Honey, are you up for a visit?"

"What?" she squeaked.

"I'm at the bed-and-breakfast. I rented a room. I'm on the third floor. I think it was an attic room years ago." Wayne rubbed the back of his head where he'd banged it earlier while unpacking his suitcase.

"Are you really here?"

"Yes."

"And this is your first trip outside of New England?"

"Yes," he answered tentatively. *What is she driving at?*

"And you did this simply to visit me?"

"Yes. Dena. Is there a problem?"

"No, no. I'm flattered. Let's book another night and spend some real time together."

Wayne chuckled. "I'm glad you said that, because I booked us both for another night."

"Pretty sure of yourself, huh?"

"I was. But, woman, you've got me wondering. Seriously, how long before you get here? I'm going stir-crazy waiting for you."

"Sorry, give me another ten minutes; I should be there shortly."

"Great. I'll wait for you in the driveway."

Dena laughed. "See you in a few."

She hung up the phone, not waiting for a response from him. Wayne clicked his phone shut, leapt off the front porch, and headed for the driveway. His heart kicked into high gear when he saw her red Mercedes driving down the rutted pathway to the seafront home.

She coasted into a parking space. "You're a nut."

"Hope you like nuts." He winked.

She smiled. "Love them."

His heart skipped a beat. *Lord, I don't think I believe in long courtships.*

❧

Dena lay back on the beach blanket and looked up at the night sky. A light breeze passed over her. She couldn't believe how one day could have started out so poorly and ended so perfectly. Wayne lay on the blanket beside her. He had flown from Portland to New York and rented a car out to the point on Long Island.

"Beautiful night," he yawned.

She yawned in response. *How is it that always happens?* "I still can't believe you actually came all this way to see me."

He rolled to his side and rested his head on his hand, his elbow extended for balance. "Honey, I love spending time with you. Besides, I might just get to see the world this way."

Dena chuckled. "Did you apply for a passport?"

"Not yet, but I've been thinking about it. Of course, I'd need some passport photos. Do you happen to know of someone who could do them for me?"

"Very funny." She sat up on the blanket, tucking her knees to her chest and wrapping her arms around her ankles. "Wayne, are we moving too quickly?"

He sat up and rested his elbows around his knees. "You know, I've been wondering the same thing. There are moments when I think we're going too slow, and then there are moments when I sit back and realize we've only known each other for a summer."

She felt a deep sense of comfort when she was with Wayne. A comfort she'd not known for years. It frightened and excited her at the same time. "Bill and I were high school sweethearts. We dated for three years, then married when he started college."

Wayne reached down and picked up a handful of sand and let it sift through his fingers. "Dena, I don't know if I'm ready for marriage."

Marriage? How'd he get—Oh, right, my relationship with Bill. "I didn't mean to imply I was talking about us getting married. Just that Bill and I dated for quite a while."

"Not that I'm suggesting we get married, either, but don't you think the three years were in part because of how young the two of you were?"

"No question. And if we were to talk about marriage, I wouldn't suggest a three-year courtship."

"Phew," he whistled.

"Oh, stop." She pushed him over to his side. "What's the game plan for tomorrow?"

"I don't know." He brushed the sand off his left arm. "What do you suggest? I'd love to see more of the area, if that's possible. The beaches are so sandy, so different from Squabbin Bay."

"A lot of beaches have sand," she teased.

"Okay, smarty-pants. You know the world; what do you suggest?"

"Well, are you driving back with me or flying home?"

"Hmm, guess it all depends on the company." He leaned over and kissed her cheek. "Driving," he whispered.

A shiver of excitement traveled down her spine. "Then I suggest we do some sightseeing and spend tomorrow night someplace else. Tell me what you've heard about in New York and New England that interests you."

"Goodness, there are so many places I've read about. I'd love to see the Statue of Liberty."

"All right. It's the other end of the island, and then some, but well worth the trip. Why don't we drive over to the Jersey side and visit Ellis Island, as well?"

"I'd love to."

"When do you need to get home?" She hoped it wasn't tomorrow night.

"I can be away for three days, but today counts as the first one."

"Gotcha." She stood up and dusted herself off.

Wayne followed suit and picked up the blanket. "I'm at your disposal, Dena."

He captured her hand in his. "Show me your world, please."

Dena's heart warmed. Perhaps a summer was enough time to know if you wanted to spend the rest of your life with a man. She firmed up her grip of his hand. "Only if you continue to show me yours. There's so much I've never seen in Maine."

"You're on."

They walked hand in hand up to the old Victorian bed-and-breakfast. A good-night kiss, and Dena found herself lying on her four-poster canopy bed. For the first time in two days, she scanned the room, absorbing every detail. It was no longer a room to spend the night in while she worked. It was a room in which she would need to make some serious decisions. *Should I sell my place in Boston and move up to Maine, like Jason suggested? Or do I want to keep my life the way it has been for the past five years?*

Chapter 16

Wayne rolled his shoulders as he drove Dena's car up I-85. Full of unspeakable emotions, he worked his way through the thinning traffic. Today had been wonderful. He'd seen the Statue of Liberty and Ellis Island many times since he was a kid—books, TV, news, and movies. They decided to spend tomorrow in Boston so she could keep an eye on Brianne.

Dena stirred. *She's an amazing woman, Lord.* He'd been tempted to pop the question today but held back. Impulsive decisions to marry weren't wise, he justified. The matter would take more time and prayer. They needed to see if they could work with her schedule.

Dena blinked her eyes open. "Hi," she yawned. Straightening up in her seat, she asked, "Where are we?"

"Not too far from the Mass border."

"We're making good time." She picked up her cell phone and dialed. "Hi, Brianne, sorry for calling so late. How are you?"

She paused.

"I'm on my way home right now. Which is why I called. I was wondering if Wayne could spend the night in your spare room."

Another pause.

"Great, thanks." She clicked the phone off.

"You're impossible."

"No, I'm thrifty. I seriously can't see you paying over a hundred bucks for less than six hours' sleep. Besides," she yawned again, "this way I can sleep with a clear conscience."

Wayne chuckled, grabbed her hand, and kissed the top of it. "I love you."

"I love you, too." She yawned again.

"Go to sleep, woman, before your yawning makes me tired and you'll have to drive."

" 'Night." She stifled a yawn.

Wayne took a swig of his now-chilled coffee. The caffeine would help him stay awake for the next two hours.

He drove for another thirty minutes when his eyes started to close. Thankfully, his cell phone rang. "Hello," he whispered.

"Daddy, it's me, Jess. I'm so excited. I'm sorry for calling so late, but I just had to tell you before I bust. I told Trev, and we've been on the phone for two hours. I'm just so excited."

Wayne grinned, then his grin slipped at the thought of a two-hour long-distance bill. "Slow down; tell me what's so exciting."

"Why are you whispering?"

"I'm trying to not wake up Dena."

"Dad?" she croaked.

"She's asleep in the passenger seat," he explained.

"Oh, sorry."

He couldn't blame his daughter for holding him accountable, especially since he also held her accountable, but it still felt a bit odd.

"Daddy, you'll never guess what I found in the mail when I got home from work this evening."

"You won the lottery?" he teased.

Dena stretched and sat up in her seat. He cupped the mouthpiece and apologized. "Sorry."

"No problem. Why don't you pull over at the next rest area and I'll drive the rest of the way?"

Wayne nodded. Jess continued in his ear. "So, what do you think?"

Ugh, I missed her big news. "I'm sorry, honey, Dena just woke up. I missed what you said."

"I got the job in Boston. Isn't that great?"

"That's wonderful, sweetheart. Is this the one you wanted? Didn't they hire someone else?"

"Yes, and yes. Apparently things didn't work out. I'm so excited, Daddy, I could burst. Isn't this great news?"

"Yes, I'm very happy for you. When will you be starting your new job in Boston?" He added the last tidbit for Dena's benefit.

"Next week. I have to give the job here a week's notice."

"I'm really happy for you; that's exciting news. Where are you going to live?"

"Trev said his parents will let me stay with them until I find a place. But I was wondering if Dena would mind letting me rent the room at her place again. What do you think?"

"I think you should ask her." He handed Dena the phone.

Dena placed it to her ear and listened. "Sure, let's start with four hundred a month for your rent. You're free to use what little food I have in the cabinets, but like before, you'll have to supply most of your groceries because I won't be around too much. As you know, I'm planning on being in Maine all next month. Same ground rules, right? . . .Good. I'll make sure your room is ready for you. I'll send a key home with your dad. I'll be on the road when you move in."

Dena said, "You're welcome," and handed the phone back to him.

"Hey, Jess, looks like things are coming together for you."

"Yeah, I'm so excited I can't sleep."

"Well, try. I'll be home late tomorrow night. Earlier if I can."

"Don't worry about me, Dad. I have to work until closing tomorrow night. I probably won't be home until after midnight."

"All right, sweetheart. Spend some time with the Lord, and I'll see you tomorrow."

" 'Night, Daddy, and thank Dena again for me."

"Okay, 'night." He clicked off the phone. "She says thank you again."

Dena chuckled. "She's welcome again. I hope she knows what she's getting into. It can't be good that the company hired someone and fired them within a month or so."

"I know. I didn't want to say anything to spoil her night. I'll bring that up to her one-on-one."

"On the other hand, it's possible the other person just wasn't right for the position."

"True. We'll have to trust the Lord, won't we?" He winked. Hadn't that been some of what Dena had been teaching him all along about grown children?

Dena chuckled. "Yeah, I've heard that a time or two."

"Are you sure about driving some?" he asked.

"Sure. Are you getting sleepy?"

"I was. It's a good thing she called when she did. I think I was starting to nod off."

"In that case, pull over now. I'll drive," Dena insisted.

Wayne laughed. "I'm wide awake right now. I can make it to the next rest area or exit, whichever comes first."

"All right."

"Thanks for letting her rent the room. Are you sure four hundred is enough?"

"It's low, but it's still my place, with my rules, so I figure she'll feel more at home for a while. She'll want her own place soon."

"But she'll need to save up for it. I'm just worried she and Trevor will make a foolish decision."

"Trust her, Wayne. She's a good kid."

"Yeah, I know." A sign came into view marking an exit in two miles.

"Have they talked marriage?"

"I don't know. Jess hasn't mentioned it. He's still living at home. Not that she isn't, also, but I've heard her mention to him a couple of times that he should be looking for his own place. He's working regular hours and has a good job. He's just content to stay at home, and I think that concerns Jess."

"It would me, also. But it's tough out there these days. Rents are extremely high, and unless you can get a group of four to rent a place together, it's almost impossible to afford anything and have money left over for food."

He flicked the turn signal on and slowed down for the exit ramp. "Yeah. I'm so proud of her."

"It shows." She tapped him on the knee. "You're a good father, Wayne. You've done well."

"Thanks. It was hard being a single parent, especially the single parent of a child of the opposite sex."

Dena giggled. "Tell me about it. I had two sons and no male role model other than memories of their dad."

"At least you had that."

"True. Didn't Jess's mother ever want to be a part of her life?"

"Not really. I talked her out of an abortion, and that made it hard for her in the small town. I can't blame her for moving away for college and never returning. She still sends Jess a birthday card and various other cards around holidays, but she has never visited with her or asked Jess to come see her."

"That's rough."

He pulled into an all-night service station. "Wanna fill up while we're here?"

"How's the gas?"

"Half a tank."

"Nah, there's more than enough to get us home." Dena opened the passenger door and slipped out of her seat. She bent down and touched her toes. "Feels good to stretch."

He unfolded himself as he got out of the sports car. He had to admit, he liked driving her car more than driving his old truck. It handled the road like nothing he'd ever experienced before. Temptation had been great to kick it up and really test how well it handled the road, but the better part of wisdom won and he drove at respectable speeds.

"She's fun to drive, isn't she?" Dena asked.

"Yeah, it is. I was just thinking how I've never driven anything that hugged the road so well."

"You should see it when she's up at really high speeds." She wiggled her eyebrows.

"How fast?" He leaned against the car and reached out to hold her. She stepped into his embrace.

"A hundred and ten, once. But only for a few seconds. I was too scared to keep driving that fast. I was out west, where you are allowed to drive insanely fast. The highway is straight, flat, and you can see for miles."

"I've heard about those roads."

"Wanna drive them with me sometime?" She leaned into him and kissed him on the cheek, then pulled away just as fast and hopped into the driver's seat. "Come on, let's get going."

Dena couldn't believe she'd gone so far as to suggest a lengthy road trip with Wayne. Were they ready to make such a commitment to each other? She questioned herself all the way home. She dropped him off at Chad's, giving him her key to their apartment. He'd stayed there before, so he knew the layout of the place.

At her own place, she adjusted the thermostat. While she was away, she had left her AC on but at a higher temperature. Enough to keep down the hot summer humidity but not enough to have her electric bill skyrocket. Having Jess rent a room would change her utility bills. Maybe four hundred a month wasn't high enough. On the other hand, she didn't pay a mortgage on the place any longer, and the kid needed a helping hand.

She stripped off her clothes and slipped under a warm shower. Her mind drifted back to the day she'd spent with Wayne. They had so much fun.

Finishing her shower, she dried off, dressed, and went to her darkroom. The nap in the car had left her wide awake. She placed the film in the darkroom and separated out her personal pictures with Wayne from the work-related ones.

She shut the door and put on the safelight. Taking a bottle opener, she popped open the metal canister that held the used film and set each roll into its own developing tank. Once done, she flipped on the regular lighting and grabbed her suitcase. She brought it into the laundry room and set a load in the machine, then went back to the darkroom.

She had developed a pattern of doing things over the years. She poured the chemicals in the proper pans then set up to make some contact prints. Normally, she'd go to bed and rest, finishing the process of selecting which shots to print and printing them. But tonight she wanted to print the ones of Wayne at the statue. Occasionally, she'd written articles to accompany her prints, and she felt there was a story in one of these pictures, if she had captured on film what he'd captured in her heart.

She worked for a couple of hours and developed some eight-by-tens of Wayne, making a close-up of his head shot with the background behind him. The contrast was incredible. The rough exterior of the lobsterman-slash-carpenter and the tear of joy, pride, and conviction in his eye, set against the backdrop of the statue were breathtaking.

The clock read four fifteen. She really should go to bed. She glanced at her computer then marched over and sat down. She tapped out a brief summary of her thoughts and went to bed.

The phone rang a moment after she fell asleep. Groaning, she reached over and answered. "Hello?"

"Dena?"

She yawned. "Wayne, what's the matter? Why are you calling me at. . ." She glanced over at the nightstand clock. "Oh dear. I'm sorry, honey. I overslept." The plan had been for her to pick him up at nine.

Wayne chuckled. "You didn't go right to sleep, did you?"

"Sorry."

"No problem. Do you need to sleep longer?"

"Probably, but I'll get dressed and pick you up in thirty minutes."

"Brianne said she could drive me over. She has some errands to run, and it won't be out of her way."

"All right. Thank Brianne for me. How's she feeling, by the way?"

"She's looking really good. A whole lot better than when I saw her the last time."

"Great. Okay, I'll see you soon. I'll make breakfast."

"Don't bother. I'll pick up something on the way over. How late did you stay up?"

"You don't want to know."

"Oh?"

"Four thirty."

"Ouch. I'll drive today."

Laughing, she answered, "Any excuse, huh?"

"You betcha. Love ya. See you soon."

"Love ya, too. Bye."

Dena threw the covers off and went to the kitchen and put on a pot of coffee. Of all the supplies she kept in the house while she was away, coffee was a mainstay. She kept a couple of unopened pounds on hand, along with several varieties of flavored coffee beans to be ground. Today she would not take the time to grind the beans. Instead, she popped the plastic lid off a can and measured the grounds into her coffeemaker.

The coffee set, she scurried back to the bedroom and dressed. She let the rich aroma of the brew filling the apartment draw her to the coffeemaker, where she poured herself a much-needed cup.

As she lifted the hot liquid to her lips, the doorbell rang. She set the coffee down on the counter and answered the door.

Wayne smiled and held out a white paper bag. Brianne grinned.

"Yum. Come on in. The coffee's ready." Dena rescued her abandoned mug and took her first sip.

"We arrived before her first cup."

"Ah," Wayne said and walked into the kitchen.

"How are you feeling, Brianne?"

"Good. Chad left this morning. He should be back tonight. The airline is putting him on a more local schedule, allowing him to come home almost every night."

"That's wonderful news." Dena took another sip of her coffee. The fuzz was beginning to lift from her brain.

"Why were you up so late?" Wayne poured himself and Brianne a cup of coffee, then set the bear claws on individual plates.

Dena yawned and stretched. "I was wide awake when I arrived so I decided to develop some pictures."

"Do you do this often?"

"Sometimes." She walked over to the table, carrying her plate and mug. Brianne and Wayne did likewise. Brianne left her items on the table and walked toward the bathroom.

"How'd you sleep?" she asked.

"Fine. I hit the bed and don't remember a thing. I woke up around eight. That's oversleeping, for me."

She bit into the bear claw. "These are wonderful, thank you."

Brianne came wandering back into the room. "These are amazing, Mom." In her hands were the pictures Dena printed last night.

"Let me see," Wayne asked, reaching out for the photos.

"If you'll agree, I'd like to send those in with an article. May I?" Dena asked.

Wayne shook his head no.

"No?"

"What?"

Dena and Brianne looked at him like he had two heads on his shoulders. "The picture is—is—too personal." He pushed the eight-by-tens away.

"Wayne, that's what makes them great photographs," Dena protested.

He knew she was right, but he wasn't about to publicly display a photo of himself with eyes full of tears. *Not this guy*, he resolved. "I don't want to discuss this further. I said I'm not interested."

Dena let out a loud sigh and sipped her coffee.

Brianne nibbled at her bear claw.

Wayne's right foot started to bounce up and down.

Another stiff minute passed before Dena cleared her throat. "Honey, before you say no, I mean a final no—I mean, allow me to show you something to see if that will change your mind. Please?"

Brianne's head bobbed back and forth from him to Dena as if she were watching a tennis match.

"Dena, I know I'm sounding unreasonable here but—"

She leaned over and placed her forefinger to his lips. "Shh. Just let me show you the other part before you completely decide against it."

He nodded his assent. There was nothing she could show him that would make him change his mind. He'd be the laughingstock of Squabbin Bay if folks saw him with a tear in his eye. Having Dena's son as his pastor guaranteed the picture would make the rounds. And that was something he just couldn't stomach, no matter what else she had to show him. He glanced over at the photograph of himself once again. *How humiliating.* At the same time, all the emotions he felt standing there at the base of the Statue of Liberty flooded back in.

"Thank you. I promise I won't bring it up again if you say no after what I show you."

"Uh-huh," he mumbled and filled his mouth with a huge bite of the sweet bear claw.

Brianne stood up from the table. "I've got to run, Mom. I'll call you later. Bye, Wayne."

"Bye. Thanks for the place to stay last night."

"No problem."

"I'll walk you to the elevator," Dena offered.

He knew she wanted to say something private, like it wasn't Brianne's fault for his ugly disposition. And she'd be right—it had nothing to do with Brianne and everything to do with Dena. How could she take such a photograph of him?

A moment later she walked back into the apartment. She stood beside him with her hands on her hips. "All right, what just happened here?"

"Nothing."

"Nothing?" she huffed then returned to her chair. "I've never seen you behave like this. What's going on here, Wayne? That's a perfectly good picture and worthy of printing. I don't understand your refusal."

"I have my reasons." *Pride comes before the fall, or something like that,* he recalled.

"Well, you keep your reasons to yourself until after I show you what I wrote."

"You write?"

"Occasionally I'll write a small piece to accompany a picture. I'm no Tom Clancy; a few choice words could cause people to look at the picture once again with a different eye, perhaps. I don't know."

She writes, Lord? How did I not know this? Here I am considering asking this woman to marry me, and I don't know something as basic as this.

Dena left the kitchen and returned with a piece of paper in hand. "It's rough, but it will give you the general idea of what I thought I should say."

Taking in a deep breath, he reached for the page and began to read. A fresh tear came to his eye. He began taking in short, gasping breaths then long, slow ones to calm down. He let the paper drift back to the table.

"You can use my picture," he mumbled and walked away. He needed air. He needed space. He walked out of the apartment building, down the slight hill, and across the street to walk along the Charles River. Water always calmed him.

"She's good, Lord."

Chapter 17

Dena didn't know whether or not to be relieved by Wayne's change of heart about using his picture. In reality, she was more confused. "What caused him to react that way, Lord?"

The kitchen now cleaned, she switched the loads of laundry she'd put in the night before, then proceeded into the darkroom to look at her contacts from the shoot. She needed to do something. *Who knows how long Wayne is going to walk off steam? If that's what he's walking off. He's obviously upset, but I don't know if he is angry or what. More like betrayed,* she guessed.

The smells of the chemicals assailed her as she walked in. She noticed a pan filled with solution. Pulling on a pair of rubber gloves, she disposed of the chemical. It wasn't like her to leave the room in this shape. She scanned the area for any other item that seemed out of place.

"Dena," Wayne hollered.

She dropped the gloves in the sink and went out to the living room. "I think we need to talk." She approached him slowly and gestured for him to sit on the couch.

"I'm sorry. I wasn't expecting to see myself crying in a photograph. I felt betrayed. It's like, I felt safe enough with you to let down my guard a little and—boom—you wanted to expose it to the entire world. I'm not used to this, Dena. Have you often used your family as models for photographs?"

"No, not really. There's been a print or two, but not many. When they were younger, I'd hang their school pictures in my studio. I had the school contract, so it was my work." She was rambling a bit. "Wayne, I'm not sure why it bothered you. I mean, it's a beautiful, touching moment. I'm pleased with how well the photograph captured your emotions. That doesn't always happen."

"Dena, I don't know how to explain this other than to simply state it. I'm a man. Men don't cry, at least not in public. You were asking to let the entire world see me cry. Do you have any idea how hard that is for a man? For me?"

"I hadn't thought about that."

He leaned back and closed his eyes. "You're right. It's a powerful picture, and your words will make a strong statement."

"Thanks, but I don't have to publish the print. I promise to keep personal moments I capture on film between you and me private."

Wayne let out a nervous chuckle. "Honey, you don't have to check with me on every detail, but I would like to see any picture of me, or us, you want to sell or put on public display before it goes out."

"Fair enough. You'll have to sign a release for the photograph to be used anyway."

"Thanks. So, now that I've spoiled our last day together, how can we redeem some of it?"

"Well, I need to drive you up to the Portland airport so you can retrieve your car. What time do you want to be home?"

"I was planning on eleven or midnight."

She mentally calculated that he'd need four hours for travel from Portland up to Squabbin Bay. Which meant he'd have to leave Portland by seven—eight, at the latest.

"What would you like to do today?" she asked.

He leaned into her and kissed her on the end of her nose. "Show me your city. I'd like to see it through your eyes."

Okay, so he has flaws. He's male; he's human, she reasoned. *But who in their right mind wouldn't want to be with this handsome, green-eyed man?* "History or contemporary?"

"Huh?"

"Do your interests lie with history or with modern-day things?"

"I have a fairly healthy interest in history, but I have seen most of the historical markers in this city on school field trips with Jess."

"All right, we'll lean to your carpenter side and visit some of the architecture."

Wayne leaned against the door casing. "Actually, I was thinking in more practical terms. Where do you like to go? What do you like to do? Where do you like to eat? Those kinds of places. What do you think?"

You're getting kinda personal. "Sounds like a plan. We'll start with a little Brazilian restaurant that has the most wonderful hearts of palm salad."

"Nothing too funky, I hope?"

"Funky? Didn't that word go out of vogue before your time?"

Wayne laughed. "Things take a little longer to make their way to us Down Easterners, you know. Especially back when I was in high school. Today, it doesn't seem to take as long."

Dena grabbed her keys and purse from the counter and looped her arm through his. "Come on, time's a wasting. This place is definitely funky. And I *am* old enough to remember using that word."

They departed her apartment with humor. "Bamboa's is really a mix of Brazilian and French cuisine. There's a huge fish tank with wonderfully colored tropical fish. The decor is loud with all the rich colors you'd find in places in Brazil."

An hour and a half later, they emerged from Bamboa's. "You were right; it was an experience, and the food was great. Now where to?" Wayne asked.

"You know, I've been wondering that all through dinner. There are so many little places I like in the city, but they are not the kinds of places where you spend time, real time, with someone. Since it's going to be another week before we see each other, I was wondering if we could just spend some downtime together."

&

Wayne sat back on his deck with a tall glass of iced tea. Dena would be arriving tomorrow for an entire month. The past ten days had been the longest in the history of mankind. At least in his history. They'd had such a good time together in New York and Boston, focusing on work seemed futile.

Jess was now living in Boston at Dena's apartment. How was it that in a few months his life had so radically changed?

His phone rang. "Hello," he answered.

"Hi, Wayne, I'm home."

"Hey, how was your trip?"

"Miserable. I missed you."

His heart took flight at those three simple words. "I missed you, too. How's Jess?"

"I haven't a clue. She appears to have moved in, but she's not here right now. I'm packing for the month. I managed to get a couple of bags packed before I left, but I need to do laundry tonight before I can come up tomorrow."

"The house is ready."

"Oh, honey, I appreciate that so much. I've been rethinking Jason's suggestion that I make Maine my residence. While I was away, Amber e-mailed me. She and David are really having a tough time. He's still not able to find work, and she's so busy working. Jason's been talking with David about some possible work in Maine. Amber could easily transfer as a nurse to a local hospital. It just seems my family needs me here."

His heart sank. He would have hoped she would have mentioned him in there somewhere. "I'll pray with you about it."

"Thanks. I appreciate it. Actually, to be totally honest, I'd like to spend more time with you, too. Is that possible?"

His heart leaped up and did a somersault. "I'd like that." He lowered his voice. "I love you, Dena."

"I love you, too. Any fears?"

"Tons, but we've been over that ground before. This next month will be a real test."

"Only way to find out is to just jump right in and live it." Wayne grinned and fired a silent praise heavenward.

"Yeah, that's why I decided to move most of my lab and files with me."

"You're kidding! Are you serious?"

"Yes."

"Dena, you've really given this a lot of thought, haven't you?"

"I started thinking about this months ago, when I made the decision to have a darkroom put in the cottage. If I were conservative with my funds, I could live off of my investments now. But I enjoy working. I have to stay active. Is there really enough up there in Maine to keep me busy?"

"I don't know, Dena. That's always been my fear. You've traveled the world. You enjoy traveling, and here I sit in a very small town with a very boring life. How can I compete with your career?"

"If you say it that way, you can't. But there's something about being up there that recharges me. I'd like to think it's the Lord and having more time with Him, but I know it also has to do with a certain green-eyed man who lives up there."

Wayne sat down on the old rocker by the fireplace. He should be rejoicing, but something about the entire weight of the state of Maine sat on his shoulders. He couldn't be responsible for Dena giving up her career. There had to be another way. She was far too gifted of a photographer.

"Wayne?"

Her calling his name jarred him back to the phone call. "Sorry, I'm—" He rubbed the back of his neck. "I don't know what to say, Dena. I don't know what to do. I want you here, but something feels off. Are you sure? Absolutely sure?"

❧

Dena wasn't sure about anything. She'd been battling herself the entire week about whether or not she was making the right decision. And driving up the interstate hadn't confirmed her decision one way or the other. David and Amber were going to rent a truck and bring up the rest of Dena's belongings this weekend. Wayne's nervousness about her changing her career plans didn't help her concerns, either. Weren't they always talking around the subject of making their relationship more permanent? Hadn't their weekend ten days ago confirmed their desires to spend more time together? What was he afraid of?

Dena drummed her cherry red fingernails on the steering wheel. She took in a long breath and eased it out slowly. Hadn't she decided last week that the family needed her? Isn't that really why she was making this change? Brianne's health continued to be a concern.

Yes, the family needed her around—or she needed to be around her family more. In either case, it was the right decision even if nothing developed between her and Wayne.

Her cottage came into view. The ocean shimmered in the sunlight. She took in a deep breath of salt air. "Home," she sighed. "When did this cottage become my home instead of my apartment in Boston?"

She grabbed two bags from the trunk and headed inside. Dropping them on the kitchen floor, she walked back to the hallway entrance to the addition. For the first time, it wasn't covered in plastic. Slowly, she worked her way into the new section and traced the edges of the woodwork with her right forefinger. "You do excellent work, Wayne. Thank you."

The Jacuzzi in the master bathroom was her next stop. The room glistened. The carpet had been put in and looked wonderful next to the stone floor surrounding the hot tub. She looked up, and there she found a skylight directly overhead. She imagined herself late at night, unwinding after a long day of work in the darkroom, feeling the warmth of the hot jets on her back as she looked up at the sky, relaxing. Totally relaxing. "Calgon, take me away," she whispered.

The idea of jumping into the Jacuzzi flitted through her mind. Then reality hit: There were more bags and boxes to unload. Not to mention that the house needed to cool down. She switched on the central air before heading out to the car for another load.

"Hi, Mom," Jason said with a box in his hand.

"How'd you know I was here?"

"Amber called. Besides, Jenny Thompson called when you got off the interstate."

"Jenny Thompson?"

"She owns a place near the four corners in town."

"Ah, but how do I know her?"

"You don't, but she knows you."

"Jason, how do you stand it? I mean, with everyone knowing everyone's business."

Jason shifted the weight of the box onto his hip. "Most folks don't pay the gossip no never mind. But there is an upside to the small community, and that's if you're in trouble, folks are always there to lend a hand. And notice when you need a hand," he added with a wink.

"I suppose Amber told you that I'm going to try living up here on a more permanent basis."

"She did."

Dena pulled another box out of the trunk and led them back into the house. "What do you think?"

"I think there's more to it than what you told Amber. Just how serious are you and Wayne, Mom?"

Chapter 18

Wayne found Dena and Pastor Russell in deep conversation, and, by the startled stares he received, he could only assume he'd been the topic of discussion.

"I was wondering if you'd like to go out for dinner," he told Dena shortly after Pastor Russell left.

"Actually, I'm beat. But you're welcome to have dinner with me. Of course, it'll be some frozen dinner or something out of a can."

Wayne smiled. "I'll take what I can get. Or I could drive to town and pick up a couple of fresh steaks for the grill."

"Are you cooking?" she asked, grabbing a suitcase.

"Sure. I'll even pick up some corn on the cob and potato salad. How's that sound?"

"Wonderful. I'm starving."

Wayne chuckled. "Honey, when aren't you hungry?" he teased.

"Hey, I resemble that," she quipped.

"Oh?" He pulled her toward him. It had been ages since they had shared a kiss. Well, maybe not ages, but eleven days was long enough. The kiss lengthened, and he felt her tension melt in his arms along with his own. He hadn't been prepared for her just moving to Maine. She'd mentioned she was coming for a month, but to just readjust her schedule and to start plans of living in the area full-time had caught him off guard.

She ended the kiss first and pushed herself away from him. He closed his eyes and mentally refocused. "I'm glad you're here," he offered, slowly opening his eyes.

"Are you? Last night, I wasn't so sure."

"Honey, I've never just up and dropped everything and changed my life around."

"Oh, didn't you? When you were eighteen, didn't you accept responsibility for Jess and take her in and care for her, giving up on your own college desires to raise a child?"

"But that's different."

"Okay, then what about the weekend in New York? That was impulsive."

Wayne stepped back and turned away from her.

"Don't walk out on me now, Wayne. We need to talk this through."

"I wasn't leaving. I was just thinking. You're right; it was impulsive. But I'm

117

worried you're giving up too much."

She reached out for his hand and led him to the sofa. "Wayne, there's a lot you don't know about my business. I can sell and resell photographs for years. It's simply being aware of what the market is looking for. I can do that far better from here than traipsing around the world."

"Really?"

"Yes. And there are other things I can do and still earn a salary. Granted, it won't be as plump of a salary as I had been making, but I would still earn a reasonable income. But I've gone a step further. I've started arranging with other photographers to kind of work as their agent, helping them with bookings and scheduling when I'm contacted for a job. And I'd earn a certain percentage of their income for that shoot."

"It's a well-laid-out plan."

"Thanks, but I still don't know where we were headed. Do you?"

"I know what I'd like, but, you're right, we are both rather set in our ways. This month will be quite a test for us."

"Yeah. Except that David and Amber are arriving this weekend with the kids. They're bringing up the rest of my stuff for the master suite."

"And?"

"And they'll probably be staying for a week. The stress has been really hard on them. I might even suggest they leave the kids and go home alone for a week."

Dena's stomach churned loud enough for the entire room to hear it. Thankfully, they were alone.

"I'm going to get you something to eat. We'll talk more when I get back."

"Thanks." She kissed him lightly on the lips. "When I was a kid and fell in love with Bill, I didn't have any fear. I do have serious doubts, Wayne. I've liked being on my own. There's a freedom in it."

"I know. I do understand. When Jess was in college, I found myself enjoying having the house to myself. I missed her, but the house was my own. The 'sound of silence' filled the air. There was a sense of rhythm in the quietness, somehow."

"Exactly. So, can we share our lives with each other?"

"I don't know, Dena. I honestly don't know. I want to, but, as with you, it's a major step."

Dena let out a half chuckle. "*Major* is an understatement."

"Yeah," Wayne sighed. "All right, I'm going now. We'll pick this up when I come back." He tapped her on her knee.

"Okay."

He left the cottage and worked his way back to town. Why was he fighting Dena's move to Maine?

You need help, ol' boy, serious help. Wayne turned into the grocery store parking lot. A few cars were parked next to the building, while a single black sedan in the center of the lot sat under the streetlight. Peter Mayhew, the elderly owner of the store, always parked under that lamp. Precious little happened in the way of crime in this small town, but the precaution had been a wise move.

"Evening, Mr. Mayhew, how are you tonight?" Wayne asked, pulling a red plastic basket from the small pile near the door.

"Fine, fine. Heard that pretty Ms. Russell's back in town. Is that so?"

"Yes, sir. She'll be staying for an entire month. You might have to stock up on some of that fancy city stuff for the lady." Wayne winked.

Peter's bushy white eyebrows rose halfway up his bald head. "Already placed an order. Pastor Russell told me she was coming last week. Any truth to the rumors that you and Ms. Russell are moving in together?"

"Not a word of it. And if you hear anyone speaking such, please let them know Mrs. Russell lives by the same standards Pastor Russell preaches."

"Pleased to hear it. Kids today just don't seem to have the same values."

It was time for Wayne to raise his eyebrows. Dena would love hearing herself referred to as a kid.

"Present company excluded, of course." Peter winked again.

Maybe moving to the city would be a better start for us if we were to get married, he mused.

"What can I get you tonight?" Peter asked.

"Two steaks, sirloin or better, if you have it."

"Delmonico cut?"

"Perfect." Delmonicos were tender, an excellent choice cut from the rib section of the cow.

He picked up a pint of homemade potato salad prepared by Pete's daughter, Mable, and a half dozen ears of corn. He paid for the order, walked outside, and slid the bag over to the passenger side of the truck. *Lord, I just don't want to get in Dena's way. Please give me peace about her decisions regarding her business.*

He pulled out into the street and turned toward the four corners in the center of town. Tires squealed. A black SUV suddenly filled his field of vision and plowed into his left side. Then he saw nothing.

❧

"Mom, there's been an accident."

"What? Who? What happened?" Dena curled the phone cord around her finger. Where was Wayne? He should have been back a half hour ago. Then it dawned on her. "Wayne?"

"I'm afraid so."

"Where is he? Is he okay? What happened?" She reached for her car keys from the counter.

"Some kids were driving too fast and ran the stop sign. The vehicle hit him on the driver's side. He's been hurt, but I don't know how badly. They're driving him up to Ellsworth now. The town doctor couldn't do much for him here, Mom. I drove up to Mayhew's Market just as they were putting him in the ambulance."

"Which hospital? Has Jess been told?"

"No one's called Jess, as far as I know. I was thinking we should wait to hear what the doctors say after they've done some tests."

"I'm going up there. Where is this hospital?"

"In Ellsworth; it's Blue Hill Hospital. I'll take you."

"No, I'll follow you. There's no telling how long I'll be up there."

"All right. Meet me at Mayhew's Market. On second thought, crews may still be cleaning up after the accident." He suggested an alternate meeting place.

"Fine." Dena grabbed her purse and ran out the door. "Oh, Lord, please keep him safe." Tears threatened to fall. *No, I can't. Not yet. I need to drive.* She set her resolve and drove as fast and as cautiously as she could allow herself.

She drove into the market's parking lot about the same time that Jason arrived. He rolled down his window. "Are you all right?"

"I'm fine. How far away is this hospital?"

"An hour and a half. Two hours with traffic."

Dena nodded. She didn't trust herself to speak. She followed Jason down the long, windy roads toward the interstate. "Who cares about schedules?" she asked aloud in the empty car. "We should just get married and follow our hearts. Life is too short. We'll work out the details somehow. Father, heal him and help us so we can be one with You," she prayed, and continued down the highway.

Inside the waiting room, she paced back and forth. Jason had a little pull, since he was clergy, and went back into the ER to discover Wayne slipping in and out of consciousness. He'd also suffered some cracked ribs. They were still checking on internal bleeding, but the doctor was very hopeful.

Dena dialed her home phone in Boston. "Jess?"

"Dena, hi. Did you arrive okay?"

"Fine. Honey, I'm sorry to be the one to tell you this, but your dad's been in an accident. He's okay."

Silence followed, then a sniffle. "Is he all right?"

"He has some broken ribs and he's semiconscious."

"Where is he? How'd it happen? I'm coming up."

"He's in Blue Hill Hospital in Ellsworth. Some kid ran a stop sign by Mayhew's Market and plowed into the driver side door. You're welcome to come up, but there's not much you can do right now. Do me a favor? If you come up, have Trevor come with you. I don't want you driving six hours by yourself with this kind of news."

Jess sniffled again. "All right. Dena, is he really going to be okay?"

"Yes, I haven't seen him yet. The doctor says it looks good. But he'll be sore for quite a while."

"Okay. Can I call you from the road?"

They exchanged numbers, and Dena began calling to ask the rest of the family to be praying, only to discover that Marie already had.

An hour later, Jason was able to go in and visit with Wayne briefly. "He barely knew I was there, Mom. You might as well go home."

"No, I want to see him. I'll wait until I can; then I'll get a room."

"All right. I'll come by sometime tomorrow and bring a change of clothes."

"Thanks, but you don't have to. My overnight bag is still in the backseat of my car."

The night dragged on. By midnight she was allowed to visit Wayne briefly.

She held his hand. Her stomach twisted and churned at the sight of him hooked up to the monitors. "Honey," she whispered and kissed him tenderly on the forehead.

His eyes fluttered open, then closed slowly. "Marry me," he whispered. He opened his eyes again and focused on hers. "Life's too short. We'll work out the schedules. Please say you'll marry me."

She kissed him again and combed his sandy blond hair with her fingers. *Lord, heal him quickly,* she prayed. "Yes, I will. I'll come back in the morning. They won't let me stay more than ten minutes. I love you."

"I love you, too."

❧

Three days later Dena stood in her darkroom and tried to put some order to her files. Amber and David brought up the rest of her files and cabinets. Those had been easy to put in place. But since she'd been living between Boston and Squabbin Bay, she had fallen behind and had a stack of filing to do.

"Mom, I hate to say this, but I think you were taking pictures of the harbor when your mind was somewhere else." Amber handed her the laptop. "I've highlighted the photos in question."

Dena looked at the foggy images. The blurred bow of a boat showed itself to be the focal point. "Ah, those are some of the photos I took while trying to capture a shot of the poachers."

"Poachers?" Amber took the computer back from Dena. "You're going to have to fill me in on that one."

"Amber," David called, "I'm taking the kids to the beach."

"Okay." Amber turned back to her mother. "The house is clear, tell me."

Dena swallowed a light chuckle then filled her daughter in about the poaching. After Wayne's accident, the police had discovered that those same teens had also been responsible for Ben Costa's house fire. Ben himself had been responsible for his boat blowing up. He'd left the gas on and a cigar still burning on the edge of his sink. But that still hadn't solved the issue of the poachers.

"Wow, and I thought your life would be too boring up here. Do you think life might be calmer in Boston?"

Dena chuckled. "You know, it might be." She reached for the photographs of Chad's wedding. "Can you sort these and place them in order? Thankfully, I made doubles and sent them to the kids so they could order the ones they want enlarged."

"Sure."

Dena opened another box and lifted out the series of negatives and contact prints from the Colorado white-water rafting trip. She labeled the file folder and placed all negatives and CDs from the trip in the folder.

"Dena," Wayne called from someplace inside the house.

"I'm in the darkroom." She got up and met him at the doorway. "Hey, what's up? How are you feeling?"

"Okay. I'm still sore, but my head isn't throbbing anymore. I hate to do this, but my dad is insisting that I spend the evening with him, something about his retirement plan. I'm sorry, but I won't be able to have dinner with you and the kids tonight."

"No problem. I've yet to meet your father."

Wayne reached over and put his hands on her waist. "You will. He's a good man but has gotten very self-centered since he retired."

"Hi, Wayne." Amber walked up from behind Dena. "Mom, these were in Chad's wedding pictures. I think they need to be filed with those other pictures of the poachers."

"You got pictures?"

"No. Well, nothing that shows who it is or even if it is the poachers."

"These are clear," Amber offered.

"They can't be the poachers. I took those before Chad's wedding."

Wayne reached for them. "May I see?"

"Sure." Amber handed over the half dozen photographs.

Dena looked over Wayne's shoulder. His hands started to shake. "When did you take these?"

"The week after the carnival, back in early May."

He let the photographs fall. "I have to go. That's my father." Wayne slowly stomped out of the house.

Dena picked the photographs up off the floor. *His father?*

Epilogue

Three months later

Dena straightened her dress and looked in the mirror. The past three months had been difficult. Dena's photographs caught Wayne's father as the poacher. Apparently, he'd gotten into gambling and lost all of his savings and then some. She smiled at her reflection. Wayne's desire to help his parents had left him destitute. Wayne had sold his house and used his savings to pay off his father's gambling debts, along with the sale of his parents' home in Squabbin Bay. Dena had grown to love Wayne even more as they worked through the situation together.

"Ready, Mom?" Amber poked her head around the door.

"Ready."

The organ music floated into the room. She'd been in this room before, primping Brianne for her wedding to Chad. Now she was doing the same for herself.

"Hey, Mom." Jess stopped short. She'd been calling Dena "Mom" for a couple of months now—ever since moving in after Wayne sold the house and moved onto his boat. "Wow, you look great. Dad's going to flip when he sees you."

Dena chuckled. "I hope not. I don't want to see the inside of the hospital again for a mighty long time." She turned to her new daughter. "How is he?"

"Better. Grandpa and Grandma are here. Grandpa is still a bit touchy about Dad having paid off his debts. Grandma is so grateful they didn't lose their condo in Florida. But I can't wait until the two of you tie the knot. I need some relief."

Dena laughed. Jess had moved back to Maine shortly after the accident. The dream job in Boston was simply that, a dream. Nothing in the office ran smoothly, the other employees didn't work well together, and everyone was out to move themselves ahead and not help anyone else. Jess's relationship with Trevor was cooling off. He wasn't interested in living in Maine, and, in fact, he had little motivation about doing anything more than was required of him. He was a good person, but Jess found him lacking in more and more areas once they were apart and she was no longer looking at him through her emotions. Dena fired off another prayer for Jess's future husband. He was out there, Dena knew, but she was glad Jessica wasn't too broken up about the end of her relationship with Trevor.

"Wow!" Amber came in with Dena's bouquet. "You look great, Mom."

"Thanks."

She and Wayne had decided on a simple wedding with no attendants. If they had allowed one of their children to stand in, they'd have to have all of them, so it had been simpler to have none.

"It's time." Marie smiled. "Are you ready, Mom?"

The fears had washed away the night of the accident. "Oh, yeah. We'd have been married a month or two ago if—"

The room erupted in laughter.

"Right, if you two ever stopped long enough to stop worrying about each other's careers. Face it, the accident was a blessing." Brianne stood with her hands on her hips, her six-month belly protruding.

Again the room erupted into laughter. "I think we could have gotten there without the accident. After all, we could have married sooner if Wayne wasn't so stubborn about. . . Never mind."

"I think he was more concerned about carrying you over the threshold," Jess offered.

Dena's eyes widened. "He wouldn't dare."

Jess laughed.

Marie took charge and encouraged everyone to take their seats in the sanctuary. Dena took a moment. Closing her eyes, she sighed and released the last of her fears over to the Lord. With total confidence, she stepped out of the small room, headed toward the center aisle, and paused. Marie signaled the organist.

The music changed to the traditional wedding march.

Her smile broadened. She took a step and rounded the corner. She caught a glimpse of Wayne's sparkling green eyes. Her heart fluttered. *Dear Lord, I do love those green eyes. But more importantly, I love the man who knows how to wear 'em.*

❧

Wayne shifted his stance upon seeing Dena walk down the aisle. He locked his gaze on hers, and they stayed focused on one another. *Thank You, Lord.*

Jason began the service. Wayne held Dena's silky hands. He couldn't believe this incredible woman wanted him above all others.

"In sickness and health," Jason said.

Wayne and Dena winked at one another.

At some point he and she said the appropriate "I do's."

"You may kiss the bride." Wayne leaned in and kissed her warm lips, then closed the distance between himself and his bride and held her, not wanting to let her go.

Reluctantly, they pulled apart. Jason concluded. "I now have the honor of presenting to you Mr. and Mrs. Wayne Kearns."

The congregation stood and clapped.

"I love you," Wayne whispered.

"I love you, too."

"So where are you taking me for our honeymoon?" Wayne wiggled his eyebrows and led her down the aisle.

She'd kept it a secret. With all the family troubles and his healing from the accident, she felt she could at least ease his burden by planning the honeymoon.

"Hawaii."

"I'm going to love being married to you. Will we be on a photo op?"

Dena giggled. "You never know."

TRESPASSED HEARTS

Dedication

I'd like to dedicate this book to all the helpful friends on the T & TTT forum. You've been so incredibly helpful to my husband, Paul, and me as we've set out to build our own Tiny Travel Trailer. Thank you.

Chapter 1

R andi!" Dorothy Grindle hollered from the back kitchen.
Randi spun around. Her foot caught, and the bowl of lobster bisque dumped all over a customer.

He jumped from his seat.

The bowl bounced on the old floorboards. "I'm so sorry." She patted the man down with the towel she wore on her apron.

"Miranda Blake, you did not do what I think you just did," Dorothy spouted as she hurried to the man draped in lobster bisque. He was well-groomed, apart from the soup. "I'm so sorry. Your meal is on us. Feel free to go home and change. We'll serve you up something special."

Randi felt the stab of Dorothy's penetrating gaze. She needed this job to hold her over. Her home Web-page-designing business was not flourishing as she had hoped it would. "I'm sorry, Dorothy. I must have tripped." Randi scanned the floor, looking—hoping—for something that would have made her lose her footing.

Clearing his throat, the customer said, "I'll clean up in the bathroom. Do you have hand dryers?"

"No, but I can lend you a clean apron to cover the damp area. And some clean towels to mop up the soup."

His brown hair, not too much shorter than her own, draped to just above his shoulders, and swayed with the nod of his head. "Great."

"Great" was not how Randi would describe his demeanor. "Controlled annoyance" fit better. The pants he wore were casual but on the upper scale of quality fabric. His wristwatch was modest, but the polo shirt and Top-Siders spelled money and summer tourist through and through. Not that Squabbin Bay received many tourists. From time to time, though, a few sailboats would pull into the harbor and spend a night or two in the area.

"Hey, Randi," Jess said with a wave as she marched in and plopped herself by a bay window. "How's it going?"

Randi shrugged her shoulders.

Jess raised her right eyebrow but didn't say another word.

Randi and Jess had been best friends since kindergarten. Jess's father had recently married one of the newest residents of Squabbin Bay. And Randi couldn't be happier for the two of them. Wayne Kearns had been the youth leader when she and Jess were growing up. As an unwed father, he had raised Jess on his own since he was eighteen. His past experience regarding sex before marriage had been a tremendous deterrent for the kids in high school. At least it had been for her and Jess.

"Randi, you can't mess up again. Once more and you're out of here. I can't afford a clumsy waitress," Dorothy muttered in a low whisper, as if to keep the customers from hearing the reprimand.

"I'll do better. I promise," Randi replied. After the lecture and cleanup, the customer still hadn't returned from the men's room. Randi took out her pad and went over to Jess.

"What would you like, Jess?"

"Nothing. I came here on an errand for Mom."

"Oh." Randi slid the ordering pad into the pocket of her apron.

"What happened?" Jess asked.

Randi slipped a stray hair behind her ears to keep it from falling in her face. "I dumped a hot bowl of lobster bisque on a customer."

"No." Jess chuckled. "Please tell me you didn't?"

"I did."

"Girlfriend, you've got to be more careful. You've got the only available job in town. Dorothy doesn't have time to train you."

"Don't remind me. She does just about every day." Randi scanned the room and visually checked on her customers. "So what's this errand for your mom?"

Randi's joy over the closeness Jess shared with her stepmother, Dena, couldn't be more complete. In the private conversations Randi and Jess had had over the years, Jess had wondered what her real, biological mother was like since she'd had virtually nothing to do with Jess's life. Now she had a woman she could talk to. Randi was relieved because she felt inept to guide Jess in her decision to continue dating her college boyfriend, Trevor. He just seemed so strange. But Jess loved him. And Randi hoped that was all that mattered.

"I'm meeting a new photographer she's interviewing," Jess said.

Jess had gotten her dream job straight out of college, but it hadn't worked out. In less than a month, she had returned disillusioned and content to stay in Squabbin Bay. Therein was the rub with Trevor. He preferred the city life in Boston and wanted her to move back. Jess hardly spoke about him.

The customer emerged from the men's room. The wet spot on his shirt and pants was enormous.

"Excuse me." Randi ran to the kitchen and procured a clean apron and some fresh towels for the poor man. Returning with the items in hand, she stepped up to his table. "I'm sorry," she said again.

"It's over, end of story. Can I have another bowl of lobster bisque?"

"Coming right up." *And hopefully not on top of you again.* Randi grinned while placing his order back at the kitchen window. Even with the huge wet spot, he was more handsome than any man should be, at least to her way of thinking. Randi gave a sidelong glance in his direction. She'd love to run her fingers through his wavy, brown hair. Normally men with longer hair didn't appeal to her, but there was something about his—Randi cut off her thoughts. He was good-looking. She had noticed. That was the end of it.

Jess walked over to the stranger's table. "Excuse me. Are you Jordan Lamont?"

"Yes, are you Jessica Kearns?" he asked.

"The one and only." Jess plopped herself down at the man's table.

What was his name? Oh, yeah, Jordan. Randi decided the best order of business was to mind her own and try not to lose her job. She should be able to do that for three more hours, she hoped, and fired off a prayer.

બ

Jordan felt so foolish sitting there wearing a big white apron. The lobster bisque would stain unless he had a chance to wash his clothes. His overnight bag was in the trunk. Dena Russell had offered him the spare room in her house for the night after their interview, but he would smell horrible and look even worse. The only redeeming factor was that Dena's stepdaughter, Jess, was now aware of what happened.

He needed this job. Thankfully, he'd left his portfolio out in the car. No telling what the lobster bisque would have done to it. Oddly enough, if the waitress hadn't distracted him so much, he would have moved out of the way before the bowl fell in his lap. She had a stunning beauty, her skin tone suggesting a rich Italian heritage. But what intrigued him the most was her eyes. If he wasn't mistaken, they were charcoal gray, almost black. It had been a long time since he'd seen eyes that dark.

"Hello? Earth to Jordan." Jess Kearns's voice broke in on his musings.

"Sorry. What did you ask?"

"If you'd like to have them make your order 'to go' so you can get out of those wet clothes and change at the house, that might help."

"Yes, yes, that would be great." Jordan jumped up and banged into Randi's tray.

He saw Jess's eyes widen saucerlike a millisecond before he felt the heat of the soup pour down his back. He spun around, and the look of horror on Randi's face said it all. Jordan couldn't contain himself and laughed out loud. "I'm so sorry." He helped steady Randi on her feet. "I was going to say make that order 'to go,' but you just did." He kissed her cheek and ran out the door.

As he approached the back end of his Jeep, he took off his wet shirt. Opening his tote bag, he grabbed a new polo shirt and pulled it on. Brushing his hair with his fingers, he fastened it with the elastic band he kept on his wrist.

Jess came up behind him. "Follow me," she said then jumped into a green pickup and turned on the engine.

He hesitated. He should go back and apologize again. And why did he kiss the waitress? He shook off the further need to apologize, slipped behind the wheel, and followed Jess down the winding roads that covered the Maine coastline. They passed a field of boulders. It looked as if someone had been planting them—there were so many—and yet he knew they were just part of the natural setting that made up Maine. He loved the rocky coast and wanted to paint and photograph as much of the area as possible. But that would only happen if he managed to get the job with Dena Russell, now going by the name of Dena Russell Kearns.

He could have managed to find the place on his own except for the last turn. There were no real markers to offset the turn toward Dena's home.

He'd driven by her studio in town. It had a large plateglass window, but other than that it appeared to be a small Victorian cottage on stilts built into the rock cliff that lined the north side of Main Street.

Jess brought her truck to a stop on the broken shell driveway and hopped out. "Bring in your bag!" she called out and marched to the side door of the house.

They had a great view of the ocean. Jordan stepped out of his Jeep and took in a deep pull of the salt air. It felt good, cool, crisp, with just enough salt and not a lot of low tide.

"Mom, I found him!" Jess hollered as she walked through the door.

Found me? As if I was lost? Grr. Not a good thing for a man who's trying to be hired as a photojournalist. Why hadn't I insisted on finding the place myself?

A woman stepped to the door. "Jordan, I'm Dena. It's good to meet. . ." Her words trailed off as she glanced at the apron around his waist.

"Sorry. I met a clumsy waitress."

"It was Randi," Jess supplied, suppressing a chuckle.

Dena smiled. "The guest room is straight back and on your right." She stepped inside and allowed Jordan entrance into the cozy cottage.

"Thank you. I'll be out in a moment."

"No problem. Would you like some iced tea?"

"Yes, thanks."

Jordan continued down the hallway to the first room on his right. He overheard Jess say, "I'm heading back to the studio to finish the bookwork."

He shut the door and placed his duffel bag on the bed of the small but comfortable room. A window faced the ocean. Jordan found himself drawn to the view. He set his hands on the sill and focused on the Atlantic past the rise of the bluff. The royal blue of the sea contrasted the sand and tall grass. He shook off the meanderings of his artistic thoughts and quickly dispensed with the damp slacks and put on his jeans. Unfortunately he had brought only one dress outfit for the interview.

He stepped out of his room and headed back to the entryway where he'd seen Dena in the kitchen. "Hi."

"Feel better?" She placed two glasses of iced tea on the table.

"Much."

"You can wash your things later." Dena sat down at the table. "I'm assuming you passed by the studio in town?"

"Yes."

"I don't do much local business yet, but I'm working on it. Your résumé showed you had studio experience."

"Yes, that's right." Jordan and Dena continued with the formalities of the interview for the next fifteen minutes.

"So what questions do you have for me?" Dena asked.

"I'm curious as to why you're hiring someone to do the work you're more than capable of? If you don't mind me asking," he added.

"Truthfully I've cut back a lot, but I'd like to pull back further. What I'm looking for is someone who can handle the local business with an occasional photojournalism job. It takes the right kind of person to live in an area so off the beaten path. Tourism is extremely limited, compared to other areas on the coast. There are two reasons for that. One, we're much farther north, so it takes a lot longer to travel here. Two, there are large tourist areas not too far from here. Personally I think Squabbin Bay is one of Maine's best-kept secrets."

Jordan nodded. The remoteness of this location had been one of the things holding him back about the job offer.

"Mr. Lamont, I've done some research on you and your work. You clearly fit my criteria, or I wouldn't have invited you up. The question is, do you think you can live in this environment? Most folks up here work two jobs. They're hardworking people with precious little to show for their efforts. That's why I'm offering the apartment on the second floor of the studio as part of the package. The lab is here in this house, which is why I had you come here for the interview."

"May I see it?" Jordan could just imagine a room the size of his bedroom having been converted into a darkroom.

"Absolutely. Follow me."

Dena Russell led him back down the hallway; but instead of turning right to the guest room, they turned left and walked past the laundry room and into one of the largest private darkrooms he'd ever seen. "Wow!"

"My husband made it for me."

He walked over to the light table. Above it were some negative strips. "May I?"

"Take a look at those." She pointed to the set farthest to his right.

"These?"

"Yes."

He turned to look for the sink and washed his hands. She smiled. Had it been a test to see if he'd reach for negatives without washing his hands? Wasn't that basic photo development 101?

Looking at negatives took an acquired skill, the ability to recognize the opposite colors for those that appeared. Oddly enough, the strip of negatives was in black and white. And the focus of the pictures looked like an abandoned fisherman's wharf.

"Print me up a couple of shots ranging from the grainy texture of the wood to the smoother, more refined photograph."

"All right. Where are your supplies?"

Dena showed him where the various chemicals were kept and the paper. She leaned against the light table and let him work. The uneasiness of the situation abated once he began the process and his mind shifted to his work. First, he made a close-up of the weathered grain of the wooden deck; then he zoomed out and recentered the frame to slightly off to the right side of the negative and printed a full-size photo. A short time later, he put the photographs in the water bath to stop the chemical reactions then hung them up to dry.

Flicking on the normal light, he asked, "What do you think?"

"You tell me."

He scrutinized each photo but settled on the one he felt confident was the best. "This one."

"Why?" Dena stood beside him looking at each photo.

"I like the contrast. It looks kinda Ansel Adams to me."

"Interesting."

He wanted to ask. *Did I get it right?* But held off. His mind flickered back to the clumsy waitress and her wonderfully alluring eyes. He wondered what they would look like in a black and white print.

"Let's clean up and go to the studio." Dena caught him in his musings. They talked as they put everything in its place in the darkroom. She was organized, unlike him. He'd love to look through her filing cabinets and see how she organized them. That was one of his weakest areas. He had logs and notes on his laptop, but apart from setting negatives aside with the date on the outside of the envelope he didn't do much organizing. It would be an honor to work with Dena Russell, even if it was only doing studio work. Then again, he could probably learn that in a few weeks. *Would I be bored with no challenge, no adventure?*

The hard fact was he needed a steady job. Income was not what he'd hoped when he left college to pursue his career. Freelancing hadn't been as profitable as he'd anticipated. To date, he owned a Jeep, a few cameras, some tubes of paint, and an easel. And his nest egg was the size of a twig. His apartment was a room with kitchen privileges that he rented from the other two guys who leased the place. At twenty-seven, he'd hoped to be further along in a career. Far enough along where he could entertain the thought of marriage. But he barely kept himself alive. He didn't earn enough to support a wife. Not that he'd found a wife yet.

"I'm glad you handle film so well. Are you equally skilled in digital photography?" Dena asked.

"Very. When I started college, digital photography wasn't financially practical for all the students. I'm grateful I was trained in both. I use digital most of the time, but I still enjoy working with the film and always have my film camera with me."

Dena gave a slight nod. "Jordan, what's your dream with regard to your career?"

Chapter 2

Randi tossed her purse on the table. *What a day!* She made it through without getting fired but only because Dorothy had seen the customer back into her serving tray and not the other way around. The man had to be a photographer, Randi figured, if his appointment was with Dena Kearns. She toed off her sneakers and pulled off her socks. Ever since she started living on her own, she found the freedom to go barefoot around the house. When she was younger, her father insisted she wear shoes all the time, or at the very least slippers, in the house. So she'd been forced to keep her toes covered for years.

She padded her way to the office, a small second bedroom. Her dad had come by and rewired that section of the cottage with up-to-date wiring and surge protection. Her computers and equipment were the tools of her trade, and unfortunately an uncontrolled charge of electricity could wipe out her system in less than a second.

Her other major expense was satellite service, giving her fast access to the Internet. Uploading and downloading took forever on dial-up. Speed and ease of working back and forth with a customer were top priority. She had lost too many customers prior to the expense. The other faster services were not available in her area and probably wouldn't be for some time. So she settled on satellite in order to continue living in Squabbin Bay. Of course, back then it had been because she believed she was going to get married. But after four years. . . well, she broke it off when she saw Cal fooling around with Brenda Scott. They married a month later, and then he split less than a year after that.

Now she wasn't sure why she wanted to stay in the area. It wasn't the fast track to success, but it was home and the place she felt the Lord would have her live. Most of her friends while growing up had moved out to go to college and simply never returned.

The phone rang. "Hello."

"Randi, you'll never believe this," her friend Susie blurted out. "There's a handsome new photographer moving to town. He's going to work for Dena Kearns and live in the apartment above the studio. I hear he's a hunk."

Susie was a bit of a gossip but always tried not to pass on bad news about others. The idea of a new man in town would have all the women buzzing.

"He is," Randi confirmed.

"You've met him? Tell me—what's he like? How'd you meet him? Are you interested? Is there room for the rest of us?"

Randi chuckled. "Whoa, girl. The man wears his hair to just above his shoulders. It's brown and wavy. I imagine he can tie it back into a small ponytail."

"Eww, I don't like men in ponytails. On the other hand, if he looks great, who cares how he wears his hair?" Susie laughed.

Randi thought back on his thick brown hair, skin tone, and the structure of his face, and her heart fluttered. "Hey, I'm sorry, but I've got a deadline, Susie. Call Jess. She's seen him."

"Sure, no problem. Talk with you later."

Randi dropped the phone in the cradle. She had a deadline, and if she didn't get this finished before midnight, she'd lose a client.

She had the new Web page design uploaded and fully functional before twelve a.m. The online appointment with her client went well. He was pleased, and the payment for the job was done immediately, also online.

The next morning, Randi set off on her daily jog around the harbor and past the inlet two miles south of her cottage. In total it was a five-mile run. Once in a while Jess would join her, riding a bike, but the hour and the exercise didn't suit her friend. Fortunately for her, she didn't have a body that would gain weight, unlike Randi. She fought the bulge every day. She ate right, exercised, and still had to work at maintaining her weight. Sometimes life wasn't fair.

Lord, it seems some folks don't have to struggle for anything, yet I have to. Why? She ran on to the last corner before the inlet. As she turned the corner, she saw a Jeep along the side of the road and a pair of jean-clad legs stretched out on the ground beside it.

Lord, no. All those television shows of criminal science investigations flowed through her mind. She squeezed her eyes shut and headed toward the vehicle. Shaking, she pushed forward. *Lord, don't let it be a dead body. Please don't let it be a dead body.*

❧

Jordan lay perfectly still, even though the morning dew was soaking through his clothes. He'd been waiting ten minutes for just the right shot. The nest of baby ducks, the mother hovering over her little ones, and the sun's rays bursting through the clouds would form a beautiful picture. His finger poised on the shutter-release button.

Just a moment more—that's it, Momma—move a little to the right—perf—
Crash! Thud!

Someone trampled the ground around him. "What—?" There she was again, that klutzy waitress with those wonderful dark eyes.

Jordan clicked off an accidental picture. He aimed the camera back to the mother duck and ducklings, but the shot was gone. The mother now sat on top of the nest, keeping the babies under her wings. Jordan clicked off a couple of pictures then turned toward his intruder.

"I take it you're fine," she said, huffing.

"Damp, but fine."

"Do you often lie down by the side of the road to take pictures? Isn't that dangerous?"

Jordan sat up and placed the lens cap on his single-lens-reflex film camera. It hung beside his digital camera around his neck. "Sometimes. Do you often trample over everything?"

"Hey, I thought you were—never mind." Randi stepped back. "Enjoy your day." She started to run down the road.

"Hey, Randi, I'm sorry." Although he wasn't quite certain what he had to be sorry for. Hadn't she interrupted his shot? Didn't he have a right to be annoyed by the intrusion?

She waved but kept running. He leaned on his Jeep for a moment and watched her strides. He lifted his digital and aimed. After snapping a couple of pictures, he rounded the Jeep to the trunk where he kept his photography equipment. He thought back on Dena's office and the shelves of lenses and cameras, all neatly arranged. *If she could see my trunk, she probably wouldn't hire me.*

The interview had gone well. He and Dena Russell shared similar tastes and eyes toward photography. He realized she'd asked him to pick his favorite of the prints to get a sense of his eye.

Her vast experience of film, lighting, and settings proved he could learn a lot from her. Just her array of cameras and lenses spoke volumes. She probably had close to a hundred lenses alone. Jordan looked down at his pitiful supply in comparison. He had ten lenses, plus four cameras—two film, two digital. If he didn't count his cell phone and the Polaroid he used when painting.

Jordan sat on the hood of his Jeep and watched the golden sun rise over the horizon. Wisps of fog rose from the water.

He lifted his digital and tried to capture the soft vapors.

The footsteps of a jogger, probably Randi, approached from the direction she had run in earlier. He had to give her credit. He found exercise boring and unfulfilling. He'd heard the talk about endorphins released in the brain from hard exercise, that it helped clear the head, helped process information faster.

"You run often?"

She crossed the road and lightly jogged in place. "Five days a week, weather permitting. Do you?"

"Only away from something," he quipped.

She narrowed her gaze.

He lifted his camera. "A bear, a moose, an occasional mountain lion, or panther."

"Really?"

"Occasionally." He held back from the urge to boast. He didn't need to impress this woman. And yet he wanted to.

"Dena's been all over the world. Have you?"

Jordan half chuckled, half snickered. "No, I've not been that fortunate. But if I understand Mrs. Kearns's history, she didn't do much until the last decade."

"True. So are you moving here?"

She stopped jogging in place and stretched. Jordan swallowed his wayward thoughts and focused his camera and his own attentions back on the stray wisps of fog rising from the water.

He decided to avoid the question, not knowing the answer himself yet. "So what do you do around here besides spill lobster bisque on people?"

He'd been attracted to this woman since he first spotted her in the restaurant. The very thought of falling for someone made his hands shake as he clicked off a shot. He groaned.

"What's the matter?"

"I messed up the picture."

"How?"

Jordan had no desire to tell her why. "Just went out of focus."

"Oh. I never could hold a camera straight. I took photography when I was a kid for 4-H, and my pictures were all blurred and washed out. I failed at developing them, too. Of course, I probably just took a lousy picture."

"What kind of camera?"

"I don't know—one of those rectangle ones from Kodak, I think. It was so long ago. When did you start taking pictures?" she asked.

"High school. Someone donated some photography equipment to our art department. The school set up a darkroom in what used to be a storage room for the science lab. Anyway, a couple of friends and I signed up. I've been hooked ever since."

"Did you go to college?"

"Yeah, but I majored in fine art. Do you know how few jobs are out there requiring that degree?"

She shook her head. She'd stopped stretching and jumping, making it easier to look back at her. "You have beautiful eyes." He clicked off a couple of pictures.

He hoped he'd captured the startled look on her face. It was so real, so innocent. Then her face contorted into the strangest expression.

"Do you do that to everyone?"

"What?" Jordan lowered his camera.

She pointed at the camera and waved her finger back and forth. "This. . . Just snap pictures of people without their permission."

"Sorry. I love your eyes. They're incredible."

Rose crimson filled her cheeks. He started to aim but lowered the camera. He slid off the hood of the Jeep and stood beside her.

He fought the urge to raise the camera.

She looked away. "I'd better get going."

"Randi." He reached out and caught her wrist.

She pulled away and ran down the road. He'd done it again, become too personal with a stranger. *Why, Lord? She is incredible. But I've photographed beautiful women before. I don't understand what's going on here. If I didn't know any better, I'd say I've fallen in love and want to make this woman mine. But that's foolish thinking. Forgive me, Lord. Forgive me, Randi.*

Randi was still shaking after she got home. She'd never had a man enter her heart so quickly, so deeply, before. Yesterday the kiss, today. . . "Lord, what just happened? I wanted to jump into his arms because he said he loved my eyes. Thankfully, with Your grace, I fought it and ran away."

She still couldn't decide if she wanted him to move into town or not. At the moment she was leaning toward no, that he should go back to wherever he came from and stay out of her path.

After years of prayer for her future husband, could she sense a connection to this man that went beyond the physical? She shook her head. Should one be that connected to another so quickly? Four years of dating Cal never produced this kind of unexplained closeness. "Okay, Lord, I need Your grace here."

She got ready for work at the Dockside Grill, which years ago had been called the Dockside Café. Then Dorothy started thinking grills were more popular than cafés and changed the name. Randi didn't see much difference in the clientele.

The wall clock read eight thirty; she had two hours to work on a Web page before going to Dockside. She sat down in front of her computer and researched a potential new client's Web page. She'd been asked to evaluate it and make suggestions for enhancing and updating the Web presence of the company.

She stopped at a popular search engine on the Internet and typed in Jordan Lamont's name. She saw only one reference to a photograph—an elderly woman with well-worn skin, a Native American. Her eyes reflected the years of life, the joys, the struggles, the pain, and the glory. "How'd he do that?" she wondered aloud. It was as if she could see into the old woman's soul. There, in the refracted light of her pupils, she saw the reflection of the photographer.

Randi clicked the computer window shut and jumped away from the computer.

Her heart felt exposed. She got down on her knees and prayed for the rest of the morning before going to work. "Please, God, don't let him move to Squabbin Bay."

Chapter 3

One month, two days, and seventeen hours since he'd moved to Squabbin Bay—and still no sign of Randi. He couldn't imagine a person could go unseen for such a long period of time in such a small town. He didn't dare ask Jess. Word had gotten back to him that she thought he might have been overly interested in Randi. On the other hand, he couldn't blame Randi for her concerns.

He'd asked for the Lord to intervene and keep their attraction to one another in control. He'd even gone so far as to pray for Randi daily. And with each passing day, he'd had an increasing wonder as to whether or not she was the wife the Lord had designed for him. But not to see her at all. . .

"Maybe it's for the best, huh, boy?" He rubbed the top of his dog's head. Duke's long, velvety ears flapped back and forth from the rubbing. Together he and the basset hound lay on an old blanket, eating fried chicken and watching the sun go down. He'd had to leave Duke at the apartment with his roommates during the interview. He tossed his faithful companion a chunk of his boneless portion. He knew the fried batter wasn't good for the poor creature, but Duke had a thing for chicken. So rather than have him try to eat the bones, Jordan had long ago given in to buying Duke his own boneless breast of chicken.

"She's a hoot, Duke."

Duke lapped his jowls and waited for another tender morsel.

Jordan wiped his hands on a wet cloth and positioned the camera on the mini tripod. Tonight was the first evening he'd had to relax and enjoy his passion for photography. He was hoping to catch a sunset using a telephoto lens with a graduated neutral density filter. He focused on the horizon but not on the sun. He'd heard too many stories of photographers ruining their eyes trying to photograph the sun. The best way he could describe it was to imagine himself holding a magnifying glass between his eye and the sun. Not a comforting thought.

He set the wide-angle lens on the digital to underexpose for a more dramatic sunset—he hoped. They sat on a western bluff of the peninsula that made up Squabbin Bay. Fortunately the peninsula was long enough that only a small spit of land protruded into the horizon. Technically it was a less boring picture to have the jagged coastline jutting out into the horizon. It gave the eye something to look at besides the sunset.

A jogger ran on the beach below. The posture of her body, the movement of her legs. . .Jordan aimed the camera at the runner. A gentle smile eased up his face. It was she, finally, after all this time. "Randi!" he hollered and waved.

She came to a sudden halt and lifted her hand to her forehead, scanning the bluff above her.

"It's me, Jordan. Jordan Lamont." He paused and added, "Dena Kearns's new photographer."

She gave a hesitant wave then continued running down the beach.

Well, that's my answer. Whatever mutual attraction or connection he'd imagined they had for one another obviously wasn't the case. He'd fallen for a woman who had no real interest in him whatsoever. "Sorry, Lord. I guess I misread You. I thought—oh, never mind what I thought. It doesn't matter. I was wrong, and I will continue to wait on You for my spouse."

Jordan quickly pushed his thoughts aside and refocused on the horizon. The sun would be coming down on the right-hand third of the viewfinder just behind the shore's jutting coastline. One of the first lessons he'd learned in photography was the principle of the thirds, which really transposed to dividing the picture into nine equal parts.

The golden rays turned a variety of colors ranging from orange to purple as earth's star settled down for the night. Jordan clicked off several shots then put the equipment away. Tomorrow was his day off, and he planned to paint. It would be his first day to paint since arriving at Squabbin Bay.

He loaded up the Jeep and whistled. "Come on, boy, let's go home." Duke ambled over. Jordan had learned long ago that basset hounds preferred to think it was their idea when to do this or that. He'd also learned food was a powerful motivator. "Want another piece of chicken?"

Duke's little legs picked up speed. His ears flapped as he ran. Once he came up to the Jeep, Jordan lifted and placed him in the passenger seat then climbed in himself. He drove out the dirt road that led to the secluded spot. At the end of the road, leaning against the gate, was Randi. He pressed the brakes.

Her arms were crossed, and the look on her face seemed stern, angry almost. "Are you following me?" She pushed off the post and rounded the Jeep. "Why were you here? Did you follow me?"

He thought back on their last encounter when he had reached out and grabbed her wrist. Time told him he'd read that situation all wrong. Very wrong, according to the attitude he was seeing right now. "Randi, I don't know what you think I've done, but I am not following you."

"Oh, really? Since when do you come to this remote location? How'd you even know about it?"

"Look—I'm sorry if I've offended you. But I came out here tonight because Dena recommended it. I had no idea you would be jogging on the beach." He wanted to beg for forgiveness, but he honestly didn't have a clue as to what he should ask forgiveness for.

"Oh." She stepped away from the vehicle.

"Good night, Ms. Blake." He wanted to toss in that he'd see her around, but it appeared that would not be received as a pleasant prospect.

She nodded and started jogging in the opposite direction. Jordan drove back toward town and his apartment. His heart felt as if it been ripped out of his chest and squeezed in a vice. "Help me, Lord. I really thought she was the one You designed for me. Of course, it was probably too soon to think such a thought. Forgive me. I just got carried away."

❧

Randi felt more out of sorts than a flounder flopping on the deck of a ship. Could she have misread Jordan on their two previous encounters? Two types of people are out there, she reasoned, those who are demonstrative and those who are not. It was entirely possible Mr. Lamont was just a touchy-feely kinda guy. But. . .weren't most guys that way? Randi groaned and plopped on the overstuffed chair in her living room. To say she'd been avoiding him since he moved into town would be putting it mildly. Not only had she changed the area where she normally ran, but she also had stopped working at Dockside Grill and taken another waitress job in Ellsworth on Route 1A. And though she'd been telling folks the tips were better, and they were, she knew the real reason—and it had nothing to do with increased pay.

Jordan Lamont scared her. "Why, Lord? Why should I be afraid of this man?" *Admit it. You're afraid of your feelings for him.*

Randi let out a frustrated groan. For six weeks, she'd been dealing with this conflict of emotions, and there was still no change. She didn't dare tell Jess. After the first time of trying to describe it to her, Jess was afraid Jordan had done something inappropriate. How could she explain it when she didn't understand herself? Her head began to throb. She'd been having headaches from all her circular thinking. "Lord, take this away. It has to stop."

After freshening up from her run, she opened her Bible and scanned the pages until she fell on the verse in Philippians 4:19. "And my God will meet all your needs according to his glorious riches in Christ Jesus." *Lord, one of my needs right now is to relax around Jordan Lamont. He scares me. Not just from the attraction, but. . .oh, I don't know. . .more like he invaded my heart and mind. How can someone I just met connect with me so deeply?* After several more minutes in prayer, Randi felt compelled to apologize to Jordan and to try to get over this fear. The invigorating night air encouraged her to walk the three blocks from her house to his. Not that Jordan knew they lived so close. Her feet seemed to get heavier with each stride, but she pushed on until she knocked on the back door to Dena's studio and the entrance to Jordan's apartment.

Within moments, he stood there with his hazel eyes and long, wavy hair. "Hello, Ms. Blake. What can I do for you?"

Such formality. "Hi. I came to apologize. I shouldn't have accused you."

"Apology accepted."

"Thank you."

"You're welcome. Is there anything else I can do for you?"

Hold me in your arms. She shook off her wayward thoughts. "No, I just felt you needed. . .and I needed. . ."

"Like I said, apology accepted. I hope you didn't lose your job at the Dockside Grill because of me."

Randi let out a nervous chuckle. "No, I found another job. Actually I only waitress to bring in a little extra income. I'm a Web-page designer."

"Really? How much do you charge?"

Randi outlined her fees and services.

"I might just hire you. I've been meaning to put together a site on the Internet for myself. What does something like that involve?"

"It all depends on what you want the site to do for you."

"Well then, once I have some extra capital, we can talk and you can give me an estimate."

"Sure. I designed Dena's. You might want to take a look at it. It might give you some ideas."

He turned his wrist and looked at his watch. "Sounds like a good idea. Well, thank you for coming by to apologize, but I have to get back to my work."

"Sure. See you around." She waved and headed home. *Well, that was an awkward but congenial conversation. Why am I so nervous around him?* she wondered. What could he be working on that involved a timer? Wasn't the darkroom at Dena's house? She looked back at the house and watched the consistent flash of a strobe light. What could he be taking pictures of with that?

She stood there and watched for a moment. What was it about this man that brought out her curious nature?

A horn honked. Randi turned and gave a weak wave. *Just what I needed now—NOT!*

⁂

Jordan stepped back from his canvas. It felt good to paint again. Especially after working with the strobe lights for the dairy farmer's ad campaign. It had taken several hours to shoot the milk splashing upward in just the right pattern for an exceptional picture. He seldom got around to painting, but living in Squabbin Bay brought out his creative juices. Today he'd decided to paint an old crab shack. In years past, the shack had been the wharf where crab fishermen would bring in their catches. Today it held a small gift store and empty docks. The salt-gray weathered boards and the reflection of the building in the shallow water seemed like the perfect scene for his first painting.

His hand froze a half inch above the canvas as Randi Blake stepped out of a small, red, compact car. He watched as she stomped inside the crab shack. One thing was certain—this woman showed her emotions. A minute later, she nearly ran out of the building. Jordan dropped his palette on the case containing his supplies. "Stay, Duke."

Running around the small inlet, he reached her car just before she turned onto the street. "Are you all right?"

She jumped and turned toward him—those wonderful charcoal-gray eyes filled with tears.

"Randi?" His heart ached to show her some compassion. "Are you okay?"

She nodded and drove off.

Okay, Lamont, that was swift. First the woman is terrified of you. Last night, she apologized, and you think—what? That she'd be interested in talking with you? Telling you her woes? Yeah, right. Jordan turned back to the one true friend he had in the world, Duke. *A man can't go wrong with a dog like Duke,* he mused.

"Hey, boy, I'm back!" he called out as he rounded the bushes that lined the road between the crab shack and the driveway to a town pier.

He repositioned himself again behind the canvas and lifted his palette and brush. The sun's light had changed. Jordan considered the new contrast of shadows and decided to continue painting it with the shadows he had already begun working with. He glanced at the Polaroid shot he'd taken when he felt the lighting had been perfect. He eased out a pent-up breath. *Why did I bother, Lord?*

Ten minutes later, a car pulled up behind him and parked. Jordan didn't turn around and look. He wanted instead to capture a couple of colors before the sun and clouds shifted once again.

"You paint?" Randi's voice tickled the back of his neck.

"Yes," he said without turning around. *Relax. Stay calm.* "Are you okay?"

"I will be. I'm sorry. I couldn't talk a few minutes ago."

"Not a problem—you don't have to explain." Jordan stepped away from the painting. It was time to turn around and be friendly. The sight of her standing there nearly took his breath away. *Lord, give me strength.*

"Jordan, I'm sorry. Can we start over?"

He gave a slight smile. "Sure." He put his brush in his left hand across the palette and extended his right hand. "Hi, I'm Jordan Lamont, and I work for Dena Russell Kearns."

Randi chuckled and took his hand. "Hi, I'm Miranda Blake."

"Miranda. I like that."

"Thanks. Only my parents tend to call me that. I've gone by Randi since I was five."

"I'll call you whichever you prefer." He gently removed his hand. "This is Duke." The dog wrinkled his eyebrows and examined this new stranger. "Say hello, Duke."

Duke let out a short, bassy *whoof.*

Randi giggled. "Hi, Duke." She extended her hand, keeping her fingers curled, and let the dog sniff her before petting him. "You're a handsome fella."

"Duke loves compliments, don't you, boy?" The low-lying critter cocked his head slightly to the right.

"He's got a personality."

"Absolutely. In fact, Duke here is the king of the castle. Just ask him."

She bent down and gave him a good rubbing. "Do you take him everywhere you go? I noticed him in your Jeep last night."

"Just about. Obviously I can't take him on some trips. But any I can, I do. In fact, do you know of a good kennel around here? I have a photo op in Connecticut next week, and I need someone to care for him. I can take him to Mystic, Connecticut, and put him in a kennel there, but I'm not sure Duke wants to spend ten hours in the car to go to a kennel."

"Not here but possibly in Ellsworth."

"Okay, I'll check around." The sun had shifted too far behind him. Jordan could not continue with his painting. He reached over and placed his brush in turpentine to clean it. Then, with a palette knife, he started to clean off the excess paints from the palette.

"I'm sorry. Did I stop you?"

"Not really. The sun has shifted. I can finish this at home just as easily as here."

"Oh. How do you like working with Dena?"

"Fine. It's a bit slow at the moment, but when we work together, I'm learning something new each time. I should have taken a job with someone like her years ago. I'd be further along in my work."

"Are you working tomorrow?"

"No, not really. Why?"

"Well, there's a carnival at the church. The youth are sponsoring—"

He'd forgotten about that. "Right—isn't that the event where Dena met her husband?"

Randi chuckled. "Yup, pie in the face, the whole bit."

"Pie in the face?"

Randi went on to explain how Wayne Kearns had crashed through the church swinging doors at the same moment Dena was going through them in the opposite direction, carrying a pie and her camera.

"Which one, 'old faithful'?"

" 'Old faithful'?" she asked.

"That's the name she calls her first SLR camera. It was a Nikon F2 photomatic. It's the camera she used to get started. It's a great old camera. Kinda wish I had one myself. But a man needs to set his priorities."

"True. Anyway, are you interested in coming? I'm working—collecting the tickets for the dunking tank."

Jordan chuckled. "I believe I heard the pastor threaten those who adjusted the switch last year so he was dunked continuously." *She attends the same church. I'll have to keep an eye out for her next time.*

"Yup. Rumor has it that John Dixon did it, but no one's saying for sure. His wife supplied the pastor with tons of vegetables last year from their garden."

"Nothing wrong with some good, old-fashioned fun."

"So you'll come?"

Is that hope I hear in her voice? "I might make it over after dinner."

"Don't. There's sure to be enough food, and the kids can really use the income. They're planning a trip to Africa this year."

"Africa, hmm. Maybe I should volunteer."

Randi laughed. "They had more than enough volunteers until folks heard the list of rules for the guardians as well as the kids. Seriously I think they have enough. And I think you'd have to wait a year before folks would let their kids go with you. You know—you're still a stranger."

"I hadn't thought of that." Jordan continued to pick up his equipment.

Randi stepped closer to his easel. "You're good."

"Thanks. I'm fair, but I hope, given some time, I'll get better."

"I'm surprised Dena didn't ask you to help with the portraits she does. She did such an excellent job last year, and with her son being the pastor, it's a given that, as long as she's in Squabbin Bay, she'll have a spot at the carnival for portraits."

"She volunteers her time on that. I'd hate to charge her." Randi stepped back and examined him as if evaluating him. *What did I say wrong that time?*

"You haven't lived in a small town much, have you?"

"No. Does it show?"

Randi chuckled. "Yes. Folks around here would never have thought of charging for their part of the carnival. You, on the other hand, immediately thought of your salary."

"Hey—"

Randi held up her hand. "My point is, your thoughts went to salary, payment for services rendered, stuff like that. Here we don't really consider it, unless we're doing our jobs for hire."

He felt reprimanded, but he wasn't certain why. All he said was he couldn't charge Dena for his services at the carnival when she wasn't getting paid herself. *What's wrong with that?*

"I'd better get going." She turned to walk back to the car.

"See ya around." He smiled. There was something about this woman. He was beginning to feel like a boat's motor oil spilled out in the water, totally unmixable and plenty chaotic. How could he ever have thought they were meant to be together? Jordan blinked as he caught a glimpse of those amazing eyes watering once again.

Chapter 4

Randi sat behind the table at the ticket booth and scanned the festival again looking for Jordan. Her heart sank a fraction of an inch. Still no sign of him. She'd hoped he'd come and join in. If the man was going to blend in, he needed to become an active part in community events. *In my not-so-humble opinion,* she thought.

"Miranda!" Her mother waved.

Randi smiled and waved back. Her mother led a group of small children over to the hippo pen. Cardboard-painted creatures drank at the fake river. Papier-mâché heads popped through the surface of the water. And on the opposite wall, one could sit on a hippo and have his picture taken. At another spot, a person could sit in the hippo's mouth. The youth had done a bang-up job on this African display. A collection jar for donations was a hollow palm tree with four-inch PVC pipe in the core of the tree and a slit in the trunk for people to put in loose change, bills, or checks.

Hidden in the shadows, poised with his camera, sat Jordan. Randi's smile brightened.

"Ten tickets, please." A small boy with short, cropped, blond hair looked up at Randi.

"Sure. Two dollars."

He handed her the crumpled dollar bills as she counted out the tickets. "Here you go."

"Thanks." He ran off and lined up, waiting for his turn at the tank. She noticed that the man sitting on the seat above the tank waiting to be dunked was Charlie Cross. Randi nodded. She looked back at the boy with his hand full of tickets and back at Charlie. *The boy must be his grandson.*

Her booth was a four-foot table with a wooden sign suspended overhead by a couple of thick fishing lines attached to the tree limb above her.

"Hey, Randi, how's it going?" Jess asked.

"Fine. Where's Trevor?"

"He didn't come. To be honest, it's over between us. I tried to keep it together, but he made it clear that, unless I moved back to Boston, he didn't see much sense in pursuing a relationship."

"Sorry."

Jess waved off the comment. "I'm over it. Mom and I had some long, heart-to-heart talks, and the truth is, for the past year, I've not loved Trevor the way a woman and man should love one another for a life of marriage. I tried to buy his affection when I first started working in Boston. Dad nearly flipped over that."

Randi chuckled. "I remember. What were you thinking?"

"I wasn't. That's what Mom and Dad pointed out. I did all the giving when it came to Trevor and me. He barely did anything. He hardly does anything. Do you know he still hasn't gotten a job and is living with his parents?"

"Ouch."

"Yeah. I love my parents, but I'm moving out as soon as I can put a down payment on a house. We decided that renting wouldn't be a wise investment when houses aren't selling at too high of a price right now."

"Are you earning that kind of money?"

"Almost. I'm working with the lobstermen to establish a co-op, and so far it looks very promising. By this time next year, we should be doing a good business. I hope anyway."

"Wow! I'm impressed. So tell me why I'm just hearing about this now?"

"Sorry. I've been working around the clock. We did decide to have you design the Web page, though."

"That'll be fun. Are all the locals in the co-op?"

"Just about. Dad's working on the last of the old salts."

"Have I seen you going out a time or two on your dad's boat lately?"

Jess chuckled. "Yeah. I think his taking me out there all those years got stuck in my veins. I actually enjoy pulling the pots and fetching the lobsters. Still not crazy about the chum for the bait bags."

"Eww. Who is?"

"Most get used to it."

"Eww. . .not."

"That's because you didn't get lugged out on the boat with your dad every morning until you were thirteen."

"Thank the Lord for small blessings."

After a chuckle Jess asked, "Can you come over Sunday after church for a barbeque?"

"Love to. What time?"

"One." Jess leaned closer. "Mom's invited Jordan. Is that a problem?"

Randi could feel the heat blazing her cheeks. "No."

"Good. Look—I gotta run. And you've got a line here. See ya later."

Randi nodded and went back to work selling tickets to the small line of children. By lunchtime, Jess returned to give Randi her first break. Jess sat down behind the ticket table while Randi picked out a lobster roll and a cold soda and sat at a picnic table.

"Hey!" Jordan called out. "May I join you?"

"Sure."

Jordan set his plate on the table and swung his leg around the picnic-bench seat. "The youth group does this every year?"

"Yup."

"Wow! That's amazing. Who's their art director? That hippo pit is great."

"Mr. Landers and Jan Dufresne. Mr. Landers is the high school art teacher, and each year one of the events is a project for the entire art department."

"Awesome. I saw fiberglass and papier-mâché."

"The fiberglassing is done by the shop teacher. That's where Jan comes in."

"You have a lady shop teacher?"

Randi chuckled. "Yeah, Jan's father was the shop teacher for many years. But he retired three years back, and she took over the job. She'd been working as his assistant for five years before that. Now her oldest son is helping. I can imagine one day he'll be the shop teacher."

Jordan took a huge bite of his lobster roll and nodded his head slowly as he chewed. His wavy hair flowed gently back and forth across the top of his shoulders. A sudden urge to run her fingers through his hair emerged again.

"What?"

"Nothing." Randi ate her own sandwich to keep herself from laughing.

"Come on. It was something. Am I wearing my food? Do I have a huge chunk of mayonnaise on my face?"

She placed her sandwich back on her dish. "No, nothing like that. That was a huge bite of sandwich."

"Oh, well I was hungry, and I love lobster." He picked up his sandwich and bit off another huge mouthful.

"I can tell."

"Do you?"

"Yes, but I've had it all my life. To me, it's like hamburger. Dad's a lobsterman, so we ate it several times a week. That and a lot of flounder. Those would get trapped in the pots, and Dad would bring them home for dinner. It was a real treat to have hamburgers or spaghetti." She took another bite, about a third of the size of Jordan's.

"Wow, I can't imagine."

"You know, back in the early part of the 1900s folks didn't eat much lobster. The market was horrible. I've heard the pioneers thought lobsters were for poor people."

"I'm not big on history. I only know what I've seen, and in New York City, I saw lobster selling for thirty bucks a pound. It was nothing to see a restaurant charge over a hundred bucks for a lobster dinner."

"Now that amazes me. As much as I consider it hamburger, I don't think I would pay a hundred bucks for one lobster."

Jordan's laughter calmed her. The more she talked with this man, the more she wanted to get to know him. Not to mention, the more she felt as if she already knew him. She sipped her cold drink.

"Nor would I. I haven't had much lobster until I moved up here."

"Watch the cholesterol if you add the butter."

"You eat lobster without butter?"

"Yup. You're eating it now without butter."

"I know, but that's because it's chopped up and cold. But. . .is it good?"

She gave the top of his hand a patronizing tap. "Yes. I'm sorry; I have to go. Jess is just watching my booth until I'm finished with my lunch."

"No problem. I want to mingle some more."

She stood up and paused. "Are you enjoying it?"

"Yes. And I'm getting to meet some of the people, especially the parents of little children. They're potential customers for portraits."

Randi sighed. "Bye." He just didn't get it about money and community. She wondered if he would ever truly fit in.

❧

He'd done it again. What, he wasn't quite sure, but he'd seen that look on Randi's face before. Jordan went back to his lobster roll and continued to observe the people. He certainly understood why folks enjoyed this fund-raiser for the teens. He'd really like to volunteer to be a chaperone, but Randi was right. People didn't know him yet and might have reservations about him being responsible for their children.

Jess came over with her own lobster roll. Since he'd come to work for Dena, Jordan found Jess to be a new friend. She'd come in to work on the studio bookkeeping while he was there. Not to mention the meals he'd shared with Dena, Wayne, and Jess at their house. "How's it going?"

"Fine. What are you responsible for today?"

"I worked before the festival to bring in enough lobsters and other seafood. Tonight we're planning a campfire down on the beach for the youth. Dad, Mom, and I went there at dawn to dig and lay out the stones for the clambake. Have you ever been to a clambake?"

"No, I can't say that I have." Jordan sipped his drink.

"They're awesome. First you dig a hole and layer the hole with rocks, generally round or oval-shaped, about the size of a football. Then you build a fire. It has to burn long and hot enough that water drizzled on the rocks will sizzle. You then remove all the coals and coat the rocks with six inches of layered seaweed. The clams go down first, then the lobsters, and on top of that you place the corn, potatoes, sausages, and so on. You cover it with canvas, and in about an hour it's all done. The key is getting those stones well-packed and very hot."

"Seems like a real art form."

Jess shrugged. "Goes back to the Pilgrims—and they learned it from the Indians."

"I've heard of a clambake but just never participated in one."

"Unfortunately tonight's bake is for the teens. It's Mom and Dad's way of thanking and encouraging the youth."

"Your dad used to be one of the youth leaders, right?" Jordan picked up the camera and took a couple of candid shots.

"Yeah. I don't know if he did it to keep me out of trouble or just because he had a passion for the teens. I think it was probably a touch of both. Once I went to college, he turned over his part to Bob Hackett, who became the church's youth pastor."

Jordan wasn't sure whether he'd met Bob yet or not.

Jess took a hearty bite of her sandwich. He did the same and finished his.

"Thanks for sitting with me. I guess I should do some more mingling. I took a few pictures of the kids playing in the hippo pool. I hope we might get some potential customers from that."

"Whoa, dude. Jordan, you have to stop thinking of this community as potential customers. Granted, they will be, but you can't think of them in those terms. I know Mom wants to see the studio succeed, but she's not interested in a huge profit thing. Think in terms of getting to know folks. Let them get to know you. That will bring in business around here, not regarding them as potential consumers."

Jordan nodded his head slowly. "Ah." *Is that what Randi reacted to earlier?* "Thanks for the tip."

"No problem. Relax. Don't stress about making such a great impression on my stepmom. She's cool, and she's happy with your work."

Jordan smiled. "Thanks."

"No problem. Later. I have a meeting with the town selectmen."

He knew Jess had a degree in business, and he knew she'd been organizing a co-op with the lobstermen of the area. She was a smart gal for someone so young. And she hit the nail on the head concerning his issues of finances and putting them in the proper perspective. God had been dealing with him about that for years. His wants, his dreams, and his general lack of funds. . .well, maybe not lack of funds—but certainly no extra.

He scanned the area and focused on Randi sitting behind the table. The wind gently blew the sign back and forth above her head. He raised his camera and zoomed in. Suddenly he noticed the line holding the sign. He dropped the camera that hung around his neck and ran as fast as he could. He tackled Randi to the ground just as the sign crashed on the table.

"Are you okay?" He brushed the hair from her face. Her deep, dark eyes opened and closed and then slowly opened again. Tiny flickers of gray in her eyes became clearer. His heart thundered in his chest.

Her eyes widened. He realized he was holding her down and jumped up. "I'm sorry," he mumbled.

Others were running over. "What happened?"

Jordan offered Randi his hand. She placed her shaking hand in his. "Thank you," she whispered.

He didn't know if it was for the hand up, for removing himself from her, or for saving her from a horrible injury. "Thank the Lord I made it in time." He turned to the gathering crowd. "The fishing line that was holding the sign broke."

"How'd you see that?" an elderly, heavily jowled man asked.

"I caught it in my camera lens. It magnifies well."

A woman Jordan knew he'd seen before spoke up. "I reckon Randi's mighty pleased by your rescue. Not that you had to tackle her as if you were at a football game. You okay, Randi?"

"I'm fine. I might bruise, and I think he knocked the wind out of me."

The crowd chuckled. Then Pastor Russell spoke up. "Better the wind than you being seriously injured." He turned to Jordan. "Thanks for being quick on your feet."

Jordan cleared his throat. "The Lord had His hand in it."

"I do believe you're right." The pastor slapped him on the back then turned toward the gathering crowd. "I need a volunteer to get a new table out here and another to take down the other line."

A few of the men jumped up and helped. Two guys put the broken table in someone's pickup truck. Whether it was going to be repaired or taken to the dump, Jordan didn't know and, quite frankly, wasn't concerned. What kept going through his mind was how scared he'd been for Randi. Not that he wouldn't have reacted the same way for someone else, but the instantaneous thought of possibly losing her ran deep. So deep that it unnerved him.

After the crowd dispersed, she came up to him and placed her hand on his arm. "Thank you."

"You're welcome."

"Jordan," she whispered, "I think we need to talk."

He agreed, but he couldn't talk yet. How could he explain to a near stranger how instantly and deeply he'd fallen in love? He couldn't. "Possibly later. I need to get back to the studio. It's been closed longer than I planned."

"Okay, later." Randi walked over to the new table.

A middle-aged couple came running up to her. "Miranda?" She embraced the woman, whom Jordan assumed to be her mother.

If time and place were different, he'd love to be alone with her, to open his heart to her. But that terrified him, as well. He walked to the studio from the church. "Lord, help me here."

Chapter 5

I'm all right, just shaken." Randi straightened her blouse and prepared to sit down behind the new table.

"What happened?" her father asked.

"Jordan Lamont, Dena Kearns's new employee, saw the string slipping or something in his camera and tackled me to the ground."

"Were you hurt?"

"No, Mom, I'm fine."

"Where is he?" her father asked.

Randi turned around, but Jordan was no longer there. "He's gone. He said he had to go to the studio and open it up."

"Ah, I'll speak with him later. You're all right?"

"I'm fine, Dad."

"Okay, then, I have to go back to the sack races. I'm calling the next event."

"I'll see you later."

Mom sat down beside her at the table. "I know you're all right physically, but you seem pretty shaken up."

"I am."

"You should be. Come have an iced tea with me." Her mother found someone else to take her place with the children, and they moved over to the refreshment area, purchased a couple of iced teas, and sat down at a private table. "Honey, you've been a little edgy ever since this Mr. Lamont moved into town. Has he done or said anything we should be concerned about?"

"No, Mom. He's fine. It was me. . .I guess. I don't know. He's very demonstrative."

"How so?"

"Well, the first time I met him, he kissed me on the cheek. That's after I spilled the lobster bisque on him a second time."

Her mother giggled. "I'd forgotten about that." Her mother paused then continued. "It is alarming that a man would kiss a stranger, but if he's, as you say, demonstrative, maybe it is just his way."

"I figured that, but I don't know. There's something more. He sets me on edge."

"Hmm." Her mother examined her a bit closer.

Randi looked down at her lap. "I'm attracted to him to the point of its being unnerving. The second time I saw him, he reached out and touched my arm.

The intimacy was so deep it scared me."

"Ah."

"Mom, it's as if he trespassed into my private thoughts, into my heart. It was scary."

"Yeah, I imagine it was. You know, we haven't spoken much about your broken engagement and what happened between you and Cal. I think it might be time."

Randi scanned the area to see just how private their conversation could be. "There's really not much to say. Cal was a cad, and Brenda got what she deserved."

"Possibly. But there is another side to that coin. What about the fact that God may not have wanted Cal to be your husband? You assumed that because you two were so compatible, it was natural for you to get married. Your father and I were thankful you both wanted to wait until Cal finished college. We felt it would give you time to realize Cal wasn't the right man—or us time to discover the potential in him as your husband. In the end, Cal wasn't the right man."

"Mom, I know all this. What does it have to do with Jordan?"

"Patience, honey. I'm getting to that. You and Cal were not as close as you thought. You were friends, but not as close as, say, you and Jess. A husband, to my way of thinking, needs to be your best friend. Cal wasn't that. Is it possible you and Jordan could be developing a friendship?"

"We are," she blurted out. "I mean, I realized I was wrong for being afraid of him, and I've tried to speak with him on more than one occasion."

"Good. I'm not saying Mr. Lamont is going to be your husband. I'm just curious about why you felt so vulnerable to him."

Randi's eyes widened. "I don't know."

"Well, pray about it. I've got to run. Thank Mr. Lamont for me for saving your life."

"Sure."

"Be careful, Miranda. Trust your better judgment."

The rest of the afternoon, she thought back on her mother's challenge regarding her past relationship with Cal. She thought about how Jordan had come to her rescue and how secure she felt in his arms. Something she hadn't felt since Cal had betrayed her.

Yes, she and Jordan had a lot to talk about. If only they could find the time and the right setting in which to do it. She was concerned about being alone with him. Not that she didn't trust him, but because her heart felt so vulnerable.

And what was his problem that he had to work 24/7?

&

Inside his mailbox Jordan found his first forwarded bill from Boston, his cell-phone bill. He slipped his jackknife in the extra-thick envelope and sliced through the paper fold. His eyes widened upon seeing the total amount due. "Three hundred and twenty dollars?"

He scanned the myriad of pages and discovered the problem. He was in an area that wasn't covered by his network's roaming fees. Unfortunately he wasn't prepared for that kind of expense this month. Moving had taken a greater portion of his savings than anticipated. Not to mention the new equipment he purchased before coming because he felt it would help him do his job better. He looked at the new 500mm zoom lens he'd just received in the mail. "Lord, should I return it or simply fast for most of the month? Not that I'm trying to make light of fasting, and I definitely could spend more time in the Word and in prayer, but. . ."

His glance flickered back to the bill. He pulled out his cell phone and called the three-digit number that connected him with his service provider. Fifteen minutes later, he had managed to get through all the sales pitches and canceled his phone service. And since he hadn't renewed his agreement last month, he wouldn't owe a fee for stopping it.

He'd have to shop around for the best service in this area.

Shaking off the unpleasantness of remote living, he pulled the digital cards from his cameras and went to work developing the candid shots he'd taken at the festival. No sooner had he loaded the images than the bell jangled over the front door to the shop.

"Hello?" a female voice called.

Jordan turned. "May I help you?"

The red-haired lady sported a healthy shade of sunburn pink on her nose and cheeks. She wore a white skirt; a striped, navy top; and Top-Siders. "I was wondering if you process digital pictures within an hour?"

"Sure can. Load the images you want printed over there." Jordan pointed to the equipment that stood against the right wall. "Or you can hand me the card, and I can take care of it for you."

"No, thanks. I'll do it myself."

"No problem. Give me a holler if you need anything."

" 'Kay."

He judged the woman to be in her early thirties.

Jordan went back to his pictures. He cropped the photos for the best four-by-six prints. He'd learned long ago to photograph a larger border on digital cameras because the enlargement process was limited to multiples of four-by-six, and an eight-by-ten could not provide a perfect ratio enlargement.

The sweet, toothless grin of a child filled the screen. She seemed familiar, but he couldn't place where he'd seen her before. Of course, with a town as small as Squabbin Bay he'd probably seen her around on more than one occasion. He printed out a four-by-six and moved on to the next print.

"Excuse me."

"How can I help you, miss?"

"How soon will these prints be ready?"

"Less than an hour. You can return later if you like."

She stepped back then paused. "Does anyone else work here?"

"No. Well, yes. My boss. But she's busy with the festival. I'm the only one today. I wasn't even open until a few minutes before you arrived."

She glanced out the front window. "All—all right," she stammered. "I'll be back in an hour."

"I'll have them ready for you."

Jordan worked on his own prints, processed a few new orders from customers then gathered the photos together for the lady's order. He thumbed through the prints, checking for quality. Seeing no problems, he set them in the envelope for small pictures and rang up the printed label, with the price tag sealing the envelope shut.

"Hey, Jordan." Randi swung open the door. "What are you doing here? Why are you working?"

"I wanted to get a start on some of the pictures I took today. It's a good thing. I've had a half dozen customers this afternoon."

Randi placed her hands on her hips. "Has anyone ever told you that you work too much?"

"No, but I take it you're about to educate me."

"How'd you guess? Come on—you're coming back to the festival with me."

"Sorry, but I can't. I have a customer who's returning for her prints. She should be here any minute."

"Fine." Randi leaned against the counter and crossed her arms. "I'll wait. Then you're closing shop and taking the rest of the day off. After all, you saved my life today, and you deserve to have some fun. You know the Lord talks about taking a rest every now and again."

"I rest."

Duke howled then, as if to protest.

"You tell 'm, Duke. Look—I've seen you for nearly a month, working every spare minute. And when you're not working, you're painting. One or the other. In either case, it is still work."

"Painting is my hobby."

"Not! You sell them. It's another form of income for you. What do you do just for fun?"

Jordan thought for a bit and realized he couldn't remember the last time he'd actually taken time off.

"See—I've got you. Now it's too late to dunk you in the tank—"

He waved her off. "Hang on. What do folks our age do around here?"

"Travel to see the movies, do something in the city. Whatever. We also get together at each other's homes. Truth is, there aren't too many of us. Most of the kids I went to school with left town for college, and they don't return, except for visits."

"Go to which city, Ellsworth?"

"Yes, have you been?"

"Can't say that I have."

"Do you like bowling?"

"Haven't done that since I was fifteen, but I'm willing to give it a try. What about shooting some pool?"

"Tim Redcliff has a billiard table in his barn. He makes it available for folks."

"You up for a game? What about asking Jess to join us? Or is she going to the clambake after the festival with her parents?"

"Don't know about Jess. Let me call Tim; then I'll call Jess."

Jordan nodded and finished his prints. He sorted through his pictures, and the sweet smile of the toothless gal landed on top of the pile. While Randi continued with her phone call, he enlarged the copy and printed out an eight-by-ten.

The red-haired lady from earlier ran in the door. "Sorry I'm late."

"No problem. That will be six dollars and forty cents."

"Here—keep the change." She plopped seven dollars on the counter, swooped up the envelope, and hustled out the door faster than she'd come in.

Randi clicked her cell phone shut. "Who was that?"

"I have no idea. Hey, who do you have cell-phone service with? I just got my bill, and I need to change providers."

They chatted while he cleaned up the area from his work.

"Jess can't make it."

Jordan paused. *Is it wise to be alone with Miranda?*

Chapter 6

Randi watched Jordan as he worked. He was so methodical, taking the time to put everything in its right place then tweaking it until it stood in perfect line or the order he wanted. She wagged her head involuntarily. This model of orderliness didn't jibe with the clutter in the back of his vehicle. "Are you always this precise?"

"Huh?"

"The back of your Jeep looks like everything was just rifled through and piled on top of each other. The counters of this shop are in pristine order. Who's the real you?"

"Ah, this is for Dena. Have you ever seen how organized that lady is? I mean, everything is in its place. I'm haphazard at best."

"Dena is organized in her lab. But her paperwork. . .well, let's just say it took two weeks before the papers, prints, and everything were well-organized in her new lab."

"Really?" Jordan's shoulders relaxed.

"Jess said when she lived in Dena's apartment in Boston the house was organized and clean, but her bedroom, which also served as her office, was overrun with papers everywhere."

"Done." Jordan beamed. "Are you sure you're up for a game of pool? Are you sore?"

"A little, but I'll be fine."

"We don't have to play tonight. You're under no obligations because I saved your life."

Randi giggled. "Not according to the town. Besides, we have some unfinished business."

"Ah, the talk."

"Yes. What happened between us today when you"—Randi scratched quote marks in the air—" 'rescued' me from that sign?"

"Are you sure you want to get into this conversation? You always seem to run away from me."

"Jordan, I was engaged for three years. Well, officially only one, but the other two were informal."

"Ah. I don't think this is a pool night. Let's go to the city and have a nice steak dinner, my treat."

"Really?" Her dark eyes rounded.

159

He reached out and took her hand. For the first time since she'd met Jordan, she didn't pull back. "Really. Call Tim and say thanks, but we've changed our plans. I'll run upstairs and get Duke some water and doggy treats."

"You're taking Duke? I don't think you can bring him in the—"

"I don't intend to take him into the restaurant. However, I've not given Duke any of my time. If he rides in the Jeep, he thinks he's spending quality time with me."

"You're a little obsessed with your dog, aren't you?"

"Probably, but he's been my best friend for years. He's a great listener, and I've never heard a rude word out of him."

She smiled then said, "I'll call Tim."

❧

Randi paced back and forth. *What have I gotten myself into?* It had seemed like a good idea to speak with him at the festival, but now she didn't feel so sure. She flipped open her phone and called Tim. Jordan ran down the stairs and hurried toward the back door, signaling to her to give him one minute. Inside the kitchen, he pulled out a couple of bottled waters for Duke and a handful of puppy treats he put in a plastic bag.

A minute later, she'd finished her call. She closed her phone and turned to see Jordan watching her, leaning on the doorframe, looking like a million bucks in casual jeans, a cotton shirt tucked in, a belt buckle that looked as if it came from a rodeo. And his hair. . . "What?"

He gave her a lazy smile. "You're a beautiful woman."

Fire danced on her cheeks.

"Are you going to run away?"

"No, but I want to."

He moved slowly toward her. "Miranda, I—" He stopped short then stepped back. She'd never been so thankful someone moved away from her.

He cleared his throat. "I'm sorry. Let's get going to dinner. Do we need reservations? It is Saturday night."

Her tongue felt dry. "No, we should be fine. We might have to wait a few minutes. No big deal."

He nodded and grabbed the keys to his Jeep from a peg on the wall. "Let's go. Come on, Duke."

The basset hound wobbled to a stand on his short legs.

"How old is he?" *On second thought, I'm glad he's bringing his dog. It will give us something to talk about.*

"Duke is thirteen. That's ninety-one to you and me."

"Wow! He's an old man."

"Yup." Jordan scooped up the dog and put him in the backseat. "He's lived with me all his life, except for my first year in college. My folks insisted I live in a dorm the first year. After that, I lived off campus in my own apartment, if you can call rooming with four to six guys your own apartment."

He held the door open for her. Randi grabbed the roll bar and pulled herself up into the high vehicle. It wasn't as high as some of those new pickup trucks, but for someone her size, it was high enough.

"I moved out of the house last year. After Cal and I broke up, I needed to be on my own. Mom and Dad were great, but I don't know—I just wanted to be on my own."

"I understand." Jordan closed the door and walked around to the driver's side. He didn't run, nor was he being exceptionally slow, but each step he took struck her as purposeful. It was confusing, trying to piece together the many facets of this man.

Sliding behind the wheel, he turned toward her. "Which way?"

Randi fought to relax her nervous stomach. "North." With only one main route into town she didn't have to explain more, which was a blessing.

❧

Jordan pushed his chair back from the table. "That was good. How was yours?"

"Excellent."

"Would you like some dessert?"

"No, I'm stuffed. Besides, I purchased a lemon meringue pie from the festival today."

"Now that sounds yummy."

Randi's eyes widened. They were onyx in the dim lighting of the restaurant. "You like lemon meringue?"

"Yup, and just about any way pie comes. I have a huge sweet tooth."

"You don't look it."

He wiggled his eyebrows. "That's because I work 24/7, as you say."

"Why is that?"

He shrugged. How could he admit he was anxious to earn the kind of living that would provide for a wife and children he didn't yet have. *For her,* he hoped. She'd been the best date he'd ever had, and this wasn't even a real date. "I have plans for the future, and it's hard to earn a lot doing photography. Truthfully, if it hadn't been for all those roommates, I would have had to get a job to help support myself."

"Dena does well."

"Yup, but she established herself when she was married."

"Actually that isn't quite true. Jess told me that when she became a widow she used the life insurance to buy the studio with the upstairs apartment. From what I've heard our pastor say in his sermons, his mother, Dena, went through some hard times the first three years after his father died. His father was a minister also, so they didn't own their own home and didn't really have much of anything."

"I knew her husband died a while back, but I didn't realize she started her business after he died."

"Yup. Photography was just a hobby before that."

"Well, she has the eye. She's good, and her name and reputation stand for quality."

The waiter, in dark pants and a white shirt, came up to the table. "Excuse me. Will that be all for the night, or can I tempt you with some desserts or an after-dinner beverage? We have several specialty coffees."

He glanced over at her and smiled. "Miranda?"

"No, thanks, I'm fine."

"Just the check, please, and would you wrap this bone in a doggy bag for me?"

"Yes, sir." The waiter stepped away.

Jordan took in a deep pull of air and let it out slowly. "Are you still wanting to talk?"

"Honestly, no. But we need to."

"Okay." Jordan slid down to the edge of the chair, stretched out his legs, and crossed his ankles. Relaxed, he wasn't; but he wanted her to be.

"Jordan, I don't know how to explain this without being horribly blunt. I like you. But I'm terrified by you, if that makes sense."

Jordan paused for a moment to collect his thoughts. "Tell me about your engagement to Cal."

"Why? What does that have to do with you and me?"

"Perhaps nothing, and maybe everything. I don't know what happened, but I suspect he dumped you. A fool, if you ask me."

Randi wrung the cloth napkin in her hands. "Yes, he was having an affair with someone I knew. Not that it's hard not to know someone in Squabbin Bay."

"Then he definitely was a fool. How have you dealt with the trust issue? I can see you've dealt with the hurt. You've moved on and made a life for yourself. But what about trust? Can you trust a man, any man?"

"I haven't had a problem around any other man, except you."

"Ah." *Because of that connection we felt for one another the second time we met. I know the feeling.* "Miranda, I like you. I'd like to get to know you better. Maybe over time you'll feel more comfortable around me. I'd like to be your friend."

Her eyes widened then closed. They told so much about her and what she was thinking. And he'd done it again. This time, he'd hurt her. "Friend isn't a bad thing."

She lifted her head and gave a slight smile. "No, friend isn't a bad thing."

"Okay, I'm clueless here. I would like a relationship, but I admit I'm terrified by the emotions I feel for you, felt for you from our second encounter. The first was unique—but not something to build a relationship upon."

Randi giggled. "I'm so sorry."

He held up his hands. "I know it was an accident. Let's not get off the subject. I thought friendship was a good place to start. Is there something wrong with that assumption?"

"My mom said something similar today. She thinks Cal and I weren't meant for one another, and I didn't see that."

"Is she right? I mean, it's obvious the guy was a jerk, but—"

"I don't know. I always blamed Brenda for the affair. They married a month or so after we broke up. He was engaged to me for years. And—"

"What was it in Cal that made you want to marry him?"

She pursed her lips then twitched them. "I don't know. I mean, I used to think it was what we were supposed to do. I'd loved him since tenth grade."

Jordan paused then asked, "Friends—meaning you and me? Can we be?"

"Yes. I think that's a good idea for now."

"Good. I could use a friend in town. Jess told me today I had to stop looking at people as potential customers."

"She told you that? Of course Jess would tell you that. But, yeah, you need to stop thinking that way."

"Noted. So can I consider you my second friend in Squabbin Bay?"

"Absolutely." She paused. "Second? Who's the first?"

He smiled. "Jess. Well, I think Duke is going to start howling soon if I don't return. The bone ought to help."

"Buying his affection, huh?"

"You could say that."

Randi seemed to relax for the first time all evening.

Jordan plopped a hefty tip on the table and escorted Randi from the room with a gentle touch on her elbow. He'd be the perfect gentleman. She needed a man who loved her enough to respect her. And with God's help he would be just that man. All in all, he decided, tonight had been a wonderful evening. He opened the front door of the restaurant.

"Duke? What are you doing here?"

Chapter 7

Randi moaned as she crawled out of bed the next morning. It had taken hours, until well after midnight, to recover Jordan's vehicle from the impound yard. He had parked in front of a No PARKING sign. She'd never seen a sign there either, or she would have warned him.

Her head throbbed from lack of sleep. She went into the bathroom and took two aspirin. Five minutes later, she was burrowed back under the covers and asleep. The next time she opened her eyes, it was well after noon. She'd missed church. She went to her laptop and downloaded the Sunday morning sermon then uploaded it into her iPod.

Showered, dressed, and feeling a lot better, she drove to the Kearns home. Jess greeted her at the door with a tall glass of iced tea. "We'd given up hope on seeing you. Jordan told us what happened."

"I never saw that sign until we found out they towed the Jeep."

"Jordan's laughing about it. Come—there're a few morsels left."

Dena and Wayne were lounging out on their deck chairs. Jordan sat beside them with a plate full of food. She really did wonder how he stayed so thin with an appetite like his. She waved.

He returned the gesture and kept on speaking with Dena and Wayne. Pastor Russell stood at the grill. Large meat patties were lined up and at various stages of completion. "Would you like one or two, Randi?"

"Two, thanks."

"Coming right up."

"Sorry about missing the service. I listened to the first part of the sermon on the way over. Sounds good."

"Digger is doing an excellent job. I can't believe he has the sermons up and ready on the Internet before I even get home. It's amazing."

"Gotta love it." Randi smiled. She'd taught Digger, aka Tommy Williams, a teen at the church, how to upload on the church's Web page and how to write the basic computer code so folks could find it.

"Absolutely." Pastor Russell scooped two burgers off the grill and placed them on a red plastic plate.

For a moment, she watched the children running back and forth to the end of the cliff that overlooked the beach then turned to find an empty chair.

"Come with me. I've got to show you something." Jess pulled her by the arm through the house and to the kitchen. On the table lay a Realtor's printout of a house.

"Is this what I think it is?"

"Yeah. I haven't seen it yet, but at the festival yesterday the Realtor handed me this printout. What do you think?"

"I think it's way too soon for you to be considering a house, but what do I know?"

Jess giggled. "Plenty. I have time to look, but staying with Dad and Mom—"

"They're newlyweds," Randi finished the sentence for her. Her mother's words came back from yesterday about her and Cal not having been that close. She never finished Cal's sentences for him. Well, except to correct him. Randi sighed.

"What?" Jess sat down in the chair. "Come on—what's going on in there? Is it the house? Am I missing something?"

"No, no, not the house. If you and your parents think it's a good idea, go for it. No, it's something my mother said to me yesterday about Cal and me." Randi glanced down at the paper again. "Isn't that Brenda and Cal's house?"

"Yeah, sorry."

Randi waved her off. "No problem. Why isn't Brenda keeping the house?"

"She's moving closer to her mother. Apparently Cal hasn't been great with the child support."

A lump flipped in her stomach. "You know, I've been getting messages from Brenda asking me to call her. I've never called back. I don't know what to say. I'm over the anger. But I still don't like her much."

"I hear ya. She's in a hard place. I'm sure she's not making anything off the sale of the house. They owned it for only a year."

"Probably not. Maybe I should return her call."

Jess put her hand on Randi's. "Forgiveness is more powerful to the person who gives it than to the one who asks for it."

"Yeah, I've forgiven both of them. I'm just not crazy about being close to either one. Of course Cal's disappeared. Brenda must be really hurting."

"I imagine." Jess took the paper and tossed it in the trash.

"What did you do that for?"

"There are other houses. Besides, I want my best friend to come visit. I wouldn't want you staying away because of who lived there before me."

"I don't think I'd have a problem with that."

"No problem. Hey, tell me—why'd you go out with Jordan? I thought you were keeping a low profile with him."

"He's a nice guy."

"I noticed."

Jordan's comment about her being his second friend in town came to mind. Randi asked, "Are you interested?" They'd had an unwritten rule that if one of them was interested in dating a guy, the other would stay away from him.

"No. He's not my type. Although he does have that handsome actor, shoulder-length hair thing going for him."

Randi smiled. "Yeah, he does."

"So what's he like on a date? Details, girlfriend—I want details."

"First off, it wasn't a date. I wanted to thank him for saving my life."

"Oh, right. Fill me in on that one, too."

Randi laughed and shared, ever so briefly, about the two major events in her life the day before that involved a certain Jordan Lamont.

"Well, I must tell you, he did better than you and showed up for service today."

"Ugh. Don't remind me. I can't believe I overslept."

"It's your first date since Cal." Jess raised her finger to hold off Randi's protest. "It *was* a date, no matter what you say. He paid. How was that a reward for saving your life?"

Randi clamped her mouth shut and pouted.

"Gotcha. By the way, he's about to come in." Jess waved toward the sliding glass door.

Randi turned to see him holding a tall glass of tea in his hand. His hair was down, and his trusty rubber band was on his wrist. His appeal went so much further than that. Their ability to talk last night about deep and hurtful events in her life wound him tighter around her heart.

"Close your mouth. You're drooling," Jess whispered.

&

Jordan eased through the sliding glass door toward Miranda. "How sore are you?"

"Not too bad. The extra rest helped."

"Good. I'm sorry I tackled you so hard."

"Don't be."

Jess popped up. "I'm going to get another burger. Anyone else want one?"

"No, thanks."

"I'm fine," Jordan said, closing the distance between him and Miranda. "You haven't touched one of your burgers. I thought they were your favorite."

A nervous chuckle escaped her lips. "Were. Now I prefer steak."

"Ah." He sat down beside her at the table.

"Dena's happy with your design of her Web page. When can we spend some time working on a proposal for mine?"

"Soon." She took a huge bite of her hamburger. Jordan loved a woman who ate in front of a man. He'd had too many dates who would eat rabbit food in public, only to go home and eat something else. If they wanted a steak dinner, they should have ordered it. But, no, they were trying to impress. Instead it only turned him off. It was another thing he liked about Miranda. He really did like her real name more than her nickname. He supposed it had something to do with Randi sounding like a guy's name. Over the years, many people had mistaken his name also.

"I'm going on a photo shoot to the Sudan next week. How about when I get back?"

Her eyes wide, Miranda nodded, still chewing her burger.

"Hey, you two, come on out. It's time for volleyball."

She groaned. "Coming."

"Are you sure you're up for it?"

"If I don't start moving, I'll just be worse tomorrow."

"All right then. I believe we've been summoned." Jordan stood up and dumped his empty paper plate in the trash.

"You don't know the half of it. Have you ever played with these guys before?"

"I'm afraid I haven't. Why?"

"Well, I know how you feel about exercise. Let's just say you're going to be hurting worse than I am now."

He could feel the blood drain from his face.

She looped her arm around his. All the blood came rushing back. "Lead on."

An hour later, Jordan sat exhausted on the deck.

"You need to start running." Dena slapped a towel on the rail beside him.

"I see you're huffing and puffing."

"Yeah, but I'm twice your age."

"Touché." Miranda laughed. "He has a thing about exercise. It's not in his vocabulary."

"Yes, it is. I just choose to ignore it."

Everyone broke out in laughter. After tall glasses of ice water, most of the guests started leaving. Jordan gave Wayne a hand cleaning up, while the women went inside to work on the dishes.

"So how do you like Squabbin Bay?" Wayne asked.

"I like it." Jordan lifted a couple of paper plates that had blown off the railing.

"Are you looking forward to your photojournalism trip to the Sudan next week?"

"Yes. I hope to get a few things settled in the studio before I leave." This trip to the Sudan was just the kind of opportunity he'd hoped to get while working for Dena Russell Kearns.

"Dena says that area of the world is especially pretty but filled with civil unrest at the moment. Have you taken to heart what she's told you regarding safety measures?"

"Absolutely. She's been doing this for a while now."

"I'm just glad you're taking the trip and not her," Wayne said. "Not that I want anything bad to happen to you, but. . ."

Jordan chuckled. "If I had a wife, I wouldn't want her going either."

Wayne smiled. "I'm glad you understand." He shoved a smaller bag of garbage into the large green one he was holding. "Looks like I'll be running to the dump tomorrow morning."

"Now that's one reason I'm glad I'm living in town. I can at least put my trash cans out for pickup."

"It's taken me a bit to get used to. But for this view I don't mind."

Jordan turned and fixed his eyes upon the dark blue waters of the seascape. The ocean seemed calm and tranquil. He took in a deep breath and let it out slowly. "Yeah, I think I could get used to no trash removal for this view also."

"Hey, you two, what's taking so long?" Dena called from the sliding glass door.

"Just admiring the view, hon. We'll put these bags in my truck and be right in."

"Actually I have to be going. Thanks for the dinner, Dena. I'll see you in the morning at the studio." Jordan took the bag he was filling and carried it to the truck. A quick handshake with Wayne, and he was off.

In the rearview mirror, he could see Dena and Wayne's house. Inside sat the one person he'd love to spend more time with. But he'd taken off most of yesterday, and the pile of work to finish before he left town loomed in front of him.

Back at the studio, he started working right away. By ten he was feeling the lateness of the night before and went straight to bed.

His phone rang. "Hello?"

"Jordan, it's Randi. There's a stranger in the bushes in front of the studio."

"What?"

"I was driving by and saw someone."

"What would they be doing in the bushes?" His mind traveled to the equipment downstairs. "Call the police." He hung up the phone, slipped on his jeans, and tiptoed down the stairs.

Chapter 8

Randi had been so embarrassed for getting the entire town in an uproar after assuming she'd seen someone in the bushes. She'd kept herself hidden for the past week—which meant Jordan was now in the Sudan and away from her silly behavior.

"Hey, Randi," Charlie Cross greeted her as she walked into the post office. "Seen any bushes lately?"

"Hardy, har, har, Charlie. I saw something."

"Probably did—a coon or something. Don't mind the teasing. You did the right thing."

"I know."

Charlie held the door open for her, and she entered the post office. "Hello, Mabel. How are you?"

"Fine, fine. Folks still giving you a hard time about last week?"

"All in good fun," Randi admitted.

"Well, if you don't mind me saying so, I think you did the right thing. I heard Georgette Townsend the other day say things were looking mighty strange at some of the rental cottages."

Randi didn't want to get into a gossip session, so she kept quiet.

Didn't take long before Mabel had all the details out. "Too many strangers living in town these days. I think there're five right now."

Jordan would still be one, and possibly Dena. Although, having married Wayne, she's probably no longer one of the five. "I know of Jordan."

"He's no never mind. He works for Dena. It's the group of folks renting the two cottages on Westwood Creek Road. I saw one at the festival, but none of the others came out."

"Well, that doesn't make them strange. Not everyone in town came out for the festival."

"True, but you'd think—oh, don't mind me. I don't know what to think. Georgette, she's the one that's all fired up about them. Not that she's called the police or anything. They haven't broken the law or nothing. They're just strangers and don't come into town much."

"Speaking of coming into town. . ." She needed to get Mabel redirected to the task at hand, or she'd be stuck here for an hour. "I need to mail these."

"Oh dear, listen to me rattling on so." Mabel weighed the mail. "That will be four dollars and eighty cents, please."

Randi handed her a five and pocketed the change. With the mail done, she headed to her waitressing job. Oddly enough, she hadn't known of strangers moving into town. She wondered when that had happened and how she had missed it. Was Squabbin Bay actually growing?

Customers passed through quickly, tips were accumulating, and Randi felt good about the day.

"Hey, Randi, how you doing?" Jess plopped down at the counter.

"Good. How's your day?"

"Wonderful. I'm all excited. The paperwork has gone through with the state. We officially have a lobster fishing co-op."

"Woo-hoo! That's great news! What can I get you?"

"A banana split. I feel like celebrating."

"Coming right up." Randi topped off another customer's coffee then scooped up an oversized banana split for Jess. "Here you go. I'll be right back." Randi checked on her other customers and returned to Jess. "So what does this mean?"

"The goal is to get a better price for the lobster in order to stabilize the market somewhat. We're also working with the hatchery to bring in more fertilized lobsters to have their eggs hatched in the safety of the hatchery then later released to keep the numbers up."

"Well, look at you. That college education really paid off."

"You know, I never thought of having a business career in Squabbin Bay, but I'm really happy doing it. It's like I have the best of both worlds. I love business and all that's involved in that, but I also love the quietness of living in a small town. This way, I can have both."

"I'm proud of you, Jess."

"Thanks."

Randi ran off to assist a customer then returned again. "You know I'm happy with my work, but I feel something is missing."

"You mean Jordan."

"No." Randi smiled. "Not that."

"So you do miss him?"

"I'm afraid so. Please tell me how I can miss a guy I don't even know."

"What is it you feel you don't know about him?"

"Everything. I don't know who his parents are. I don't even know where he grew up." Randi took a cloth and wiped down the counter, removing the dishes and money first. "I wish I didn't have to work two jobs."

"Ah, I know what you mean. But apart from my stepmom, who do you know that doesn't?"

"Well, Pastor Russell doesn't."

"Okay, that's one. Who else?"

"I'll admit there aren't many, but wouldn't it be nice just to work one job?"

"Yeah, but that brings its own distractions, as well. I didn't work long in the corporate world, but it was long enough to know you can't trust anyone. Personally, I don't want to live like that."

Randi pulled the salt and pepper shakers out from under the counter and started filling them. "I don't either, and I'm not saying I want to work in the corporate world, but I'd love to have one job support me, you know."

"Yeah, I know." Jess took a spoonful of ice cream. "Speaking of one job, look at Jordan. He's working two, as well. Have you heard from him?"

"No. We don't have that kind of relationship."

"You will. I can tell." Jess stirred her melting ice cream with a spoon then looked straight at Randi. Randi pulled her gaze away from her. "You love him, don't you?"

"Jessss." Randi spilled some salt onto the counter.

"Randi, number five is up," the short-order chef called from the kitchen through the half wall.

"I'm coming." Randi walked toward the pickup window.

"You and I will have to have a serious talk. How about tonight?"

"Can't." Randi passed Jess and brought the order to the table and checked with a few of the other customers before returning to the counter. "Tomorrow night I'm free."

"I'm not. I have a special meeting with the youth going on the mission trip." Jess had gotten involved with the youth group since she'd moved back to Squabbin Bay.

Randi hadn't felt so inclined. Her ministry revolved more around technology, and her contribution was working with kids like Digger to enable them to help the church. "You know, Jordan would have loved to go along on that."

"Yeah, but you're right. Parents would have been concerned. Maybe next year." Jess polished off the last of her ice cream. "That was yummy."

"Good—you deserved it."

"Speaking of the youth mission trip, how come you didn't volunteer?" Jess wiped her mouth with the paper napkin.

"I didn't have the funds, and I have a couple of clients who have scheduled a Web-page overhaul for that month."

"Ah. Well, maybe you can do it next year."

"Maybe." The thought of her and Jordan being on a mission trip together gave her a sense of joy. He obviously loved missions. The photo op he'd been sent on to the Sudan was for a Christian mission. Dena was going to do the job, but at the last minute she had asked Jordan if he'd take her place. She refocused on Jess's question. "How about Thursday morning?"

"Done. I'll meet you at your place after I come in from fishing."

Randi waved off Jess's attempt to pay for the banana split and paid for it herself from her tips. Fishing for lobsters wasn't Jess's only occupation. She knew her best friend was fishing for answers regarding Jordan.

Randi only wished she had them.

æ

At home, Jordan wiped off the African dust from his cameras and lenses—after a long and warm welcome from Duke, who'd been staying with Jess in his apartment. The purchase he made before moving to Squabbin Bay paid off. Each day he'd gone out with four cameras. One film, two digital SLRs, and another small digital for wide-angle shots if he couldn't frame a picture with the other three. He prayed that the pictures he'd taken—of civil unrest, matching the turbulent winds that kicked up the desert sands—would cause folks to pray more and give more to the various charities trying to help the Sudanese people. He knew the trip had been a life-changing experience for him. On the flight home, he'd decided that all profit from the pictures would go to various Christian missions working with these people.

Tomorrow he'd have to take the cameras completely apart and clean them. Tonight he needed to stay awake long enough to adjust back to his time zone. He'd been grateful for the opportunity, but he definitely liked his own country. He sat down at his computer and viewed the myriad of pictures he'd taken, stopping at the one of a militia gun to the head of a Sudanese woman, whom they claimed was a rebel. A knot squeezed tighter in his gut. If he hadn't been there, the woman would have lost her life. The child at her breast held no meaning to these men. What mattered to them was whether or not she was a rebel, and if so, she would be killed.

Jordan shook off the memory. "Thank You, Lord, that they didn't shoot her. Lord, continue to protect her and her child." He had never wanted to be a war correspondent–type photographer. War and crimes of passion were not his kind of picture. Sorrow and hurt were, and he could see the worries for this child and his future flick through the woman's eyes in a nanosecond.

He stared a bit longer at her brown eyes. Memories of Miranda's dark eyes flooded in. His mind drifted from one place to another. He closed his eyes and opened them slowly. He was home, safe, and forever changed. "Teach me, Lord, all You would have me learn."

Glancing at the clock, he lifted the phone and called Miranda. She answered on the second ring. "Hi, Miranda. It's me, Jordan."

"Hi, Jordan. When did you get back?"

"An hour ago." They talked for a few minutes; then he asked the question he'd called for. "Would you be up for a cup of hot cocoa and a stroll down at the point?"

She hesitated. "Sure."

His confidence soared.

"Let me finish up with this client. I could be ready in thirty minutes."

"All right. I'll pick you up in thirty." Jordan hung up the phone. Miranda was the first person he wanted to share his thoughts with. *Is she ready for that kind of relationship, Lord? I don't want to push her.*

He put Duke in the Jeep then drove to her house with a thermos full of hot cocoa and a cooler with some ice water. Hesitating, he rubbed his hands back and forth on the steering wheel then closed his eyes. "Lord, help me to be myself and not mess up."

"Talking to yourself?" Miranda stood beside the passenger door in a pair of jeans and a dark T-shirt. "Hey, Duke."

Duke woofed and lapped his jowls.

Jordan wanted to swoop her up into his arms and hug her. Instead he simply smiled. "Hey, there. It's good to see you."

"Same. So what's up?"

"I wanted to share with you my experiences in the Sudan."

She slid into the bucket seat beside him. "Cool. I want to hear all about it."

Jordan slipped the vehicle into gear and headed out to the point. "It was awesome but terrifying at the same time. The stories are brutal, but the mission work has been fruitful. They've put in wells, which completely changes a community."

They talked all the way to the point. "I don't think I'll ever be the same."

"There's something more, isn't there?"

"Yes. Let's go down to the beach first."

"All right."

He knew she was thinking it had to do with their relationship, which it didn't. But then again, maybe it really did. "I need to walk this out. Come on, boy. You need the exercise."

"And you don't like exercise."

He chuckled. "Sometimes a man just has to." They walked down to the shore's edge, leaving their shoes farther up the beach. Duke waddled behind, stopping every now and again to sniff at a clump of seaweed. "I had an encounter with the radical forces in Sudan. You're aware they'll kill a person who has converted from Islam to Christianity, right?"

She nodded.

"We were forced to stop at an impromptu checkpoint by radical forces. They questioned us at gunpoint and let us go when they discovered our journalism passes. At the same time, a woman was being taken away with her child. They said she was a rebel, and perhaps she was—I don't know. But deep down in my gut, I know that if I hadn't been there with all my cameras and the entire group with me, they would have killed her right there on the side of the road."

"Oh, my." Miranda reached out and placed her hand on his arm. "What happened?"

"I don't know. I pray she's safe, but I honestly don't know. Sometimes we just have to leave things in God's hands."

"Yes, you're right, but are you okay?"

"I think so. It was so raw and real. I know it is going to change me permanently in some ways. How, I'm not certain. I'm still in a bit of shell shock. If it hadn't happened on our last day, maybe I would have worked it through some more. But we were on our way to the airport."

"Another reason they probably didn't kill her."

"Quite possibly. There was a look in her eyes. . .I don't know. . .I can't describe it."

"What is it with you and eyes?"

"Huh?"

"Sorry. I didn't mean for it to come out that way. But ever since I met you, you've mentioned my eyes. And the one photo I found on the Internet done by you was of this old Native American woman, and in her eyes was a reflection of you. It was a great pic, but kinda strange."

Jordan smiled. "That's my great-grandmother. I was in college and won an award for that picture."

"Really. You're an Indian?"

"Fourth generation, if you count from my great-grandmother. That was a special day in celebration of our heritage. In truth, my great-grandmother lived in the city with my great-grandfather and then with my grandmother. My great-grandfather was a professor. Later he went into real estate. He was white. My grandmother is of a fair complexion, and my mother is even fairer. And, as you can see, there isn't much melanin in me. Well, except for this tan I picked up in the Sudan."

"Wow! You're Native American?" she repeated.

"One eighth, yes. Does it matter?"

"No, I just don't know much about you and your family."

Jordan rolled out a blanket he'd carried down on top of the cooler. Duke sat in the middle. Miranda sat on the opposite side. "I didn't spend much time with my Indian cousins. But once a year we would go to various tribal ceremonies. It was required as long as my great-grandmother was alive. I continued even after she died."

"I'm sorry. This took us off the subject you wanted to talk about."

"You know, it might be related. You mentioned my interest in eyes. I've always seen them as the window to one's soul. In the picture of my great-grandmother, my reflection was superimposed on the pupil. I actually could see myself, but the reflection wasn't clear, so I played with the image and placed myself in there. It was a comment on my great-grandmother's love for me, as well as my love for my heritage."

"There's so much we don't know about one another."

"Miranda, there are a lot of things. We haven't had the time." He wanted the time; he wanted to get to know her better. His life experiences flooded to the surface. All of a sudden, he wanted to share everything he'd learned and gone through in life, his relationship with God, his family.

Jordan reached over and took her hand. "Miranda, I want to be your friend."

"That's my problem," she said. "I want more."

Jordan's heart thudded in his chest. *Calm down. Count. One, two...*

"Jordan?"

Chapter 9

Randi tightened her grip on Jordan's hand. After what seemed like an eternity, he opened his eyes. "I do, too." He paused. "You were the first person I wanted to share my experiences with."

"I've missed our time together. Is it possible to be just friends?"

"I think your mother is right. Friendship is key to a healthy marriage." His eyes widened. "Not that. . .I mean. . . ," he stammered.

Randi let out a nervous giggle. "I understand."

"Miranda?" His voice calmed her. She liked the sound of her name coming from him. "And you're afraid to let me close because of what Cal did to you?"

She nodded.

"Come here." He opened his arms for her.

She hesitated for a moment then stepped over to him and leaned her head against his chest. Sweet relief washed over her like the waves brushing up against the shore. It felt good to be in Jordan's arms.

"I will make you a promise. I will not cheat on you. If our relationship is not right to pursue any longer, I promise to be up front with my feelings and concerns. Okay?"

"You can't know how you'll feel—"

He placed his finger on her lips. "I promise, Miranda. I want what is best for both of us."

She kissed the tip of his fingers. How did he know the right things to say? She wrapped her arms around him. For the first time in longer than she could remember, she felt at peace. Then she heard him pray.

"Father, be with us and guide us as we seek Your will for our lives. Help us to keep You as our central focus even when we want to put ourselves or one another ahead of You."

"Amen." Randi pushed away from his embrace. "So tell me more about your trip to the Sudan. Did you capture any wildlife? Go on a safari?"

They talked for an hour until the air started to chill. "Would you like some hot chocolate?"

"Yes, but I really need to get home. I need to finish my client's Web page."

"Speaking of Web pages, when can we start working on mine?" Jordan got up from the blanket and extended his hand to help her up. He set the cooler to the side and lifted the blanket. Randi grabbed hold of the corners, and they shook it out together. Duke sat there and watched them. "Duke, get up. It's time to go."

Randi draped the folded blanket over her arm. "How about tomorrow afternoon after I get home from work? Can you have some photos ready for me by then?"

"Sure. Digital?"

"They're easier to work with, but we can scan prints."

"All right. I've been giving some thought to overall design and layout."

"Good. Visit a bunch of different photographers' Web sites and see what you like and what you don't. Then we'll have a better idea of a design just for you."

Jordan smiled.

"What?"

"I love the way you brighten up when you talk about your computer work. It's not the same as when you talk about waiting on tables." He propped the blanket on top of the cooler then picked up both.

"Waitressing is necessary to help pay my bills. Web designing, I hope, will grow enough to make a living. I'd love to work only one job."

He headed toward his vehicle. She and Duke followed. "That's not very commonplace in this area, is it?"

"Nope. We're hardworking people, but I'd rather do my hard work in the Web designing."

"I hear ya. I can't wait until I earn enough to support a family."

Randi stopped. "How much do you believe you need to earn before you can have a family?"

"I'm figuring enough to support my wife and kids with full insurance. I don't have insurance for myself yet. Also, I'd like to buy an old Victorian house and renovate it as a wedding present."

"Sounds nice. But more than likely, you won't be getting married until you're forty-five."

He placed the cooler in the back of his Jeep. "Why? I want to provide well for my family. Is that too much to ask? I'm not asking to be the richest man in the world, but I do want certain things."

She raised her hands to his protest. "I'm not saying they are unreasonable, but shouldn't you think in terms of finding the right person then working with the Lord and her to provide the rest?"

He frowned. She hit a nerve and knew it. *Friendship might be as far as things could ever go between the two of us.* Money was something she worked for to provide the necessities. And, while she may want to plan for the future, she apparently figured she had plenty of time to do it.

"You're not into preparing for the future then." He hoisted the basset hound into the vehicle.

"Not really. I know I'll need to someday. But right now, I'm more concerned with earning enough to work only one job."

"I was raised to plan for the future."

"How so?"

"Both of my parents were very strict about preparing for college and encouraging me to be debt free within a year or two out of college so I could prepare for marriage."

"And are you prepared?"

"No, at least not where I'd hoped to be. My education is paid off, and I have a nest egg for purchasing a house, but it's tied up. I don't spend it."

"I have a hundred and fifteen dollars and twenty-six cents in my savings." Jordan chuckled. "Do you tithe?" He turned on the engine and started off.

"Of course."

"Start tithing another ten percent and put it in your savings each week."

"I can't. I won't be able to pay my rent. Wait. I thought you didn't have much. I mean, didn't you say you didn't have a lot and couldn't afford your cell-phone bill?"

"I don't count my savings as money I can touch," Jordan said. "Once it is in there, it is no longer a part of my thinking for my daily use."

Maybe I have been too lax with my finances. "You're serious, aren't you?"

"Absolutely. That's why I have to have a certain income before I consider marriage."

Yup, just friends. "Wow! I don't know if I could live that way."

"Try it—you might like it."

"I'll think about it."

He pulled up to the curb in front of the small cottage she rented. Even Jess, she recalled, was thinking of buying rather than renting. *Have I been all wrong about my money, Lord? Should I have kept living at home and saved up to buy a house?* "Good night, Jordan, and thanks for the evening. It's—it's been interesting."

" 'Night."

❧

Jordan slapped the steering wheel. "Why did I have to bring up money? Our values are so dissimilar."

The night had gone well until he'd brought up his desire to be able to provide for a wife and family before he married. But she did have a point with regard to searching for the right woman. He didn't agree it had to be first. He could still save and plan for that day even before he met the right woman. *The problem is—is she the right woman?* If so, he was definitely not financially ready for her. And could they be right for one another when they differed so much on financial issues? "What do you think, Duke? Would Miranda and I be fighting constantly over where and when to spend the money? Or, in her case, why save?"

Duke laid his head on his paws and hiked up one of his eyebrows.

"Okay, maybe that's unfair to her. She did say she intended to save for the future—just not today."

And what was his nest egg? Just a few thousand dollars he'd hoped would be four times that amount by now.

Lord, I know my overplanning is a problem, and I'm trying to trust You; but if Miranda is to be my wife, I'm not ready for her. What can I offer her?

Jordan went to bed that night and woke with the same question recycling in his brain even as he arrived at work.

"Good morning, Jordan." Dena poured a cup of coffee from the coffeemaker in the back room of the studio. "How was your trip?"

"Good, but I need to clean my cameras."

Dena chuckled. "Goes with the territory. Can I see your proofs?"

"Sure." Jordan brought up the folder with the photographs he'd downloaded. "I'll need to go to your darkroom and develop these later." He plopped six film canisters on the counter.

"Film does have its advantages."

"Yes, but I got some great shots with the digital." He loaded the picture viewer on his laptop and left the chair for Dena to view.

"Wonderful. These are great." *Click, click* went the computer keys. "What's this? This is powerful, Jordan. Look at her eyes."

On the screen was the shot of the Sudanese woman and child. The next shot panned out, revealing the gun to her head.

"I don't mind admitting it was a terrifying experience."

"Praise the Lord you came back in one piece."

"Yes, but I keep praying for this woman. I don't know if she's still alive or if they've killed her."

Dena paused for a moment. "I have an idea. Let's put this photo on my Web site, credited to you, of course, but make it free to be broadcast all over the net, with a prayer request for her and her child."

"I'd love to, but I signed a waiver with the magazine for the mission that sent me. They have first rights on all pictures taken."

"Ah, I forgot about that clause. I've signed a few of those myself a time or two."

Jordan poured himself a cup of coffee and held it in his hands. "Dena, may I ask you a personal question?"

"Sure. What's on your mind?"

"When you married your first husband, had he saved for your future?"

"Bill?" Dena chuckled. "No, we were poor college students, and he was heading to grad school. It was basically hand-to-mouth our entire marriage. We did manage to take out a term life insurance policy on him once we started ministry, and that's what helped me buy my first studio with an apartment upstairs. Why do you ask?"

"My parents have ingrained in me that I should be able to provide for my wife and family before I get married. Even possibly have our house purchased before that."

"And you're nowhere near those goals?"

"Right. Don't get me wrong. You're paying me a fine salary, and to toss in the apartment saves me a bundle. But—"

"You couldn't provide for a family on your current income," she finished for him.

Jordan nodded. He'd been doing a lot more of that since meeting Miranda; it was her habit to nod instead of reply, and now he was doing it, too.

"Sit down." She patted the chair next to hers. "I didn't have extra until my children were grown. I took on assignments once they were in college. I was fortunate; I have a good eye and was in the right place at the right time. To me, that was divine intervention. It isn't because of what I did or didn't do. It was a matter of God's timing for my life. On the other hand, life got so full with all the traveling. I was forgetting my family. I wasn't really forgetting them, but I didn't spend much time with them. I've learned that having money is almost as difficult as not having money. But this isn't what you're dealing with right now, is it?"

"No, it's the goals I've set for myself. I'm wondering if I set them too high."

Dena smiled. "This is probably coming up because someone, namely Randi, has caught your attention."

"In part. On the other hand, it is something I've been dealing with the Lord about for quite a while. It's hard not to go by the plan. To let go and let God."

"God is a God of order, right?"

He nodded in agreement.

"And He's wired you to be precise with regard to finances. That means He'll work with your natural talent and challenge you to trust Him when the numbers might not add up."

"But how?" Jordan wiggled in his seat. "No, wait. That's not the right question. While I was in Africa, I decided to give the profits from the pictures to the Sudanese missionary work there."

Dena smiled.

"That's so unlike me. I tithe, I give, but I've never given up all I'm going to earn for something like that before. If I continue to do that, I'll never have enough to get married."

"And there is your real problem. You are trying to step out in faith, and yet your logical mind is telling you, you can't pay the bills if you do this, right?"

"Right." *I know all this, but I obviously need to be reminded.*

"I can't judge whether you've done the right thing by deciding to give those profits to that ministry. It is noble and truly sacrificial. But I can tell you from my own personal experience that when I've given in that way, God's met my needs in other ways. I have volunteered my time and profit for many events over the years, like the festival, and God's always supplied my needs. And, in most cases, He's given me more than I needed."

Jordan closed his eyes. "Trust and faith."

"Most things boil down to those two issues, don't they?" Dena placed her hand on his shoulder. "With regard to Randi, do the same. If it is God's will, He'll work out the details. If it isn't, He'll work that out, too."

"You're right. It's just that. . ."

"You love her—I know. I've seen that look before." Dena winked. "Now let's get to work."

"The day is awasting." Jordan stepped up to the counter and went to work on the studio's computer. They continued through the morning.

"Can I see your candids from the festival?" Dena asked a while later. "There wasn't time before you left."

"Sure." He pulled up the folder, and Dena went through his pictures.

"This girl is a cutie."

Jordan glanced over. "Yeah, I don't know who she is. No one picked up her picture at church after the festival."

"Well, that shot is a keeper. Can't sell it without a release form from the parents, but you could put a copy of it on your Web page. When is that going up?"

"Randi said we could work on it this afternoon."

"Great. Well, look—I'm meeting Wayne for lunch, and then we'll be out for the next couple of days. We're going to Boston to visit the kids. Feel free to use the lab whenever you need to."

"Thanks. I'll probably go over there this evening."

"No problem. Call Jess and let her know. She's going to house-sit for us."

They said their good-byes, and Jordan glanced back at the picture of the girl with the toothless grin he'd taken in the hippo pool. She was cute, and the shot wasn't too bad either. He added it to his list of pictures for his Web page.

He answered the ringing telephone. "Hello?"

"Hey, Jordan, it's Randi. Can you come to my studio today rather than my coming there? Some time-sensitive items are due in before the end of the day, and the customer wants them on his Web site yesterday."

"That'll be fine. Should I bring some lunch?"

"Nah, I've already eaten. Bring your own if you like. Otherwise, I'm good."

"Okay, I'll see you later." Jordan gathered up his photographs, called in a take-out order from the Dockside Grill, and fetched his laptop and photo CDs, just in case he missed something.

"Duke, guard the fort. I'll be back shortly."

Duke raised his head inquiringly then settled his chin on the floor in resignation.

Jordan ran over to the grill and paid for his lunch. As he crossed the street toward the studio, he noticed a thin man peering in the studio's front-door window. "May I help you?" Jordan asked as he approached.

The man ignored him and walked back to his car. Jordan walked faster to catch up. "Can I help you?"

"No, thanks, I was just looking for my wife."

"Okay." Jordan turned to see the man drive away in a silver Volkswagen Bug with out-of-state plates.

Back at the studio, he turned the sign around and posted his return by 3:00 p.m. He hoped his absence wouldn't mean any more loss of customers.

Chapter 10

Using the templates she had put together for other Web pages, Randi had the basic design of Jordan's done later that evening. The time would be in the graphics and giving an honest representation of Jordan and his work.

Jordan's homework for the night was to develop information on digital photography, his area of expertise. This would set his Web page apart from Dena's.

She crawled into bed much later than planned, but that was the way it happened from time to time. She was thankful she didn't have to go to work the following day.

Early the next morning, she went out for her five-mile run down by the point and came upon Jordan's Jeep. She searched the area but didn't see him. She continued running down the point to the marshy shoreline. There she found him, kneeling in muck with his camera aimed toward the sunrise. "You're nuts."

He turned and smiled then went back to his picture taking.

She wouldn't disturb him again. Thoughts of their second meeting flickered back in her mind. He'd been aiming his camera on a mother duck and her ducklings, and she'd messed up his shot. She picked up her pace and headed away from Jordan and his camera. After circling around and heading back toward home, she found him standing in the middle of the road, his pants soaked with mud and his arms across his chest. Duke looked out from the front seat, perfectly clean and definitely content.

"You do have a way of distracting a man."

"You were in the muck."

Jordan laughed. "Yeah, but it was a clean shot between the rocks in the harbor."

"It might be." Randi stopped jogging in place and stretched. "It's still nuts. You're going to have trouble getting that smell out of your jeans."

"They'll wash."

"They will, but they'll still smell for a while unless—"

"Unless what?" He inched closer to her. "Is there some secret ingredient to cleaning your clothes from the tidal marshes?"

"Most folks don't go mucking around in them without their hip boots. Those hose right down."

Jordan looked down at his shoes. "I might need to get a pair of those."

"If you're going to be playing in the muck, you will."

"All kidding aside, I'm wondering if you would like to have breakfast with me."

"Sure. Where?"

"My place. I'm going to try to wow you with my culinary skills."

"Do you have any?" Randi's eyes immediately widened in self-recrimination. She hadn't meant to be so flip with him.

"I can handle a few things. But I do have one ace up my sleeve over most men who don't know how to cook."

"What's that?" She inched toward him.

He leaned into her. His gentle voice tickled her senses. "You'll have to come and see."

Gooseflesh rippled down her spine. "All right. What time?"

"Give me forty minutes to clean up."

Randi stepped back and started back down the road. "I'll see you there. Remember—I eat well."

"That's one of the things I love about you."

She lost her footing momentarily but regained it. *Love—he said love, Lord.*

❧

Jordan made it back to his place in record time. He added a cup of vinegar to the washing machine. He didn't know what secret washing ingredient Miranda had in mind, but vinegar cut a lot of smells. Of course, he would have to rewash or else smell like a dill pickle for a few days. He took the fastest shower he'd ever taken and returned to the kitchen. He whipped up a batch of crepes then ran back to his room and finished dressing. He buttoned the last button on his shirt by the time she knocked on the back door.

"Wow! You clean up well."

He brushed the back of his teeth with his tongue for one final check. "You're not so bad yourself."

Miranda came in and walked to the kitchen area. "So what's the big surprise? Hey, Duke, how you doing, boy?"

Duke ambled over to her and nuzzled in for his free loving. Jordan wished he were in Duke's shoes. Jordan pulled back his hair and wrapped it behind his head. "Patience. It involves blueberries, but I still have to wash them."

"Blueberries are always good."

"And whipped cream."

"Even better." She sat down at the table. "I finished a basic layout for your Web page last night."

"Wonderful. I'll take a look at it after breakfast. Oh, I forgot to tell you—Dena loaded a picture I took of a little girl at the festival to her Web site."

"Really? How come?"

"She loved it. There's a copy of the print I blew up for the parents on display in the studio. No one claimed it, so I can only assume they don't attend the church."

"More than likely. Did Dena recognize her?"

"Nope. Maybe you'll have better luck."

"I might, but I'm getting old enough that I don't know all the grammar school–age kids."

Jordan pulled out his crepe pan.

"Crepes? You know how to make crepes?"

"Oui. It was one of the things I learned in French class. I think it might have been the only day I paid attention actually."

"You—I can't believe it." She leaned on her elbows. "Were you a good student in school?"

"Fair. I didn't care much for school. I liked art and some of my other classes, but I just did what was required to get through. In college, I discovered I had to buckle down and study if I was going to graduate." He removed the plastic film he'd placed over the batter earlier. "Are you a big crepe-eater?"

"If they're stuffed, four, please."

"Yes, they'll be filled with whipped cream and blueberries."

Randi licked her lips and closed her eyes. "Sounds heavenly."

Jordan turned back to the stove. "So what are your plans for the day?"

"Work. What about you?"

"Same. I have some film developing I need to do at Dena's. I'd hoped to do it last night; but I called Jess too late, and she'd already retired for the evening. I hope she's not working too hard."

"With regard to Jess, she'll be okay once the co-op is launched. Are the pictures of the Sudan?"

"Yeah, I shot a few rolls of film."

Jordan dipped the pan into the batter then flipped it over and placed it on the warm burner. Moments later, the crepe was ready to be turned over. He repeated the process.

"You're really good at this."

"It's the pan. It is amazing what happens with the right equipment."

A brisk knock on the front door of the studio rapped in his ears. Jordan glanced up at the clock. "Miranda, would you keep making the crepes while I take care of the customer?"

"Sure."

Jordan went to the front door and opened it. "May I help you?"

"I'm sorry to barge in like this, but that picture in the window. . . That's—that's my daughter. Where did you get it?"

Jordan glanced over at the little girl sitting in the hippo's mouth. He had it displayed with several other shots of the children from the festival. "I took it at the festival. Would you like it?"

"Yes, please." The woman's red hair overflowed her decorative scarf.

"No problem. It's on a mat but not framed yet."

"It's fine just the way it is."

Jordan reached over and pulled the picture from the window. "Here you go."

"How much do I owe you?"

"Nothing. Consider it a gift from Community Church."

"Thank you."

"Have a nice day."

As he watched the woman scurry off, Jordan remembered her as the same woman who had come in during the festival for one-hour film developing.

"What was that all about?" Randi asked as he entered the kitchen.

"Remember the collage of photos I put together of the festival and hung in the studio window?"

Miranda nodded.

"A mother saw her daughter and wanted it."

"She couldn't wait until you were open?"

"She's always on the run. She might be hyper—who knows? Now how are you doing?"

"Just about finished cooking up all the batter."

"Great. I'll make some blintzes for later."

"Blintzes?"

"Rolled-up crepes stuffed with cream cheese and other things. You make them ahead of time and freeze them."

"Hmm. Just how many French classes did you take?"

"Actually, blintzes are Yiddish."

"Hebrew class?"

"Nope, a neighbor." Jordan smiled. He relieved Miranda of her duties and finished making the crepes, filling them with whipped cream and blueberries and then sprinkling some powdered sugar over the tops.

Jordan set the plates on the table and joined her. He grasped her hand. "Father, direct us in our relationship and lead us in Your design for our lives. In Jesus' name, amen."

"Amen." Miranda took her fork and cut off a large piece. She sighed with pleasure. "These are excellent. You can cook breakfast for me anytime."

Jordan's mind sprinted to the future, to a vision of the two of them married, living happily with one another, and him making breakfast for them and their children. Jordan opened his mouth and filled it to avoid sharing his heart and dreams with Miranda at this time. He didn't want to scare her again.

Chapter 11

R andi!"

Randi spun around at the sound of her name. Her spine stiffened. The subject of many sleepless nights and far too many hours on her knees appeared in all her blond, blue-eyed beauty. Randi nodded in acknowledgment then turned back in the direction she had been going.

"Randi, please," Brenda pleaded.

It had been well over a year since she and Cal had been married. Randi even told Jess she'd forgiven Brenda, but. . .

Randi came to a halt. She decided to face the backstabbing. . .

Forgive me, Lord. Help me. "What do you want, Brenda?"

"I want"—Brenda's eyes started to water. She hoisted the six-month-old child higher on her hip—"I want to apologize. It was wrong for me to date Cal while you two were still engaged. I knew it, but I ignored the truth and walked right into a horrible situation."

Randi shut her eyes for a moment then opened them, counting, *One, two, three.* "I forgave you a long time ago."

"Yeah, right. Look—I admit I was wrong. I didn't mean to hurt ya. It just happened. And look where it got me. At least you can be thankful you're not the one with a child and no husband."

"Brenda, I'm sorry Cal ran off on you, but what does that have to do with me?"

"Nothing. Everything. . .I don't know. Cal always blamed me for breaking you two up."

Randi shook her head. "Cal likes to blame others for his actions. That isn't to say you didn't play a part in his affair, but he shouldn't be blaming you. He was the one engaged." It felt good to say those words out loud.

"Yeah, my mother says if he walked out on you, he was more than likely going to walk out on me, too. I didn't believe her, but she was right."

"What are you going to do?"

"We hired a lawyer to track him down for child support, but the lawyer said not to hold out for much. He said even if they find him and require him to pay the child support, he still might not pay. Knowing Cal, he won't."

Randi's heart went out to Brenda. "How are you going to support yourself and the baby?"

"Mom's going to watch Tyler."

Randi's heart cinched. That was the name she and Cal had picked out for their first son.

"I'm going to work part-time and finish my college degree. Dad's going to help me with tuition and stuff. After a couple of years, I should be able to provide for Tyler and myself."

"Your folks live near Portland now, right?"

"Yeah, Daddy's working for the hospital there." She shifted Tyler. He had Cal's eyes. "I'm sorry, but life has bitten me—"

"Brenda, the Lord will help you," Randi said, cutting her off. She'd felt many times as if Brenda had gotten what she deserved, but the child didn't deserve a father who had abandoned him. Admittedly, at this very moment, Randi realized her "forgiveness" of Brenda and Cal was not complete. *Lord, forgive me.*

Brenda snickered. "God helps those who help themselves. And so help me, if I ever get my hands on Cal, I'll—"

"I'll be praying for you."

"You know, that's the problem Cal had with you, all that high and mighty stuff. I'm no saint, but at least I don't believe I can't do anything in life, that I live at the whim of God."

"It isn't at God's whim. It is a matter of submission, giving everything back to the Lord and trusting Him."

"Where was your God when Cal was cheating on you?"

Randi wondered why all this anger was coming at her when Brenda had started out with an apology. "Cal cheating on me was not God's doing. God got me through, and I'm a stronger person now. Bad things happen in this world, Brenda. It's how we choose to live with those bad experiences that make or break us as human beings."

"You really believe all that stuff we learned in youth group with Mr. Kearns, huh?"

"Yup. And, trust me, it's helped me deal with you and Cal going behind my back."

"I wasn't the only one."

"I know." *Stick the knife in deeper. Lord, I don't understand why I'm going through this conversation with Brenda. She isn't even repentant. Not really.*

"You do? Cal said you didn't have a clue."

"As I look back now, I can see all the lies. But Cal was right—I didn't know then, or how many other women there were. I chose to overlook his lies and believe him in spite of what was happening around me." *No wonder I have trouble trusting Jordan.*

The baby started to cry.

Randi looked down at him. "Is something wrong?"

"He's hungry. I need to feed him." She glanced at her son. "Randi, I know I've been saying this all wrong. I am sorry for what happened between me and Cal and what it did to you. But I love my son. How could it have been so wrong?"

Randi took in a deep breath then let it out slowly. "Come on inside and you can feed Tyler."

"Are you sure?"

"Yeah, come on in." Randi let the one person in the world she despised most into her cottage, allowing the Lord to crumble the wall she'd built up for so long. She felt sorry for the woman and her child and knew they needed to get acquainted with Jesus. "Iced tea?"

"Sure, thanks." Brenda's knees shook as she sat down on the sofa.

Randi went to the kitchen then returned in time to see the baby nursing hungrily. "Here you go."

Brenda knitted her eyebrows together and peered at Randi. "Why are you being so nice?"

⁂

Jordan's Web page was fully designed and operating in three days. Miranda had done a wonderful job. She also included a blog for him to post pictures for people to comment on. The little girl with the great smile and no front teeth was the first photo he put on his blog. Today he noticed Randi had added a couple, as well. The work at the studio crawled along. Apart from customers coming in to have their pictures developed, they had no other studio work. Dena said it would pick up in the fall with school pictures. Jordan hoped she was right. He knew what came in, he knew his salary, and the two weren't that far apart. He set up an easel in the rear corner of the studio to work on between customers.

The crab-shack wharf was taking shape on canvas. He decided to go with high tide and reflect the building in the water below. He dabbed the titanium white and added a touch of cobalt blue and left the colors unmixed on his brush. With a careful hand, he dotted the water below.

The bell over the door chimed. Jordan turned to see a man with short, cropped, black hair and a form-fitting T-shirt and jeans walk in. "Can I help you?"

"Yeah." He inhaled a deep pull on a cigarette and breathed out the smoke. "Wife said you took this." He held up a photo of a young boy playing in the hippo pool.

"Yes, sir. Would you mind putting your cigarette outside?"

He took another pull and stepped outside to place his cigarette in a planter box. "I was wondering if you could make copies."

"Sure can. What do you need?"

The man went over the various photographs Jordan had taken of his son then placed an order. "I'd like these by tomorrow. Is that possible?"

"I can have them ready in an hour."

"Really? Awesome. I'll be back."

Jordan processed the man's order. The phone rang. "Hello?"

"Hi, Jordan, it's Dena. I'm wondering if you're up for another trip? Jamie

Stewart had to cancel at the last minute, and I have family plans. I'll understand if you can't."

"When?"

"You need to leave on Friday night and fly out of Boston or possibly pick up a flight from Bangor. It's a three-day shoot in Niagara. You could drive if you want."

"No problem."

"There's one more thing. Jamie was taking an assistant because of the multiple shots required. Do you know of anyone who could go at such short notice?"

His mind flickered to Miranda. "No, I'm afraid not."

"All right. I'm sure you can handle it by yourself. You know what? Fly—don't drive. You'll be exhausted at the end, and flying home will feel much better."

"Yeah, but I'll still have a six-hour drive from Boston."

"True, but you could spend the night there. Your old roommates or parents could put you up, right?"

"More than likely. Don't worry, Dena. I'll take care of it." *I could use a visit with my folks.* "Oh, by the way, I had the first return customer from the candids I took at the festival."

"Excellent. You only charged for the prints, right?"

"Yes. We've discussed this before." He was beginning to understand small town logic, but it still bothered him not to make a profit on those prints. Then again, he'd had a lot of hits from the picture of the toothless-grinning girl on the Internet, and that was another freebie. Comments to his blog were along the lines of "What a beautiful smile," "Gotta love those freckles," and so on. A couple even inquired to know the child's name. He was thankful he didn't know and wrote back accordingly. Whether he'd received any orders because of that shot, he didn't know. But a few pictures had been requested from some of his previous work.

"Jordan, I'm sorry. I know this is a hard adjustment, but you're going to have to trust me on this."

"Dena, I do trust you. And I'm beginning to see the logic, although I'm not sure how it will all work out."

"It'll work out. Okay, I have to run. Contact me when you return."

Jordan gave his salutations then tapped out Miranda's phone number and reached her answering machine. "Hey, Miranda, it's Jordan. I'm afraid I can't make our dinner date Friday night. Dena's asked me to fill in for someone on a job. I'm going to Niagara." He glanced up at the calendar. "I'll see you in a week."

Jordan arranged for Jess to take care of his dog while he was gone. Duke enjoyed being on the water after spending a week with Jess during his trip to the Sudan. Jordan went back to his painting of the crab shack. He dipped his brush into the linseed oil and then a tiny dab of cerulean blue.

The jarring sound of screeching brakes, followed by the thump of one car hitting another, sent him running from his easel and out to the street.

Chapter 12

Randi eased out a pent-up breath. "Brenda, I'm not all that nice. But God's been working on me and my anger toward you and Cal. Jesus loves you, and I'm called to love as He loves. I'm not a saint, and I can't do it on my own. But I do have compassion for you and Tyler. . .even Cal. He's missing out on his relationship with his son."

"I can't believe I fell for his lies."

Randi let out a nervous chuckle. "I'm with you there. I'm sorry he walked out on you."

Brenda sniffled. "He said I wasn't you."

"Brenda, you can't judge yourself from what Cal said. And you certainly can't judge yourself from me. The Bible tells us how God believes we're all wonderfully made and of His redeeming love for us. No matter what happened, He still loves you."

"How?"

"That's kind of a mystery to all of us. But we have His Word, and we have His actions—sending His Son to die for us—that proves He does love us and forgive us."

"I'm scared, Randi. I don't want to live with my parents, but I have no other choice. I can't allow Tyler to suffer for my mistakes."

Randi thought for a moment. "You know, your love for Tyler is like God's love for us. Your parents' love for you is the same. They warned you about your relationship with Cal, but they are allowing you to come back home, to provide for you and your child, even though you didn't listen to their counsel. Isn't that how God deals with all of us?"

Brenda wiped the tears from her cheeks and looked down at her nursing son then back at Randi. "I knew if I came to you, you would help me sort this out. All this Jesus and God stuff is really real to you, isn't it?"

"Yup."

"Just like Mr. Kearns."

Randi nodded.

"I should have listened to him about that sex before marriage stuff. I thought he was so. . .well, I won't say it. But I really thought he had a few marbles loose just 'cause he had to raise Jess on his own. Now I'm in the same boat. Oh, I married Cal after I was pregnant, but he left me, just like Jess's real mom left her."

"They will be helpful people for you to talk with about raising Tyler without a father."

"I suppose. I just don't know if I can go through all that Jesus stuff. I mean, I'm glad He's real for you and all that, but I'm still not sure He can do anything for me."

Randi rubbed her hands together for a moment. "Pray, Brenda."

"I'll think about it."

Tyler slurped and rolled back his eyes. A knot tightened in Randi's stomach. The longing for her own child increased. She and Cal had planned on having children right away. Then her mind kicked back to something Jordan had said about children and how he wanted some. But not until he and his wife could afford them. She glanced back at Brenda. "Thinking things through and praying are the best things you can do."

"I didn't mean to stay so long." Brenda caressed Tyler's soft brown hair. "I'm leaving town today, and I've been trying to speak with you for so long."

"Why?"

"To apologize."

Randi nodded. "I realize that, but you've said you were sorry before. Why do you suppose you had such an urgent need to speak with me before you left town?"

Brenda turned away. "Because I tried to take Cal away from you," she muttered.

Randi already knew that from the gossip of others and even from what Brenda had said earlier, but it was good for her confess it. "You're on the road to recovering your faith, Brenda. You do believe in Jesus. You're just afraid to surrender your life to Him."

"I never wanted to live in Africa."

Randi chuckled. "Not everyone is called to be a missionary and go to Africa."

"I know but. . .oh, I don't know. It sure felt good to party and. . .well, you know."

Actually I don't. Thank You, Lord, for giving me the strength to resist Cal. "If sin didn't feel good from time to time, how would it be tempting?"

Brenda chuckled for the first time. "You sound like Mr. Kearns."

Randi smiled. "Yeah, I suppose I do. But it is still the truth."

"Yeah. I've gotten myself into quite a mess. But I don't want that for Tyler."

"Go to your parents," Randi said. "Do what you need to do to provide for your son, but get right with the Lord, Brenda. Nothing else will get you through some of the long hard days you have ahead of you. And, trust me, you'll be tempted to fall for the first guy who wants to provide for you and your son. Don't. Fall for the man the Lord will provide for you."

"Didn't you think Cal was that man for you?"

"Yes, but I've learned since that I wasn't trusting the Lord. I was just assuming Cal was the guy because that's what I thought I wanted back then. I don't now."

"No, I've seen you with the new photographer. He's pretty hot."

Randi's cheeks flamed. "Yes, he is."

"Do you like all that hair?"

She remembered his hair tickling her arm as he kissed the back of her hand. And then again when he'd worn it down at breakfast. "Yes, oddly enough I do. It fits him."

"That's so weird. Cal's is so short."

Randi hadn't made the comparison. Was she attracted to Jordan because he was so different from Cal?

Tyler finished nursing. An awkward, silent pause passed between them. Randi stood and walked to the window. From her cottage window, she could see the harbor. In the street below, people were running toward the center of town.

"Something's happening."

&

Jordan sat on the curb, paintbrush still in hand. He watched as the volunteer firemen used the "jaws of life" to remove a man trapped in his car.

"How come you aren't photographing this?" a crusty old fisherman called out from the crowd.

"Huh?" It had never entered his mind to grab his camera. If it had been a year ago, instinct would have taken over, and he would have grabbed the camera and cell phone. He would have been calling a major newspaper in the Boston region as he took the picture and then working his way down the list until one of the newspapers wanted his shots. With Dena working as his agent and with the more laid-back routine of living in Down-Eastern Maine, he realized he was more concerned with the individual who was trapped in the car than earning some money from someone else's misery. Not that he'd ever been that kind of photographer. But income was income, and generally he took any opportunity he could get.

"Ain't ya workin' for the newspaper?"

"Nope."

"Bet they'd pay to have a picture of this. That man in the car there is someone well-known in these parts."

"Thanks, but I'd rather be praying for his safety."

"Ah, prayer ain't a bad thing."

Jordan smiled and stood up from the curb. The volunteers worked methodically, cutting the car door and using the "jaws of life" to lift the roof high enough to pull the victim out. The driver of the car had run into the back end of a freight truck with a hydraulic lift on the rear, crushing the roof.

The bloody driver moaned. Jordan lifted another prayer for him, as he had been doing since seeing the wreck ten minutes ago. Jordan looked back at the truck then the car and noted how fortunate the driver was to be alive.

"Jordan, what's happening?" Miranda came running up, followed by a woman with a baby.

He held out his arm, and she drew close in his embrace. He sniffed her hair and felt ever so grateful she was safe. He explained what had happened. Miranda peered at the car.

The woman with the child gasped. "Oh, no!"

"Who is it?" Jordan asked.

Miranda left his embrace and steadied the woman. Jordan followed suit and took the baby from her arms. "That's Cal's father, Mike Collins, in the wreck. This," she told Jordan, nodding toward Brenda, "is Cal's wife and child."

"Cal, as in—" He cut off his question. This was no time to ask hows or whys.

"I need to call my parents," Brenda said.

Jordan reached for his cell phone then remembered he no longer had one. "You can use the phone in the studio."

Miranda led Brenda back to the studio. Jordan held the little boy in his arms and followed behind them. "Hey, there, little one, I'm Jordan. Who are you?"

The baby greeted him with a drooling grin.

"His name is Tyler," Miranda said as she opened the door for Brenda to go in.

"Phone's on the counter." Jordan turned back to the child. "Hey there, Tyler. Would you like to play with a ball?"

The baby thumped Jordan's chest with his tiny fists. "I'll take that as a yes." Jordan put him on the carpeted area and pulled out a box of toys they kept on hand for children while they set up to take their photos. He glanced away and saw Brenda was on the phone. "What's going on?"

"I'll explain later."

"Okay."

"Is he alive?" Miranda asked.

"Yes, he's fortunate," Jordan replied. "There's a lot of blood, but there always is with a head wound. The firemen were on the scene within a few minutes."

"Good."

He had a thousand questions for Miranda, and looking at Brenda and Tyler he knew something had been transpiring between the two of them. But he'd wait. He'd give her the time she needed to tell him what was going on and why they were in one another's company. He took it as a sign that Miranda was moving on from the hurts of the past, giving him more hope for their future. Yes, she was going to be his wife one day; she just didn't know it yet. And he'd learned long ago not to tell a woman that before it was time. Back in college, a friend of his told a gal on their first date that they would marry one day. She ran away from him faster than a rocket lifts off from Cape Canaveral.

He picked up his camera and focused on Tyler. He was a handsome child. *Click.* He took a shot. *Click.* And another. Just then, Duke edged his nose around the doorway at the stairs to his apartment. Jordan held up his hand. Duke sat down and waited.

Brenda hung up the phone. "Mom's going to call Mrs. Collins and let her know about the accident. Do you think he'll be all right? Should I go to the hospital?"

Jordan thought it odd she was asking Miranda for help.

"I don't know," Miranda said.

"How are you?" Jordan asked. Perhaps if he understood what Brenda's thoughts were at the moment, he could better understand what to suggest.

"Freaked out. Mom said he was probably coming to take Tyler away from me."

"Why?"

"Ever since Cal left they've been trying to get custody of Tyler. They say I can't support him. That's another reason I'm going to my parents' house."

"Why don't you have a seat? Can I get you something? A cup of tea?" Jordan offered.

"No, no, I'm fine. I've imposed long enough. Bye, Randi, and I'll think about what you said."

"Bye. And I'll be praying for you."

"Thanks." Brenda picked up Tyler and headed out of the studio then turned around. "And thanks for the use of the phone."

Then she was gone. They stood there for a moment in silence. The ambulance siren signaled its departure. Jordan rubbed the back of his neck. "What's going on?"

"She came by to apologize."

He edged up beside her. "How are you?"

❧

Randi sighed. "In the words of Brenda, 'freaked out.' I'm glad she's moving in with her parents. I was able to share about the Lord with her, and, for the first time, I no longer have that bitter taste in my mouth when I think about her and Cal. I'm sorry it happened, but in the end I'm over being hurt by his actions." She glanced out the window at the wrecked vehicle then back to Jordan.

"Do you think Cal's father was going to take the baby?" Jordan asked.

"It's possible. Cal's family has done fairly well. Consequently they kinda live by their own rules—which I should have seen ages ago but didn't. I guess I was so taken by the fact that Cal said he loved me that I overlooked a lot of things, including how his parents spoiled him. I don't think they'd be the right people to raise Tyler."

"What about Brenda?"

"I think she's grown up a lot since she became a mother. If you had asked me before she had the baby, I would have said no way. Today I think she's on the right track. It would be better if she trusted the Lord, but that's between her and God to work out."

"I've missed you." Jordan stepped closer to her.

Randi's legs felt like Jell-O. "It's only been a couple of hours, if that."

"I know." He wrapped his arms around her. "I still missed you."

With all the strength she could muster, she stepped out of his embrace. "Do you think this is wise?" Duke came over and sat on her foot as if anchoring her to stay put.

"Honey, I love you. Seeing that man in the car, my first thought was, I'm glad it wasn't you. I didn't think about getting my camera. . .nothing but you. Are you ready to be more than friends?"

Randi closed her eyes. *He confessed his love; should I?* She opened her eyes and slowly focused on the sparkling hazel of Jordan's. "I want to."

Jordan beamed. "Good. Then may I kiss you?"

Prickles of gooseflesh rose up and down her spine. She took a half step toward him and traced his lips with her finger. He kissed it gently. "Yes," she whispered.

He leaned over, and Randi closed her eyes.

"Jordan?" The front door of the studio slammed open.

Randi's eyes flung open.

"Randi?" Jess stood there with her hands on her hips. "Did I. . . ?" Her words trailed off. "Sorry," Jess mumbled. She turned and marched out of the studio.

"What was that all about?" Randi asked.

"I don't know, but her timing leaves a lot to be desired."

Maybe. The moment had passed. Randi slipped out of Jordan's embrace.

"Miranda?"

"We should see what Jess wants."

"Uh, sure. Whatever you say." Jordan went after Jess.

Randi tried to regain her footing. She knelt down and patted Duke. Was she really ready to involve herself with that level of commitment to Jordan? She still didn't know him all that well. Could she truly trust him? What were his parents like? An image of Jordan and her in their own home with children in the living room and the two of them preparing breakfast in the kitchen flickered through her mind.

Is he the one?

Chapter 13

Jordan packed his bags and flew out to Niagara Falls the next day. Jess's interruption had ended the kiss before it happened. Miranda pulled out of the studio faster than an old-fashioned camera flash burning the powder in the trough. And to be confronted by lovers strolling arm-in-arm all over Niagara on the Canadian side of the falls just reminded him of what they didn't have.

He was still puzzling over this when he flew back to Boston three days later. He'd thought of calling Miranda at least a hundred times, but he never got up the nerve. The fact that he no longer had a cell phone made it even more problematic. And she couldn't call him, with no number where she could reach him. But something still didn't feel right. Should he call? Or should he wait patiently for Miranda to be over the pain Cal had caused her?

On the other hand, Brenda's uninvited visit and Miranda's reaction to it indicated she was ready to move on. But then again, she had left the studio before he returned with Jess. This circular thinking was getting him nowhere. He took the T and walked up the hill to his parents' home. They lived a few blocks from Fenway Park. Cars lined the streets. *The Red Sox must be playing tonight.* A person could watch the game from his parents' roof.

He took the steps two at a time and knocked. His mother answered. She looked good, and her smile sent a wave of peace through him. "Hey, Mom."

She pulled him into a bear hug. "It's good to see you, Jordan. We've missed you."

"I've missed you, too. What are you cooking? It smells good." He stepped into the front hall.

"New England boiled dinner." She closed the door behind them. The coolness of the air-conditioning felt wonderful.

"My favorite."

She winked. "I know. But your father enjoys it, too."

"Where is he?"

"Down in the basement. Go put your bag in your room. I'll tell him you're home."

"Thanks." He hadn't lived at home for years. It seemed strange that his folks still called it his room, especially since it had become his mother's craft room. But there in the corner sat the twin bed and dresser he had used since he was two years old. He glanced at the table and looked over her newest scrapbook.

It held pictures of him and his siblings when they were young. He thumbed through the beautiful pages she had designed and laid out. His mind filled with childhood memories, page after page.

"Jordan!" his father's voice boomed through the room. "Good to see you, son."

"Good to be home, Dad."

"So you're working more with this Dena Russell?"

"Yup, I have a nice, steady income now."

"Wonderful. Aren't those"—he pointed to the scrapbooks—"great?"

"Yes, she's done an incredible job."

"I think so, but, then again, I didn't mind just looking at the pictures in the plastic sleeves. Can you tell me why the pictures from the sixties are turning color?"

"It was the process they used back then. You can have them scanned and restored. I can do it for you if you'd like."

"That would be wonderful. Your mom's had duplicates made of most of the photographs before she puts them in the books. Not to mention duplicates so each of you kids can have your own copies."

"You mean I'll get to have these one day?"

"Absolutely. They'll be good to have especially when you have children. On the other hand, they'll be even better to have for me to show my grandchildren."

"First, I need a wife."

"That would be helpful. So tell me more about this gal in Maine. Randi, I think her name is, isn't it?"

Jordan took in a deep pull of air. "Yeah, it's Randi. Miranda is her full name. I love her—I really do—but she's been hurt by a fiancé who ran around on her. At least she found out before they married, but it still has her in a tailspin of sorts. I know she doesn't fully trust me."

"Trust develops over time, son. Give her a chance. She'll come around if she's the one the Lord has in mind for you."

"I think she is, Dad. And I'm trying to be patient."

"But that's not really your strong suit, except with photography."

Jordan chuckled. "Yeah, except with photography. So what are you working on in the basement?"

"I've taken up a new hobby," his dad said. "I'm learning how to make stained glass."

"Wow! How are your fingers?"

"Ha, ha. I've only nicked 'em a couple of times. Cutting the glass is the easy part. Laying out the design and using the copper foiling is tough, but I'm starting to get the hang of it. After that, I'll work on learning how to use the lead. The copper foil, though, is your mother's favorite."

Jordan was happy his parents found hobbies to keep them busy. He knew retirement was only a few years away for them, and he loved the idea that they kept active. "Lead on—I'd love to see what you've done."

As they passed by the kitchen, his mother called out, "Don't stay down there too long! Supper will be ready in fifteen minutes."

"Not a problem, Mom. I'm starved."

"You won't have to call me twice for dinner," his father added with a smile.

Jordan quieted the laughter that bubbled up inside him. Once his father was in the basement, it took a lot of prodding on his mother's part to get him to come up for dinner.

They rounded the corner, and both ducked as they went down the narrow basement stairs. One thing about old houses in the Boston area—they generally were made in the 1800s when stairways were put in some of the tightest spots of a house. Jordan lifted his hand and reached out to the carrying beam that had beaned him more times than not when he was growing up and moving too quickly.

"Tell me more about Miranda. What does she do? Look like? And why do you love her?"

Nothing like his father to get to the heart of the matter. "She's beautiful—inside and out. She has these wonderful dark gray eyes."

"Like your great-grandmother's?"

"Yeah."

"Interesting. Do you have a picture?"

"On my laptop. I'll show you after dinner."

"I'd love to see your work. Have you looked into the real estate in Squabbin Bay?"

Jordan chuckled. "I haven't, but I guess you have?"

"Absolutely. The market hasn't moved much in years up there. The area seems to be just far enough away from the general tourism routes that it is still secluded and underdeveloped."

They continued talking until his mother called them for dinner. Jordan enjoyed the time with his parents. He found it helped to settle him down, to continue being patient with Miranda.

❧

Driven by distraction, Randi paced back and forth in her cottage. Jordan hadn't come home from his Niagara trip yet. Jess had said he might spend the night in Boston, but she had no contact information for him. "E-mail! Why didn't I think of that before?" She thumped her head and sat down at her desk.

Pulling up Jordan's contact information, she typed his e-mail address into a new mail window then proceeded to type.

"*Dear Jordan. . .*" She paused. "Dear" seemed too formal. She hit the delete key and held it down until all the letters were erased then tried again. "*Hi,*

Jordan. . ." Her fingers paused again on the keys. Why was it so hard to type a simple e-mail? What did she want to say anyway? *"I miss you."*

"I'm sorry I ran out of the studio when Jess showed up."

Nah, that wouldn't do. Her desire for the kiss had turned the instant Jess walked in on them. All the old fears resurfaced. There was no question she was attracted to Jordan, and the attraction went way beyond his looks. She loved their time together, loved being able to talk so openly with him. But she was afraid of being vulnerable once again. A few days ago, she was confident in moving on. Today she still was. . . But thinking back on the near kiss. . .as much as she wanted it. . . Fear wrapped its ugly head around her logic.

Randi deleted the e-mail. She should wait until they could speak one-on-one.

The computer flashed that she had incoming e-mail. It was from Jordan. She smiled and opened it.

Hi, Miranda,

This is just a quick e-mail to let you know I'll be back in town tomorrow evening. I'm wondering if we can go out to dinner. Please let me know. Also I'll be bringing up some of my earlier work. I thought we might be able to put some of the photos on my Web site and others in stock-photo archives.

See you soon.
JORDAN

Randi reread the e-mail. Then she reacquainted herself with some of the various Web pages that kept stock-photo archives and the costs for those services and checked into their search capabilities. She smiled to herself, thinking about how this stuff made her parents' heads spin. They didn't understand the computer world and her career. They knew it could be a great benefit for those who used it regularly; they just didn't happen to be such people. She wondered if Jordan's folks kept up with computer technology. Even as techno savvy as she tried to keep herself, the industry kept growing at a rate too rapid to keep fully abreast of everything going on.

Two hours later, Randi had jotted down some practical ideas for Dena and Jordan in producing their own network of archives. Tomorrow she would put together a proposal for them to consider. She glanced at the clock. It was midnight. Time to go to bed. She had work in the morning.

At work the next morning, Randi's mind buzzed with further possibilities for Dena and Jordan.

"Waitress!" A man waved his arm. "I need some more coffee here."

Randi grabbed the brown plastic handle of the glass coffee carafe and headed to the gentleman's table.

A baby at the next table knocked a plate to the floor then started crying.

Randi poured the coffee then bent down to clean up the mess.

"I'm so sorry. He never does this at home."

"How old is he?"

"Eleven months." The young mother's smile brightened.

Randi turned to the baby. "Well, you're a cutie." *Even though you toss your plate. What is she thinking, giving a baby his own plate? What's the age when a parent should do that?*

"Miss, where's our order?"

"Should be coming right up. I'll check on it in a moment." Randi finished cleaning up the baby's mess and headed to the kitchen. She blew a strand of hair from her face. "What's up with these people this morning?"

"Order's up," the cook replied. "Just one of those days."

"Ayup," she drawled out in her heaviest Maine accent. Randi washed her hands, dried them off, and went back into the restaurant. She placed the recent order on her tray and headed toward the customer's table.

Lord, I'd really like to be working only one job.

The phone rang. A moment later the cook called out, "Randi, it's for you!"

❧

"Hi, Miranda. I won't keep you, but I wanted you to know I was home. How are you?" Jordan had longed to hear her voice.

"Busy. It's good to hear from you, but I'm afraid I've got to run."

"Okay. What about dinner tonight?"

"Seriously, I don't want to see the inside of another restaurant."

Jordan's heart sank. Maybe she was having second thoughts about their relationship. "All right. Call me when you can."

" 'Bye."

He heard the click of the phone and the electronic hum that followed. He pressed the OFF button and replaced the portable phone in the charger. The bell above the studio door rang. Jordan looked up.

"Hello, Sheriff. How can I help you?"

"Afternoon, Jordan." The sheriff was holding a sheet of white paper. "How was your trip to Niagara?"

"Fine." Did everyone know his comings and goings in this small town?

"Dena said you'd be back sometime this afternoon."

Jordan nodded. The tiny hairs on the back of his neck rose. This wasn't the average customer visit. "What's up?"

"Well, now, that's what I came to talk with you about. Dena said you may have taken this picture at the church fair." He handed Jordan the shot of a girl, with only her face appearing in the picture.

"Yes, sir."

"Have you met her parents?"

"No, sir. I don't believe so."

The sheriff inched his cap further up his head.

"Is there a reason you posted this picture on the Internet?"

"It's a great shot. The girl is adorable. Aside from that, no. Why?"

"Hang on. Let me ask the questions."

"Yes, sir." Jordan's legs started to shake. He'd done nothing wrong, he hoped. So why did he feel as if he was about to be arrested? He looked at the picture again. He couldn't place where or when he'd taken it because the headshot blurred what little there was of the background.

"Jordan, relax. Let me rephrase that. Do you have any other photographs of this child with her parents or of the child speaking with anyone else?"

"No. . .well, I don't know. I can check. I took hundreds of shots that day."

"That would be helpful. This girl looks like a child who was abducted from her home a few months ago."

"Oh, no. Please say it isn't so. She seems so happy."

"Yeah, it is quite a smile. I'd appreciate your going through your pictures from that day."

"No problem. I can pull them up right now."

"Wonderful. Mind if I look over your shoulder?"

"No, not at all."

Jordan pulled up the folder on his computer and loaded the photos from that day. One by one, they clicked through every photograph. Twenty minutes later, they had found no other pictures of the girl. Not even that one. "I'm sorry, Sheriff. I'm not even sure when I took this if it isn't in my computer. It must have been at the church fair. I haven't had an occasion to take other pictures of children playing except then. It's possible the picture was accidentally deleted when I was giving Miranda copies of pictures for my Web page."

The sheriff put his hand on Jordan's shoulder. "No problem. You've done a lot just by taking this picture and posting it on the Internet. The parents are 99 percent certain this is their daughter, but they also received a ransom note a few days after the fair. It had been mailed from the same town the child had been taken in."

"Weird."

"Absolutely. I'm inclined to think the girl is with some family or with someone who was close to the family, in order for her to be so happy. But, then again, I saw a few of my kids in those photographs, and they were having a great time, too. When I'm not on duty I'll come around and order a couple of prints of my kids. But right now, I have to get back with the FBI missing persons unit."

"I understand. I wish I had taken more photographs of her."

"That's all right. No one knew. I'm going to ask around and get folks to check their personal photographs. Does that machine keep track of all the photographs it's printed?"

"Yes, but it's temporary, in case the customer wishes to have another set of prints made. But apart from that, we don't keep those files for long. No more than a week."

"I was afraid of that. Okay—keep your eyes peeled. But don't say anything on the Internet. We don't want to warn the abductors that we're aware they were in the area. With it being a festival, they could have just been traveling through."

Jordan nodded. The way the sheriff's blue eyes focused beyond Jordan, he could tell the officer was already mentally moving on in his investigation.

"Should I remove the picture from my Web page?"

"Let me get back with you on that. I'd like to see what the FBI profiler has to say."

"All right."

"Relax, Jordan. We know you simply took a picture."

Jordan nodded. What could he say? That he was relieved he wasn't a suspect? At the same time, he was also upset he was even considered a possible suspect. On the other hand, Dena must have put the police at rest about him. Once the sheriff left, Jordan called her. "Hey, Dena. Why didn't you tell me about the girl?"

"Sheriff asked me not to. He wanted to see your reaction. I filled him in on when and how you took that picture."

"Thanks."

"Jordan, I also told the sheriff you were on an assignment at the time of the kidnapping. I'm thankful I had your time-dated photos from your resume to prove where you were then. You're not a suspect, Jordan. The police just needed to be certain."

Jordan let out a pent-up breath.

"You feel crummy, don't you?"

"Absolutely."

"If you need to clear your head, I can come down to the studio for the rest of the day."

"No, I'm fine. It's only a few hours before closing."

"All right. Would you like to come for dinner tonight? I'd love to take another look at your Niagara photos."

Jordan hesitated. Miranda didn't say yes, and she hadn't said no. In fact, she had basically ignored him. "Sure, I'd love to."

"Great. I'll have Wayne bring us some lobsters."

"Count me in for two."

Dena chuckled. "Great. Come on over after you close the studio."

They said their salutations, and Jordan went to work getting caught up on the orders that had come in over the weekend. In the corner of the studio stood his painting of the crab shack. *Maybe I can get back to that soon.*

A couple of customers later, he'd finished sorting the files from the Niagara trip. It had been for a tourism brochure for the state of New York and the Niagara chamber of commerce.

He tapped out a proposal for an article on his trip to Niagara for some travel magazines. If he sold the pictures and the article, he'd have enough to get a new cell-phone service.

He packed the box of negatives he'd brought from his parents' house in the Jeep to make use of Dena's darkroom. It seemed like ages since he had developed a film picture. Even so, several of the shots he'd taken in the Sudan had been printed. Duke sat in the passenger seat on the way to Dena and Wayne's home. Even the natural beauty of the place didn't appeal to him. All he could think about was Miranda and why she was avoiding him again.

Chapter 14

Randi pushed the button to play her messages as she toed off her shoes. Tonight she would not run. More than likely she wouldn't be running in the morning either. She was sore from head to toe. Every now and again she had one of those days that, no matter what she did, it was never enough for the customers. It was as if all the customers had conspired to take a "nasty" pill before entering the restaurant. In any case, today had been one of those days. A long, hot soak in the tub was top priority.

"Randi," said a voice on the answering machine. "This is Joe from Down-Eastern Solutions. There's a major problem with our Web site. We need you to take care of it ASAP. Call me as soon as you get this message."

Randi glanced up at the clock. She ran to her desk, located the phone number for the company, and placed a call. While she waited for the phone to connect, she pulled up their Web site. What appeared was something totally different, totally inappropriate.

The company's answering machine came on. Randi left a brief message then called Joe's cell phone.

"Randi, it's about time. Where were you?"

"At work. Sorry. What happened?"

"I don't know. We hired a kid to take care of the everyday uploads, and the next thing I know. . ." Joe went on to explain the disaster that was now his Web page. He gave her the contact information for "the kid," and she called him. Fortunately he was only a fifteen-minute drive away and would come over to try to figure out what went wrong.

Then she placed a call to the host servers of the Web site and verbally worked out a new user name and password. It appeared that someone had sabotaged the Web site. It was rare but did happen from time to time.

Randi glanced at the clock again. She had five minutes to wash her face and freshen up before Michael Robert, aka "the kid," arrived. She whirled through the cottage and pulled a cold piece of pizza from the refrigerator along with a soft drink. No sooner had she taken a bite than Michael Robert knocked on her door.

By two in the morning, Down-Eastern Solutions was up and running, and Randi's day ended in much the same way it had begun. It wasn't until her head hit the pillow that she remembered she hadn't called Jordan back. Nor had she answered his question about going out to dinner that night. Randi's stomach twisted. She tossed and turned until she finally fell fast asleep close to dawn.

ॐ

"Miranda, open up." Her mother was pounding on the door. "Miranda?"

Randi pushed herself off the bed and went to the front door. Her eyes squinted from the bright sunlight.

"Thank the Lord you're all right. I've been trying to reach you for hours. What's the matter? Are you sick?"

"No, I was sleeping."

"Honey, it's three in the afternoon. We were supposed to go out for a late lunch at two today."

"Three?" Randi yawned. "Sorry, Mom. I was up until two this morning fixing a client's Web page."

"Miranda, you have to stop working two jobs. This is killing you."

"I'm fine." She yawned.

"And I'm a monkey's uncle. Go get dressed. I'll make you some coffee."

"Thanks."

Dressing helped wake her up. Randi returned to her mother and the kitchen a few minutes later.

Her mother chuckled. "You look much better."

"Thanks." Her mother poured the coffee into two cups. Randi joined her at the kitchen table. "I'm sorry about lunch, Mom."

"No problem. You just scared me when you didn't answer your phone."

"I didn't hear it." Randi grabbed the phone and checked for a dial tone. It was there, and she hung it up again. "I didn't fall asleep until dawn."

"Oh, honey, I'm sorry. Do you need to go back to bed?"

"No, I have other work to catch up on."

"All right. Should I go pick up something from the café? I see you haven't had time to shop."

"Sure, that would be nice. A seafood salad for me."

"Okay, I'll be right back."

Randi gave the cottage a clean sweep while her mother went to town and picked up their lunch. She took a few minutes to download her e-mail and was thankful to find no emergencies pending. She also realized she had no messages from Jordan on her answering machine or in her e-mail box.

Jordan. She needed to call him to apologize. She picked up the phone just as her mother walked back in. She replaced it on the charger.

"So tell me about Jordan. What's going on with the two of you?" Her mother put their salads on the table.

Randi sat down after bringing some napkins to the table. "Nothing to tell. We're just friends."

"Right. I wasn't born yesterday. Come on, honey. I've seen the way you look at him."

"Mom, don't you think that until I have something to tell, it should be my own private affair?"

"Maybe, but we live in a small town, and folks are asking me. They saw you leaving his apartment one morning."

Randi's head dropped. "He invited me for breakfast."

"I know, dear. I found that out from Georgette. Heard he made crepes."

"So what is it you want to know?" she asked sharply. "You seem to know it all already."

"Miranda, don't take that tone with me. I'm not trying to be a busybody. I'm concerned. I'm your mother, and I know how hard it has been since you and Cal broke up."

"I'm sorry, Mom. I know you're not trying to tell me how to live my life. And with regard to Jordan, I don't know. We seem to get close; then something happens, and we start fumbling over our words. I'm still nervous, I guess. I want to trust Jordan, but it's hard. Not that he's done anything."

"But Cal breaking your trust has made you leery."

"Exactly." Randi took a forkful of salad and hoped her mother would understand that she didn't want to go too deeply into her feelings for Jordan.

"Jess said Brenda came by for a visit."

"Yeah, that was really hard. You can say you've forgiven someone, but when you're face-to-face with that person, it's hard to believe in giving out grace. Do you know Cal named the baby Tyler? That's the name I picked out when we were dating."

"I can't figure out Cal." Her mother paused with her fork halfway between her mouth and the plate. "If he was so in love with you, why did he cheat on you? And why leave his child like that?"

"Brenda said her in-laws are trying to get custody of Tyler."

"That's sad. I hope they can arrange a visitation plan. Brenda needs to raise her son. But Cal's parents want to see their grandson. Maybe when Mike Collins gets out of the hospital they can work it out."

"Maybe." Randi ate another bite of her salad. "Mom, Jordan wants to be more than friends."

❧

Jordan sat back. The canvas glared at him. Nothing seemed to be going right since returning from Niagara. Miranda hadn't called, and he'd been rethinking his interest in her. He'd broken one of his rules—not to get involved with a woman until he could take on the responsibility of a wife and children. At his present salary, they'd be eating macaroni and cheese every other night. Miranda deserved better.

"Miserable" described the mood he was in. But time would heal the tear in his heart. He must have misunderstood when he felt God was leading for her to be his wife. How foolish he had been to think he knew the mind of God or

God's will for his life.

He glanced back at the canvas. The calm sea had changed to a raging storm on the horizon, just like his own life. A storm hovered around him, nothing really settled. He'd even gone so far as to wonder if he should have taken the job with Dena. How would his life be if he'd stayed in Boston? Would he have landed more contracts with various advertising companies? Dropping his cell service had been an impulsive mistake. No one knew how to reach him. His old roommates had moved out, and that number no longer existed. He was stuck in the boonies with no one to love and tired of feeling sorry for himself.

He tossed the brush in the thinner and left his easel. Walking over to the front bay window, he scanned the area. Duke came up beside him and put his front paws on the window sill. Jordan rubbed the top of the basset hound's head. "Did I make the right decision to move here, boy?"

The summer tourist season was in full swing, and while it doubled the local population, it was a far cry from being a tourist town. Few came to the area with more touristy towns so close by. But there were the exceptions—families who used to live here or whose grandparents lived here. Now they vacationed in the quiet coastal town in the many summer cottages that lined the hills overlooking the harbor.

Sheriff McKean pulled up in front of the store. He marched toward the door. Jordan reached it before him. "How can I help you, Sheriff McKean?"

"Did you take these?"

Jordan examined the photographs. "Yes."

"Jordan Lamont, you're coming with me."

"What do you need?"

"You don't get it, son, do you?"

"No." Jordan looked back at the photographs. He'd taken them the first or second week he moved to Squabbin Bay, of a child digging for clams while her mother lay on a blanket keeping a watchful eye over her. Jordan examined the picture again. It was the same girl.

"Come on, son. I don't want to arrest you and have to bring you out in cuffs."

"What? You can't possibly believe I had anything to do with that girl's kidnapping."

"Evidence says you're a prime suspect. Not only do you have a picture of the girl, but now you have two. The first was easy for someone to believe you, with so many people at the church festival. But this picture proves you saw Lucy Tomisson before that. The investigators also claim it was a couple, a man and a woman, who kidnapped her. Tell me, where is she? And who is your accomplice?"

"Sheriff McKean, it wasn't me." He wanted to ask how the police found this picture, because he hadn't published it. It was in his personal gallery on his computer. Jordan scanned the studio. His laptop was behind the counter. "Do you mind telling me where you got that picture?"

"Your Web site."

"I didn't—" He bit off his words. If he claimed he hadn't put the picture on his Web site, he might give the impression he had something to hide. "Miranda must have uploaded it."

"Look—I don't care how it got there. But the FBI wants to speak with you ASAP, and they're at my office. You're obviously involved with this case, son, whether innocently or not. I'd like to take your word for it; but you're new here in these parts, and, well, I can't vouch for you."

Jordan swallowed hard. Thoughts of getting a lawyer before being questioned flew through his mind as several television episodes of police shows and movies flickered in instant replay.

"Sheriff McKean, I'll be happy to go there with you, but I have the equipment here to blow up the image."

"They have their own."

"Right. Duke, watch the place. I'll be home soon." Jordan stepped back, grabbed his laptop, and took his first-ever ride in the backseat of a police cruiser. What hit him first was the missing knobs on the rear doors. The bars across the front seat, protecting the officers from criminals, were the second. His heart sank. Fear washed over him. Jordan closed his eyes and prayed. Instantly logic took over. He hadn't been arrested; he was simply being brought in for questioning.

Father, give me peace and the right words to speak. Help me, and help the police find this missing child.

&

Randi punched in Jess's number on her cell phone. "Jess, it's me. Do you know why the police arrested Jordan?"

"What? When? Are you sure?"

"I just saw him riding in the back of Sheriff McKean's car."

"I don't have a clue. Let me ask Mom. Mom. . ." The word diminished into nothing. Randi figured Jess had covered the phone with her hand.

Moments later, Dena Kearns's voice came through the line. "Randi, it's Dena. What's going on?"

"I don't know. That's why I called Jess. Do you have any idea why the police would arrest Jordan?"

"No, but we can't assume he's been arrested."

"Dena, Sheriff McKean doesn't take people for joyrides in his car." Randi shook her head. She'd done it again—fallen for a man who was not trustworthy. "Dena, I have to go. If you didn't know, I'm glad I could tell you."

Randi used to pride herself on not being judgmental. But today she felt better knowing she hadn't completely fallen in love with Jordan Lamont.

Whoever he was, he certainly wasn't the man for her. She had already dealt with one liar in her life, and she didn't need another.

That isn't fair to him, a voice whispered in her head.

Randi paused, looked around to see if someone had spoken then continued walking back to her cottage. She had left her mother convinced she wanted to step out in faith and trust Jordan—only to see him being whisked away in the sheriff's car. *Lord, it isn't fair.*

You're the one not being fair, she argued with herself.

By the time she arrived at the cottage, Jess was sitting in her driveway. "What's going on?" She stood there with her hands on her hips.

"I'm just glad I found out before I was hurt again."

"Randi, you're talking nonsense. You don't know why the police arrested—or if they even arrested—Jordan. You're running scared, and you're not making any sense."

"Drop it, Jess. I can't do this."

Jess relaxed her stance and came up beside Randi. "We need to trust Jordan. He's a good man, Randi."

"I'd like to, but I can't. I just can't."

"Okay, how about a glass of iced tea?"

"Sure."

Jess came inside and didn't say a word while Randi poured two tall glasses of iced tea and sat down at the table.

"Randi, he's not Cal."

"I know, but. . ." *But what?*

"Look, Randi—it's me. I've gone through you and Cal. I know you're afraid, but why don't we wait to see what's going on?"

Randi wrapped her hands around the cool glass of iced tea. It felt good to feel something, anything, to jar her back from the instant betrayal she felt seeing Jordan in the sheriff's car.

Jess reached over and placed a loving hand on her shoulder. "Why don't we pray about this?"

Randi didn't want to explain that she already had. Instead she gave a quick nod of her head and closed her eyes.

"Father, be with Randi right now. Give her the knowledge she needs to trust Jordan or the strength to walk away from him if he's not the man You have designed for her."

Tears edged Randi's eyes.

Chapter 15

Jordan rubbed his neck as he answered for the fifth time, "No, sir. I do not know these people. I took the picture on April 17th."

"Mr. Lamont, I understand this is frustrating to you, but you do see our problem. You are the only person to have pictures of this child since she was taken from her school," the senior FBI agent said. He pushed back the few remaining hairs from the top of his head.

Why do they do that? Jordan promised himself he would never do that if he started losing his hair. "Yes, sir, but you have the wrong man. If you'd just let me scan through my files, perhaps I have another shot that shows a clearer image of the woman."

"My partner is taking care of that."

Jordan closed his eyes. Something about privacy and needing a warrant popped into his head. On the other hand, Lucy Tomisson's life was at stake. He could put up with a few discomforts. "I can locate the file more easily." He made one last offer.

The agent simply ignored him and looked back at the two blown-up images of the girl. The face of the woman on the beach was hidden by her floppy hat and long hair. *Lord, help us find this little girl.*

"Talk me through your file system." The younger agent, perhaps right out of training, came in holding his laptop.

"I sort my photographs in various ways. Mostly by topic, for easy recovery if someone requests a picture. I also keep a record with a thumbnail sketch of the file as well as a backup of the original file on CDs at home. Search for rev48."

"What does that mean?"

"Revelation chapter four, verse eight. It's where John is writing about the four living creatures in heaven that have eyes all around their heads."

The young agent scrunched his nose. The older man rubbed his hands across those long, thin hairs. Jordan shrugged it off. He'd done that as his own code, a sort of protection if anyone were to try to find his files. Not that anyone would, but "rev48" didn't sound as if it could be that important to the casual looker.

"Got it," the young officer replied. An expletive passed through the man's lips. "What's the password?"

Jordan looked to the senior officer. "Can I type that in privately?"

"Can't you just change it when we're through with it?"

Jordan sighed.

"Jordan," Sheriff McKean said. "Give it up, son."

"You do realize I am aware of all my civil rights being violated here. I have the right to refuse to help. I have the right to call a lawyer. The least you could do is be respectful of my privacy."

"Mr. Lamont, we're not trying to violate your rights. We're simply trying to find a child who has been kidnapped."

"Yes, and you believe I'm a prime suspect. In which case, I have the right to seek legal counsel and to refuse to let you search my computer openly without a warrant."

The young agent slid the computer away from him. "Fine. Call the judge."

"Look—I am simply asking to keep my password a secret—" Jordan stopped himself. "Fine. The password is 'rjjakm79.'"

"What does that stand for?" Sheriff McKean asked. "I'm not familiar with that biblical book."

"It stands for Roger, June, Jordan, Adam, Katie, and Michael, and seventy-nine is the year my parents got married."

"Ah."

"I'm in." The young agent rubbed his hands together. His eyes sparkled. *He truly believes I'm guilty, Lord.*

"Now go to April of this year. You'll see a listing of all the pictures I took according to the series. If you read them off, I'll be able to tell you which set that picture came from."

"Flowers, trees, birds, shore, mountains, family at play—"

"That's it."

"It's not linked to the photos." The agent's shoulders slumped.

Jordan closed his eyes and prayed for the Lord's grace one more time. "No, they are not linked. I simply keep an accounting in this file of what series I took that month. Now find 'fapme.'"

"What is this, Fort Knox?"

"No, but it is my livelihood. Open the folder 'fapme' and select to read the group as a list."

"There're about two hundred photos here."

"I honestly can't tell you from here which photos to look at. But you can select them all and hit the open apple key and the letter *O* key, and it will open all of them so you can simply click through them."

"You'd think with you being a professional photographer you'd use the better software."

Jordan resisted the cutting remark he wanted to say and simply replied, "It's on there. I don't upload all the raw files to it."

"Oh," the younger agent mumbled.

"Now, while Agent Wilkes is looking, would you mind going over the details one more time with me?" the older agent asked.

Yes! he wanted to scream in frustration. Jordan turned toward the sheriff, who was putting his hat back on his head. "I need to go out on patrol."

"I want you here!" Jordan demanded. "I'm here of my own free will, but I need a witness, just in case."

The sheriff removed his hat and sat down again. "All right."

"Now as I was asking. . ."

❧

Randi fought with herself all day knowing she should give Jordan a chance to explain what happened. But why go through that kind of misery? Would she ever be able to trust someone again? Had Cal robbed her of being able to trust people? No, she still trusted many people. But men, especially single men, or rather men she wanted to date, were the problem. Jordan was the only man she wanted to date.

Randi huffed as she lay down on her bed for the night. Jordan hadn't called. Not that she expected him to. But then again she did. She wondered if he was still down at the police station and fought the desire to check after Jess went home.

She wanted to trust him. She prayed he was the man she thought him to be. But then she had prayed for Cal, too. And what did she and Jordan really have in common with one another? She loved to run; he hated to exercise. He spent hours in the mud just for a picture. She wouldn't be caught dead playing in the muck of low tide.

She woke to the same thoughts the next morning. After a hearty run, she went past the studio and saw no evidence of Jordan being awake. Back at home, she readied herself for work. Just as she was about to leave, her phone rang.

"Hello."

"Hey, Randi. It's Cal."

"Cal?"

"Yeah, look—I'm in the neighborhood, and I wanted to speak with you."

Randi thought it odd that Cal would be in the area a couple of days after Brenda moved down to Portland. Obviously his parents or someone was keeping him well informed. "What do you want to talk about?"

He hemmed and hawed. "I'd prefer to speak in person."

"Cal, I don't have anything to say. And if you're thinking I might be interested in getting back together with you, you're sadly mistaken."

"No, no, it's nothing like that. I heard Brenda spoke with you before she left town."

Randi rolled her shoulders to work out the building stress. "I have nothing to say about that."

"Come on, Rand. It's me. I need your help here."

Her mind flew back to the issue of his parents trying to get custody of the baby. "No, Cal. I'm not getting involved."

"But, Rand, I'm not allowed to see my own kid."

"Maybe you should have thought about that before you ran off and left Brenda and the baby alone. Cal, for once in your life, be a man. Support your child and do the right thing by Brenda. Stop fooling around and take responsibility for your own actions."

An expletive flew through the phone lines. "I knew I couldn't count on you—a woman scorned and all that."

"Cal, stop it. This has nothing to do with you and me; this has to do with you and how you treat people. You're a spoiled kid who's never grown up. Try growing up and being a man." She hung up the phone and ran out the door and headed for the car. She knew his pattern. He would call again. He would continue to badger her until she did what he wanted her to do.

Getting behind the wheel, she turned the ignition and drove off to nowhere in particular, ruminating over how her personal life couldn't get more miserable. She prayed Cal would not continue his normal pattern and move on.

She thought about calling her mother and telling her about Cal's call. She thought about calling Jess. Instead she called Jordan. On the fourth ring, the answering machine picked up. Randi snapped her phone shut. Could she really trust him anyway? Out of the corner of her eye, she spotted Jordan's vehicle at the police station.

Randi's entire body shook. She tightened her grasp on the steering wheel and headed out of town. Why couldn't life be simpler?

❧

Four hours later, the lunch rush was in full swing at the restaurant. Randi's feet ached. Her mind buzzed about Jordan, Cal, and Brenda. She knew without asking Cal that he wanted Randi to give him some kind of information that would allow him to get custody of the baby. Or rather for his parents to get custody. No judge in his right mind would give custody to a father who had deserted his wife and child, would he? No. Any parent who could do that once could do it again. At least she hoped such logic would prevail in the courts and not Cal's parents' way of paying for what they wanted.

Randi said another prayer for Brenda and the baby. Brenda was changing. Cal showed no signs of change.

The bell over the restaurant door rang. Jordan stood there with two men dressed in black business suits. All she could think of was the movie *Men in Black*. "Miranda." Jordan came up to the counter. "Honey, it's good to see you."

"Who are your friends?"

"They're with the FBI. They'd like to talk with you."

Me? She wanted to scream.

"They have some questions for you."

"Miss Miranda Blake?"

"Yes." She nodded and balled up the dishcloth she held in her hand.

"Please advise your superiors that we need to speak with you."

Randi stepped back to the kitchen. "Jake, there're some men—"

"We know." Jake slapped the spatula on the grill. "Send them in to me."

"Okay."

Randi went back to the FBI agents. What could Jordan have done to get the FBI involved? "My manager wants to speak with you. He says to go back there."

The counter bell rang. "Randi, pick up for table four."

"Excuse me."

Jordan couldn't believe Miranda's manager had convinced the agents to sit down for lunch and wait until the rush was over. They ordered Reuben sandwiches and ate without saying a word to one another. Jordan also couldn't believe they still didn't trust him. *Once they sit down with Miranda, I hope they'll see I've been telling the truth.*

Miranda came to the table. She looked worn-out and suspicious. She must have heard they'd taken him to the police station yesterday. Squabbin Bay was a small town, and news traveled quickly. Unfortunately the truth about why he'd been brought in would not spread. Only rumors. He'd been ordered not to talk about it.

"Mr. Lamont, would you please excuse us?" Agent O'Malley rubbed the crumbs off his white shirt.

"Sure." Jordan stood.

"Don't go too far," Agent Wilkes added.

Jordan nodded and left the restaurant. He'd wait outside for them. The piercing look he'd received from Miranda when he left gave him a good idea what she was probably thinking.

He couldn't blame her, with what had happened between her and Cal. *On the other hand, doesn't she know me well enough to know I'm not like that?*

Jordan leaned against the black sedan. They hadn't even allowed him to drive his own vehicle. He scanned the area looking for a telephone booth. He spotted a phone on the corner of a building a half block away. He wanted to talk with Dena. The sheriff had promised him he would call her, but she should hear everything from him.

He reached into his pocket and pulled out two quarters then tapped out Dena's number. On hearing her answering machine, he left a detailed message of the events over the past couple of days. Jordan still hadn't been arrested, but he wasn't free to leave either. He was heading back to the restaurant when he noticed an art supply store down the street. He could use some more oils for his painting. He rounded the corner in time to be tackled to the ground.

Wilkes whispered in his ear, "I told you not to run off."

Jordan groaned. "I was going to the art supply store."

"Yeah, right. I know you're involved here. I just can't prove it. Yet. You're not going anywhere—got that?"

Jordan had had enough. "I want a lawyer. Now. I've had enough. I've cooperated with you all the way. I've given you more information than you had. And yet you still suspect me. I want a lawyer now. I know my rights."

Agent Wilkes pulled him up from the ground. "You gave up your rights when—"

Agent O'Malley had followed Wilkes out and gave the younger agent a stern look of reproof.

"I did not kidnap her," Jordan repeated.

"We'll see." Wilkes slapped handcuffs on his wrists and started back to the restaurant.

"What are you doing, Wilkes?" Agent O'Malley demanded.

"He was running away."

"I doubt it. Take off those cuffs."

"But, sir."

"Wilkes!" Agent O'Malley bellowed.

Agent Wilkes removed the cuffs. "I'll get you yet," Wilkes whispered. Then he added in full voice, "He lawyered up."

"I would have done it yesterday. Let's get back to Squabbin Bay."

He could see Miranda standing near the window, her eyes filled with tears. She turned and ran toward the back.

"May I make a call?" Jordan asked.

"Sure," Agent O'Malley said. "We'll wait for you in the car."

Jordan went to the payphone by the door in the restaurant and dialed his parents. "Dad, I can't explain right now, but I need a criminal lawyer ASAP."

Jordan scanned the room for Miranda. "No, Dad, I'm fine. I'll explain later. Just contact who you can and have them send a lawyer to the Squabbin Bay police station."

"Are you sure you're all right?"

"Yes. It's a misunderstanding. But one man is convinced I'm guilty. I really can't talk right now, Dad. Please call one of your lawyers and have them connect with someone in my area."

"All right, son. You be careful, okay?"

"I will. I'll be fine. But please pray for the situation. An innocent life could be in danger."

"Son, I wish you hadn't said that. Now I'll be fretting all afternoon until you can explain."

"I will as soon as I'm able. But I'm all right. I'm just tired of the nonsense from this one agent."

"Agent?"

"Please, Dad, no more questions. I have to go."

"Oh, all right. I'll get Larry right on it."

"Thanks."

Miranda stepped from the back kitchen with a tray of entrées.

"Miranda—"

"Stay away, Jordan."

"What?"

"Just stay away. I can't handle this right now."

Jordan lifted his hands in surrender. Deep in his heart he'd known she would respond this way. He had to trust that the Lord would work things out. Unfortunately God's timing was always slower than his own, or so it seemed.

Chapter 16

Wild thoughts ran through Randi's mind. Why would the FBI want to question her for putting a picture on Jordan's Web site without his knowledge? Why didn't they believe him? She'd found the picture of a child playing on the beach with the mother watching in his files of photographs and uploaded it. It was a touching picture. She'd even taken just the face of the child and blown it up to a full-size print. But the agents said the little girl had been taken from her parents. They obviously suspected Jordan of being a part of the kidnapping, which didn't make sense.

When she got home, she searched the Internet. After hours of hunting, she found a Web site with a picture of the girl Jordan had photographed then followed up on that information and found news releases about Lucy Tomisson's abduction. Randi's stomach twisted just thinking about it. Why would anyone steal a child?

One thing was clear—it was not an act Jordan would have participated in. No matter what Agent Wilkes said. Jordan wasn't that kind of man—which made her wonder if she should be questioning his actions, either. "Father, bring clarity to this situation."

She reached for the phone to call Jordan then pulled her hand back. As much as she wanted to talk with him, she was still unsure if it was the wisest move to make. And why hadn't he called her? Shouldn't he be home by now? Glancing at the clock, she decided it was too late to call anyway.

Instead of going to bed, she worked for a few hours on some of her clients' Web pages. By midnight, she finally went to bed and fell into fitful slumber. The battle of trusting Jordan waged on in her dreams for a second night.

The next morning, she woke tired and sore. Today she would run the full five miles before getting ready for work. Yesterday she'd run only three. She needed the release of endorphins in her brain to kill off the pain. She finished her five miles, showered, dressed, and ran out the door to go to work when she saw Cal sitting against the hood of her car.

"Cal?"

"Hey, Randi."

She walked to her car door. "Excuse me, but I have to go to work."

"Rand, I really need your help."

You really need the Lord's. "I can't help you, Cal."

"Don't you understand? I won't be allowed to see my son."

Then you should have thought about that before you left your wife. "I can't help you, Cal. Speak with Brenda. She's your wife."

"That's the problem, isn't it? You won't help me because I wouldn't marry you."

Anger rode up her spine. "To be honest, that is not why. Your problems with Brenda are your problems, not mine. I don't want to and won't have anything to do with you."

"I don't get it. All those thoughts and plans we put together for years. How can they die just like that?"

"Cal, you have a problem. First of all, you couldn't be faithful to me in our dating relationship."

"I—"

She held up her hand to stop him then continued. "Second, you're forgetting you're married to the mother of your child. What have you done to try to make that relationship right? How can you fix your marriage? I'm not interested in marrying you and haven't been for a long time. You and I were a mistake. I just assumed we'd naturally get married when we were older. But that wasn't meant to be."

"But, Randi, I still love you."

"You don't love me. You love yourself. Put your wife and child first. Try that and see if your life changes."

"I am thinking of my child first. If he comes and lives with me, I'll see him almost every day."

"Almost? Just listen to yourself. You aren't thinking straight. Who's more important, you or the child?"

Cal opened his mouth then stopped.

"I know you were going to say you then thought I wanted to hear 'the child.' You don't get it. Why don't you go talk with Pastor Russell? Maybe he can help you understand."

"I don't need God."

"Oh yes, you do. Look how wonderful your life has turned out without Him. You're a man who would run out on his family. You'd leave your wife and child hungry rather than be responsible for them."

"I knew there was a reason we never got married."

"Exactly. We weren't meant to."

"No, it's because you think you're so special and holy. Why don't you get off your cloud and come live with the rest of us?"

And to think he came to me for help. Give me grace, Lord. "You're right. I am special. I'm a child of God, and He loves me so much that He died for me. He lives inside me and helps me deal with"—she didn't want to be spiteful—"deal with situations in my life that aren't always pleasant."

"Randi, look. I didn't come to argue with you. I simply wanted you to testify that I'm a better parent for Tyler than Brenda."

Randi chuckled. "I'm sorry, Cal, but I can't do that. In my book, you aren't." She opened the car door and slipped inside before Cal could respond then rolled down the window. "Don't get a court order, because I will not help your case."

Cal stepped away from her car. *Lord, please get through to him. He needs You. He needs to grow up.*

She turned the key and started the engine. Putting the car in reverse, she backed down the driveway and onto the street then shifted into drive and headed toward work. She saw Mabel pushing her shopping cart out to her car and waved. The older lady smiled and waved back.

Randi clicked on her cell phone and auto-dialed Jordan's number. On hearing the answering machine, she hung up and continued on to work. *He couldn't possibly be at the police station still, could he?*

❧

Jordan couldn't thank his father enough for the quick response of finding him an attorney. To say the attorney was happy with how cooperative Jordan had been with the authorities was an overstatement. Legally, Jordan should not have given them so much freedom. Morally, he felt as if he had no choice. But with Agent Wilkes out to prove him responsible, an attorney was necessary to protect him. They spent a little over an hour reviewing the past two days; then the attorney excused himself, and five minutes later Jordan was walking out of the police station.

"Thank you." Jordan extended his hand.

"My pleasure. Remember—if they call you in again, you call me. My office is in Ellsworth. But I've informed them that if they need to speak with you again, they are to contact me and I'll get in touch with you. Don't say another word. I understand your wanting to help them find the little girl. But Wilkes is convinced you're guilty. Be very careful."

"I will." Jordan put his hand in his pocket to retrieve his keys and touched the business card the lawyer had given him. He hoped he would not have to use it.

He returned to the studio and went to work. Dena had everything in order, and tomorrow there would be an early morning studio appointment for a family portrait. He glanced down at the number. Ten people. He hoped they were older and able to listen to instructions; patience would be in short supply after the grueling time with Agent Wilkes.

It felt good to be working. Dena had covered for him, but he wanted to keep working for her. He prayed she still trusted him.

The next day the family arrived, and the session went very well. Dena came in and went over some of the bookwork while he finished up with the family. After the last person left, she spoke up. "You were good with them."

"Thanks. I was concerned the weariness of the past few days would get the better of me. I'm just grateful the baby was sleeping most of the time."

Dena chuckled. "I hear you. So what's happened with the police investigation?"

"If they would leave me alone and try to find Lucy, it might help."

Dena's eyes widened. "They think—"

"Not all of them—just one," he interrupted. "He thinks I must have been a part of everything and that my pictures were going to be used somehow for the ransom."

"Oh, no. Why would he think that?"

"Because I unwittingly took another photograph of Lucy Tomisson."

"What? When?"

"About the second week I was here. I was just out taking photos when I came across this mother and child at the beach. The girl was in her glory. The mother seemed happy, but something in her eyes seemed more distant. Looking back, I'd say she was thinking about what she'd done or how much time they'd be spending with the child. Unfortunately the photo does not capture the woman's face. I can't wait until the police find Lucy alive and leave me out of it."

Dena settled into a chair. "Wayne and I were going on a shoot next week in Florida. Do you want me to find someone else to cover it?"

"May I?" He smiled. The getaway would be nice. "Joking. I know the sheriff wants me in the area."

"Would you like Wayne to speak with the sheriff? They go a long way back."

"No, I'm fine. I called my dad and had an attorney sent to the station after the second day of Agent Wilkes's not bothering to look at any information, except to twist things so it looked like I was guilty. I gave them two days of my time without a lawyer to try to help. After that, I'd had enough."

"I doubt I would have given them more than an hour." Dena stood up and patted him on the back. "Hang in there, Jordan. The Lord will get you through."

Jordan respected Dena's faith and appreciated her confidence in him that he wasn't a suspect in her eyes. He wished he could say the same for Miranda. Her suspicious, dark gray eyes from yesterday still haunted him. "He's what I'm trusting in. If you wouldn't mind, I'd like to go over to the point where I took those pictures. It would be nice if the lady and child were there again."

"Do you think it wise to go? Wayne and I have been on a stakeout before. Maybe we could lend a hand, as well."

"You know, if we could set up a team to stake out the area—"

The phone rang.

"Hello," Dena answered. A moment later her face paled, but she said nothing. She motioned for a pen. Jordan reached for one and handed it to her. She wrote something down then handed it to Jordan.

He read the note. *FBI is listening.* His temper rose another notch; then he told himself to settle down. Agent Wilkes believed him guilty. The man had to follow his leads. Unfortunately it wasn't helping that little girl. He hoped Wilkes would move on and look for Lucy Tomisson's real abductors.

"Sure, Sally, we can work that out. Tell Brad he can come to my place this evening. Wayne would love to see him." Dena paused and gave Jordan a thumbs-up.

Something was going on with this phone call. Who was Sally, and how would she know the FBI was listening in on their conversation?

"Great. See you tonight." Dena hung up the phone. "Jordan, on second thought, we probably should leave it to the authorities to investigate." She scribbled down another message. *Play along with what I say.*

"You're probably right. I just wish I could do something for that little girl." Jordan read the next note. *Tonight—my house with Sheriff McKean.* Jordan nodded his agreement.

"I know. But we can pray."

"I've been doing that since the first visit from the sheriff." He wanted to say so much more but figured he shouldn't.

"Well, I've done my bookwork. I need to get ready for Brad and Sally coming over tonight. Wayne and I will go to Florida as we've planned. I'm sure things will work out here."

"I know they will. I'm innocent."

"I know, and eventually Agent Wilkes will know, as well." She smiled.

Jordan held back a chuckle. He could have so much fun knowing Agent Wilkes was listening. But then again, that would let Wilkes know he was exposed.

"I'll call you later."

"Sure."

"Do we have any scheduled appointments for the rest of the day?"

"Nope."

"Good. Why don't you finish that painting today and take your mind off things?"

She pointed to the photograph on his computer of the abducted little girl.

"You know, that doesn't sound like a bad idea. I could use the relaxation."

Dena left after a brief hug and slipped her cell phone into his hand. Cell phones were one of the easiest devices to listen in on. He slid it into his pocket. He understood he was to meet the sheriff at her house tonight, but only after he spent the rest of the day out at the point, painting, waiting, praying that Lucy would show up. He grabbed his portable easel and paints and headed out the door. He loaded the Jeep, forcing himself not to look at the street. "Come on, Duke."

"Randi, it's Jess," Randi heard on her cell phone.

"Hey, Jess. What's up?"

"First, I'm wondering how you are after the other night."

"I'm fine."

"Yeah, right, and you're ready to run the marathon this week."

Randi chuckled. "Okay. I'm okay. I'm trying to look at Jordan in a better light. I had a visit from Cal this morning."

"Cal? What does that cad want?"

"He wants me to testify that he'd be a better parent for his child than Brenda."

"No way."

Randi checked the rearview mirror then glanced at the road ahead of her. "That's basically what I said to him, as well."

"I want to hear all the details, but I can't talk long. You need to come to my house tonight. Something major is going on, and Jordan needs our help. Well, actually a little girl needs our help."

"Wait. What are you talking about?"

"You know Jordan was speaking with the sheriff, right?"

"Yeah, and they came to see me at the restaurant, as well."

"Oh, man. Look—one of the FBI agents is out to get Jordan. The sheriff doesn't buy it, and he wants to find this little girl ASAP. For her sake as well as to clear Jordan of any wrongdoing."

Randi's heart went out to him.

"Anyway, they're listening to Jordan at his place."

"They bugged the studio?"

"Not exactly. They have one of those listening devices where they can sit in the car and aim it at the area they want to listen to. It looks kinda like a gun with a minisatellite dish on it. The whole town is in a buzz over it. Jordan's out at the point painting. We're hoping they're going to stop watching him after a few hours and start looking for the girl. Mom gave him her cell phone. She's going to call him later on this evening and ask him to bring the phone by our place. The FBI can't listen at our house unless they come closer in on the driveway. Sheriff McKean is coordinating this. Anyway, come to my place tonight."

"I'll be there."

"Great."

Randi wanted to ask more questions but kept it to one. "Is this all my fault?"

"Huh?"

"I put those pictures on his Web site. I thought it was a beautiful picture of a family's emotional bond."

"Randi, this isn't your fault. Maybe it's God's way of helping this little girl. You and Jordan didn't know she'd been abducted. This could be what saves her and returns her to her family."

Randi's eyes filled with tears. She pulled into a store parking lot to get a grip on her own emotions. "Can I call him on your mom's cell?"

"No, they can listen in on a cell-phone call."

Randi's stomach flipped. How could they believe Jordan guilty? How could she?

Chapter 17

Jordan sensed that the car driving back and forth on the road behind him was probably Agent Wilkes. He forced himself to concentrate on the bluff in the foreground of the painting. He wanted to go to the beach where he'd taken the picture of the child but knew that if he did, the FBI would take him in for questioning again. So he settled on an area one would drive past to get to that beach. Dena's phone weighed heavily in his pocket. He wasn't sure why he had it but knew it involved something about the meeting with the sheriff tonight at Dena's house.

Jordan put down his brush and set it in the jar with thinner. He wiped his hands and grabbed his camera. He clicked off a couple of shots from where he was painting then walked over to the water's edge and concentrated on the various tidal pools formed from the outgoing tide. Inside them, he found baby shrimp, horseshoe crabs, and minnows. He had no reason to photograph these pools, but it seemed easier to get lost in photography than in painting at the moment. He knelt down and switched his digital to macro settings and worked his way down the beach. Each pool had its own unique characteristics. Two-thirds of the walls around the pool in front of him now were granite rock. The last third was thick, coarse, brown sand. Inside the pool, a row of snails lined a crack in the rock. At the other end of the granite edge, a colony of baby mussels held on to the rock's edge with their brown, stringy beards. A small starfish wrapped itself around an even smaller baby clam. Just then a baby eel popped out and attempted to take the clam away from the starfish. Jordan clicked off some rapid pictures, hoping to catch the eel in action.

He watched closer as the barnacle on the rock face opened to catch the plankton that was also trapped in the pool. It always amazed him how creative God was when He crafted the various life forms on this earth. Not that he had a heart for barnacles, since they could tear the bottom of a person's foot when walked on—not to mention the infection that could set in if the wound wasn't cleaned well. But they served a purpose somehow. He didn't know what that purpose could be, though, since barnacles were the bane of most boat owners. Jordan smiled and snapped a few more pictures. Then he added some different filters to see the difference they would make on the tidal-pool shots.

Eventually Duke got tired of waiting for him and came moseying down the shoreline, disturbing the tidal pools. Jordan chuckled and took some pictures of his four-legged buddy. He found a small piece of driftwood. "Fetch, Duke."

Duke lifted his head and watched as the stick landed in the water. Slowly he ambled over to it and picked it up. Basset hounds weren't known for their speed, and the years had taken their toll on Duke. He still loved to fetch, but one or two tosses were all the old boy could handle.

"Atta boy, Duke." Jordan gave the dog a hearty rubdown. "At least you still love me."

Duke slobbered kisses over Jordan. "All right, boy. That's enough."

An hour passed before he knew it. Relaxed, he and Duke walked back to his easel. Jordan knew he was boring Agent Wilkes, but there seemed to be some poetic justice involved. Jordan's smile broadened as he dipped his brush in a blend of color that resembled the rock in the shadow of the bluff.

His mind drifted to Miranda. She was like that rock, hidden in the shadow of her past relationship with Cal. *Lord, help her move on and trust me, please.*

He hadn't sensed Agent Wilkes for quite a while. He turned toward the road and glanced up and down. Not seeing anything, he returned to his painting.

A short time later, Dena's cell phone rang. He checked the display and saw the word *Home.* "Hello?"

"Hey, Jordan, did you find my cell phone?"

"Yeah, I was going to drop it off later this evening. Need it sooner?"

"Nope. Later is fine."

"I'll bring it over as the sun starts to go down."

"That will be great. Can I add you to our supper list?"

"Do you have enough? Can I bring anything? You know I won't turn down a home-cooked meal."

Dena chuckled. "Nah, Wayne will fire up the grill, and I have everything else under control."

"Thanks for the invite. I'll see you later."

"Great. Bye." Dena hung up the phone.

Jordan hoped Agent Wilkes would get the message. He'd been tempted to use the phone and call Miranda, but it wasn't his, and he still hadn't ordered a new service yet. He really needed to do that.

Plus, he wasn't sure she wanted to talk with him yet. The haunted look in her eyes still caused a shiver to run up and down his spine. *Lord, please help her.*

❧

Randi wiped the tears from her eyes and drove the rest of the way home. She passed Jordan's driveway only to see his vehicle wasn't there. At home, she opened her computer files to the job she was contracted to do for Jess and the lobstermen co-op she had put together.

Dena had supplied some great photographs to go on the Web site. Randi tweaked the header of the Web page to be a collage of various shots of the lobster industry with a huge, five-pound, steamed lobster on a platter in the center. It made Randi's stomach rumble just seeing it.

Remembering she'd been too upset to eat much for a few days, she raided the fridge. As she grabbed a lobster roll her mother had left the day before, she remembered the picture she'd put on Jordan's Web site. The FBI had removed it, but she had her own copy. She opened the picture on the computer and stared at it. She knew exactly which beach Jordan had photographed. Grabbing the sandwich and keys, she headed for the point. As she approached the bend in the road out to the point, she noticed a dark sedan parked on the side of the road. Around the bend, she found Jordan's Jeep and him sitting at his easel. She pulled over. "Jordan!" she called.

He turned and jumped up from his easel.

"Miranda, what are you doing here?"

"I know where you took that picture. I put it on the Internet. It's the same picture, Jordan. I blew it up for the facial shot. I'm—"

Jordan held his finger to her lips. A shiver of joy spread through her. He leaned in closer and whispered, "I don't know if I'm being watched."

The dark sedan popped into her mind. "There's a car around the bend."

"Ah, I'm not surprised. I was hoping Wilkes would be bored by now."

"I think he's asleep."

Jordan laughed. "Come." He held her by the hand and led her down to the beach. When they were down at the water's edge, he brushed her hair away from her face and gazed into her eyes. "I do love your eyes."

Miranda blinked. His own hazel ones captivated her attention. She raised her hand and pulled the elastic band from his hair and wove her fingers through the long, wavy strands. "Do you know how much I've wanted to do that ever since I've met you?"

Jordan held her tighter. "I love you. I'm sorry about what is happening. But, trust me, I've done nothing wrong."

"I know," she whispered. "I'm sorry for not trusting you."

Jordan squeezed her. She felt his protective love encircling her. "I've never been so afraid of losing anyone's respect as I have been about losing yours."

"I'm sorry."

"I had a visit from Cal this morning."

He pulled back and held on to her shoulders. "What happened?"

"He wanted me to testify that he would be a better parent than Brenda."

"You've got to be kidding. Does this guy have no clue? He ran off on his wife and child. What is he thinking?"

"He isn't. He's always had what he wanted. He smooth-talked me for years. Maybe losing his son will help him grow up. I don't know. But what really bothered me was that he thought I would let him back in my life."

She felt Jordan stiffen.

"Relax. It's okay. I handled it. He knows I'm not interested in being involved with him."

Jordan caressed her cheek. She leaned into his fingers. She'd never felt so close to Cal as she did to Jordan. She closed her eyes, and her voice caught. "Jordan, I love you."

Jordan scooped her in his arms. "Miranda, you don't know how long I've waited to hear that. Woo-hoo!" he hollered and spun her around.

Duke howled in unison.

She held on as joy flooded her senses. A peace, a connection with Jordan, cemented within her. He was the one her soul longed to unite with. All the fears and doubts from the past melted away. She kissed his cheek. He stood perfectly still and eased her back down onto her feet. "Kiss me," she whispered.

"With pleasure." Their lips met, and a deeper sense of connection and oneness fused within her. Her pulse raced. Slowly she pulled away and rested her head on his chest.

Neither of them spoke. They stood there for a moment, caught in the intimacy of the moment. Then she pulled back and looked into his eyes. "I love you."

"I love you, too."

Jordan stiffened.

"What's the matter?"

"Agent Wilkes is standing behind a tree."

She'd forgotten he'd been out there following Jordan. Watching. A wave of nausea swept over her at the mere thought. Randi swallowed. "Should I go? I'll be at Jess's tonight."

Jordan stepped back. "I'll see you later."

❧

Jordan opened and closed his fist several times as he watched Agent Wilkes stare at Miranda while she walked to her car. He followed at least ten paces behind then went to his easel. He had no desire to paint, not now, not when he should be with Miranda. But he had little choice. The only thing he was happy about was that the agent wasn't holding his listening device and could not have heard the conversation between them.

He sat down at the easel and picked up a brush. Dipping it in the burnt sienna and mixing it with a touch of green, he placed the brush next to the bush he was painting in the foreground. He'd never sell this painting. The best he could hope for was to scrape off what he had done and paint over the canvas. There was nothing of interest in the painting. And if he couldn't find anything in the picture, a customer sure wouldn't.

He decided to change the picture to a surreal painting instead of the more traditional impressionist one. It fit his mood better. Moments later, a surrealist image of Wilkes's head, protruding out of the stone bluff, developed on his canvas. Jordan laughed and continued with the wild rendition.

An hour later, he finished the painting. Picking up his gear, he loaded his Jeep and walked over to the agent's car with the canvas in hand. "Here ya go, Wilkes. Enjoy!"

"Hey, what—? I don't look like that."

"Perhaps not, but it sure felt good painting you that way. Have a good night."

Wilkes pulled out of his parking place before Jordan reached the door. By the time Jordan drove back to town, he expected the agent to be stationed outside his apartment. As he drove past the sheriff's office, he noticed Wilkes's car and the sheriff's parked outside.

Instead of going home, he headed back out of town for Dena and Wayne's. Dena's red convertible Mercedes was parked out front alongside Wayne's four-wheel-drive pickup.

"Jordan," Dena greeted him at the door. "Come in. You're early."

"Agent Wilkes is at the sheriff's station. . . ." His words trailed off. Sheriff McKean sat on the living room sofa. "Sheriff."

"Relax, son. Remember, I called this meeting."

"What about Wilkes?"

"He's doing some busywork at my office. I had my secretary draw up a list of recent home purchases in the area."

Jordan sat down on the rattan chair in the corner of the room.

"Jordan, can I get you anything?" Dena asked. "Soda? Iced tea?"

"Iced tea will be fine."

"Good. Wayne has the steaks marinating, so we should be eating in an hour," she said and headed into the kitchen. "A few more will be coming in a half hour."

He wanted to ask who and why but simply nodded.

"Jordan," the sheriff said. "First off, I don't believe you're guilty. And I do believe you had a wonderful idea in staking out the point. But with Wilkes convinced you're part of the child's abduction, I think it best if we organize and stake out the point in shifts. After all, if that little girl is in my territory, I want to find her. I certainly don't want to spend days talking to the same person over and over again."

Jordan sat back and smiled. "Thanks for the vote of confidence."

"I'm glad you called the attorney. If you hadn't, I was going to do it for you. Enough is enough."

"I don't mean to be telling you your job, sheriff, but aren't you breaking some laws by informing me I was being listened to?"

"Nope. He didn't get a court order, which means he's disobeying the law. I pointed that out to him when I radioed him to come in from his surveillance."

Interesting. "If Agent Wilkes feels he's above the law, I'll need to be careful he doesn't fabricate my involvement."

"I don't believe he'll do that. But I do want to be careful you are with someone at all times."

After a knock at the door, a half-dozen people came in. Most Jordan didn't recognize. Among them were Sally, the sheriff's secretary; and her husband, Doug. Jim Baxter he'd seen a time or two in church. And a Bob and Marie from someplace. Jordan didn't catch their last name or their connection. He shook hands and sat down.

After thirty minutes, the house was full. It was established that six teams of two would go out on four-hour stretches. Miranda walked in the door as Wayne finished cooking the steaks on the grill. In the end, Jordan learned that most of the people were volunteers for Squabbin Bay's fire department and other emergency services.

Miranda sat down beside him at the picnic table and slipped her hand into his. "Hi." She kissed him on the cheek.

"Hi. I'm really sorry Wilkes busted in on us."

The lilt of her laughter caused his heart to skip a beat. "Do you think he has a tape?"

"What?"

"Might be fun to listen to it several years from now."

Jordan roared with laughter. Everyone turned and faced them. Miranda buried her face in his chest. "Sorry."

By the end of the night, Jordan felt so welcomed and a part of this community that he never wanted to go back to the city. He understood completely why Dena had moved up here. And with God's blessings, he and Miranda would have the same joyful reasons in the future.

The sheriff's radiophone rang. "Sheriff McKean, Agent O'Malley here. We have a lead. Can you come in?"

Chapter 18

Randi snuggled up beside Jordan as the sheriff took the call. "I'll be right there." Sheriff McKean turned toward the group anxiously awaiting further information. "Nothing to tell, folks. But you'll need to take care of one last order of business in my absence. Who's spending the night with Jordan?"

The sheriff left without another word.

"I have the dead-man's shift at the firehouse tonight. Sorry. I can do it tomorrow though," Jim Baxter offered.

"I can do it," Steve Healy called out. "Do you snore?"

Jordan chuckled. "Not that I'm aware of."

Randi wondered and hoped she would find out one day. The thought caught her up short. She'd just kissed Jordan, and now she was thinking marriage. *Get a grip, girl.*

Wayne Kearns smiled. "Let's take this one day at a time. Let's stop and have a word of prayer for this little girl."

Everyone joined hands, and Wayne led them in a brief but touching prayer. As folks started to leave, they made their way to Jordan and gave him their individual support. Randi couldn't have been more proud of her hometown.

Jess pulled her aside and out to the deck. "So what's going on with the two of you?"

"Nothing."

"Girl, this is me you're talking to. Give."

"We made up this afternoon."

"I'd say made up. You believe him, don't you?" Jess sat on the rail of the deck, smiling. She seemed so content.

Randi prayed Jess would find what she'd found in Jordan. "Jess, I love him."

"That was pretty obvious. So come on—details."

"Ask Agent Wilkes. He might just have it on tape."

"No." Jess jumped back to her feet. "For real? Video or audio?"

"Audio, I think." A smile spread across her face to think that Agent Wilkes might have a video of her and Jordan's first kiss.

Jess laughed. "You kissed him, didn't you?"

"I'll never tell."

Jess's laughter increased. "You don't have to. And to think the first time you met the man you dumped two bowls of lobster bisque on him."

Randi giggled. "Don't remind me." She paused. "Might be fun to have it at the wedding."

"Wedding?" Jess's voice must have carried into the house, because everyone stopped talking. Then Randi noticed Jordan. She shrugged her shoulders, and Jordan smiled and went back to his conversation.

"Not yet, but maybe down the road."

"He must be some kind of a kisser for you to think marriage after just one."

"I've had several thoughts, but it isn't time yet."

"Right. You're bad—you know that? One kiss and you're sunk. But I have to agree he's a far better choice than Cal."

"Don't even go there."

"Unbelievable. I'm so glad you didn't marry him."

"You and me both. I feel sorry for him. I hope he finds the Lord and saves his relationship with his child."

Randi peeked into the living room. Only a few people remained. Jordan and Steve Healey were among them. He kept glancing out at her. "Jess, I want to talk with Jordan. Can you drive my car home tomorrow?"

"Sure."

Randi handed her keys to Jess. "Thanks."

They joined the others in the living room. "Can I get a lift home with you, Jordan?"

"Absolutely. But what about—?"

She held her finger to her lips, gave the international "sh" sign, then turned to Steve. "Did you come here on your motorcycle?"

"Yup."

"Can Jordan meet you at his place?"

"Well, I don't know. The sheriff said we weren't supposed to leave Jordan alone."

Randi slipped her arm around Jordan's elbow. "He won't be alone."

"Ah, well," Steve stammered.

Wayne Kearns cleared his throat. "Miranda, I believe you can use the telephone to talk with Jordan. And considering all that's been going on, it might be best that you two not spend too much time alone. If you catch my drift."

Perfectly. She wanted to scream.

Jordan placed his hand over Randi's. "Excuse us for a couple of minutes."

He led Randi out to the deck. "Honey, what's going on?"

"I'm sorry. I just want to spend time with you."

He wrapped her in his arms. "And I, you. But—" He kissed the top of her head.

Randi sighed. Her head was buzzing with conflicting emotions. "I'll call you after I get home."

"Good. Everything is going to be all right. Trust me."

Randi let out a nervous giggle. "I do."

Jordan's emotions had run the full gamut today. He could only imagine Miranda's had done the same. Wayne Kearns in his not-so-diplomatic way was right; they shouldn't be alone tonight. Caution seemed to be the word for the hour.

Steve had followed him home from the Kearnses'. They talked briefly; then Steve sat down on the sofa and watched the Red Sox win. Jordan placed a call to Miranda and planned to meet her for breakfast in the morning.

Jordan took a hot shower and allowed the pulsing water to work out the remaining tension in his back. Even though the sheriff believed in him, the fact still remained that Agent Wilkes believed him guilty. And the very real possibility existed that he could be set up if the agent went rogue. *Please, Lord, prevent that from happening.*

He called his father and told him about his developing relationship with Miranda. "Dad, I want to marry her."

"Well, congratulations, son. Would you like your great-grandmother's engagement ring?"

"Really?"

"Sure. Let me check with your mother. Hang on." His father covered the phone with his hand. "Mom's all excited. She's picking up the extension."

"Jordan, is this the same girl you were talking about when you were here?"

"Yes."

His mother giggled. "I thought so. Your great-grandmother would love for your wife to wear her ring."

"I think Miranda would like it, too. It isn't your traditional engagement ring."

"No, it isn't," his father agreed. "But if her eyes are the same color as your great-grandmother's, I'd say it would be as beautiful on her as it was on your great-grandmother."

"Yeah, I believe so."

"So when do we get to meet our new daughter?" his mother asked.

"We're not married yet. I haven't asked her."

"All in good time, son," his father said. They talked for a few more minutes, and Jordan agreed to take a trip down to Boston with Miranda when things were settled in Maine concerning the missing child.

He hung up the phone, and it immediately rang. "Jordan, it's me."

"Miranda?"

"Yeah. Listen—I remembered something Mabel said to me. I'm going to check it out."

"Miranda, what are you going to do? Don't do anything foolish. Call Sheriff McKean. Tell him what you're thinking. What are you thinking?"

"Mabel said something about new neighbors. I'm going to check out the neighbors."

"Miranda, don't. Let the police handle it."

"I'll be careful. I'll just visit Mabel."

"Honey, it's late. How late does this woman stay up?"

"Half the night."

"Miranda, please—let the sheriff do this."

"I'll be careful."

"I don't like it. Please stay home."

"Jordan, you need to trust me."

Jordan groaned. This was the issue she had with him, and now she was turning the tables on him. "I still don't like it."

"I'll be fine. I grew up playing over there. I know all those roads."

"Be careful."

Jordan started to pace. He rubbed the back of his neck. He didn't like this. Not one bit. Duke watched him without moving. His eyes simply rolled back and forth, not missing one of Jordan's steps.

"I will. I love you."

"I love you, too. That's why I want you to be careful."

"I know, and I will. I'll call you in the morning."

"Call me when you return."

"It will be late."

"I don't care. Call me."

"Okay. Love you. Bye."

Jordan hung up the phone and fell on his knees. "Dear Lord, protect her."

❧

Randi ran down the dirt road and over to Mabel's house. No lights were on. She wouldn't wake the older woman. She ran past the various houses that made up Mabel's neighborhood. A large dog barked. Randi kept running. Seeing nothing, she ran back to her car and called Jordan on her cell.

"Hey, it's me."

"Where are you?"

"At Mabel's. Everyone's asleep down here."

"Of course they are. It's midnight. Go home, Miranda. I'm not comfortable with you being out there."

"Okay." She turned on the car engine and popped the car into gear. "I'm heading home now."

In her rearview mirror, she saw a porch light come on at one of the houses. She continued to head back toward town.

"Miranda?"

"Huh? Oh, I'm fine. Sorry. A porch light went on. I was trying to catch someone in the rearview mirror."

"Honey, call Sheriff McKean."

"I will in the morning. 'Night, Jordan. Sorry for the disappointment."

Jordan let out a nervous chuckle. "I'm glad you're all right. These people abduct children for money. They can't be real nice, reasonable people."

She hadn't really thought about that. She'd only been thinking about Jordan and how to help him. "You're right. I'll call the sheriff."

"Good. I'll see you at breakfast."

"I'm looking forward to it." They hung up, and she called the sheriff's office. The answering machine came on. She left a detailed message about what Mabel had said about her new neighbors and hung up.

By the time she returned home, Agent Wilkes was standing at her door. "Are you insane?"

"Good evening to you, Agent Wilkes."

"Look, lady. I don't care what you think of Jordan Lamont or me, but you can't go running off in the middle of the night looking for trouble. Didn't your parents teach you anything?"

"Nothing happened. I'm fine."

"This time. But what's to prevent you from doing something as foolish again in the future?"

"I don't need a lecture from a man who doesn't obey the rules either."

"Excuse me?"

Randi paled.

"Do you have a videotape of Jordan and me kissing?"

"What? Who's feeding you this stuff?"

"I was hoping you might. Be nice for our memory book in the future. Look—I'm fine."

"I can see that. Miss Blake, I need your word you'll stay out of this investigation. We can't have you tipping off the suspects."

"Are you saying you believe Jordan?"

"I won't go that far, but he obviously doesn't have the child."

He relaxed his stance. "By the way, for the record, I do have a judge's order now to listen in on Jordan's phone conversations. And if something had happened to you tonight, you'd have been glad I did. Fortunately the sheriff knew who you were talking about and headed out there."

"I didn't see him."

Agent Wilkes laughed. "You jogged through the neighborhood."

Randi's legs felt like rubber.

"Stay out of there, Miss Blake. For the sake of the child, stay away."

"Yes, sir."

Randi walked past Agent Wilkes into the house. She wondered who else had seen her out there. She hadn't noticed anyone. She showered and went to bed. What had she been thinking?

Chapter 19

Tired from a restless night, Jordan went to the kitchen to prepare breakfast. The idea of Miranda trying to find the child last night in the dark on her own caused an ulcer to develop in one night. Well, maybe not a full-blown ulcer, but close.

He had a frying pan in one hand and a mixing bowl in the other when Steve Healey walked in. " 'Morning."

"Did you sleep well?"

"Not exactly. Couches and I never seem to get along all that well. How about yourself?"

Steve was probably a few years younger than his dad. *I should have offered to sleep on the couch.* "Sorry you were so uncomfortable. As for me, nada. Miranda decided to go out to see someone named Mabel in search of her new neighbors." Jordan set the frying pan down on the stove, placed the mixing bowl on the counter, and pulled out some eggs, milk, cheese, onions, peppers, ham, and potatoes.

"Miranda?"

"Sorry. Randi." He set the refrigerator items on the counter next to the mixing bowl and fetched his cutting board and knife.

"Oh, right. As for Mabel, that would be Mabel Bishop. She's eighty-something and doesn't look a day over sixty-five. She works at the post office." Jordan set a mug of black coffee in front of Steve. "She has more energy than most people half her age, me included."

Jordan searched for the grater in the lower cabinet where he kept it. "I'd like to meet her one day."

"You probably will. Whatcha cooking?" Steve picked up the coffee and sipped it, not bothering to add cream or sugar.

"I thought I'd make some hash-browned potatoes and an omelet. Mir— Randi is coming for breakfast. If you have the time, I'd love to make you something. A thank-you for being my babysitter last night."

Steve laughed. "I was out pretty quickly. But I'm glad I could help. I appreciate the offer for breakfast, but I should get going." He hesitated.

"Are you sure? Can I fix something for you to take with you? At least let me give you some coffee to go," Jordan said. Having found the grater, he placed it on the counter on top of the cutting board.

"Nothing, really." Steve hesitated. "I'm not sure if I'm supposed to wait here until someone else comes."

"Oh." The idea of having to have someone with him around the clock hadn't appealed last night, and this morning it annoyed him. "I'm fine. Miranda will be here shortly. What could go wrong?"

"You're sure?"

"Absolutely. Go on."

"Okay, catch ya later." Steve finished his coffee, put on his faded Boston Red Sox cap, and headed out the door.

Jordan went back to work organizing his breakfast with Miranda. All the prep work was done when the phone rang.

"Hello."

"Jordan, this is Sheriff McKean. We caught them early this morning."

"Praise the Lord! Is the little girl safe and unharmed?"

"She's safe."

Jordan knew Lucy Tomisson had been kidnapped for ransom, and usually the victims were kept in good health, unlike other abductions. "I'm really glad to hear this. Does that mean I'm clear of any charges from Agent Wilkes?"

The sheriff chuckled. "More than likely he's trying to pull his foot out of his mouth right now. I hope this is the end of it for you. And, more important, it's the end of it for this child. Her parents should be arriving up here in about four more hours."

"I'd love to photograph that reunion."

"I'll keep that in mind."

"Sorry, Sheriff. I was speaking out loud. I'm not asking to be an intrusion on their family time. I just know there will be some mighty happy faces on both parents and child."

"More than likely. All right. I've got a lot of paperwork to complete, but I thought you'd like to know."

"Thanks. I appreciate it."

Jordan hung up the phone. "At least I don't have to have a babysitter any longer," he thought aloud. Jordan made several calls, letting his parents, Dena, and others know the child had been found. He waited to tell Miranda in person.

Just then she knocked on the screen door, still wearing her running clothes. "Jordan, did you hear?"

So much for the surprise. "Yes, the sheriff called."

"Isn't it wonderful!" She stepped through the back door and into the kitchen.

"Yes, it's an answer to our prayers. Come here." He opened his arms.

"No, no, I can't. I'm all sweaty. I just wanted you to know."

"Thanks. So should I hold off on breakfast?"

"Oh, no, I forgot. I'm sorry. I ran seven miles this morning. Agent Wilkes scared the living daylights out of me last night."

Jordan's spine went rigid. "Why? What did he do? What happened?"

"Oh, nothing. He informed me that the sheriff and others saw me jogging through Mabel's neighborhood last night." Miranda walked over to the window. "I didn't even see them. What if the criminals had been watching and had seen me? I could have—"

Jordan closed the distance between them, wrapping her in his arms. "Shh. It's all right. You're okay. Nothing happened." *Not that it couldn't have.* Fear washed over him at the thought of losing her. His heart pounded. His mind filled with an urgent desire to ask her to marry him, right now, right here. Then the sensible part of his mind kicked in and told him now was not the time. Soon, but the right time and place needed to be prayed about and certainly planned. Didn't all women want a special proposal?

Miranda snuggled into Jordan's embrace and released a pent-up breath. She leaned against him for a moment then jumped back. "I'm so sorry. I forgot. I soiled your clothes."

Jordan reached out and pulled her back. "They'll wash. Kiss me."

Miranda giggled and complied.

&

Randi ran home and got ready for work. Jordan made her breakfast to go and wrapped her omelet in a soft tortilla so she could eat and drive at the same time. She wanted to cancel going to the restaurant, but she still needed the money to pay her rent. Her savings were beginning to add up; with any luck, she could start considering purchasing a home instead of renting. She was thankful for Jordan's suggestions on how to handle her finances. All she needed was a small cottage for herself. Then it hit her. What about a home with Jordan? Children? Oh, yeah, a small cottage would not be enough.

The rest of the day, she entertained thoughts about marrying Jordan, imagining arguing over how they should wait and get to know one another better.

She wanted to get together with Jordan that evening, but she had to work on the Web pages for her clients. At home, she sat down with a sandwich, a glass of iced tea, and her computer. An hour later, she heard a knock at her door.

"Hey."

Jordan stood there, as handsome as ever.

"Man, I love your eyes."

Randi giggled. He'd been obsessed with her eyes since the first day they met. "Come in. I'm working, but I can visit for a while."

"I was hoping you'd say that."

"So what's happening with the missing girl? Have you heard anything?"

"The parents came to town this afternoon. They're staying at Montgomery's Bed-and-Breakfast for the night. No one has released to the media that she's been found. They're going to do that tomorrow so the family can have a day without media interruption."

"And, of course, the FBI will want to question the child."

"Of course," Jordan grumbled.

"He was only doing his job," Randi reminded him gently.

"I know. But I hope he treats the little girl much better than he did me."

She walked over to him and kissed his cheek. "He will. They've been trained in how to help the victims."

The doorbell rang. Randi excused herself and went to answer it. Agent Wilkes stood there with his shoulders squared. "May I speak with Jordan Lamont, please?"

"How'd—?" She stopped. They wouldn't still be listening in on them, would they? "Jordan!" she called back to the kitchen.

Jordan came to the door. "Agent Wilkes? What can I do for you?"

"May I come in?"

Jordan looked at Randi. She nodded. What else did one say to the FBI?

"Mr. Lamont." Agent Wilkes looked like a hermit crab that was afraid to come out of its shell. "I want to express my apologies for anything I said or did during the course of my investigation that caused you anxiety. I was wrong. I made assumptions and didn't examine all the facts. I'm sorry. And I know it's a little too late, but I want to thank you for taking those pictures. Without them, we wouldn't have little Lucy."

"You're welcome. And you're forgiven."

"Thank you." Agent Wilkes cleared his throat. "Sheriff McKean has asked for you to come down to Montgomery's Bed-and-Breakfast. The family would like to meet you. Oh, and they asked for you to bring your camera."

"Al–l–l–l ri–i–ight," Jordan said, drawing out the words. "Can Miranda come also?"

"Yes, both of you are part of why we found the little girl."

"We'll be there shortly."

"Very good. And seriously, I am sorry for giving you such a hard time. I don't know what came over me. I promise it won't happen again. We could have lost her if—"

Jordan placed his hand on Wilkes's shoulder. "It's all right. She's alive, and the Lord allowed us to find her. That's all that matters."

Agent Wilkes gave a halfhearted smile and nodded before walking out the door.

"Do you have your cameras?" Randi asked.

Jordan laughed. "You don't know me all that well yet, honey, but the first thing you need to know is that I always have at least one camera with me, and generally two or three."

Randi came up beside him. "Well, we'd better go, because I have a lot of work to do today."

He wrapped his arms around her and yawned. "Nighttime can't come soon enough. I didn't sleep much last night."

"You're not the only one."

"No, I imagine the sheriff and his crew are wasted, too. And tomorrow the media will descend on Squabbin Bay, and the locals won't know what to do with 'em."

ॐ

They met with the grateful parents for a brief visit and had a chance to get acquainted with Lucy. Jordan took some publicity photos and planned to make copies available to the media in the morning. At midnight, they released the news that Lucy Tomisson was safe and sound, along with details of her rescue.

The family had listened to the advice given by other families in similar circumstances. Jordan's pictures would be the only ones released to the media. Randi hoped the media would respect the family's wishes. Considering it wasn't a high-profile case, a horde of journalists and photographers wasn't trying from every angle to take a picture of the family. By the time the father gave the press conference, Lucy and her mother were safe and sound in another town out of reach.

The next few weeks kept Randi and Jordan squeaking out moments of time for one another. With fall approaching, she made plans to show him Acadia National Park. They packed a cooler and headed south. One day after they married, she hoped to go camping with Jordan at the park.

With his Jeep packed, they drove down the highway. "So tell me what it is about Acadia that you love? I've seen pictures, and it looks awesome, but why does it interest you?"

"I love camping, and it's just like, well, the perfect example of Maine's rustic coast. I don't know why it's such a special place to me. My family and I have gone there so many times over the years. We love it."

"Hmm, I'm looking forward to it. Of course, it could be you love it because of the memories."

"No doubt."

"Oh, by the way, my parents are looking forward to our visit next week."

"I can't wait. I'm terrified, but I can't wait." Randi squirmed in her seat.

"Terrified? Why?"

"Because they're your parents."

"They already like you."

She smiled. "So you say."

"Hey now, have I ever steered you wrong?"

ॐ

The ring weighed heavily in Jordan's pocket. He hoped and prayed today would be the day for another favorite memory for Miranda in Acadia National Park. Today was the first full day they'd managed to have with one another since Lucy Tomisson was found.

"No." Miranda pulled her legs to her chest and held them. It amused him that she was so nervous at the prospect of meeting his parents.

"Miranda, I love you."

Her smile brightened. "I love you, too. I can't believe how busy we've been the past few weeks."

"Neither can I. I'm truly sorry Lucy was kidnapped from her home, but it has helped launch my photojournalism career. Dena says she's booked me on several shoots, and many more are pending."

"How long will you be gone?" Her voice sounded sad.

"Each shoot is different. Is it a problem?"

"Jordan, I don't want to come across like a wet sponge, but how often will you travel? I mean. . ."

"How often will I be home with you?"

"Yeah, if we get married."

Jordan smiled. *If* was no longer a question in his mind, but rather *when*. "I'll take only as many trips as we agree upon. Before we marry, I'd like to accept as many assignments as possible. My first obligation is to Dena and the studio, so I can't take more than two or so a month."

"I'm only starting to get a handle on how a photographer makes money, but are these trips that worthwhile?"

Jordan chuckled. "Most of the time, yes. Some trips, like the one to the Sudan, won't produce a lot of income."

"Jordan, what's changed? When we were first getting to know one another, you told me about your plan to earn so much and have a house *before* you marry. Are you expecting us to wait years?"

He tightened his grip on the steering wheel. "No, I'm not wanting to wait years. But I do think a little planning and some savings would be helpful, don't you?"

"Yes. In fact, you'll be happy to know I started a savings account after you challenged me, and I'm happy to say I have a nice little amount set aside."

"Wonderful. Money issues have been a problem for me for as long as I can remember. I appreciate my parents' influence, but they drummed it into my head for so long it's almost second nature to me. I'll always be a planner, but I'm trying to be more flexible."

"Oops. Sorry. Turn right up here."

Jordan turned into the entrance to the park. Without question, the area was stunning.

"There's no way for you to see the entire park in one day, so I thought we'd hike up Cadillac Mountain."

"You're bound and determined to have me exercise, aren't you?"

She wiggled her eyebrows. His stomach flipped. "Probably." She winked.

They drove up Park Loop Road and parked. "What about Duke?"

"He'll be fine. Trust me," she said as she bounced out of the vehicle.

TRESPASSED HEARTS

"Come on, boy. We're in for it today." Jordan attached a leash and knew he'd be carrying Duke most of the way. His stubby little legs could not keep up with Miranda's sleek ones.

"You tricked me," Jordan protested. The road went right to the top of the mountain.

"Possibly."

"Wow! It's an awesome view."

"Yeah, it's pretty amazing." Miranda beamed. "There's such variety here. The ocean, the mountains, the sandy beach, the rocky beach, little streams—it's all here in one spot. There's a place over there"—she pointed to her left—"where the waves splash against the rocks and the water spews out like a geyser."

"I would love to see it." *Man, I hope she doesn't want a long engagement.*

She placed her hand in his. "I want to show you. I want. . ." She paused then continued. "Jordan, I know we don't see eye-to-eye on financial matters. Is this going to be a problem for us?"

He wrapped her in his arms. "I wondered that myself a while back. I don't believe it will be, if we are honest and open with one another about our feelings and agree on how to handle our differences ahead of time. I told you about my parents encouraging me with regard to my income before marriage."

She nodded.

"Well, it turns out I misunderstood what they were telling me. They set an example, and I took it as gospel."

"So are you saying you can consider marriage before you buy your own home?"

Jordan let out a nervous chuckle. Duke barked. "Yes and no. I'm wondering if we could start looking for a place together."

"I'd love to help you look."

"No. I mean—Miranda, I'm getting this all wrong. Hang on a minute." He released her and bent down on one knee.

Miranda's eyes widened. The deep pools in her eyes glistened. "What I'm trying to say is, I'm not perfect. I have many flaws. I don't have a huge income. But would you do me the honor of becoming my wife?"

Miranda blinked twice.

Jordan reached into his pocket and touched the small gold band that had belonged to his great-grandmother.

"Miranda?"

She started to shake. "Are you sure?"

"Absolutely. I've known since the second day I met you that I wanted you to be my wife."

Miranda swallowed hard.

Jordan's fingers started to sweat holding the ring.

"How long of an engagement?"

Jordan let out a nervous chuckle. "I wasn't planning on a long wait. But it's up to you. You can set the date."

"Tomorrow?"

"If you wish. I'd marry you right here and now."

"Jordan, are you sure? Absolutely, positively sure?"

"Yes. I love you, Miranda Blake, with all my heart and soul. You make me complete. Please say you'll marry me."

"Yes! Yes! Of course I will."

Jordan jumped up and took her in his arms. His lips captured hers, and the kiss deepened. Duke pawed at them then barked. "Sorry, boy. But what do you think of Miranda being your mom?"

Duke barked again.

Miranda giggled. "You'd better tell him he's not coming to the wedding or on the honeymoon."

Jordan held her close. "Of course he won't. He'll be house-sitting. So, seriously, when do you want to get married?"

"Tomorrow. But I think our parents would have a fit."

"Agreed." Jordan fingered the ring once again. "Miranda, I have a ring. It belonged to my great-grandmother. As you saw in the photograph, her eyes were as dark as yours. My great-grandfather bought her this ring to go with her eyes. I'm hoping you'll like it and accept it as your engagement ring. If you want the traditional diamond I'll understand, but. . ." He pulled out the ring and slipped it on her finger.

"Oh, Jordan, it's beautiful."

A black pearl encircled by tiny diamonds made up the unique ring. "You like it?"

"Yes. It's beautiful. This was your great-grandmother's?"

"Yes. Great-grandfather told the story of searching the world for his perfect mate and the perfect ring for her. Now, we all know he was not a world traveler, but he loved to make up exotic tales of searching for the love of his life. When he found her, he gave her the black pearl because it was rare, and he cherished my great-grandmother as a rare jewel. Miranda, you're that same rare jewel I've searched my whole life for. Please accept this ring as a token of my love for you and how special you are to me."

Her eyes filled with tears. Unable to speak, she simply nodded her head. Jordan kissed her delicate pink lips again and thanked the Lord for such a special woman in his life.

Epilogue

Randi stood in Pastor Russell's office waiting for Jess. Jordan's brother, Adam, had called her out of the room moments before. Randi never could have believed she'd be this nervous waiting for the organ to play. Jess opened the door.

"Is everything all right?" Randi asked.

"Yeah. Um, how big of a deal is it for Duke not to be at your wedding?"

"You're kidding, right?"

Jess shook her head.

Uncontrollable laughter spilled out. "Of course he'd bring Duke. How did Jordan get Duke past Pastor Russell?"

"Uh, he didn't."

"Huh?"

"Well, it's my fault really."

"Jess?"

Jess shrugged. "He just seemed like part of the family, and since Pastor Russell is my mom's son and my stepbrother, what can he do to me?"

"What have you done, Jess?" Jess was her maid of honor. Randi just smiled and wondered if maybe she should have made a different choice.

"Trust me—he'll be good."

Randi shook her head. "You're one of a kind, Jess."

"So are you, Randi. I'm so happy for the two of you."

"Thanks."

The organ music started to play. Randi's mother stood in the doorway. "Everything all right, dear?"

"Yes, Mom, thanks." Her mother blew her a kiss and left.

Jordan's parents were wonderful, too. She had loved them from the moment she met them.

Jess looped her arm around Randi's.

Her father slipped through the door. "Miranda, you're beautiful. You take my breath away."

"Thanks, Dad."

Jess squeezed her arm and kissed her on the cheek then left the room to line up for the processional.

"How you doing, kiddo?" her dad asked.

"Fine."

"That nervous, huh?"

"Does it show?"

"A little. But, hey, it happens to all of us. Once you're standing next to Jordan and you take his hand, it will all wash away. At least it did for your mother and me."

Randi kissed his cheek. "Thanks, Dad. I love you."

"I love you, too, sweetheart. But it's time."

He led her through the door and down the hall. The organ music shifted to the traditional bridal march. Everyone stood. Randi looked down the aisle. Jordan stood there as handsome as ever, his hair tied back. Duke sat beside Jordan, wearing his own bow tie and tuxedo tails. She smiled. Jess was right. Duke belonged here.

Jordan's smile broadened. Her gaze stayed fixed on his. Today they would unite as one. Today they would break down all the barriers of their hearts, no longer trespassers but welcomed and honored guests

At the altar, she whispered, "I love you."

"I love you, too." He held out his hand. And it was as her father had said—all fears washed away.

Today was the beginning of their future, and Randi couldn't have been happier.

SUITED FOR LOVE

Dedication

I'd like to dedicate this book to all eight of my grandchildren:
Jonathan, Joshua, Leanna, Serenity, Matthew, Kayla, Jeremiah, and Hannah.
God's grace has blessed me with a wonderful husband. Then He blessed
us with three children who have turned around and blessed us with the
eight of you. My prayer for each of you is that you will find the gift of a
spouse who is suited for loving you and Him. God bless you all.
Love, Grandma

Chapter 1

S top!" someone screamed.

Crack. The sound of wood scraping underneath Jess's boat hull caused her to frantically search the water from port to starboard. She put the engine in neutral. Pieces of a red kayak slithered past. Arms and the upper body of a man surfaced. Jess jumped overboard. *Dear Lord, have I killed him? Oh God, please help.*

She reached the man and flipped him onto his back. Shifting her body out of the foul-weather gear and losing her boots, she reached across the man's chest and swam with him to the dock. Time was of the essence.

A couple of fishermen joined her at the dock and pulled the limp man out of the water. Jess climbed onto the pier. Immediately she checked his airway and began performing CPR.

"We called the paramedics, Jess," Bill Hayden reported.

Jess counted, inhaled, and blew the fresh air into his mouth. *Please, Lord.* She held back the tears.

She began chest compressions and counted to thirty. Two more breaths, then back to chest compressions. "One, two. . ."

The man sputtered. Saltwater flowed out of his mouth. Jess turned him to his side to allow the water from the man's lungs to continue to pour out. He opened his eyes. They were a rich royal blue with shafts of gray radiating from the pupil.

Jess's hands shook. "I'm sorry. I'm so sorry," she mumbled.

The man coughed.

She rubbed the man's back for a moment, hoping to ease the strain the coughing dealt his body. "Anyone got a blanket?" she called without lifting her eyes. He convulsed. She was shaking. "Dear Lord," she whispered, "please!"

The intensity of the sirens caused Jess to look up toward the street. It was low tide, and the paramedics would have to carry him up fifty steps to reach the ambulance. Seemingly half the town lined Squabbin Bay's rocky cliff harbor, which looked like so many other coastal towns in Maine. A large, meaty hand fell on her shoulder. "He's going to be all right, Jess." The firm, even tones of her father's voice calmed her.

The paramedics made it down the long dock with a body board in tow. As soon as they arrived, she left the stranger in their care. Jess rubbed her face with her cold hands. May was not the time of year to go swimming in the North

Atlantic. She trembled—whether from the shock of the accident or the frigid water, it didn't matter. She'd nearly killed a man. How could she have missed a bright red kayak?

"What happened?" Josie Smith asked. Josie had worked for the fire department as a paramedic since before the time Jess fell off the monkey bars at school and needed stitches. At eight, having to ride in the ambulance had been a rather cool experience.

"I don't know. I never saw him until after I heard the boat crunching the hull." Jess shook off the horrible image and sounds that flickered through her mind.

"Jess?" Todd snorted. "You?" Todd was her age. He had gone right from high school to training for the fire department. She and Todd had been rivals for various athletic titles while in grammar school. In high school Jess had discovered her femininity and lost interest in running and climbing ropes—unlike her best friend, Randi, who ran five miles every day, until she was eight months pregnant.

"I didn't see him. I don't know where he came from." She hesitated. As a kid she'd won more awards for water safety than the rest of her friends. "I must not have been paying attention," she mumbled.

Todd grabbed his walkie-talkie and reported the injured stranger's situation. Jess stepped back. He was out of her hands now. She prayed he would be all right. Her father came alongside, wrapped her in a towel, and pulled her into his embrace just as her stepmother, Dena, arrived at the top of the dock. Dena had been married to Jess's father for the past two years. A lot had happened in that time. Jess had just finished college and moved to Boston, only to discover her job experience didn't bode well with her Down-Eastern ways. The struggle for success meant being less than honest with her coworkers, and that was something Jess couldn't adjust to. So she'd come home and within six months started forming a co-op for the local lobstermen in much the same way that the cranberry farmers had done decades ago.

"What happened?" her father whispered.

"I honestly don't know. I put the boat into a slow approach to the dock and— smack—I ran into him. I didn't see him, Dad. I swear."

"Kayaks are low riding."

Jess scanned the harbor. Another lobsterman was on board her boat, *Jessy*, and bringing it back to the dock. "Did our *Jessy* drift in toward the rocks?"

"Probably scraped a barnacle or two off. Don't fret about it. Do you have a change of clothes on board?"

"Nope."

"Foul-weather gear in the harbor?"

"Yup." She scanned the remains of the red kayak.

The paramedics started to carry the stranger up the long walkway of the floating dock. Due to low tide, it was quite a climb. A few others helped. Jess looked back at the sinking debris of the kayak. *What have I done?*

❧

Krispin moaned and pushed himself up on the recliner. *Of all the stupid things to have happened.* He let out a long gasp of air. Unable to deal with the conflicting emotions between whether to wring his aggressor's neck or hug his savior for her quick thinking, he groaned again. He'd rented this remote cottage in a little-known place to have peace, not to be smashed into pieces.

For the past seven years, he'd been working his way up the corporate ladder. Finally, with a little luck, he'd made it to a senior position in the company. But he felt empty, alone, and couldn't understand why. He had all he ever wanted, and then some, but life wasn't adding up. "Now this," he muttered and leaned over to pick up the phone.

On the second ring, his secretary answered, giving the usual formal greeting.

"Hi, Amanda, it's me."

"Mr. Black, how are you? How's your vacation?"

"Fine, fine. Actually, no, it isn't fine. I've had an accident. Is Gary in?"

"Yes, sir. Are you all right?"

"Mild concussion," he admitted, but he wouldn't confess to her he was lucky to be alive. The office would have it blown out of proportion by the time he was due back on Monday. . .*three days.* He wouldn't be back by Monday. He knew that before the accident. The injury just gave him a good excuse.

"Krisp, you all right?" Gary seldom showed any real concern for anyone apart from how it would affect business.

"I'll be all right. But the doc said I shouldn't drive for a few days, especially not the long distance back to Manchester from here."

"Gotcha. What happened? And what clients do I need to know about for next week?"

Krispin filled him in. He rubbed his throbbing temples and closed his eyes. "Gary, I hate to do this, but can I call you back later? I'm feeling a little nausea coming on."

"TMI." Gary groaned. "Take another week; we'll cover for you."

"Thanks, I could use it."

"Should I send Maureen up?"

Krispin squeezed his eyes closed. Gary had been trying to set Krispin up with Maureen for ages. He dated her on occasion but only when he had no other option. Maureen was Gary's younger sister. Nice enough gal, but they had nothing in common—except Gary. "No thanks. I'm going to be busy taking care of a lawsuit, I'm sure."

Gary whistled. "Betcha end up owning that boat."

"More than likely." And that's the way it was in his world. Fight until the person next to you drops or you bring him to the poorhouse. But how could he

251

sue her after she saved his life? "Later, Gary."

"Later."

Krispin waited to hear the disconnect before clicking the OFF button of the cordless phone. He didn't need to sue her. He could let it drop. "I suppose a new kayak would be worth the pain and suffering." He leaned back in the chair.

A gentle knock on the door woke him. It took a few moments to get to his feet and catch his bearings. He went to the door and saw a honey-haired woman with a timid smile on luscious pink lips staring at him. "Hello?"

"Hi, I'm Jess Kearns. I. . ." She looked down at the wooden planks on the small deck. "I'm the one who ran you over."

"Ah." He didn't remember her being this beautiful. Of course he never really got a good view of her. "Come in; you've saved me the trouble of tracking you down."

"Yes, sir. I've brought my insurance information. I hauled the kayak out of the harbor, but it's not repairable."

"I can imagine." He didn't want to be angry with this woman, but he was. "Have a seat."

"No, thank you." She handed him a piece of paper. "Here's all the information you need to know."

He scanned the sheet. "My lawyer will be in touch." He dropped the paper onto the table.

"Lawyer? Won't it be easier just going through the insurance company?"

"I'm planning on suing you, Ms. Kearns. You nearly killed me."

Tears filled her eyes. His stomach knotted. *Why'd I say that?*

"I'm sorry. You're welcome to sue me. I don't have much, but anything I have is yours." She scurried past him and out the door.

Krispin stood there for a moment. *How odd. Doesn't she know that she's admitted guilt? No lawyer would have trouble taking her for all she's worth.* "Wait," he called out.

She kept running and then jumped into a red Mercedes convertible.

"She doesn't have anything? Yeah, right!" Krispin reached for the phone to call his lawyer, then paused. *She said I could have it all. Do I want that?*

❧

Jess couldn't believe her ears. The man wanted to sue her. While she didn't own much, she may well have put her father into jeopardy, and possibly Dena. *Dear Lord, protect my parents from my careless actions.*

She fretted the entire drive home. After she told her parents the news, they called their attorney and prepared for the lawsuit. Her father's lobster boat and business were worth a small amount, but Wayne and Dena had previously taken steps to incorporate their various businesses so that if one should fail, they wouldn't lose it all. Five hours later Jess had a computer printout of the worth of the lobster business, her mortgage, a statement of personal worth, another copy of the insurance policy, as well as a statement from the lawyer regarding his contact information. A plastic container of Dena's homemade chicken soup sat on the passenger seat beside her as she drove up to Krispin Black's house for the second time that day.

A faint light glowed in the living room of the rental cottage. Jess used to play here with her girlfriends years ago when Mindy's parents owned the cottage. But like so many others, they had moved farther south and sold the property.

She knocked on the door. No answer. Peering into the living room, she looked for any signs of life. He lay on the recliner with a cup in his hand. She watched his body tense, then relax. The cup dropped to the floor. He didn't respond.

Jess opened the door and walked in. She took his pulse. It seemed steady. His hand suddenly clutched her wrist. "What are you doing here?"

"I. . .I came to bring you the information for the lawsuit."

"What?" He jumped up from his chair, then collapsed.

"Do you have a concussion?"

He nodded his head and groaned.

"Sit back. When was the last time you took your medicine?"

"I don't know." A glazed look clouded his blue eyes.

Jess flipped open her cell phone and called Josie. Within minutes Jess was told what to look for and to give the word if she needed any further help. Josie would be right over.

"Have you eaten?"

"I don't think so."

Jess looked through the small kitchen. A half-eaten, stale bagel sat next to a very cold cup of coffee. "Breakfast," she mumbled. Finding a pot, she heated up the soup and went back to the living room. She looked into his eyes, his incredibly handsome eyes, and swallowed.

"You like?" he purred.

Jess closed her eyes and prayed. She hadn't dealt with a man like this in years. She ignored his question and pushed on. "What day is it?"

"Friday." He glanced out the window. "Possibly Saturday. How late is it?"

"Not that late, Mr. Black. I have some soup heating on the stove. Do you have a wife or someone to watch over you?"

"Nope. You offering?"

"Jesus wouldn't want me to ignore your condition. I'll call my dad and he'll come over."

"Your father? Don't bother. I thought. . ."

"Mr. Black, I'm fairly sure I know what you thought, but I'm not that kind of a girl. I'm sorry you were injured at my hand, but please show me some respect."

Krispin Black scanned her face, then closed his eyes. "You're right. I apologize. It was terribly rude of me."

"Apology accepted. Let me get your soup." She left him and called her father. He couldn't come but would find someone right away. Placing the bowl of warm soup on the dinette, she asked, "Are you able to make it to the table on your own?"

"I think I can manage."

Jess held herself back as she watched the proud man work his way over. They sat in silence as he ate.

"Thank you." He pushed the bowl away. "That was thoughtful."

"You're welcome." She reached for the pile of papers. "Here's all the information you'll need for your lawsuit. Our lawyer's name and contact info is on top."

He scanned the pages. "It's not your boat?"

"No, it's my father's."

"And he's willing to give up on this without a fight?"

She smiled. "I didn't say that. He's hired his attorney. But they knew you'd order to obtain this information, so we just prepared it in advance."

"You're nuts." He paused. "Sorry."

"No, we're not nuts, we're Christians. And I was at fault." She paused for a moment, then looked directly into his eyes. "You don't believe, do you?"

"Nah, never had much use for religion. Didn't see the point. It's all right, I mean. I'm not against it or anything. But if there truly is a God, why would He concern Himself with the likes of me or anyone else in the world?"

Jess smiled. "Because He loves us."

"You really believe all that stuff?"

"Yup."

Krispin gently wagged his head back and forth.

"You can call it my Christian love that brought over these papers and that soup and the friend who's going to spend the night with you to make sure you're okay."

"Why would you do that? I mean, I get the Christian thing, but I told you I was going to sue you." The disbelief was written all over his face.

"Krispin. . ." She paused. A desire to reach out and touch him caught her by surprise. "I honestly did not see you as I was approaching the dock. I must have looked down for a moment and missed your entering the waterway in front of me. I'm just thankful I was able to save you. I don't think I could live with myself knowing I killed a man." She pulled her hands back to her lap. *Lord, what do You have in mind here? Did this accident occur to bring this man to salvation? Your will, Father, not mine.*

"Jess—you did say your name was Jess, right?"

She nodded.

"Fine. Jess, you're a beautiful woman but definitely weird."

"More than likely." Her cell phone rang. "Excuse me." She answered the call from Jordan, her best friend's husband.

"Jess, it's Jordan. Randi and I are on our way."

"Great, thanks." Closing her phone, Jess passed on the information. Jordan worked for her stepmom. He was the newest resident of Squabbin Bay. Of course in a couple months he would lose the title because Randi, Jess's best friend since she was five, would be having a baby, making him or her the newest member of the small seacoast community.

Krispin pushed his chair out from under the table. "I'm fine. I don't need a babysitter. It's not necessary."

"Actually"—she placed her hands on her hips—"I think it is. You didn't eat, and I suspect you haven't taken your medication. Someone needs to look after you, and I can't. Sorry." There was a peculiar attraction to the man, but she couldn't run with such thoughts, and she certainly couldn't enter into a relationship with someone who didn't believe the same as she did. No, it was best if she and Krispin never saw one another again. "If you have any questions, you can contact our attorney."

"Thank you."

"I'm sorry."

"You've already said that."

I know, but I still feel guilty. "Good night, Mr. Black. I'll be praying for you."

He opened his mouth to say something, then closed it.

Jess slipped out of the cottage before she said another word or gave thought to her foolish feelings. *It must be the guilt I'm feeling, Lord.*

Chapter 2

Krispin drummed his steering wheel, feeling like a fool, waiting in the Squabbin Bay Community Church parking lot on Sunday afternoon. How he'd ever committed himself to having dinner with Randi and Jordan, he'd never understand. Of course they'd hoped he would come to church and join them before they went to the Dockside Grill. He inhaled the lightly seasoned salt air and calmed himself. Finally, people slowly streamed out of the church, laughing and talking with one another. His memories as a child were of hustling into the car to get home for dinner. And the memories of family fights to and from church still turned his stomach in knots.

Person after person, family after family came out, actually happy to be with one another. Jess came out with her parents, he could only assume. And tagging behind them were Randi and Jordan. All five were in a lively discussion. Jess's eyes met his, and she sobered, then nodded her head in his direction. Randi waved.

Krispin gave a weak wave in return.

The man he assumed to be Jess Kearns's father came up to his car. Krispin braced himself for the oncoming wrath. The prospect of a lawsuit and losing his boat and income probably had him in an uproar. Not that Krispin was going to sue. He'd pretty much decided not to after listening to Randi and Jordan talk about the community. He'd learned the red Mercedes belonged to Jess's stepmother.

"Hello, Mr. Black." Mr. Kearns extended his hand. "I'm Wayne Kearns. Jess is my daughter."

Krispin gave a firm handshake but didn't say a word.

"Randi and Jordan just told us they invited you to dinner with them. You're welcome to come with us, as well."

Krispin's mouth went dry. "Ah, thanks, but no." *Why are these people being so nice?*

"No problem—thought I'd ask."

Wayne Kearns's strides were long and confident as he stepped back to the small group of people. The man was large enough to squash someone if he wanted to, Krispin mused, as Randi and Jordan parted from their friends and headed toward him. Jordan opened the passenger door and sat down. "I'll show you the way. Randi's going to drive our car."

"I could follow."

"Nah, she told me Jess wanted some private time with her. They grew up together. They're pretty close."

"I don't think you told me. . . ." Jordan chattered on. "What do you do for a living?"

They enjoyed some light conversation on the way to the restaurant, Krispin's hands nearly sliding off his steering wheel. *Why am I so nervous?*

"We're here." Jordan pointed to a gray, weathered, shingled building that sat on the edge of the rocky cliff overlooking the harbor.

The same harbor where he'd almost drowned. His hands remained firmly gripped on the steering wheel as if holding on to life. . .his life. It could end so suddenly. Krispin shook off his musings. *No need to dwell on such thoughts.*

"So—what do you recommend?" Krispin closed the door of the car and hoped he sounded calmer than he felt. He watched Randi drive up with Jess. His stomach flipped. He felt trapped. Did he see her as the grim reaper?

"Lobster bisque is one of my favorites." Jordan chuckled.

There had to be some inside joke going on that he didn't understand. Randi joined them, but Jess, he noticed, walked away from the restaurant.

"I'm not partial to lobster."

Jordan sobered. "No problem. They have several different dishes to choose from."

Randi came up beside them; Jordan looped his arm around his wife's shoulders. It would be nice to find someone who made his life complete. An image of Jess Kearns floated through his mind. He turned his gaze back to the harbor. Nope, that woman was dangerous, in more ways than one.

"Shall we?" Randi motioned for them to go into the restaurant.

Krispin found the Dockside Grill charming, fitting for the area. He noticed Jess's parents eating quietly in a back corner, their gazes locked on one another. *Aren't they curious about me? Doesn't it bother them that I'm going to sue? Or threatened to sue,* he amended.

"Krispin," Randi spoke, "did Jordan tell you this is where he and I met?"

"No, he left out that tidbit. Why don't you tell me?"

Randi elaborated on how the two of them met over a spilled bowl of lobster bisque. Now Krispin knew the inside joke and chuckled along with his hosts.

After lunch they went to the studio where Randi showed off Jordan's work. He was a good photographer, Krispin had to admit. They could use someone like him in his office.

"Have you ever thought of working closer to civilization?" Krispin asked.

"Started in the city. . .it's been more profitable here. The money was fair, but the other benefits far outweigh life in the city. At least for me." Jordan winked at his wife. "Of course I was straight out of college and full of myself back then, but I like it here. Plus, Randi and I want to raise our children in Squabbin Bay."

Krispin had learned yesterday that Randi was expecting their first child which, from her expanding waistline, now seemed obvious. "Would you be interested in some freelance?"

"Possibly. You'd have to talk with Dena. She arranges my schedule."

"Is she an agent?"

Jordan nodded. "Of sorts. She's actually a far better photographer than myself. But she's semiretired and concentrating on her marriage and family over career these days. Perhaps you've seen some of her work. Her name is Dena Russell."

"Doesn't ring a bell." But apart from Ansel Adams, Krispin knew no other photographer's name.

"Too bad. Here, let me show you." And for the next thirty minutes Krispin was treated to some of Dena's photographs.

Krispin slipped his hands into his pockets and placated his host—until he spotted a picture so terrifying he gasped out loud.

❧

Jess picked up another pebble and tossed it onto the water. It skipped four times before it sank. In her younger years, she and her father had played for hours, skipping stones and talking. She rocked gently back on her heels, remembering. Yesterday after their Sunday lunch, Jess, Randi, and her stepmother had talked about Jess's frustration with wanting to be a good witness to Krispin. After her experience with Trevor, her college boyfriend, she was leery about getting involved with any man, and certainly didn't want a relationship with one who didn't believe in God.

She replayed the accident over and over in her mind, trying to figure out where he'd come from and why she hadn't seen him cross her path.

"Jess?" Krispin Black's smooth baritone voice played down her spine.

She turned toward the voice as her back stiffened, forcing herself to remain neutral to any emotions she might have. "Mr. Black."

"You didn't come to lunch yesterday."

How'd he know I was out here? "Are you tracking me down?"

"No. Well, yes, I suppose I am. I'm going to be staying an additional week and was wondering if you'd be interested in going out to dinner with me?"

Jess snickered. "You're suing me *and* you want me to go out to dinner? Is this for a tactical advantage at the trial?"

"There won't be a trial. Most lawsuits are handled out of court."

"I don't get it." Jess placed her hands on her hips. "We're more than willing to compensate for your losses, so why sue?"

Krispin shrugged and looked down at his feet. Slowly he lifted his head and locked his gaze with hers. A smile rose on his lips. "Tell ya what. If you go out with me, I won't sue your dad for his entire company."

"Blackmail?"

"Now, did I say anything about blackmail? I'm merely suggesting that if you'll give me the pleasure of your company, I'll reduce the scope of the lawsuit."

"Mr. Black, I'm sorry to say I don't like you. Why would you even care to go out with me?"

He reached out for her, then held back. Or she stepped back. Jess wasn't exactly sure.

"You nearly killed me, Ms. Kearns. The very least you could do—"

"I also saved your life," she interrupted. "I am not duty bound to go out with you. There's no attraction," she mumbled.

He squinted.

"What I mean to say is that while you might be a handsome enough man, your personality is limited. And there is the issue of my Christian faith, which you don't share. I will not date a man who does not believe as I do. Once was enough," she confessed. *Why'd I say that?* she chided herself.

"I'm really a decent person, once you get to know me."

"I suppose that's in the eye of the beholder." Jess stepped away from the water's edge. She didn't like being rude to anyone, but Mr. Krispin Black grated her nerves, in positive and negative ways.

"Touché." He bowed and turned back toward the parking lot. Halfway to his car, he turned around again. "I won't sue your father."

"Thank you." Tears threatened to fall. For the past three days, she could think of little else except how she had not only ruined her father's business but nearly killed a man, as well.

"I really didn't see you," she choked. "I'm so sorry. I am glad I was able to save you."

He nodded. "Thanks. I shouldn't have been so hard on you. Life's been a. . ." A word Jess would have preferred not to hear escaped his lips.

"Sorry," he apologized. "I've done well in business. The language goes with the territory."

And made you hard as nails. "I'll pray you find more joy in your life, Mr. Black," she said softly.

He plopped down on the beach right where he'd been standing. "I don't get it. Why? I've been miserable to you, to your family. Why do you care?"

Admittedly she had found it hard to care a few moments ago. But now, seeing a more humbled image of the man, her heart was drawn to him. She took a tentative step forward, then stopped. "Because if not for God's grace, I'd be the same as you."

"You?" He snickered. "You have no idea what the corporate world is like."

Jess shook her head. He had her compassion for only a moment. "Mr. Black, do you realize how big your ego is? You make judgments about people without knowing them. You're automatically assuming I've never been in the corporate world, which is a wrong assumption. I was once as driven as you are. Thankfully, it didn't last long. Don't get me wrong, Christians and Christian CEOs have a place in business, but it is a hard line to walk. I was drawn to success first, the Lord second, and possibly even lower, before. . .well, never mind."

"Jessica, I'm sorry."

She nodded rather than say something she would regret. "Have your lawyer contact me when you're ready to file." Jess marched to her car, leaving the man full of himself and his shoes and britches full of sand.

"God, only You can do something with that man. I can't."

Krispin felt as useless as the piece of driftwood lying on the beach in front of him. He'd once had a life. But recently he'd been drifting on the sea, tossed and turned and aged by the world. Had he really turned into a man with such an inflated ego that he prejudged people, and poorly at that?

He grabbed a fistful of sand and let it stream through his fingers, repeating the mindless process several times. Was there really a God who held people? Who held the world, the universe, in the palm of His hand? Randi and Jordan thought so. So did Jess. It was obvious that her family did not respond to his threat the same way a normal person would. *At least not a normal person in my world,* he amended. They'd be looked at as wimps. But Wayne Kearns was no wimp.

Brushing off the sand from his hands, he scanned the horizon. The sea was a royal blue spotted with outcroppings of small green and rock islands. He couldn't sue Jess. As much as Gary, his senior partner, and everyone else would expect him to, he just couldn't. He owed her his life, even if she was the one who had nearly killed him. If she hadn't saved him, he'd be dead now. Krispin paused on that thought. *And what would death be like for me, if there is a God?*

A shiver of fear slid down his spine. He looked toward heaven and cried out, "Are You really up there?"

Not hearing an answer, he paused and listened for a moment longer. Still nothing, except the gentle roll of the surf hitting the shore. He left the beach unsure of life in a way he'd never experienced before. He'd come to Squabbin Bay to find answers. Instead he found more confusion, more pain, more honesty. Was he really a self-centered egomaniac? Not that Jess had said it in quite those terms, but he certainly understood what she'd implied.

Chapter 3

Jess gasped, tightened her grip on the shopping cart, and pulled it around the corner. Meeting Krispin Black at the beach yesterday had been bad enough, but to see him in the aisle of the grocery store forced her to retreat. Originally she had planned on doing her shopping on Friday, but running over Krispin Black's kayak had unraveled her. With the lawsuit against her looming, she had spent a sleepless night. While it was true she didn't have much, she had managed to purchase a home nearly a year ago. It took four months to work out the paperwork, so technically she'd only owned the house for eight months. There wasn't much equity, but she'd be starting from scratch if Mr. Black did sue her.

"Hello, Ms. Kearns," Krispin said with a smug smile.

"Hello." Jess pushed her cart farther down the aisle. She didn't need anything in this one, having already been down it. She reached for another can of black olives anyway.

"I read over your financial information. You said you didn't have much. You own your own home, Ms. Kearns."

"I have a mortgage, which has only had eight payments made against it out of 360. So if you call that owning, yes, I have a house." She paused and put the can back on the shelf. She also had her deposit and closing costs. "Will you be suing for possession of my house?"

"I can't see the advantage of owning your mortgage."

Jess relaxed. She'd given up trying to understand her attraction to him. Instead she felt it best to simply avoid him as much as possible. But in a town as small as Squabbin Bay, she wasn't sure how easy that would be. "How long are you here for?"

"Originally just the weekend. But because of the accident, I've taken the entire week off."

Jess nodded. Being Tuesday, that meant he'd be in town for four to five more days. And if he was kayaking. . . "Mr. Black, I'd be happy to loan you my kayak while you're visiting our area."

"Seriously?"

"Yes."

"Why?" He raised his eyebrows. His neatly trimmed, dark brown hair didn't seem to match the stubble showing on his face.

"Because it's the right thing to do. And you should get back on the water as

261

soon as possible. I don't know what kind of fears you might have after what you've been through, but I can't imagine it will be too easy for you to go back into the water."

He squared his shoulders. "I can handle it."

"I'm sorry, I don't mean to be telling you your business. I just thought you might like to go kayaking while the weather is agreeable. A front's due to come in tomorrow, and well, you won't be able to kayak on the ocean."

"I hadn't heard the weather forecast. Thank you. If you don't mind, I'd like to take you up on that offer."

"No problem. I'll deliver the kayak to your cottage after I'm done shopping." She turned, placed both hands on the cart, and continued down the aisle. If she worked quickly, she could get to his place before he returned. She hoped.

"What about dinner?"

She stopped short. If nothing else, Krispin Black was a determined individual. Jess could easily see how he'd made his mark in the corporate business world. "I believe we had this conversation yesterday."

"Nothing has changed?"

"Nothing has changed."

"Farewell, Ms. Kearns."

Jess simply nodded. *Finally.* Her shoulders slumped. She was done with Krispin Black. Well, done for the moment. The pending lawsuit still loomed on the horizon.

She scurried to the checkout, went home, and loaded her kayak on the roof of her car. It was a beat-up, old Volkswagen Bug from the sixties that her father managed to keep running from spare parts found in the junkyard. Because it was a classic car, she hoped to refurbish it someday. But other things had been more important, like saving for the house, furniture to put in the house, and supporting the lobstermen's co-op. For the past two years, she'd been working hard at establishing the co-op. The profits from last year were marginal. This year, with the continuation of good weather and healthy catches, they expected to make a good profit.

The phone rang as she opened the screen door to the back porch of her house. She wrestled the bags of groceries into one arm and picked up the cordless phone. "Hello."

"Hey, Jess, it's Myron Buefford."

"Hi, Myron, what can I do for you?" Myron had moved up to Maine from Louisiana thirty years ago after a hurricane had wiped out his shrimping business. He figured while Maine was colder, it seldom had hurricanes. Nor'easters were another matter. But he and his family had settled in. His kids had developed a linguistic blend of Southern and Down-Eastern twang. Myron, on the other hand, still spoke as Southern as if he'd just moved up.

"We heard about the accident and pending lawsuit. We're wondering if ya'll would come to a meeting of the co-op tonight with your attorney. We want to make sure Mr. Black can't own the co-op."

Jess stood rigid for a moment. *Could Krispin Black end up as a member of the co-op? Dear Lord, please say it isn't so.* Then the thought hit her. Incorporation was one of the points her stepmother had made when they were establishing it. "Myron, I think the co-op is covered with the way we set up the Articles of Incorporation, but I'll willingly meet with all of you. And if my lawyer can't be there, I'll ask his take on all of this."

"Thanks, Jess. We all know it was an accident, and the man has to be out of his mind to want to sue. I'm sorry for your troubles, and no one wants y'all out of the co-op." He paused. Jess could see Myron, in her mind's eye, brushing the few strands on top of his head to the back—a gesture he'd been making since she was a little girl and he had a full head of hair. "But we've all worked real hard to establish it."

"Myron, I'll be there. Trust me, I've worked too hard to let this co-op fall into the hands of someone else. I believe we took care of this when we incorporated, but let's be sure."

"You're not upset?"

Jess could hear Myron's wife, Shelia, mumbling something in the background. "Myron, I really understand. I'll do whatever I can to protect the co-op."

"Thanks, Jess. I knew you'd understand."

More than he realized. She'd met with Krispin Black several times now and knew he would be relentless in his pursuit of anything he put his mind to. Unfortunately he didn't put his mind on God. Jess shook her head and ended her conversation with Myron. After she'd put away her groceries, she drove the kayak over to Krispin Black's house. His car was in the drive. Her heart sank. If only he were still at the store.

The back door to his rental cottage squeaked open. "Thanks for bringing the kayak by. Are you certain about the loan, Ms. Kearns?"

"Yes."

"Fine-looking kayak. I don't recognize the brand." His gaze traveled the breadth and length of the long, slim, one-man kayak.

"Dad and I built this about ten years ago."

"Nice." He pulled his gaze from the boat back to her. His royal blue eyes sparkled. "You built this?"

"Yes, with my father. We used to go kayaking every year until I went to college. Unfortunately, I haven't used it enough lately."

"What a shame. It's a fine-looking vessel." He knelt down and passed his hand over the top of the hull. The boat was a wooden-strip kayak with a fiberglass hull. "I don't get to go as often as I used to, either."

"Price of growing up, I guess."

"Or our obsessions. Mine's work. What's yours?" He stood and faced her again.

Jess suppressed the desire to get to know Krispin. *Or did the Lord put him in my life for me to witness to him?*

"What?" She shook her head in confusion. "Look, Mr. Black, I'm uncomfortable speaking with you. One minute you're talking a lawsuit, the next you're asking me to go out with you. Forgive me, but I need to go. I hope you enjoy the kayak. Just leave it here when you go back home, and I'll pick it up." Jess scurried back to her car.

"So your charity only goes out with regard to your possessions?"

She stopped and turned toward him. How dare he accuse her of not showing the Lord's love to him! She placed her hands on her hips, opened her mouth slightly to rebuff him, then closed it. Why should she get into an argument? "Enjoy your stay in Squabbin Bay, Mr. Black."

Jess slipped behind the wheel. Her hands and body were trembling. It wasn't fear, exactly. The shakes seemed more to do with her controlling her anger. *How dare he presume to judge my faith!*

ᐧ⬩

Krispin had done it again. Whenever Jessica Kearns came near him, he put up more defenses than the US Army fighting terrorists. *Why?* He honestly didn't have a problem with her and her religion. It just wasn't something he cared about one way or the other. And apart from the cost of a replacement kayak and his medical bills, he didn't need remuneration for the accident. But he continued to fluster Jess with the impending lawsuit. *Why?* Truth was, he would have sued her for every cent he could a year ago. Krispin let out a deep sigh. A year ago. That's when all his dissatisfaction with life began. And whatever he'd thrown at Jessica Kearns, she didn't retaliate. She simply went the extra mile and provided all the information he needed. She offered her home. . .what was she thinking?

He watched the old Volkswagen Bug sputter down the road. The answers he was looking for weren't in Maine; they were back home at work, at his studio apartment, where his life had taken the wrong path. Yes, he needed to return home. Then he could put everything back into its proper perspective.

Inside the cottage he packed his bag, then left an envelope with a healthy tip for the maid service and a note that Jessica Kearns would be back to pick up her kayak in a few days. He drove through the heart of Squabbin Bay. People were chatting with one another. Lobstermen were working on the docks. Wayne Kearns waved as Krispin drove past. Krispin pulled over into a graveled parking spot.

Wayne Kearns left his dock and walked over toward the car. "What can I do for you, Mr. Black?"

Krispin stared down his opposition. "Tell Jess I am only asking for damages and that I'm leaving town, so she can pick up her kayak."

"All right. But didn't she just take it over?"

"Yes. Uh, something came up. I'm heading home earlier than expected."

Wayne Kearns nodded. "Tell me something, Mr. Black. Why did you pick Squabbin Bay for your vacation?"

"I've been under a lot of stress at work and wanted a nice, quiet place to reevaluate my position with the company." Krispin rubbed his hands on the steering wheel.

"I guess the accident changed all that."

Krispin nodded.

"I'll pray you'll make the right decision, Mr. Black."

"A rugged outdoorsman like yourself takes stock in that God stuff?"

Wayne Kearns's smile brightened. "Yes, I do. Wanna talk about it?"

"Not really. I mean no offense. Religion never seemed to matter before. Life is life. You work hard, do your job, be nice to folks, and eventually die one day."

"I suppose that's how your life is. Mine, well, I don't think I would have done so well if I hadn't found the Lord. Jess was nearly two, I was nineteen, a single father, and my life was controlling me. I worked to provide for Jess. I spent every free moment I had with her. I loved her so much, yet something was missing. At first I thought it was that I didn't have a wife. But the answer wasn't in finding more women and a mother for my daughter. The answer came to me when I didn't know what else to do, when I finally gave up trying to do my best and constantly falling short. Truthfully, if I hadn't found God and surrendered to Him, I wouldn't have made it as a single father."

"Where was Jess's mother?"

"She was sixteen when she got pregnant. She agreed to let me keep the baby and raise her. Terry finished school, went on to college, and eventually made a new life for herself. She wasn't ready to be a mother. Not that I was ready to be a father, but I had the advantage of having a mother who would watch Jess while I was working. If it hadn't been for my parents, I wouldn't have made it financially or emotionally. Jesus gave me a peace, a confidence, the strength to go on. And I'm probably sounding like I'm preaching here a bit, but the Bible is a good handbook on how to really enjoy life. After all, God is the creator of life."

Krispin wagged his head. "If you believe all that stuff, I suppose. It just seems archaic to me."

"You know, you're right. You can't get much more archaic than with God."

"I can see where Jess gets it from."

Wayne narrowed his gaze and leaned a little closer. "I raised her in the church, but she had to find her own way to let God in and give Him the chance to rule over her life. God doesn't have grandchildren, only children, meaning we all have to accept Him as our Father. There isn't a grandfather clause in Christianity."

Krispin raised his right eyebrow. Hadn't his parents always told him he was a Christian, that they had baptized him as a baby? That he had his fire insurance if there was a hell? "So you don't believe everyone is going to heaven? *If* there is a heaven," he amended.

"Nope. It's a choice, Mr. Black."

"Jordan said something similar the other night when they watched over me because of the concussion."

"Not surprised. He has a pretty solid faith."

"Is everyone in Squabbin Bay like you guys?"

Wayne chuckled. "No. But we have a good-sized church, and we're a fairly strong-willed people when it comes to our faith and living it out. Actually, we can be strong-willed a lot of the time, even when we shouldn't be."

Krispin shifted in his bucket seat, then slid his hand around the steering wheel again. He didn't want to insult the man, but he had to admit he would make any minister proud. Krispin knew Jordan worked for Wayne's wife as a professional photographer and had a huge respect for both Wayne and Dena. Jordan had said Dena's first husband had been a pastor, just like her son was the pastor of the Squabbin Bay Community Church. So it made sense that she'd remarry someone who had a faith equal to that of her first husband. . . if she respected her religion. He supposed it worked for this blended family. "Hey, I'm happy for you, Mr. Kearns. You raised a fine daughter, even if she is dangerous behind the wheel of a boat."

He saw the muscle in Wayne Kearns's jaw move slightly. "For the record, Jess has been driving that boat since she was four, and she's never had an accident. Unfortunately accidents do happen, Mr. Black. I'm sure, over time, Jess will get over nearly killing you. But I think you should be thanking the Lord that she had her wits about her and jumped in and rescued you, rather than securing the boat first. I think that's what saved your life. And given time, I imagine Jess will get over this and be comfortable behind the wheel once again."

"Forgive me; you're right. Thank Jess again for me. I'd better go."

Wayne tapped the lower part of the window doorframe. "All right, Mr. Black. Travel safely."

"Absolutely." Krispin put the car in reverse. Wayne stepped away from the vehicle. Krispin hesitated for a moment, then pulled out. The sooner he put Squabbin Bay in his rearview mirror the better. As uncomfortable as he'd gotten with his life back home, it didn't compare to what he was feeling now. He'd never been so confused or on edge, even when he'd gone through the investigation from the gaming commission regarding the technology he'd written to protect their online Web sites from intruders. While everyone knew of Internet thieves, few had slipped under the radar like the one who got through one of Krispin's encryption programs. Thankfully it was the first layer of encryption, and they'd only escaped with bogus files. The creative thinking he'd put into his program had earned him a partnership in the company. The intense scrutiny made him question why he was living like this.

He drove down the winding road that led out of Squabbin Bay to Route 1, which he'd take to Ellsworth. There he'd pick up Route 1A to Bangor, then Interstate 95 South toward home.

"Why did I pick Squabbin Bay? No one recommended it. I simply threw a dart at the map and it landed there," he reminded himself. He'd taken to speaking to himself out loud inside the car. It was a way to sort out what was important, what he needed to remember, and besides, he had no one else to talk with.

Chapter 4

A month later Jess found the letter from Krispin Black waiting in her mail-box. It included his ambulance bill, his hospital bill, and the receipt for the kayak he'd purchased. When he'd left town, Krispin had told her father that he wouldn't be suing her. But she couldn't believe it was true, not until she opened this letter. The actual bill was less than a thousand dollars. She was only paying the co-payment and the cost of a new kayak. What she didn't expect to see in the letter was "plan two," as Krispin called it.

"Jess, if you're willing to help me build a kayak just like yours, I'm willing to absorb all the costs. Can you help me?" He then listed all his contact information.

Jess dropped the paper. He lived in Manchester, New Hampshire. That was an easy four-and-a-half-hour drive. "No way, I'll pay." She stomped over to the phone and called her father.

"Hello," he answered on the second ring.

"Hi, Daddy."

"Hey, Jess, what's up?"

"Krispin Black's bill came in the mail today. He's asking for less than a thousand."

Her father sighed. "Thank the Lord."

"Yeah." Jess paused and curled the cord around her finger. "Daddy, he gave me an alternative to paying the money."

"What's that?" His voice sounded tight.

"He asked me to help him build a kayak like mine."

Her father snickered. "He doesn't quit, does he?"

"No." She'd been open with her parents about Krispin's insistence on going out to dinner. "He lives in Manchester, New Hampshire. I can't be spending nine hours on the road—"

"There is that. But I think it would be better to simply keep your distance from the man."

"I agree. Besides, the cost is nothing compared to what it could have been."

"True. I'll have Dena write a check in the morning, and you can put it in your account and pay him off."

"No, Daddy. I appreciate it. But I have to pay for this myself. It will be tight, but I can do it."

"Are you sure?"

"Yes, sir." It had taken her the better part of a year to learn how to control her spending and her finances, but she'd done it. Of course using her father's credit card to buy her boyfriend expensive gifts right after graduation from college taught her some heavy-duty lessons, as well. But thankfully she had learned quickly and didn't have any debt, except for her mortgage.

"All right. Thanks for calling, and I'm glad Mr. Black was a man of his word."

A smile curled on the edges of her lips. Yes, Krispin Black had done exactly as he'd said he would. He'd even charged her less than what he could have. "Talk with you later, Dad."

She pushed the OFF button on her phone and walked back over to the letter. She opened her laptop computer and typed out an e-mail to Krispin Black.

> *Dear Mr. Black,*
>   *I received your letter today. I'll be sending you a check in a few days.*
>
> > *Sincerely,*
> > *Jessica Kearns*

Jess hesitated before she sent the e-mail. He'd given her his contact information the night of the accident and again in this letter. She hadn't given him her e-mail address. Did she want him to have it? She paused, thinking on the matter. It would make it easy for him to contact her. But what other contact would they have? Once she sent the money, their association would be finished.

Jess hit the SEND button. For better or worse, she sent it. She could always change her e-mail address or simply not read anything he sent in the future. She sat at the computer for a moment longer, scrolling through her in-box. For the most part, her personal e-mail entailed little notes from friends. There was an e-mail from her biological mother.

> *Hey Jess,*
>   *I'm sorry it took so long to get back with you. Yes, I'm looking forward to your visit. The kids are excited to see their big sister. I'm glad you're doing okay after the accident. What a terrible thing to go through. I'm really glad your faith brings you so much comfort.*
>   *I have our entire time together planned out. We'll be going...*

Jess scanned the itinerary her mother had laid out. If nothing else, Terry, her bio-mom, was organized to the hilt, which was where, she supposed, she got her organizational skills. Her father wasn't unorganized, but he wasn't a neat freak. His record keeping consisted of a container here, a folder in the filing cabinet there, and a couple of coffee cans for each of his business receipts. That was how it had been for years, until Jess had taken over that part of the business while she was in high school, and then again once she returned home from college.

Maintaining a relationship with her bio-mom had been very strained during all of Jess's high school and college years. But for the past two years, since her mom got a computer and discovered the Internet, contact was less strained but still not what it could be. It felt good to have some connection with this woman. She recognized a few of her characteristics in Terry.

Truthfully, she and Terry would never have a real mother-daughter relationship. The most Jess hoped for was a friendship, and that seemed to be getting better. The weekend visit with her mother would prove to be the true test of their new relationship.

Dena, her stepmother, was more of a mother than anyone else had ever been. The fact that they had begun their relationship when Jess was finishing college made it awkward at first to think of this woman as her mother. The plus side of all of this was Dena had raised three kids and knew how to have a good relationship with all of her adult children, even her in-law children. Jess could talk with Dena, and with all Jess's heart, she loved and respected her stepmom.

Terry had been sixteen when she got pregnant, and her parents had not been nurturers. They had even moved away from Squabbin Bay right after Terry finished high school. They had never acknowledged Jess's existence. Instead they encouraged Terry to have an abortion. They never wanted their daughter tied down to a child, certainly not one born out of wedlock. Jess honestly didn't hold any resentment toward these people. They just never factored into her life. Her father's parents had been wonderful grandparents whom she loved dearly.

Jess's thoughts drifted back to the screen, and she typed in a reply to her mother. Her in-box contained an e-mail from Krispin Black. Hesitantly she clicked it open.

Dear Jess,
    Thanks. Take your time with the check. I won't be replacing the kayak for a while.

                                                Krispin

Jess relaxed her shoulders. "Thank You, Lord. He didn't push the idea of my helping him build a kayak."

Krispin pushed himself away from his desk and looked out his office window. The building his company now owned had once been a linen factory. Below was the Merrimack River, the power source that had kept the machines working for many years. He loved that about the old building. His office, like the rest of the others in his company, was a totally contemporary one. High-tech lighting, furniture, computers, and lots of white, black, and stainless steel metal with wooden-framed windows and cream-colored walls. It was a blend of the old and new.

Gary tapped on Krispin's office doorjamb. "Krisp, got a minute?" His voice sounded more subdued than usual. Of course the fact that Krispin had only four more days with the company might have something to do with it.

"Sure." Krispin put the tiny flash drive in his pocket. He'd backed up all of his files to download onto his computer. While he'd given his resignation a few days after returning from Maine, he had agreed to work as a consultant from time to time and to be the technical advisor on some of his more sophisticated encryption programs.

By the time Krispin walked out into the hallway, Gary was striding into his office. Gary was like that, always business, all the time. Gary hadn't so much as flinched when Krispin had handed in his typewritten letter.

"Come in, close the door," Gary said as he settled in behind his glass-topped desk.

Krispin sat down. "What's up?"

Gary closed his eyes and paused. "Krisp, I thought you'd have changed your mind by now. Please, tell me what I need to do for you to stay with the company. Name it, and it's yours."

Krispin leaned back in his chair. "I've lost my edge, Gary. I'm no good to you or the company."

"Hogwash. Look, you can work from home. . .from across the world. I don't care. I don't want to lose you. You saved our bacon too many times. I need that brain of yours working for me."

"Gary, you have my word. I've signed all the contracts. I'll never reveal the codes. You know that."

Gary folded his hands and padded his thumbs together three times. It was one of those habits his partner exhibited under stress. Gary's showed up when he wasn't getting his way. "I know. Besides, I'll sue you for everything you've got and your future earnings if you *ever* break one of our contracts."

Krispin's spine tightened. A flicker of Jessica Kearns displaying the same reaction when he threatened to sue passed before his mind's eye. *Interesting.* "You and I both know that will never be the case; that's why you agreed to buy my portion of the company."

"That's the part that bugs me, Krisp. After all this time, you allowed me to buy you out. You could have held on to your share, maintained your interest in the company. If you did that, I wouldn't have had nightmares every night for the past three weeks. What gives? You and I have been at this for seven years."

"All the more reason to trust me, don't you think?" Krispin shifted in his chair.

Gary narrowed his gaze. "Is this that God junk you've been philosophizing about?"

"No." *Was it?* His mind hadn't been able to settle on anything about anything since leaving Squabbin Bay. "Nah, I was considering this when I left for vacation, Gary, and that was my first vacation in five years. I'm burned out."

Gary raised his hands in surrender. "All right." He lifted a small bundle of papers. "Here's the check and the contracts. Have your lawyer go over them. Legal's gone over them with a fine-toothed comb, but you need an attorney. I won't have it any other way."

"All part of the corporate process. Not a problem." Krispin took the pages from Gary. "Gary, I do appreciate all that you've done for me and my career."

Gary nodded. "Don't make me regret my decisions, Krisp."

"You won't. And I promised to be available for consultations."

"You and I both know that will only last for a short time. The industry changes too fast to be out of the loop for more than six months."

"I understand."

"So on a personal note, where are you going? What are you going to do with yourself?"

Find myself? How sixtyish does that sound? "I've rented a cottage for the summer months in Maine."

"That must have set you back a bundle."

"Not too bad." Squabbin Bay was remote enough that summer rentals were easy to come by. Not that Krispin felt inclined to tell Gary that secret tidbit he'd discovered quite by accident while searching for a place last month.

"Well. . ." Gary held out his hand. Krispin got up and shook it. "I'll see you around."

"Thanks, Gary."

Gary nodded, picked up his phone, and punched in a number. Krispin left the room like so many other times before, unsure of his place in the company. That was just Gary's way. Some of the folks who had come to work for them had quit because they didn't like Gary's personality, or lack thereof. It never bothered Krispin, never until today. Why now?

Because it's directed at you, he reminded himself, and exited Gary's office as swiftly as possible. Twenty steps later he was alone in his office, looking down at the Merrimack River. Krispin leafed through the pages and looked at the six-figure sum on the check. In two years it would have been three times as much. Was it worth it? Was Squabbin Bay the only place he could deal with this God issue?

He'd given up on not believing. God seemed plausible, but Krispin knew he had to change his life. He wasn't even thirty years old and already feeling like he'd lived a lifetime with little or nothing to show for it. All his accolades meant nothing in the grand scheme of things. If he wanted to, he could have worked, or still could work, on encryption programs from any remote location that had a strong Internet connection. He knew from Randi and Jordan that the only high-speed access to the Internet in Squabbin Bay was provided by a satellite service. He'd been working on computer programming since he was twelve. Mathematics he understood. He had even downloaded the Bible onto his iPod. God stuff

. . .well, that didn't make sense.

He glanced at the check again. If frugal, he could live for many years off this check. Or he could invest the money. He didn't need to decide at the moment. His phone rang, jarring him back to the office work that still needed to be done before he left the company.

Five calls later and at least an hour on the computer, everything in his office was purged of his personal information. Once he removed the couple of boxes containing his personal belongings, there would be little evidence that he'd worked here for the past seven years. He looked at the family pictures that used to sit on a small table between two chairs. His parents stood arm in arm with a picture of Haleakala Crater on Maui in the Hawaiian Islands. The crater supported no vegetation, no life, just rock and rubble from the old volcano. He'd thought it odd they would see the photo as picturesque, but then again, he'd given them the trip as an anniversary present.

He picked up the simple wooden frame and brushed the glass with his thumb. He loved his family, but he wasn't close to any of them. They'd been brought up to be totally independent of one another. Conversation at the table that involved getting to know what one or the other had been doing rarely happened. They ate together because that was the rule of the house. But conversation wasn't a part of it. Conversation at a dinner table took on a whole new meaning when he went to college. Everyone talked. People gathered in small groups and talked about everything. The first few months Krispin offered little into the conversations. But slowly, as time passed, he'd speak more and more, to the point where he decided he liked this level of conversation. He discovered that many families used that time to connect with one another. He wondered if Jess experienced that with her family. Somehow, he imagined they probably did. Mr. Kearns didn't seem like the kind of man to keep his personal opinions to himself. The day Krispin left Squabbin Bay, he'd given Krispin a lot to think about.

"Hey, Krispin." Judy Enwright stood at the door. They had dated several years ago. But Judy had wanted more than a casual relationship. He decided from then on he wouldn't date any of the women who worked for the company.

"Hi, Judy. What can I do for you?"

"Just wanted to say good-bye." Judy stepped closer. Her eyes burned with desire. Krispin turned around and picked up one of the boxes as a shield.

She reached out and placed her hand on his arm. "Since you're no longer going to work here, whadaya think about us getting back together again?"

No way. "Judy, I'm flattered, but I'm leaving town, leaving the state. Long-distance relationships never work out."

"What about. . ."

"Judy, thanks, but no thanks."

"Well, I never!" Judy huffed.

Krispin tried to soften the blow. "Judy, you and I weren't a good match. I'm sorry. You're better off trying to find the right man than just any man. I'm sorry I used you."

Judy's eyes watered.

Krispin put down the box and cradled her in his arms. "I'm so sorry. It was a mistake."

Judy sniffed. "I know. But. . ."

"Shh, don't you worry any more about this. I'll be praying for you to find someone." At that moment Krispin knew he really would be praying for her and for all the other women he'd used in his past. He felt like a cad, totally unworthy of anyone's love. He had abused love, used love to get what he wanted. He had never really loved anyone. "I was horrible to use you that way. I'm very sorry."

"You pray? I thought you didn't have any use for God."

"I don't. I mean, I didn't." Krispin released Judy and picked up the box. "Judy, I don't know much about God, but I'm trying to learn."

"Is this why you're leaving? To go find God like a monk or something?"

Krispin let out a nervous chuckle. "You know, Judy, I hadn't thought about it like that before, but I guess you're right. I'm going to live like a monk."

"Man, that's just crazy."

"More than likely, but I'm not good enough for anyone right now. I can't function in business, and my personal life is zilch. I don't know who or what I believe in at this point in time. Trust me, you're better off not knowing me."

Judy laughed. "You weren't that great to begin with."

"Gee, thanks."

Judy laughed again. "See ya around, Krispin. I can't picture you living like a monk. Good luck."

Krispin knew he was getting into this God stuff probably a little too deeply. Then again, maybe not. Hopefully he'd find the answers he was looking for. He hadn't found them in success, in women, in adventures—everything he'd experienced in life to this point had left him dry and unfulfilled. *Why?*

Chapter 5

Jess clicked the power switch to the winch, which pulled the pot out of the water and up to the side of the boat. The power winch and pulley were something she'd purchased to make her life a little easier. Her father had hauled the pots up by hand for years, but even he admitted to liking the new system.

She hoisted the metal cage on board, took out the four lobsters, and placed in a new bait bag. The boat rolled with the waves. Her sea legs held, and all was right in the world. Krispin Black was no longer a threat, and the monthly meeting of the co-op last night had breathed a collective sigh of relief. No one was more grateful than Jess.

The memory of Krispin, pale faced, lying on the dock, floated back into her mind. It had been six weeks since the chilling event, and still his image was as real as when it actually happened. Flashbacks came more than once a day. She blinked away the image and praised the Lord that Krispin Black was still alive. "Lord, thank You again for helping me spare Krispin's life. Be with him right now, Lord. Make him aware of You and Your love and grace for him." She had started praying for Krispin that way right after he left town.

She was grateful to see no more messages from Krispin Black in the weeks since he'd replied to her e-mail. The check had been mailed to him yesterday morning, a fact that the entire co-op had been pleased to hear. All thought Mr. Black to be a fair and honorable man. Of course they didn't know of his rude suggestions. Dena and her father knew, but no one else. Jess hadn't even told Randi, though she rarely saw her old friend anymore. Marriage and expecting a baby had a way of changing a person's desire to hang out with single friends. Or maybe it didn't change the desire but kept a young woman busy with other, more important things. She and Randi still talked, just not as often.

"I need a new best friend." Jess plopped the lobster pot back into the Atlantic. Krispin's image popped back into her mind. Jess laughed out loud. "No way."

She finished with the last pot as the sun stood over the horizon and started to warm everything with its golden rays.

"Jess, come back," the radio crackled.

Jess picked up the old bulky gray microphone. "Hey, Dad. Over."

"Just thought I'd warn you before you came in this morning. Word has it Krispin Black is back in town. Rented the same cottage for the summer. Over."

Great. "Thanks. Over."

"Jess, are you going to be okay with this? Over."

"I'll be fine, Dad. Thanks for letting me know. Over."

"Over and out."

Jess returned the mike to the hook. If she could go days and weeks without speaking with her best friend, then it ought to be as easy as sliding on ice to avoid Krispin Black. And that's what she intended to do.

❧

Two weeks later, Jess caught her first glimpse of Krispin Black in the grocery store.

"Hello," he said as he walked past her, pushing his cart farther down the aisle.

"Hi," she replied. A bit stunned that he didn't say anything else, she felt tempted to turn her cart around and follow him. But she remembered their last conversation in this very store. Jess finished her shopping and headed out to the car.

As she placed the last bag into the trunk and pulled down the hood of her VW Bug, she saw him nearby, getting into an old, completely restored Mustang. *Daddy's dream car,* she mused. "My dad would be so jealous if he saw your car."

Krispin chuckled. "I picked it up when I was fourteen from an older lady who had saved it for her son when he went off to fight in the Vietnam War. I mowed her lawn and took care of her hedges for two years to pay for the car."

"Impressive. You didn't strike me as the mechanical type."

"I'm not." He leaned against the side of his car and folded his arms across his chest. "But I wanted that car. Rot and decay had taken their toll after twenty years, but I've enjoyed refurbishing it."

"Why are you here?" she blurted out, and slapped a hand over her mouth.

"It's all right, Jess. I understand your reluctance to have me in the area. I want to apologize for my behavior before. It was crude, rude, and socially unacceptable. I came here to reevaluate things."

But why here? she wanted to ask, deciding against it. There was no sense getting to know this man further. "See you around."

Krispin nodded and immediately turned away from her. *Is he trying to stay away from me as much as I'm trying to avoid him?*

❧

Krispin squeezed the steering wheel, trying to rein in his frustrations. He'd been debating moving to Squabbin Bay ever since deciding to try and live his life like a monk. He knew Jess would be a temptation to break the commitment. She was more beautiful than he remembered. On the other hand, given the opportunity, they could become friends, he was certain of that. But he wasn't ready to handle friends. He wasn't ready to handle much of anything yet.

Ten days earlier he'd managed to get up the nerve to confront his questions of faith, the Bible, and religion in general and had met with Pastor Russell, the pastor of the same church where he had met Jordan and Randi the Sunday after the accident. Not knowing where else to go, he settled on that church because he trusted the few people he'd met from there. During that meeting Pastor Russell had led Krispin in a prayer of commitment to God. His body trembled at the awesome leap of faith he was making, yet a peace washed over him unlike any he'd experienced before.

But Krispin had put off going to church in order to avoid seeing Jess. He prayed for her daily. He knew she wouldn't appreciate his presence in town. Not that he would blame her. His suggestive tones and comments had been completely out of line. But it felt good to apologize to her.

He turned the key, and the engine roared to life. Earlier that morning, he'd signed a lease to rent one of the old warehouses. He didn't have a place to build a kayak at his cottage and found the old fishing warehouse to be perfect for his needs. The closer it came to building the boat, the more nervous he felt about being able to do it. He'd never done anything like it before. Restoring the car had been easy. He'd simply purchased the refurbished parts and put them in. If he couldn't do it, he had hired someone who could.

This project he planned to do by himself with a little help from an online forum for kayak builders. He'd read and reread all about building the small boats. He now owned enough tools to make any carpenter proud. Learning how to use the tools would take a lot more practice. Purchasing a bunch of wood to get a feel for cutting and gluing seemed the practical way to go. With any luck he'd be able to build something that would float. In truth, he'd love to have someone show him how to use the various tools. Thankfully, detailed videos and instruction manuals could be found on the Internet, not to mention the home makeover shows on television.

Krispin drove to the cottage he had rented for the summer. He had sublet his condo in Manchester for the next six months. If all went well in Squabbin Bay, he'd stay the full time. If life in this secluded area didn't work out, he'd relocate someplace else for a while. His desire was to stay put until he understood what having God in his life meant. He understood he was going to heaven, but living the Christian life day to day would prove difficult, he imagined. So many of his worldviews were turning upside down. Some blended well with scripture, like being kind to people, not murdering anyone, and other basic moral truths. But the reality that his morals weren't the same as God's standard was hitting him hard. He felt an even greater responsibility to all the women he'd known. And truthfully, he knew he wasn't worthy of someone like Jessica Kearns. From everything he'd seen and heard around town, she was a good, clean, and wholesome person. Unlike himself.

When he arrived at the cottage, he found the red light of his answering machine flashing. He pushed the button. "Hi, Krispin, it's Pastor Russell. I'm having a barbecue at my house tonight. If you'd like to come, you're more than welcome. Call me."

Krispin froze. Should he go to such an event? He felt too unworthy to be around the pastor and his family. Krispin picked up the phone and dialed the pastor's number.

"Hello," Pastor Russell answered on the first ring.

"Pastor Russell, Krispin here. Thanks for the offer, but I'm busy tonight."

"Oh, all right. Maybe next time."

"Yeah, maybe," Krispin mumbled.

"Krispin? Is everything all right?"

"Yeah, I'm fine. I've been reading the Bible like you suggested. I'm still having trouble understanding some of it, but I'm seeing more and more of my life as being unfit for God."

"Ah, well, just remember, your sins were forgiven when you asked Jesus into your heart. Everything from your past has been wiped clean. In fact the Bible tells us God throws our sins into the depths of the sea. In other words He forgives and forgets."

"How? I remember them."

"Because He, being God, is able to forgive and forget. We, being human, have a hard time doing that. Even harder is forgiving ourselves for the things we've done." Pastor Russell paused. "Krispin, would you like to talk some more about this? I've got an hour I can spare before family arrives."

"Thanks, but I'll be fine. I'm sorry to impose on your time."

"Like I said before, you're not an imposition. If you change your mind, you're still welcome to come for dinner."

"Thanks. I appreciate the offer."

"You're welcome. Forgive yourself, Krispin. You're a new creature in Christ. Your slate has been wiped clean."

Krispin couldn't quite put his head around that thought. But it made sense on some level. A hard drive can be wiped clean, but what was on it was still there until it was written over many, many times. Just how clean was God's hard drive? "Thanks, I'll keep that in mind."

They said their good-byes, and Krispin went to work putting his groceries away, including the two frozen dinners he had purchased. Eating out, even ordering takeout, was getting boring in Squabbin Bay. Lobster wasn't his favorite food. He could purchase a steak rather than go to the Dockside Grill. Cooking for one had never been one of his favorite things to do. Girlfriends and dates had come in handy with regard to dinners. Picking up fast food for lunch, ordering with the others in the office, all seemed to work just fine and provided an eclectic menu. Adjusting his eating habits was just one of the many obstacles involved in moving to a place so far away that it boasted only one traffic light—a blinking one at that—and one grocery store. Secluded places like this were good for vacations for someone who hadn't grown up here—but not regular life.

On the other hand, those were the very reasons he'd come to such an out-of-the-way place to reexamine his life and priorities. He sighed. Living here would definitely be an adjustment.

ﾞ♠

Jess watched Jason set the phone in the cradle. "You invited Krispin Black to dinner?"

"Yes, is that a problem?"

How do I answer that? "Well, kinda."

"Jess, I know he threatened a lawsuit."

Jess waved it off. "That isn't the problem."

"Then what is?"

"Nothing. Never mind. Is he coming?"

"No, I don't believe so."

"Okay, whatever." Jess scurried off. *How do you tell your pastor, who's also your stepbrother, your fears of being attracted to such an ungodly man? You don't,* she reminded herself, and went back to the kitchen to help her stepbrother's wife. "Hey, Marie, what can I do to help?"

"Grab the potatoes off the stove and drain them, please."

"Sure." Jess took the hot pot over to the sink and poured the contents into the colander. "What else?"

"How are your potato salad skills?"

"I've gotten much better since I learned Dena's recipe."

"Great, make that. The family loves it."

Jess chuckled. "Where's the bowl?"

"Third cabinet on your right. Everything else is in the fridge."

"Got it." Jess went to work. She wanted to ask Marie why Jason would be inviting Krispin Black to the family picnic. Of course the man needed salvation, and with Jason's job, it probably went hand in hand, him wanting to reach out to a lost soul. *But still. . .why now? Why here?* She was filled with so many questions. She wasn't afraid of Krispin. She was afraid of her own reactions to him.

"Hi, Marie. Hi, Jess." Dena walked into the room, carrying a pan of double-chocolate brownies and a two-gallon cooler of grape lemonade, and set them on the table.

"Hi, Mom," Marie and Jess said in unison.

"So what can I do, Marie?" Dena went straight to the sink and washed her hands.

"Marinate the steaks."

"No problem."

"I'm so—o—o glad you decided on beef tonight," Jess purred. "I've seen too much seafood lately."

Dena chuckled. "Your father can still lobster, Jess. You don't have to do it every morning."

"Yeah, I know, but I don't have too much to do with the co-op right now. Come fall, Dad's going to have to go out pretty near every morning."

"You've spoiled him. He probably won't want to lobster."

Dad came in carrying a huge watermelon and kissed all three women on the cheek. "Hey now, I resent that remark."

Jason followed him in. "Amber and David should be here in a couple minutes."

"Chad and Brianne will be here after she finishes feeding the baby," Dena offered.

Dena's cheerful smile set Jess thinking back on all the planning and how much it meant to Dena to have the entire family together. Oddly enough, Jess felt fully a part of this family. Dena had a way of doing that. Unlike her own mother, Terry. Their visit last week had been strained on several occasions. Jess felt like Terry was trying too hard. Terry's other children and husband weren't all that thrilled with Jess's visit. And despite their obvious discomfort with her visiting, she knew she'd go to her bio-mom's house for a visit again. But she didn't have the same sense of belonging and being a real member of the family like she did here.

"Hello, anyone in here?"

Jess's eyebrows lifted. "Grandpa?"

She turned toward the doorway where her grandfather stood, nodding and grinning warmly. Grandpa and Grandma Kearns hadn't come back to Squabbin Bay since the lobster poaching charges against him had been dropped.

Jess left the potato salad and ran to her grandparents. "Grandma, Grandpa." She hugged them hard. Tears edged her eyes. "It's so good to see you."

"And you, sweet one." Grandma Kearns smiled.

"I love you, princess. I'm sorry." Grandpa hugged her. He'd been guilty of gambling in Florida and had lost just about everything he owned. Jess's father had to bail him out financially, leaving her dad with no money going into his marriage with Dena. At first Grandpa had been bitter and angry. Then as time passed and he got the help he needed, he accepted he was addicted to gambling and had ruined his retirement, life, and reputation. If the community of Squabbin Bay hadn't loved him so much before he had his problems, he would have served a lot of time in prison. In the end, he was doing well. And Grandma Kearns now handled the finances.

"Grandpa, I forgave you a long time ago. You know that."

"I know. I just wanted to say it in person."

Her father placed his hands on her shoulders. "Hey, Mom, Dad. It's good to see you."

"Good to see you, too, son. How's that pretty wife of yours?" Grandpa Kearns winked.

"She's just fine. How was your trip, Mom?"

"Fine. I'm a little stiff, but your father stopped just before we got here so we could walk around a bit and stretch our legs and joints." Jess's father gave his mother a kiss on the cheek.

Jess thought back on all the hurt that her father had gone through when he discovered his own father had been the cause of everyone's misfortune that summer. *Forgiveness is a wonderful gift, Lord. Thanks.*

She slipped away from her father and grandparents and made her way toward the kitchen. The house buzzed with people as everyone arrived. Six children, eleven adults, two dogs, one cat, and a pet frog running about made up the entire gathering. Jess loved her family. And they loved her. What more could she want?

A man who loves me, her heart cried out to God. *Not just any man, the right man,* she amended. Trevor had proved to be such a huge disappointment in the boyfriend department that she didn't even want to date anymore.

The doorbell rang. Jason went to answer it. Jess glanced up to see Krispin Black. She swallowed and walked back to the kitchen.

Chapter 6

Krispin paused. He'd tried to avoid Jess by coming early to explain his actions about not accepting the pastor's invitation, yet there she was . . . *I should have known better.* "Welcome, Krispin. Let me introduce you." Pastor Russell pulled him through the front door while shaking Krispin's hand.

A whirlwind of names swirled around him as he greeted each one. "I'm sorry to intrude, Pastor Russell. But I was wondering if I could borrow you for a moment. I promise it won't take too long."

"Sure. Excuse me, folks." Jason Russell escorted Krispin to his private office in his home. Once inside the small room, Krispin's palms began to sweat. "Pastor, I need to confess something to you."

"Relax, Krispin. Take a seat. What do you feel you need to confess?"

"I turned down your dinner invitation because of Jessica Kearns. You probably know I threatened to sue her."

Pastor Russell nodded.

"Well, it's worse than that. I made a crude comment to her, suggesting a way she could pay me back without using money."

"I see. So you're avoiding church in order to avoid Jess?"

"Yes. I don't want to make her more uncomfortable. I knew it was a problem returning to Squabbin Bay, but I also knew that if I were going to find the answers about God, I'd find them here. Should I leave town?"

"Have you apologized?"

"Yes, but. . ." Krispin rubbed the back of his neck. "It's not that easy. I'm attracted to her. She's a temptation to my newfound faith. I've been attracted to her from the moment my eyes focused and saw her leaning over me. But I can't have a woman in my life."

"I understand. I'll speak to Jess."

"No, please don't. I mean, I don't want her to think I became a Christian to have her. I can't see how I'd be worthy of any woman's love, but if God sees fit one day, I'd like the woman, even Jess, to be able to see my faith in Christ first. Does that make sense?"

"Yeah, it does. All right, I won't tell Jess. And I'll be mindful to invite you when Jess isn't coming, how is that?"

"Wonderful." Krispin sighed and got up from his chair. "I won't keep you from your family. I just couldn't live with myself, deceiving you."

Pastor Russell extended his hand. "Thanks for filling me in."

Krispin took the proffered hand. "Thanks for not knocking me out for my crude remarks to Jess."

Pastor Russell tightened his hand around Krispin's. "I'm human, Krispin. And I understand you weren't saved, but even by human standards, that was a very rude proposition."

"Yes, sir."

"Remember, she *is* my sister."

"Yes, sir."

"Good. Now, go on home, and I'll handle the family."

"Thank you." Krispin exited the house by way of the front hall, missing the glances from the living room. As he closed the door behind him, he saw Jess with her hands across her chest and a stance that meant she wasn't about to be bullied around. "Hi, Jess."

"What was that about?"

"I needed to apologize to Pastor Russell for turning down his dinner invitation."

"Why?"

Krispin swallowed. He wasn't ready for this conversation. "It's personal, Jess. Can we leave it at that?"

Her eyes widened. "Why are you here, Krispin?"

"I just told you."

"No, I mean here in Squabbin Bay."

"It seemed like the right place to be."

"What about work?"

"I sold my partnership back to the others."

"Why?"

"Jess, forgive me, but these things are my personal matters, not yours."

She opened her mouth, then closed it. "You're right. I'm sorry."

"Jess, I do have one question for you. Would it be a problem for you if I went to church?"

"You?"

Krispin looked down at the ground and scuffed his shoe against the pavement. "Yeah, me. Would you have a problem if I attended here?"

"Ah, no, I guess not. Are you sure?"

Never more sure of anything in my entire life. "Yeah, I'd like to hear Pastor Russell preach."

"I can't stop you from coming to church, Krispin. It's a free country. You can go to whatever church you like."

"Thanks, I promise to stay out of your way. Good-bye, Jess."

"Bye."

Krispin felt her penetrating gaze sear his shoulders as he walked back toward town and to his cottage. All in all, things went very well. He didn't confess to Jess that he was now a believer. He'd rather have her see it in his life.

ze

Jess returned to the family with a million questions. The first and foremost was what was going on with Krispin Black. He seemed almost lost, but not really. He didn't seem as arrogant as he had after she'd nearly killed him. Had she caused the man to lose his drive, convictions? *Dear Lord, say it isn't so.*

"Jess, what's the matter?" Dena came up beside her and wrapped a loving arm around her shoulders.

"Hey, Mom, sorry."

"Is it Krispin Black?"

Jess nodded.

"Did he do anything?" Jess felt Dena stiffen.

"No, nothing like that. He seems different. Less of a man somehow. I'm afraid the accident took away who he was."

"You know the Lord could have used that to get ahold of him."

"I suppose. He's just so unsure of himself. He didn't make one leering comment."

"Well, that's a good sign."

Jess chuckled. "I guess it is. I've just come to expect a certain behavior from him, and when I didn't see it, it bothered me."

"Honey, I'm glad he wasn't rude again. But I still don't think it's wise for you to be alone with him."

"Oh, I agree. It's just that Jason invited him to dinner tonight."

"Jason? Why would he? Oh, he doesn't know."

"Right."

Dena sighed. "Jason has a very open heart to so many. He's so much like his father in that respect. They see a man in need, and they reach out and go the distance, plus some, to help. I guess Jason saw that need in Mr. Black."

"Yeah. Krispin asked if I had a problem with him coming to church. I told him it was a free country. But I wanted to tell him to go someplace else. I'm not very loving, am I?"

"You're being cautious. I tell you what, if Mr. Black comes to church, why don't you sit with your father and me?"

"I might just do that."

"Good. Now it's time to get back to the family. Clear your head, say a prayer, give yourself a moment, then come back and join us. By the way, I think Brianne's pregnant again. She's looking awfully pale. But they haven't said anything yet."

Jess chuckled. "You get pleasure out of that, don't you?"

Dena laughed. "Not that she's sick but that I have another grandbaby on the way, you betcha. Another one to love and spoil and let the parents do the raising."

"What about when it's my turn?"

"Oh, honey, I'll love your children just as much as I love my other grand-children. You're so much a part of my family I can't imagine you not being here."

"Thanks, Mom. That means the world to me."

"Terry blew it last week?"

"Afraid so, but she doesn't have a clue. She loves her family, but there really isn't room in her life for me at this time. Maybe someday. I have the mother I never had; my life is full."

Dena hugged her. "I love you, sweetheart. Remember, when all is said and done, your father and I love you very much."

"I know, and I appreciate it."

Dena smiled and winked. No words were spoken, but Jess knew Dena saw into her heart, her longing to be a wife and a mother, to have her own family one day. "It'll happen, Jess. Trust the Lord."

Jess sniffed. "I am."

Dena gave Jess a kiss on the cheek and left her to finish putting her emotions back in place. *Thank You for my family. For Dena, she's such a special gift, Lord, to Dad and to me.* Jess paused, then asked, *What's going on with Krispin Black?*

❧

Krispin found himself aware of Jess in the congregation but refused to give her more than a passing thought. Instead he prayed for her on a regular basis. She seemed relaxed enough when he walked past her and nodded hello.

It had been three weeks since the family dinner invitation from Pastor Russell. And they had had three more discipleship meetings. Pastor Russell wanted him to become part of the mentor program in the church, where they teamed up seasoned Christians with new converts. The available men at this time were Wayne Kearns, Jordan Lamont and a Greg Steadman. Krispin had been praying over the choices. He liked Jordan, but his baby was due in the next few weeks. Wayne seemed like a silly idea, being Jess's father. So Krispin settled on Greg Steadman. Greg was also a lobsterman and had a wife and six kids. They were hard-working people, and Krispin was sure Greg didn't understand business. Not that Greg needed to, since he worked for one of the larger fishing companies. He sometimes went out for weeks at a time, which was a drawback for being Krispin's mentor, but Pastor Russell explained that those long sea voyages happened during the winter months, not the summer.

So Krispin found himself pacing back and forth in his shop, waiting on Greg Steadman, his mentor. The old wooden planks that made up the flooring were thick and uneven from years of use.

The large door creaked open. A man with burly shoulders and a huge brown beard stood in the doorway. "You Krispin?"

"Yes, are you Greg Steadman?"

"Ayup!"

Krispin wanted to groan. Greg seemed to be your stereotypical Maine fisherman. "Come on in. The AC is on."

"Feels like it. Whatcha working on?"

"I'm trying to make an ocean kayak using strips of wood."

"A strip-built kayak—awesome. Got some plans?"

"Yes, over there."

Greg walked over to the makeshift table of a couple of sawhorses and a sheet of marine plywood. "Sweet. Ever build one before?"

"Nope, have you?"

"Nope, but I've wanted to. Mind if I lend you a hand?"

"That would be wonderful. I'm still learning how to use these tools."

Greg scanned the workbench. "Nice tools. All new?"

"Afraid so."

"Hey, don't apologize. So what would you like to ask me?"

"I don't know. I guess the first question is how does this mentor thing work?"

Greg sat down and brushed his beard with his hand. "I've found that the best way to approach this is to start by being friends, and through the friendship, you'll have the freedom to ask me questions. I'll challenge you from time to time on your prayer life, scripture reading, and attendance in church, if necessary, but the key is honesty between us. If I can't make a meeting, I'll be frank with you. I have six children, a wife, and things come up. Not to mention work. My summers aren't as busy. I want you to be totally honest with me, as well. Can you do that?"

"Yes, I think so. Am I supposed to tell you all my sins?"

"No. You're welcome to tell me anything you need to discuss. But I don't need a biography. Pastor says you're a computer programmer who writes encryption codes. And until recently you owned a part of a company."

"Yes. I started writing programs when I was twelve."

"Man, I could never have done that. Math and me never got along real well. My daughter, Lissa, she's a snap at it. She's nine and my oldest."

"Has she been tested?"

"Ayup. The school said she scored a ninth-grade level in the third grade. How is that possible?"

"It's possible. I started algebra when I was in the fourth grade."

"Do you think Lissa should be taking algebra next year?"

"Only if she wants to. On the other hand, private lessons might be better. It was really hard on me in school to be an overachiever. The other kids weren't as excited about my math as I or the teachers were."

"I wouldn't want to have her picked on in school." Greg looked back at the tools. "So tell me why you're building a kayak. To replace the one Jess Kearns ran over?"

Krispin let out a nervous chuckle. "Yes and no. I need something different to work on. I don't know if woodworking will do it, but I'm burnt out with computer programming. Don't get me wrong, I still can do it. I just don't have the passion for it that I once did. After I achieved all that I set out to, I felt empty."

"Ah, I hear ya. That's when you started searching for the answers to life and found the Lord, right?"

"Yes, but that hasn't totally changed how I feel about my work."

"Well, my daddy always said a man can't do much better than to work with his hands. At the end of the day, he has something to show for all his hard work. I think woodworking might just be the ticket. I'm no craftsman with woodworking, but I can saw a straight line and use a router and a few of the other tools you've purchased. Would you like some help?"

"That would be wonderful, yes. I do believe I could use your help."

"Great. I'll come around nine tomorrow morning, and we can get started. What do you want to learn first?"

"The table saw, then the planer."

"Not a problem." Greg looked over at the wood. "Just how many kayaks do you plan on making?"

"One."

Greg whistled. "Do you know you have enough wood for two, possibly three?"

Krispin chuckled. "I figured I'd make a lot of mistakes."

"Ah. Makes sense. Okay, I'll see you in the morning." And just like that, Greg Steadman left. Krispin sat down on the stool and replayed the entire conversation. Greg was an interesting guy. There was more to him than his rough exterior would suggest.

"I think I'm going to like working with him, Lord. He's down to earth and a straight shooter. Something I haven't had a lot of experience with in the business world. Thanks for sending a man who's going to stretch me."

❧

Jess flew through the house, looking for her binoculars. Krispin Black was holed up in one of the old warehouses on the other side of the harbor. She hadn't been sure she'd seen him going in and out of the old building a couple times, but today she could see his Mustang outside and knew he was there. What he was doing? She didn't have a clue, but she wanted to find out.

It made no sense, him wanting to live in Squabbin Bay. And while he'd been right, it wasn't her business to know what he was doing here, she certainly couldn't just sit by and wait. What was her obsession with this man? The fact that she nearly killed him made her feel like she had a certain responsibility toward him, which was foolish, or so she told herself over and over again.

She had no business spying on him. She stopped looking for the binoculars and sat down in the easy chair in the living room. Her Bible was on the side table. She pulled it into her lap and started to read.

Father God, why is Krispin Black living in Squabbin Bay? She paused long enough to wait for an answer, hoping she'd hear God's voice on this. Instead she looked down at her open Bible and found a verse she read many times before. Jeremiah 29:13: *"You will seek me and find me when you seek me with all your heart."*

Father, have I not given You all of my heart? Is this why I'm so bothered by Krispin's presence in town?

Lord, what is in my heart that I haven't given over to You? I've confessed my attraction to Krispin. I know he's not saved, and I won't get involved with him. Are my feelings for Krispin keeping me from giving You all my heart? Lord, I'm afraid of him. I'm afraid of my reactions to him. He seems so different. Is it my fault? Did the accident cause this change in him?

"Oh, Lord, forgive me for not trusting You with Krispin. Help me get over my obsession with him."

"Jess?"

Jess turned to see Randi standing at her back door with her hand on her protruding stomach. "Jess, help me, please."

Jess jumped up. "What's the matter?"

"I think I'm in labor."

"Oh no!" Jess ran to the back door and helped her best friend in. "What happened?"

Randi chuckled. "What do you mean, what happened?"

"I'm sorry. Why do you think you're in labor?"

Randi's body convulsed.

"Oh dear, don't worry. I'll call Jordan. Where is he?"

"In Boston."

"You've got to be kidding!"

Randi shook her head. Jess rolled her eyes heavenward, grabbed the phone, and called the fire department. Then she left a message on Jordan's cell phone and called Randi's parents. Jordan's return call came in at the same time Randi's parents and the ambulance arrived. Randi held on to Jess. "Jess, you've got to come with me. I need a coach."

"Randi, I'm no coach."

"You're the closest thing I've got. Stay with me, please."

"Okay, but only until Jordan gets back." *Lord, help Jordan get back in time.*

Randi's water broke, and Jess nearly fainted. *O Lord, help me. There's no way I'll make it through this.* Randi squeezed Jess's arm. "Help me breathe, Jess."

"Breathe? Oh, you mean like those prenatal breathing exercises."

Randi nodded. Jess held on to Randi's hand. Together they breathed the first level of Lamaze breathing technique. She remembered the second level, but the third and fourth totally escaped her memory. Frankly, she hadn't paid that much attention when Randi had showed them to her when she and Jordan were taking the prenatal classes.

Josie Smith took Randi's pulse and other vitals. "When is your due date, Randi?"

"End of August."

"Guess this little one doesn't want to wait." Josie smiled. "You're doing fine. I need to check the dilation."

Randi nodded. Jess's eyes widened, then she turned to the gathering crowd. "Everyone out, now!" Jess demanded.

Josie and Randi chuckled. Josie added, "It's her first. Trust me, I've delivered quite a few little ones over the years. You're doing fine, Randi."

"Thanks, Josie."

"Where's Jordan?" Josie asked while doing the examination. "Three centimeters. You've got some time."

Randi let out a pent-up breath. "Thanks. He's in Boston. We thought we had enough time."

"Apparently the little one wants to see her or his mommy and daddy now." Josie covered Randi, then removed her plastic gloves.

"What's wrong with Jess?" Jess heard a winded male voice call out.

"Ain't Jess; it's Randi. She's having a baby," someone from the crowd called out.

"Oh," he mumbled. At that point Jess recognized the voice of Krispin Black. "Where's Jordan?"

"Boston," said another.

"Where are they taking Randi?" Krispin asked again.

"Blue Hill Hospital in Ellsworth, most likely." Jess couldn't help but notice Krispin's curiosity in this entire event.

"Jessss!" Randi cried out.

"I'm here, Randi. I'm here." Jess held on to Randi's hand and followed the EMTs out the door and into the ambulance. Krispin was on his cell phone as she got in. *That's odd. Who would he be telling?*

Chapter 7

K rispin walked away from Jess's house as they wheeled Randi into the ambulance. "Jordan, it's me, Krispin Black. I imagine you're trying to get home for Randi right away."

"Yeah, how'd you know? Never mind. It's Squabbin Bay."

"Right. Look, I have a friend who owns a chopper and lives in Boston. Would you like me to call him?"

"Yes."

"Okay, I'll call you right back." Krispin clicked through the address book on his phone, found Michael James's private phone number, and dialed. A few minutes later Krispin had the location and directions finalized with Michael. Krispin called Jordan and passed on the information.

"Thanks, Krispin. I appreciate it."

"No problem. I'll take care of the fuel expense, unless you barter with Michael for some photos. He's always needing some promotional shots."

"All right, thanks again."

"As a favor to me, I doubt Michael will even bother charging you, but I've always offered."

"Gotcha. I'll see you later. Thanks again, Krispin."

"You're welcome." Krispin headed back to his shop. He wanted to go to the hospital and wait to hear how Randi was doing but knew it wasn't his place. He'd have to wait in town like most of the folks around here.

Greg was leaning against the doorframe. "So what happened?"

"I'm sorry I'm late. Randi Lamont went into labor."

Greg chuckled. "I know that. You forget we live in a very small town. I also heard you called out wondering what happened to Jess. What's going on with you two?"

"Nothing. I'm not worthy of her."

"Worthy?"

"Yeah. You know some of my past. Well, when it comes to women, I've had more than my share. According to God, a lot more. Anyway, I don't think I have the right to consider marriage when I've messed up so badly and hurt so many."

"Hmm, so how do you see Jess?"

"She's pure, untouched by the world. She deserves better than me."

Greg chuckled. "Well that's probably true, but you're missing a point."

"What?"

"You're redeemed. As in you've been forgiven of all the wrong things you've done. You stand before God as one free from the past because you've repented and given your past to God."

"I know, but—"

"Ain't no buts about it. You're redeemed, same as she. So tell me again why you can't have a relationship with Jess?"

"You mean besides the fact that she nearly killed me the first time we met?"

Greg roared with laughter. "Yeah, besides that. Oh, and the fact that she saved your life."

Krispin laughed. "That, too." He walked over to his table saw. "You said you'd teach me how to use this today."

"Fair enough, but you and Jess is not a closed subject."

"It is if I'm not ready to talk about it."

"I'll give ya that." Greg joined him at the table saw. "You see this plate?" He pointed to the small plate that had a long, narrow slit where the blade came through. "If we remove it, like this, we have access to remove and tighten a blade."

Greg continued the demonstration, and by the end of the day, Krispin was cutting, raising, and lowering the blade and knew just about every piece of the saw. He found Greg to be a good teacher—patient, never belittling him for what he didn't know. Which was quite a lot. He only knew which tools to buy because of the various articles he'd read online and from the kayak-building forum where folks listed the tools they used for their projects.

"Tomorrow we'll work on the planer. All this wood needs to be planed to the same size."

"Right." Krispin looked over at the rectangular frame. He'd assembled it but didn't have a clue as to how it worked. He knew he would put the boards in one way, and it would automatically feed them out the other side, but how the blades were to be set, he didn't know. Tonight he'd read up on the instruction manual for the planer and the router. Both needed to be learned.

Greg left, and Krispin cleaned up the sawdust from all the cutting he'd done. He liked the feel of the wood in his hands and the various textures of the different kinds of wood.

The door creaked open. Without turning, Krispin asked, "Did you forget something?"

"Not exactly." Jess's voice resounded in his ears.

"Jess. I'm sorry, I thought you were someone else."

"I gathered. What are you doing in here?"

"Cleaning up." He knew it was a glib answer, but he really preferred that she stayed on her side of Squabbin Bay and not his. "How's Randi?"

A sweet smile rose on her lips. Krispin turned back to sweeping up the sawdust.

"Randi is fine. Jordan arrived in time to relieve me. I've never been so grateful. Having babies is messy business."

"I wouldn't know myself, but I'm glad I'm a man. Has the baby arrived?" Krispin dumped the full dustpan into the garbage can.

"Not yet. The doctor said it could still take some time." Jess walked around the room. "What are you building?"

"A kayak, I hope."

She glanced over at the pile of wood. "You have enough material here for several."

"I figure I'm going to be making a lot of mistakes."

"Ah. Krispin, I need to know why you're here. I know it probably is none of my business. . . ."

Krispin put the dustpan and broom aside. "Jess, I will leave town if you're that uncomfortable with me living here."

"As much as I'd love to say yes to your leaving town, it isn't my place to do so. I'm thinking we should talk a bit, maybe get to know one another."

"Why are you so uncomfortable around me?"

She leveled a gaze at him that would have tumbled a brickyard with its intensity. And he understood it had been his forward nature and rude comments. "Jess, I promise never to speak that way to you again. I was out of line, completely out of line. I'd like to say I was out of my mind. But I wasn't. I'd become a man who thought mostly of myself. Please forgive me."

She paused for a moment, then released her gaze. "All right. But it will be awhile before I can trust you."

"I understand."

"You're letting your hair grow out?"

Krispin shrugged his shoulders. "I guess. I've kept it so short for business. I figured I could skip seeing the barber for a couple months."

"It looks like it's going to come in curly."

Krispin chuckled. "You don't know the meaning of my name, do you?"

"Afraid not. What is it?"

" 'Curly hair.' The way my mother tells it, she and Dad took one look at my full head of curly hair and named me Krispin. Before I was born, they were planning on naming me Walter."

"Krispin is much better."

"Thanks. I've been happy with it. It's unique, and because of that, I think it's helped give me an edge in business."

"Speaking of business, don't you have a partnership in a company?"

"*Had.* I sold out."

"Why?"

Krispin fought the desire to tell her he'd become a Christian. Jess needed to see the change in him before he told her. *Actions speak louder than words,* his father always said. "Let's just say, I wasn't very happy with my life."

"Secrets?"

"Omissions."

Jess pouted. She had a beautiful pout, he decided. "Well, I'm going home. I've got to lock up now."

"Oh, sorry." Jess bolted toward the door. "Krispin, why did you come running over to my place when you saw the ambulance?"

"I'd hate to have anything bad happen to my rescuer," he admitted.

"You seem different." Jess reached for the door.

"I am. And I think it's for the good."

Jess gave a slight nod of the head. "Yeah, I like this new you much better than the one I pulled out of the harbor."

Krispin smiled and fought off the desire to say, *I aim to please*, knowing it would make him look superficial in her eyes. But he did want to please Jess. His prayers for her grew with intensity each passing day. He'd fallen in love with Jess—no longer with the vile selfishness of his past but with a healthy respect for her and a desire to see her succeed. He wanted to ask her out to dinner but knew she'd take the invitation the wrong way. Instead he simply said, "Good night, Jess."

"Night, Krispin."

≥≈

The next morning Jess got up thirty minutes earlier to gather in the lobsters. By midmorning she was done. She went home, showered, and drove to the hospital to meet Randi and Jordan's little one. The joy on the parents' faces was so contagious Jess also beamed. "She's beautiful," Jess whispered.

"Yeah, she is." Jordan clicked off a couple of pictures of Jess, Randi, and Ella Ruth, Squabbin Bay's newest resident.

"Would you like to hold her?" Randi offered.

"Love to. Do I need to put on a gown or something?"

"No, just wash your hands; that will be fine." Randi handed her daughter over to Jess with a gentle kiss on the forehead.

Jess cradled the tiny bundle in her arms. "I don't think I've ever held someone so tiny."

A long moment of silence filled the room, broken only by Jordan's clicking of the camera. "How do you put up with that?"

Randi laughed. "I'm still getting used to it."

"It looks like she'll have Randi's dark eyes." Jordan beamed. "See how black the irises are?"

Randi had a very unique characteristic in her nearly black eyes. And Jess knew that Jordan had always been fascinated by them. They reminded him of his Native American great-grandmother. "They're beautiful."

"Mom said my eyes were black when I was first born, too," Randi admitted.

Ella Ruth started to squirm. Her little fists poked out of the blanket. Her face scrunched up, and a little yelp came out.

"Must be feeding time." Jess handed the baby back to Randi. "She's very beautiful. You guys must be so pleased."

"The Lord's blessed us. She's fine. They're watching her bilirubin count to make sure her liver is working fine, but all indications are that she'll be able to leave the hospital with Randi tomorrow."

Jess stayed a few minutes longer. But Ella Ruth was hungry, so Jess left to allow Randi to breastfeed her baby.

The desire to have her own little one occupied her thoughts on the drive home. She'd never been one to ooh and ahh over an infant, but this one hit closer to home. Her best friend was now a mother. Jess didn't even have a prospect for a husband.

She went to the office and worked on co-op business until old Ben Costa came in. "Hey there, Jess. Is your dad around?" Ben had retired a couple years ago, but he kept his boat and a couple pots just to keep himself busy.

"I believe he's out at the old Ford place. What's up?"

"Nothin' really. Just saw your grandpa in town, and I wanted to make sure he was aware."

Jess sighed. Her grandfather's summer of stealing the other lobstermen's lobsters had been hardest on her father, but Ben had suffered a lot, too. Even worse, that same summer, a couple of teens running fast and loose had set his house on fire. Then old Ben himself had left his cigar burning and the gas on in his boat, and he had lost that, as well. Thankfully, Ben's insurance covered a large portion of his losses. "We know. Daddy has Grandpa and Grandma living at the house with them."

"Has he been able to kick that nasty habit?"

"Yes. Grandpa goes to Gamblers Anonymous regularly, and Grandma takes care of the finances."

"Good. Your grandpa was a good man. Nothing like sin to cloud a man's judgment. Well, that's all. I just wanted to be sure."

"No problem, Ben. Come by any time."

Ben waved as he shuffled down the steps. For a man in his seventies, he was spry enough. Jess noticed he held the railing tightly as he took each step. At the same time, she noticed Krispin Black walking into the Dockside Grill. She wondered if he ever cooked for himself. She'd seen him many times coming out of the restaurant with a meal to go.

Jess looked back at the quarterlies. The income this year was better than last. The number of lobsters harvested was a bit more, but not too much more. One thing Jess had learned early on was not to glut the market with too much lobster.

Mark Bisbee ran the warehouse for the co-op. Jess placed a call to him. "Hi,

Mark. How's it going?"

"Fine, fine. Orders are coming in steady. And so far we've had enough lobster to meet the needs."

"Wonderful. Did you receive the order I faxed from the Weathervane Restaurants?"

"Ayup, got it right here. You gave them a mighty nice price."

"Yeah, we'll lose a nickel a lobster, but I think the size of the order will keep us in the black."

"No doubt. They have restaurants in three states now, and they're still growing. They like getting the freshest lobsters they can."

"And we aim to please. Thanks, Mark. Keep me posted."

"Will do. Talk with you later. Bye."

Jess listened to the disconnection hum for a moment, then placed the phone back in its holder. With her work done, she looked out at the harbor. The ocean was calm. The prospect of paddling her kayak through the waters seemed like a good idea. She locked up the office and ran over to the boathouse where she and her father stored their kayaks along with all their fishing equipment during the summer months. Within minutes she was dressed in her wetsuit and carrying her kayak over her head to the small dock.

Once inside, she paddled her way through the harbor and over to Krispin's warehouse. She pulled the boat up onto the small dock outside his building and knocked on the seaside door.

A moment later, Greg Steadman appeared. "Hi, Jess. What can I do you for?"

"Uh, I was looking for Krispin."

"He's here. Hang on."

Greg slipped behind the gray weathered boards that made up the door. A couple of minutes later, Krispin appeared. "Hi, Jess. What's up?"

"I thought maybe you'd like to go kayaking with me. But I see you're busy."

"Afraid so. Greg's teaching me how to use a router."

"Ah. Well, I won't keep you. See you around." Jess headed back to her kayak.

"Jess?"

Jess turned back.

"Thanks for the offer. Maybe some other time."

"Of course."

Why, why, why, did I do that? He's going to think I'm chasing him now. Stupid! Stupid! Stupid!

Jess worked her way out of the harbor and to a small island that she and Randi used to play on when they were younger. They had made a small hut out of driftwood. Jess found the remains of a childhood castle and the makings of a new fort by some other child. Upon closer inspection, some of the missing wood had come from their castle. Jess smiled.

She sat down on a rock and drew in the sand with a stick. She wasn't a child any longer. The days of kings and queens, princes and princesses were long gone. She was a woman, alone in this world. Alone for the very first time. She scanned the harbor. Boats of all different shapes and sizes painted the horizon. She knew most of the people on those vessels, so why did she feel so alone?

Her father was married now. Her best friend was married and had a baby. The co-op didn't demand every waking minute she had, and even lobstering only took up a small amount of her time each day. She was bored. Alone and bored was not a good combination in Squabbin Bay.

Was it time to send out her résumé again? Was it time to go back to corporate America and enter the business she'd gone to school for?

The co-op still needed her, she argued. She had a place in Squabbin Bay. So why was she so uncomfortable here now?

The ever so delightful image of Krispin Black flooded her senses. *Lord, it isn't fair. Why am I attracted to men who don't put You first in their lives?*

Chapter 8

Krispin watched Jess paddle away. *Why does she keep coming around?*

"Penny for your thoughts?"

Startled, Krispin turned back toward Greg. "Sorry."

"What's the matter, Krispin? Have you not forgiven yourself?"

"It's not that. I've been trying real hard to avoid Jessica Kearns. And now she's stopping by. Why would she do that?"

Greg chuckled. "Oh, I don't know. Maybe she likes you."

"She's afraid of me."

"Pardon?"

Krispin sighed, then filled Greg in on his and Jess's conversation yesterday.

"So let me get this straight. You promised not to say or do anything crude, rude, or socially unacceptable to her, and you're confused by her appearance here this morning?"

Krispin nodded.

"Seems obvious to me. She's attracted to you."

"But—"

Greg raised one of his beefy fingers. "You're redeemed, Krispin. But if you were as rude as you said you were, I imagine your bigger problem will be getting past her father."

Krispin plopped down on a stool. Going head to head with Wayne Kearns, confessing his sin toward his daughter, struck him as both undesirable and impossible.

"Tell ya what. I'm going to go home now. Give this matter some prayer and thought. Wayne has a real talent with wood. You might want to ask for his help."

Krispin shook his head no. "I asked for you to be my mentor."

"I wasn't saying I'd stop being your mentor. You're a good man, Krispin. Your heart has changed since the day of the accident. Relax and give yourself a break. I'll see you tomorrow."

Greg left without a further word. Krispin sat in a quandary. He liked Jess. No, he loved Jess. But he had to admit he didn't feel good enough for her. Compounding the problem, he respected Wayne. What father would want to know the unholy thoughts a man has entertained or, in his case, said to his daughter? Yet was it the right course of action? Should he apologize to Wayne? Should he seek Wayne's blessing to pursue a relationship with Jess? Should he even consider a relationship with Jess?

Yesterday he thought they could be friends. Today the very thought of it scared him.

He spent the next few minutes in prayer, then closed up the shop and went home. What he didn't expect to see was Wayne Kearns's truck in his driveway. His posture was noticeably rigid.

"Mr. Kearns."

"Mr. Black," Wayne's voice strained.

"What can I do for you?"

"I want to know what kind of a game you're playing with my daughter, Mr. Black. You've seemed to convince Pastor Russell you're a changed man, but frankly, I don't see it."

Krispin sighed. "What exactly are you not sure of? Would you like to go inside while we talk?"

Wayne nodded. "Look, I'm sure you're a good enough person. You did drop the lawsuit. . . ."

"I never filed one," Krispin interjected.

"Right. Okay, but why did you come to Squabbin Bay?"

Krispin let out a nervous chuckle and held the door open to his cottage. "Because of you."

"Me?"

"Yeah. It's a long story. Well, perhaps not that long. But would you like a soft drink or something?"

"Sure. Got any beer?"

"No. You drink beer?"

"No, but I was checking if you did."

"Ah." Krispin held the door of the refrigerator open. "Here ya go. You're free to search my cabinets, too. Now if you'd come at the time of the accident, that would be a different story."

"Gotcha. Let's sit down, Mr. Black."

They went into the living room. Wayne sat on the couch with his legs spread and elbows resting on his knees. "Jason says you've prayed for salvation. Why?"

"Because I came to realize I wasn't happy with my life. I've had fortune and fame, as they say. Although my fame is really in the work I've done, but I've lived a lifestyle that was very worldly. Things came easy for me. . .too easy. But I was empty. And my short time in Squabbin Bay showed me another side of life, the ability to be content with little, to enjoy who and where you are. And frankly, your words drove me to reconsider my life."

Wayne relaxed. "So you've really given your life to the Lord?"

"Yes, sir. You can ask Greg Steadman. He's my mentor, and he's been helping me in the shop."

Wayne smiled. "I already spoke with Greg."

Krispin knitted his eyebrows. "Then why—"

"I'm a father concerned for his daughter. Jess shared with Dena, and I know you propositioned her on more than one occasion."

Krispin felt his face grow hot with humiliation. "I'm really sorry. I was totally out of line."

"Yes, you were."

"Mr. Kearns, I am attracted to Jess. But I don't want a woman in my life right now. I don't think I can handle it."

Krispin felt the weight of Wayne's scrutinizing gaze.

"I think you may be right."

Krispin relaxed.

"What is the status of your relationship with Jess?"

"Nothing more than casual friends, if that."

"Mr. Black, I'm not blind. I saw Jess at your warehouse yesterday and then again today with her kayak. And the whole town is buzzing about how you ran over to her place, concerned that something had happened to Jess when Randi went into labor."

Krispin bent his head low and collected his thoughts. "Jess came to me yesterday and today. The concern for her welfare is genuine. I do care for her. But as I said, I don't think it is wise for me to be considering having a relationship. I want to get my life right with the Lord first." *And I'm still not confident that God would allow me to have a wife*, he silently added. "Also, I told Jess I'd leave town if it was too uncomfortable having me live here."

"I see. Let's talk about that. If you came here to try and refocus your life, have you done that? I accept your confession in believing in Jesus Christ now, but is that all you needed to accomplish by coming to Squabbin Bay?"

Krispin had given this a lot of thought. "Mr. Kearns, can I be perfectly honest with you?"

Wayne nodded.

Krispin poured out his heart—his fears, his frustrations, the things he'd been learning and reevaluating in his life, everything that had been spinning in his mind for the past year and especially during the three months since the accident.

"Krispin, you've come a long way. I'm happy for you. But you must realize you're not the only person who's led the kind of life you did before you got saved. I myself was no gem. God forgives completely. You need to forgive yourself."

"Greg said something very similar."

"If you like, you can feel free to call me if you're dealing with any serious temptations."

Krispin's face reddened.

"It's Jess, isn't it?"

Krispin swallowed. "Yes."

"When Dena and I first started to get to know one another, we dealt with some strong emotions waking up in both of us. You should do just fine if you give the matter to the Lord and give it a lot of prayer. He'll help, trust me. I know from firsthand experience."

Krispin felt even more embarrassed, if that were possible. "I don't know if Jess feels the same way about me. We hardly know one another."

"Trust the Lord. If He's designed the two of you for marriage to one another, then it will happen. If not, He'll give you the strength to get past your affections for her right now."

"How can you be so blunt about this? It's your daughter we're speaking about."

"It is my daughter, but I learned not too long ago I had to trust her to make the right choice, and so far, she has.

"Now, tell me about the strip-line kayak you're building with Greg."

And just like that the subject changed. Krispin decided he liked Wayne Kearns and respected him even more.

❧

The following day, Jess sat down at her computer and punched in her password. Something was wrong. She opened her e-mail. It had been downloaded recently. The fine hairs on the back of her neck began to tingle.

Jess's hand shook. This computer was tied into the co-op's computer. Someone must have been on her computer. Why? She looked over the various files. She gathered the backup disks from the past three months, then called Randi.

"Hey, Randi, how are you? How's the baby?"

"We're both doing well. It will take a bit to get used to no sleep, though."

"I've heard that. Hey, I hate to cut this short, but I'm in a bit of a jam here, and I'm wondering if you can help me out." Jess went on to explain.

"First, call the sheriff. Second, call Krispin. He's an encryption software genius of some sort. He doesn't know it, but I checked into him. He's considered an expert in the field."

"Really?"

"Yup, and I'm sure he can tell you how your system was breached and how to fix it."

"All right. Do you have his phone number?"

"Sure, hang on." Randi was gone from the phone for a moment. "Here ya go." She gave Jess his home and cell phone numbers.

"Thanks, Randi."

"You're welcome. I think it's probably a couple of local kids. But still, you can't allow anyone to break into your system like that."

"Right. I'll talk with you later. 'Bye."

Jess hung up and called the sheriff, then left a message on Krispin's cell phone to come to the co-op as soon as possible. She headed to the office to check the computers at the co-op.

She was surprised to see Krispin Black waiting outside the office when she arrived.

"Hi, Jess. What's the problem?"

"Randi says you're an encryption expert."

"I write encryption software. Why?"

"I think someone broke into my home computer."

"Oh boy, any money missing?" Krispin asked.

"As best as I could tell, no. Can you help?"

"I can try. First, do you have backup copies?"

"Right here." She lifted the small bundle of disks.

"Good, let's get to work." He held the door open and let her pass.

Jess watched as Krispin fired up the computer. Within minutes, he had a bunch of numerals and digits that didn't make any sense to her. Jess left him to do his job and went to the desk to sort through the mail.

"Morning, Jess. What seems to be the problem?" Sheriff McKean said as he entered the co-op.

"I think someone broke into my home computer."

"Interesting. How do you know this?"

"My e-mail had been downloaded when I wasn't home. Krispin's looking on the office computer to see if anyone's tampered with them."

"All right. Keep me posted on Krispin's discoveries. He is qualified, right?"

"According to Randi, yes."

"Good enough for me. I'll see you later."

Three hours later, Krispin got up from the computer. "Jess, you're fine. I only saw remote access from your home computer, nothing else."

"What time? Can you tell that?"

"Not with this software. I've uploaded a better encryption software package and changed all your access passwords. You can change them again after I leave." Krispin handed her a small piece of paper.

"If anyone got in, it would have been through that computer. Do you keep your doors locked?"

"No. I guess I should, huh?"

"If you're going to have access from your home computer to this one, yes. However, I'll need to encrypt your home computer, as well. At the moment, no one can enter this computer without your permission, and that means even looking at pop-up windows on the Internet."

"How much do I owe you?"

"Nothing. It's my own program; not even my company had access to this one. However, the password is twenty-five digits. You'll need to keep the key handy but in a safe place."

"Twenty-five?"

"I can reduce it, but until we find out who's trying to get in, I felt higher encryption would be wiser."

"You're right. Sorry."

"Also, I cleaned up your hard drive. You should notice it running faster." Krispin smiled.

"You're good at this, aren't you?"

"I have a knack."

Jess laughed. "I'd say that was an understatement. Okay, why don't I take you to my house and I'll fix us some lunch while you work on my home computer?"

"I'd love to, but it will have to be later. I have an appointment for lunch."

"Sure, just let me know when, and I'll work around your schedule."

Krispin placed his hand on the doorknob. "Thanks for calling me, Jess. I'm glad I was able to help."

"Thanks for coming. I was so scared someone got into the financial records or even to the bank account information."

"You're safe now. But you might want to speak with the bank and change your account information, just as an extra precaution. They can give you a new account number in no time and transfer the funds over."

"I'll go to the bank right away. Thanks again, Krispin."

"You're welcome." Krispin left and went to his car.

Jess watched with interest. He seemed more confident today. As if things were falling into place for him. Jess prayed a short prayer of thanks for Krispin and asked the Lord to continue to draw Krispin close to Him.

&

Krispin hurried over to the shop and met Greg just as he was about to pull out of the parking lot. "Hey, sorry about that, Greg. Jess had an issue with her computer."

"No problem. The wife's looking forward to meeting you. I hope you like lobster salad."

Krispin smiled. "Yes." Whenever he did leave Squabbin Bay, he probably wouldn't be eating lobster for two years.

"Great, 'cause she made minestrone soup."

Krispin roared. "Thanks."

"I remembered you said you liked it well enough but it wasn't your all-time favorite food."

"Touché."

"Follow me."

Krispin settled back behind the wheel and followed Greg in his old pickup truck. They passed through town and drove out past a huge field peppered with boulders. Greg's home was set back in the woods and up a windy dirt road. Krispin would have to wash and wax his car this weekend.

Pine trees lined the path. A two-story clapboard house painted white with blue trim spread across the clearing. Kids' toys littered the front yard. A couple of bicycles leaned against the front steps. No one would doubt a truckload of children lived in this house.

Their home was humble but clean. The kids were bright, and Lissa, Greg's oldest, knew her math just like her father had said. Bryan, Greg's seven-year-old son, brought in a boat he'd made from a couple of pieces of wood. "See, it floats, too," he boasted.

"Wow, that's great. Maybe you can come and give your dad and me a hand at the shop."

"Really?" Bryan turned toward his father. "Can I, Dad?"

"Since it's all right with Mr. Black, then maybe someday. You need to mind your mother."

"Yes, sir." Bryan ran off to play with the others.

"Mr. Black, can you show me how to do algebra?" Lissa asked.

"Now kids, give Mr. Black some space. Lissa, he's here for lunch, not to be your math tutor."

"Sorry, Daddy."

"I'll be happy to show her a few things. Does she have a book?"

Lissa pulled out a book from under her chair. "Right here. Mommy got it from the library for me after Daddy told her that it was all right for me to learn algebra."

Krispin chuckled. "Okay, how about after lunch? I'll spend a few minutes with you before I go."

"Thank you, Mr. Black. That would be awesome."

Jayne, Greg's wife, set a bowl of minestrone soup and some homemade rolls of Portuguese sweet bread beside him. "Thank you, Jayne. You don't know how good it is to have a home-cooked meal."

"You're not a cook, Mr. Black?"

"Call me Krispin, and no, I'm not."

"I thought most men were these days." She served Greg, then the children, then herself. *The perfect hostess,* he mused.

"I never had time for it. I ordered out a lot. But in Squabbin Bay, take-out eateries are limited."

Jayne laughed. "That's stating it mildly. It took me a few years to adjust to life up here."

"Where were you from?"

"I met Greg in college. I grew up near Hartford, Connecticut."

"A city girl."

Jayne giggled. "Not anymore. I've been countrified, as they like to say."

The meal progressed with light chatter. They were a happy family. After the meal, Krispin sat down with Lissa and helped her to understand the first chapter. Doing the algebraic problems wasn't difficult, but helping her understand concepts behind how to use the math problems took a bit longer than he expected. On the other hand, she was only nine years old and had an incredible mind for mathematics.

He returned to town and went over to the co-op to see if this was a good time for him to work on Jess's computer. It was a typical Northeastern-type cottage that had been converted to a place of business, with grayed weathered shingles and white trim paint around the windows. It had been built into the side of the cliff overlooking the harbor.

Krispin got out of his car and strolled up the walkway to the open front door. Jess stood face-to-face with a stranger, medium build and brown hair. As Krispin watched, the man leaned over and kissed Jess.

"Jess?" Krispin's heart stopped.

Chapter 9

Krispin," Jess gasped. "Trevor, back off."

"Come on, Jess. I'm sorry. Please say you'll get back with me," Trevor pleaded.

"No. Now back off!"

"You heard the lady," Krispin said in a firm voice.

"Is he the reason you won't get back together with me?" Trevor demanded but took a couple steps away from her. Jess had never been so happy to see Krispin.

"Mr. Black and I are friends."

"Right, and I was born yesterday."

"Trev, it's over. It has been for over a year, so why are you here? Never mind, I don't want to know. Go back home to Boston, Trev."

Krispin planted his feet and puffed up his chest. Jess saw she had a defender if needed. If anything, dating Trevor had taught her that he had no backbone. He would not go up against Krispin Black or any other man, for that matter.

"I thought—"

Jess stopped him. "It's over, Trev. I don't love you. Go home."

Trevor started to take a step toward her, then cast a second glance at Krispin and headed out the door. "You'll regret this, Jess."

"No, I only regret the time I spent with you," she mumbled after he walked out the door.

"I'm sorry you had to see that," she said, turning to Krispin.

"Who is he?"

"An old boyfriend from college. Thanks for coming when you did. I was about to smack him."

"I'd be happy to oblige."

Jess laughed. "Seriously, I appreciate your coming in when you did."

"Divine intervention," Krispin said and turned to watch Trevor's departure from the door window.

"Is he gone?"

"He's pulling out now."

"Good." Jess crumpled in her seat. "I loved him once."

"What happened, if you don't mind me asking?"

"He wanted me to live in Boston. But it's more than that. He wouldn't get a job out of college. He's been living off his parents ever since. I guess they got wise and kicked him out. He's incredibly lazy. I never saw it when we were in school. He did his schoolwork and even worked a part-time job. I don't know what happened. Once we were out of school, he changed. And to think I almost . . ." Jess let her words trail off. Confessing her past relationship with Trevor to Krispin Black seemed totally inappropriate.

"What?"

"Never mind."

"Right, okay. I came by to see if you wanted me to work on your home computer."

"Yes, that would be great. Let me finish a couple of things; then I'll take you over to my house."

Krispin sat down and picked up one of the annual reports of the co-op and thumbed through it while she finished off a couple of e-mails.

"I'm ready."

Krispin placed the report back on the small table.

"What do you think?"

"Interesting. So you founded the co-op?"

"Yeah, it's based off what the cranberry growers did years ago when they formed their co-op."

"It's a sound plan. You might want to consider. . ."

"What?"

"Sorry, force of habit. I don't know your business. I was just thinking speculatively."

"I'm all ears."

"No, Jess. I shouldn't get involved. It's your business, and you're doing a fine job."

"Thanks, that means a lot."

They got in their cars, and Krispin followed Jess. She kept watching her rearview mirror. The man remained a mystery. It took less than ten minutes to get to her place from the co-op. Jess let him inside the cottage, then left to go to the grocery store. "I'll be right back," she called from the door as he settled in at the computer.

≈

Krispin found the problem. Someone had been on Jess's computer the day before. Whoever it was had made three password attempts before figuring out her password. His thoughts drifted to Trevor. If he was as lazy as Jess said he was, he might have been after some quick cash from Jess.

Krispin looked to see if Jess's bank records had been accessed by her computer yesterday. They had. But by her or the intruder? Krispin got up from the computer and started to pace. He picked up his cell phone and looked at his incoming calls. He called the number that Jess had called from earlier today. The house phone rang. Krispin hung up.

SUITED FOR LOVE

He went back to her computer and found a Trojan program that would silently run in the background and gather all her financial information. It had been installed yesterday. To the best of his knowledge, it hadn't been accessed for its information yet. Krispin deleted the nasty program and installed his encryption program on her computer.

Jess returned. "Hey, how's it going?"

"Jess, someone has been on this computer."

"What?"

"I found evidence they tried three times for your password, then they got into the portal to the co-op's computer. I checked your online banking records. One log-in occurred yesterday. Was that you?"

"No. Wait, yes. Last night."

"Okay, that's the only instance I found. However, as with the co-op's bank account, you should change your account information, as well."

She glanced up at the clock. He did, also. Five of five was too late. "I'll do that first thing tomorrow. I'll have Dad go lobstering in the morning."

"Jess, I don't want to scare you, but you have all your information on this computer. Someone could steal your identity with the information on here."

"I knew I should have bought a Mac."

Krispin laughed. "There is that. However, I've put my encryption program on here and another twenty-five-digit password."

Jess sighed.

"Hey, I could have made it forty-nine digits."

"No way. I'd never use the thing. Please tell me you're just scaring me."

"True, I am scaring you. You could take some simple steps to protect yourself, and you won't need a twenty-five digit password forever. The more difficult encryption is to protect you because someone has tried and succeeded. What I find odd is that nothing is missing. However, I did find a Trojan horse program that would gather all the information they would need, like credit card numbers, bank numbers, your social security number, and things as harmless as your e-mails to your friends. All of that is to say I don't know who is after your information or what information they are after. It could be somebody just after the co-op information. Or it could be more personal. I hate to ask, but is Trevor capable—"

"Trevor? Nah. Well, wait, he does lug his computer around with him every-where he goes. I thought he was always playing games online, though."

"It might not be him. And if he's after money, why would he have waited, when he had access to your accounts?"

"Because I don't have that much in my account right now."

"Possibly." Krispin tapped the top of the computer. "You're safe for now. Please lock the house when you're gone."

"I will. I promise."

"Good. I'd better be going."

"Krispin, I bought a couple of steaks. Would you like to have dinner with me?"

Krispin paused. He'd love to, but was it wise?

"I want to thank you for all your help."

"Jess, I don't—"

"Shh, I know the fear. I have my own. But we'll sit on the front deck of the house. We'll keep ourselves in view of everyone."

"All right. I have to go home for a few minutes, though. Is that a problem?"

"Not at all. Why don't you come back in an hour? I should have everything done by then."

"Can I bring anything?"

"Not this time. Maybe next."

Krispin left the house and sat behind the wheel of his car, his hands shaking. "Dear Lord, give me strength."

❧

After Krispin left, Jess thought better of the two of them being alone and picked up the phone. "Hey, Mom."

"Hi, Jess, what's up?"

"I need a favor. I've invited Krispin to dinner tonight. He's coming in an hour. I'd like you and Dad to be praying. And could you swing by at around nine? I want the safety check."

"I guess we could. Are you sure you want to do this?"

"Yeah, he's been a huge help today." Jess started to prepare the dinner. "Plus, Trevor came to the co-op today."

"Trevor?"

"Yup. He wanted to get back together."

"Oh, Jess, what did you tell him?"

"Before or after he kissed me?"

"He what?"

Jess sighed. "Mom, I can't believe I loved him. His kiss meant nothing to me. It was interesting seeing the look on Krispin's face when he came in and saw Trevor forcing himself upon me."

"What did you do? What did he do?"

"Krispin was the perfect gentleman. But he would have decked Trevor if I'd asked him to. I would have decked Trevor if Krispin hadn't come in. I was savage. That is, I was until I saw Krispin. Mom, isn't it kind of weird the Lord would use someone like Krispin to protect me?"

"It's weird, all right. But He used a donkey to speak to Baalam."

"True," Jess agreed, laughing. "Mom, tell Dad Krispin encrypted the co-op's computer as well as mine. He's some kind of expert in encryption."

"I'll let him know. And Jess, we'll be over sometime tonight. I won't guarantee it will be at nine."

Jess smiled. "Thanks. I appreciate it."

"You're welcome. Be careful, sweetheart."

"I will. I promise." Jess hung up the phone, grateful for the relationship with her stepmom. Dena had been the one to get Jess to see Trevor's faults and the problems with their relationship.

With the potatoes rinsed and in the oven, she flipped the steaks in the marinade and then started on the salad. She opted for a spinach and purple cabbage salad with a honey-mayo dressing. It was simple and easy to make. She'd only started learning how to cook since Dena had married her dad. She'd never had an interest in cooking before then. Instead, she used to pride herself on knowing all the delivery numbers in town.

ᐤ

Krispin pushed his dish away. "That was wonderful, Jess. I can't believe I've had two home-cooked meals in one day."

"Two? What was your first?"

"Greg Steadman and his wife had me over for lunch."

"They're a lovely couple."

"Yeah, and they've got a great bunch of kids."

"Do you like children?"

"Well enough. Truthfully, I hadn't given having children much thought." *Could I be a father one day? Would the Lord allow such a thing? That would be a huge blessing.*

"Randi having her baby has made me start to consider it. When Trevor and I were together, we thought eventually, one day. But neither one of us was in a hurry to have children. Of course back then I was going to run a Fortune 500 company in ten years, according to my plans."

"What changed?"

"The job. I discovered a certain amount of self-centeredness goes hand in hand with that kind of work. At least in the company I was working for. To be successful, you surrendered to the company at the expense of your life, and your personal goals were to get ahead at the expense of those around you. I guess if I had stayed in it, I would have found a way to work within the system, but after someone stole my idea and ran with it, it kind of let the wind out of my sails. Even when I could prove it was my proposal, the boss didn't care. He rewarded the thief. Can you believe that?"

"Yes, unfortunately. Let me guess, he was considered innovative."

"Yeah."

"Temp's dropping," he observed, changing the subject.

Jess looked away.

"I wasn't suggesting we go inside. I should be going."

"Krispin, no, I'm sorry. You've been the perfect gentleman, but—"

"But the first impression I gave you of myself still has you on pins and needles.

Not a problem, Jess. I'm amazed that you even want to be alone with me."

"God's grace," Jess mumbled.

"I understand." Krispin stood up. "I'd offer to help with the dishes, but I think in this situation, it's best if I just leave."

"Krispin, thanks for all your help today. I don't know what I would have done without it."

Lost your identity or worse. "Not a problem. Again, thank you for such a wonderful dinner. I'll return the favor sometime, after I learn how to cook."

"Try the Food Network. It's been a huge help to me."

Krispin chuckled. "I'll try that. Good night, Jess."

"Night, Krispin."

He got to his car just as her parents drove up behind him in the driveway in the same Mercedes he'd seen Jess driving right after the accident.

"Hello, Mr. Black." Wayne extended his hand.

"This town's gossip line is something," Krispin grumbled as he accepted the proffered hand.

Wayne pulled him closer. "Actually, Jess asked us to swing by as a precaution."

Krispin felt the heat rise in his cheeks again. *So Jess doesn't trust me. I can't blame her, Lord.*

"I was just leaving." Krispin slipped behind the wheel of his car.

"Krispin," Dena Russell said as she came up beside his window. "We brought a game. Why don't you stay?"

Krispin's jaw tightened, then relaxed. He'd done everything in his power to have these people not trust him. Why was he overreacting? *Because you know you've changed, but they don't.* "Mrs. Kearns, I really appreciate the offer, but I need to get home. I've been out all day."

Dena stepped back. "Maybe another time."

"That would be nice. Good night." He saw Jess give a weak wave from the front porch. He knew he shouldn't be upset. But he couldn't help it. His past would keep him from having a future. He'd known it all along. Tonight he'd come face-to-face with that truth. He might be redeemed and certain God had forgiven him, but Jessica Kearns could never truly trust him.

Chapter 10

Jess felt bad for having invited her parents to come over—not because it wasn't the right thing to do, but because she hadn't told Krispin she'd invited them. The next few days passed with little or no contact from him. His new encryption software seemed to be working well. She still didn't like typing in twenty-five digits as her password, but then again, it was worth it.

Today, however, she was determined to make things right between them. Jess marched over to Krispin's workshop and reached for the old steel handle before noticing the brass padlock. Locked. She scanned the area for his car. Nothing. She headed back to the co-op and went to work, wondering how she could reconcile this situation.

Five hours later, she saw him drive through town with his car loaded with bags of groceries. Jess smiled.

She dialed his cell phone. "Where have you been shopping?"

Krispin chuckled. "You see me drive past?"

"Yupper. What's going on? Is there a huge sale at the store that I don't know about?"

"Nope, I went to Ellsworth and did some shopping after watching two days of the Food Network."

"You don't believe in doing things slowly, gradually working up to them, do you?"

"Guilty, I'm afraid."

Jess chuckled.

"Jess, would you like to come over and help me? I'm planning on cooking several meals ahead of time. Plus, I've got this new recipe for bruschetta that looks absolutely marvelous and a snap to make. What do you say?"

"Uh. . ." She paused.

"Jess? I'm not mad about the other night. After I had time to think about it, I understand why you called your folks. I would have appreciated a heads-up, but I understand. Look, I have enough food here to invite your parents to dinner, as well. What do you say?"

"Sure. Do you have all the pots, pans, and utensils you need?"

"I think so. I purchased a bunch of those, too."

"You're unbelievable."

"I believe in getting the proper tools for the job, even if I don't know how to use them yet. So when can you get here?"

"A half hour."

"Great, call your folks and invite them. Tell 'em I have no idea what's on the menu yet."

Jess laughed. "They'll love that."

"Good. See you soon."

By the time Jess arrived at Krispin's, he had taken all of the bags out of his car. Jess shut his open trunk as she headed to his back door. She knocked.

Krispin opened the door with his right hand, holding a bunch of green grapes in the other. "Hi, come on in."

"Have you ever frozen those whole?"

"No, why?"

"They're really good frozen in the hot summer. Very refreshing." Jess chuckled. "I was in college before Dad confessed that it also made them last longer 'cause I didn't sneak as many."

Krispin laughed along with her. "I'll have to freeze some. How do you do it? Pack them in a baggie?"

"Not at first. You place them on a cookie sheet, freeze them, then put them in a plastic bag or some other container. They're really good in sparkling cider, as well."

Krispin smiled and handed her the grapes. "Okay, you're on grape detail. Freeze half. The rest I need for the chicken salad and to munch on, of course."

Jess took the grapes. "Do you have a colander?"

"The strainer thingy?"

"Yup."

"In the living room in one of the bags on the sofa."

Jess walked over to the couch and found it littered with all kinds of kitchen equipment. "Wow, you've bought some really nice stuff. Just how much money did you make when you sold your share of the company?"

"Enough, but I purchased this with other money. I deposited that settlement check in a high-yield account for a couple months while I decide just how I'm going to invest it. Most of it I'll put aside for retirement so I won't have to pay taxes on it. I honestly don't know what I'm going to do yet, so I'd rather leave it untouched and in reserve until I have a definite direction."

"Why'd you leave your business? Why not a leave of absence?" Jess fished through the bags and pulled out the colander, then went to the sink and washed it.

"I burned out. I went five years without a vacation. Often I didn't even take the weekend off. I worked all the time."

"I kinda felt that way after college. I didn't want to see another book or take another test or write another paper for the rest of my life. A year later, I'm working on articles of incorporation and writing articles about why we should band together and sell our lobsters through a co-op."

"College was a snap compared to the last seven years. The first three years after school, work was easy. I went to work, did my job, got really good at what I did, and began the promotion process. Gary and I started to consult more often. He kept raising my position within the company, and then last year, something I'd done as a backup to my encryption program saved the company from a huge lawsuit and at the same time put us in the media spotlight. The flip side of that was I had every hacker in the world trying to break my codes. I was working nonstop trying to stay one step ahead of the hackers. It was a horrible year for me." Krispin pulled out a cutting board and retrieved a new set of knives from the sofa. "Should I wash these?"

"Always. Anything you buy from the store for food prep should be washed before you use it. You don't know who might have sneezed on it in the store."

"Now that's gross." Krispin held the package by the tips of his fingers and carried it over to the sink.

"Those are nice knives."

"The set that comes with the cottage are horrible. I couldn't slice a tomato without squishing it."

"What are you making? And I'm done with the grapes. What do you want me to do next?"

"Okay, I'm going to make this bruschetta recipe. Would you take those boneless chicken breasts and bread them?" He turned around and fished out a container of preseasoned bread crumbs. "In the drawer under the oven, you'll find a baking dish you can use."

"All right."

"Are your folks coming?"

Jess laughed. "Yes, but they're a bit surprised."

"Did you explain to them it's going to be a wild night of experimental dishes?"

"I think that's what surprised them the most."

"I figure we can take Jordan and Randi a couple of meals after we're done. After I make the bruschetta, I want to marinate the steaks. Oh, the recipe for the chicken with the bruschetta is on the counter. I bought a grill. We'll need to assemble it though. I thought we could make shish kebabs."

Jess continued to laugh. "I've never met anyone like you."

"Thanks, I think."

"Let me call Dad and tell him to bring his toolbox, or did you buy the wrench and screwdrivers to put the grill together?"

"Ah, I didn't buy those." Krispin hesitated. "I do have some at the shop. What kind do I need?"

"Don't bother. Dad will bring his."

"If you say so." Krispin started cutting the small grape tomatoes into tiny pieces. "What kind of potato or rice should we make for supper?"

"What are we having: the steak, chicken, or the shish kebabs?"

"All three?"

"Rice for the shish kebabs, baked potatoes for the steak."

"Okay, how do we bake potatoes?"

"You're serious, aren't you?"

"Yeah. They didn't cover making those on TV."

"Three-fifty for an hour in the oven."

They continued working on all kinds of food and various meals for the next thirty minutes. When her parents arrived, they were put right to work. By the end of the evening, they had made stuffed mushrooms, chicken bruschetta, shish kebabs, twice-baked potatoes, wild rice, corn on the cob, a tossed green salad, and had a roast cooking in the oven for roast beef sandwiches.

Krispin set aside two plates for Randi and Jordan. He also learned that his refrigerator wasn't big enough for all the food he'd purchased. Some went home with Jess, and some of the meat went home with her parents to put in their freezer.

She reflected on the wonderful evening, thinking about how she had never enjoyed cooking so much. Tonight she had seen in Krispin a passion for life that she'd never seen in him before. She liked it. His enthusiasm was contagious. She found herself still grinning when she settled between the covers to go to sleep in her own home. *Lord, he's amazing. I pray I'm being a good witness for You. Father, please help him find You. I think he's searching, Lord. I think he's even curious about You. He seemed to hang on every word Dad spoke when he was talking about the joy in knowing You. Please, Father, bring him to You.*

a.

Krispin blew off the sawdust, then stood up tall and stretched his back. A reflexive moan followed. He never knew working at a counter for several hours would so strain the lower back. Of course he'd been discovering all kinds of muscles since moving to Squabbin Bay. Woodworking took one set; cooking took another. He'd had a blast with Jess and her parents last night. He couldn't wait until they could do it again. But every time he had looked over at Jess, his stomach did a flip. He needed to take this friendship very slowly.

"Hey, Krispin." Bryan, Greg's son, came running through the shop door. "Is it okay if I work with you and Daddy today?"

"Sure."

He ran out the door as fast as he'd come in through it. "Daddy, Krispin says it's okay."

Greg walked through the door with the boy in his arms. "Are you sure, Krispin? You mentioned at the house he could come, and he's been bothering me every day."

Krispin chuckled. "No problem."

"Great." Greg lowered the boy to the floor. "Go get your wood and tools, Bryan."

The boy scurried off again.

Greg walked over to the worktable where Krispin had laid out the purple-heart strips. It was one of the more costly woods, but he felt the purple color would make great accent lines on the kayak.

"I love that wood," Greg said.

"Yeah, I'm really glad I decided to purchase the couple of boards."

"Would you like me to start sanding the yellow or red cedar strips?"

"Red, then the yellow. Thanks. That would be helpful."

Bryan came waddling in with his arms full of wood scraps. "Whatcha making, Bryan?"

"Daddy says we ain't got no money for expensive Christmas presents—"

"Bryan!" Greg scolded.

"Sorry, Daddy. I'm making Mommy a box to put things in."

"That sounds like a wonderful present."

"If I build it here, Mommy won't know, and Daddy says we have four months before Christmas. Course, once school starts, I can't do much buildin'."

Krispin held back a grin. Then he thought about Bryan's statement. Just how tight were the Steadmans? "Greg, I can pay you for helping me work on the kayaks."

"No, no, we're fine. We're always tight just before the season starts. Truth is, Bryan likes building things, and I felt it would be a good idea for him to make some presents this year."

"Understood. But I know I'm not going to use as much wood as I bought since you've been helping me out. So why don't you build yourself a kayak, too? I have more than enough wood."

Greg stroked his beard. "A canoe might be better for me and the family."

"Great, you make whatever you'd like. I'm sure we have plenty of wood for the two of us."

"You're certain? I wouldn't want to take the wood from you."

"Trust me, I'm certain. I don't think I could make another in the three months I have left in Squabbin Bay."

"Where ya going in three months?"

"I don't know."

"Daddy, can I help you build the canoe?"

"That would be up to Mr. Black."

Bryan pleaded with puppy dog eyes. "If you're well behaved, I don't have a problem, but you have to mind your father and me. There are some dangerous tools here."

"I will, I promise."

"All right."

For the next couple hours, the three of them worked hard. By lunchtime Bryan had reached his max. "I'll take him home. Krispin, are you sure about the wood?" Greg asked.

"Absolutely. And by the looks of it, I have more than enough fiberglass material, as well."

Greg extended his hand. "Thanks, Krispin. That's mighty generous of you."

"You're welcome. I can't tell you how much I appreciate your help and friendship."

Greg nodded. He scooped his worn-out son in his arms and carried him out the door. "I'll see you tomorrow."

Krispin looked at all the strips of sanded wood and all that remained to be sanded. He didn't think he'd make another one of these again, but he was glad for the experience. He was learning all kinds of new things. More importantly, Greg used the process to show him how God continued to sand off a person's rough edges. For the first time in Krispin's life, he was glad he wasn't God and in control. On the floor lay a broken and rough-cut piece of wood. *That was me a few months ago.* On the table were some pieces that had gone through the planer, nicely cut and semirefined. But they were nothing compared to the very smooth pieces that he and Greg had already sanded. The odd thing was that they would be sanded again and again before the kayak was finished. "Lord, you've got quite a project on your hands with me."

"Krispin?" Wayne Kearns called from behind the closed door.

Chapter 11

Jess strained over the side of the boat to try and get a glimpse of what her father was doing in Krispin's shop. It was the second day in a row she had seen him enter the shop in the early afternoon. Truthfully, she had no reason to be on her boat, except to try and get a bird's-eye view into the shop's harbor doorway. He had to be helping Krispin with his kayak, she figured. Something, in all honesty, she'd love to be working on with him. The memories of making her kayak with her dad so many years ago flooded back every time she thought of Krispin making his.

For two days she'd been trying to come up with an excuse to get together with Krispin again but had come up with nothing. Jess turned from the starboard side of the boat and headed to the dock. She went back to the co-op and continued to work on next spring's advertising campaign.

Other small lobster fishermen were starting to contact the co-op to talk about joining the group. She'd had two inquiries so far this week. If the co-op continued growing at this rate, she'd have to start working full-time. The question was, when would the co-op be able to pay her salary? The balance between donated time and salary needs were quickly becoming a matter of discussion for the board of directors. And even then, she wasn't sure if she could handle everything in the office by herself much longer. She knew she could use a secretary or an administrative assistant, but the income didn't warrant it.

Jess scanned the preliminary ad campaign. It seemed flat, unengaging. Jess tapped the desk with her pen. "What's missing?"

"Me." Trevor stood in the doorway, beaming.

"Not!" Jess shook off her startled expression. "What are you doing here? What's going on, Trevor? When we broke up, I didn't hear from you. It's been well over a year now. What gives? When we were dating, I couldn't get you to come up for a visit, and here you are twice in a matter of a week or two."

"Now, Jess, hang on. Before I returned to the city, I thought I'd take one more stab at getting back together with you."

"Why? Nothing's changed."

"I've changed."

"Really. Would you be willing to live in Squabbin Bay?"

Trevor took a tentative step toward her desk. Jess stood up and held out her hands. "You stay right there, Trev."

"What's going on, Jess? You never were afraid of me before. I've got a job."

317

"Where? Doing what?"

"I'm a traveling salesman. Would you like to buy some knives?"

"No. Trev, I'm glad you've got a job. I'm glad it's working for you. My not living in the city was not the only thing wrong with our relationship. And you not wanting to get a job was another, but not the only reason, although that was major."

Trevor stepped back toward the door. "I think I've heard this conversation before. On that note, I'll take my leave. Tell me this, Jess. Are you happy?"

"Yeah, I am."

"I'm glad. Don't hate me too much, Jess. We had some good times."

Jess's spine relaxed. "Yeah, we did. Good luck with your job, Trev."

"Thanks. Hey, here's my business card if you ever decide you might like to buy some of these knives. They're pretty pricey. But they're excellent quality, with a lifetime guarantee." Trevor pulled a card out of his pocket.

Jess walked over and took it. "I'll keep it in mind."

Trevor turned the knob and opened the door. Looking back at her, he asked, "So are you dating the bodyguard?"

"Huh?"

"The guy that wanted to knock me into next week the last time I was here."

"Krispin? No."

"Ah, just curious. I'm sorry I blew it before, Jess. I hope you find the right person someday."

I do, too. "Same for you, Trev."

Trevor nodded his head and left. She had loved him once. He had seemed like the perfect Christian gentleman to blend with her. But she'd changed during college, too. It took graduating, having trouble getting the right job out of school, and then getting the dream job to show her the emptiness of that life she was headed for. It took coming home and getting grounded once again to show her who she really was in Christ. In the end she wouldn't have been happy married to Trevor. They looked at life and family in very different ways.

She thought about Krispin and what he had shared the other night about his life, his career, the emptiness of it all. *Dear Lord, thanks for saving me from that life. I could have gotten caught up in work and left You behind. Father, help me keep You central, even with the demands of the co-op pressing in on me.*

❧

Krispin scanned the shop. It had grown in use. Greg and his son Bryan were hard at work on their canoe. Wayne Kearns was spending a huge part of the day working on numerous projects since Dena had gone on a photo shoot for a few days. And Krispin had his kayak starting to take shape in his corner of the room. Krispin had also given Greg and Wayne their own keys to the shop.

But Krispin wanted to go home and work on the newest recipe he'd decided to make from watching television. Cooking, for some odd reason, was really appealing to him, more than he'd ever thought possible. "Wayne, I'm going to put some shrimp and steak on the grill tonight. Would you like to join me?"

"I'd love to, but I'm having dinner with my folks before they return to Florida."

"How much longer will they be here?" Greg asked.

"Labor Day weekend. After that, they'll fly back to Florida. It's been a good visit."

"Glad to hear it."

Krispin knew the basic story from Jess. Greg had filled him in on some of the details regarding the townsfolk dropping as many charges as they could if Wayne's father got help for his gambling problem. It seemed odd, at first, to hear how the town would pull together behind an individual who had hurt so many. But what surprised him the most was that Wayne had sold his house and paid off all his father's debts, including what had been stolen from the lobstermen in terms of lost revenue. He was broke when he married Dena. Dena, who drove a Mercedes. Krispin wondered if he'd ever have the kind of love and forgiveness that Wayne and his family had demonstrated toward his father. It was so different from the world he'd been living in for the past ten years.

"Penny for your thoughts?" Wayne asked.

"Sorry, just thinking about my past, how I approached life."

"A lot to think about?"

"Yeah. I don't think I'll ever be as forgiving as you."

Wayne let out a nervous chuckle. "Let's hope you never have to."

Krispin paused. Didn't the Bible talk about God's grace being sufficient for whatever trials we encounter? *Where will I go and what am I going to do with myself after my six months are up?* "Wayne, my lease is up in November. Would you be interested in taking it over?"

Wayne rubbed the back of his neck with a handkerchief. "Let me think on that. A shop to work on some cabinets would be nice. We don't really have the room at the house. What's the rent?"

They discussed the lease arrangements Krispin had made with the owner, then went back to work. Greg and Bryan left first. Krispin put away his tools and cleaned up the shop, except around where Wayne was still working. "I'll lock up," Wayne offered.

"Thanks." Krispin left. The cool, crisp air of early fall invigorated him. A thought to invite Jess for dinner breezed through his mind. He sat down in his car and tapped the steering wheel, debating whether or not he should invite Jess to dinner tonight. Deciding to throw caution to the wind, he placed a call on his cell and turned the key.

"Jess, it's Krispin."

"Hey, what's up?"

"Dinner, my place, steak and shrimp on the grill. What do you say?" He glanced in the rearview mirror before putting the car in reverse.

"I'd love to, but I can't. Sorry."

They said their good-byes, and he dialed Randi and Jordan's only to find that they were busy, too. He passed a roadside stand and grabbed a couple of ears of corn. He'd throw the second steak in the freezer and eat the shrimp instead.

His phone rang as he drove up the scalloped-shell driveway. "Hello."

"Krispin, it's me, Jess. There's a problem with my home computer. I have dinner plans with Dad and my grandparents tonight. Can you come by and fix it while I'm out?"

"Sure, what's it doing?"

"It won't turn on."

Fear sliced through his backbone. Someone had tried to retrieve the Trojan horse program he had found on her computer. "All right. Where will you leave a key?"

"I'll drop it off on my way out to my parents' house."

"Okay, see you in a few."

"Great, thanks."

He clicked his phone shut and debated whether or not he should have told Jess that someone probably tried to break into the computer. Not wanting to worry her, he decided to keep that to himself until he knew for sure.

Krispin grabbed the corn and headed to the kitchen. *Should I warn her, Lord? What if the intruder is in the house? Is she in danger?*

He dialed Jess's house. It rang. . .no answer. He paced back and forth in his kitchen. It rang a second time. . .still no answer. "Pick up, Jess." Third ring, again no answer. "Come on, Jess." Fourth ring. He hung up and called the sheriff.

"Sheriff McKean, it's Krispin Black. I'm concerned about Jessica Kearns. I just called her house and there was no answer."

"Now, son, just because she's not—"

"Sorry, she just called me, said her computer wouldn't start up. I put a safety in the computer program I installed that has the computer look like it won't turn on if an unauthorized person tried to access her computer." He didn't have time to explain everything. "Look, what if whoever broke into the computer is in the house? Couldn't she be in—"

"I'm on my way. You sit tight."

Krispin hung up the phone. Unable from the time he was thirteen to just sit tight when his elders told him to, Krispin got into his car and drove over to Jess's. As he turned into her drive, he saw the sheriff's car parked beside hers. The sheriff stood outside the back door, talking with Jess. Her hair was wrapped in a towel, and she was dressed in a terry robe she held tightly across her chest. She glanced over at him and frowned.

Oh boy. He responded with a wave.

Jess turned back into the house. The sheriff approached him. "You don't listen well, do you?"

"Sorry. Shower?"

"Ayup. Look, Krispin, I don't mean to be telling you your business, but you should have told Jess what could have happened with her computer."

"I didn't want to alarm her."

"Instead you alarmed me and had me come over and roust her out of a shower."

"Right. I'm sorry."

The sheriff tapped the upper part of the door. "She told me to tell you to wait and she'd hand you the keys." He walked toward his car.

"Thanks, Sheriff." Krispin's mind swirled. How could he make things right with Jess? *You could start by telling her you believe in Me.*

His body went rigid. Had God just spoken to him?

He placed a call to Pastor Russell.

"Hello?" Marie, the pastor's wife, answered.

"Hi, Marie, it's Krispin Black. Is Pastor Russell free?"

"Sure, let me get him."

Krispin tapped the steering wheel, waiting for the pastor. "Hi, Krispin. What can I do for you?"

"Pastor Russell, I'm wondering if you ever hear God's voice." *How do I explain this?* "It was like a voice in my head."

"Yes, I've had that experience. The caution is to test what the voice says and make sure it's not telling you something contrary to the Bible."

From everything Krispin had read in the Bible so far, this wasn't contrary. In fact, several places in it said to tell others that you believe in God. "Okay, thanks."

"Is that it?"

Krispin chuckled. "Yeah. Pretty dumb question, huh?"

"No, actually there are many who never 'hear' a distinct voice from God. Pray and seek the Lord, Krispin. You're doing well."

"Thanks."

Jess opened the back door.

"I've got to go, Pastor. See you Sunday."

"Bye." Pastor Russell hung up.

Krispin started to shake. He wanted to tell Jess, but he'd also wanted her to see the changes in him and recognize what had taken place in his life for herself.

"Krispin, why didn't you tell me about the program?"

"Sorry. I didn't want to scare you."

Jess leaned in toward him. "I'm not a child who needs to be protected."

"I'm sorry, Jess. I didn't mean to offend you. If you remember, I had to run off after I installed the security program. I simply forgot to mention it. I can fix it, but it does mean that someone probably came into your house."

"I understand, and the sheriff checked the exterior before you arrived. Krispin, it isn't your job to protect me."

But I want to. "I know. I'm sorry. It won't happen again."

She leaned back on her heels and handed him the keys. "I've got to go. I'm going to be late as it is. Call me if you find anything on the computer."

"I will."

Jess left his side and slipped behind the wheel of her car. The cold metal of the keys felt like the coldness around his heart. Jess didn't love him, at least not like he loved her. He went inside, sat down at her computer, reset the security program, and left in a span of fifteen minutes.

Back at home, his appetite faded. He put a sandwich together and saved the steak and shrimp for another time. Tomorrow he'd have to tell Jess the full truth of why he had come back to Squabbin Bay and that he was now a Christian.

Chapter 12

The brisk early morning air lapped Jess's cheeks as she walked to her car. The only noise was the swooshing of her foul-weather gear sounding like a huge, thick pair of rubber gloves walking down the street. They made their final *squeak* as she sat down behind the wheel of her car and drove to the harbor. Walking down the steep incline of the dock due to low tide, she held on to the rail. She glanced over to the spot where she had run over Krispin and his kayak.

She closed her eyes and paused for a moment, saying another prayer for him, then added, *Lord, help me forgive myself for not seeing him that day.* For the past two weeks, she'd been avoiding him.

The shadow of a man's profile stood on the deck of her boat. The muscles on the back of her neck tightened. "Hello?"

"It's me, Jess."

"Krispin?" Jess relaxed.

"Yes. We need to talk."

She came toward him. "What are you doing here?"

"You've been avoiding me. I decided to take matters into my own hands and came where I knew you would be." He rubbed his arms.

"Are you cold?"

"A little. There's a lot of moisture in the air."

"How long have you been here?"

"An hour. I wasn't sure when you would arrive, so I came early." He took a step toward her. "Jess, I'm sorry about the computer program, calling the sheriff."

Jess snickered. "Krispin, that's not the problem."

He paused for a moment. "May I go out with you this morning so we can talk?"

Did she want to be alone with him, really alone? "You can trust me, Jess."

"All right. But you'll need some foul-weather gear. It's too cold without it. Let me get Dad's from the shed." She went over to the small shack standing on the end of the dock that abutted the granite cliff walls lining the harbor and reached for her dad's yellow, foul-weather gear. Her gear was orange. She'd chosen the different color to stand out from others.

"Thanks."

"Just slip them on over your clothing. I'm afraid Dad's boots won't fit you, though."

"That's all right. These will help."

"You get dressed. I need to make the boat ready." Returning to the shed, she grabbed the chum buckets and set them on the edge of the dock. She gathered some extra nets for the pots in case she found any that had been destroyed.

Krispin loaded the chum buckets on deck. "These stink."

Jess laughed. "You haven't smelled anything yet." Grabbing a couple more chum bags, she headed back to the boat.

The engines came to life with a roar at the twist of a key. She set it in neutral and started to cast off.

"Can I help?"

"No, thanks. I have this down so I can pretty much do it in my sleep."

"Ah." Krispin turned and sat down on the bench on the port side of the boat.

Stepping back on board, Jess got behind the wheel and shifted the lever into reverse. Slowly the boat pulled away from the dock. She circled around in reverse, then pushed the throttle into forward and headed out of the harbor. The gentle ribbon of first light shone on the eastern horizon.

"Do you get up this early every morning?"

"Only on Tuesdays. The co-op needs a lot of my attention on Tuesdays."

"How is the co-op doing? Any more attempts to access your computers?"

"No. And thank you for fixing them."

"You're welcome." He stood on the deck and came up beside her. "Jess, I don't know what I did, but I'm sorry."

"Krispin." She paused. It was time to confess. He needed to understand why she couldn't see him anymore. "It's not you, it's me."

"No, it's me. I know how rude I was to you the day you saved my life."

"It's not that, Krispin."

"No, I suppose it isn't. Look, before you say anything, I need to tell you something. I've been fighting it for a long time, but if I don't tell you soon, I'm going to explode. Well, I don't think I'll explode exactly."

"You're rambling."

"Right, sorry. Okay, here's the deal. I came back to Squabbin Bay to find God."

"What?"

He took in a deep breath and let it out slowly. "Your father challenged me the day I left. Life had gotten very boring and complicated. I wasn't satisfied by what I'd earned, done, or even who I was anymore. I didn't enjoy the competitiveness of my industry any longer, and I knew my company would suffer if I wasn't driven the way I had been before. Anyway, all of that is to say that the accident and what your father said made me reevaluate my life—where I was headed and why I was here. I didn't tell you because of what you said to me before."

"What?"

"That you wouldn't get involved with a man who didn't believe like you did. I didn't want you to think I became a Christian so I could date you."

Jess started to giggle. "Does my father know?"

"Yeah, sorry. I asked him not to say anything. I wanted you to see a change in me, not have me tell you. But ever since that night when someone tried to access your computer, I've known I was supposed to tell you. In fact, I was going to tell you the next morning, but I couldn't find you. Then it just got easier and easier to avoid you because you were avoiding me. But it really hasn't been all that easy. I keep being encouraged by the Lord to tell you. I couldn't resist any longer, and that's why I staked out your boat."

Jess clenched the steering wheel, aiming for the red light that marked the port side entrance to the harbor. "You're truly saved?"

"Yeah, sinner that I am."

"So that's why you've been visiting with my stepbrother? And Greg Steadman?"

"He's my mentor."

"Unbelievable."

"What? Why? Can't a guy like me get saved?"

Jess relaxed. "No, it isn't that. What's unbelievable is what I was going to confess to you."

"Shoot."

"Krispin, I had to tell you I couldn't see you anymore because. . ." Should she confess it? *But if he's saved, what's the problem?*

"Because you're attracted to me?"

"Right," she admitted.

"I avoided you for that very reason. And I'm still not sure that you and I should see a lot of each other. I still have a long ways to grow as a Christian. I'm not sure we should get too involved at this point in time."

Jess looked at the compass. It was her only navigator at this time of day. She set out on her heading, glanced at the clock, and worked her way down the western shoreline. She had to concentrate on where she was going. If she gave in to her emotions, she'd get distracted by their conversation and lose her bearings, and they'd be out far longer than they should be.

"Jess?"

"Sorry. I'm not sure what to say. I think we need to get to know one another better."

"I agree. Being friends is a good place to start." The wind and chop of the water grew with intensity as they left the confines of the harbor. The hull bounced hard on the water. Jess steadied her sea legs and positioned for the impact.

Krispin slipped and grabbed the helm, keeping himself from falling.

"Sorry. I should have warned you."

"No problem. Look, I'm not just attracted to you. Wait, that didn't come out right. Hang on." He paused. Jess held back a grin. She knew exactly what he was thinking, but it was too soon. Too soon for them to consider a life with one another and too soon for him as a new Christian to consider marriage.

"I'm not saying this right, but here it goes. I'm not just physically attracted to you. I'm attracted to you as a person—who you are, how you do things, the way you smile. The way you look at life. The way you treated me after I was so horribly rude to you. All of that and so much more. I even love the way you gently nibble your upper lip when you're concentrating on something."

"I do what?"

"You roll your upper lip slightly and press your lower lip against it, like so." She watched him do the very thing he just described. "I do not."

Krispin chuckled. "Yes, you do. I've seen you. I'll point it out next time."

"Well, you have a few personality traits of your own, you know."

"Oh really? Like what?"

The horizon was brightening behind them. "For example, you rub the back of your neck when you're not sure what to say or do."

Krispin pulled his hand down from the back of his neck.

"All right, I'll give you that one."

They bounced along with the waves for a couple of minutes, neither knowing what to say next. *To admit I'm attracted to him before I really get to know him* . . . Jess shook off the thought. "What are you going to do with yourself once you leave Squabbin Bay?"

"I don't know. One thing is certain, I won't be going into boat building. Greg and his son's canoe is farther along than mine, and I had a two-month head start."

"I enjoyed building mine with my dad, but only because I was building it with Dad. I do have a few skills that have helped me repair a thing or two around the house, though. I'm certain I wouldn't have known what to do if I hadn't built that kayak with Dad."

"And I'm learning how to use power tools. Never used any before, not even in shop. The school budget was cut that year so all the guys who signed up for shop got to take an extra music or gym class. Or we could have taken home ec, but that was a sissy class in my neck of the woods."

"Where'd you grow up?"

"Outside of Manchester, a small town called South Hooksett. The sun's coming up."

"Yeah, by the time I reach the first pot, the sun is cresting the horizon. See that bluff?" She pointed to the largest bluff jutting out from the shore farther up. "That's Mom and Dad's place."

"Nice location."

"Yeah. Dena rented it from the previous owner, but when he decided to put it on the market, she bought it and had Dad put the addition on. One thing led to another and boom—they got married."

"You seem happy with your stepmother."

"Very. She's the mother I never had. I visited with my bio-mom earlier this summer; it was the first time since Dena and Dad married. It was odd. I don't have any real connection to her. I mean, there are things in my temperament that I realize I got from her genes, but the most we'll ever have in common is an occasional friendship where we connect every now and again. I don't fit in her world. Truthfully, I never fit in her world at all."

"My folks are still married, but we're not very close. I love them, but they aren't the kind of people who make great friendships with others. They tend to be lost in themselves. Even when we were small children, they seemed to leave us behind and go off with one another. Eating meals together was done in silence. They never asked questions. I envy the relationship you have with your family. I'd never have known you weren't Dena's daughter by the way you all respond to one another."

"I had a great relationship with my dad. He spoiled me rotten. Fortunately, he worked hard for the little money he had or he would have gone overboard with expensive gifts I didn't need. Instead, he gave of himself by being the dad at every school event, going out with the Girl Scout troop events. Trust me, he was the only father at those events, except the father-daughter banquets. Scouting always brings out the mothers. Even Boy Scouts have den mothers. My dad was the first man, and probably the last, to attend such functions. And the girls were horrible to him. They'd giggle and tease him. He'd pitch his tent on the other side of the campground just to get some sleep at night. Anyway, Dad took me everywhere and did everything with me. When I was sixteen, I wished he'd go away. Thankfully he didn't, and I'm a better person because of it."

"I like your dad. He tells it like it is."

"Yeah." She slowed the engine and shifted it to neutral. "Here we go."

"What can I do?"

"Nothing, just watch."

"Okay." He crossed his arms and stood with his legs apart. Jess smiled. He'd gotten a handle on his sea legs.

"Seriously, watch me so you can see what I'm doing."

"Okay."

She fished the buoy out. "First, I hook the rope with this gaff hook. Then I place the line into this pulley. With the push of a button, it reels in the pot. I had Dad buy these, and I love them. I don't have to haul up each pot by hand."

The winch hummed, and the rope spooled up. "From this point"—the pot hung above the water—"I pull the pot over here and slide it on this table, like so."

"How many pots do you have?"

"Only two hundred."

"But you've got six lobsters in there."

"Not all the pots will have lobsters. See this one?" She held a mother lobster upside down, her eggs fully coating her tail. "She goes back. Those black circles are eggs."

"Awesome."

"You haven't been around sea or country life much, have you?"

"Nope. We lived in South Hooksett, but my folks had us in Manchester schools. By the time I was ten, I was in a private school. Country life is something I know little about."

"All right. But this is country on the sea, and people who grow up on the shore are different than plain old country folk."

"Hmm, I have a lot to learn."

"You betcha. Now for the nasty part." Jess flipped open the bucket of chum.

"Gross! What is that?"

"Rotting fish."

"Double gross. What are you doing?"

"Lobsters are bottom feeders, scavengers. They eat what they can find on the bottom of the ocean. Generally, that's dead fish."

"Yuck. I knew I didn't care for lobster for a reason."

She laughed.

Jess reached her hand into the chum bucket, and Krispin leaned over the side of the boat and nearly lost his breakfast—no wait, supper. He hadn't eaten this morning. The smell was the most foul he'd ever encountered.

"The smellier, the better."

She placed the chum in a bag of what appeared to be cheese-cloth-type material and tied it down on a spike in front of the net where the lobsters were housed.

"You do this every day?"

"Just about."

"Man, how can you stand it?"

"You get used to it."

Not on your life. "Isn't there fake bait or something you could use?"

"Nope. Real stuff. You can't fool a lobster."

She lifted a panel in the center of the boat. Water lapped against the hull. "What's that? Are we sinking?"

"A holding tank. We sealed off a section of the boat hull and vented it to the ocean. The lobsters stay alive even if we can't unload them right away. Most don't do that, but one winter Dad and I had nothing better to do, so we made it out of fiberglass and wood."

Krispin eased in for a better look. He had to admit, he was still timid around the water. But for Jess, he'd do anything. Well, anything but touch that awful chum. Thankfully, she wore gloves. He shuddered just thinking about that smell.

"Once the pot is ready, we toss it back in and move on to the next one."

"You do this a couple hundred times?"

"No, only one hundred, then tomorrow the other half."

"I'm amazed. That's a lot of work for a little return."

"Maybe. But it is honest work, and unlike yourself, a lot of people like lobster."

"True. Supply and demand."

"Ayup," she said in her Down-Eastern accent. "You said you went into computer programming because you liked numbers."

"Yeah. Then as I got older, I found ways to make those numbers cash numbers. I liked that even better."

"Okay, wrap your head around this. If I catch an average of a 150 to 200 lobsters every day, that's 6 times a week, and each lobster pulled in an average of $12 a piece wholesale, how much can I earn in a year?" She paused. "Oh, and figure in for only 40 weeks."

"Okay. At 150 lobsters per day, six days a week, that's 900 a week and 36,000 a year. Earning $12 per lobster, that's $1,800 per day, for a grand total of $432,000 a year." He whistled. "I thought you were poor, relatively speaking."

"I said I didn't earn much. Here's the thing: We don't average that much per sale. For the bigger orders, we can get as little as $6 for a pound-and-a-half lobster. Some online businesses are selling their lobsters for a premium price, but they're buying them from the fisherman for a lot less. That's the reason I started the co-op: to try and get a better price for our product without going through the roof so that a typical lobster dinner doesn't cost what it costs in New York City."

"We'd order them from a caterer for our corporate parties. Lobster isn't cheap."

Jess continued to pull up pot after pot.

"Basically, you're saying you have a lot more earning potential than you're currently doing."

"Yes. But it's not only about the profit. It's also about making it a more steady income."

"Why only forty weeks?"

"We don't lobster in the really bad winter months. Even with foul-weather gear, you freeze out here. Commercial fishermen go all year, but they can be out on the sea for a month and bring in a hefty salary. But that isn't the kind of a life I want to live. Have you seen some of those programs about those dangerous jobs? Lobstering is one of them, for the commercial fishermen."

"I can imagine." Krispin was enjoying the warmth of the sun's rays as it came up over the horizon. Jess fascinated him. How could she do this day after day and still like it? "Jess, do you honestly enjoy doing this?"

Jess reached into the bucket and pulled out another brown, bloody, chunky handful of rotting fish. Krispin held on to his stomach. *Lord, help me get over that smell.*

"Yeah, it's crazy. I know. A woman who likes lobstering. I like being out on the water. Four years of college and little time on the ocean showed me how much I missed it. But when I moved to Boston and started working in the city, the commute wasn't quite as early as when I get up for lobstering, but it was early enough. Still dark in the morning when I'd leave, I'd smell diesel and road grime. Here I smell the ocean, feel the wind on my face, roll with the waves. . . . It's more peaceful."

"Yeah, but the smell?" Krispin held his nose and waved off the stench of decaying fish.

The lilt of Jess's laughter caused him to relax. "I know. I said the same to Dad, year after year. Trust me, Randi thinks it's odd, too.

"So," Jess continued, "tell me more about your newfound faith."

Chapter 13

I'm still putting the pieces together," Krispin said. "I believe in God and that He has a perfect plan for me. Jesus and His need to come to earth and die for my sins is more real to me than it was the day I asked Him into my heart. But I'm still not sure of my purpose in this world. Before I found the Lord, my life wasn't adding up. I'd done all you were supposed to do, and then some, and still I wasn't satisfied. In programming that's a good thing, because you constantly have to rewrite and build new and more powerful components to the software. But for life, it left me feeling empty and alone. Truthfully, I don't feel that much different. There's a calmness inside me. No, it's more like a contentment, a sense of peace that everything will work out fine."

Jess watched as Krispin's face turned a light shade of green. "Are you all right?"

"I will be, I hope," he muttered.

"Okay, the key is to not think about it. The chum is simply what is needed to catch lobsters—the bait."

"I've never been one for fishing."

Jess fastened the bait bag around the spike in the center of the pot. "How do you feel about fishing for men?"

Krispin chuckled. "I'm getting more comfortable with the idea. I don't want to be one of those guys who tells everyone that they need to be saved. I mean, it's true they need to know Jesus and accept Him as their Savior, but—I don't know, I've never been the salesman type. I let others in the company do that. I was more involved with the day-to-day numbers and code to write the software."

"So what made Jesus real for you?" Jess closed the pot and plopped it back in the water.

She went to the helm and switched gears; the boat's propellers churned the waters off the stern. "Hang on, we're heading back in. Come, sit up here next to me. You won't be as cold, and hopefully the smell will remain behind us."

Krispin navigated to the seat next to hers.

"So are you satisfied now?"

"I'm confused more than anything. I know I'll go back to work eventually. I'm too young to retire, and what I made off of the sale will hold me for a while but not the rest of my life. I liked work, just not the stress of the partnership. I'm the kind of guy you can lock in a room with a computer, and I'd be happy for days. But the past few years, I've dealt with the clients more, and I discovered I liked having a social life. A few years back, when nerds were cool, I suppose that's when I started changing from the quiet geek to the rude, crude, and socially unacceptable guy I was when you first met me."

Jess smiled. He didn't seem the same man at all. She couldn't put her finger on it, but he seemed almost depressed, and certainly not as confident as he had been. "Krispin, who is the real you? I mean, when you were a kid, what were you like around other children?"

"I never really had childhood friends. School was a snap for me. I was bored. So I read or worked on math problems. I was doing algebra by the fourth grade. You know, I've never really fit. At work I was popular because of what I offered the company. College was a bore. I didn't have to work hard to get the grades, so I started to party all the time, and that's back when geeks were popular with the girls." He paused for a moment.

The hull of the boat jumped and banged against the waves. Jess glanced back at the compass heading.

"Since I became a Christian, I don't seem to fit in anywhere again. I feel kind of like the young school boy in the private academy, in my room, enjoying my study, but not enjoying my life."

Jess reached over and placed her ungloved hand on his arm. "You need to start enjoying life."

"Yeah, but I. . .well, I feel so guilty. The things I found pleasure in before don't even interest me now."

"Ah, okay. Let's correct that. Why don't you meet me for an evening kayak ride in the harbor? You can use Dad's."

A slow smile eased up his handsome cheeks. *Lord, if this man is who you've planned for me, keep him around. If he's not, move him soon. I don't think my heart can take it.*

"All right. Can you come back to my place for dinner?"

Jess paused and wondered if she had the strength to visit and not give in to moving their relationship too quickly forward.

As if reading her mind, he offered, "You can invite your folks or anyone else to join us. I don't mind."

"No. It'll be all right. Let's just promise ourselves we won't move too quickly, too soon."

The small lines that ran across his forehead when he thought intently on things furrowed. Slowly he nodded his head. "Yes, let's keep each other accountable that way."

&

Krispin feared he shouldn't have revealed so much of his confusion. *Father, go before us and help us. Help me determine what is right and holy in our relationship,* he prayed.

He still had many of the same questions he had before he asked Jesus to come into his life. The difference was he was content with not knowing. But he was a babe in the woods when it came to understanding how to relate to others on a personal level. It was one thing to be the handsome guy pursuing a new conquest, but to be an honorable man in pursuit of a wife. . .that was totally new to him. He'd avoided marriage in his former lifestyle and made his aversion to it clear to the women around him. Now, he still felt shame for his past. How could Jess ever love him with that hanging over him?

They were pulling back into the harbor. "Thanks, Jess. I'm glad I came out."

"Me, too."

"Can I lend you a hand once we get into port?" he asked, hoping the answer would be no if it came to that chum bucket. His stomach rolled just thinking about it.

Jess chuckled. "No, thanks. Dad will be around soon to lend me a hand. Then I've got to run home, clean up, and go to the office."

Jess slowed her approach. It seemed slower than the other fishermen. "Are you still having problems about running over me?"

Jess's knuckles whitened as she tightened her grip around the steering wheel.

"Jess, I was just as much at fault as you were. I wasn't looking and had been under the pier just before you hit me."

"What?"

"I had taken my kayak under the pier to get a look at some of the sea life living on the pilings. I pulled out without thinking. My mind was on work and the problems I was having with the company. I wasn't thinking about where I was or what I was doing. You couldn't have avoided me. I'm certain of it. I owe you my life, Jess."

"Then why. . ." Her words trailed off.

"The lawsuit?" he finished for her. "Because I was a cad."

Jess nodded.

One of those awkward moments passed between them, until the boat gently rubbed against the pilings. Krispin jumped up and took the stern line with him. He secured the rear line of the boat while Jess moved up to the bow. He took off the yellow foul-weather gear and laid it on the bench of their fishing shack. "I'll see you later, Jess."

Jess came up beside him. Her honey-wheat hair glistened in the morning light. Her blue eyes dazzled him. Krispin swallowed. He wanted to kiss her. He refused to act on such an impulse.

Placing her hand on his chest, she whispered, "Thanks for telling me that. I've had many a sleepless night trying to figure out how I—"

He reached out and pulled her close. "Jess, I'm so sorry. Please forgive me."

Jess nodded her head against his chest. "I do."

His heart wanted to burst. The woman he loved, the woman he'd been so incredibly rude to, was in his arms and forgiving him for the cad he had been. "Thank you for saving my life, Jess. My soul," he whispered.

Jess pulled away first. Krispin stepped back. "I'll see you later."

Jess smiled. "Later."

Krispin hiked up the walkway back to the street level of the harbor. He turned back to see Jess working. When she pulled the bucket of chum out of the boat, his stomach flipped once again. He needed a shower and a nap.

His cell phone rang. "Hello?"

"Hi, Krispin. Pastor Russell here."

"Hi, Pastor. What's up?"

"I was confirming that you would be giving your testimony in church tomorrow morning."

"Yes." *Another reason I had to tell Jess the truth—before she heard my public testimony.*

"Great. I'll see you later."

"Later?"

"I take it you've forgotten the meeting of the men and their mentors tonight? A barbecue at the church."

Krispin let out a nervous chuckle. "Afraid so. I'll be there."

"See you soon."

Krispin said good-bye and immediately called and left a message on Jess's answering machine that he had to cancel their evening plans. Although he definitely would prefer to be in Jess's company, perhaps it was wise that they not be alone together too often after declaring their attraction to one another.

Later that evening, he found himself pleasantly surprised, enjoying the company of the men around him. Wayne stood at the grill with Pastor Russell. Greg Steadman came up to him with a plate brimming with food and an inch-thick stack of napkins. "Now don't you tell my wife. She says I could stand to lose twenty pounds."

Krispin chuckled. "My lips are sealed."

"Good." Greg sat down beside him. "I saw you went out on the boat with Jess this morning. Are you two dating?"

"No," Krispin answered a bit defensively. "We're friends. But we're talking about the possibility, maybe bringing our relationship to the next level. Do you know she still feels guilty for running over me?"

"I suspect she will for a while." Greg picked up a rib and bit into it. Barbecue sauce stained the edges of his beard. Krispin now understood the large pile of napkins Greg had brought with him, as he automatically wiped his beard after every bite.

"I told her on the boat."

"Told her what?"

Krispin sighed. "That I am a Christian. I didn't want her to hear my testimony in church tomorrow without having heard it from me first."

"Makes sense. But what about her seeing you live a different lifestyle first?"

"I tried that, but for the past two weeks, she's been avoiding me. So I thought it best to get it out in the open once and for all."

"Krispin, you told me you didn't become a Christian to get the girl. Are you still sure?"

"Yeah, I'm sure. God is real, and I've noticed a change in my life. Although some of the changes aren't all that pleasant."

"Like?" Greg continued to eat.

"I had a strange childhood."

"You mentioned that. But what in particular is striking you now?"

Krispin paused, scanned the area, and noted that Wayne still stood by the grill. Krispin lowered his voice. "When I was a child, I never learned to socialize with the other children. I was a loner. I liked it. Or rather, I preferred it over being teased about being so smart. When I went off to boarding school, I didn't know anyone, and it basically stayed that way until college, when I discovered a certain popularity with the women.

"Anyway," Krispin went on, "fact is, I really don't know how to act around a woman that I'm not trying. . .well, you know."

"Are you trying to with Jess?"

"Oh no, never! I mean. . ." Krispin stumbled over his words. "I respect her too much. I would never try to. . .you know."

Greg smiled and nodded.

"Yeah, I know. When Jayne and I met, I had similar ideas. The thing to do is to pray about it. God will give you the wisdom, the control, and the understanding in how this will all work out."

"I wish He'd just tell me and get it over with," Krispin mumbled.

"You and just about every other Christian on the planet. That's what trust is all about."

"But if the Bible is right, I have way too many wives as it is now. How do I reconcile what I've done in the past with who I am now?"

"You're forgetting that forgiveness clause. All your sins—and I do mean *all* your sins—have been forgiven."

Another man was heading toward the table—Jim or John or something like that. Krispin couldn't remember. "Hello," he said. "Would you care to sit here?"

"Josiah, take a load off." Greg pointed to the chair beside him. "Josiah, meet Krispin. Krispin, Josiah."

The two men shook hands. Krispin went back to his meal. "Josiah here has an incredible problem," Greg said. "He's about to go to prison."

"Sorry to hear that."

"I deserve it. I conned my grandfather out of his life savings. He has nothing left. The only downside is that I can't earn the money from prison to take care of him. My family won't speak to me; my wife left and returned to her parents. Last I heard, I was going to be a father in a month, but my wife isn't communicating with me."

"Ouch."

"Yeah. 'If you do the crime...'"

"You do the time," Pastor Russell said as he sat down beside Krispin. "You're turning yourself in tomorrow morning?"

"Yes. Today is my last day as a free man. However, the sheriff says I'll be coming to church with him in the morning 'cause he doesn't want to watch the cell, which means I can give my testimony before I go in."

"Wonderful. Tomorrow's service will be very different."

Krispin forked his coleslaw. He wondered what kind of a testimony Josiah had. He couldn't imagine stealing from someone, let alone from his own grandfather, and leaving him with nothing.

"Grandpa says he'll be here in the morning, too."

"Good," Pastor Russell answered without much of a reaction.

Krispin watched as Josiah ate his food. He seemed content going to jail and remorseful that he was leaving his grandfather in such scrapes. "What does your grandfather do?" Krispin asked.

"Lobstering, now. When he was a young man, he worked at the granite quarries."

How old is his grandfather? Krispin's thoughts flooded with memories of the early morning hours, the cool damp air, the weight of the lobster pots being pulled on board. *How can an old man do what Jess does?* he wondered.

"What about yourself, Krispin? Aren't you the man Jessica Kearns ran over with her boat?"

"Yes, but it wasn't only her fault. I should have paid more attention."

"More than likely. Most folks know well enough not to try and outrun a motorboat with a paddle." Josiah smiled. "Seriously, dude, what are you doing here? Didn't you threaten to sue Jess, her father, and the co-op?"

"Only Jess." Realizing he was being defensive, Krispin added, "I saw something in her and her father that made me curious about God."

"I wished I'd paid more attention when Mr. Kearns was my youth leader. I wouldn't have ruined so many lives. But enough about me. I've got the next five years to think about it. Word on the street is you're some kinda computer genius or something."

"I wrote software. I'm not a computer genius."

Greg smiled and placed his hand on Josiah. "Math is easy for him, like it is for my Lissa."

Josiah held a cob of corn in his hand and thought for a moment, then narrowed his hazel gaze on Krispin. "How do we know you're not the one that tried to break into Jess's computers?"

Krispin's spine stiffened; then he relaxed a fraction. "Frankly, you don't. But in my line of business, I have to be above reproach. I've been investigated more than once and have always stood the test. If I were not a man to be trusted, no one would buy our software. It's not just me that needs to trust in my abilities and honor. All of my clients have to trust me. And for what it's worth, I'm bonded." Krispin stood up. "Excuse me, I'm going to get some more corn."

He took a couple of steps, then turned back and leveled his gaze on Josiah. "To add to all the professional accolades, I now have Jesus in my court. God knows it wasn't me, and He knows who it was. I don't have to worry anymore with Him on my side."

Chapter 14

Jess caught herself wiggling in the pew as she waited for the morning service to begin. *Face it, girl, you've been wound up tighter than a rope spun around the propeller.* All night she'd been thinking about Krispin's confession and wondering how she hadn't picked up on the change in him. She had noticed he no longer behaved like a Neanderthal and that he was actually a kind and considerate person. Like when he asked his friend to fly Jordan back to Squabbin Bay in time for him to be at Randi's side for the birth of their baby. She had seen how generous he'd been to Greg Steadman and his family and how helpful he'd been to her with her computer problems. All in all, he did not seem to be anything like the man she had pulled out of the harbor those many months ago.

A smile of pleasure crossed her lips. She couldn't wait to tell Krispin of her observations. Admittedly, she had been overly guarded on the boat, fearful that it was another manipulative ploy on his part. But throughout the day and night, more confirmations about Krispin's faith and actions became clearer, along with her own guilt for not really trusting him. *Forgive me, Lord.*

Jess glanced over to the front pew where Krispin and the others sat waiting to give their testimonies. Krispin's gaze locked with hers. His deep, royal blue eyes sent a shiver of excitement through her. She lifted her hand to her chest and gave him a discreet wave. Krispin beamed.

Jess's stomach flipped. An instant flash of. . .what? A dream, fantasy, prophecy? A vivid image of Krispin standing in the front of the church as she was walking down the center aisle to become his wife went through her mind's eye. *Could he be? Lord, is he the one?*

"Good morning, Jess." Her father sat down beside her.

"Where's Mom?"

"She'll join us later. Jordan was up all night with Randi and the baby, so he asked Dena to fill in taking pictures for the testimonial part of the service."

Jess scanned the sanctuary. Over on the right side of the building, she saw her stepmother with a camera in hand and another around her neck.

"Dad, can Krispin join us for Sunday dinner?"

"Sure, except I believe Greg has planned a meal for his mentorees after the service."

"Okay, maybe another time."

"Are you two dating?"

"No!" she blurted out, perhaps too defensively.

Her father's beefy hand went over her own. "It's okay, sweetheart. I like him."

"I do, too. He's nothing like the man I first met."

"And that's a good thing." He squeezed her hand. "If Krispin asks you to join him for dinner, you're excused from the family meal."

Jess's smile brightened. She kissed her father on the cheek. "Thanks, Daddy."

"You're welcome."

The music started to play, and the worship leader stood up. Jess put all dreams and fantasies aside and concentrated on worshipping the Lord. Krispin floated into her mind only every other minute after that.

Krispin's mouth went dry. He couldn't sing. He could barely stand up. *Lord, help me say the right words. My testimony needs to be about You, not me.*

Josiah's testimony came first. Krispin sat while he listened to Josiah confess his sins to his grandfather and the entire congregation.

"I'm afraid I have another confession." Josiah turned his gaze toward the area where Jess sat. "Jess, I'm the one who broke into your computer." The congregation gasped audibly.

"I needed some money. I thought I could get enough cash to hold me over for the summer through the co-op's financial records." The congregation rustled in their seats. "I wanted to help my kid, ya know?"

"Sheriff, I suppose that means another trial?" Josiah asked.

"More than likely," the sheriff replied.

"Jess, I'm truly sorry. I didn't mean to break your computer. I'll add that to my list of things to pay back."

Jess sat silently and nodded.

Josiah had grown up in the community. Krispin saw from the faces of those in the congregation how much of a disappointment Josiah had been to the folks who cared about him.

Josiah continued. "I don't know what else to say except, I'm sorry. Pastor Russell and Mr. Steadman have made me see how selfish I've been. Grandpa, I'm sorry. I don't know how, but I'm going to get the money back for you. Jesus has forgiven me. . .I know that. But I want to be the man you would be proud to call *Grandson* once again. I love you." Josiah's voice cracked, and he left the pulpit and sat down.

Krispin rubbed the sweat from his palms on to his slacks before he stood up. "Good morning," he said from behind the pulpit. "Most of you don't know me. My name is Krispin Black. I'm from New Hampshire, and I found the Lord here. Many of you know that Jessica Kearns ran over my kayak with her lobster boat several months back."

The congregation let out a nervous chuckle. Krispin reached out and held the pulpit to keep his knees from buckling.

"Besides saving my life that day, she put me on the path to the salvation of my soul. You see, I had no use for God. I wasn't even sure there was a God. Instead I saw Him as a helpful crutch for others to lean on to get them through life. Well, you know what? He is. I finally came to realize I made a mess out of my own life. I found fortune and fame in my little corner of the world, but it left me cold and empty. My parents love me, but they loved themselves more. I was not a priority for them. Their own lives were more important to them, even while I was a small boy. I'm not saying that to blame them for how they raised me. But the way they expressed their love was very cold and distant, so I grew up with that same coldness.

"When I threatened Jess with the lawsuit, it was out of anger and from a way of life I'd been used to living. That's what you did in my world. You sued anyone for any inconvenience, including any you might have caused yourself. The truth is *I* was at fault that day. It wasn't Jess's fault. I wasn't paying attention and darted out from under the dock without looking.

"I know this sounds odd, but I'm grateful that Jess ran over me that day. I can see the Lord's hand was in it. You know, they say there are some hardheaded people in this world, and you have to hit them over the head with a two-by-four to knock any sense into them. But I'm especially hardheaded. God had to use an entire boat to get me to stop and reconsider my life choices."

The congregation gave a collective chuckle.

"I'm here today to proclaim I believe in God the Father, the Son, and the Holy Spirit. They live together as one, and Jesus is in my heart. I don't deserve Him or His love, but I'm thankful for it." Krispin let go of the pulpit and took his seat next to Josiah. The congregation burst into applause. Krispin bent his head in prayer. *Father, to You belongs all the glory. I'm the unworthy vessel. I'm not suited for this love, but I accept it. Thank You.*

The rest of the service was a blur. Krispin's mind stayed focused in prayer for God to be praised, not the people who were giving their testimonies.

❧

Jess couldn't wait for the service to end. She wanted to give Krispin a great big hug. He deserved love. He deserved to be loved, and with God's grace, she would be the one to love him in the way he'd never known before. Her heart ached to be able to speak alone with him, but she knew the next few hours would be taken up with a brief reception after church and then the meal at the Steadmans'.

Jess stood with the congregation when instructed by the worship director. The room filled with the voices of people enjoying the presence of the Lord, His praises, and good friends and family. After the benediction Jess worked her way through the congregation to shake Krispin's hand, as well as those of the others who had given their testimonies, including Josiah Wood.

"Hey, Jess. I'm sorry," Josiah said.

"You're forgiven. And you didn't break the computer. It was part of an encryption program to shut it down when someone attempted to get in one too many times."

"Oh. Well, like I said, I'm sorry. I have no idea what the penalty will be for breaking and entering."

"Neither do I." Jess held back from telling Josiah that she wouldn't press charges. Frankly, she didn't quite feel he was completely repentant. There was a marked difference between his testimony and Krispin's. Then again, it could be her own emotions shading the events. In either case she'd have to pray about it and ask for some wise counsel on whether or not to pursue legal action.

She shook Josiah's hand and moved over to the one she most wanted to speak with. Instead of taking his hand after the person in front of her moved on, she gave Krispin a huge bear hug and whispered in his ear, "You did well and gave the Lord His due."

Krispin pulled out of her embrace but continued to hold her shoulders. Their eyes searched one another's for a moment. "Thanks, Jess. That means a lot."

"I wanted to invite you to the Sunday family dinner, but Dad says you are probably going to the Steadmans'."

"Afraid so. Why don't I call you later?"

A line was gathering behind her. "Absolutely. Talk with you later." Jess moved toward Pastor Russell.

The afternoon passed with the speed of a slug crossing the sidewalk. Jess left her parents' house and returned to her own in time to receive Krispin's phone call.

"It's good to hear your voice, Krispin."

"Jess, I know this sounds horrible, but would you skip working with the youth tonight to go out with me?"

Jess giggled. "I don't have to skip out. The youth have a special event with another church's youth group so I didn't have to go. They had enough drivers and adult supervisors."

"Excellent. I mean. . ."

"Shh, I know what you mean. Please come over as soon as possible." Jess ached to share all that was in her heart, everything she hadn't spoken yesterday morning on the boat. For whatever reason she knew she loved Krispin and believed the vision she saw during church was God's way of saying it was okay to love him. She'd been afraid of her attraction for so long. Now she could allow it to grow and become what God intended for them as a couple.

Jess paced the living room as she waited for him to drive up. When she saw his Mustang turning in the drive, she ran out to greet him.

Krispin turned off the engine and slipped out of the car and into her arms. "Oh, Jess." He leaned down and kissed her.

Jess received his kiss and returned it, cradling his face in her hands.

Krispin broke away and held her. "I guess that answers the question."

I love you, Krispin. "And asks a whole lot more." Her heart beat wildly with love and fear.

"Definitely. Let's go inside. This town talks far too easily as it is."

Jess looped her arm around his elbow. He tensed for a moment, then relaxed. They walked to her house without a word spoken between them. She wondered about his hesitancy, then thought about what he said the day before, about his parents, about their lack of demonstrative love. *Was Krispin not so inclined?* "Are you afraid of physical touch because your parents weren't demonstrative?"

"No." He paused. "Jess, you have to know the whole truth about me before we can seriously consider a relationship. And once you do, you might not want to be anywhere near me."

Chapter 15

Krispin placed his hand over Jess's in the crook of his elbow. He didn't want to lose her, not now, not after everything he'd been through. But he knew she would have a serious problem being with a man like him, a man with a very stained past.

"Jess, my past—"

"Is in the past," Jess interrupted.

"Yes, I know. But you should know the extent of how bad it was."

"Krispin, you've already told me you were loose with women."

"Please, sit." Krispin released his grip and watched her gently settle on the sofa. He sat down beside her.

Jess sighed. "Krispin, we come from different backgrounds. But this morning I accepted once and for all that your faith is genuine. What happened back then were bad choices."

Krispin got up and paced. "You're not making this easy for me."

"Why? Because I forgive you? Am I supposed to ask how many? Am I supposed to ask what their names were? Is that really all that important at this time? Maybe later on, after we start dating and consider. . ."

"Marriage?" he supplied for her. "That's just it, Jess. I don't want to get involved with anyone if it isn't someone the Lord intends for me to marry. Look, I know the Lord forgives me. And I'm trying to forgive myself, but I know we can't enter a relationship without you knowing the truth about my past."

"All right. Tell me what you need to tell me."

Krispin sat down beside her once again. For the next fifteen minutes, he told her all he felt he should about his wrong choices and experiences, then concluded, "I'm sorry, Jess. I had no idea how God felt about marital love."

Jess closed her eyelids for a moment, then opened them slowly. "Krispin, I forgive you. You need to forgive yourself, and you should ask the Lord to forgive those other women for their part in the past sins."

"What are you suggesting?"

"Dad told me that he never felt truly forgiven for having gotten my bio-mom pregnant until he asked the Lord to forgive her. He'd taken the full responsibility for his actions upon himself. He forgot that Terry, my bio-mom, also chose to sin. Once he asked the Lord to forgive her for the part she played in their relationship, he finally felt really free from the past."

Krispin thought for a moment. He'd never asked the Lord to forgive the women he'd been involved with, only forgiveness for his part. *Is that why I'm still not feeling free from the past? Lord, forgive them.* "I never thought about that."

Jess smiled. "Now, let's change the subject. Tell me more about yourself, about your desires and dreams for the future. I want to get to know you better."

Krispin laughed. "You're incredible, Jessica Kearns. Do you have all night?"

"No, I have to work early tomorrow morning."

He popped up off the couch. "What time do you go to bed normally?"

"Nine."

He glanced at his wristwatch. "We have two hours. Are you hungry?"

"Nope. Just to know more about you."

"As I want to learn more about you. Let's do this: You ask a question, and I'll answer it. Then I ask the next question. Fair?"

"Sounds fair," she said. "What's your favorite color?"

"Brown."

"Brown? Why brown?"

"Nope, it's my turn." He smiled.

She turned and sat cross-legged on the couch and faced him. "Shoot."

"Well, I can tell by the decorations in your house that blue is your favorite color, which works well with your eyes, so I'm not going to ask that. Let's see." He paused with a hum. "I got it. What was your favorite toy growing up?"

"Oh man, you're going to cringe at this one, but it was a large Tonka truck that my neighbors had in their backyard."

Krispin chuckled. "A real tomboy, huh?"

"Yes, plus that's a second question, so I get two. Why brown, and what was your favorite toy, besides a computer?"

"I like brown because it reminds me of wood, especially wood that's been stained. I guess it's because of the old library I'd spend so much of my time working in when I was a kid. As for a toy besides the computer, that would be my dirt bike. It was risky and adventurous. Plus my parents hated it. Mom feared I'd break a leg. Dad just hated the noise. I liked it, so they let me keep it. Obviously they didn't buy it for me. My grandfather did."

Jess laughed. "I had a few of those presents over the years. I think my CDs of teenybopper music just about killed my father. Of course Grandma said it was payback for all the heavy metal rock they had to endure when Dad was young."

They talked until nine. At last Krispin stood up. "It's time for me to go."

"Krispin, this has been nice. Thank you." Jess walked him to the door.

"The pleasure was all mine. Good night, Jess."

She leaned toward him. He reached out and combed her silky, honey-blond hair with his fingers. A knot the size of a CD lodged in the pit of his stomach. Jess reached up and brushed his face with her knuckles. A cord of warmth wrapped itself around his heart.

Jess touched his lips with the tip of her finger. "May I?" she whispered.

Unable to speak, he blinked his agreement. Her soft velvet lips gently pressed against his. His heart pounded in his chest—not because of wild excitement, but because it was a beautiful, chaste kiss. It said more to him than any other kiss he'd ever known. He knew at that very moment, Jessica Kearns loved him with a love so profound and pure it made him weak in the knees. *How? I don't...*

Jess pulled away. He opened his eyes. "Don't question God's forgiveness." She winked and stepped back. "Good night, Krispin."

Krispin slipped out the door and stood for a moment or two on the small landing that made up her stairway before his head cleared enough to remind him that he looked like a fool just standing on the woman's doorstep.

❧

Jess spent an hour in prayer before going to sleep, asking that the Lord would protect her thoughts and memories in the days to come. What Krispin had shared was limited, but she knew enough of the world to know what kind of a lifestyle he had led. In thinking back on the first time she had met him, it fit perfectly with her first impression. But he was a changed man, and he was sincere. And after the vision this morning in church, combined with the impact of their first two kisses, she knew beyond a shadow of doubt God was bringing them together. By His grace, she felt certain they would be married one day.

Thinking about that the next morning brought a smile to her face when she passed the spot in the harbor where she had run over Krispin and his kayak.

Her day flew by quickly. It was four in the afternoon when Krispin came into the co-op.

"Hey there, handsome. What brings you here?"

"You." His smile brightened up his eyes.

"What's up?"

"Nothing. I just thought I'd like to get a better feel for your passion with this co-op to understand you better."

"Sure. What would you like to know?"

"Nothing in particular. If you don't mind, I'd like to observe you while you work. I can check out your computers so you won't notice me."

Jess laughed. "Right. I haven't had any further trouble with the computers, but what Josiah said yesterday has me a little concerned."

"Everything's probably fine, but I'd like to check on the software I installed that recorded all the transactions on the computer."

The phone rang. Jess answered and waved for Krispin to go to work on the computer. The voice on the other end said, "I'd like two hundred one-and-a-half- to two-pound lobsters by Wednesday and another five hundred by Friday. Can you handle that order?"

Jess clicked a few keys on her keyboard. "Sure. What's your name? Have you ordered from us before?" She went on with her work and continued with the order. As she finished up with her call, Tom Wood, Josiah's grandfather, entered the co-op and engaged Krispin in a conversation.

"Hi, Mr. Wood," Jess interrupted. "What do you have for me today?"

"Not much." He handed her the inventory sheet from the holding tank.

She read the chicken scratch of the counter. "Fifty one-and-a-half- and twenty two-pounders. That's not too bad."

"Maybe not. I kept a couple for myself." The age spots on his hands were getting larger, she noticed. His hands shook a little.

"Can I get you a cup of coffee to warm your blood?" Krispin offered.

"That'd be right nice of you, thank you." Mr. Wood sat down. Jess went behind the desk and inputted his information.

"Are we still good for payment the end of the month?" Tom Wood asked. Krispin handed him a cup of coffee.

"If you're tight, I can give you an advance, Mr. Wood," Jess offered.

"I was hoping I could hire an attorney for Josiah, what with the new charges the sheriff is going to be adding on after his confession in church. I'm sorry he went after you, Jessica. You're a fine woman, and you've done a lot for us. I just don't understand that boy. Pastor is hopeful he's on the right trail this time. But I don't know. I've seen him repent before. Only time will tell."

Jess didn't know how to respond.

"Mr. Wood, if I were you, I'd hang on to your money as long as possible. It will take awhile for the sheriff to file the charges. Plus the public defender can take care of those."

"I probably should. I've given that boy the shirt off my back." He stopped from admitting anything further.

"Mr. Wood." Krispin put a loving hand on Mr. Wood's shoulder. "Wait on the Lord for this one."

"I suppose you're right. You really meant all you said yesterday, didn't you?"

"Yes, sir."

"Good, I hope you stick to it." Mr. Wood sipped his coffee and put the mug on the edge of Jess's desk. "I'll hold off until the end of the month."

"All right. Remember, if you need it, I can work something out."

"I'll be fine." Mr. Wood got up to leave.

Krispin called out to him as the old man ambled outside. "Hey, Mr. Wood. Wait up."

Jess watched from the store window to see a smile break across Mr. Wood's face. The two men shook hands and then Mr. Wood leaned into the cab of his truck. Krispin pulled out his wallet and gave him what looked to be a twenty-dollar bill. Jess laughed and went back to work. Krispin truly was a changed man. Who would pay twenty bucks for a lobster that he didn't even like to eat, except a man with a mission to do good for others. *Yes, Krispin Black, you and I are meant to be together.*

Krispin put the large, three-pound lobster on the passenger seat of his Mustang and called Jess on the phone. "Hey, I'll be right back."

"What are you going to do with that lobster?"

"I thought about dumping it in the harbor. But then I remembered that Jordan loves these things with a passion, so I'm going to take it over to the Lamonts."

"Hang on; let me lock up and go with you."

"All right." Krispin closed the phone and got behind the wheel of his car. He gently grabbed the greenish blue crustacean and put him on the backseat of the car.

Jess bopped out of the co-op, her face lit with a contagious smile. "So, have you named him yet? You really shouldn't. You could get too attached."

"Ha-ha. I have no intentions of naming a lobster. I feel bad for that old man. He's been left with nothing. I think he needed money for more than hiring a lawyer for Josiah. I'd like to do something for him, but I don't know what."

"The church has a benevolent fund. If you know of someone in need, you tell the elders or pastor, and they give a love gift."

"That's not enough. This poor man lost his house because of Josiah."

"Not quite. Josiah doesn't know this, but between the church and the co-op, we managed to help Mr. Wood get a second mortgage on the house. As long as he keeps making his payments, he's got a place to live."

"And Josiah doesn't know this because. . ."

"No one is completely certain he's turned around yet. What's really scary is that if Josiah had gotten into the co-op's computer, he would have seen what we did to help his grandfather. He would have been a target again. Until there's more evidence of a changed life, no one wants Josiah to know."

"Makes sense. Still, I think Mr. Wood is hurting financially."

"Maybe. He probably spent the last of his cash on Josiah before his grandson went to prison. Mr. Wood is a good man, but he's got a huge blind spot when it comes to Josiah. You know what hit me in church was how different your testimony was compared with Josiah's. Josiah said he was sorry. He confessed to breaking into my house and computer, but he didn't give God any glory for the changes in his life. You, on the other hand, spoke little about what you'd done and more on what the Lord had done. It hit me then that Josiah still needs to put God first in his life. But at the time, I thought it was possibly me, unfairly misjudging his confession. Thinking about it now, I think maybe my impressions were right."

"Maybe, but it isn't our place to stand in judgment."

"No, but we are to be wise. And wisdom says to wait and see if Josiah is being sincere this time."

"On that, I totally agree."

"We're here." Krispin drove into Jordan and Randi's driveway. They were staying in the apartment above the photography studio. "Your stepmom owns this place, right?"

"Yup."

"I Googled her name. She's pretty famous," Krispin commented and reached behind him. "C'mon, Fred," he joked. "Uh-oh, I named him."

Jess let out a belly laugh. "What?"

"Fred."

"Well come on, Fred, you're going to make Jordan a happy man," Jess called out, walking up to the doorway of the apartment.

❧

Fred was a hit with Jordan. They stayed for a few minutes and played with the baby. Back in his car, Krispin asked, "Can I make you dinner?"

"Anytime," she quipped.

"Good. I'm enjoying the cooking."

"When I was in college, I was the take-out queen. As I told you before, Dena turned me on to cooking. I'm starting to like it, but not with the same enthusiasm as you have."

"We can learn together."

"I'd like that." Jess reached over and placed her hand on his. Krispin turned his hand and curled his fingers around hers. She brought his hand up to her lips and kissed the back of it. "I love you," she confessed.

He opened his mouth to blurt out the same when his cell phone rang the too familiar ring of his ex-partner in business. He answered. "Hi, Gary, what's up?"

"I need you. We have a huge emergency."

"What's the problem?"

"Something is wrong with the main components of several of your encryption codes. I know you're off somewhere finding yourself, but I really need you, man. The techs here have only been making the problem worse. I'll triple your pay. I need you for a month, possibly less."

"This isn't a good time, Gary."

"I don't care what it takes. Get here, and get here now. You gave your word you'd stand behind your product, and it is failing miserably. Get here by tomorrow morning. I'll hire a jet, if need be."

"All right. I'll be there in the morning."

"How about yesterday?"

"Okay, I can get there shortly after midnight. I'll need a room. I've sublet my apartment."

"Trust me, you won't have time to sleep. I'm setting you up in a secure and sealed-off room. You won't have access to any outside numbers."

"No way. I need an outside line, even if it is just the Internet."

"Separate unit?"

"Of course."

"Fine. I'll see you at midnight."

"What's the matter?" Jess knitted her brow. "You've got to go?"

"I'm afraid so, Jess. I don't want to, but I gave my word. I have to help."

"That's not a problem. I understand."

Krispin drove past his house and toward hers. "I'll drop you off. I'm sorry."

"Shh, don't you worry about it. I'll see you when you get back."

"Jess. . ." How could he tell her he might not be coming back for a month? With all the clarity that could come from a divine revelation, Krispin realized he might not know what he was going to do the rest of his life, but it would include Jessica Kearns. *If she'll have me.*

Chapter 16

Thirty days later, Krispin had still not returned. A weekly e-mail from him wasn't giving Jess a whole lot of satisfaction. She made arrangements with Myron Buefford to run the co-op in her absence while Dad took care of the lobstering. Jess drove up to the software company that Krispin had worked for, and even owned a portion of, before settling in Squabbin Bay. But had he really settled? He'd been gone for so long and—

She stopped the circular thinking that had plagued her for weeks.

Jess parked next to his Mustang and walked into the building. Its modern art and stainless steel statue in front glistened in the bright afternoon sun. The windows were three stories high. If a building could look high-tech, this one sure did.

She marched up to the receptionist.

"May I help you?" The woman had straight black hair pulled back in a bun. Her gray pinstripe suit declared all business.

"Yes, could you please tell me where I can find Krispin Black?"

"Do you have an appointment?"

"No."

"Well, I'm sorry, Mr. Black is not seeing any customers at this time."

"I'm not a customer." Jess narrowed her gaze. She wanted to say she was his fiancée, but nothing had ever been said about such a relationship, and she wouldn't presume it upon him. "Would you please just tell him that Jessica Kearns is here to see him?"

"Jessica Kearns." The woman wrote the name down, then popped her head up and scanned Jess from head to toe. "You're Jess?"

"Yes. Can I see him?"

"Uh, yeah. I guess so. Take the elevators to the third floor and take a right. His office is on your right. You can't miss it. It's the corner office."

"Thanks."

"You're welcome." She grinned as if knowing a secret. Whatever it was, Jess really didn't care. She wanted to see Krispin, and she was only a few feet away from him. *If this elevator would move.* Jess rapped her fingers on the stainless steel plate that housed the buttons for the various floors, having already punched in the number three. Impatient, she tapped it again. The doors closed. The floor jerked, then seemingly nothing until the door swooshed open on the third floor.

She walked down the hallway to the last office. Inside she found him with his back to the door. "Krispin?"

He jumped up and banged his knee on the keyboard. "Jess?" He ran up beside her. "Oh, honey, you're a sight for sore eyes."

Jess giggled and held on to him tightly. "So are you. I've missed you."

"And I, you. It's been horrible here. But I think I've finally created a new system."

"Krispin, I just want to hold you."

He held her close and kissed the top of her head. Joy filled her. "How long can you stay?"

"A couple days."

"I'll get you a suite."

"A suite?"

"Don't worry, it's a trade-off with the hotel. When we have customers we want to treat well, we put them in this suite. We manage the hotel's security software. It's a fair trade. The cost for me is that of renting a regular hotel room."

"All right. How long before you can take a break?" Jess asked and stepped out of Krispin's embrace.

He looked back at his computer, then back at her. He was pale and at least ten pounds thinner.

"Have you been eating?"

"A little. I've been shut up in a solitary room for days. I finally worked out the bugs and got through. It's an incredible program, Jess. The next level in encryption."

"I thought Gary asked you to fix a problem, not create a new program."

"I forget you don't understand all this stuff. Sorry. I fixed the problem. But what happened meant that all our other encryption programs that had those same components were vulnerable to this hacker. Replacing the software program with a totally different matrix seemed the logical course of action for the future. The stopgap I finished in a week. If the hacker's as good as I think he is, and if he's dedicated, he'll probably figure this one out in three months, possibly six. But that gives Gary's crew time to develop the new software they've been working on."

"I see."

Krispin chuckled. "I can tell by the glazed look in your eyes that I lost you. Suffice it to say, it's fixed, and the new and improved model should keep folks safe for a while."

"If you say so." Jess shook her head in disbelief. "You really are good at this stuff, aren't you?"

"He's the best," a deep male voice from behind her answered. She turned to see a man in his early thirties leaning against the doorway. "So you're Jess, huh?"

Krispin wrapped his arms around her. "The one and only."

She could feel Krispin's smile even if she couldn't see it.

"It's a pleasure to meet you. I'm Gary Ladd, owner of this company, and I'd be in your debt forever if you'd convince this man to come back to work for me. I've offered him fifty percent of the company, his own hours, and still he refuses."

Jess stilled in Krispin's arms. *He shouldn't be giving up his future, Lord.*

"I'm renting the suite for her."

"Not on your life. I'm paying. And I'd like you to take her out to the finest restaurant and put it on my credit card. Remember, you're unemployed. I'm not."

"But you're paying me three times the normal rate for the past month. I think I can afford to take my girlfriend out to dinner."

"Okay, I'll give that—you can afford it. Allow me to give you this gift."

"We'll think about it," Jess answered for him.

"That's all I ask." Gary turned his wrist. "Gotta run. It's a pleasure to meet you, Jess. Stop by again tomorrow. Perhaps we can chat some more." And he was off.

"Is he always like that?"

"Yes."

"Wow, he must take some getting used to."

"Most couldn't handle his abrupt changes in persona. By the time I was in the upper ranks of the company, I'd already seen how he operated, and it didn't bother me. He and I got along well. He truly does want me to come back. I'm not surprised, but I'm not really interested. I don't mind doing limited projects like this for him. But I don't want to have to be put in lockdown for weeks at a time. It's not healthy."

"No, you look horrible. I mean. . . " Jess stumbled over her words. "I mean, you don't look as healthy as when you left Squabbin Bay."

"I'm not. Besides not eating right, I've been working day and night to get this done, so I could get back to you. Jess, I've missed you so much. E-mails only made it more difficult to concentrate. That's why I didn't send you many. I'm sorry."

"Now that I'm here with you, everything is fine."

"Hang on a minute, and I'll take you to the hotel."

"I can find it."

Krispin chuckled. "I know you can. It's basically across the street. I want to get out of here, though, and I don't want you out of my sight."

Jess's heart jumped. "I'm all for that."

Within a couple minutes, they were locking his office and heading down the hallway, walking arm in arm. It was hard to believe how much she missed this man. Inside the elevator he leaned down and kissed her. Jess savored the moment and held on until they heard applause coming from behind them. She felt the heat rise in her cheeks. How'd they not noticed the doors had opened? She wanted to crawl under the floorboards and hide. Krispin wrapped a protective arm around her and escorted her out of the building.

⁊

Inside her suite Krispin removed his shoes and gazed over the cart of food he'd ordered from room service. "Honey, do you want ice cream later?"

Jess came from behind the closed door of her bedroom. Her hair was damp from the shower. "What did you order?"

"A little of everything." He handed the waiter a substantial tip.

"Thank you, sir. Can I get you anything else?" The waiter smiled and waited for a response.

"No thanks. We'll call if we have any other need."

"Very good, sir. Ask for Ramone, and I'll take good care of you, sir." Krispin knew he could count on Ramone getting him and Jess anything they desired tonight. Krispin closed the door. Jess's beauty took his breath away.

As if reading his mind, she ran to him and wrapped her arms around his neck. "Kiss me before I faint," she begged.

She didn't have to ask twice. He kissed her with the fervor of all the love he had for her. It had been growing day by day for the past month. Whoever had said absence made the heart grow fonder certainly nailed it for the two of them. "Marry me, Jess," he blurted out.

"Yes," she answered.

Then it hit him: what he had asked and what she had responded with. The realization struck him at the same time it dawned on her. An awkward silence filled the room. "I love you, Jess. I want you to be my wife, if you'll have me as a husband."

"I want to be your wife. But there's so much left unsaid between us. So much we don't know about one another yet."

"Agreed. How do we approach this situation now?"

"We could marry ASAP. Dad told me to be very careful and guard my heart so as not to be too vulnerable while we're alone together."

Krispin laughed. "I can see you paid attention."

She jabbed him in the ribs. "Let's eat. We'll figure this out as we go along."

"Excellent idea."

Jess took the hotel's white china plate and sampled the different cheeses and fruit, then placed the steak with mushrooms and onions on her dish. Krispin did the same and added a bowl of cream of asparagus soup.

"Be careful not to eat too much. How many meals did you skip?"

"Way too many. You look great, though."

"Thanks. The shower helped." She sat down on the sofa and put the plate of food on the coffee table. "Krispin, why didn't you call me?"

"I was afraid if I heard your voice I wouldn't be able to concentrate on the project. I was trying desperately to finish it so I could get home to you. I told Gary if I didn't finish it in two more days, I was leaving for a visit. I'm so glad to see you."

"Krispin, we should get married, just not tonight."

"Agreed. Don't you need to get blood tests or something first?"

"Not anymore. But you do need a marriage license, and we have to pick that up at the town hall."

"We could find a minister to marry us tomorrow," Krispin hinted.

"And who's going to tell my father we eloped?"

"I get your point. What if we call them and ask them to join us?"

Jess took a forkful of steak and chewed it thoroughly before she spoke. "I think I know why you're so good at writing software—you stick to it. Which will be a good thing in marriage. However, I've always dreamed of getting married in Squabbin Bay at the church, the white gown, walking down the aisle, a flower girl, the whole bit."

Krispin swallowed the chunk of apple he'd just bitten off. "How much time do you need?"

"Honey, there's a lot of work at the co-op right now. I can't see myself getting married until next June."

"June? That's like seven months away."

"Exactly."

Krispin sobered. "If you want to wait seven months, I think I'll take a couple of jobs Gary offered me. They will take a couple of months."

"Why?"

Krispin swallowed hard. "Jess, that's a long time to be close to you without something else to occupy my thoughts."

"Yes, so? Oh!" Her eyes widened. "Okay. What about you helping me at the co-op?"

"Doing what?"

"There's a ton of things. I know we could be better organized. The software we have doesn't fully integrate all the information to the various areas I need to retrieve it, so I'm inputting the same information two or three times a day."

"I can handle that. So could we get married in November? If I take that on?"

"That's next month."

Okay, I'm missing something here. He thought of a movie he'd seen about what women want and remembered a line about proms being all about the dress. "Jess, how much time do you need to get the dress, set up the wedding the way you'd like? I want you to have the wedding you've always dreamed about."

Jess giggled. "Daddy would die. He'd have to work a third job to pay for it."

"Seriously, Jess, what do you want? I'll do whatever it takes to make that day special for you. And I can pay for it. Your father doesn't have to."

There was a long pause. "You know what? I'm not thinking about this right. You're willing to give me everything I want, and I haven't offered to give you anything you want. What do you want, Krispin?"

"Only one thing: to be your husband. I don't care how the process happens. I just want to do it right."

"What about your parents?"

"I'll find them and let them know. I'm pretty sure they'll come, if they can be reached." Krispin resumed eating. So did Jess.

After a few minutes, she said, "How about if we get married a week before Thanksgiving?"

"Seriously?"

"Yeah. I know the photographer, so that's not a problem. We can have it at the church, and we can have it catered or have folks bring potluck."

Krispin wiped his mouth with the linen napkin. "We'll cater."

"How many invitations for your friends from here?"

"Probably no more than a dozen, if that. If you've noticed, no one came out to visit with me."

"Do you think Gary would come?"

"If he can still do business on the side."

"He can't be that bad, can he?"

"Just about. But he'll come, and he'll bring his wife."

"He's married?"

"Yeah. I never could figure how he managed to keep a wife, but he does, somehow. Are you sure, Jess?"

"Yes, I'm sure. Now hurry up and finish your dinner. I want to go out and spend some time in your city."

"Okay. What about careers, Jess? Are you willing to leave Squabbin Bay, lobstering, and the co-op if some opportunity came up for me to work somewhere else?"

Chapter 17

Jess fought all night with the question Krispin had asked her before they went out. She avoided the answer, saying something lame like she'd deal with it when the time came. But the time was now. Krispin had excellent opportunities to stay with this company. He meant a lot to them and their future. How could she possibly pull him away from all of that?

She'd gone to work with him in the morning in order to retrieve her car. Today she sat in the suite, bored and alone. She thought about going shopping, but that wasn't the answer. This was what life would be like with Krispin. He'd go to work, she'd stay home and do what? Raise babies?

Jess wanted children, but that wasn't her only goal in life. She had a business degree and would like to continue using it. *I wonder if I could find a job in this company? But what about the co-op? I can't desert them now. Perhaps in a year, when we're really established, but right now seems too soon, Lord. What should we do?*

She picked up her cell phone and called her stepmother. "Mom, it's Jess. I need some help."

"What's the matter, Jess? Are you all right? Krispin didn't—"

"Oh, no, nothing like that. He asked me to marry him."

"Congratulations! Wait—are you happy about that?"

"Yes, but, oh—I don't know. He's got great career opportunities here. They love him, and he's a valuable member of their staff, Mom. I just don't feel like I can take him away from this. And then there is the co-op. I can't leave it now. It's too fragile."

"I see. You know, Jess, your father and I had similar problems before we got married. I had a career that took me all over the world. He wanted to stay in Squabbin Bay. In the end, we worked it out. If Krispin is the right man, it will work out."

Jess sighed. "I know. We talked about eloping but figured Dad would have my head. Plus, I still would like to get married in the church."

Dena let out a nervous chuckle. "Sweetheart, I know the pain of trying to decide. Unfortunately, I can't answer this question for you. You and Krispin have to work this out."

"Yeah, I suppose so. It's just that I was hoping you could tell me what to do."

"I can tell you what not to do. And eloping would fit in there somewhere, only because your father would like to attend and give his blessings on his little girl's wedding, not to mention the rest of us." Dena paused. "Jess, I truly understand the agony you're going through right now. But try to be patient and wait on the Lord."

"Mom, here's the thing. Krispin doesn't want to wait a long time. He's more concerned about not sinning. What do you think of the weekend before Thanksgiving?"

"I understand. Your father and I didn't wait a long time either. But—"

"I know, you were older. I had a vision the Sunday morning that Krispin gave his testimony. I saw us getting married in the church."

"Honey, I don't doubt that you love Krispin or that he loves you. I don't even doubt that the Lord is behind this. What concerns me is the time you haven't had together to become friends. It's that friendship that will get you through the ups and downs of life. And marriage is hard work. I love your dad with all my heart, but there are adjustments we both have to go through."

"I know what you're saying is right. I just don't want to hinder Krispin's career."

"That's Krispin's choice, as it is your choice about the co-op. You say it is at a critical time, but the fact of the matter is the co-op can move on without you, if you let it go. I'm not saying it is the right thing to do, I'm just remembering back to my own decision-making process. Letting jobs be done by others rather than myself was a hard thing to allow. You created a good co-op. You could let someone do the daily running of the business and still stay on the board to help oversee the growth of the company, couldn't you?"

"Yeah, I suppose I could. But who could do my job?"

Dena laughed. "I don't know. I do know one thing: It won't be your father."

Jess joined her stepmom in the humor of that statement. Time was precious to her parents, and she knew it. "Thanks, Mom."

"You're welcome. Please tell me I can tell your father the news."

"Nope, I'll do it. Right now."

"Great, 'cause I don't think I could have kept this a secret."

They ended the conversation, and Jess called her father on his cell phone. He didn't pick up, so she left him a message to call Dena for the news. Then she reached for her purse and headed out of the suite to take in some of the sights of the city.

❧

"Krispin, this is incredible."

"I'm pleased, but you and I both know it won't take long before someone is able to crack it. In my opinion you need to get some of the younger guys working with this right away so they can take it to the next level."

"I understand. Krisp, please reconsider and come back to work for us."

"I can't. It's not a healthy environment for me."

"True, you don't look so hot. Okay, what about this? I keep you on retainer, and you work from wherever you are."

"I'll think about it. I'm not like you, Gary. I can't separate my work and my personal life. I get too obsessed with it. I couldn't do that to Jess. I honestly don't understand how you manage to have a successful marriage."

"That's because she and I run in very different circles. She has her work; I have mine. You notice we don't have children. Neither one of us wants to give up the time it would take to raise kids. It works for us."

"I know Jess would like to have children one day—not right away, but one day. She's really quite an intelligent businesswoman. She put together—"

"The co-op, yeah, you told me. And what's that encryption program you put on her server?"

"You checked?"

"Of course. I always check into my competition, and frankly, Jessica Kearns is my competition. However, I can see I won't win against her. Promise me you'll seriously consider the idea of going on retainer and working remotely."

"We'd have to talk about it further. And I'd limit myself to only a couple projects a year."

"You can't live on that, can you?"

"It would be tight. However, I'll probably agree to a certain percentage of the profit from the program sales."

Gary shook his head in disbelief. "You'll do all right. You're still a wise businessman."

"I learned from the best." Krispin winked. "Gary, I know you think I've gotten all holy and stuff, and perhaps you're right. But trust me, I have more peace now than I've ever had in my entire life. And at the same time, I have more issues with no answers or quick resolutions. It's weird, but Jesus really does help."

"If you say so. Look, I don't mean to brush you off since you started talking religion again, but I do have an appointment in three minutes. Thanks for this. I don't know how to pay you back for it."

Krispin chuckled. "You will. Here's my bill." Krispin tossed an invoice over to him.

Gary's eyes bulged. "Wow, that's triple?"

"All except the percentage of sales for this product. That's at the same standard I used to earn."

"I guess you can only work on two or three projects a year."

Krispin smiled. "Thanks, Gary."

Gary initialed the invoice and handed it back. "You're worth it, man. Call me once in a while."

"You'll be getting a wedding invitation."

"Louise and I will be there."

"Great. God bless." Krispin walked out of Gary's office a new man. It wasn't the same as when he'd left the company all those many months ago. Instead he was standing the victor, knowing he was walking the right path in the right direction—and into the arms of the woman he loved. Life couldn't get any better than this.

He pulled out his cell phone and called his parents. The service said they were out of communications range. He left a message, telling them he'd be getting married in November and asking them to return the call as soon as they could.

Somehow it didn't surprise him that they weren't available to hear the news. *Father, try to reach my parents. They're good people, just self-absorbed. Help me deal with them.*

Krispin walked to accounting and waited for them to process the check. Ruthie Martin stood at the printer, waiting for it to be printed. "Mr. Black, I hear you're getting married."

"Yes, Ruthie, I am."

"Congratulations. Is it this woman from Maine that everyone's been talking about?"

"Yes."

Ruthie smiled and retrieved the check. "Wow! I'm sorry, what you're paid is none of my business."

"That's all right." Krispin took the proffered check and folded it in half.

"Will you be coming back to the company? Everyone's been wondering."

"No, I'll probably do some side jobs and come in for emergencies. But let's hope there aren't any more emergencies."

"Yeah. Everyone talked about you being here, but no one really saw all that much of you. You came to work before anyone else, and you left after everyone else."

Krispin didn't want to tell her of the numerous nights he never left. "Goodbye, Ruthie."

"Good-bye, Mr. Black." Ruthie sat back down at her console and began typing. Krispin walked out and looked back at the tall office building they had built five years earlier. Back then he had been a junior-level partner. He knew his programs were the backbone for the early growth of the company, but it would take a team of programmers to bring the company further up the software chain to become the best in the world for encryption.

A slow smile eased up the corners of his mouth. It no longer mattered to him if he was the best in the world. He was content to be the best man he could be for the Lord and for Jessica. He flipped open his phone and called her. "Hey, where are you? I'm done."

The lilt of Jess's laughter felt like warm honey on a sore throat. "You won't believe this, but I'm at a bridal shop."

"Oh, really? Did you find anything you like?"

"Uh-huh. I'm standing in front of the mirrors with it on."

A rush of emotions hit Krispin all at once. He could picture her standing in front of three mirrors dressed in white. "Jess, I love you."

"I love you, too, Krispin. The saleswoman is here. I'll call you in a couple minutes."

"Sure. I'm heading to the hotel suite."

"Let's meet for lunch."

"Okay. Go to Richard's Bistro—it's on Lowell Street—say in thirty minutes?"

"Make it forty-five."

Krispin chuckled. "No problem. See you there." He drove down to Lowell Street and parked outside a jewelry store. Glancing at his watch, he made a quick detour inside. Finding mostly secondhand jewelry, he decided to look but not purchase. The thought of giving Jess a "used" engagement ring didn't set well. It would be one thing if it were a family heirloom, but this would never do.

"Can I help you, sir?"

"I was looking for an engagement ring, but I'm looking for something new."

"I understand. We have a fine variety of rings. What some of my customers have done is purchase the ring here and have the stones reset in a new setting."

"Hmm." Krispin scanned the glass counter. "Why is this diamond almost yellow?"

"That's a rare type of diamond. Be warned of the imitations out there. . .stones that have been chemically altered."

"How can you tell the difference?"

"You can't, but an honest jeweler can. There are also pink diamonds."

"May I see the yellow diamond ring?"

"Sure." The gentleman took a key ring from his pocket and opened the cabinet. A small, white price tag dangled from the ring. Krispin glanced at it, then refocused his gaze. "Is that the correct price?"

"Yes. It's actually a steal. Brand-new can run from five to forty thousand for that carat. The clarity of the stones accounts for the higher figure."

Krispin handed the diamond back. The idea of a beautiful ring for a beautiful woman thrilled him. The idea of her fishing with a ring of such great value seemed foolish. "What do regular diamonds go for?" Krispin could feel the sweat beading on his forehead. Marriage was going to cost him big-time.

❧

Jess sat down beside Krispin at the restaurant. It had taken her the full forty-five minutes to dress and worm her way out of the store. The saleswoman unsuccessfully tried to convince her that seven thousand dollars was appropriate for a woman like her to spend on a wedding gown. *Not!*

"What's the matter?" Krispin asked as she settled into the chair.

"Nothing."

"Did you like the dress?"

Jess sighed. "Yes, but there's no way I'm going to spend seven thousand on a dress. I'd rather save it for something more important."

"Seven isn't too bad. You should have seen a price tag I saw earlier. Did you know that yellow diamonds could cost forty thousand?"

"Please tell me you didn't spend that! Did you?"

"No. I'm far more practical than that. It was a pretty ring, but not that pretty."

"Phew."

Krispin reached over and held her hand. "Jess, let's pray."

Jess nodded. And Krispin began. "Father, guide us in the decisions we're going to be making over the next few days. Help us to make the right choices. I want to give Jess the kind of wedding she has dreamed of, but help us be practical in choosing what, when, and how much."

"Father," Jess added, "please help us to be in agreement with one another and not to be sidetracked by what others think or believe is acceptable for a marriage ceremony. Amen."

"Amen." Krispin's rich baritone voice spiraled down to the depths of her being. She could feel herself calming.

"So what is the normal price for a wedding gown?" he asked. "I already have a tux, so that isn't a problem."

"You own your own tux?"

"Yeah, it seemed practical at the time. I had several events where I needed to rent one, so I simply purchased it. Anyway, what kind of a dress do you want?"

"I loved the one I had on. It had all sorts of fancy beading and just sparkled wonderfully in the lights. I could see myself in it. But then again, it seemed too, oh, I don't know, rich for my taste. I'm basically a jeans and sweater type of gal. Don't get me wrong, I like nice clothes, and I love the feel of fine silk against my skin but—"

Krispin held up his hand. "I understand. One of the reasons I didn't buy the ring was that I just couldn't picture the ring on your finger while your hand was diving into that chum bucket."

Jess laughed. "I wear gloves."

"I know, but still, it wasn't the kind of jewelry you would wear on the job. Personally, I'm looking for a simple gold band that tells the world I'm married, and that's it. I'm not interested in impressing anyone. I do want to get you an engagement ring, but I want to be practical about it. What would you feel comfortable wearing every day?"

"Probably just a solitaire. . .nothing huge, just a simple-cut ring."

"Yeah, that's what I was picturing, too. Good, we have similar tastes."

Jess squeezed his hand. "I told Mom. I couldn't reach Dad."

"I called my parents, as well, but could only leave word on their answering service."

"Krispin, I've been thinking. Are we making the right decision? I mean. . ." *What do I mean?* "I can see us getting married one day, and I understand your desire to marry quickly, but. . ."

"You need more time?" He rubbed the top of her hand with the ball of his thumb.

"Yes. . .no. . .maybe. . .I don't know. All I do know is that it isn't right for you not to work in the place where you shine. As for me, I'm hesitant to leave Squabbin Bay, not because of the area, but because of the co-op."

"Jess, I have no intention of moving back into the rat race that I was once in to help develop this company. I can, and probably will, develop more software for them. However, I've got to learn how to stop working." He leaned in closer. "Here's the thing. I'm obsessive when it comes to developing new programs. I don't break away as often as I should. I couldn't do that to you."

"So what are you saying?"

Krispin closed the few inches between them and kissed Jess's forehead.

"May I take your order now?" the waiter interrupted.

Jess pulled away. She'd been so focused she'd forgotten their surroundings. Krispin ordered a cold steak salad for both of them. After the waiter left, he said, "I'm saying I don't have to work for anyone except myself. I can develop the software and sell it to Gary. He'll package and sell the programs. I don't want the headache of business. I simply want to be creative and write the programs."

Jess smiled. "Mom suggested I should start letting other people work for the co-op."

"Is that what you want to do?"

"No. I like working. I like planning and moving the co-op forward."

Krispin laughed. "The very things I really don't like in the business world."

"Yeah, I guess we're opposites there."

"Look, Jess, I'll wait as long as you want to get married. I love you, and I can't believe God is allowing me to find a wife. I simply am not worthy of it. You deserve better."

She laid a finger to his soft, warm lips. "Shh, we've been over this. You're suited for love just as much as everyone else. I love you, Krispin, and I love the man you have become."

"I'm glad I'm not the man you first met. But, Jess, there are parts of me that are still that man. I'm not perfect. I've changed but—"

"You're perfect for me," Jess finished his statement.

"You know how to tickle my ears. So are we still on for the Saturday before Thanksgiving?"

"Yes. Where do you want to go for our honeymoon?"

"Hmm, I haven't thought that far. Where do you want to go?"

"I love camping, kayaking, and all those outdoor things, but I'd really love to go to Italy—to Venice. I've never been there, and a city on water intrigues me."

"Venice it is. Do you have a passport?"

"Yeah, Mom insisted on it, saying she'd like for all of us to travel together sometime."

Krispin sat back. The waiter approached and placed their steak salads down in front of them, then disappeared. He picked up his fork, then laid it back on the table. "Let's pray."

Jess slipped her fingers into the palm of his hand. She loved the feel of his touch. She could see herself getting old and gray and still cherishing holding this man's hand. The Lord had answered her prayer and brought the perfect man into her life. A man with an unworthy past but standing on the promises of God, washed in the blood, and fearfully and wonderfully made to be her life partner. *Thank You, Jesus.*

Epilogue

Jess slipped her hand into Krispin's, then turned to her father. He lifted the veil and kissed her on the cheek. "I love you, sweetheart."

"I love you, too, Daddy."

Krispin squeezed her hand and gave Wayne a wink. Pastor Russell continued with the wedding service. "Dearly beloved, we are gathered here today. . . ."

Her eyes met Krispin's. The confessions of love and fidelity were spoken with such truth and honesty Jess had no doubt this man would keep his word to her and to God. Her love for Krispin deepened as she professed her love to him.

"Krispin, you may kiss your bride." Pastor Russell smiled.

Krispin cradled her head in his hands. "I love you, Jess."

"I love you, too."

Their lips met. A deep warmth of excitement, passion, and completeness filled out the kiss. Oh yes, she was one with this man and would be for the rest of her life.

Slowly the sounds of the cheers and clapping from those watching penetrated their senses, and Krispin pulled away. His fingers slid down her arms and entwined hers. They turned and met the congregation.

"May I present to you for the first time, Mr. and Mrs. Krispin Black."

Jess's smile filled her face. Krispin's did the same.

The old pipe organ cranked out the traditional wedding recessional, and Krispin led her down the aisle, past his parents, past hers. In the row behind her father and stepmother was her bio-mom, Terry, with her husband and children. Jess smiled. Terry actually seemed comfortable being there.

Krispin pulled Jess into his embrace once they stepped into the foyer. "I love you, Mrs. Black."

"I love you, too."

"What did your mom say about her matron of honor present?"

"She and Dad were floored. I can't believe you worked it out for them to join us the second week in Italy."

"Well, you said your father wanted to travel more, and I know Dena's been there before, so she'll be a great tour guide."

"Honey, that isn't why you invited them, is it?"

"No, it isn't. But I love the togetherness of your family."

"I know, and that's what I told them. They're excited and will be joining us."

"Great. Besides, your stepbrother, Chad, got us a fantastic rate. Oh, by the way, he and his family will be joining us, as well."

"What?" Jess's knees felt weak.

"I rented a large villa for the second week. There are six bedrooms, so I figured we had room to invite the rest of the family to join us. I know that Amber and David would never be able to afford a trip like this, and neither would pastor, so I figured with the rate Chad was able to get, we could afford to bring the entire clan over with us."

"You're kidding!"

People were gathering to shake their hands and congratulate them. "Nope. I figured it would be fun to have a family Thanksgiving in Italy."

"Do Mom and Dad know?"

"Probably by now. I had the family keep it a surprise from you and your parents. I had to check with them to see if they could arrange their schedules to join us. It took some work, but they'll all be able to come."

"Just how much money did you make last month?"

Krispin leaned over and whispered in her ear. Jess's eyes bulged. "You're kidding!" she said again.

"Nope."

"So you could have afforded that forty-thousand-dollar ring?"

"Yup. But this trip is better than that ring, right?"

Jess started to giggle. She giggled all during the receiving line. Not only was Krispin Black suited for love, he was the giver of love to others. As they walked back into the church for the wedding photos, she said, "You're nuts, you know."

"Absolutely. Nuts about you and nuts about a forgiving God who has blessed me beyond all I could ever hope for."

"I love you."

"I love you, too." They stood arm in arm and posed for the cameras. Jess's heart swelled yet again with love for this incredible man. And for an incredible God who would, and could, take away all the hardness of the world and make vessels suitable for His love for others.

A Letter to Our Readers

Dear Readers:

In order that we might better contribute to your reading enjoyment, we would appreciate you taking a few minutes to respond to the following questions. When completed, please return to the following: Fiction Editor, Barbour Publishing, Inc., P.O. Box 719, Uhrichsville, OH 44683.

1. Did you enjoy reading *Harbor Hopes* by Lynn A. Coleman?
   ❏ Very much. I would like to see more books like this.
   ❏ Moderately—I would have enjoyed it more if _____
   _____
   _____

2. What influenced your decision to purchase this book?
   (Check those that apply.)
   ❏ Cover   ❏ Back cover copy   ❏ Title   ❏ Price
   ❏ Friends   ❏ Publicity   ❏ Other

3. Which story was your favorite?
   ❏ *Photo Op*   ❏ *Suited for Love*
   ❏ *Trespassed Hearts*

4. Please check your age range:
   ❏ Under 18   ❏ 18–24   ❏ 25–34
   ❏ 35–45   ❏ 46–55   ❏ Over 55

5. How many hours per week do you read? _____

Name _____

Occupation _____

Address _____

City_____ State_____ Zip_____

E-mail _____

continued . . .

Vanishing Point

"Van Gieson evokes the desert beauty of New Mexico with meticulous care . . . [and] manages to keep the reader guessing throughout." —*Publishers Weekly*

"Besides her professional skills at plotting and conveying the fascination of Southwestern scenes, Van Gieson also excels at a witty depiction of the academic world in which Claire Reynier does not quite fit." —*Amarillo Globe-News*

"Intriguing . . . Van Gieson describes the character and colors of the canyon lands with her deft sense of place, making the beauty and danger of the land vivid and palatable." —*Mystery News*

"A classy new mystery series . . . moves confidently from one reasonable plot development to the next, incorporating in the action a nice sense of place." —*Arizona Daily Star*

"In Van Gieson's hands, issues involving family, the 1960's, academia, and the Southwest converge, giving us another characteristically fine read, leaving our quietly resolute, solitary heroine to deal with the evanescence of things." —*The Bloomsbury Review*

"I loved it! It's even better than *The Stolen Blue*." —Fred Harris

The Stolen Blue

"Van Gieson's back—and better than ever. Don't miss *The Stolen Blue*." —Tony Hillerman

"An intricate puzzle that kept me guessing until the last piece snapped into place. A terrific mystery with a savvy and totally likable sleuth." —Margaret Coel

"A very entertaining book, and a promising new series." —*Arizona Daily Star*

"A beguiling mystery filled with fascinating and likable characters. Ms. Van Gieson proves she is a powerful storyteller." —*Midwest Book Review*

"An engrossing read. Just the thing for book lovers to curl up with." —*Las Cruces Sun-News* (NM)

"A book-lover's delight . . . ingenious . . . a great new series." —*Romantic Times*

"A lovely book. . . . Claire Reynier is a wonderful character." —Mysterious Women

"Engaging. . . . The setting infuses the narrative with the Southwest's richness." —*Tucson Weekly*

"A quick-paced, enchanting, modern whodunit." —*Albuquerque Journal*

"A captivating and absorbing, highly readable, stay-with-it-till-you're-done mystery." —Fred Harris

Also by Judith Van Gieson

Confidence Woman
Vanishing Point
The Stolen Blue

LAND OF
BURNING HEAT

A CLAIRE REYNIER MYSTERY

Judith Van Gieson

A SIGNET BOOK

Land of Burning Heat is a work of fiction, but it is based on historical fact.

SIGNET
Published by New American Library, a division of
Penguin Putnam Inc., 375 Hudson Street,
New York, New York 10014, U.S.A.
Penguin Books Ltd, 80 Strand,
London WC2R 0RL, England
Penguin Books Australia Ltd, 250 Camberwell Road,
Camberwell, Victoria 3124, Australia
Penguin Books Canada Ltd, 10 Alcorn Avenue,
Toronto, Ontario, Canada M4V 3B2
Penguin Books (N.Z.) Ltd, Cnr Rosedale and Airborne Roads,
Albany, Auckland 1310, New Zealand

Penguin Books Ltd, Registered Offices:
Harmondsworth, Middlesex, England

First published by Signet, an imprint of New American Library,
a division of Penguin Putnam Inc.

First Printing, February 2003
10 9 8 7 6 5 4 3 2 1

 REGISTERED TRADEMARK—MARCA REGISTRADA

Printed in the United States of America

PUBLISHER'S NOTE
This is a work of fiction. Names, characters, places, and incidents either
are the product of the author's imagination or are used fictitiously,
and any resemblance to actual persons, living or dead, business
establishments, events, or locales is entirely coincidental.

For my stepfather,
Richard Zieger

ACKNOWLEDGMENTS

Many thanks to Irene Marcuse, Lou Hieb, Julie Mars, Ann Paden, Mike Clover, and Maria Senaida Velasquez Huerta. I am blessed to have such knowledgeable friends who were willing to read the manuscript of *Land of Burning Heat* and share their expertise in many areas including Judaism, academia, the history of the New World and the Old, the Spanish language, and the town of Bernalillo. Any errors that survived their careful readings are the author's. Thanks to Erwin Bush for exploring Bernalillo with me, to my agent, Dominick Abel, and my editor, Genny Ostertag.

I am deeply grateful to Jerome Aragon for sharing his family's fascinating story.

I cared for you in the desert,
in the land of burning heat.

Hosea 13:5

Chapter One

During the break before summer session Claire Reynier walked across the University of New Mexico campus, enjoying the quiet time when the students were gone and the campus reverted to the staff. With no students and backpacks to dodge, Smith Plaza felt larger. It was noon and the sun was directly overhead. The longest shadows she cast were the half-moon beneath her visor and the darkness under her feet that made her feel there was another Claire, a reverse Claire, who extended into the ground and mirrored her footsteps from the other side. The sun warmed her shoulders and the top of her head. It wasn't searing hot yet, not so hot that she wanted to stay inside until dark, but hot enough to make her long for rain. As she approached Zimmerman Library, a massive pueblo-style building, her reflection was visible in the glass doors. In this light she saw more silver in her hair than gold. She looked slim enough in her pale summer dress, but knew she would look even slimmer if she straightened her back. She made the correction before she stepped into the library's familiar shelter.

She walked through the gallery, which had an ex-

hibition of Mexican photography from its sepia be-
ginnings in the nineteenth century, when itinerant
photographers posed families in a stiff and formal
way. She passed the nearly empty Anderson Reading
Room. The young woman manning the information
desk didn't glance up from her book. Claire crossed
the hallway and went through the wrought iron gate
into the Center for Southwest Research, grateful as always that she worked in such a beautiful place. She
walked down the office corridor. Through the interior
window that faced the hallway she was startled to see
a woman she didn't know standing inside her office.

"Hello?" Claire asked, wondering whether the
woman was a student. She wore a dark red skirt and
top and platform shoes that brought her up to
Claire's height. She had the slenderness of a stalk
that swayed in the wind, but the thick-soled shoes
kept her grounded. Her hair was black and pinned
up on top of her head with a spiky plastic clip. Her
eyes were large and amber colored. The skirt was
slinky and calf length. Her matching T-shirt had a
golden butterfly embroidered across the bodice. The
woman had a delicate, exotic quality Claire was unable to place. Her looks could have been Hispanic,
Native American, East Indian, Middle Eastern, Asian,
or a mixture of any of them.

"Are you Claire Reynier?" she asked.

"I am."

"My name is Isabel Santos." She extended a hand
with rings embellishing nearly every finger.

Claire shook her hand, then circled her desk and
sat down behind it, motioning for her visitor to do
the same.

Isabel went to the visitor's chair and perched on
the edge. "A woman at the Bernalillo Historical Soci-

ety referred me to you. She said you were an expert on old documents."

"May Brennan?" Claire asked.

"That's her. I moved back from California to the family home in Bernalillo this spring. One of the bricks in the floor was loose. I tripped on it when I got up last night to go to the bathroom, and I pulled it out. I was digging out the sand to make more room for the brick when I found something."

Claire knew that brick floors were often laid on a foundation of sand in New Mexico houses. "What?" she asked.

"An old wooden cross with a hole in the bottom. I picked it up and a rolled-up piece of paper fell out. The cross had been hollowed out so the paper could fit inside." Isabel had a red suede purse dangling by a strap from her shoulder. She opened it and removed a piece of paper.

The archivist in Claire noticed that the paper was white and crisp and new. "Is that what you found?" she asked, doubting that there could be anything of value to the center on such white paper.

"No," Isabel replied. "The paper I found was really old and dry. I didn't want to mess it up by moving it around so I copied what it said."

She handed over the paper. Up close Claire could see that it had blue notebook lines and that the writing on it was as round and symmetrical as a schoolgirl's.

" 'Todo sta de arriva abasho,' " she read. " ' El fuego o el garrote. Dame el fuego. Adonay es mi dio.' "

"Is that some kind of old Spanish like Castilian?" Isabel asked. She spoke the word "Castilian" with a contemptuous lisp, then laughed. To speak Castilian Spanish was considered arrogant in parts of New Mexico.

"It might be an archaic form of Spanish," Claire said. "*Arriva* could be a variant of *arriba*. *Abasho* could be a variant of *abajo*."

"As in 'everything is up and down'?" Isabel asked.

"Or 'upside-down,' " Claire said.

"And *garrote*? What does that mean?"

It was Claire's nature and her job to be careful, but she knew all too well what *garrote* meant. In English or in Spanish it was an instrument used to strangle people during the Inquisition. *El garrote* was considered kinder than *el fuego*—"the fire"—being burned at the stake. The distinction had always seemed a subtle one. In either case the victim ended up dead. She explained to Isabel what *el garrote* meant.

"And *Adonay*? What is that?" Isabel asked.

"The Spanish version of the Hebrew word for God," Claire said. "Are you sure it said *dio* and not *dios*?"

"Yes. That seemed weird to me because we always say *dios*."

"The Spanish Jews said *dio*; for them there was only one God."

"You think this was written by a Jew?" Isabel said, balancing on the edge of her chair.

Yes was Claire's thought, but the archivist's response was, "It could have been. The language could be Ladino, the language used by the Sephardic Jews, which was a combination of Spanish, Arabic, and Hebrew. These words appear to have been written by a Jew who faced the Inquisition."

"Was the Inquisition practiced here?"

"No one was actually killed in New Mexico, but people were garroted and burned at the stake in South America and Old Mexico, where the Inquisition was practiced until the wars of independence."

"There was a Marrano in our house." Isabel

laughed, puckering her lips like she had bitten into a piece of rancid meat.

Literally "Marrano" meant swine, but it was also a word used to describe Jews who converted to Catholicism during the Inquisition. The more polite word was "converso."

"If this was written by a Marrano then why was it hidden inside a cross?" Isabel asked.

"It's possible the person who wrote it thought a cross was the last place anyone would look or the author was trying to pass as a Catholic. Is your family Catholic?"

"Are you kidding?" Isabel said. "Is the pope? We have the last name of the saints. My brother's first name is Jesus."

Pronounced "haysoos," it wasn't such an unusual name in Spanish. "How long has your family had the house?" Claire asked.

"Forever. My grandmother grew up there."

"An ancestor might have buried the cross under the floor."

"My ancestors were not Jewish."

"Was the document signed?" Claire asked.

"Yes. It was signed 'Joaquín.'"

Joaquín was a common enough name in the Spanish-speaking world, but the further back one went in the New World the fewer Joaquíns there were until the number became minuscule and then there were none. One of them once made the statement that the number of real Christians in the New World could be counted on the fingers of one hand. If that Joaquín had written and signed this document it would be extremely valuable: The story of how it got to New Mexico and under the bricks in Isabel Santos's floor could be written later. The most important thing at this point would be to safeguard the document. Exposing it to the light after years in darkness could be ruinous.

"I'll need to see it to be sure," Claire said, "but it could be a document of enormous historical significance. If it is, we would love to have it here in the center." She didn't think she was being unduly acquisitive. The center had the facilities to preserve it and make it available to scholars.

"Who is this Joaquín?" Isabel asked.

"There was a Jewish mystic named Joaquín Rodriguez who was killed by the Inquisition in Mexico City in the late sixteenth century."

"If the paper is that old, it would be *very* valuable, wouldn't it?"

"It could be," Claire admitted, knowing that much as she would love to have it in the center, there were other institutions and collectors who could pay more.

"I'll have to think about it," Isabel said, putting her hands on the edge of her chair as if preparing to push off.

"Of course," Claire replied, reluctant to see her leave. "The document could be fugitive to light. You should get it in a controlled environment as soon as possible. We have the optimum conditions here and would be happy to preserve it and protect it until you decide what to do."

"I'll get back to you, okay?" Isabel stood up, wobbling for a second before she found her balance on the platform shoes.

"I can come out to your house and take a look at it if you like," Claire said. She didn't want Isabel to leave the center, but didn't know how to keep her. As a mother of two grown children she saw a fragility in Isabel that made one want to shelter her, as well as a determination to go her own way that would make mothering difficult.

"Okay. I'll let you know what my family says. Thanks for talking to me." Isabel left without reclaiming her note.

Claire watched her walk away swinging her purse with a long, bare arm. It seemed to pick up momentum as she walked.

Once Isabel had disappeared around the corner, Claire made a copy of the note and locked the original in the bottom drawer of her desk. Then she walked down the corridor in the other direction, noticing as she passed several empty offices that most of her coworkers were out. She was pleased when she got to Celia Alegria's and found her working on her computer. Celia, who was determined not to let the library turn her into a brown bird, often wore velvet to work. It was too hot for velvet and today she had on a yellow linen dress and a necklace that was a string of turquoise birds in flight. All the color at CSWR seemed to be concentrated in Celia's office. The folk art posters on the wall and the shrine to Frida Kahlo on her bookshelf made the point that she remained in touch with her Mexican heritage.

Claire stepped into her office and shut the door behind her.

"Harrison?" Celia asked, looking up from the computer and raising her eyes to the ceiling. Harrison Hough, their prickly boss, was a frequent source of annoyance. Closing the door was a signal that Claire would complain about him.

"Not this time," Claire said, handing her the copy of Isabel's note. "What do you make of this?"

Although Spanish language and history had long been a subject of interest to Claire, Celia had a Ph.D.

in history and had studied in Mexico and Spain. "The language is Ladino. I'd say it was written by a Jew who faced the Inquisition, but that person didn't write it on twenty-first-century notebook paper," Celia said.

"A woman named Isabel Santos brought it to my office referred to me by May Brennan of the Bernalillo Historical Society. She claims she found the original document inside a cross buried beneath the brick floor of her house in Bernalillo."

"Have you seen the original?"

"No. Is there any way of telling whether this was written in the New World or the Old World by the content?"

Celia studied the note. "Not really. The Inquisition was practiced many places—Old Spain, New Spain, Peru, Colombia. The Spaniards didn't just kill Jews either. They killed Muslims, Protestants, even Catholics who had strayed. In theory the Holy Office of the Inquisition punished lapsed Catholics. In 1492, all the infidels had to convert to Catholicism or leave. Some Jews and Muslims converted but with varying degrees of conviction. Supposedly, converso families weren't allowed to emigrate to the New World, but some did. The ones who went on practicing Judaism in secret became known as crypto Jews. There is no record of anyone ever being killed for practicing Judaism in New Mexico. We have that distinction. But crypto Jews were not allowed to own property or to hold water rights here. If they were found out they would lose their water rights, which could be a death sentence."

"What if the document was signed 'Joaquín'?"

"Just 'Joaquín'?"

"That's what Isabel said."

"Well, if it was signed 'Joaquín Rodriguez' I'd say

it was written by the Jewish mystic who was killed by the Inquisition in Mexico City in 1596 except that he wasn't burned at the stake. He was garroted. His death is well documented. The Spaniards kept detailed records of everything they did. If it's just Joaquín, I don't know. There could have been other Joaquíns who were burned at the stake during the Inquisition. Supposedly Joaquín Rodriguez converted and was saved from the fire, but his sister Raquel was incinerated. She went to her death screaming at her Inquisitors. She was even more passionate about her *dio* than Joaquín was. And he was pretty passionate. Often crypto Jews were not circumcised as infants because that gave them away. When Joaquín was fifteen he circumcised himself with a pair of scissors in the Rio de los Remedios." Celia grimaced at the thought. "If you had a choice, which would you choose? The fire or the garrote?"

"Does it matter? Either way you're dead."

"Most people preferred strangulation when given a choice. Burning takes longer and is more painful. The special collections library at Berkeley recently acquired a treasure trove of Inquisition documents, the largest collection of Mexican Inquisition papers in this country. The fact that this person chose the fire might indicate that this wasn't written by Joaquín Rodriguez. There are some scholars who could help you. Peter Beck at Berkeley is a leading scholar of the Mexican Inquisition. Your friend August Stevenson in Santa Fe authenticated the documents for Berkeley. But you'd have to have the original before you could establish anything definitive."

"I hope I can get it," Claire said.

"Of course you can. What was this doing buried under the floor of a house in Bernalillo?"

"I don't know."

"It could have been there for hundreds of years. It could also have been put there more recently. If you bring it to the center, Harrison will want to establish for sure that it wasn't stolen. You know Harrison." She rolled her eyes again. "Have you said anything to him yet?"

"Not yet."

"It might be better to wait until you actually have the document in hand. Once Harrison hears about it, he'll get greedy. You won't have any peace until he has it in his fingers. There's no guarantee we're going to get it, is there?"

"None," Claire admitted. "Isabel said the family has been here a long time. I'm hoping a state-sponsored library will appeal to them."

"It might," Celia said. Her silver bracelets clinked as she rubbed her fingers together in the universal symbol of greed. "But money might appeal to them even more. There are plenty of places able to raise more money than we can. Berkeley has deep pockets. We'd lose but it would be fun to see Harrison get into a pissing contest with them."

"Even if the document isn't originally from Bernal-illo, it was found there, which makes it in some way a part of New Mexico history. The center is where it belongs," Claire protested.

"You're right," Celia agreed.

"It would be good for the center. It would be good for New Mexico."

"It would be good for you," Celia said, getting up and giving her friend a hug.

Chapter Two

The next day Claire had a luncheon to attend in Santa Fe. She called August Stevenson and asked if she could stop by and see him afterwards.

"Of course," he replied. "I'd be delighted."

It was the response she expected, but she still enjoyed hearing it. August had a distinguished career in document verification in New York City before moving to Santa Fe, supposedly to retire. He was well into his seventies now, but as far as Claire could tell he'd barely slowed down. Instead of documents finding their way to him in New York City, they found their way to him in Santa Fe. August had helped her before with an important document. She respected his expertise and trusted his discretion.

He lived a few blocks from the Plaza in a quiet neighborhood that tourists rarely visited. After her luncheon Claire drove there and parked in front of August's small brick house. It took him a long time to answer the doorbell, but she knew he was on his way when she heard the shuffle of slippers against the wooden floor.

"Claire, my dear," he said, swinging open the door, staring at her through the thick lenses of his glasses and giving her the impression that he was peering out through the water of an aquarium. "Very good to see you."

"Good to see you, August."

"Come in."

He turned and shuffled down the hallway with Claire following him. His broad, hunched back and slow movements reminded her of a tortoise. When they reached his office, he lowered himself into a leather desk chair. Claire sat in an armchair.

"How are you?" she asked.

"All the better for seeing you. And how are things at the library?"

"Good," Claire said. They had more to say about their work than about their personal lives, so she got to the point. "I just came across a very interesting document I'd like to ask you about. A woman named Isabel Santos who lives in Bernalillo found it under her brick floor. May Brennan referred her to me."

"And how is May?" August asked. "I hear she is getting a divorce."

"It happens to the best of us," Claire said. "May will get over it sooner or later. Isabel didn't actually bring me the document, but she wrote down what it said."

August sniffed with contempt at the photocopy Claire presented. "Well that and four dollars will get you a cup of coffee at Starbucks. You know I rely on quality of paper and ink to establish the age of a document and on writing style to establish authenticity." Claire had the sense that he was pulling up his tortoise shell and retreating inside. "This looks like it was written by a schoolgirl."

"I know," she soothed. "Of course you need the original document to come up with anything definitive, but in this case the content is so unusual I thought it might provide some clues." Claire didn't want to tip her hand by telling him she knew he had authenticated Inquisition documents.

He held the paper at arm's length trying to find the right perspective through the thick lenses. He pushed it away, pulled it close, scrunched up his forehead, and studied it for some time before he said, "The content suggests it was written by a Jew who faced the Inquisition. Which Jew, which Inquisition, I couldn't say. A few years ago I examined some documents for UC Berkeley that involved the Mexican Inquisition. The documents were in private hands and Berkeley wanted to be sure they were authentic before purchasing them. The Spanish kept impeccable records, although perhaps they shouldn't have. The Inquisition was a despicable affair, one of the most despicable affairs in a long human history of despicable behavior. Humans are monstrously cruel creatures. Some people were burned at the stake in Mexico, the most famous of whom is Raquel Rodriguez, who remained a fervent Judaizer up until the moment she was consumed by the flames. If there really is an original document and it was written by Raquel Rodriguez . . ." He put the paper down and stared at Claire through the deep-water lenses. "Well, that would be a find indeed."

"Isabel said it was signed 'Joaquín.' "

"Just 'Joaquín?' "

"That's what she said."

"Ah, to have the original in my hands." August thumped his desk in frustration. "Raquel had a brother, a Jewish mystic named Joaquín, who was garroted."

Claire knew all this but she kept quiet, waiting

to see in what direction August's thoughts would lead him.

"I authenticated the document that described his execution. He converted at the last minute and was given the favor of being garroted."

"Isabel told me that she found the document inside a hollowed-out wooden cross."

"I suppose it's possible that the document was concealed in a cross that ended up in New Mexico. It may have been written on handmade paper imported from Europe, which could survive for hundreds of years in New Mexico's dry climate. The Inquisition was heating up in Mexico City at the end of the sixteenth century. It has long been believed that some Jews whose names appeared on the Inquisition lists came north with Don Juan de Oñate's expedition in 1598. Few questions were asked of anyone willing to make the arduous journey into unknown territory. There are samples of both Joaquín and Raquel's handwriting extant. It would be very easy to establish if he wrote these words if only I could see the original."

"Isabel said she would get back to me."

"Keep after her. This could be a very important find. I'd hate to see it go to some wealthy collector or to Berkeley. You, of course, have many years to make wonderful discoveries. But me?" The slowness of his shrug demonstrated the weight the carapace on his back had become.

After she left August's house Claire negotiated her way across The City Different in her pickup truck. She owned a truck because she needed one to transport books, but it also made a statement about the

kind of strong and adventuresome person she was—
or wished to be.

Santa Fe was founded in 1610 on the model of a
Spanish colonial city with streets radiating from a
central plaza and a cathedral a few blocks away. It
was to be expected that the Spanish would build a
city resembling the ones they came from. What always surprised Claire was that they would cross an
ocean and find a place so similar geographically to
the one they had left behind. History was never very
far away in New Mexico, which was one of the
things she liked about it. She enjoyed the sensation
of moving from one century to another.

On her way out of town she stopped at twenty-
first-century Wild Oats to buy granola and bagels.
As she checked out she noticed the clock on the wall
said four-fifteen. Wondering whether there was any
need to return to her office at CSWR at this point or
to just go home, she checked her voice mail from the
cell phone in her truck. Talking on a cell phone was
a private matter for Claire. She wasn't a person to
walk up and down the aisles discussing what to buy
for dinner. Besides, she had no one to discuss dinner
with. She found a message from Isabel Santos on her
voice mail saying, "I want to talk to you again. I'll
be in Albuquerque tomorrow and will stop by your
office."

Claire left the parking lot and drove down St. Fran-
cis Drive to the interstate. It wasn't long before she
was out of the city and into the wide open spaces of
I-25. She saw a cluster of lenticular clouds hanging
over the Ortiz Mountains and one had been twisted
into the perfect symmetry of a corkscrew. She inserted a cassette of the Indian rock group Red Thun-

der into her tape deck. The backdrop of drums and chanting and the ease of the drive left her mind free to wander. It headed back to southern Europe and northern Africa, the region that was the source of the Inquisition. There was a time when Muslims, Jews, and Catholics lived in harmony, but that ended and the Inquisition began, forcing Jews and Muslims to convert, leave the Iberian Peninsula, or be persecuted.

Claire had taken a semester off when she was in college and spent some time traveling through Spain and Morocco with an Italian man named Pietro Antonelli in a Volkswagen van that broke down in every country they visited. She had recently tracked Pietro down on the Internet to the University of Florence, where he taught. Now that she had his E-mail address, she had been composing E-mails in her mind, but she hadn't arrived at the perfect phrasing yet. To help the process she popped out Red Thunder and inserted Andrea Bocelli. Listening to the Italian tenor and composing an E-mail to Pietro made the time pass quickly. When she reached the Bernalillo exit, a few miles north of Albuquerque, she turned off, thinking she might not have to wait until tomorrow to speak to Isabel.

She stopped at a convenience store on Route 44, went to the pay phone, and flipped through the phone book that dangled beneath the stand. If Isabel had recently returned to Bernalillo, her phone number wouldn't be listed yet. But Claire expected there to be other listings for Santos and she found three: Chuy and Tey in Bernalillo and Manuel in Placitas. She called the two in Bernalillo, getting no answer at one and voice mail at the other. She wrote down the addresses, then went inside the store to ask the clerk for directions.

The young woman with a mane of curly brown hair was busy talking on the phone. Claire stood in front of the counter feeling invisible while she waited for the conversation to end. Realizing that being empty-handed offered no inducement, she picked up a newspaper and placed it on the counter. The clerk hung up. Claire paid for the newspaper and asked if she knew where either address was. She didn't know Mejia Street, where Tey lived, but directed Claire to Calle Luna, the address for Chuy.

"Thanks," Claire said.

"Sure," the girl replied, picking up the phone again.

Claire drove south through Bernalillo on Camino del Pueblo looking for the turnoff that led to Calle Luna. The Sandia Mountains in the east were the color of slate, mirroring the color of the clouds that had formed over the West Mesa. It was the time of year when clouds began to build up late in the day, but rain rarely fell until later in the summer. Claire thought of this as the waiting-for-rain season, when the earth seemed to be holding its breath in parched anticipation. Camino del Pueblo was once El Camino Real, the royal road that led from Mexico City to Santa Fe, traversed by a long line of oxcarts, horses, settlers, friars, and conquistadores, traversed now by trucks and motorcycles and SUVs. The road was lined with churches, a courthouse, a hardware store, a bar, restaurants, and storefronts, but a few blocks behind it were quiet streets and open fields. Claire turned off Camino del Pueblo and followed the directions to 625 Calle Luna.

The street ended in a cul-de-sac beside an irrigation ditch. As Claire turned the corner she saw that the cul-de-sac was filled with one ambulance and a swarm of white-and-brown Sandoval County Sheriff's Department cars. She hoped that 625 wouldn't turn out to mark the end of Calle Luna, but as she followed the numbers down the street she had the ominous sensation that it would.

Chapter Three

Claire saw the number 625 set in tile in an adobe wall, parked in front of it, and got out of her truck. The house was in the northern New Mexico style with a pitched tin roof ending in a porch. The walls hadn't been stuccoed and she could see straw sticking out of the adobe. The yard was full of police officers. One of them saw her and walked down the path.

"Can I help you, ma'am?" he asked. He was young with a stocky build and a thick black mustache. He had a tough-guy appearance but his manner was deferential. "I'm Detective Jimmy Romero."

"Is this 625 Calle Luna?" Claire asked, thinking it was a stupid question but not knowing what else to say.

"Yes. And who is it that you're looking for?"

"Isabel Santos."

"You mind telling me why?"

"My name is Claire Reynier. I work at the Center for Southwest Research at UNM. I met Isabel when she came to see me yesterday. She found a document buried under the house that she thought might be of interest to the center."

"What kind of a document was that?"

"A historical document. You need to tell me. Has something happened to her?"

"The house was robbed and she . . . well . . . Isabel Santos is dead."

"Oh, no." She turned toward the house. It had a beautiful, verdant setting but it was an unpretentious house. "What would anybody want to steal from here?"

"We don't know yet," Detective Romero answered.

"I need to speak to the person in charge of the investigation," Claire said. "There was a phone call on my voice mail from Isabel this afternoon."

"What did she say?"

"That she wanted to see me tomorrow."

"Do you know what time that call was made?"

"I left my office at eleven. It was sometime after that. The time will show up on my caller ID."

Detective Romero asked her to wait in the yard while he talked to the investigation commander. Claire sat down at a picnic table under a cottonwood tree, watching the activity going on around her but feeling detached and isolated from it by a bubble of shock. How could Isabel, so full of life and potential yesterday, be dead today? Detective Romero spoke to a police officer on the porch, then went inside the house. A friendly black dog walked up and rested its nose in Claire's lap while she scratched its head. The field around the house had been irrigated with water from the irrigation ditch and was green with alfalfa. Horses grazed at the far end.

A man stepped off the porch and walked over to Claire. His hair was streaked with gray and he had a middle-aged spread. He wore jeans and a T-shirt decorated with the feathered logo of Santa Ana Star

Casino. His hand had the curve of a container. Today it held a Dr Pepper.

"I'm Chuy Santos," he said. "Isabel's brother." Up close his eyes were large and full of pain.

"Claire Reynier," she replied. "I am so sorry to hear about Isabel. I can't believe anything like this could happen to her. She was such a bright spirit."

"Are you a friend of hers?"

"No. I just met her. I'm an archivist at UNM. She came to see me about a document she found. Is this where she was living?"

"Yes."

"Is it your house?"

"It belongs to all of us." Chuy sat down on the bench on the other side of the picnic table. The dog went to him and he patted its head. "What document are you talking about?"

Claire wondered if she would betray a confidence by telling him, but decided that when a document was found in a house that belonged to a family, the document belonged to the family. She pulled Isabel's note from her purse and showed it to Chuy. "She didn't actually show me the document, but she wrote down what it said and brought it to me."

Chuy took a sip of his Dr Pepper and studied the document. "That's my sister's handwriting, but I never saw anything like this anywhere."

"She said she was going to discuss it with the family."

"She didn't discuss it with me," Chuy said, "and I'm her family. My sister went to California to get away from all of us. She comes back, starts getting her shit together. Now this . . ."

Paramedics came out of the house bearing a body on a stretcher. They loaded it into the ambulance and drove away. A man who left the house with them came over to the picnic table. He wore slacks with a sharp crease and a white shirt with sleeves so carefully rolled they appeared to be creased, too. His hair was black. He was slim and rather elegant, Claire thought, wondering if he might be the investigation commander.

"Hey, bro," Chuy said.

The man put his hand on Chuy's shoulder and Chuy gripped it with rough, callused fingers.

"This is my brother, Manuel. Damn, I forgot your name already," he said to Claire. "I'm not playing with a full deck right now."

"I'm Claire Reynier. I met Isabel yesterday. I feel terrible about this," she said.

"It sucks, don't it?" Chuy said, taking a loud sip from his Dr Pepper. It seemed to Claire that he became coarser after his brother appeared, but Manuel was smooth enough to make most people seem coarse in comparison. She placed him as the eldest sibling with Chuy in the middle and Isabel as the youngest. He had her amber eyes, although they lacked her warmth. His eyes were on remote. The dog wagged its tail but stayed away from the creases in Manuel's pants.

"Thank you for your concern," he replied.

"Claire here said Isabel found a paper in the house. She wrote down what it said and took it to UNM."

"Is this it?" he asked, taking the paper and reading it.

"Yes," she said.

"And how do you interpret this?" Manuel asked, handing the paper back.

"It appears to be something written by a Jew during the Inquisition."

"*Híjole*," said Chuy.

"Where did she say she found it?"

"She said there was a loose brick in the floor. She pulled it out and found a wooden cross buried in the sand with the document inside. If I saw the original document it would be easier for me to judge how authentic it was, but she didn't bring it to the library."

"I didn't see anything like that in the house, did you?" Chuy asked. "It's a mess in there. Stuff was thrown everywhere."

"Could you tell if anything is missing?" Claire asked.

"The TV, the stereo, stuff like that," Chuy said.

"It was a local kid," Manuel said, "looking for drugs and guns. My sister walked in and surprised the thief. The most dangerous part of a robbery is interrupting one."

Detective Romero stepped out of the house and motioned to Claire. "Lieutenant Kearns will see you now," he said.

Chapter Four

Claire left the Santos brothers at the picnic table and went to talk to the lieutenant. He had a rumpled, jowly face, bristly reddish brown hair, and eyes the pale blue of an eastern sky. Claire had been way off the mark when she thought the immaculate Manuel Santos was the investigator. Lieutenant Kearns's pants had never known a crease and his short-sleeve shirt was wrinkled. His arms were thick with rusty hair.

"You wanted to talk to me?" he asked.

Claire handed him her card. "Isabel came to see me about a document she discovered in the house. I did some research and found out it could be quite valuable. She left a message on my voice mail today saying she wanted to see me. I stopped by this afternoon."

Lieutenant Kearns turned the card over his fingers. "Do you have any ID?" he asked.

In Claire's experience, when a middle-aged woman was noticed at all her respectability was taken for granted, but she opened her purse and produced the driver's license and UNM card that proved her identity.

"Do you have a copy of the document?" Kearns asked.

"I have a copy that Isabel made in her own handwriting." Claire handed it to him.

"Have you seen the original?"

"No."

The lieutenant frowned at the paper, squeezing a few more wrinkles into his forehead. "What does this mean?"

"I think it was written by a Jew about to be killed by the Inquisition."

"That would make it what? Three, four hundred years old?"

"If it is from the New World. If it's from Spain it could be even older."

"Could something like that survive for centuries?"

"Under the right conditions."

"Is there a market for it?" The lieutenant squinted into the sun breaking through the late afternoon clouds.

"Yes, but I'd have to do more research to tell you exactly what that is and I'd need to see the original. Isabel told me it was inside a wooden cross she found beneath the brick floor. Did you see a wooden cross in the house or an old document?"

"No, but we weren't exactly looking for a cross or an old document. We're doing a room-to-room, plain-view search. It appears to be the typical crime scene of someone lookin' for something they could use or fence quick—drugs, guns, jewelry, money, cell phones, VCRs, stuff like that. We see this kind of robbery every day in Sandoval County. It can turn tragic if the owner has the misfortune of walking in on the perp."

In Claire's experience people were also capable of

killing for rare and valuable objects not so easy to
fence. She knew that once she got back to her office
and the shock of Isabel's death wore off, guilt that
she had not gotten here sooner would fill the chasm
created by the death. To stumble on the crime scene
was deeply disturbing, but she would feel worse if
she left here without taking advantage of the opportunity being offered.

"The document Isabel described could be very valuable to the family and to historians," she said. "If
it is here, it needs to be preserved. I might be able
to help your investigation by looking through the
house. I may be able to pinpoint where she found it."

Lieutenant Kearns leaned against the wall and
studied her. Claire supposed he wondered if she
could really be useful to his investigation or if she
had some other agenda for getting inside the house.

"I am an archivist," she added. "I work with historical documents."

"I need to go inside and make a few calls,"
Kearns said.

Claire waited, wondering just whom he was calling. A superior? Someone he knew at UNM? The
campus police? She hoped the phone calls wouldn't
lead to Harrison, her boss. The last thing she'd want
him to know was that she was at the scene of a
criminal investigation.

Kearns came back outside. "All right. You may
look, but that's it, and you've got to cover up your
hands and feet."

He produced a pair of plastic booties and plastic
gloves and Claire put them on. He opened the door
and they stepped into darkness and chaos. Policemen
in brown uniforms swarmed all over the living room.
When they saw Claire the buzzing stopped. Kearns

explained why she was there and they resumed their investigation. Sofa pillows had been tossed on the brick floor, drawers were emptied and the contents spilled out, an end table was tipped on its side, a lamp smashed. The wreckage struck Claire as the work of a crazed or reckless thief or someone trying to create that impression. Beside a heavy wooden table there was an outline on the floor where the body had been. The red suede bag lay within the outline. The image of a single platform shoe tipped on its side jumped out at her from the clutter, an image likely to return in the middle of the night. Claire saw no religious objects in the room: no crosses, milagros, or images of the saints.

"Isabel told me she tripped over the brick on her way to the bathroom," Claire said. "May I?"

"Go ahead."

She followed the hallway leading to the bathroom and the bedroom. The bathroom seemed untouched but the bedroom was as chaotic as the living room. Pillowcases had been ripped from the pillows. A shawl had fallen or been tossed from the bed to the floor. The drawers and the closet had been ransacked.

"Petty thieves follow a pattern. They go to the closets and bedside drawers first, looking for guns," Lieutenant Kearns said.

The destructiveness of the theft made Claire despair about the condition of the document if it was ever found. Movement was one antidote to depression and she made herself start at the bed and follow the path Isabel would have taken to the bathroom. All the bricks she saw were in place, but the shawl concealed part of the path. It was a red Spanish shawl with deep fringe as vivid as Isabel herself.

"Could we move this?" Claire asked.

Lieutenant Kearns called in Detective Romero, who had put on plastic gloves. He gathered up the shawl with a movement as gentle as an embrace and put it on the bed. As the bricks came into view, Claire felt the thrill of discovery. The brick that Isabel had moved was obvious. The others were embedded in sand, but one was framed by the dark outline of space.

"That must be it," Claire cried, pointing toward the brick.

Detective Romero knelt down, inserted the blade of his pocketknife into the crevice, and began working the brick out of its space. Claire's hopes were that the cross and document would surface beneath the brick. She wanted to pace away her anxiety while Romero worked, but she forced herself to stand still, clenching her hands into fists. Eventually he wiggled the brick out of its space. The sand had settled and formed a pocket under the brick, but to Claire it was a void. The cross and the document were not there. She squeezed her fists tight and then she let go.

Romero placed the brick on the floor, then moved his hand around the edges of the void. "This pocket goes under other bricks," he said. "Do you want me to continue?"

"Yes," Kearns said.

The adjacent bricks were packed together. Romero began digging out the sand that separated them. It was slow, painstaking work. Claire understood why Isabel hadn't searched any further after she found the cross. Although she felt like sinking onto the bed, Claire forced herself to stand and watch. She was intrigued by Romero's absorption in his work. Lieutenant Kearns went back into the living room. Although that room bustled with police activity, Romero created an island of quiet around him. He moved with the precision of an archaeologist and Claire wondered if he'd had any training in that area. As the bricks came out he piled them on the floor. The pocket grew until it ended in a depression about two feet wide. Romero dusted his hand across the top of the sand to feel if anything else was buried without actually disturbing it. His hand felt something and he began to gently brush the sand aside to expose it. Claire had become as focused on his search as he was, wondering if the cross had slid under here. His movements were light as a feather as he brushed the sand.

She held her breath while something began to emerge. As Romero continued brushing the sand aside, she could see that it wasn't the weathered wood of an old cross. It became a knob and then it turned into the joint of a finger. He brushed a little further and the shape of a skeletal hand, white and mournful as a pietà, appeared in the sand. For a moment he and Claire stared at each other, stunned into silence. Then he stood up and called for Lieutenant Kearns.

"You'll wanna take a look at this," he said.

Kearns came back into the room holding a plastic evidence bag.

"I'll be damned," he said, staring into the sand.

"You want me to continue?" Romero asked. "There could be a body attached to this."

"No. If those are old bones we need to call in the Office of the Medical Investigator's forensic anthropologists." He held up the evidence bag for Claire to see. "We found a cross."

It was about six inches long, weathered wood with a few specks of green paint.

"Where was it?" Claire asked.

"In the purse lying on the floor."

"The one inside the outline of the body?"

"Yes. The strap was over her shoulder. The purse must have slipped under her as she fell."

"She may have been trying to protect the cross," Claire said.

"Maybe," Kearns replied.

Claire wondered if Isabel had been planning to bring the cross to her at the center. She hesitated to ask the next question. "Was the document inside the cross?"

"No." The lieutenant turned the bag upside down to show her the hollow in the bottom of the cross. There was room for a document, but the space was empty.

Her disappointment was balanced by the excitement of the hand under the floor. For the police that investigation was just beginning, but in her mind the two finds were linked. "It's possible that the document Isabel found belonged to this body," she said.

"You're getting ahead of yourself," Kearns replied. "We don't have a document and we don't have a body. All we have is the skeleton of a hand."

Claire knew she was about to be dismissed. The lieutenant extended his hand. "Thank you for your help," he said. "We'll call you."

"Please," Claire said.

Kearns asked Romero to escort Claire to her vehicle. They walked through the living room and back outside. The Santos brothers had gone to the far side of the house and were leaning against a truck talking to an elderly woman. Claire wanted to tell them about the hand beneath the floor, but that wasn't her job.

"Thanks for your help," Romero said, echoing his boss. He opened the door of her truck for her.

"Let me know what develops, please," she said.

"We will."

Chapter Five

Claire drove down Calle Luna and reversed her path to Camino del Pueblo. From here she could see that the clouds on the West Mesa had darkened and thickened. Although they appeared to be heavy and pregnant with rain, she doubted it would come so soon. June was the waiting season, not the rainy season. She headed north, turned right, and got on the interstate again, relieved that the rush hour was over and traffic was relatively light. She felt too drained to deal with heavy traffic. She debated whether to go home but decided to return to her office, replay Isabel's message, and think about all that had transpired.

By the time she parked and went into the center, anyone who had been there during office hours had gone home. Her office was dark and, on the surface, exactly as she had left it at eleven a.m. She turned on the light and checked the caller ID screen. Isabel had called at one p.m. and the number she called from was on the screen. She compared it to the numbers she had written down and found it to be the one listed for Chuy in the phone book. Isabel had said her brother was named Jesus and Chuy could be a nickname for Jesus. Before replaying Isabel's message, she turned off the light to sit in darkness. In Claire's experience dimming one sense heightened the others. Listening in the dark could make hearing more acute, but she heard nothing in Isabel's voice that she hadn't heard earlier. Isabel sounded eager but not anxious or frightened or threatened. She didn't mention the purse, or the document, or the cross.

As Claire played the message over and over in the darkness, Isabel assumed the hallucinatory vividness of a dream. Claire could almost smell the fragrance of her skin and hear the rustle of her skirt. She saw the platform shoes, the red purse, the golden butterfly embroidered on the T-shirt. She had a mother's sense that she should have kept Isabel from danger and couldn't stand being in her office another minute. But before she left she turned on the light and checked the drawer in her desk where she had put the original of Isabel's note. It was still locked. The note was in place. The copy was in the hands of the police. Even so, Claire made another copy and took it home, locking the original back in the drawer.

When she finally fell asleep that night, she saw red and gray in her dreams: a red skirt, a skeletal hand, a gray cross, the dancing flames of an auto-da-fé. In the morning she found a sage stick and took it to work. She was sitting at her desk with the fragrant sage in her hand when Celia walked into the office.

"You look exhausted," Celia said.

"I am."

Celia took the sage stick from Claire and sniffed it. "What are you planning to do with this?"

"I'd like to burn it to exorcise the spirit of Isabel Santos from my office."

"I heard about her on the news this morning. The newscaster said she walked in on a robbery at her home."

"The house is a wreck," Claire replied.

Celia stopped her examination of the sage stick. "You *saw* it?"

"Isabel left a message on my voice mail that she wanted to talk to me. I went to her house on my way back from Santa Fe. The Sheriff's Department was all over the place. They let me in and I directed them to the loose brick where the cross must have been. A detective started digging and the skeleton of a hand appeared in the sand."

"Does that mean there's a body connected to the document?"

"I don't know if there is a body. Maybe it's only a hand. The investigation commander called in the OMI."

"Was the document found?"

"It hadn't been when I was there," Claire said. "They found the cross but the document wasn't inside. The house was such a wreck I hate to think about the shape it would be in if it was in the house."

"If," echoed Celia.

"If," repeated Claire.

Celia put the sage stick back on the desk. "If you burn this it will set off an alarm and alert Harrison. You don't want to tell him about Isabel Santos, do you?"

"No. He'll think everything I touch here turns to murder."

"Was she a positive spirit?"

"Yes."

"Why not keep her spirit around? Maybe you'll learn something from it."

"Maybe," Claire said.

Celia said she had to be at a meeting and left. This was the first time since they'd met that Claire hadn't noticed what Celia wore.

She expected Lieutenant Kearns to get in touch with her but it was Detective Romero who called that afternoon. He said he wanted to meet her in her office as soon as possible. They made an appointment for early the following morning; she didn't want her coworkers or Harrison to see a policeman in her office.

When the detective arrived at seven a.m. Claire was waiting at the information desk to let him in. Romero's tough looks reminded Claire that the boys who got in trouble when she was in high school often became cops later on, that there was a connection between the criminal and the cop, the suspect and the prosecutor, the hunted and the hunter.

"Thanks for meeting me, ma'am," he said.

It was only recently that Claire started being called ma'am, and she was amused by it. "You're welcome," she replied.

"This is such a beautiful building," Romero said, looking up at the rows of vigas in the high ceiling of the great hall. "I took a few courses here after I got out of high school, but then I got married, had a kid, got a job. I used to think I'd like to be an archaeologist."

"You looked like one when you were searching in the sand."

"I went on a few digs, and I enjoyed it. Maybe I'll come back someday, finish up after I retire."

He was young to be thinking about retirement, but people with government jobs were people who were

willing to put their futures on hold. The death of
Isabel Santos made Claire doubt the wisdom of putting anything on hold. She walked Romero down the
hall to her office, flipped on the light switch, and
chased the resident spirit away.

"Have you established what killed Isabel?" she
asked.

"Apparently she tripped and fell—or was pushed—
against a table. Her neck landed hard on the edge
and ruptured an artery. That can happen if you hit
it just right. The force of the fall and the state of the
house indicate there was a struggle. A gang member
named Tony Atencio who lives in the neighborhood
and has been in trouble before was seen running
down the ditch that afternoon. We brought him in
for questioning. Can you tell me what time Isabel
called you?"

Claire brought up that information on her caller
ID screen and showed Romero that it came in at one
p.m. She accessed the message for him and said, "Isabel doesn't sound distraught to me."

"She doesn't," Romero agreed.

"Do you know what time she was killed?"

"Chuy Santos called 911 at three-thirty to say he'd
found the body. All we can say for sure is that she
died sometime between one and three-thirty. According to the phone records, you were the last person she called that day."

"Did you find the document anywhere?"

"No."

"Isabel must have told somebody else about it. I
know she talked to May Brennan at the Bernalillo
Historical Society; it was May who referred her to
me. It's possible she gave Isabel some other names."

"We'll check it out," Detective Romero said. "We need the original of the words she wrote down for you."

Claire unlocked the drawer and handed the paper to him.

He stared at it. "What is your interpretation of this?"

"The language is Ladino, an ancient combination of Hebrew, Spanish, and Arabic. My translation is 'Everything is upside-down. The garrote or the fire. Give me the fire. Adonay is my God.' I've shown a copy to an expert here and one in Santa Fe and the consensus is it was written by a Jew who faced the Inquisition in either the New World or the Old."

"My grandmother says Jews came to New Mexico in the old days. They kept to themselves and practiced old customs. They didn't eat pork but sometimes they slaughtered a pig and hung it outside the house so no one would suspect. As time went by they began to forget that the reason they kept the old ways was because they were Jews."

"Did you grow up in Bernalillo?"

"Yes. I've lived there all my life."

"Do you know the Santos family?"

"I know Isabel went to California. I know Chuy likes to gamble. I know Manuel is a lawyer who lives in Placitas. The Republican party is preparing to run him for the statehouse."

Claire hadn't heard that. "Tell me about the hand you found. Did it lead to a body?"

"Yes. The OMI forensic anthropologists dug it out. They can tell how long it was buried there."

"Was anything else found?"

"Just the skeleton."

"Would the OMI consider turning it over to the Smithsonian? They have the best resources for establishing how old it is and where it came from."

"Usually the OMI handles the old bones themselves. There'd have to be something special for them to call in the Smithsonian."

"The document Isabel found makes this case special."

"It might if we had a document," Romero pointed out.

"You could begin by asking the Smithsonian to examine and date the cross," Claire said. "I don't know of anyone in New Mexico with the ability to do that." She was trying to capture the interest of the archaeologist in Romero.

"I'll talk to Lieutenant Kearns about it," he said.

"Maybe the old bones can tell us something about the more recent death."

"Bones make good witnesses. They never lie. But I have to tell you that Tony Atencio is looking pretty good to us right now. We picked up some prints and fibers at the crime scene. We'll see if we can get a match."

It was eight when he left. Claire wondered if it was too early to call August but she went ahead knowing that most older people slept little and woke early.

He answered so quickly his hand might have been resting on the phone waiting for a call. "Claire," he said, clearing his throat with the hoarseness of a smoker, although he claimed he hadn't smoked for years. "How are you, my dear? Was that *your* Isabel Santos who was killed in Bernalillo?"

"I'm afraid so," Claire said.

"The news reports say that she walked in on a

theft. Do you know what happened to your document?"

"Not yet."

"It wasn't in the house?"

"The police haven't found it."

"A robber would never know its worth. Could she have sold it before this happened?"

"It's possible, but who would she have sold it to?"

"Some rogue collector. UC Berkeley. Unlike other universities we know, Berkeley will do whatever it can to keep scholars happy." He cleared his throat again, more for effect than from necessity.

Claire had been thinking theft, but she supposed it was possible that Isabel had sold the document. If so the buyer should come forward. The money should have been deposited somewhere, which would be easy for the police to establish.

"There's more," she said. "A skeleton was found under Isabel's house near where the cross and document were. The OMI's forensic anthropologists are investigating."

"That raises all sorts of intriguing possibilities, especially if the skeleton brought the cross and document to Bernalillo."

"It does," Claire agreed. "Is there anything in the documents you verified that might be helpful to me or the investigators?"

"There's a lot about the persecution of the Rodriguez family. Whether it would be helpful or not, I don't know."

"Would you be willing to make copies of the relevant documents for me?"

"Of course. I'll put them in the mail today."

"Thank you," Claire said.

"My pleasure," August replied.

Chapter Six

The documents were waiting for Claire when she got home after work on Friday. Her house was stifling after baking in the sun all day. She let the cat out, turned on the cooler, and microwaved a bowl of leftover pasta for dinner. Then she took August's documents outside to her courtyard. Her house had a small backyard with a long view across the city and the Rio Grande Valley to the West Mesa. The sunsets were a glorious play of shadow and light but the view could be too vast. Claire felt her thoughts might float into the faraway spaces and never return. For concentration she preferred the enclosed space of her courtyard. There were times when she enjoyed hiding behind the courtyard's high walls, which reminded her of a medieval cloister. She had a datura plant that had volunteered to live on one side of her courtyard. On the other she had planted an herb garden of rosemary, sage, and oregano.

She sat down on the banco, opened August's package, and found a note from him saying that he had spoken to the Inquisition scholar Peter Beck and that Beck doubted Joaquín Rodriguez had ever written the document Claire described. According to Beck it was well documented that Joaquín Rodriguez had converted and been garroted. Claire returned August's note to the envelope. Just like a scholar, she thought, to deny the existence of something that might contradict his scholarship. She didn't know Peter Beck, but she knew other scholars and she knew how committed they became to the positions that earned them their reputation.

Having dispensed with scholars, Claire turned to the photocopies of the documents written in the ornate penmanship of the sixteenth century. Flowery language matched the elegant handwriting. Her Spanish was good enough for a short document but too laborious for a long one. Fortunately August had enclosed the translations he had used in his authentication process. Authenticity was established by dating the paper and the ink and by comparing these documents to other official documents. One needed to know the content to do an effective comparison. It was hard for Claire to imagine people spending their time faking Inquisition documents, but she knew that forgers would fake anything they thought they could sell.

As she read the translations Claire learned that there had been three Rodriguez siblings: Joaquín, Raquel, and a younger brother named Daniel. The records of the Inquisition of Joaquín and Raquel were enclosed. There was no record of Daniel's fate, leading Claire to wonder if he had escaped the Inquisition. Perhaps he had been a less fervent Jew or a more convincing Catholic. No Spaniard was allowed to emigrate to the New World without at least pretending to be a good Catholic. Some came with the hope that they could abandon the pretense as they moved farther away from the church.

As Claire read on she learned that the Rodriguez family was accused of Judaizing by a neighbor in Mexico City. Once people were accused the Inquisitors were quick to incarcerate them and confiscate their property. The only way the accused could save themselves was to convince the Holy Office of the Inquisition that they had repented and embraced the church. Although they were both tortured on the rack, neither Raquel nor Joaquín repented. Both were convicted of apostasy and "relaxed to the secular arm," meaning they were turned over to the civil authorities for public execution. Raquel was burned alive at the stake.

Joaquín was accused of "making jokes about Our Lord Jesus Christ and insulting Our Lady." Although he was a baptized and confirmed Catholic, he reverted to his family's Jewish beliefs "like a dog who returns to his vomit."

Joaquín responded that he obeyed only the Law of Moses. His God "cares for me in the desert in the land of burning heat, and brings water, honey, and oil from the rock. He will welcome me into heaven with strumming harp and clicking castanets. Starve me, break my body on the rack, but my faith remains gold in the treasure chest of my mind."

He was sentenced to be led "through the streets on a saddled horse with a crier telling of his crime." Someone in the crowd stepped forward and Joaquín spoke words that were interpreted as a conversion. When he arrived at the marketplace of San Hipólito, he was garroted until he died, and then his body was taken to the *quemadero*—the "burning ground"— put on the fire, and burned to ashes.

Claire liked to believe the words *dame el fuego* were truly Joaquín's last words and wishes. The Joaquín she'd just read about wouldn't have converted out of fear of the fire. The elegant handwriting and the poetic language described a barbaric act, one of many that had been committed in the name of somebody's God.

The light had faded in the courtyard. Claire looked up and saw the red glow of the planet Mars hanging over the Rio Grande Valley. Tonight was the dark of the moon and there was nothing in the sky to diminish Mars's light. The red planet, considered the ruler of war, action, and aggression, was at its closest point to Earth in many years. Claire knew mankind was capable of vicious acts. However, blood spilled in the heat of passion and war, blood spilled over lust or fear or territory, was more understandable to her than blood spilled in a cold and calculated public execution. It took time for the Holy Office of the Inquisition to try and execute the lapsed Catholics. At any time in the long process, the Inquisitors could have shown compassion and tolerance, but they never did. The Inquisition continued for centuries in the Old World and the New. In Claire's mind it was one of Christianity's darkest chapters. Her heart was with the passionate Joaquín Rodriguez who had wanted nothing more than to worship his God.

Her cat, Nemesis, startled her by jumping off the courtyard wall and landing in the herb garden, releasing the fragrance of oregano and rosemary. He meowed and rubbed against her legs, indicating he wanted to go in.

Claire took him inside, sat down on the sofa in her living room, and turned on the light. Along with the Inquisition documents, August had sent copies of prints depicting the Inquisition of Raquel Rodriguez. With her breasts bare she was dragged in front of

her black-robed, black-hatted Inquisitors. She was
burned at the stake dressed in a *sambenito*, the yellow
cloak and pointed hat Jews were forced to wear. The
executioners' faces were well hidden by black hoods
as they fed the flames. It was a horrifying image, not
one Claire wanted to take to bed with her.

She looked through the documents again, trying to
find something in the elegant wording to erase the
image of Raquel being burned at the stake, something trivial or stupid or even humorous. There was
a kind of black humor in the wording of the documents. She found her diversion at the end of the
"Inquisition Case of Joaquín Rodriguez" but it wasn't
particularly humorous. The document concluded
with a list of witnesses to the execution. She'd
skipped over the list earlier, thinking the names had
no significance. This time, however, one name leaped
out at her from the list, the name of Manuel Santos.
He was one of the grim, sanctimonious, black-robed
men who had watched Joaquín Rodriguez burn to
cinder. And this was the name of Isabel Santos's
brother.

Claire put down the document and began pacing
from one end of her house to the other, wearing a
path through the gray carpet. Nemesis watched from
the sofa, flicking his tail. She had wondered if the
skeleton under the bricks was a Rodriguez who had
come north with Joaquín's last words hidden inside
a cross, possibly even with the Oñate expedition. It
was a wise time for a Jew to escape Old Mexico.
Claire had never considered that the bones could belong to an Inquisitor or the family of an Inquisitor.
It was possible that Joaquín's encounter on the way
to the stake was not as it was described in the Inquisition record. It was possible that the church hadn't

been able to convert Joaquín Rodriguez and had garroted him to save face, in which case the Inquisitors
would not want his last words to be known. Had
the record keepers, too compulsive to destroy them,
buried them on the frontier?

Joaquín's Inquisition had happened over four hundred years ago. Would anyone care about having an
Inquisitor as an ancestor at this point? Usually vil-
lainous relatives became less evil and more picturesque as time went by. But Inquisitors were a special
class of evil. Did the Santos brothers know they were
descended from one?

Those weren't thoughts that led to a good night's
sleep either. Claire went to her office and turned on
the computer, thinking that writing her thoughts
down could help her get rid of them. As she typed,
she thought about the deep, dark evil of the Inquisition, an evil that had sprung from one of the most
harmonious periods in history. Prior to the expulsion
of the Muslims and Jews from Spain, the Iberian Peninsula had experienced an incredible flowering in the
arts and the sciences. The scientific achievements and
art that came from that period were remarkable.
Claire thought about the symmetry and beauty of
the Alhambra. She remembered sitting in the tiled
courtyard with Pietro Antonelli, eating oranges, listening to the tinkling fountain.

If there was anything that could take her mind off
the Santos and Rodriguez families, it would be Pietro. There was the risk that he wouldn't remember
her or wouldn't answer her but if she didn't write
him she would consider herself a coward. The dark
of the moon marked the end of one phase, which led
to the beginning of another. The red glow of Mars
encouraged action. She typed the E-mail she had

been composing in her head, trying to keep it brief and to the point. She told Pietro about her grown children—Eric was working in California, Robin studying in Boston—her divorce from Evan, her new life in Albuquerque. She said her work had recently caused her to think about Spain and North Africa and to wonder how he was. Before she could reconsider all the reasons why she shouldn't do what she wished to do, she typed his E-mail address and hit the send button.

Chapter Seven

She woke up early wondering what time it would be in Florence. Before she heated a bagel, made a cup of coffee, or drank a glass of orange juice, she checked her E-mail to see if there was a response. Nothing but the usual collection of porn and credit card offers. She began to realize how big a step she had taken with one small E-mail. Would it condemn her to look for an answer first thing in the morning, last thing at night, and every hour in between? It wasn't the first time she felt like a teenager when it came to middle-aged romance. She had been in her late teens when she met Pietro, but in some ways she'd been more mature about love then than she was now, more secure about her looks and more optimistic about her ability to love and be loved back.

To convince herself that she wasn't obsessed with getting a reply, she decided to do some work while she was on-line. She poured a glass of juice, returned to the computer, went to the *Albuquerque Journal*'s Web site, and typed in the name of Manuel Santos. The most recent article came up on the screen. Manuel made a statement expressing his sorrow at his sister's death and declaring that the state needed to get tougher on crime. Claire scrolled through earlier articles, learning that he had been in the news for years in a small way. He was a partner at a large, well-known law firm, and an active member of the Republican party. When a prominent Republican came to town, Manuel Santos was at the politician's side. When there was a fund-raiser for the party, Manuel was there. He was prodevelopment, anti–government spending, not particularly concerned with protecting the environment. There were photos with his attractive blonde wife and two adorable children. Manuel and his family lived in the hills of Placitas, where subdivisions with large lots looked down on the interstate, the fast food strip of Route 44, the Santa Ana Casino, and the town of Bernalillo. Santos was the type of Republican with Hispanic roots that the party had been courting. Claire wondered if he'd also be willing to turn his back on his roots.

She checked her E-mail one more time, then logged off the Internet. After breakfast she called May Brennan.

"Hullo." May answered the phone in a voice that had a dull echo like it came from an emotional cellar.

She was getting a divorce and Claire knew what a miserable experience that was. She could also sympathize with any guilt felt about the death of Isabel Santos.

"May," she said. "This is Claire Reynier. Are you all right?"

"I've been better. And you?"

Been worse, Claire thought, remembering the dark days of her own divorce. "I'm all right, but I'm upset about the death of Isabel Santos."

"Me, too. I gave her your name. I gather she came to see you?"

"She did. Are you free for lunch?"

"I was planning to work at the Historical Society today, but I could take a break."

"The Range?" It was Bernalillo's best-known restaurant.

"Not there. Too busy. Too noisy. There's a new microbrewery called Milagro on Route 44 just before the Santa Ana Casino. Can you meet me there at noon?"

"Okay," Claire said.

She allowed herself to check her E-mail just once more. Nothing from Pietro.

May was sitting at the table sipping a beer when Claire arrived at Milagro. The brewery was at ground level. The dining room was on the second floor. It was large and bright with brick walls painted white and an IMAX view of the Sandias. Cedar trunks went from the floor of the brewery to the roof, making the dining room feel like a tree house.

May was alone, but Claire had the sense that the gray moth of depression sat beside her, a companion that could drive all others away. Sometimes people had to isolate themselves in order to recover from a wound. Most people healed eventually and got back in circulation again. Reaching out to Pietro was a sign that Claire had finally healed from her divorce. But some people's wounds went too deep to ever heal. It was too soon to tell with May. Claire knew her ex-husband was a drinker who had been rude and abusive. He had berated May publicly about her weight.

May wore no makeup, not even a touch of blush. The bright light at Milagro didn't flatter her pasty skin. Her hair was long and gray and piled carelessly

on top of her head. She didn't get up when she saw
Claire. Claire bent down and gave her a hug, noticing
that May felt thick and lumpy as a pillow stuffed
with straw.

"Good to see you, May," she said.

"You're looking well," May replied.

"Thanks. I feel good. There is life after divorce,
you'll see."

May sighed. "I hope so. Going through it is a
nightmare."

"Are you going to do all right financially?"

"Not if Rex can help it."

The waitress brought menus and took their drink
orders. A designer beer for May. A lemonade for
Claire.

"I feel terrible about Isabel Santos," Claire confided when they were alone again.

"Me, too."

"What do you think happened?"

"She walked in on a robbery by Tony Atencio, according to the Sandoval County Sheriff's Department."

"He's only a suspect. Nothing has been proved
yet."

"No, but Tony's a gang member and he has been
in trouble ever since he dropped out of middle
school."

"Did you talk to the Sheriff's Department?"

"Yes. Lieutenant Kearns visited me. They found
the call Isabel made to the Historical Society in her
phone records. I told Kearns I had referred Isabel to
you, but they already knew that you'd been
involved."

"Was I the only person you referred Isabel to?"

May's eyeglasses dangled from a cord around her

neck. She put them on and studied the menu before she answered Claire. "No. After she saw you she came to the Historical Society and told me you said the document was related to the Inquisition. She asked me if I thought it was valuable and I mentioned Peter Beck and Warren Isles. Peter is an expert on the Inquisition. Warren is a collector in Santa Fe. I thought the document should go to the center, of course, but it was her choice."

"Do you know if she contacted them?"

"No. I gave her the names and numbers. I don't know what happened after that."

"Did she show you the document?"

"No." Her eyes went back to the menu. "The fish and chips are good. I'd recommend them."

"You're a historian. Weren't you curious? Didn't you want to see the original document? Weren't you tempted to go to her house?" Claire wasn't willing to let May slide by hiding behind the menu.

"I'm not as curious about things as I used to be." Her eyes—with or without the glasses—were dull as soot. "I tried to do you a favor, Claire. If you weren't interested in the document, you could have passed it on to someone who was."

"Actually I was very interested. The police haven't found the document in Isabel's house and I'm worried about what happened to it."

May wrapped her words in the ellipses of disdain. "Well . . . you know the Sandoval County Sheriff's Department . . ."

"Have you ever been to the Santos house?"

"Of course."

"Do you have any idea how old it is?"

This was a subject May was more willing to talk about. She became animated as she spoke, more like the woman Claire had known, a woman who was interested in her work and proud of her expertise. She put down the menu and let the glasses on the velvet cord drop back to her chest. "It's a hundred years old. The Santos family has been in Bernalillo since the very beginning. That property was once the family hacienda and they built and rebuilt on the same site. Lieutenant Kearns said a skeleton was found under the brick floor but he didn't know how old it was yet. It could be a family member. The first Manuel Santos came to New Mexico with Oñate's expedition. The family settled in San Juan but eventually ended up here, although it isn't known exactly when. Records were destroyed during the Pueblo Revolt."

"The Spaniards all left then, didn't they?"

"Presumably. Although it's possible some of them made peace with the Indians and hid out until the area was conquered again. The Spaniards lived in widely separated family groups. It would have been hard to survive in Bernalillo in the early seventeenth century without getting along with the Indians. Sometimes Spaniards returned to their original homesteads."

"Have there been Manuel Santoses in Bernalillo since that time?"

"No. The name Manuel didn't get passed on in every generation. Most of the current Santoses aren't very interested in their own history. The latest Manuel hasn't given his son the name."

"There was an Inquisitor in Mexico City named Manuel Santos in the late sixteenth century."

"There was?" May seemed startled. "I didn't know that."

"August Stevenson gave me copies of Inquisition

documents dated 1596 with the name Manuel Santos on them."

"I'm sure Manuel would love to have it known that he was descended from an Inquisitor. That would really help his campaign. That and his gambling brother." May's voice was marbled with sarcasm but she laughed. It was the first laugh Claire had heard from her in a while. "But it's unlikely the two Manuel Santoses are related. An Inquisitor in Mexico City at that time would have been a powerful person. Why would someone with that kind of power leave for el Norte?"

"I don't know," Claire answered. "Have you ever come across evidence that any crypto Jews settled in Bernalillo? Maybe the conflict between the Rodriguez and Santos families played out again here."

"Nothing tangible," May said. "There is talk that the old ways endured in some families. That they burn candles in secret on Friday night, that they don't eat pork, that they sweep to the middle of the room. Even though I've lived here for forty years and know more about the history of the place than most people, I'm still considered an outsider. Anyone who secretly practices Judaism wouldn't admit it to me. I don't know why anybody needs to keep it a secret in this day and age, except that devout Catholics in the family would rather not know."

"Sometimes people fall into the habit of secrecy," Claire said. "And are unwilling or unable to stop."

"Sometimes," said May. She saw the waitress approaching. "If it's all the same to you I'd like to order now."

"All right."

May ordered the fish and chips. Claire got a duck-and-spinach salad. While they waited for the food to arrive, Claire's thoughts returned to Isabel Santos. "Did you know Isabel well?" she asked May.

"Not really. I saw her occasionally when she was growing up. She was a pretty girl with a lot of spirit. She had problems with drugs when she was younger. It caused a rift with her family, especially her brother Manuel, who's always been concerned about his image. She fell in love with an Anglo guy in California, but eventually she came back. It seemed like she'd made peace with her family and was settling down here."

"Are the parents still alive?"

"No. She was raised by her grandmother, who lives in town."

When the lunch arrived the portions were enormous. May's plate overflowed with fries and fish. Although there was more than enough for two, she ate every bit.

Chapter Eight

After lunch Claire drove east on Route 44. The strip from Santa Ana Star Casino to I-25 was one of the places in New Mexico that combined the best of the past with the worst of the present. There was the casino, the convenience stores, the gas stations, and fast food restaurants. But there was also the Coronado State Monument, a quarter mile away from the strip by road but much further than that in spirit.

It was one of Claire's favorite places in the state. Although named for a conquistador, it was more of a monument to the peaceful Kuaua people who lived on the banks of the Rio Grande when Coronado's expedition arrived in 1540. Most of the pueblo buildings were now in ruins. The kiva had been restored and could be entered by a wooden ladder, but the original frescoes had been removed and taken inside the Visitor's Center, a building designed by John Gaw Meem, the architect who designed the library where Claire worked. She felt a sense of shelter and timelessness in a Meem building. As she walked through the Visitor's Center she passed a child-sized suit of armor. Historical figures cast such long shadows it was surprising to be reminded that people were smaller four hundred years ago. She went out the back door and followed the path around the pueblo ruins. The comments of the conquistadores were imprinted on signposts stuck in the ground. In 1540 Pedro de Casteñada wrote about Indian women grinding corn, "A man sits at the door playing on a fife while they grind, moving the stones to the music and singing together." In 1610 Perez de Villagra wrote, "They are quiet, peaceful people of good appearance and excellent physique, alert and intelligent. . . . They live in complete equality, neither exercising authority nor demanding obedience."

Claire left the pueblo and walked down to the riverbank. Kuaua women were excellent swimmers and easily negotiated the treacherous currents of the river. In summer it had a wide, gentle flow and Claire liked to sit on the banks and watch it wander. She had a favorite spot sheltered by a cottonwood and she sat down there. The view here was south to the Sandias, not gentle mountains from any perspective, but from here they seemed even rockier and more jagged than they did from her house. Traffic crossed the bridge on Route 44, but the rippling water drowned out the sound. Coronado was close to the sprawl of Albuquerque, yet removed by the sense of being in another time.

Claire's mind regressed to the sixteenth century. It was 1598, almost sixty years after Coronado, before the Spaniards returned in any numbers. Settlers and friars came north with Oñate, and at some point after that a Manuel Santos settled in Bernalillo. Could it have been Manuel Santos, the Inquisitor, or a relative carrying a cross with the last words of Joaquín Rodriguez inside? What would that mean to the current Santos family?

As Claire watched the water, the sun beat down on her back. From the beginning of civilization mystics had gone into the land of burning heat seeking enlightenment. She thought about Joaquín Rodriguez circumcising himself on the banks of the Rio de los Remedios—the courage, the pain, the sense of release and acceptance that could come from obeying a covenant of his God. His blood might have flowed into the water and blended into the current in the same way the waters of one river flowed into another when their paths came together, in the same way that people merged when they followed the same God.

Her thoughts moved on to May Brennan eating enough for two. She sympathized with her confusion and her pain about the divorce, but she wondered if despair was clouding her vision. She was bothered by the sense that May hadn't told her everything she knew. The May she knew would have insisted on seeing the original and gotten to Isabel's house even before Claire did. Claire stood up, took one last look at the free flowing river, and walked back to her truck.

She took Camino del Pueblo south through Bernalillo and when she got to 711 Camino del Pueblo, the building that housed the Sheriff's Department and other county offices, she parked and went in. The building had been renovated and given a false front that reminded her of a Western movie set.

She stopped at the front desk and asked for Detective Romero.

"He's not in," a soft-spoken policewoman replied. "Would you like to speak to Lieutenant Kearns?"

Claire had to say yes, although she doubted Lieutenant Kearns would be as interested in the historical elements she'd uncovered as Detective Romero.

The woman rang Kearns and he walked down the hallway toward Claire. His clothes were very plain and rumpled. His posture had the weary droop of an old shoe.

"Ms. Reynier," he said, "what are you doing in Bernalillo?"

"I had lunch with May Brennan today. Then I went to Coronado Monument. It's one of my favorite places in New Mexico."

"Never had a chance to go there myself. One of these days. Well, come into my office."

Claire followed him into the office, listening to the buzzing noises of a police station, thinking of it as the hive the force returned to at the end of the day weighted down with evidence found all over Sandoval County.

"Have you found the document yet?" she asked.

"Not yet."

"May told me you contacted her about the phone call Isabel Santos made to the Historical Society. She said she gave Isabel and you the names of Peter Beck and Warren Isles. Have you been in touch with them?"

"We're working on it," Kearns said, leaning against his desk and watching her with pale eyes, waiting to see where this was heading.

"It could be that Isabel contacted them, maybe even sold one of them the document." She didn't want to imply she could do his job better than Kearns could by suggesting that if there'd been a sale there could be a deposit somewhere.

"We haven't found any evidence to suggest she contacted anyone but you and May."

"It's such an important document. It's hard to imagine any historian or collector hearing about it and not going to Isabel's house as soon as possible to see it. I did."

"We don't know that the experts May recommended ever heard about the document, but as I said we're working on it."

"Could you ask May if she contacted anyone?" Claire felt like a yappy little dog. She didn't like to think she was barking at Lieutenant Kearns's heels, but there was a lot at stake here, including her own reputation.

Kearns responded to her assertiveness by stepping behind his desk. "She says she didn't." The late afternoon sun followed him around the desk, beaming through the window, lighting up the rusty hair on his arms and turning the lines in his face from fissures to canyons.

Claire wondered if it was doing the same to her and stepped away from the light. "If a substantial amount of money was deposited in Isabel's or the Santos brothers' accounts, that would be on record, wouldn't it?"

"We have to have some reason to suspect there was a sale before we can go looking at people's bank accounts," Kearns said. "We don't even know that there was a document. May couldn't confirm it and you never actually saw it either, did you?"

"To me the content is confirmation. I don't see how Isabel could have made it up."

"It might be confirmation to a historian. A policeman needs something more tangible than a description," he reminded her.

"The cross could tell you more."

"We're investigating. The OMI identified the skeleton as a man, by the way. Sex is relatively easy for them to establish. For one thing a man's forehead has more slope than a woman's. It will take longer to determine the age and origin of the skeleton. It's old, but they don't know how old yet."

"I asked Detective Romero if the Smithsonian could be called in."

"They usually only participate in exceptional cases like ones that involve Paleo-Indian artifacts."

"I think this is an exceptional case," Claire said. "I've been researching Inquisition documents and I discovered that there was an Inquisitor named Manuel Santos who witnessed the execution of Joaquín Rodriguez in Mexico City. May told me a Manuel Santos was part of Oñate's expedition and was one of the first Europeans to settle in Bernalillo."

"There could have been more than one Manuel Santos, no?"

"There were very few Europeans in the New World in the late sixteenth century." Claire persisted although she felt discouraged about convincing a man who worked in Bernalillo without ever visiting the Coronado Monument of the relevance of anything that happened here four hundred years ago.

"Even if Manuel Santos's ancestor was an Inquisitor, that's not a crime at this point," Kearns said.

"It could have provided a motive for Isabel's death."

"To you Tony Atencio may be an uninteresting suspect but to us he's a gangbanger with a record. We found his prints in the house. He tried to sell Isabel's VCR to a buddy of his, and the buddy ratted on him. We had enough evidence to charge him with burglary and keep him in jail."

Claire thought she could be stating the obvious, but she did it anyway. "Maybe someone else fought with Isabel and she fell. Maybe Tony Atencio found her dead and took advantage of an opportunity."

"Maybe," Kearns said in a weary voice that lacked conviction. He turned to the window and asked, "You think it's going to rain?"

"No," Claire replied, recognizing the meaningless phrase that marked the end of the meeting.

"Either Detective Romero or I will be in touch," Kearns said.

Chapter Nine

Claire got in her truck and continued on through Bernalillo. She wasn't planning to go to Calle Luna, but when she saw the turnoff she acted on impulse and swung a right. The decision was made so quickly that she didn't have time to flick her turn signal. The driver of the car behind her leaned on his horn. His irate face was visible in her rearview mirror. She had learned much about the Santos family since the last time she was here. She wanted to look at Isabel's house again and see how it appeared through the lens of her new knowledge.

She wondered what it was like when Manuel Santos first came here with an oxcart full of possessions. There would have been paths but no roads. The only buildings were the Indian settlements along the Rio Grande. Before the river was dammed in the twentieth century, the bosque and the valley were a wide floodplain. Buildings had to be on higher ground to survive. Houses were built of native materials. The people were smaller then, so the houses were constructed with low doors and no windows. Only the very well cared-for buildings from that period survived. Mud houses were organic and eventually they sank back into the ground from which they had come. The first Santos dwelling might have stood on the spot of the present dwelling or it might not. It would be difficult to prove.

May might have more knowledge of the Santos family history than they did themselves but it wasn't so unusual for a family to lose touch with their own history. Genealogy was an interest that families drifted in and out of and that was partially a function of age. As people got older and concerned with their own mortality, they became more interested in their ancestors. Claire knew that the Reyniers had arrived in New Amsterdam in 1650 on a ship called the *Gilded Otter*. They had a French name but they traveled to the New World on a Dutch ship.

She turned onto Calle Luna. As she neared the cul-de-sac at the end of the street she saw a Ford pickup parked in front of Isabel's house, a truck with lots of hard miles on it, a bed full of holes, a body full of dents and dings. It had once been white but was now layered with brown dust. Claire was debating whether to turn around in the cul-de-sac or to stop when she saw Chuy Santos hunched over and yanking out weeds in the yard. It was hard labor in New Mexico in June when the earth was as fixed as concrete and unwilling to let go of its scrawny progeny. Weeding came easier after a hard rain.

As Claire parked, Chuy heard the gravel crunch and looked up, rearranging his expression once he saw who it was.

"Hey," he called.

"Hello," she said, climbing out of her truck. The black dog that had been sitting on the ground watching Chuy work stood up and wagged its tail.

"How's it going?" Chuy asked.

"I'm all right. How are you?"

"Been better," he said. "Been a whole lot better." He seemed to be shaking something off his back as he walked over to Claire. "There's nothin' I can do for my sister now except clean up the place and pull out the weeds. We had the funeral in Our Lady of Sorrows. I wanted to scatter the ashes here or in the river, but Manuel says we're Catholics even though he's the only one who goes to church, so the body has to be buried in the cemetery."

"You have my deepest sympathy," Claire said.

"*Descanse en paz*," Chuy said.

"Do you live here?" she asked.

"No. I live down the road. Isabel lived here by herself and that son of a bitch Atencio knew that."

"Has the document been found yet?"

"Nope," Chuy said.

"I've been doing some research. I came across some interesting things about your family history."

"Oh yeah? Like what?"

"I told Isabel that the paper she found under the floor could have been written by a Jewish mystic in Mexico City named Joaquín Rodriguez. I read about Joaquín's Inquisition and learned that it was witnessed by an official named Manuel Santos."

"*A la.*" Chuy slapped his forehead. "You're saying our illustrious ancestor who came here with Don Juan de Oñate and the person my brother was named after was an Inquisitor?"

"It's possible," said Claire, the careful archivist, wondering how she would feel if she heard similar news about her own ancestor.

Chuy surprised her with a laugh that was short and sharp as a bark. "We've been called many things, but an Inquisitor? That's a new one. It would piss my brother off to hear that, but me? I wouldn't give a shit if it was true. Hell, my given name is Jesus and our last name means saints, but in spite of our name none of us are descended from saints. We're all mutts like Blackie here. Scratch a New Mexican and you find Spanish blood, Moorish blood, Inquisitor blood, infidel blood, Marrano blood, Indian blood, and who the hell knows what other kind of blood? Maybe even some white dudes' blood." He laughed. "Four hundred years in this state and people are still worryin' if they have *limpieza de sangre*. We all bleed red, but none of our blood is pure. Every one of us has dirt on our hands." He looked down at his own hands covered with yard dirt. Then he rubbed his nose and transferred some of it to his face. "I'm ready for a cold one," he said. "And you?"

"All right," Claire replied. She didn't want a beer, but she hoped to keep Chuy talking. She sat down at the picnic table and the dog followed. She patted his head while she waited. The phrase "we all bleed red" was familiar. She tried to place it and concluded she had come across it in a novel she'd read recently about Albuquerque gangs. By the time Chuy returned with the Coors Light, the dog's head had settled in Claire's lap.

"Negrito," he said. "Get your goddamn nose out of there." He gave the dog a shove. The dog moved away but with a wag of its tail indicating it intended to come back.

Claire took a sip of the beer. "Do you know if Tony Atencio was a gang member?" she asked.

Chuy shrugged. "I don't know for sure that he was in a gang, but he's a gangster."

"Do you think he is capable of killing Isabel?"

"Sure, why not? Who else could have done it?"

"If the document is what I think it is, it could be very valuable."

"Who knew about it," Chuy asked, "but you and May Brennan? Isabel didn't tell me."

"Did she tell Manuel?"

"Not that I know of."

"It's possible Isabel consulted someone else. May gave her the names of two experts in the field."

"Possible," Chuy said, sipping at his beer.

"What do you do?" Claire asked.

"Me? I've done a lot of things. I was earning my living at the Santa Ana Casino until they cut me off." He laughed. "Gambling for a living isn't very secure, but hey, when is life ever secure? Two bodies in our house in one week. First Isabel and then the skeleton under the floor. Now I learn that our ancestor could be an Inquisitor. Are those OMI dudes gonna be able to tell us that?"

"Lieutenant Kearns said the skeleton was a man."

"Why didn't he tell me? The bones were found in our house." Chuy guzzled the beer and put the can down. It thumped the table with a gimme-a-refill sound.

"I'm sure he'll tell you. He just happened to see me first."

"How do they know it was a man?"

"Men have more slope to their forehead."

"Just like the monkeys, right?" Chuy stood up. "How about another beer?"

It was late in the day. Darkness approached and cast its shadows before it. Dusk was quiet at this time of year before the cicadas started their evening shrill. Claire stood up, too, putting down her nearly full beer. "I should go," she said.

"Stop by any time," Chuy said. He kept up the

wise guy banter, but his shoulders sagged when he stood, as if he was carrying the weight of his sister's death. When Claire looked in his eyes she saw the brown bleeding into the white.

She took the back way home through Sandia Pueblo. When the pueblos allowed development at all, it nibbled at the edges of their land near population centers. There was no development on Sandia land between Bernalillo and Albuquerque, only fields where cattle grazed, a cottonwood bosque on the west and the Sandias on the east. The sun had moved behind the West Mesa, taking with it the dazzling light and leaving behind a more subtle landscape. It was the hour when the mountains seemed to want to speak. Claire thought if she could only listen carefully enough she would hear. The shadows created a backdrop and the space allowed room for her imagination to wander. It took her far away from fingerprints and VCRs.

She checked her E-mail when she got home and found offers to consolidate her debts and to connect her with hot college studs but nothing from Pietro Antonelli.

Chapter Ten

On Sunday she woke when daylight came through her bedroom window. Skipping her morning tai chi, she let Nemesis out, followed him into the yard, and tended her roses. Gardening was a form of meditation and the best time to practice was early in the morning when there was still a lick of coolness in the air. During the night the temperature dropped thirty degrees in the desert but the heat returned as soon as the sun crawled over the mountain. Claire's house was in the foothills of the Sandias and still in deep shadow. She watered the roses and deadheaded the spent blossoms, enjoying the coolness left over from the night. The Don Juans were a deep, dark red, the color of love, the color of blood. The dead petals fell to the ground and spun away in a gust of wind.

She hated the thought that Isabel Santos was dead. She would hate it even more if the death had been caused by anything as trivial as a VCR. She knew that most murders were impulsive, provoked by alcohol and/or anger. A former Albuquerque policewoman told her the police were thrilled if they came across a crime scene where the murderer had given it more than five minutes thought; they liked to occasionally be given a challenge. As she nipped off the roses, Claire considered whether she had selfish reasons for hoping the cause of Isabel's death was not the interruption of a petty robbery. She had a mother's response of not wanting to see a young person die and a thinking person's response of hating to see death be meaningless. There was also the issue of guilt. She had no reason to feel guilt if the thief had been after a VCR. She needed to feel guilt only if the thief had gone to Isabel's house looking for the last words of a mystic named Joaquín. That death could have been prevented by bringing the document into the secure shelter of the center.

The sun had come over the mountain and burned the coolness from her skin, but dark-of-the-night emotions lingered. She remembered the words "Everything is upside-down. The garrote or the fire. Give me the fire. Adonay is my God." She knew Isabel had not made up those words. Claire was convinced there had been an important document under the floor of Isabel's house. Either it had been destroyed or the person who possessed it now had not come forward. Tony Atencio had provided the police with little incentive to look further. They needed evidence to motivate them. Claire wondered where that evidence would be found. She went inside, made herself a cup of coffee, and called August Stevenson.

"And how are you this fine morning?" he asked.

"I'm struggling with the death of Isabel Santos," she replied.

"I'm sure you are."

"I talked to May Brennan and Lieutenant Kearns yesterday. The boy they have in custody is a strong suspect, but the police haven't charged him with

murder yet. May said she gave Isabel the names of
Warren Isles and Peter Beck, but there's no evidence
she contacted either one of them. Can you tell me
anything about these men?"

"I know Peter Beck by reputation only."

"And what is that?"

"That he knows more about the Mexican Inquisition than anyone else in this country. Warren Isles
lives in Santa Fe. I hear he has deep pockets and has
been buying up documents related to New Mexico
history. John Harlan could tell you more about that."

"How did he come into his money?"

"Selling mutual funds. Have you ever noticed how
people with boring jobs turn to history? New Mexico
history will relieve boredom like that of no other state."

"It has been lately," Claire said. "If someone offered the document to Isles without revealing its
source, do you think he would buy it?"

"It's possible," August replied. "I would consider
that unethical myself, but ethics may not be an issue
with Warren Isles." Before he bid her good-bye he
gave her a warning. "If you're thinking that someone
killed Isabel Santos over a document related to the
Inquisition, you ought to consider what that person
would do to you. The Inquisition is a grim subject.
Anyone who spends too much time thinking about
it is likely to have a dark side. My advice would be
to turn the names over to the detective and go back
to your regular job."

Sleuthing had become her regular job, Claire
thought, but she thanked August for the advice and
hung up the phone.

On Monday she checked her messages and mail at
the center, then went to Celia's office and found her

adding a bottle cap magnet to her Frida Kahlo shrine.
Frida Kahlo was a Mexican artist who had a short,
painful, but brilliantly creative life. She painted her
way out of a horrible accident and a difficult marriage to the philandering Diego Rivera.

"Another tribute to Frida?" Claire asked her.

"Yes," said Celia, who today was wearing a gray
linen dress and a necklace made of silver elephants.

There was a portrait of Frida Kahlo inside the bottle cap. Even in this scale her eyebrows looked like
ravens in flight. Claire considered the clothes and the
shrine to be a form of rebellion against the restric-
tions of academia. Celia was very good at her job
and she had tenure. She couldn't be fired, but she
could be pushed aside, given an office in the basement and nothing to do if someone like Harrison
Hough took a dislike to her. Playing up her ethnicity
could be an insurance policy. Even Harrison
wouldn't dare create the appearance of getting rid of
a woman for being too ethnic.

Celia found the perfect spot for the bottle cap, then
turned to Claire and said, "What's up?"

Claire told her about the visit to May Brennan.
"What do you know about Warren Isles and Peter
Beck?" she asked.

"I've seen Warren at historical conferences but I
never met him. He's a dough boy with soft, white,
greedy hands. If the document is ever found, he'd be
a good person to buy it and donate it to the center,
if he could be talked out of keeping it for himself.
His name on a plaque in the library might give him
an incentive."

"And Peter Beck?"

"His scholarship is impeccable. As a person, he's
a prick, but that goes with the territory, doesn't it?

The bigger scholars get, the more arrogant they become. He knows everything there is to know about the Inquisition in the New World, but he's so pedantic he manages to make even evil and cruelty boring. His book is duller than dust. Speaking of pedants, you haven't said anything about this to Harrison yet, have you?"

"No."

"Don't."

"May also told me that the first person in the Santos family to settle in Bernalillo was named Manuel and he came north with Oñate. Manuel Santos is also the name of an Inquisitor who witnessed the execution of Joaquín Rodriguez. I came across that in a document August sent me."

"I suppose it's possible Manuel Santos, the Inquisitor, or a relative came north with Oñate, but you'd have to wonder what would motivate a family in a position of power in Mexico City to leave it for the wilderness of el Norte."

Claire went back to her own office with no warning from Celia to be wary of Inquisition experts or anyone else. It wasn't Celia's nature to be careful.

Chapter Eleven

When Claire left work she usually went out the back door to the parking lot behind the library, but tonight she planned to attend a reading at the bookstore so she left by the main door and walked across Smith Plaza. It was evening, there was a light breeze, and shadows danced on the wind. The man walking across the plaza had something rarely seen in Albuquerque—style. His well-fitting suit made him seem out of place. Suits were seen occasionally at UNM, but they rarely had style. Suits at UNM bagged at the elbows and the knees. The man had a self-possession that made the near-empty plaza seem like a stage for his solitary walk. He was slim. He held his head high. He had black, wavy hair. Many would consider him good-looking, but the quality Claire noticed most was his focus. His name was Manuel Santos.

"Can we talk?" he asked when their paths met in the middle of the plaza.

"All right," she replied.

They stood still for a minute considering where to go. Manuel was Claire's height, although he had appeared taller at a distance. Since this was her territory it was up to her to name a suitable place. She was done with her office for the day. It was too nice to go back inside. She suggested they sit by the duck pond and they walked to a bench that overlooked the water. Manuel sat down, leaned against the corner of the bench, and draped his arm across the back. It settled into the curves of the wood as naturally as a snake nestling on the branch of a tree.

"Chuy told me you came to the house," he began.

"I did."

"What is this talk about us being descended from an Inquisitor?"

"I did some research into the document Isabel found, and came across a record of Joaquín Rodriguez's Inquisition in 1596. One of the officials who witnessed the event was named Manuel Santos. According to May Brennan, a Manuel Santos came north with Oñate's expedition and was one of the first settlers in Bernalillo. Did you know your family was descended from a settler who was part of Oñate's expedition?"

"Of course," Manuel said. "But I never heard that our ancestor was an Inquisitor. Do you have any proof that the name isn't just a coincidence?"

"No, but if the document Isabel found was written by Joaquín Rodriguez, it would establish a link between the two men."

"There is no proof there ever was a document. There is only your word." He looked like a lawyer today and now he began to sound like one.

"Of course there's proof," Claire said. "There's the note in Isabel's handwriting. The authenticity of her handwriting is easy enough to establish."

"I'm not denying that, but the note you produced

was not signed 'Joaquín Rodriguez' or 'Joaquín' anyone else. It wasn't signed at all."

"Isabel told me it was signed 'Joaquín.' "

Manuel didn't need to say the words "hearsay, inadmissible"; his hard amber eyes said it for him. They were Isabel's eyes in shape and in color, but not in warmth of expression. "For all we know Isabel wrote that note in your office and those were words you asked her to write."

He remained cool in his lawyer's suit but Claire began to sweat in her summer dress. She hoped her face wasn't flushing to reveal her anger. "That's not true," she said.

"We found no notebook with lined pages in the house."

"The police found the cross. There was a skeleton beneath the floor."

"They found nothing inside the cross. It's not so unusual for an old house to have a skeleton buried underneath it."

"If the skeleton belongs to a member of your family, that could be established by DNA testing."

"Yes, but that would require samples of current DNA for comparison. Why would I want to subject myself and my family to that?"

"Because you care about what happened to your sister and you want to know the truth."

Manuel's eyes demonstrated how hard lawyers could be while his hand tightened around the railing on the back of the bench. "I know the truth. My sister walked in on Tony Atencio while he was robbing our house and he pushed her. She fell, hit her neck against the table, ruptured an artery, and it killed her. It's brutal. It's stupid. But that's the way crime is."

Was this the truth of his sister's death? Claire wondered. Or the spin a politician chose to give it?

"You would be doing my family and Isabel a service if you dropped all this business about Inquisitors and Jews."

"The document Isabel described could have enormous historical significance. Don't you care about finding it?"

"For me and my family, seeing that Tony Atencio pays for his crime is a priority. Finding the document is not."

Before Claire was able to reply, a backpack-toting student approached them. For a split second it occurred to her that backpacks could be considered a weapon and that she and Manuel might be in danger, but then the student smiled and said, "Excuse me, but are you Manuel Santos?"

"Yes?" Manuel replied.

The student extended his hand. He had the short blond hair and earnest manner of a Mormon missionary. "I'm Charlie Bowles, president of the Young Republicans Club on campus. It's such an honor to meet you."

"My pleasure." Manuel smiled a professional smile and shook the student's hand.

Claire had been wondering whether Manuel Santos the slick politician would surface. She wasn't surprised he could turn on the charm when he wanted to, but the quickness and completeness of the change were as startling as a lightning flash.

"Would you be willing to speak to our group sometime?" the student asked.

"Of course," Manuel said. He handed a business card to him.

"Thank you," the student gushed, taking the card and walking away.

It took longer for Manuel to turn off the charm than it had taken to turn it on. Still basking in the glow, he turned toward Claire. "Are we done?"

"Yes," Claire said.

"My family will be suffering from the death of my sister for a long, long time. We would be grateful if you would let us deal with our grief in our own way."

She remained seated on the bench while Manuel walked across the plaza accompanied by his shadow. Smith Plaza wasn't that large, but it was bordered by the massive library building. When it was empty it reminded Claire of public spaces in Mexico, the plazas where the Aztecs ripped the still-beating hearts from their prisoners, the Spanish slaughtered the Aztecs, the Inquisitors tied Jews to the stake and burned them to cinder. There had been plenty of violence in New Mexico, too, but there was no record of it ever being the public spectacle it had been in Old Mexico. She wondered about the effect of Isabel's murder on Manuel Santos's career. To Claire it was a dark stain that could widen and spread like ink on a blotter, but a random murder by a petty criminal might have familiar reverberations and evoke sympathy in voters. It was the kind of violence that could—and all too often did—happen to anyone. A murder related to hidden documents and family secrets would be harder to understand and explain.

When Manuel had reached the far side of the plaza, climbed the stairs, and disappeared from view, she went back to her office. She still intended to go to the signing at the bookstore, but there was something she needed to do first. She skimmed through the addresses on her computer to see who she knew at the Smithsonian. Over the years her career had created a web of contacts. She came across the names of several people she knew, but the one she knew best was Sarah Jamieson, who had once been an anthropologist at the University of Arizona. The Smithsonian had offered her a good job and she had reluctantly left the dry heat of the desert for the steamy heat of Washington, D.C. It was two hours later in Washington and Sarah might be home from work.

Claire dialed the number. When the answering machine came on, she said, "Sarah, this is Claire Reynier. I was wondering if—"

"Hello."

"Sarah?"

"Claire. How have you been? It has been years, hasn't it?"

"Years," Claire said. "How are you doing? Are you liking the Smithsonian and Washington?"

"Pretty much, but I miss the desert. It gets in your blood. I hear you're at UNM now."

It wasn't exactly the Smithsonian, but Claire liked it. She told Sarah about Isabel Santos, the cross, the document, and the skeleton found under the house. "It would be incredible," she said, "if that skeleton could be traced and connected somehow to Isabel's death."

"Bones don't lie," Sarah said, "and neither does DNA."

"Do you know any of the forensic anthropologists at the Smithsonian?"

"I know Harold Marcus. He's the best."

"The Sandoval County police told me that the

Smithsonian only gets involved in exceptional cases and ones having to do with Paleo-Indian artifacts, but my impression is they don't want them to get involved. The OMI here is territorial. The Smithsonian has better resources and has a better chance of finding out what happened than anyone else. If they got interested in the case, how could local law enforcement say no?"

"Would you like me to mention it to Harold?"

"Yes, but . . ." Claire feared she was exceeding her authority.

"I won't say you're suggesting the Smithsonian get involved, only that you told me about a very interesting case."

Sarah had an intuitive understanding of people and was good at management. Claire was not. Claire had never learned how to persuade other people to do her bidding. "Thanks," she said.

The conversation moved on to work, old friends, and ex-husbands, ending in a promise to get together soon. It was a sincere promise, but they both knew it was unlikely to happen unless something brought one to the other's city.

As Claire hung up the phone she had the sensation that she wasn't the only person working late at CSWR, that someone had been wandering through the corridors.

"Hello," she called, but there was no answer. She gathered up her belongings and left her office. As she locked the door behind her, she heard the gate that led from the library to the center creak open and shut. When she went through the door and entered the library herself, she found the great hall empty.

It was still light as she walked across campus. Usually the bookstore closed at six, but this was a special event honoring a well-known woman writer from South America. She gave a passionate reading that went on longer than Claire expected. She waited in line afterwards for a signed first edition.

When she left the bookstore, night had fallen. Except for an occasional megaphone of artificial light suspended beneath a streetlamp, the campus was dark. As she passed by the construction site that had once been the Student Union, she became aware that she was very much alone. She enjoyed that rare sensation during the day, but it wasn't so pleasant at night. Student escorts were available after dark, but she never would have called one. This was where she worked and spent much of her time. In a way it was her home.

As she headed toward the steps that led down to Smith Plaza she heard footsteps behind her that seemed to echo her own. When she took a step, the echo took a step. She didn't want to turn around and give the impression that she had noticed or was afraid. She continued walking. The footsteps continued following. When she reached the steps she took a diagonal path, turned her head slightly, and glimpsed a man in the glow of a light. She turned back toward the library and began descending the steps at a rapid pace. The man was still walking on level ground. Their footsteps got out of sync, but it sounded as if he, too, had picked up his pace. It became a syncopated beat rather than a literal echo. At any time someone could have come out of the library or the Humanities Building, but no one did. Claire and the man remained the only people within sound or sight.

She began to cross the open space of the plaza, where there was no cover. In a sense the openness provided protection. Whatever happened here could be seen from the library, if anyone was watching. Still she kept on walking as fast as she could without appearing to be running away. The footsteps stopped and once again the only sound she heard was the beat of her own feet. The lights from inside Zimmerman Library spread across the steps and beckoned.

She crossed the plaza, climbed up the stairs to the library, and let herself in through the glass doors. Zimmerman wasn't buzzing with activity at this hour, but it was in operation. Students manned the information desks. A guard sat on the bench. She looked through the door that faced the plaza and saw no one. The man had stepped back into the shadows or had turned and walked away.

She could have asked the guard to escort her to her truck in the back lot, but to ask for help would mean admitting that she thought she'd been followed, and she wasn't ready to do that. Besides, the guard appeared to be half asleep. She walked around the corner to the ladies' room, took her key chain from her purse, and inserted the keys between her fingers with the sharp ends protruding. She walked out the back door toward the parking lot with her keys at the ready but no need to use them. No one was on the walk; no one was in the lot. She got in her truck and drove home.

Chapter Twelve

After work the next day she went to see her friend John Harlan who was an antiquarian bookseller at Page One, Too. Their friendship dated back years to the time when they were both married. John had become a widower. Claire had gotten divorced. There was a possibility that they would become a couple after they both became single, but it hadn't happened yet. John was seeing another woman. Claire was waiting for a message from Pietro, which resembled waiting for a message in a bottle. She thought about him as she drove through the traffic to Page One, Too. What was she expecting to hear anyway? The chances were overwhelming that Pietro was married. In her more detached moments she wondered if she daydreamed about him because he was in some ways a known quantity, or was it because he lived in Italy and was most likely unavailable? They had parted many years ago with regret but no bitterness on her part. It was safer to contemplate reuniting with a long-distance lover she had once known than moving forward with a person who, as a lover anyway, was unknown.

"Hey, Claire," John said when she entered his office, which, as usual, was piled high with books and papers. He stood up, brushing his hand across the top of his head, giving it an electrical charge. "How's it going?"

"I'm good. And you?"

"Not too shabby."

"How's Sandra?"

"Fine," he said.

Claire thought she would prefer a little more enthusiasm if she were Sandra.

"Have a seat. What's on your mind?" he asked, sitting down himself and preparing to play the role of book dealer psychologist. Claire knew that psychology often came into play when buying and selling books, particularly when coaxing people to part with their books.

"How do you know anything is on my mind?"

"You look worried."

"I do?"

"Yup."

"Tell me what you know about Warren Isles."

"He's a good customer. He's interested in New Mexico history. He's got a lot of money."

"How did he get his money?"

"By coaxin' old ladies to part with theirs, persuading them to invest in mutual funds during the boom years of the nineties. Trust me." He laughed. "Getting old ladies to part with their money is not as easy as you might think." He leaned back in his chair. "What is your interest in Warren Isles?"

"Strictly professional," she said. "Have you heard about the murder of Isabel Santos, a young woman who lived in Bernalillo?"

"There are a lot of murders in New Mexico," John said. "What's special about this one?"

She told him the story of Isabel Santos and the document she found.

"You think the document was stolen from her?"

"It might have been."

"What good would that do a thief? It would be like having a stolen Van Gogh. You'd have to keep it in the closet; you'd never be able to show it to anybody. That would take all the fun out of owning it, wouldn't it?"

"May Brennan gave Warren's name and number to Isabel. Is this a document he would want to add to his collection?" she asked.

"It's possible. He's been buying up a lot of stuff related to New Mexico history and paying a good price for it. He's especially interested in the Penitentes."

"Would this be considered New Mexico history or Old Mexico history?"

"I'd say both if it was found in New Mexico. You're sure that the document Isabel found was written by a Jew?"

"Yes."

"You know the Penitentes were—and still are—very secretive. It's a tight brotherhood that flourished in remote New Mexico villages. They meet in their moradas, their places of worship. They say their prayers; they conduct their rituals; they reenact the Crucifixion. The church frowned on their practices. The Jews had to be secretive about their practices, too. Both groups were outside the control of the church. They lived in areas where the padres seldom visited. Some of the ephemera I sold Warren speculates that the Penitentes allowed the Jews to worship in their moradas. No one except for those involved will ever know if that is true or not. It may be interesting to speculate, but you're never going to find out the truth about a people who practiced their religion in secret for centuries."

"I didn't realize you knew so much about the subject," Claire said.

"If you want to become an expert on a subject quickly, this is a good one. It is so shrouded in secrecy you can claim anything you want to claim. Who's to deny it?"

"Peter Beck? He's the leading scholar of the Mexican Inquisition."

"Now there's a fun job. Can you imagine spending your working hours thinking about all the innocent people the Inquisition slaughtered in the name of God? Would you want anything to do with that God?"

"I have very little to do with him," Claire confided. "But the concept of a masculine God still exists in my psyche. I don't know why I do it, but when I'm worried or in trouble I find myself consulting with him and bargaining with him."

"Conditioning," John said. "In Texas where I grew up we were raised in the Baptist tradition of a masculine God. It's hard to break away from that. It probably wasn't all that different in Tucson. You were raised an Episcopalian, right?"

"Right."

"When you're a Protestant the differences between the denominations seem large, but once you break away, they all look pretty much the same. Catholics are another story. People don't break away. Once that church gets a hold of a person it doesn't let go. They still have a tight grip in New Mexico."

Claire never knew where a conversation would go when she visited John. The piles of books and papers and the clutter in his office made it a comfortable place to sit and chat. She also never knew when a conversation would be interrupted. A customer appeared at the door and ended this particular conversation.

"Nice talkin' to you," he said to Claire, standing up to greet the customer.

"You, too," she replied.

Checking the E-mail when she got home had become as routine as letting the cat out. That night she checked it again to find an extensive selection of credit card offers. She made herself a salad and was sitting down to eat it when the phone rang. She checked the caller ID box and saw ANONYMOUS, one step up from UNAVAILABLE. Occasionally ANONYMOUS was a real person instead of a computerized phone dialer that reached five hundred thousand people a day. On a whim she answered. The line was full of the static caused by distance and time.

"Hello? Is this Claire?"

"Yes."

"This is Pietro. Your old . . . friend, Pietro Antonelli." She knew that the minute she heard his voice.

"Pietro. It's so good to hear from you. How are you?"

"I'm fine. And you?"

"Fine."

"It was such a wonderful surprise to get your E-mail. You are living in New Mexico now and working at the university library?"

"Yes."

"I teach American literature at the University of Florence. It was so amazing to hear from you after all this time. I've thought about you often and wondered how you were."

He had taken the step of calling her. Now she had to plunge into cold water to find out what his marital status was. "I got divorced a few years ago and started a new life. I'm doing well now. I have two grown children. My daughter, Robin, is in graduate school at Harvard. My son, Eric, is in the computer business in Silicon Valley in California. Do you have any children?"

"I have a daughter, Sophia, who is sixteen. She is very beautiful."

"I'm sure she is." Did his daughter have his brown eyes? she wondered. "And your . . . wife . . . ?"

"My wife . . ." His voice seemed to come from an island of sorrow, someplace in the middle of the Mediterranean, where the tree limbs remained bare and women in black wailed a constant lament. "My wife has cancer. It has been difficult. That's why I didn't answer you sooner. I couldn't put it in an E-mail."

"I'm sorry, Pietro. It must be awful."

"It's hard to talk about."

"What kind of cancer?"

"Of the breast." Pietro sighed into the line and changed the subject. "Tell me about your work. You said you were doing something involving the Iberian Peninsula. Something that reminded you of the time we spent together. It was a very special time."

"It was," Claire agreed. She noticed how fluent his English had become. Pietro's English had been a rather charming struggle when she knew him. "Your English is excellent now."

"I teach American literature. I had to become absolutely perfect."

"Do you remember the day we spent at the Alhambra? The time we spent looking for the Jewish quarter in Barcelona?" The souk in Rabat? The snake charmers in Marrakech? The blue doors in Essaouira?

"I remember it well. You were so beautiful then, Clara."

He was the only man who had ever called Claire beautiful. The best she ever got from her ex-husband was "nice dress" or "Did you get a haircut?" Even the name Clara, which sounded clunky in English, sounded melodic in Pietro's voice.

"Thank you."

"It's true."

"I came across a document that appears to have been written by a converso who came to the New World and was killed by the Inquisition in Mexico City. It was found buried under an old house here. It got me thinking about Old Spain. To me the Alhambra is a symbol of the time when Jews and Muslims and Christians lived in harmony. Why are those periods so rare in Europe?" She didn't expect Pietro to be an expert on the subject, but she was interested in his point of view.

"There are too many people grasping for their piece of pie in Europe and the Middle East. Too much remembered hatred. Too many old grudges. The religions of Abraham are like siblings who never stop squabbling. When anything bad happens people revert to tribal warfare. They mask it in religion, but it's tribal warfare. That has always been the promise of America, a wide-open country that could absorb the overflow. I like America. I've been there several times since I last saw you."

"Really?"

"Yes. I go to academic conferences, mostly on the East Coast. I've never been to the Southwest."

"There's still plenty of wide-open space here."

"Someday, I hope. Well, I must go, Clara. It was wonderful to hear from you. I will e-mail you my address in Florence. If you ever come to Italy you must visit. If I can help you with your research, please let me know."

"I will."

"Ciao, Clara."

"Ciao, Pietro."

After she put down the phone she wasn't hungry anymore. She dumped her salad down the disposal, went outside, and walked along the rose wall. When she reached the dark red Don Juans she got lost in her thoughts about Pietro. How perfect his English had become. How sad he sounded. How awful that his wife had cancer.

Claire took a pair of shears and began cutting the Don Juans until she had an armful of dark red flowers. She took them inside and arranged them in a vase, thinking what a nice gift the roses would be for Pietro's family if only there were some way to get them to Italy in time to arrive red as blood and full of life.

Before she went to bed she checked her E-mail again and found Pietro had sent his home address. She clicked the return button and sent her own address. She considered adding a line saying she had some roses she wished to send but was afraid that would be inappropriate.

It was also inappropriate to be fantasizing about a former lover whose wife had cancer. When she got in bed she lay awake for a long time wondering how the youthful Pietro she had known had been marked by his wife's illness and the passage of time. No one could remain isolated forever from pain and the vicissitudes of life.

Chapter Thirteen

In her profession no one could remain isolated from egotism and arrogance for long either. She was reminded of this on Friday when Peter Beck called her at the center.

"Claire Reynier?" he asked.

"Yes?"

"Peter Beck. I'm in New Mexico to meet with Lieutenant Kearns of the Sandoval County Sheriff's Department. Your name came up in connection with the document Isabel Santos found. I'd like to get together with you. Could you meet me at Flying Star for coffee this afternoon? Say at three?"

"All right," Claire agreed. "How will I know you?" She assumed Peter Beck would be recognizable as a scholar, but he might not be the only scholar at the Flying Star.

"I'll know you," he said.

He was sitting at a table when Claire arrived. True to his word he recognized her as she walked in the door and signaled that by standing up. She waved and went to the counter to order a lemonade. When she got to the table, Peter Beck was seated and did not stand up again. Claire assumed that once was sufficient for him.

"Have we met before?" she asked, sitting down herself. If she had met Peter Beck she would have remembered; his reputation made him larger than life. He was also rather unusual looking. The outlines were unexceptional: tall, thin, with the limp, gray ponytail of a middle-aged professor who never forgot he'd been a student in the sixties. He was dressed rather elegantly for a professor in a slate blue silk shirt, but it was the face between the outlines that really distinguished him. Peter Beck had narrow eyes, high cheekbones, and a prominent nose with an aristocratic hook. It was a thin, angular face except for the mouth. Beck's mouth had full, sensual lips that drooped when he wasn't speaking. It was a face that combined WASP arrogance with renegade bravado.

"I've seen you at conferences," he said. "You are an archivist?"

"Yes."

As he dropped some sugar into his espresso, his spoon clinked against the side of the cup. "You spoke to Isabel Santos?"

A waiter brought Claire a tall glass of lemonade. She thanked him and sipped it through the straw. "May Brennan gave her your name, my name, and Warren Isles's name as people who might be interested in the document she found."

"Is Warren Isles an expert on the Inquisition?"

"He collects documents relating to New Mexico history. Isabel came to my office to see me," Claire said. "She copied the Ladino words she saw on the document and gave them to me."

"What exactly were those words?"

"Didn't Lieutenant Kearns tell you?" Claire assumed Kearns would have been interested in the opinion of an Inquisition expert. Peter Beck was the foremost expert, but she didn't see any need to reinforce his ego by saying so.

"Yes, but I'd like to hear it from you."

She had no desire to try Ladino in the presence of Peter Beck so she repeated the words in English.

"What makes you think the language was Ladino?"

"The use of the words *arriva* and *abasho*."

"Couldn't that be archaic Spanish?"

"Possibly."

"And why did you think those words were written by Joaquín Rodriguez?"

"Isabel told me it was signed 'Joaquín.'" Claire felt like a graduate student presenting her thesis to a skeptical committee. No doubt Peter Beck had been on numerous committees and was skilled at turning Ph.D. candidates to quivering lumps of Jell-O. She didn't have a Ph.D. and anticipated that sooner or later Peter Beck would remind her of that fact. "Were there any other Joaquíns killed by the Inquisition?" It was a question that Peter Beck was capable of answering, but he didn't.

"Joaquín Rodriguez converted as he was led through the streets of Mexico City, and he was garroted. He didn't choose the fire," he said.

"I know he was garroted. August Stevenson authenticated the documents and he gave me a copy of Joaquín's 'Inquisition Case.'"

"Ah, well, that makes you an expert." Peter Beck's lips smiled slightly. His eyes remained narrow and of indeterminate color. His nose seemed to extend until it dominated his face. If he were Spanish, Claire was sure he would be speaking perfect Castilian.

He was trying to humiliate her and she was determined not to let that happen. "I'm not an expert but I am capable of reading a document," she replied. "The 'Inquisition Case' says someone in the crowd stepped forward and Joaquín spoke words that were interpreted as a conversion. Maybe that's what the church wanted to believe. Maybe the church staged the meeting because they were unable to convert Joaquín Rodriguez. It's possible they garroted him to save face and faked the conversion to demoralize the other Jews in Mexico. It's possible the words in the document Isabel found were his last wishes."

"That's not what happened," Peter Beck replied, raising his cup to his lips and sipping deliberately. "When faced with the prospect of being burned alive, Joaquín did the reasonable thing and converted to Catholicism."

"When was Joaquín Rodriguez ever reasonable? He was a mystic who died for his beliefs, a man who circumcised himself with a pair of scissors in the Rio de los Remedios."

Peter Beck grimaced as if someone had taken the scissors to him. "Unpleasant as circumcision must have been, the pain couldn't compare to the torture of being burned alive. Joaquín Rodriguez chose to be garroted."

"Are you aware that a man named Manuel Santos witnessed Joaquín's Inquisition?"

"Manuel Santos was an official in Mexico City who witnessed numerous Inquisitions."

"Manuel Santos is the name of Isabel Santos's brother as well as her ancestor who came to New Mexico with Don Juan de Oñate."

"It's not the same person. Manuel Santos was a person of power with no incentive to leave Mexico City. He later became corregidor. His name appears on Inquisition documents well into the seventeenth century. There was obviously more than one."

"Did he have a son?"

"I've seen no record of that."

"Perhaps the skeleton will reveal more."

"You mean the one the police found under Isabel Santos's floor?"

"Yes."

"Lieutenant Kearns mentioned it. The possibility of any connection is remote."

"I'm hoping the Smithsonian will get involved; they're able to date and place skeletons with considerable accuracy."

"Why would they get involved?" Peter Beck's eyes widened enough to let in some light and show their true color. Gunmetal gray.

"It's a skeleton that could be of considerable historical significance. It could be the first Spanish settler in Bernalillo or someone who is linked to the document."

"It's more likely to be someone with no links and no historical significance. The Smithsonian is more interested in Paleo-Indian artifacts than insignificant Spanish settlers in Bernalillo, New Mexico."

Peter's disdain made Claire even more determined to get the Smithsonian involved.

"Lieutenant Kearns asked me if I thought the document Isabel described was authentic and valuable," Beck said. "It's only fair to tell you what I told him. I'm flattered that May Brennan recommended me as an expert, but I never heard from Isabel Santos and I never saw any document. Furthermore I don't believe Joaquín Rodriguez ever wrote the words Isabel gave you. If the document existed at all, it was written by someone else and of dubious value. I pointed out that Lieutenant Kearns didn't actually have a document, only a few lines of Isabel's handwriting on a slip of paper." Beck leaned back and waited for Claire's reaction.

"Do you think Isabel had the knowledge or ability to make those words up? She wasn't a scholar."

"Maybe she didn't. Maybe someone else did. You spoke to Isabel. You've shown a layperson's knowledge of the subject."

"You can't be suggesting that I made it up." Claire tried to hide her anger by sipping her lemonade, which was tart but not tart enough.

"You know quite a bit about Joaquín Rodriguez, a man who is far more obscure than he ought to be. You read his 'Inquisition Case.' You saw a connection between the name of a witness and the Santos family."

"I learned all that after I saw Isabel's document," Claire pointed out.

Peter Beck's cavalier shrug and supercilious smile suggested the timing of that was open to question.

"What possible motive would I have for making up such a document?" Claire asked.

"Career advancement," Beck said. "Some people advance in academia by scholarship; some do it by making attention-getting discoveries. You could call that the short track. It takes a long time and considerable effort to earn a Ph.D. It doesn't take very long to do a bit of research and manufacture a shadow of a document. Crypto Judaism is a hot topic in New Mexico these days. Everybody is coming out of the woodwork claiming to be a Marrano. Anyone who makes a discovery in that field is sure to receive attention. I passed that information on to Lieutenant Kearns, by the way."

You supercilious son of a bitch, Claire thought. She had spent enough time in academia to have learned not to express such thoughts at the moment she had them. "That's totally ridiculous," was the only comment she allowed herself.

"Is it? Well, Lieutenant Kearns said the evidence points to a petty theft, not a document theft. Isabel apparently had the misfortune of walking in on the robbery. The Sheriff's Department has the robber in custody. Most likely that will be the end of any investigation into document theft. I hope this will be the end of your attempts to insert yourself into my field."

His eyes were full of cold contempt. He had no trouble expressing icy anger. Claire wondered if it was the only kind he was capable of expressing.

"If you will excuse me, I must be going. Pleasure to meet you, of course," he said.

"Of course," said Claire. She watched as he finished the dregs of his espresso and stood up, watched as he walked across the room. She waited until he was out the door and then she got up, too, left Flying Star, and walked down the street to her truck. Only when she was inside the truck with the windows closed, the doors locked, and the air conditioner running did she grab the steering wheel and say out loud, "You supercilious, coldhearted, mean-spirited son of a bitch."

Saying it once wasn't enough. When she got back to the center she went into Celia's office and said it again with embellishment and feeling. "Peter Beck is an arrogant, self-centered, coldhearted, mean-spirited, supercilious son of a bitch."

"What did you expect from an Inquisition scholar?" Celia responded. "Kindness? Tolerance? Generosity?" She was wearing purple today, a rich, deep, defiant purple, the color of irises and kings.

"Intelligence," Claire said. "Doesn't intelligence imply tolerance? Is it too much to expect that from an intellectual?"

"There are different kinds of intelligence," Celia pointed out. "There is the left-brain, rational kind that does research, solves problems, and likes to dominate. Then there is the right-brain, intuitive kind capable of creating art and understanding another human being. That's intelligence with compassion and heart."

"He's definitely lacking in that."

"I have a friend at Berkeley and she says Peter has been pushing the arrogance envelope there. They know even more about arrogance at Berkeley than they do here. It's the best state university in the country and they never let anyone forget it."

People pushed the arrogance envelope all the time in academia and all that ever came of it was bitching and bitterness among coworkers. It was nearly impossible to fire a person who had gained tenure.

"Why were you talking to Peter Beck?" Celia asked.

"He came to New Mexico to talk to Lieutenant Kearns and after that he wanted to talk to me."

"What about?"

"He questioned my motives and he tried to cast doubt on me and the authenticity of Isabel's document. It contradicted some of his assumptions about the Inquisition of Joaquín Rodriguez. He implied that

I might have made the document up in an attempt to further my career."

"Here's another word for your list—prick."

"Thanks. I'll remember that. It would help if the original could be found."

"Are the police still looking for it?"

"They were, but they might not be anymore after Peter Beck told them he doubted its existence. It would be a shame if that happens because then the original may never be found. Evidence and an important piece of history will be lost. I wondered from the beginning if Isabel could have been killed over the document. If that's true and the police stop looking for it, they'll never find the real killer. Or is this just what I want to believe?"

"It's hard to accept that Isabel was killed in a stupid robbery over a VCR."

"Is it really any different than being killed in an intelligent robbery? After you're dead, does it matter how you died?"

"It matters to the living," Celia said. "My advice is to trust your instincts and keep on looking for the document."

"Thanks," Claire said.

"*De nada.*"

Claire left the office feeling grateful that Celia at least had never doubted the existence of the document. As she walked down the hall she felt she had left the world of Technicolor to reenter the world of black and white, left the swirling world of dreams in motion for the static world of print. Celia's office was full of posters, shrines, and milagros. Claire's was full of shelved books, black words on white paper. Celia acted as a thorn in the side of the somber center, although the thorn came with a rose attached.

Claire saw her own role as the interpreter of other people's actions, a person who brought her own muted colors but an active imagination to the words others had written.

Chapter Fourteen

On Monday Harold Marcus called from the Smithsonian. "Ms. Reynier, Sarah Jamieson told me you've come across some interesting bones. Over the years I've examined many remains, but I've never found anything in the United States connected with the crypto Jews or with the Inquisition. The combination of the skeleton and the document presents an interesting challenge. I'm an Ashkenazic Jew myself. The Sephardic Jews settled in Spain and Portugal. The Ashkenazic Jews come from Eastern Europe."

"It would be wonderful if you got involved," Claire said. The OMI forensic anthropologists were good, but they weren't the Smithsonian.

"I'm going to a conference in California this week. I could stop by Albuquerque on my way back. Would you have time to meet with me if I do?"

"Absolutely."

"I'll give the OMI's office a call and see if they could use some help."

Claire believed a call from Harold Marcus would open the door in any but the most territorial medical investigator's office.

* * *

She had no qualms about meeting him at the center, where there could be an excess of curiosity about her visitors. She still hadn't told Harrison about the murder of Isabel Santos. If anyone questioned Marcus's presence, all she needed to say was that he was with the Smithsonian. She could think of any number of reasons why she might talk to the Smithsonian having nothing to do with murder. When the student manning the information desk called, she walked out to meet Harold Marcus. He was a plump man, shorter than Claire, with rosy cheeks and a pleasant expression. A fringe of white hair circled a bald spot on top of his head.

"Ms. Reynier," he said, taking her hand and smiling. "It's a pleasure indeed to meet you."

"Please. Call me Claire."

"That was my mother's name. To me it means clarity and light," Harold said. "I hope you can shed some light on this skeleton that came out of the darkness under Isabel Santos's floor."

"I hope *you* can."

"Let's put our heads together," Harold said.

A promising approach, thought Claire, as she led the way down the hall to her office listening to Harold wheezing behind her. She attributed the heavy breathing to the altitude of Albuquerque, the weight of Harold Marcus, and/or a respiratory problem. When they reached her office, he sat down in the visitor's chair and exhaled with a sigh. She went behind her desk and sat down, too. Standing next to Harold made her feel too tall, too blonde, too WASP. She could never get away from being a WASP, but her perception of her tallness and her blondeness depended on whom she was with. If she and Harold were going to put their heads together in any way, she preferred to do it when they were seated and she wasn't towering over him.

"What is the altitude here?" he asked.

"A mile."

"Is that all? It feels like ten."

"Have you examined the skeleton yet?" she asked.

"First I needed to convince the medical investigator, Joan Bannister, that I could be of help. Usually we get involved after they contact us."

"Did she agree?"

"Yes. We have advanced techniques for establishing the origin of a skeleton." He smiled at Claire. "So I got to look at your old bones, which appear to date from the early seventeenth century. Joan has established that the person was a young male. I examined the growth plate line on the tibia and reached the same conclusion she had—the man was in his early to mid-thirties. Even if he did live on the frontier in the early seventeenth century, that's young to die. I didn't see any broken bones or obvious signs of warfare or foul play. We'll need to do more work before we can establish the cause of death. Although the hair and nails have turned to dust, we found a few threads of fabric attached to the rib cage that I will examine further. It is entirely possible given the time and place of death that the man was an Indian. We can determine that through bone chemistry and by strontium testing of the tooth enamel. The teeth are in good shape and intact. Tooth enamel is formed in early childhood. It reflects the food and water consumed in youth and can tell us where a person grew up."

"You can tell where a person from the seventeenth century grew up just by testing tooth enamel?" Claire was incredulous.

"We can. Once the test is completed we will know

whether our young man grew up in Spain, Old Mexico, New Mexico, or somewhere else."

"That's amazing."

Harold smiled again. His enthusiasm for his work gave him the warm, steady glow of a pilot light. Studying the dead took him into the darkness, but his intelligence transformed the experience. Claire was beginning to feel better than she had since Isabel died.

"I convinced the medical investigator to take me out to the site," Harold said.

"What did you find?"

"Nothing new. The investigators had dug extensively in the area around the body, but nothing else was uncovered. The fact that our young man was buried without a coffin may help to date his death or establish his ethnicity. Native Americans didn't use coffins. I'll have to do some research to establish when the settlers began using them. In the early days, they may have been too poor for wooden coffins. I understand that the settlers left in the Pueblo Revolt, but that some of them returned to their homesteads. Houses may well have been built over and over again on the same site. On the other hand, there may have been no floor or no house either when our young man was buried."

"Does your work ever deal with murder?" Claire asked.

"Of course. Those tend to be the most interesting cases. Forensic anthropology has made great strides in recent years," he continued, "but sometimes we need more than forensics to make an identification. Documents and history can help." Harold's eyes were full of curiosity. "Enough about me," he laughed. "Tell me what *you've* discovered."

Claire showed him the copy of Isabel's note.

"What language is that?" he asked.

"Some say old Spanish; some say Ladino. I believe it to be Ladino."

"But you don't have the original?"

"No. The original document has vanished."

"That's unfortunate because our document people could tell a great deal from the paper and the ink. Sometimes the acidic ink on these old documents eats right through the paper and turns it to lace."

"Isabel said she found it rolled up inside a wooden cross also buried under the floor. She told me it was very old and very dry. She copied the words down because she was afraid of moving the document and damaging it. I'm afraid that it was destroyed in the robbery or that it has fallen into the wrong hands and is not being taken care of."

"I'm sure you are," Harold said with so much sympathy that Claire felt he was reaching across the desk and patting her hand. "I've read that some of the Jews imprisoned in South America in the sixteenth century wrote their thoughts down on corncobs. One of them went to his death with those writings wrapped around his neck. Corncobs have been known to last for many centuries in the right environment, but whether the writing on them would last I don't know. If a document was hidden inside a wooden cross and buried under a floor, that would help to preserve it. We are going to examine the cross from the Santos house, date it, and determine its origin.

"I've long been interested in the story of the Sephardim. My family is from Eastern Europe, but I grew up in Rhode Island. I used to go to the Touro Synagogue in Newport. It's the oldest synagogue in

America, founded in 1658 by Sephardic Jews who came to New England via the Caribbean."

"It's strange to think that a synagogue could be founded in Newport at a time when Jews were being burned at the stake in Mexico City."

"They were different worlds back then, far more than a country apart. Little is known about the Inquisition in the New World. This investigation could teach us more about that dark chapter and create a wider awareness of Joaquín Rodriguez, who certainly deserves to be better known."

The dialogue with Harold reminded Claire how pleasant intellectual endeavor could be when there was a common purpose and ego was left outside the door. "I came across something interesting in my research," she said. "The Santos family is descended from a man named Manuel Santos who came north with Don Juan de Oñate. It is believed that some of the people in Oñate's expedition were crypto Jews whose names had appeared on the Inquisition lists. One of them might have brought the cross containing the last words of Joaquín Rodriguez, but Manuel Santos is also the name of a man who witnessed the execution of Joaquín Rodriguez. I have a copy of the 'Inquisition Case.' I made one for you."

"Thanks."

"I've been told that Manuel Santos the Inquisitor remained in Mexico and witnessed further executions."

"The skeleton could be that Manuel Santos's son."

"If he had a son. If that's the case, why were the words of a Jew hidden in the house of the family of an Inquisitor?"

"That's for us to find out. With the cooperation of the present generation it's easy enough to establish whether the skeleton belongs to a member of the Santos family."

"They're reluctant to claim an Inquisitor as an ancestor; the latest Manuel Santos is running for state senator."

"Do you know anyone else in the family?"

"I met Manuel's brother."

"Would he be willing to provide DNA for testing? Can he tell you any more about the family history?"

"I'll talk to him," Claire said.

"It's also possible that we will find no connection between the document, the cross, and the bones, that it is coincidence they ended up under the same floor. The young man who surfaced might not be related to the Santos family at all."

"I know," Claire said, feeling her optimism crawling out the open door.

"This may not have any relevance to the skeleton under the floor, but it's something I'm curious about," Harold said. "If crypto Jews came north with Oñate, what was their life like?"

"I'm not an expert," Claire warned, "but I've learned that there were times during the end of the sixteenth century and the middle of the seventeenth when the Inquisition in Mexico actively persecuted Jews. However, much of the time they seemed to be ignored. They lived in remote villages the padres seldom visited. It is believed that they kept to themselves, intermarried, and went on practicing their religion in secret. They continued to speak the old language. Their diet and customs were called 'the old ways.' As time passed and they went on practicing their religion in secret, some of the crypto Jews lost touch with why they were doing it."

"There's no reason to be secret anymore, is there? Why not come forward and join a local synagogue?"

"Actually there are a number of reasons. It is considered double jeopardy to be both Jewish and Hispanic. If you throw in being a woman, that makes it triple jeopardy. These are all groups that have felt oppressed at some time. By now some family members have become devout Catholics. Over the centuries the families have developed the habit of secrecy. Their Judaism is very private, very personal, not something they want to share with outsiders. The religion that they practice has its roots in the Middle Ages, and they may not feel connected to modern-day Judaism."

"I've always felt that the oppression of one Jew should unite all Jews," Harold said. "Over the centuries we've faced everything from insult to annihilation."

Claire remembered the insults and stereotyping when she was in high school and wondered if Harold had found it as oppressive as she had. Jewish boys were supposed to be smart, ambitious, and unathletic. WASP girls were expected to be pretty, pleasant, and dumb. Young women were sought after for that reason. The dumber they acted the more popular they became. They were status symbols but it was a role she hated. It was a relief to grow older and be able to develop and express her intelligence.

"A blow against one of us should be a blow against all," Harold said.

It was the ideal, Claire thought, but it might not be the reality. Sometimes religions were as divided internally as they were threatened by external forces.

"Compared to the other religions, there are so few

of us," Harold said. "There are a billion Muslims now, two billion Christians. Yet there are no more Jews in America now than there were ten years ago. Many people marry outside the religion and their children are lost. If you come across anybody in your investigations who is willing to talk about the old ways, I'd be interested in meeting with that person whether it has anything to do with the Santos investigation or not. I'm always interested in learning more about Judaism and connecting with other Jews. This is a little-known chapter back East."

"Of course," Claire said.

Harold stood up and shook Claire's hand. "It was a pleasure meeting you. Good luck with your work."

"You, too."

"I'll let you know what story the old bones have to tell."

"Thanks," Claire said.

She walked Harold out to the information desk.

When she got back to her office she called Chuy Santos.

She heard someone lift the receiver and pause before speaking. "Hello," a woman said in a voice that seemed rusty from lack of use.

"Hello," Claire replied. "I'm looking for Chuy Santos."

"Oh, Chuy," the woman answered. "Chuy's not here. He went to the Santa Ana Casino. To collect his paycheck, he told me."

"My name is Claire Reynier. I work at the Center for Southwest Research at UNM. Would you ask him to call me? He has my number at work, but I'll give you my home number, too."

"Of course," the woman said, taking the number down. "I will tell him to call you the minute he gets home."

Chapter Fifteen

It was hot outside when Claire left the library at five-thirty, even hotter when she got in the truck that had been baking all day in the sun, so hot she could barely touch the steering wheel. She drove across campus and was on University Boulevard before the air conditioner had cooled the cab down. Her house was stifling and full of dead air when she got home. In midsummer the days were long and full of sun. She let Nemesis out, turned on the cooler, and went outdoors herself. She checked the courtyard where the datura was extending its antennae and preparing to bloom, then went to her backyard to water the roses. The front of her house faced east toward the Sandia Mountains, which provided a backdrop for the reflection of the setting sun and the rising of the moon, but her backyard faced the long view across the city over the Rio Grande Bosque into the vastness of the West Mesa. The weather usually came from the west and tonight thunderheads were building over Cabezon Peak. Claire couldn't remember exactly when it had rained last, but it had been months. The ground, the people, the vegetation, even the air itself, held their breath longing for rain. The prickly pear and ocotillo in the foothills were parched and layered with dust. She had the sensation she had every summer that she was waiting for something she believed would come but feared might not. The sky seemed promising tonight. The clouds were darkening and the wind was picking up.

The clouds left their encampment on the West Mesa and marched across the valley preceded by a wind that reminded Claire of Pueblo feet thumping the earth and raising clouds of dust. It picked up speed as it climbed the Heights, leaped the fence, and swirled into her backyard. The rose branches shimmied. There was a flash of lightning and a crack of thunder. The ambient light shifted from daylight to dusk. Nemesis ran for cover, but Claire stood still and waited on her back step for the smell, the taste, the joy of the rain. She wanted to hear it ping the roof. She wanted to see her wilted plants spring back to life. She wanted to feel rain run through her hair and down her face, washing away death, sadness, heat, and dust. When the downpour started she would go inside, turn on Vivaldi's *Four Seasons*, and watch the rain dance in her courtyard.

There was a crack of thunder. The wind paused from its dervish whirl for the moment of stillness and silence preceding the rain. Claire waited for the precipitation, expecting the first drops to splatter the walk. It began with one drop, and then another. And then it ended. The clouds and wind passed right over the house and climbed the mountain, taking their gift to a higher elevation. In the mountains there would be a ground-soaking rain, but in the foothills it was over. Tonight had only been foreplay, reminding Claire that the monsoon promised rain many times before it delivered.

She went inside feeling she'd been let down by an indifferent lover, thinking that only the parched would pin their hopes on the weather. People on the East and West Coasts didn't sit and wait for rain. They didn't dance in the drops when it finally came. She wondered whether she had any food in her house that could compensate for the desertion of the rain, something dark and inspiring like chocolate. She rarely had chocolate in her house because whenever she had any, she ate it immediately. She found a ripe, rich mango and peeled it. *Mangos de oro*, they were called in Mexico. She remembered eating one in Guanajuato impaled on a stick like a Popsicle, the fruit carved to resemble the folded petals of a flower. She cut the mango into slices and slid them into her mouth on the tip of the knife.

She would have to water the roses now, but she put it off until morning. It was too disappointing to go back outside and see the dust on the flowers and leaves. She glanced at her answering machine and saw a blinking red light. Thinking it might be Chuy, she pushed the play button and heard John Harlan's Texas twang.

"Hey, Claire, John here. Looks like it's finally gonna rain. Damn, we need it, don't we? I'm gettin' together with Warren Isles Friday and was wonderin' if you'd like to meet the guy. Give me a call."

She called him back and learned the meeting had been scheduled for the Tamaya Resort Hotel on the Santa Ana Pueblo north of Bernalillo.

"He's one of those guys who will only deal face-to-face and one of those Santa Feans who will only come to Albuquerque when he has to go to the airport," John said. "But he's a good customer and Tamaya is a beautiful place. Have you been there?"

"Not yet." The resort, a cooperative effort between the Santa Ana Pueblo and the Hyatt Regency Hotel chain, had opened recently to rave reviews. Claire wanted to see it, and she hoped Warren Isles might know something about the missing document, so she agreed to meet them.

"Do you want me to pick you up?"

"I'll meet you there. I have some stops to make in Bernalillo."

"See you then," John said.

On the afternoon of the meeting, the interstate was clogged with traffic, giving Claire time to study a sky so clear and blue it gave the impression rain was a foreign language. She left I-25 at the Bernalillo exit and took Route 44 through the fast food strip, remembering the tranquility of Coronado Monument only a quarter mile away.

She passed Santa Ana Star Casino and turned at the next light, eventually ending up on a one-lane road about as wide as her truck, not a road she'd want to navigate after a couple of drinks. At least it was surrounded by desert that could provide an escape route. Claire smiled at the first road sign that read SPEED LIMIT 24 MPH and again at the next one reading 17 MPH, thinking this had the subtle, offbeat quality of Indian humor. The Santa Ana land stretched from Route 44 along the banks of the Rio Grande into the Jemez Mountains.

A magnificent stretch of bosque was visible from the hotel. Claire passed the golf courses where water sprinklers ticked, and parked in the lot. A worker who cruised the lot in a jitney offered her a ride to the door of the sprawling building. The exterior was monumental but unexceptional. The beauty of the building became evident once Claire was inside. Every detail from the furniture, the floors, the vigas, the lights in the ceiling that resembled the skin of drums, had been carefully thought out. The artwork showed a subdued and subtle taste—Edward Curtis prints, Emmi Whitehorse paintings, photographs of Indian dancers by David Michael Kennedy, priceless Indian rugs framed and hanging on the walls. She passed through the lobby furnished like a large and elegant living room with sofas arranged around fireplaces and tables for playing board games. She entered the bar and found John Harlan nursing a Jack Daniel's.

"Welcome to my new home," he said.

Claire had been to John's home and knew it to be a dark cave of a town house bearing no resemblance whatsoever to the elegant and expansive Tamaya.

"How do you like it?" John asked.

She admired some oversized prints of horses' heads on the wall. "It's beautiful," she said.

"Warren's not here yet. Get yourself a drink and we'll sit outside."

Claire ordered a glass of Chardonnay and they took their drinks to the deck, sat down, and looked across a field to the cottonwoods on the banks of the river and the jagged gray Sandias beyond. The farther north Claire traveled in the bosque, the steeper the peaks of the Sandias appeared. She liked the way the branches of the cottonwoods curved and rambled like country roads. It was a lovely place to sit, watch the light change, and make small talk with John, but she didn't like to be kept waiting. When fifteen minutes had passed she got annoyed. Fifteen turned to twenty and even laid-back John glanced at his watch.

"He'll be here soon," he said. "You can count on

Warren to be twenty minutes late and twenty dollars short. That's how he lets you know he's an important guy."

"Do really important people have to do that?"

"Nah, but they get in the habit and sometimes they do it anyway."

A child on the deck jumped up and down and cried out, "Look."

A coyote trotted across the field. Other people on the deck stood up to ooh and aah. The coyote loped along ignoring its audience and the fuss it had created with an indifference so complete Claire found herself admiring it. Warren Isles chose that moment to show up at the table. He was a large, plump man with soft skin and a sliver of a smile that appeared to have been pasted on. Dough boy wasn't a bad description; neither was Michelin Man. Warren's skin had a rosy glow, and his hair was damp as if he had just stepped from the shower or the sauna. Had he been enjoying the spa while they waited? Claire wondered. Taken a sauna on their time?

John saw it differently. "You get stuck in traffic?" he asked.

"I never see any traffic between here and Santa Fe," Warren replied, oblivious to John's sarcastic innuendo. "Traffic picks up at Bernalillo. One reason I never go south of here unless I have to. I came down this morning, had lunch at Corn Maiden, spent the afternoon. You must be Claire Reynier." His smile curved a little higher.

"Claire, meet Warren," John said.

Warren signaled to a waiter and ordered a glass of ancient Scotch, the oldest Scotch likely to be found anywhere in this state. He sat down in the empty chair and said "Howdy" to Claire. "John told me you're interested in the history of Bernalillo."

"I became interested when Isabel Santos told me about a document she found under her floor."

"The last words of the Jewish mystic?"

"Yes."

"It was very kind of May Brennan to give her my name. I would have been quite interested, but unfortunately I never heard from Ms. Santos. Lieutenant Kearns questioned me about the document she described. I told him that given the age and the scarcity of documents in New Mexico pertaining to the crypto Jews, it could be very valuable indeed if it turns out to be authentic. I told him that no one had offered such a document to me, but if anyone did I would let him know immediately."

"I'm glad that you agree with me that the document is valuable," Claire said. "Peter Beck at Berkeley told Lieutenant Kearns that it wasn't." Claire herself wondered whom Kearns was more likely to believe. Both men seemed to be quite impressed with their own knowledge.

"I can't speak for Peter Beck, but Kearns seemed to think I was the expert in the field," Warren said with a self-satisfied glow. "I pointed out that I am not an expert in the Inquisition, but I do have one of the finest private collections of historical documents in the state of New Mexico." His aged Scotch arrived and he sniffed delicately before taking a sip. "Excellent," he said.

John grinned at Claire from across the table while Warren savored his expensive Scotch.

"I am very interested in the story of the crypto Jews here and collecting documents pertaining to that subject. There is nothing rarer. The subject is so secret, documentation is very hard to find. I have tried to talk to some of the old families, but they won't open up to me. If the document Isabel Santos found turns out to have a connection to New Mexico's Jews, I want it."

Claire supposed that what Warren Isles wanted, Warren Isles got, but if she had knowledge about ancient and secret family traditions, the acquisitive Warren Isles was the last person she would want to share it with. She didn't trust his soft hands with their fat, greedy fingers. She didn't trust the practiced half smile used to coax valuables from women who might do better taking the long view and holding on to what they owned rather than entrusting it to Warren.

"I have the same problem with the Penitentes. They are very secretive," he said.

"John said he sold you some ephemera that implied the Penitentes allowed the Jews to practice in their moradas."

"It was an obscure article published years ago in a historical journal. John sold it to me for an outrageous price."

"Now Warren," John drawled, "you know I never sell ephemera—or anything else—for more than the market will bear."

"Right, and I am the bear market." Warren laughed at his own joke.

"Are you still in the investment business?" Claire asked.

"I've been cutting back, but I haven't retired. If you're looking to invest, I can do right by you. Women don't pay nearly as much attention to their investments as they should, often holding on when they ought to be selling."

Claire felt she gave her investments no more or no less than their due. When she inherited money, she studied, analyzed, consulted, invested, and forgot about it. She didn't need the money now. She didn't want to be buying, selling, trying to time the market, and paying a broker a fee for every transaction. Warren Isles was the type of broker she avoided, one who took advantage of women who didn't pay as much attention to their investments as they should.

"If you're looking for investment advice, I have a very good track record."

"I'm content with my mutual funds," Claire said.

"Well, if that ever changes, call me." Warren took a card from his pocket and handed it to Claire. "Call me, too, if you should come across the original Joaquín Rodriguez document. That's something I would be very interested in."

"All right," Claire said, thinking the last place she would want to see that document end up was in Warren Isles's dough-boy hands, although she was encouraged that he believed there was a document. It was more encouragement than she'd gotten from other men she'd talked to.

John took out his briefcase to show Warren the articles and journals he had brought, the unbound material known to dealers as ephemera. Claire was reminded that she happened to be sitting at the table with a couple of dealers who had come to Tamaya to buy and sell. They began to discuss the quality and haggle over the price. John loved to deal and negotiate. His ears picked up and his eyes had the keen wariness of a coyote's.

But the negotiations soon bored Claire, and she turned her attention to the natural world, scanning the field for another glimpse of the coyote. It had vanished. The child who had spotted it had gone inside with his family. The brilliant sunshine and sharp shadows were fading. She looked toward the sky and saw clouds moving in, hazy, ephemeral wisps—not the towering thunderheads that promised rain but clouds that hung in and obscured the horizon. They had crossed the bosque and were climbing the Sandias when Warren and John finished making their deal.

They all stood up, shook hands, and left the deck. Warren now had a briefcase full of ephemera, and John's was empty. They walked through the living room, and the families playing board games made Claire think of an elegant country home on a summer weekend.

"Can we walk you to your car?" John asked. "Or do you get a ride in that golf cart?"

"Neither," said Warren. "I have a dinner engagement."

They shook hands and said good-bye at the hotel door.

Chapter Sixteen

John walked her across the parking lot to her truck. The time of day, or the hazy weather, or the deal he'd made with Warren—something had put him in the mood for confidences.

"I'm not seeing Sandra anymore," he said to Claire as his feet crunched the gravel.

"What happened?" she asked.

"She wanted a different kind of man. Somebody who would make a lot of money and take care of her."

"Unrealistic to expect that of a book dealer."

"True." John laughed. "But I did well today. It's the Warren Isleses that keep the wheels of this business turning."

One reason that Claire stayed out of it. She felt a refreshing moisture in the air. "I was in touch with an old boyfriend of mine over the Internet," she said. "I met him in Europe when I was in college. He teaches at the University of Florence."

"Oh?" said John.

"His wife has breast cancer."

"Why did he get in touch with you?"

"He didn't. I contacted him. I didn't know about his wife."

"Spending years watching a person die of cancer is a sad and lonely business. You don't want to be disloyal, but you're ready for some love and companionship when it's all over."

Claire didn't know that Pietro's wife was dying, but she knew that John's wife had died a lingering death. "Is that what happened to you?"

"Not according to Sandra. She says I'm still thinking about my wife."

"Are you?"

"To the point where I couldn't love someone else? I don't think so, but that person isn't Sandra."

It was more open than they had ever been with each other. When they arrived at Claire's truck, she didn't know what to say until the sky took charge and left her speechless. She pointed toward the Sandias.

The sun had set beyond the golf course. The departing rays illuminated the clouds, embracing the mountains and turning them into a radiant pink mist. Claire had never seen a sunset so fluid and mysterious. The Sandias were rarely shrouded in mist.

"Exquisite," John said.

There was nothing left to say. They waited for the light to fade and the clouds to turn gray again. Then they got in their respective vehicles and drove away. As she negotiated the narrow road out of Tamaya, Claire felt that the thoughts she and John had just shared had taken them ever deeper into friendship and even further away from romance. Once a man became too good a friend, once she started confiding in him about other men, it became difficult to think of him as anything but a friend, although in this case a very valuable one.

After a few miles on the Tamaya road, she returned from the sublime to the commercial and was back on the strip that housed nearly every fast food restaurant known to man as well as the Santa Ana Star Casino. Wondering why Chuy Santos had never called her back and if she might find him there, she pulled into the casino parking lot and walked to the building. As soon as she opened the door she was assaulted by smoke and layers of noise. The bottom layer was background music with an unidentifiable beat and lyrics. Above that a repetitive ding, ding, ding emanated from the slot machines. That sound was punctuated by the clang of coins dropping into a metal receiver. Change? Winnings? Claire didn't know. If it was winnings, the clang should have been followed by exclamations of joy instead of more dings. There was hope in this casino, but little joy.

She walked up and down the rows of slot machines searching for Chuy. Most people played alone with a cigarette in one hand and the other on the machine. Many were older women who had little to lose. Women who were put off by Las Vegas felt welcome in New Mexico's more intimate casinos. They sucked their cigarettes and pushed the buttons like automatons. One woman appeared to be linked to her slot machine by a chain. It only took a few minutes for Claire to long for escape. If she still believed in hell, this would be it.

She gave up on the slot machines and went to the tables. A bunch of men were clustered around one table tossing dice, laughing and joking, adding

human sounds to the mechanical noise. She found
Chuy hunched over a green-felt blackjack table while
a dealer prepared to deal him a new hand.

"Hey," he said. "What are you doing here? You
play?"

"I called you a few days ago and the woman who
answered told me you were at the casino. You never
called me back. I happened to be at Tamaya, and I
stopped here on my way home."

"That was Grandma Tey you talked to. I've been
staying at her house. What the hell." He signaled
"no more cards" to the dealer. "I'm on a losing
streak anyway. You want to go somewhere and
talk?"

"Yes," said Claire.

Chuy's cell phone was on the table. He picked it
up and led the way to the cafeteria with a shuffling
walk. The restaurant was open to the casino and offered little relief from the smoke and noise.

"You want anything?" Chuy asked. "I'm getting a
soda for my Dr Pepper jones."

"I'd like a lemonade if you can find one."

Chuy went through the cafeteria line and came
back with a lemonade and a Dr Pepper.

"Sorry I didn't get back to you sooner," he said,
lowering himself into a chair. "I've been busy."

Doing what? Claire wondered. "I thought you had
stopped gambling."

"I did, but then I got lucky and I started up all
over again." He put his cell phone on the table.
"What was it you called me about?"

"Have you heard anything new about your sister's death?"

"Nada."

"Is Tony Atencio still in jail?"

Chuy shrugged. "Far as I know. I haven't seen him around anyway."

"I've learned a lot since I last talked to you."

"Yeah? Like what?" The light in his eyes reflected the gambler's belief in endless possibility.

"Lieutenant Kearns talked to the two experts May Brennan recommended to Isabel, and so did I. I don't know exactly what they told him, but Peter Beck, who is the leading Inquisition scholar, told me he doesn't believe that the Manuel Santos who witnessed the Inquisition of Joaquín Rodriguez is your ancestor."

Chuy slurped his Dr Pepper. The bells in the casino continued their pounding, relentless beat. "Why not?"

"He said there was no incentive for an Inquisitor to leave Mexico at that time. This particular Inquisitor became a corregidor and was involved in other executions after your ancestor arrived in Bernalillo."

"That ought to make my brother, Manuel, happy now that he's the great brown hope of the Republican party. But our ancestor could have been Manuel Santos, the Inquisitor's son, if he had a son."

"It's possible, but that expert doesn't think so."

"Do they know how old the skeleton was when he died?"

"Early thirties, I've been told."

"Who's the other expert?"

"A man named Warren Isles, a wealthy collector from Santa Fe, who buys historical documents. I just had a drink with him at Tamaya. I thought he might have heard something about Isabel's document, but he claims he hasn't."

Chuy's cell phone rang and the sound was barely audible above all the bells and whistles in the casino.

It was the rare place a cell phone could ring without being annoying. "Hey, bro," Chuy said. "I can't talk to you now. I'm busy." He paused to listen. "What do you care what I'm doing? I'll have to call you later." He hung up.

"Did Lieutenant Kearns tell you that the Smithsonian has gotten involved in dating and identifying the skeleton?" Claire asked.

"Kearns don't tell me nothin' he don't have to tell me. That's cool that the Smithsonian is getting involved, isn't it?"

"I talked to Harold Marcus, a forensic anthropologist at the Smithsonian. The skeleton has been dated to the early 1600s. It might or might not be your ancestor."

"Hell, it could be an Indian. No one in my family likes to admit that we don't have *limpieza de sangre*, but why couldn't we have an Indian ancestor?"

"If you do, it's more likely to be a woman." Claire knew that Spanish men were more likely to marry Indian women than the reverse.

"I guess."

"Marcus will do more tests. He told me that by testing the tooth enamel he can tell where and when the skeleton grew up."

"Is that right?" Chuy said.

"Yes." Claire was getting to the difficult part. She wished she were in a quieter place where she could concentrate and get the phrasing of her question right. "The one way to establish for sure whether or not you are related to the skeleton is by DNA testing and comparison. Would you be willing to do that?"

"I don't mind."

"Your brother said no."

Chuy laughed. "When my brother says no it means *nunca*, if you know what I mean."

Claire knew.

"Maybe you ought to talk to my grandmother," Chuy said. "If she says yes, Manuel might go along with it."

"Would you mind?"

"No. I don't mind. Let me give her a call." Chuy dialed a number. "Hey," he said. "It's me, Chuy. I'm at the casino. I got a lady here from UNM who wants to talk to you. The same lady Isabel talked to." He listened for a while, then said, "Okay. I'll send her over. I'll be home later." He put the phone down. "She says come on over."

"It's not too late?" Claire asked. It would be convenient to stop on the way home but she didn't want to keep an elderly lady up.

"Nah," Chuy said. "She's too old to sleep. She loves to talk anytime. Here's how to get there. You go back to Isabel's house and follow the ditch road. It's the house on the other side of the field. Grandma Tey will be waiting for you."

"Thanks," Claire said.

"No problem. Now, if it's all right with you, I have to get back to work."

"Okay," Claire said. She watched Chuy shuffle back to the blackjack table and lay down his chips. She finished her lemonade and walked out through the casino.

As she pushed the outside door open, feeling she was about to be released from a noisy prison, she was greeted by the fresh smell of rain. She put out her hand and felt the touch of a gentle rain, the kind the Navajo called a female rain. Where did it come from? she wondered. The clouds she'd seen hugging the Sandias earlier had not been rain clouds. Rain was always welcome in New Mexico and she opened her arms to it. "Hello, rain," she said. If she were at home she would have stayed outside, watched it dance in her courtyard and let it wash away the sadness and the dust. She didn't want to show up at Tey Santos's house dripping wet, so she hurried back to her truck and clicked on her windshield wipers for the first time in months.

Chapter Seventeen

The rain and wind picked up speed as Claire drove through Bernalillo, forcing her to turn the wipers from intermittent to medium. Isabel's death had been an undercurrent tugging at her emotions and her memory, but the minute she turned the corner onto Calle Luna it swelled into a wave. Death had a way of receding, then rushing back whenever the memory of the deceased was reactivated. Claire thought of Isabel as a crushed butterfly, a bright and vibrant spirit who should never have died so young. Despair about her loss was mingled with frustration that the death seemed so pointless.

As Claire approached 625 she thought she saw a light flickering in a window. But when she reached the house, it was dark. She stopped and watched through the rain beyond the windshield wipers. Isabel's presence was strong, but Claire saw no other vehicles and no activity around the house. The windows were all dark. The light might have been a reflection of her headlights or a projection of her imagination. It was dark enough here to give her second thoughts about visiting Tey. On the other hand, people were more likely to confide and agree in the intimacy of a dark, rainy night.

She drove to the end of the street and turned onto the ditch road that passed behind Isabel's house. The road was made of dirt and was about as wide as the road into Tamaya, wide enough for one vehicle. But here she didn't have the option of escaping into the desert. On one side there was a ditch full of water, on the other a drop-off into the field that surrounded the house where Isabel died. The field had been bull-dozed lower than the road so when the ditch water flowed in, it wouldn't flow back out again. The road had the slickness of a surface that was about to turn to mud. The weeds stood high as a child beside the ditch. The arm of a cottonwood hung across the road, and branches full of wet leaves scraped the roof of Claire's truck.

Visibility was poor in the darkness and the rain. Claire clicked on her brights, but that only deepened and lengthened the shadows. She thought she saw a shadow lumber onto the ditch road. She blinked, try-ing to clear her imagination. The shadow turned toward her and she faced an SUV with the headlights off and darkness as a driver. The only lights along the ditch were her headlights, and the SUV seemed drawn to them like a vengeful bat. Claire felt trapped in a high-stakes gamble. The SUV gave no indication of intent to stop or turn away. Braking might stop her truck, but it wouldn't stop the oncoming vehicle. Her options were to dive into the ditch or into the field or to face a head-on collision. She was in a state of slow-motion suspension, but the SUV was getting so close she could almost hear it beating its wings.

She focused on the sounds and the feel of the dan-gers—the sickening impact and shattered glass of a

crash or the splash and water pouring into the cab
if she turned into the ditch. She swung the steering
wheel toward the field. The truck lurched across the
lip and stumbled into the field like a horse with a
broken leg. While she struggled to regain control, it
careened into a picnic table, smashing it to kindling.
She swung the wheel to the left, crashing into the
trunk of a cottonwood. The glass on her side of the
cab shattered on impact and fell to the ground. Her
engine died. The headlights went out. Claire was all
alone in the middle of the Santoses' field with no
protection. She felt around the cab searching for her
cell phone. Through the broken window she saw the
SUV turn onto Calle Luna with its high beams on
and continue down the road.

Claire found the cell phone and punched in 911.
She gave her name and location to the operator, relayed what had happened, and asked if it would be
possible to send Detective Romero.

"We send whoever is on duty," the operator
replied.

Feeling like a stationary target inside the cab of
her truck, Claire climbed out. If the SUV returned,
she could disappear into the darkness on foot with
the cell phone in hand. She left the truck behind,
found her way to the portal of Isabel's house, and
stood under it listening to the rain drumming the tin
roof. In the heat of the day she wouldn't have imagined that she could be so cold, so wet, so soon. She
tried to see through the windows into the house, but
it was darker inside than out. She shifted her weight
from one foot to another searching for warmth, listening for any sound beyond the rain. She heard a
rustle, a displacement of water beside the house. She
heard motion, the jingle of a collar, and Chuy's dog

came around the corner, poked her with a cold nose, and began to lick her arm.

"Are you alone?" she whispered, grabbing his collar and holding tight, hoping the dog would provide some protection if a person came out of the darkness.

The next sound beyond the rain was the whine of a distant siren. As it got closer, she saw the lights of a Sheriff's Department vehicle flashing like a strobe.

The car parked. Leaving the headlights on, two cops stepped out.

"Over here," she called.

They turned their flashlights toward her, and she wondered if she looked as damaged as she felt.

"Are you all right?" a policewoman called.

"I think so."

Claire released the dog and he ran off to greet the police. As they approached, Claire became more illuminated, but they disappeared into the darkness behind their flashlights.

"That's a nasty cut you've got," the woman said.

"Where?" Claire's arm was covered in blood. "I didn't even notice."

By now the policewoman was at her side. The flashlights had turned away from Claire's eyes and she could see how petite the woman was. She took hold of Claire's arm and examined it. "It's a nasty cut but it looks like a flesh wound. I'm Deputy Anna Ortiz and this is my partner, Deputy Michael Daniels."

Her partner was a burly man several inches taller than Claire with a pushy, aggressive manner. "What happened here?" he asked.

He moved in close while he questioned her, as if sniffing her breath. Drinking was an issue when someone drove off a road, but denying an accusation that hadn't been made yet would do Claire no good. She kept quiet about her glass of wine.

"I was on my way to Tey Santos's house on the ditch road when someone in an SUV pulled out of the field with no lights on and ran me off the road. I lost control of my truck when I turned, and I hit the tree."

"Why were you on this road?" Daniels asked.

"This is the way Chuy Santos directed me."

"Chuy? How do you know him?"

"I knew Isabel. I came here to see her on the day she died. I've been talking to Detective Romero and Lieutenant Kearns about the case."

"Is that right?" The deputy was standing too close, invading Claire's private space. "So what brought you here tonight?"

"Chuy sent me to talk to his grandmother. I thought I saw a light on in Isabel's house as I drove down Calle Luna. As far as I know, her death isn't a closed case yet. Is there any possibility of getting Detective Romero to come over and look at the house?"

"I'll give him a call," Deputy Ortiz said.

While they waited for Romero, the policewoman took Claire back to the car, turned on the inside light, and began filling out a report. Daniels stayed outside, circling the house and property with his flashlight, looking for evidence. He came back and said, "I saw SUV tracks climbing the embankment on the south side of the house. No sign of breaking and entering."

Detective Romero approached quietly. He pulled up next to the police car, stepped from one vehicle to the other, and sat down in the backseat. He wore jeans and a T-shirt that emphasized his hard, muscular arms. His hair was cropped so short he appeared to be bald. He was younger than the police officers, but he took command with his soft-spoken manner.

"Are you all right?" he asked, examining Claire's arm. "That's a bad cut. Do you want me to take you to the emergency room or call a paramedic?"

"I'm okay," Claire said. "It doesn't hurt. I'll clean it up when I get home." The blood had clotted and caked, which stopped the bleeding. "I'm sorry to call you out at this hour."

"No problem. Tell me what happened."

He turned on his tape recorder and she repeated her story, wondering as she did whether she was giving it any change in emphasis or detail because he was the listener.

"So you think the attempt to run you off the ditch road was deliberate?" Romero asked.

"Yes. The SUV came right at me playing chicken. There would have been a head-on collision if I hadn't turned off."

"Did you see a license plate or anything else that would help to identify the vehicle?"

"It was big and black. That's all I saw. I couldn't even tell if it had a driver. There was nothing but darkness behind the wheel."

"Did anybody know that you would be driving the ditch road tonight?"

"Chuy Santos knew. He told his grandmother. I don't know whether he told anyone else."

"When did you talk to him?"

"I saw him at the Santa Ana Casino about an hour ago. He had his cell phone with him. Someone called and he said, 'Hey, bro.' "

"Anybody could be a brother to Chuy, especially when he's had a few drinks."

True, Claire thought, but he only had one blood

brother. "He sounded annoyed that he'd been interrupted."

"Could you tell if Chuy had been drinking?"

"I don't think so. He didn't act drunk. He was drinking a Dr Pepper while I talked to him." She knew Detective Romero and didn't mind raising the issue of her own drink with him. "I went to Tamaya before I met Chuy and had a glass of wine there with Warren Isles, one of the experts May Brennan recommended to Isabel. I'm sure it has worn off by now."

"One glass of wine will keep you well below the legal limit. Did you tell Warren Isles where you were going?"

"No."

"Did you see what kind of car he drove?"

"No."

"Tell me why you were going to see Tey Santos."

"I've been talking to a forensic anthropologist from the Smithsonian and he asked me to see if I could find someone in the Santos family who would allow them to do a DNA comparison to the skeleton's DNA. I thought I saw a light inside the house as I drove down Calle Luna, but when I got here, it was off. Would you be willing to go inside to see whether anyone has been there?"

"Let's do it," Detective Romero said.

They left the car and walked across the yard with the cops trailing behind. Romero stepped around the house and turned his flashlight on the truck. It was the only truck Claire had ever owned, the trusty Chevy she bought right after she split up with Evan. It was her symbol of an independent new life, and she was more attached to it than a grown woman ought to be to a truck. Seeing it smashed made her feel that she had failed. The damage to the truck bothered her far more than the gash on her arm.

"The front end is pretty beat up," Romero said. "We need to get the vehicle towed back to the shop to investigate further. I can give you a ride home."

"Thanks," Claire said.

He had skeleton keys in hand when they reached the front door, but tried the knob before using them. The door swung open. He ordered Claire to stay outside, pulled out his weapon, stepped through the door, and flipped the light switch. Deputy Daniels followed. Deputy Ortiz remained with Claire.

Romero called out "all clear" when the search was completed, and Claire and Deputy Ortiz went inside. The house wasn't as chaotic as it had been earlier, but it wasn't orderly either. A rug had slid or been kicked sideways; the sofa pillows were askew; a closet door was open. Two candles on the mantelpiece had burned down, dripping wax all over their candlesticks and leaving a faint smell of smoke in the air. The mirror over the mantel was covered by a black cloth. Why? Claire wondered. So the glass wouldn't reflect what had gone on here? She stared at the covered mirror. In the depths of the black cloth, which absorbed light rather than reflected it, she saw an image of Isabel swaying like a reed in her platform shoes. She saw the golden butterfly embroidered on her shirt. She saw someone give Isabel a hard shove, but she didn't see Tony Atencio. Was it the person in the SUV? Did Isabel have some thing or some knowledge that person wanted? She saw Isabel fall and hit her neck against the table. She saw her land on top of her purse. Claire cringed.

Romero tapped her shoulder with a light touch. "You okay?"

"Yes," Claire said. "But being in this house reminds me of Isabel."

"Her death was terrible," he agreed. "It's one of the old ways to cover the mirrors in black when a person dies as a sign of mourning."

"I didn't know that. Is Tony Atencio still in jail?" she asked.

"Yes."

"The person in the SUV couldn't have been him."

"Not him, no, but it could have been one of his homeboys."

They walked down the hallway. The mirror in the bathroom was also covered in black.

They moved on to the bedroom, which now resembled an archaeological dig. The bricks had been pulled out and stacked to the side and there was a deep hole in the middle of the room. Most of the dirt had been carted off. Romero sat on his heels and stared at the hole with his hand hovering over the dirt as if he longed to be digging in it himself but knew that was forbidden. The law that said digs were reserved for scientists wouldn't have stopped a criminal. Claire saw signs of recent activity. There was sand on top of the remaining brick floor, and marks that appeared fresh inside the dig.

"Has the OMI been here recently?" she asked Romero.

"I don't know when they were here last," he said.

"Harold Marcus with the Smithsonian told me he came out here with them a few days ago."

"It might have been then."

"Do you think whoever ran me off the road was here?"

"Someone was inside the house," Romero said. "Someone lit the candles and let them burn down, but that could have happened hours ago. It could have been a family member. Let's give the officers the opportunity to examine the house and I'll take you home."

Chapter Eighteen

They took the back road through Sandia Pueblo and didn't see another vehicle between Bernalillo and Albuquerque. The rain fell softly now and clouds scurried across the sky, indicating the storm was moving on.

"Best rain we've had all summer," Romero said. "Only rain we've had all summer."

"Usually I love the rain, but this was the wrong night to be out in it."

"Tony Atencio is still our prime suspect, but if someone did go back to the house it might open other avenues of investigation. A connection between Isabel's death, the robbery, and the old bones would pretty much eliminate Tony. That's a guy more interested in scoring drugs than in history."

"He may have gone to the house after Isabel fell and taken advantage of an opportunity. That would explain the fingerprints."

"True."

"Have you found a match for the fibers?"

"No. I hear you've been doing some historical research."

"Some," Claire admitted.

"What have you found out?"

"I told Lieutenant Kearns that Manuel Santos is the name of a man who witnessed the Inquisition of Joaquín Rodriguez. But that particular Manuel Santos went on witnessing Inquisitions after someone else named Manuel Santos arrived in New Mexico in 1598."

"It could be a son. The bones have been traced to the early seventeenth century by the OMI, and the Smithsonian traced the cross to roughly the same period."

"I hadn't heard about the cross."

"That's the advantage to being a police officer. We get the good news first. We also get the bad news first." Romero stared straight ahead at the road. Claire couldn't see him well in the darkness but she imagined he smiled when he said that. "We can find out easily enough if those bones are Santos bones if the family agrees to DNA testing."

"It was what I intended to talk to Tey Santos about. If she doesn't agree, can you make the old bones part of the current investigation? Can you insist that the Santos family submits to DNA testing?"

"Not really," Romero said. "There's nothing to indicate the man under the floor died of unnatural causes. Even if there was a crime, it could be four hundred years old."

"Is covering the mirrors a custom everybody followed in the old days?"

"I'll ask my grandmother," Romero said.

They reached the wide turn onto Tramway and Romero took it, heading east toward Claire's house in the foothills. They passed the new Sandia Casino, an enormous building in the style Claire thought of as *nuevo pueblo grande*, a pueblo enlarged and embellished. She went to the casino once because the deck in the back was a good place to watch the full moon rise above the Sandias. She had to walk through the casino to reach the deck and was impressed by the high ceilings, the architecture, the decoration, and the state-of-the-art air filtration system. It was the only casino in which she'd been able to breathe. If she was ever going to gamble, this was where she would go. But Santa Ana was expanding, too, and when it was finished it was likely to equal or outshine Sandia.

There weren't many people Claire enjoyed riding with. From what she knew of cops they were cowboys behind the wheel, but Detective Romero was a calm and steady driver. It might have been the rain, the darkness, the fact that he was behind the wheel, the threat she had faced—something in this moment made her want to confide in him. His gentleness opened doors Lieutenant Kearns's businesslike manner left closed.

She began with gambling. "The last time I saw Chuy he told me he had stopped gambling, that the casino had cut him off, but now he's back again, so his debts must have been paid. He said he got lucky. What does that mean? If he wasn't gambling, he didn't get lucky in the casino. So where *did* he get the money to pay off the money he owed?"

"His brother, Manuel, has the money if that's how he wants to spend it."

Claire hoped she wasn't about to cross a line. The Santos and Romero families were native New Mexicans with similar backgrounds. She was an outsider, a woman from Arizona who lived in the foothills in a neighborhood known as the White Heights. "If it was Manuel, why would he choose to pay off Chuy's debts now?"

"Why do you think?" Romero asked.

"I'd hate to think it was to keep him quiet. A valuable document that was in the house when Isabel died disappeared at a time when Chuy needed money."

"You think Chuy or Manuel are capable of killing their own sister?"

"I don't know. You know more about killers than I do. For me the question is more whether they would take advantage of their sister's death."

"We've talked to the experts May Brennan recommended and we haven't found any evidence that a document was offered for sale."

"If one of them bought it, would he admit it? Experts are practiced at concealing their sources. You might learn more by talking to May Brennan again."

Romero swung the car into the long, lazy curve where Tramway headed south, holding tight to the wheel. "Why her?"

"May isn't as practiced at the art of deception as Peter Beck and Warren Isles. She says she didn't speak to them herself, but maybe she did." It was skirting closer than Claire liked to come to accusing an old friend of concealing the truth.

"Why would May hide the fact, if she did talk to them?"

Although Claire was sitting down, she felt like she was thinking on her feet. Thoughts about Isabel's death had been percolating for a while but this was the first time she'd allowed these thoughts to rise to consciousness. "Because she's depressed. Because she's not thinking clearly. Because she may be on drugs or alcohol. Because she might have done something she feels guilty about. She might have revealed information that put Isabel in jeopardy. You could question her more thoroughly. You could find out what kind of a car she drives."

"I suppose you want us to find out what kind of vehicles Manuel, Chuy, and Warren Isles drive, too."

"Chuy drives a beat-up Ford truck. I've seen it. As for Manuel he came to see me at UNM and his manner was edgy."

"What did he want to see you about?"

"He didn't like the idea that his ancestor might have been an Inquisitor. It wouldn't be good for his career. He made it clear that he wanted me to stop looking into it."

They reached the road that led into Claire's subdivision. Romero followed her directions and turned left. The moon hanging over the mountains was draped in a black cloud. The cloud slipped off. For a second the moon was in full light before another cloud drifted over it. There were times Claire liked the complexity of a moon seen through clouds better than the black-and-white contrast of an unambiguous sky.

"Maybe we ought to give you a badge and let you run the investigation," Romero joked.

"I'd follow up on the document if it were up to me, but Kearns doesn't believe there was a document, does he?"

Romero searched for the right words. "He believes what the evidence supports."

"Do you think the evidence supports a document?"

"Let's say I'm open to the possibility. I'm not a person who needs to see something to believe in it."

Claire directed him to her house and he parked in front. "Do you have another vehicle you can use?" he asked.

"No."

"Are you going to be all right if I leave you here without one? It'll take a few days to examine your truck and then it will have to be repaired. I can recommend a mechanic in Bernalillo, if you like."

"Thanks," Claire said. "I'll rent a car tomorrow."

She felt a kind of current in the car. The kind caused by a man rescuing a woman from danger? Or was it that they were alone in a car at night and Claire was about to return to an empty house? She hoped her house was empty. Whoever had run her off the road had had plenty of time to come here. She thought of inviting Romero in, asking him to check the house, offering him a cup of coffee, but wondered if that would be appropriate. She liked him, his tough exterior and his gentle interior, his openness to the old ways, his respect and consideration for her. He treated her as an equal, not as an older person, or a white person, or an academic. He treated her as a woman, but not in a demeaning way. But she didn't know if she ought to be leaning on a detective at all, especially one who was at least twenty years younger than she was.

"I'll walk you to your door," he said.

"I'm okay," Claire replied.

"I'd like to check your windows and doors. Someone ran you off a road and almost killed you. There are people who knew where you were going. People who could find out where you live. We need to be sure that no one came here."

"All right," Claire agreed.

She went to the front door and inserted her key in

the lock, which turned as smoothly as it always did. Nemesis, startled to see her with a man, arched his back and circled Romero warily.

"Nice house," he said.

"I like it," Claire replied.

As soon as they entered, she could see that the alarm had not been activated. She turned it off and walked through the house with Romero examining every window and every door. He even beamed his flashlight outside. Although the ground was still wet from the rain, he found no prints.

"You're okay," he said. "No one has been here. Lock the dead bolt after I leave, make sure all the windows are locked, too, and turn on the alarm."

"Would you like a cup of coffee for the drive home?" It seemed the least she could offer under the circumstances.

"No, thanks. Is there anyone you can call to come and stay with you?"

"I'll be all right," Claire said.

"Well, I need to get going." He handed her his card. "Here's my cell phone number. Call if you have any problems."

Bernalillo was so far away, Claire thought. Anything could happen by the time he got back to the Heights.

"Don't worry," he said, as if she had somehow communicated her thoughts. "I'll pass the call to someone close by."

"Thanks for bringing me home."

"I'll check in with you tomorrow."

She stood in the doorway and watched him walk to his car. Then she shut the door, snapped the dead bolt into place, and walked through the house making sure every window was locked. She turned on the alarm and went into the bathroom to wash off her arm. It was caked with dried brown blood that turned red again when the water hit it. She watched the bloody water swirl down the drain, remembering the deliberateness of the SUV as it headed straight for her. Was the driver trying to wipe *her* out or aiming at whoever happened to be in the way? Once the blood had washed off she could see that the edges of the cut held together and stitches wouldn't be needed. She treated it with antibiotic cream, then she got in the tub and soaked away the dirt and pain of the day, resting her arm on the side of the tub so as not to wash away the cream. Nemesis was being a nudge by scratching at the door.

"Go away," she said.

He did but when she got into bed she found him curled up on her spot. She slid him gently to the far side of the bed. He could be a nuisance, but on a rainy night it was nice to climb into a warm bed. She expected that sleep would be a long time coming and she would have time to replay the events of the day, anticipating that at any minute a window would break and the alarm would sound.

She began at the end of the day and worked her way back. One positive element was that she had connected with Romero again. Kearns was in charge and to approach Romero directly was to go behind his back. But Romero's intuitive side, his connection to the community and the past, could solve this crime better than Kearns's no-nonsense outsider attitude. She admitted to herself that she liked Jimmy Romero better than Kearns. Kearns seemed to see her as a pest. Romero saw her as a person. It was a comforting thought. Nemesis purred in the bed beside her. She fell asleep and didn't wake up again till morning.

*   *   *

Claire's first thought on waking was that a bird was singing outside her window. Her second was that her arm hurt. Her third was that something was missing. She ran her tongue around her mouth searching for a hole as if she had lost a tooth. Then she remembered her truck had been impounded by the police somewhere in Bernalillo. She was without wheels.

"Damn it," she said, jumping out of bed.

A startled Nemesis leaped out of bed behind her, landing on all fours.

Before she even brewed coffee, she got on the phone and made arrangements to have a rental car delivered. It was an expensive solution, but she had to have a vehicle. Being stuck in her house with no transportation left her feeling trapped and abandoned. Being without her truck left her feeling bereft. It was stupid to care so much about a truck, but this truck represented more than transportation—it represented a life that didn't depend on an untrustworthy husband.

Once the arrangements were completed she made herself a bowl of granola and a cup of coffee and sat down at the dining room table. The phone rang. Considerate of Jimmy Romero to call so early, she thought, picking it up.

"What happened to you last night?" Chuy Santos asked. "When I got home, my grandma told me you never showed up. Through the trees she saw all kinds of police lights at the house. The police told her you'd been in an accident."

"When I drove down the ditch road someone pulled out of the field in a black SUV and ran me off the road."

"*A la,*" said Chuy. "Were you hurt?"

"I cut my arm. My truck was bashed in. I ran into a tree."

"Hey, a truck can be fixed. Be glad you're okay."

"Had anybody been to Isabel's house that you know of?"

"Not that I know of," he said, but he paused before he said it. "I need to go over there and check it out myself. Grandma still wants to talk to you. Could you come by this afternoon?"

"Is there another way to get there?"

"Sure." Chuy gave her directions by the regular roads. "I want to talk to you, too. I'll be back around three."

"See you then," Claire said.

A few minutes later Detective Romero called. "I tried you earlier, but I got a busy signal."

"That was Chuy Santos. He wanted to know what happened last night. He heard I'd been in a wreck."

"Was everything all right last night?"

"Fine. I'm going to Bernalillo this afternoon to talk to Chuy and his grandmother."

"You got wheels?"

"Yes, a rental car is on the way."

"Lock up before you go. I'll be at the station this afternoon."

It was an unusual experience for Claire to have a man concerned about her safety, and she rather enjoyed it. Her own son, who had been putting all his energy into a start-up company in Silicon Valley, called her once a month.

Chapter Nineteen

Claire left at one-thirty to go to Tey Santos's house in a generic white rental car, the kind of car that could be seen in every airport parking lot. Other types of rental vehicles were available but ninety percent of the rental cars she saw resembled hers. At every stoplight and turn she missed her truck. She could have been anybody in the rental car, but in her truck she was a book scout, an archivist, a person with a taste for adventure.

She wanted to drive by Isabel's house to see the damage and make sure her truck had been towed away, but she was afraid Chuy would be there cleaning up the yard and she hoped to see Tey first. She followed his directions and circled around the block on paved roads to get to Tey's, thinking this route was easier to follow than the one he'd given her, wondering why he'd sent her down the ditch.

Tey lived in a small adobe house sheltered by a sprawling cottonwood. A willow tree that was a cascade of leaves stood behind the house. A dog who could have been Blackie's sibling was lying in the yard when Claire pulled into the driveway. It wagged its tail when it saw the car but didn't bother to get up. Water from the ditch kept Tey's property green and fertile. Claire passed a well-tended vegetable garden as she walked toward the door. Between the stalks of corn, she saw tomatoes, chile, beans, and squash, crops that had been growing in the Rio Grande Valley forever. One section of the garden was devoted to herbs. Claire identified mint, oregano, rosemary, sage, and the tall stalks and umbrella-shaped yellow flowers of anise. She knocked at Tey's wooden door.

"Hello?" Tey called.

"Hello. I'm Claire Reynier, the woman Chuy sent to see you."

"Okay," Tey said, opening the door.

Claire faced a tiny elderly woman wearing a faded cotton dress and leaning on a cane. Her face was as warm and wrinkled as a dried peach. Her black eyes had the alertness and curiosity of a hawk. Her nose had a prominent hook. Her white hair was pulled up in a bun on top of her head. Tendrils escaped and tumbled down to her shoulders.

"Come in," she said.

The house smelled like something baking. Claire thought she caught a whiff of marijuana but decided it had to be another herb.

"I'm so sorry about Isabel," she said. "I only met her once, but I liked her very much."

"After her mother and father died, she was a daughter to me. She had problems and went to California. I was so happy when she came back home." Tey's gnarled fingers clutched the top of her cane. "That terrible, terrible boy killed her."

"Are you sure it was Tony Atencio?"

"It was him. He's a very bad boy. Even my dog didn't like him and growled when he walked by.

Sonny started barking when he heard him running down the ditch that awful day."

"Did you see or hear anything else that afternoon?" Although Tey was an old woman, she'd given no sign she was hard of hearing. Her body might be slowing down but her mind and senses seemed sharp.

"Nothing."

"Chuy said you heard about the incident last night. I was driving here along the ditch when a black SUV pulled out of the field and tried to run me off the road."

"A SUV? What is that?"

"A sports utility vehicle." Tey's expression remained confused, so Claire added, "It's a cross between a car and a truck. Do you know anyone with a car like that?"

"I think Tony Atencio had one. Would you like some yerba buena tea?"

"I would. Thank you."

"And a cookie?"

"Yes." Claire sat down at a table covered with a flowered plastic tablecloth while Tey prepared the mint tea. "Yerba buena" translated literally into "good herb." "When the SUV ran me off the road into Isabel's yard, I hit a tree."

"Don't worry, those cottonwoods, they are very old and very strong like me." She smiled and her skin crinkled. "You can't hurt them."

"I called the police. That's why you saw all the lights."

"Even in the rain they were very bright."

"I thought I saw a light inside Isabel's house when I drove by. The police went inside later to investigate. The door wasn't locked."

Tey put the tea down on the table along with a plastic bear full of honey and a plate of cookies. "Why lock the door now that my sweet *nieta* is gone?"

"Could anyone else have gone inside the house?"

"Yes, but why would they? There's nothing left to steal."

"Do you go there?"

"Often. I talk to my Isabelita. For me she is still alive in that house."

"I felt that way, too," Claire admitted. "Someone left candles burning."

"I did that."

"Did you cover the mirrors in black?"

Tey nodded. Her hands resting on the table had the bulbous joints of rheumatoid arthritis. "It's the old way, *las costumas antiguas*, something we do. It's not good to be looking in the mirror when someone dies. My mother taught me those ways. I wanted to teach Isabelita, but I didn't have the time. Have a cookie." She handed the plate to Claire.

She bit into the cookie. "These are delicious. Did you use anise from your garden?"

"Yes. It's a good plant."

"You have a beautiful garden. Has your family lived here for a long time?"

"For four hundred years," Tey said, "God has kept our garden green. The first Santos came here with Don Juan de Oñate."

It was the door Claire had hoped would open. "Did you know that there was an Inquisitor in Mexico City in 1596 with the name of Manuel Santos?"

Tey's eyes were fierce. "That person is not my ancestor. My ancestor was not part of the Inquisition."

"You know about the skeleton that was found under the floor?"

Tey nodded, shaking loose a few more tendrils of hair.

"That man lived in the sixteenth and seventeenth centuries. He was in his thirties when he died. He could have been Manuel Santos, the Inquisitor's son."

"No," Tey said, placing one gnarled hand over the other. "He could not."

"The medical investigators could find out if he is your ancestor by testing your family's DNA."

"DNA? What is that?"

Trying to explain DNA was daunting, so Claire settled for: "The medical investigators can take a piece of hair or skin or even saliva and compare it to the skeleton. They can tell from that if people are related, even people who lived four hundred years apart."

"The investigators can do that?"

"Yes, but they need your cooperation and your permission."

"I will have to ask my grandson. He is the one who has the Manuel Santos name." Claire felt the door had closed again; she knew what Manuel would say.

"Do you know anything about the document Isabel found or the cross?"

"Nothing," Tey said. "I never even saw them. She told you, but she didn't tell me. I will never understand that."

"Maybe she didn't have time."

"Maybe. The police have the cross now."

"Do you know who has the document?"

"No." Tey pushed herself away from the table to stand up. She went to a canister on the kitchen counter, picked out a stem, brought it back to the table, and dropped it into her tea. "My arthritis is hurting me," she said. "It does that when it rains."

"What's that?" Claire asked, expecting to discover another good herb.

"Marijuana," Tey replied. "It's very good for the arthritis. I grow it myself between the cornstalks."

"Here?"

"Why not? It's my land. I was born here. I grew up here. I came back after that no-good man I married left, and took the Santos name again. What are they going to do? Arrest a ninety-two-year-old woman and put me in jail with that Tony Atencio? Wait till they see what I would do to him."

Claire was reminded that people who lived to a ripe old age had a strong will. "Do you smoke the marijuana?"

"Only when the pain is very bad." The dog in the yard began to yip. "That's my grandson. That's the way Sonny barks when he hears Chuy."

"Don't get up," Claire said. "I'll let him in."

"Chuy can let himself in," his grandmother said.

Claire stood up anyway, went to the window beside the front door, and watched Chuy park his truck and walk across the yard. The dog stood up, wagged its tail, and let Chuy scratch its head.

"Whose car is that, Grandma?" he asked as he pushed open the door. He was wearing his Santa Ana T-shirt and jeans that were caked with dry mud.

"Mine," Claire said.

"*Hola*, Chuy," Tey said.

"*Hola*." Chuy bent over, kissed the top of her head,

then turned to Claire. "I thought you said you were coming later."

Claire could think of no excuse for her early arrival so she changed the subject. "Were you at the house?"

"Yeah."

"Was my truck there?"

"No. It was gone, but I could see the scar where you hit the tree. That must have hurt."

"I cut my arm," Claire admitted. "How did the house look?"

Chuy shrugged. "Looked the same to me. I didn't see any SUV tracks in the yard. The only tracks I saw went from the ditch to the picnic table to the tree, like the truck had had too many beers."

"Have a cookie, Chuy," his grandmother said.

He took a cookie from the plate, snapped off a piece, and crunched it in his mouth.

"The police saw the tracks last night," Claire told him.

"Did they?" asked Chuy. "Well, maybe it was one of Tony's homeboys who went back to check the place out."

"What kind of vehicle does your brother drive?" A lawyer living in the hills of Placitas would likely have an SUV, Claire thought.

"Manuel?" Claire saw ambivalence toward his older and more successful brother ripple across Chuy's fluid features.

His grandmother was quick to remind him that Manuel was Chuy's brother. "Your brother does not drive a black car," she said.

"Right. His SUV is gray," Chuy said. "A black car like that drove by yesterday afternoon when I was in the yard, but I couldn't see who was inside it."

Tey's sharp eyes told Chuy his statement had not gone far enough.

"My brother was home last night anyway," he added. "I called him and then I went up there after I left the casino." He looked to his grandmother for approval.

She nodded.

Claire thought that Manuel could easily have been at Isabel's house while Chuy was still at the casino, but she didn't say so. A wall of family solidarity had gone up and shut her out. She couldn't tell if this was a knee-jerk reaction to an outsider, if the Santoses had something to hide, or if they just valued their privacy.

The marijuana in Tey's tea hadn't dulled her mind. "The medical investigators want to compare our bones to the old bones to see if we are related to an Inquisitor. I said we would have to ask Manuel."

"Sure, Grandma," Chuy said, sitting down next to his grandmother and putting his hand on top of hers. "If that's what you want."

Claire saw this as a signal that it was time for her to go. She thanked Tey for the cookie and tea and said good-bye.

In her white rental car she drove out of the yard. In a way the car was cover, but the cover had been blown now that Chuy had seen it. She couldn't drive by Isabel's house anymore without feeling that she would be noticed. She had been wanting to visit Isabel's grave and this seemed like a good time. Tey and Chuy were occupied; she wouldn't have to worry about running into them at the cemetery. She'd be free to think her own thoughts about the death of Isabel Santos.

*   *   *

Claire drove through the town of Bernalillo. The cemetery wasn't where she thought it should have been—beside Our Lady of Sorrows Church. It was below the on-ramp to the interstate. It didn't seem like a very desirable location, but the cemetery was established long before the interstate. She had seen it many times but had never stopped. She turned off the side road from Route 44. Just past the cemetery a lot full of trailers advertised with a large sign that it was having a sale. The sign was tied to the fence and snapped in the breeze. Claire parked and entered the cemetery, surprised by the bright reds, pinks, and yellows of the artificial flowers that covered the graves. She'd been expecting a duller, grayer place.

She liked to visit old graveyards; she saw them as an illustrated collection of poetry and short stories. Stories could be found in the names and dates of the departed: the men who had survived wars, the men who hadn't, the women who had died in childbirth, the children who had died young, the people who had lived to a ripe old age even in the hardest of times. People didn't live any longer now than they ever had, but a higher percentage of them lived to an advanced age. There was art in the symbols carved into the more elaborate tombstones—the birds, the crosses, the intertwined wedding rings— art in the ceramic figures left behind and in the weathered wood of the oldest markers. Poetry could be found in the epitaphs, many of which were in Spanish. Claire saw *juntos para siempre* (together forever), *descanse en paz* (rest in peace), and one she especially liked, *para el mundo eras uno, para nosotros eras el mundo* (for the world you were one, for us you were the world).

It was intriguing to think her ashes would eventually be scattered in the water or the wind, blending into the elements without a marker now that she no longer had a husband to lie beside in eternity. It would also be reassuring to be buried in a family plot beside her mother and father, her grandparents and the generations before them, people she never knew but would always be related to by the substance of her bones. Someday, if her children made no deeper connections in the course of their lives, they might lie next to her, too. This cemetery celebrated family and she envied the people here who would be *juntos para siempre.* But for her it was a dream. Her family had been in America almost as long as the Santoses, but the Reyniers had never settled in one place long enough to have a family plot that went back several generations. Reyniers were scattered across the country from New York to Arizona. Unless Claire was willing to start her own dynasty, for her it would be the water or the wind.

But the Santoses were deeply rooted in New Mexico and Bernalillo, and Isabel would be buried near her ancestors. Claire went to her grave and found it marked with a brand-new tombstone. "Isabel Santos," it said, *"descanse en paz."* Hearts were carved into the stone, but Claire would have preferred the symbol of a butterfly. The artificial flowers on the grave were the right color—dark red, the color Isabel wore when she visited CSWR. A pebble sat on top of her tombstone. There were other people in the cemetery, but their attention was focused on the newly departed, not on Claire. She picked up the pebble and balanced it in her hand, thinking that holding it might tell her something, that being tactile would be better than being intellectual or emotional. It was hard not to get emotional at Isabel's grave, thinking she had already begun the process of turning to dust, hard not to feel that if she had only been in her office when Isabel called, if the document had been safely stored at the center, her death might have been prevented.

Claire took strength from the solidity of stone. Did people put pebbles on graves because stone endured? She knew people who collected stones because they liked the color or the markings or because a stone reminded them of a place they had been. The pebble in her hand was an ordinary gray stone crisscrossed by white lines, but if she stared at the lines hard enough and long enough, they took on the shape of mist and clouds. She replaced the pebble, trying to put it exactly where she had found it.

Her hand dropped to the top of the tombstone and she let it rest there, saying a final good-bye to Isabel Santos, whispering, "Rest in peace. *Descanse en paz.* If there is anything I can do to make sense of your death, I will."

Other members of the Santos family were buried near Isabel. Most had tombstones with names, dates, a cross, and *descanse en paz* chiseled into them. The names Ester, Isabel, Manuel, and Jesus occurred several times. Sometimes Claire came across families and couples buried together. Isabel's parents had died within two years of each other and their cross was marked with intertwined wedding rings and the epitaph *juntos para siempre.* Sometimes individuals were buried alone. There were other tombstones with pebbles on them. While she stared at the Santos tombstones she heard the trailer sign flap, flapping in the wind.

She moved away from this section and wandered into the far corners of Our Lady of Sorrows Cemetery where the markers were older and more primitive. Wooden crosses were attached to the fence or lay on the ground. If they had ever been inscribed, the inscriptions had weathered away. It made it difficult to tell how far back the cemetery went. The oldest dates Claire found were nuns who were buried here in the 1880s. It made her wonder where all the bodies from the 1600s and 1700s were.

A jackrabbit jumped out of the weeds and stared at her. In the very back corner Claire found the tombstone of Isabel Santos de Suazo, who also died young in 1890. Twenty years later her husband Moises Suazo was buried beside her. This was the oldest Santos tombstone in the cemetery. It had no cross. This tombstone was decorated with an open flower with six petals. There were lines in the middle of it that looked like musical notes arranged in the shape of a W. It was either a stamen or a symbol that Claire couldn't read. Beneath the flower she saw the curved arms of a candlestick. This etching was rougher and lighter than the professionally carved flower and looked as if it had been added later by hand.

When she was back in her rental car Claire sketched on a piece of paper the markings she had seen. Then she drove to the police station to ask about her truck.

Chapter Twenty

Romero didn't have his own office. He shared the room with several other detectives. The phones were ringing, people were talking, but Claire felt he tuned it all out and focused on her. His eyes were warm and sympathetic.

"How is your arm?" he asked.

"Fine," she said.

"You'll get your truck back soon," he said. "The SUV must have tapped your truck's tail end as you went into the field. We found some paint marks that could help to identify it. We're checking Atencio's family and homeboys to see if any of them own a matching vehicle."

"Were the paint samples gray or black?"

"Black."

"Manuel Santos owns an SUV." Chuy had said that vehicle was gray, but Claire wasn't sure she believed him.

"How do you know that?" Romero asked.

"Chuy told me. I went by there this afternoon." Claire didn't consider it her civic duty to tell Romero that Tey Santos had been sipping marijuana stems she raised in her vegetable garden.

"I'll look into it," Romero said.

Although Claire hoped he would, she wasn't convinced; a wall seemed to go up whenever she mentioned the name of Manuel Santos, possibly because he was a local boy who had made good. "I asked Tey if someone had been in the house and covered the mirrors. She said she did."

"That's the kind of thing *abuelas* do."

"Did you ask your grandmother about it?"

"Not yet."

"She told me she lit candles while she was in the house. She leaves the door unlocked; she says there is nothing left to steal. Tey thinks Tony Atencio is a very bad boy and that he killed Isabel." It seemed only fair to pass that on.

Romero made no comment.

"She said she would ask Manuel about comparing their DNA to the old bones, but I'm sure he'll say no."

"We can't make them unless we can establish that the old bones will help solve the current crime. Considering that the bodies are separated by four hundred years it's a very long shot."

"I know," Claire said. "After I left Tey's I went to the cemetery to see Isabel's grave. Someone had put a pebble on top of her tombstone. Is that one of the old ways, too?"

"I don't know." He shrugged. "Maybe in the old days when people were too poor to afford flowers they brought stones."

"Maybe," said Claire. "I came across the tombstone of another Isabel Santos, who died in 1890. That one had flowers and a candlestick carved into the stone. Have you ever heard of her or the man she was married to, Moises Suazo?"

"No. How's the rental car working out?"

"All right."

"I'll give you a call when the truck is ready." He stood up, signaling that the meeting was over.

"Thanks," Claire said.

She drove home through Sandia Pueblo, where the road was lined with the faces of wildflowers. Recent rains had rejuvenated them, but even when it hadn't rained for months, flowers bloomed in New Mexico. It could be a harsh place, but from May to November there were wildflowers beside the roads. Anyone who couldn't afford to buy artificial flowers could easily pick real flowers. But real flowers didn't last. Stones and artificial flowers did. Was that why people put them on graves?

She poured herself a glass of Chardonnay when she got home, took it into the living room, sat down on the sofa, and stared out the window at the Sandias where the piñon and junipers were sprouting shadows. She had a phone call to make and she wanted to have her thoughts in order before she did. It was early evening here, nighttime where she was calling. She didn't have the home phone number of the person she hoped to reach, but she got it from information. She hoped he would be home and wouldn't consider this an intrusion. She hoped she wouldn't wake him up.

"Hello," he answered in the grouchy tone of an animal disturbed in its lair.

"Harold. This is Claire Reynier."

"Oh," he replied. "And how are *you*?" The grouchiness disappeared from his voice. Harold Marcus seemed genuinely pleased to hear from her.

"I'm good. I hope I didn't wake you."

"No, it's only nine o'clock here and it's Saturday night. I can't go to bed at nine o'clock on Saturday even when I have nothing better to do. What's on your mind?"

"Have you learned any more about the skeleton?"

"Well, let's see, bone chemistry indicates he's a Caucasian. He died in the early seventeenth century when he was in his thirties, apparently of natural causes. I don't have the results back on the tooth enamel so I can't tell you where he grew up. The logical choices would be Spain or Mexico."

"I went to the Bernalillo cemetery today to visit Isabel Santos's grave. Someone had placed a pebble on top of her tombstone."

"That's interesting." Claire only had his voice to go on, but Harold seemed fully awake now. "It's an old Jewish custom to leave a stone at a grave."

"Why do they do that?"

"It's a sign that someone has been there."

"I found the grave of a woman named Isabel Santos who died in 1890 and was married to a man named Moises Suazo."

"It's a Catholic cemetery, isn't it?"

"Yes."

"Catholics aren't likely to name their children Moses."

"The tombstone didn't have a cross but an etching of an open flower with a stamen in the middle that might be a symbol or a letter. I drew a picture."

"Can you fax me a copy?"

"Yes."

"How many petals did the flower have?"

"Six."

Claire heard the excitement of discovery in his voice. "I've seen similar flowers in other Sephardic cemeteries. It could be a representation of a six-pointed star. The Star of David appears on Jewish tombstones, although in the past a six-pointed star wasn't exclusively a Jewish symbol."

"I also saw a candelabra carved on the tombstone, although it was lighter and rougher than the other carving. It may have been added later by hand."

"How many arms did the candelabra have?"

"Nine."

"That could make it a menorah. It would appear that Isabel the Saint married Moses the Jew. In the nineteenth century Ashkenazic Jewish merchants settled in New Mexico, but Suazo is a Spanish or Portuguese name, which would make Moises a Sephardic Jew. Nowadays when there are interfaith marriages, all too often the man forgets he's a Jew and takes the religion of his wife. That's one reason there are so few of us. But the tombstone would suggest that Isabel was the one who converted. Did they leave any heirs?"

"I didn't see any children buried nearby. Isabel Suazo died when she was only twenty-two. Chuy Santos sent me to his grandmother's house last night. Someone ran me off the ditch road into a tree in Isabel's yard."

"Were you hurt?"

Claire considered her bruised arm. "Not really, but my truck was damaged. I thought I saw a light in Isabel's house when I drove by. After the accident I went into the house with the police. Candles had been burning and the mirrors were covered in black. I went to the grandmother's today and she told me she had covered the mirrors and left candles burning in the house."

"Jews burn Shabbat candles on Friday nights to

mark the beginning of the Sabbath. Covering the mirrors in black after a death is an old Jewish custom. Mourners are not supposed to be thinking about vanity. Mourning is only supposed to last for seven days, but people here may have lost sight of that. What is the grandmother's name?"

"Tey."

"That could be a diminutive of Ester, and Esther was the Hebrew queen of Persia."

Claire liked to hear his excitement grow and know that someone else shared the joy of discovery.

"There were several Ester Santoses in the cemetery."

"Here's what I think," he continued. "I think Isabel Santos married into a Jewish family. Somehow the last words of Joaquín Rodriguez ended up in the hands of the Santos family, maybe through the Suazos. The Rodriguezes and the Suazos could be related. Both names have a Portuguese connection and some of the Sephardim went to Portugal before emigrating to the New World."

"Have you learned any more about the cross?" Claire asked.

"It was made in Mexico in the late sixteenth century. It's from the same period as the bones, but so far that's the only way we can connect them. It's possible the bones belong to a Suazo, and the Santos family moved into a Suazo house."

"There's another possibility." Claire's mind had leaped ahead of Harold Marcus's, but she'd had more time to think about what she'd learned in the cemetery. She was in New Mexico looking at the mountains that inspired big thoughts, whereas he was likely to be in a suburban house where the only view was of his backyard. She had learned when solving problems related to her work that sometimes it was best to return to the premises that had been taken for granted and reexamine them. "Suppose the first Manuel Santos to arrive in New Mexico was connected to Joaquín Rodriguez and brought the cross and the document with him. Maybe the Santoses were Jews before they came to New Mexico. Maybe the marriage between Isabel and Moises was an intrafaith marriage."

"Well, all the forensic techniques in the world won't tell me whether the skeleton belonged to a man who was circumcised. Strontium testing of tooth enamel could tell me if he spent time in Portugal as a boy. If he did, it would be an indication of Judaism, but it wouldn't be proof. And the question remains, how do you explain the family having the name of a saint and an Inquisitor?"

"I can't," Claire said. "But I'll keep trying."

"I'll do what I can to speed things along here. Do you think the Santos family has been telling you all they know?"

"Not entirely."

"Perhaps if you tell Tey what you've discovered, she'll tell you the whole truth."

"Perhaps," Claire said.

She said good-bye to Harold, hung up the phone, and went to her window. The shadows on the mountain had begun to merge with the twilight. Soon the creatures of the night would be slipping out of their nests and their dens—the owls, the bats, the snakes, and coyotes. In Harold's mind there was a line between truth and untruth and the methodological approach could put the facts into one column or another. But that wasn't the way Tey Santos would look at things.

Chapter Twenty-one

Claire revisited Tey the following morning while the bells of Our Lady of Sorrows called the people of Bernalillo to church. Claire expected Manuel to be at the service but not Tey. Claire didn't know where Chuy would be, although the casino was always a possibility.

When she pulled into the yard, she was relieved not to see his truck. Tey was in the garden among cornstalks that were taller than she was. To be able to maintain a house and a garden at the age of ninety-two was a major accomplishment. Claire attributed Tey's long life to living in and caring for this fertile spot.

She stopped tending the corn and leaned on her cane when she saw Claire. "*Hola*," she called. "It's a beautiful morning." She didn't seem at all surprised that Claire had returned.

"*Hola*," said Claire. "Do you have any time to talk to me?"

"I have nothing left but time," Tey said. She maneuvered her way out of the cornstalks and headed for a bench parked under the willow tree. Claire followed and sat down beside her. The temperature was already in the nineties, but it was ten degrees cooler in the shade of the tree. Willows drew a lot of water and were rare in New Mexico. This one seemed to be converting groundwater into a waterfall as the leaves cascaded around them, creating a sheltered, private place, a good place to share a secret.

"You have a lot left," Claire said. "You have a house, a garden, a dog, a family."

"*Verdad*," Tey said. "And God gave me this nice tree to sit under."

"It's lovely here." Claire could have easily spent the morning exchanging pleasantries with Tey, but she was afraid Chuy would show up, and there were things she preferred to say when he wasn't around.

"I went to the cemetery after I left here yesterday to pay my respects to Isabel," she began. "Someone had placed a pebble on top of her tombstone."

Tey's black eyes were alert, but she said nothing.

"I walked around the graveyard and came across a grave for Isabel Santos de Suazo and Moises Suazo. They shared a tombstone and it had a six-pointed flower carved on it with a symbol inside. When I got home I called a friend who is Jewish." She had decided not to mention the Smithsonian at this point, thinking that the institutional connection might put Tey off. "He told me that he has seen similar flowers on Jewish tombstones, that it is an old Jewish custom to leave a stone at a grave."

"What else did he tell you?" Tey asked, clutching the top of her cane.

"It is also a Jewish custom to light candles on Friday nights to mark the Sabbath, and to cover the mirrors when someone dies. That Tey is a nickname for the Hebrew name Esther."

Tey seemed to be stepping into the truth and blinking her eyes at the light. She said without hesitation, "*Somos Judíos.*" We are Jews. "I am named for Queen Ester. That name has been in my family forever."

It was where Claire's investigations had been leading, but she was so startled to hear Tey say so that she felt the bench was tipping and spilling her into deep water.

"Our ancestors were Jews," Tey said. "Sometimes we named a son Jesus so no one would know. For years we always married Jews, but now there are hardly any left. The make-believe Catholics became real Catholics. If those bones under the house belong to our ancestor, they are the bones of a Jew. But that's all I know. I don't know anything about Manuel Santos before he came here. I don't know why he had the name of a saint and an Inquisitor. I never heard of Joaquín Rodriguez until Isabel told you about that piece of paper."

"Did Isabel know you are Jewish?"

"No. I am the only one who knows that now. When I die the secrets go with me. The women pass on the religion and the tradition of the Jews. When they are old enough we tell the young women, but Isabel died before I could tell her. Now there is nobody left to tell."

"Chuy and Manuel don't know?"

"No. They may think they know a little, but they don't know everything."

"Would Manuel be upset to find out? He's a devout Catholic, isn't he? Wouldn't it be hard now to think of himself as a Jew?"

"It would be hard," Tey agreed. "Because his wife is very Catholic. At first the Jews had to pretend to be Catholic. We could lose our land or our life if anyone found out. But as time went by some people became real Catholics and forgot where they came from. Some families gave a son to the church so the church wouldn't know they were Jews. If you could read, they thought you were a Jew. We were called the people of the book. If a son became a priest he could read the Old Testament and bring it home. In the old days when they were both in hiding from the friars, the Penitentes let the Jews practice in their moradas. They chanted in the old language."

"Do you ever want to go to a synagogue and connect with the Ashkenazic Jews?"

"No," Tey said. "It's not the same. They are white people who drive big cars. We have been hiding from the church, lighting candles, speaking the old language, never eating pork, sweeping to the middle of the room, practicing the old ways, doing things in secret for four hundred years. We are not like the other Jews. It hurts me when I hear other Jews are hurt and killed. *Adonay es mi dio.* His words are in my heart. I am part of them, but I am different. It's too late to change that."

"I could put you in touch with my Jewish friend Harold Marcus at the Smithsonian. I know he would love to talk to you."

"I don't want to talk to him. I don't want to talk to anybody. I am only telling you this because you are a woman I can pass my story on to and you knew my Isabelita. There is a mezuzah in her house, very old. Would you like to see it?"

Claire supposed "mezuzah" was a Hebrew word, but she didn't know what it meant. "What is it?" she asked.

"It's a little box with a prayer inside." Tey gripped the top of her cane and prepared to push herself off from the bench. "Let's walk. It's a nice day."

"Are you sure?" Claire asked. "I'll be happy to drive."

"No. It's good to walk. I say His words sometimes when I walk along the road."

Tey stood up and led the way, refusing any help as she climbed the ditch bank. Her pace was steady as a tortoise but much slower than the pace Claire kept when she walked. She checked her impatience by cranking up her powers of observation. The ditch road was shaded by the branches of cottonwoods. The sun broke through the leaves and dappled the path, giving it the shifting reality of a pointillist painting. The weeds were high beside the ditch. The sun hadn't touched the wild pink morning glories yet and they were still in bloom. A duck flapped its wings and lifted out of the ditch, which was brown and muddy from the recent rains. Claire could see the water ripple and hear it lap against the banks. They came to the carcass of a dead bird in the road. Tey stopped and poked it with her walking stick.

"A coyote did that," she said. "They come here at night. When my dog hears them he cries and asks to come inside."

The ditch was a watering hole, where animals came to drink, to eat and get eaten. During the night it was wild and dangerous, a place where Claire herself had felt hunted. But in the morning it was green, fertile, and peaceful, far removed from the noise and danger of the street. Along here nothing appeared to have changed for centuries. Claire was glad they had taken this walk so she could remember the ditch as it appeared now and not as a place where an SUV had pursued her in the rain.

After her comment about the coyotes, Tey kept silent and focused on picking her way down the dusty road. As they approached the old house Claire offered her arm and helped her down the path that led to the embankment. The rain had washed away any tracks. As soon as she was on level ground again Tey let go of Claire's arm. They walked to the door. Tey took keys from her pocket and unlocked it.

"Chuy locked the house yesterday," she said. "We can't leave it open anymore with all those bad boys around."

The light was dim inside the house, but Claire could see that the mirrors were still covered.

"The closet door is open," Tey said. "Was it open when you were here?"

"Yes."

"It was closed when I left. I always keep it closed." She went to the closet, reached around the door, and slid her right hand along the inside of the doorjamb. "The prayer is supposed to be on the doorpost of the house, but my grandmother hid it here. It's gone," she cried. "Our little mezuzah is gone. Look."

She placed Claire's hand against the doorjamb, and she felt a hollow section a few inches long carved out of the wood.

"The mezuzah had a prayer inside that kept this house safe. And now my Isabelita is dead and the mezuzah is gone. This is not a place for people to live anymore."

"Was it still here after Isabel died?"

"Yes. I felt it Friday when I lit the candles."

"Did Chuy or Manuel know about it?"

"No. It's hidden here. You can't find it unless you know where to look." Tey made her way to the sofa and sank into the cushions. Claire felt that the spirit that had kept her so fierce and strong was escaping along with the dust from the cushions.

"Help me find out who took it," Claire said. "It could be the person who ran me off the road. It could be Isabel's killer."

"You think we are related to this Joaquín?" Tey asked.

"I don't know if you are related, but I think you are connected in some way. You used the same phrase Joaquín used—*Adonay es mi dio.*"

"It's what my mother said, *descanse en paz.* Why didn't my Isabelita show me what she found? Why did she tell you and that May Brennan?"

"Maybe she didn't have time to show it to you." It was a lame explanation, but the only one Claire could offer at the moment.

Tey's tired shrug implied she didn't believe it either. "That May came to see me once to ask me about the grave of Isabel Suazo, but I wouldn't tell her anything. It was none of her business. You think those bones that were under the floor will tell us something?" she asked.

"They might."

"Okay. Go ahead. Take my blood; do your tests. Find out what you need to know." She pulled up her sleeve and offered a scrawny bare arm to Claire.

"Someone else will have to do the tests," Claire said.

"I will tell Chuy and Manuel the family story. They're big boys; it's time they knew. No one is going to take our land now. You find out what happened to my Isabelita. You think she was killed for being a Jew? They stopped killing us for that long ago."

"I don't think she was killed for that. I think she was killed because someone wanted the document she found, but the police want to believe it was Tony

Atencio. You need to go to them. Tell them every-thing. Tell them about the mezuzah. Detective Ro-mero is a local boy. He knows something about the old ways."

"What is his first name?"

"Jimmy."

"I think I know Adela, his grandmother. Okay, I will call him."

"Let me get my car and drive you back to the house."

"Okay," Tey said.

"Will you be all right here? Do you want me lock the door?"

"I'll be all right. What can anybody do to me now? I heard about an old woman in Chama. A bear came into her house looking for food and killed her. To be killed by a bear or a robber—what's the difference? When you're old, dying in your own house is not a bad way to go." She thumped her cane against the floor. "If that robber comes back, I'll make him sorry he killed my Isabelita."

"I'll be back soon," Claire said.

She hurried along the ditch, too busy thinking about Tey to notice much except that the sun had landed on the wild morning glories and the blossoms had shriveled.

Tey had moved outside and was sitting under the portal when Claire returned. She seemed to have re-gained some of her spirit. "Not my day to be killed by a bear or a robber," she said.

When Claire dropped her off at the other house Tey said, "You find that killer for me."

"I'll do my best," Claire said, "but you need to call the police."

"Okay," said Tey.

*   *   *

As she drove home through the Sandia Pueblo, Claire thought how often one generation forgets the past, leaving the next to search and reinvent. If knowledge was passed down from one generation to the next, she would know all about her own ancestors. As it was, she knew next to nothing. She liked the phrase "people of the book" and identified with it. Not because she had a Jewish connection. When the Reyniers fled Europe they were persecuted for being Protestants and by now they were very lapsed Protestants. But Claire was a book person who turned to the written word for solace and for answers. The question she needed to answer was whether Isabel had been killed because the Santoses were people of the book. The long arm of the Inquisition could not have reached out of the past to punish Isabel in the twenty-first century, but there might have been some other connection. Had Isabel learned the Santoses were descended from Jews, and was that what she called to tell Claire? Was she intending to bring the cross and the document to the center? Could someone else have learned of the connection, like May Brennan, Peter Beck, Warren Isles, or her own brothers? Could Joaquín Rodriguez's last words have remained somewhere in Isabel's house? Had someone gone back to the house for the document or the mezuzah, been surprised by Claire, and run her off the road? Did that someone know she was coming?

It might hurt Manuel's standing with the church and his career to have his Jewish background come out, but would he kill his own sister to suppress that information? Maybe he had meant to warn and not to kill. Maybe Isabel had fallen and hit her neck during a struggle over the document. Claire hadn't had any physical altercations with her own brother as an adult, but they'd had plenty when they were growing up.

She visualized the same scenario with Isabel's other brother. Suppose Chuy found out about the document, learned it was valuable, and needed money to pay off his gambling debts? Isabel refused to give it to him and they struggled. If the document had been sold, it might be hidden but at least it would be preserved.

Claire wondered how the police would react to learning that the Santoses had a hidden Jewish connection. Romero was more likely to find it relevant than his boss. Claire had to consider whether she had any business pursuing a line of investigation if the Sandoval County Sheriff's Department rejected it. Was it egotism on her part to think her experience and knowledge could ask and answer questions they could not?

Chapter Twenty-two

When she got home, she turned on the cooler, let the cat out, took the documents August had given her to her courtyard, and set them on the banco. Before she began to read she picked the dead flowers from her datura, which grew faster with less encouragement than any plant she had ever seen. A few summer showers and it covered the floor of her courtyard and climbed the wall. On the night of the full moon she had as many as fifty flowers. As the tendrils approached her front door, she had the sensation that one night they would turn the knob, slither into the house and down the hallway, enter her bedroom, and wrap themselves around her neck in the same way the Inquisition had reached out of the past.

It was one hundred degrees or more in the courtyard. The sun had been beating on the adobe walls all morning. The bricks soaked up the heat and reflected it back at Claire. She went into the kitchen and poured herself a lemonade with ice. She took the drink outside and sat down in a sliver of shade in the corner where the banco met the house.

Last night's white satin datura flowers had turned

brown and shriveled in the heat and the light of the sun, yet the plant had to absorb the sun's energy in the daytime to blossom at night. Mystics of many religions had gone into the desert to find their visions in the dryness and the heat. But the temperature in the desert dropped thirty degrees once the sun went down. What happened to a mystic's vision in the darkness? Did it blossom into something pure and white or did it develop long tendrils that reached out to garrote the nonbeliever?

What Claire disliked about religion was that the burning heat of vision too often turned into a heated passion for destruction. She thought about all the slaughter that had been carried out in the name of the God she knew, the Christian God: the Jews and Muslims garroted and burned at the stake, the millions of Indians killed during the conquest. It had happened elsewhere in the names of other gods, but she knew more about this part of the world. She knew all the ways in which the conquest had been despicable. What kind of a God would allow millions of people to be slaughtered in his name? It was not a God she could connect to.

She sipped her lemonade, sank deeper into the shadow, and read through the documents, fascinated once again by the relationship language had to events. In this case elegant language described horrific events. She read that Joaquín Rodriguez was "relaxed to the secular arm" and led through the streets on a "saddled horse." Someone stepped out of the crowd and Joaquín spoke words interpreted as repentance and conversion. He was garroted until he appeared dead, then burned to a cinder. The events were witnessed by Manuel Santos, among others. Claire wondered about the sincerity of the conversion that allowed the church to strangle Joaquín before they burned him. Was it a true conversion or a convenience that allowed the church to save face? She wondered about the relationship between Manuel Santos the Inquisitor and Manuel Santos the settler. Manuel Santos the Inquisitor had to be a Catholic in good standing. Manuel Santos the settler had been a pretend Catholic. What was the connection between the Santos men and Joaquín Rodriguez? Why had Joaquín's last words turned up hidden inside a cross under a house owned by the Santos family? The Spanish kept detailed records of everything they did, but to find a particular record could take months of searching through archives written by hand in a language in which Claire was not fluent. She looked through the other papers August had given her. Raquel had gone to her death at the stake screaming at the Inquisitors. Daniel was never tried, too young perhaps to be judged by the Inquisition.

Another place to turn was the scholar Peter Beck's exhaustive, pedantic, duller-than-dust study, which should be on the shelves at Zimmerman. She put that off till the next day, went inside, and called Harold Marcus.

"Hello," he said. "What's it like out there?"

"Hot."

"Ah, for the dry heat. It's so humid here I feel like I'm swimming. If only I had gills. Did you talk to Tey Santos?"

"Yes."

"And?"

"You were right. Tey is a diminutive for Ester. She lit the candles, covered the mirror, and put the pebble on the tombstone. A mezuzah hidden in a closet in Isabel's house disappeared, and she showed me the hollow in the doorjamb where it had been. She admitted that the Santoses are Jews."

The line crackled as if an electrical storm danced somewhere between N.M. and D.C. "I knew it. The symbol you saw in the flower on Isabel Suazo's grave could be a shin."

"What's that?"

"It's the twenty-second letter of the Hebrew alphabet and first letter of Shema, the prayer Jews say. It means 'Hear O Israel, the Lord is our God, the Lord is One.' Tey Santos is living history. I want to meet her, bring along a tape recorder, record her experiences while she is still alive. Can you arrange it?"

The scientist in Harold had surfaced, eager to put Tey under a microscope. "It's a very personal, private matter," Claire said. "Tey's family has been practicing their religion in secret for hundreds of years. It's not something that's easy for her to talk about. She doesn't see much relationship between her religion and modern-day Judaism, although she does feel a connection to the Jewish people."

"She's an incredible resource. We can't let her go to waste."

Actually she's a person not a resource, thought Claire, not someone you want to subject to the methodological method. "She won't agree to talk to you." Her voice assumed the deep-freeze tone WASPs used to put people in their place. "The religion is passed down from woman to woman in the Santos family. One reason Tey talked to me is that I am a woman. She wasn't able to tell the story to Isabel before she died, so she told it to me. I'd be violating a confidence if I sent you to talk to her. She used the same phrase Joaquín Rodriguez did, by the way—*Adonay es mi dio*."

" 'God' in the Spanish singular."

"She said sometimes they named a son Jesus as protective cover. Her grandson is named Jesus."

"They named boys Adonay, too. You don't see people naming their son God in English."

"She told me the Jews were known as the people of the book."

"We followed the Old Testament. There was a time when it was considered a sign of Judaism to be able to read," Harold said.

"You'll be happy to know that she agreed to a DNA test."

"That's good. We'll know then whether she's related to the old bones. I'll set it up with the OMI. We still won't know for sure whether the skeleton is Manuel Santos, but it would be a reasonable assumption given the date of the bones."

Reasonable assumption wasn't enough for Claire. "I want to know for sure. I want to know how Joaquín Rodriguez's last words ended up under the floor of Isabel Santos's house. I want to know if there's a connection between the two Manuel Santoses. Is there anyone there who could help?" The Smithsonian was the place people turned to for American history, but she didn't know what information they'd be able to provide about the Mexican Inquisition.

"I'll ask around and see what I can find out," Harold Marcus said.

"Thanks," Claire replied.

She hung up the phone and stared out her window at the piñon-studded mountains, wanting to share her discovery with someone who would understand how much it meant to her. She had visited Barcelona

with Pietro, sighed with him under the Bridge of
Sighs, walked along Las Ramblas and down a narrow
calle lined with the fluid shapes of an Antoni Gaudí
building, gone to the house of the alchemist, explored
the old Jewish quarter without finding any trace of
Sephardim. Barcelona was a city that kept its secrets,
which was one of the things she liked about it.

She went to her computer, opened a file, and com-
posed an E-mail. "Pietro," it began.

> I've discovered that the Santos family is descended from
> conversos. Their ancestry must go back to medieval
> Spain. They have been living in New Mexico and prac-
> ticing Judaism in secret for four hundred years. It has
> been a wonderful discovery for me.

Her eyes returned to the window. What to say
next?

> Do you remember the time we spent in Barcelona
> searching for the Jewish quarter? Kissing under the
> Bridge of Sighs, going to the harbor to see the statue
> of Columbus, and imagining his voyage to the end of the
> world? Do you ever wish we could go back there again?

It wasn't the appropriate communication to send
to a man with a sick wife. And "if someday his wife
were to die" was not a thought she should allow to
enter her mind. There were times when being a
WASP woman felt like being shipwrecked on a remote and vacant island. She couldn't imagine Pietro's
life in Italy would ever be a vacant island. Full of
family and chaos, maybe, but never empty.

As E-mail was not an exact science and anything
written had the possibility of being inadvertently
sent, Claire deleted her message and turned toward

the window. The sky remained an unfettered blue. If it was going to rain, the thunderheads would be building by now. She picked up the phone to call John Harlan, who knew something about remote islands of the heart, but she changed her mind, put the phone down, went outside, and followed a path that led through the foothills into the mountains. Eventually it reached the top of the peaks, but she only went to the elevation where high desert cactus segued into piñon-juniper forest. She sat down on a favorite rock and stared at the line where pinon and juniper turned to stone at a higher elevation. Her eyes focused on that spot while her mind focused on the empty place where people turned to God.

Chapter Twenty-three

When she got to work in the morning she looked up *The Inquisition in Mexico* by Peter Beck on the computer. There were numerous books on the Inquisition in general but few on the Mexican Inquisition. She wrote down the call number for Peter's book. That afternoon she walked through the stacks following the numbers until she came to the Bs and Peter Beck. His book turned up exactly where it was supposed to. It was a massive volume, heavy enough to serve as a weapon.

After dinner that evening she sat down on her sofa and opened Peter Beck's exhaustive and exhausting opus. She went first to the copyright page and learned that this was a first edition published ten years ago. It had remained the definitive study, still in use as a textbook, still earning a royalty for Peter Beck. She turned next to the last page to see how long it was—1235 pages. Each one of these pages was packed with the small, dense print of a university press book. No space breaks, no dialogue, no white space on the page. The length was formidable, the subject depressing, the style stultifyingly dull. There were many things she would rather be doing than reading Peter Beck's plodding prose—washing the dishes, watching the news, vacuuming the carpet, polishing her silver, talking to her cat.

An index made the job easier. There was an extensive bibliography listing sources in Hebrew, Spanish, Portuguese, Latin, French, German, and English, establishing that Peter Beck's knowledge was encyclopedic and his scholarship impeccable. Claire skimmed through the bibliography, encountering one of her all-time favorite books—*History of the Conquest of Mexico and History of the Conquest of Peru* by the nearly blind scholar William Prescott. He had marvelous material to work with—criminals and kings, Cortés and Montezuma, Pizarro and Atahuallpa, rooms full of beaten gold ornaments, captives with their still warm hearts ripped from their chests. Prescott's imaginative and evocative style did it justice.

Peter Beck's material wasn't quite as marvelous and it demonstrated the cruelest, most self-righteous and inhumane side of human behavior. His material had the potential to be revealing and interesting, but his style got in the way. Claire consulted the index and turned to the first entry of the name Rodriguez on page 562. It was at this point that Joaquín's uncle Tomás arrived in the New World and quickly established himself as a trader. He petitioned the court to bring in family members from Portugal and Spain to expand his trading network. The request was granted even though the Rodriguezes were a known converso family. The crown was willing to overlook their ancestry as long as Tomás remained useful to them. The family members he brought to Mexico included Ester, Raquel, Joaquín, and Daniel, the wife and children of Tomás's deceased brother David, who had lived in Portugal. Unfortunately for the family,

Tomás became too successful. Fearing his power and coveting his wealth, the Inquisition arrested him in 1594, confiscating his property and letting him languish in jail until he died of natural causes.

Joaquín Rodriguez came under suspicion as soon as Tomás was arrested. He was questioned, then released. A year later he was arrested again when a neighbor accused him of being a fervent Judaizer. Joaquín learned at age fifteen that his ancestry was Jewish and he became passionate enough about it to circumcise himself in the Rio de los Remedios. He was tried for the crimes of heresy and apostasy at age twenty-five in 1595. He refused to repent, but eventually, under repeated torture on the rack, he gave up the names of his mother, Ester; his sister, Raquel; and his brother, Daniel. Raquel was twenty-two at the time and Daniel was sixteen. Raquel was burned at the stake in 1596. Joaquín and his mother were garroted. Daniel was considered too young to be tried for the crime of heresy and was assigned to the care of a Catholic family after his own family was incarcerated. That was the last entry Claire found for Daniel Rodriguez. She wondered whether his new family succeeded in turning him into a good Catholic. She wondered what effect seeing his family executed had on a sixteen-year-old boy.

It was the material of a soaring and epic novel but Peter's prose kept it grounded. Claire longed for the graceful similes and metaphors of Prescott or some of the flowery, elegant prose of the "Inquisition Case of Joaquín Rodriguez." She had read that document several times by now and she was sure that Peter had read it many more times. The only difference she found in his book was based on an eyewitness account that Claire hadn't encountered. In this version Joaquín rode to his death on a saddled horse with a green cross tied between his hands. A young man stepped out of the crowd also holding a cross and embraced Joaquín. The two men spoke to each other in soft voices. As Joaquín was led to the burning ground, the young man confronted the witness Manuel Santos to tell him that Joaquín had repented and converted, which was enough to save him from being burned alive. The young man may have been known to Joaquín but his identity was never established. Between the lines Claire saw that the inability to identify him galled Peter Beck.

The Rodriguez martyrs—Joaquín, Ester, and Raquel—were given a single chapter in a long and brutal history. The Inquisition continued with varying degrees of severity until the wars of Mexican independence. There were long periods when crypto Jews were more or less ignored interspersed with times when they were actively persecuted. After this chapter the Rodriguez name did not appear again. No mention was made of Joaquín's last words, although Peter quoted liberally from his journals. The only Santos Claire found in the index was Manuel the witness, who later became corregidor. His name reappeared from time to time until he participated in his last Inquisition in 1614, proving that he was not the same Manuel Santos who came north with Oñate's expedition.

Claire put down the book and checked her watch, surprised to learn that it wasn't bedtime yet. She had expected to be kept awake well into the night, but the index made her job easier. Peter Beck had spent years on the Mexican Inquisition and had researched and written the definitive book. Still it was impossible to answer every question relating to an auto-da-

fé that went on for hundreds of years. She wondered
if he had moved on to another project when he finished *The Inquisition in Mexico,* or if he continued
searching for previously undiscovered material, assuming he was willing to concede that there was any
undiscovered material. Even if he wasn't, people
might have come to him with new information once
the book was published.

As she still had an hour left before bedtime she
decided to search the Internet to see if Peter or anyone else had come up with new material relating to
Joaquín Rodriguez. She went to the Google search
engine, typed in the name Joaquín Rodriguez, and
got 23,322 replies. The *o*s in "Google" stretched
across her screen, each one representing a page of
entries. Her allotted hour could extend to a week or
a month if she let it. Scrolling through the list she
discovered that many of the entries were in Spanish,
some were in Portuguese, others were in French.
Since Google offered instant translation Claire tried
it out on a Portuguese entry; she found that language
more difficult to read than either French or Spanish.
Instant translation got the literal essence of the words
but missed all subtleties of rhythm and meaning.
Some of the mistakes were amusing. The overall
clunkiness of the prose reminded Claire of Peter
Beck's style. She visualized his brain as a computer
program trying without success to imitate the sub-
tlety of a human mind as it organized his volumi-
nous research. A thought like this convinced her it
was time to go to bed.

Nevertheless she continued scrolling through the
list without opening any more Web sites. The beginning sentences told her if they were about Joaquín
Rodriguez, the Jewish mystic who was killed by the

Inquisition in 1596. She skipped ahead to page 20, then 30, then 40. The deeper she delved into the entries, the further removed the Joaquín Rodriguezes became from the Inquisition. She found doctors named Joaquín Rodriguez, students, writers, and on page 50 she found one who was a Colombian drug lord. It was sad to see the name of the poet and the mystic affixed to a drug dealer and to think the men might be distantly related. She moved on the very last *o* in "Google" and found a Joaquín Rodriguez who was a scientist in São Paulo, Brazil. Even on this page, however, she found listings for her Joaquín. In fact she had found him on every page she searched. To eliminate all entries she would have to search every page and look at all 23,322 of them. That was impossible, but she wasn't ready to stop either. She had the hunter's heightened awareness of being on the scent. The clock in the lower right-hand corner of her computer screen was marking time but she avoided looking at it.

To narrow her search she added the name Manuel Santos to Joaquín Rodriguez. This time she only got a thousand hits and a number of them were references to articles Peter Beck had written. Some were entries on syllabi for courses he and others had taught. There were numerous Web sites, but she found only five articles. She opened them, read them, found nothing new.

Nemesis came into the room, meowed, and rubbed against her leg saying it was past bedtime. She stopped for a minute and looked at the window. Had she gone outside she would have seen the distant warmth of the stars, but her window had the impermeable blackness of her computer screen after it was turned off. Except for the yellow light of her desk lamp, her room was dark; her house was dark. She was sure her neighbors' houses were also dark. Her office was a boat adrift on a sea of dark. She stretched, shook the sleep from her brain, said "in a minute" to Nemesis, and started another search.

This time she entered the name of Daniel Rodriguez, ending up with 20,200 entries, most of which belonged to a baseball player. Some were the same articles she had found in her previous search. It was getting later. She needed to narrow her search even further.

Giving it one last go-for-broke search before turning off the computer, she combined the names Daniel Rodriguez, Joaquín Rodriguez, Manuel Santos, and Peter Beck, which should have been complicated enough to eliminate all the *os* from "Google". To Claire's surprise she got a response, the URL for the syllabus of a course in Mexican history taught by a professor named Richard Joslin at Berkeley. On his supplemental reading list was an article titled "The Identity of the Man in the Crowd at the Inquisition of Joaquín Rodriguez" written by Peter Beck and published in the *Historical Journal of the Americas*, which Claire knew had lost its funding several years ago and was no longer being published. Professor Joslin had made a notation below the title saying "Daniel Rodriguez, Joaquín Rodriguez, Manuel Santos. An interesting theory, but the facts didn't support it." That remark struck Claire as the kind of not so subtle put-down at which academics excelled, although they were more likely to say it in class than put it in writing on the Internet. She knew Peter Beck would love to read that an article he published was not supported by fact. If it had been in his power he was likely to have deleted the notation and closed the Web site. She printed the page so she would have the information at hand in the morning. While she waited for it to print out she wondered about the upstart professor who would dare criticize Peter Beck on a syllabus, searched some more, and found he was no upstart but a man who'd had a long and distinguished career as a history professor before retiring from Berkeley.

She did another search using the title of the article but nothing else came up. She searched for the *Historical Journal of the Americas* but found no Web site. Apparently the journal had gone out of business before the Internet boom compelled scholars to put everything they had ever read or written on the Web. She felt she had come to a wall as impermeable as the darkness of her window, and allowed herself to look down at her computer clock. Three-thirty a.m., even later than she had expected. She was still burning with the fire of her computer chase, but she had to go to work tomorrow. She shut off the computer and went to bed wondering what Peter had discovered that earned him a put-down from a respected scholar.

Chapter Twenty-four

She spent the rest of the night chasing those thoughts around the bed, finally falling into a deep sleep a half hour before the alarm went off to jangle her awake. She climbed out of bed knowing she would face the day through the dull haze of exhaustion and her nerves would have a ragged edge. Lights would be too bright, noises too loud. People would violate the perimeter of her private space, which extended a couple of feet beyond normal. She had to go to work. Staying up most of the night searching for a document was no excuse to take the day off. The best way to get through days like this was to keep the blinds drawn, the door shut, and do routine work on the computer. She had an extra cup of coffee before she left the house and another when she got to the center.

She was sitting at her desk staring at a blank computer screen, trying to lasso a thought that remained out of reach, when someone knocked at her door. She was tempted to ignore it and pretend she wasn't in, but the visitor knocked again.

"You in there?" Celia asked.

The one person Claire didn't mind seeing today was Celia. "I'm here," she said. "Come on in."

Celia swirled in wearing a black dress accented by a liquid silver necklace and a slew of silver bracelets. "What's up? You look like you were awake all night."

"Most of it," Claire replied.

"Doing what? Dancing? Snuggling?"

"I wish," said Claire. "It was a computer search."

"You can do that all day. Nights are for snuggling and dancing." Celia made a cuddling motion and her arms rattled, making Claire wish she weren't wearing so many bracelets.

She had a husband to snuggle with. Claire did not. Even when Claire had a husband, he wasn't a snuggler. "I was hot on the trail of a document," she said.

"Did you find it?"

"Not exactly. Tey Santos told me on Sunday that her family is descended from crypto Jews. Her given name is Ester."

"That's an amazing discovery."

"I meant to tell you yesterday, but you were out. She still practices some of the old ways, like lighting candles on Friday night and covering the mirrors when someone dies. She used the same phrase Joaquín Rodriguez did—*Adonay es mi dio*. Isabel died before she could pass the knowledge on to her. She took me back to Isabel's house to show me a mezuzah, but it had been stolen."

"That kind of information usually isn't shared with outsiders," Celia said. "Tey must have found you simpatico."

"It could be because I'm a woman and after Isabel died she didn't have anyone else to tell it to."

"You're a good listener, a rare skill these days."

"Am I?" Claire asked. In her tired state listening seemed like a skill that was beyond reach.

"Of course." Celia picked a paperweight from Claire's desk and balanced it in her hands. "What document were you looking for?"

"I read Peter Beck's book last night, the part about the Rodriguez family and the Inquisitor Manuel Santos."

"*That* kept you up all night?"

"No, I was done by nine, but I came across something I hadn't known before. A cross was tied to Joaquín's hands as he was led through the crowd on the way to the *quemadero*. A young man holding another cross exchanged words with him and then he spoke to Manuel Santos. That event was interpreted as the conversion that saved Joaquín from being burned alive at the stake."

"The church would have interpreted a sneeze as a conversion at that point if it would save face."

"Maybe I was reading between the lines but it seemed to annoy Peter Beck that he wasn't able to identify the young man. I did a search and found an article he wrote titled 'The Identity of the Man in the Crowd at the Inquisition of Joaquín Rodriguez' published in the *Historical Journal of the Americas*."

"That publication is history now. That's an article that would have been read by six people even when the journal was still being published."

"It makes it difficult to find. Here's the reference I found for it on the syllabus of a course taught at Berkeley." She handed the printout to Celia, whose bracelets clinked as she reached across the desk to take it. "Don't you think it's unusual for a professor to criticize an article he recommends even if it is only on his supplemental reading list? He might be willing to say that in class but to put it in print?"

Celia read the syllabus. "It would be unusual for this professor. Richard Joslin was a wonderful man with a generous spirit, highly respected, but then he developed Alzheimer's and had to retire. It was a great loss to the department."

"Where is he now?"

"In a home somewhere, I'd say. Some kind of Alzheimer's theme park if he's lucky. Alzheimer's patients are happier if they live in an environment that reminds them of their past, someplace where they can eat comfort foods, wear bell bottoms or Bermuda shorts, and listen to the old songs."

"Maybe my own mind was gone in the middle of the night, but when I read in Peter's book that the young man embraced Joaquín, I had the thought that they exchanged crosses and the young man ended up with Joaquín's cross with his last written words stating that he would not convert to Catholicism." In the fuzzy haze of exhaustion, the conclusion to that thought seemed to have lost the definition it had last night.

But Celia, wide awake and full of energy, reached the same conclusion. "And someone brought that cross to New Mexico and it ended up under Isabel Santos's floor?"

"Yes."

"Then who was the young man?"

"I wish I knew. Tey Santos agreed to DNA testing, so eventually we will know if she is descended from the skeleton found under the floor. It's possible that person brought the cross to New Mexico, but how would you prove it? You can't get fingerprints from a skeleton. It will also be hard to determine whether that skeleton is Manuel Santos, the settler, or not, but if he turns out to be Tey's ancestor he's a crypto Jew. The question is how could there be a crypto Jew named Manuel Santos and an Inquisitor named Manuel Santos living in the same time and place? Even now it's not that common a name."

"Sometimes crypto Jews took the names of prominent citizens as protective cover."

"But the name of an Inquisitor?"

"Why don't you just call Peter Beck and ask him what he said in his article?"

"I don't trust him. I don't like him. He'll accuse me of inserting myself into his field. If he intended to tell me about the article, he had plenty of opportunity to do so the day I met him."

"He may have been embarrassed that his scholarship was challenged by Richard Joslin."

Claire wondered if Peter Beck was capable of embarrassment. "Maybe," she said. "There are other ways of finding the article."

"I'll see what I can do."

"Thanks."

Celia pushed her bracelets aside to consult her watch. "I have to go to a meeting. Talk to you later."

"Okay."

She left the office, shutting the door gently behind her, leaving Claire with the rest of the day to fill. Although she wanted to spend it entering boring data on the computer, she needed to track down Peter Beck's article. She thought about her datura plant putting out runners and creeping along the ground, opening its satiny blossoms to let bees, moths, hummingbirds, whatever happened to be flying through the night, settle in. She needed to send out feelers herself.

First she put out an interlibrary loan request. Then she called Harold Marcus and told him her theory about the crosses. "Interesting," he said. "I'll see if anyone here can track down the article."

Then she called August Stevenson and asked him to keep an eye out for it. "Delighted to help," he said.

She wanted to talk to John Harlan, too, but decided to visit the store after work. The other people she needed to call—May Brennan and Detective Romero—were more problematic. She didn't know whether Tey had kept her promise and talked to Romero. Then there was the issue of why May hadn't told her she'd spoken to Tey about the grave of Isabel Suazo.

She dialed May's number at the Bernalillo Historical Society.

"Oh, Claire," May replied in a weary, put-upon voice. "How are you?"

"Fine," Claire replied, thinking her own voice was a blanket thrown over a teddy bear cholla.

"That's nice."

"I was with Tey Santos over the weekend and she told me you asked about Isabel Suazo's grave."

"It was a couple of years ago. She told me she was a good Catholic. I wasn't going to argue with her."

"Did you have any reason to argue with her?"

"Not really. I was just gathering information, that's all. People are always asking me for information about the crypto Jews. Isabel Santos married a Jew. I thought there might be some connection. Look, Claire, it's busy here. Can I call you back?"

"Please."

After that unproductive conversation, Claire called Detective Romero on his cell phone to ask if he had spoken to Tey Santos. "I got a message from her yesterday," he said. "But I haven't had a chance to go over there. I'll get back to you once I talk to her."

"Thanks."

That left Claire with nothing better to do than enter data onto the computer. She kept her door closed and her blinds drawn and at noon she put her head down on the desk and went to sleep. She woke up feeling her head had been screwed sideways. She stretched to get out the kinks, then she had lunch—another cup of coffee, an apple and a granola bar—and went back to entering data on the computer. At three she received a call saying there was someone at the information desk to see her. She walked out and found Detective Romero in his brown uniform.

"I happened to be in town," he said. "I hope you don't mind my stopping by."

"Of course not," said Claire. "Come into my office."

She led him down the hall and shut the door behind them, thinking this happened to be a good time to talk to Detective Romero. Her door and blinds had been closed all day. Whatever attention that would attract had already been attracted. She had inadvertently created an intimate atmosphere. As he sat down she remembered how relaxed Jimmy Romero had looked in jeans and a T-shirt the night he drove her home. It was a thought she should have checked at the door.

"I called the mechanic before I left Bernalillo. Your truck will be ready in a day or two."

"Yea," Claire said.

"Getting tired of the rental car?" He smiled.

"Very."

"I went to see Tey Santos and she told me they are Marranos, which was why she lit the candles and covered the mirrors. She said her old ways are Marrano ways."

Claire tensed when she heard the word "Marrano." Literally it meant swine. Sometimes people used it in an ironic way to refer to themselves, but it was as derogatory as "nigger" or "wetback" or "beaner" or all the other insulting names people called each other. "She told me that, too. I thought you should know."

"When I talked to her before, she was convinced that Tony Atencio had killed Isabel, but now she doesn't think so. What changed her mind?" He leaned back in his chair and his eyes lit on Claire.

"A mezuzah was stolen from Isabel's house Friday night. Did she show you where it was hidden?"

"Yes."

"Whoever took it may have been the person who ran me off the road."

"Possible," Romero said.

"It couldn't have been Tony," Claire said.

"No, but it could have been one of his homeboys."

"How would a homeboy know where to look, and what would he want with a mezuzah?" she asked. "It's not likely to have any monetary value."

"It might," Romero said. "Anything has value if it's old enough, and according to Tey it was very old. The other things stolen from the house didn't have much value."

"Except for the last words of Joaquín Rodriguez."

"We don't know yet if that document *was* stolen or what its value is," Romero pointed out. "We haven't found any evidence that it was offered for sale."

The image of him in casual clothes faded as he took the official line. Today Detective Romero

seemed very much a police officer. Perhaps he was
putting on his armor for his next call. "Did you find
any evidence that the dig had been disturbed?" she
asked.

"The OMI archaeologists looked into it. Someone
had sifted through the dirt, but we don't know who.
Family members were in the house. It could have
been one of them. Tey agreed to have her DNA analyzed and compared to the skeleton."

"So she said."

"We're setting it up with the OMI and they will
work with the Smithsonian. That man died four hundred years ago. It will be interesting to know if he
is a Santos but I don't see how it will help solve
Isabel's death. It's unlikely anyone killed her just for
being a Marrano."

"May Brennan had reason to think the Santoses
were crypto Jews. A couple of years ago she asked
Tey about her background."

"It would be hard to get my boss to consider May
a suspect, if that's what you're suggesting. She's been
in Bernalillo for a long time. She's the town
historian."

As a middle-aged white professional woman she
didn't fit the criminal profile. It was the same profile
Claire benefited or suffered from, depending on her
point of view at the time. She'd thought before that
the profile was a good facade to hide behind. In fact
it almost gave one license to commit a crime.

"For me it goes back to the document," she said.
"I believe someone wanted Joaquín Rodriguez's last
words. Isabel got in the way and got killed. The mezuzah in Isabel's house proved that the Santoses had
a Jewish connection, and the killer didn't want that
fact known. I read Peter Beck's book last night. He

described Joaquín Rodriguez's execution. Joaquín had a conversation with a man in the crowd who held a green cross, maybe even the same cross we found in the house. I'm wondering if that man ended up with Joaquín's last words and brought them to New Mexico. Beck published an article about the identity of the man, but I haven't been able to locate a copy."

She'd been hoping to pique Romero's interest in the historical aspects but sensed failure as he shifted his weight from one side of the chair to the other.

"It's interesting," he said, "but it doesn't compare to having a gangbanger in custody who tried to fence Isabel's VCR."

"Have you found any record of Isabel depositing money or calling anyone who might be a suspect?"

"No deposits and the only people she called were you and family members."

"You could examine *their* records."

"They'd have to be suspects first."

"What about May Brennan? Have you examined her bank account or phone records?" Claire's despair over Isabel's death was greater than her guilt about implicating May.

"She'd have to be a suspect, too," Romero said. "What you've come across is real interesting for a historian and an academic, but I don't think Lieutenant Kearns will see it as motive for homicide." He moved to the edge of his chair. "Anything else? I need to get going."

"That's it," Claire said.

She walked him out to the exit and said good-bye. He hadn't seemed totally unsympathetic, just busy, preoccupied about his boss like anybody else with a job. She was glad her own boss was at a meeting, and she didn't have to worry about him seeing her with a policeman. On her way down the hall she glanced at the wall clock. Four. She couldn't stand another minute in her hermetically sealed office. It was either open the door and the blinds, let the world in, or leave. She picked up her keys and her purse and left.

Chapter Twenty-five

On her way home she stopped at Page One, Too to see John Harlan. He wasn't a historian, but his work took him into the past. When she told him about her conversation with Tey Santos, he ran his hand over the top of his head, making his hair stand up like it had been electrified.

"You're lucky to find someone who would talk to you about that subject. It's not information they reveal to just anybody."

"I don't know if I'm lucky or unlucky. I think the Santoses' background has something to do with Isabel's death, but it's hard to get the police to see it that way."

"A gangster in the hand is worth a lot of speculation in the bush," said John.

"She also told me the Jews were known as the people of the book."

"Just like you and me," John said.

Claire sat down, cleared a space on John's messy desk, and rested her arm there. "I read Peter Beck's book on the Inquisition last night."

"Is that why you look so tired?"

Do I look that bad? she wondered. "Not exactly.

Beck's description said Joaquín Rodriguez was led through the streets to the burning ground with a green cross tied between his hands. He encountered a young man also carrying a cross. Something about that encounter convinced the Inquisitor Manuel Santos that Joaquín had converted, and it saved him from being burned alive. I did a computer search for more information and discovered that Peter Beck published an article in *Historical Journal of the Americas* titled 'The Identity of the Man in the Crowd at the Inquisition of Joaquín Rodriguez.' "

"But you couldn't find the article?"

"I put out an interlibrary loan request but haven't gotten the article back yet. Sometimes it takes a while."

"And you want me to help?" John had the ability to spot a customer from across the room. He turned his nose up like he'd caught the scent of a rare and sought-after document.

"Right."

"Is it ephemera?"

"That would depend on how you define ephemera."

"I define it as printed material that doesn't have a spine thick enough to display writing."

"Then I would say that it is. As I remember, the *Historical Journal of the Americas* didn't have a spine."

"Do you care if I ask Warren Isles? If the article has anything to do with New Mexico, he may have picked it up somewhere. That journal occasionally published articles about our state, which would be enough for someone as obsessive as Warren to collect every issue."

Warren Isles gave Claire the same uneasy feeling as Peter Beck. She didn't trust either one of them.

"I'd rather you didn't. Warren will connect you to me, and if he has anything to hide, I don't want him to make that connection."

"Warren has a devious mind, but I can see right through him. If he has anything to hide, I'd know it."

"It would be better if you didn't contact him."

"Okay. I suppose you've got some reason for not asking Peter Beck himself."

"I don't trust him either."

"He teaches at Berkeley, right?"

"Right."

"Combine Berserkeley with academentia and what do you get?"

Claire's brain was too tired to wrap itself around that crazy thought. "You tell me."

"Double jeopardy, double insanity."

And what would that produce, Claire wondered, a paranoid schizophrenic? Alzheimer's could be considered a form of insanity, too, she supposed, as the mind slipped further and further from its moorings.

"What are you doing for dinner?" John asked.

Claire hadn't gotten to dinner yet. She was so tired all she had thought about was going home and going to bed. "I'm hoping I'll find something delicious in my freezer."

"You want to stop at Emilio's? It's on your way home."

"I'm so tired."

"Have a glass of wine. It'll revive you for a little while."

"Okay," Claire agreed.

She waited for John to finish his business; then they walked across the parking lot to their vehicles.

As she reached for the door of her rental car, John said, "Wait a minute. Where did that come from?"

"Did I forget to tell you that my truck was in a

wreck?" Claire asked, wondering what else exhaustion had caused her to forget.

"How'd that happen?"

"Someone ran me off the ditch road on Friday night. I had just passed Isabel Santos's house on my way to Tey's. I wasn't hurt, but my truck was wrecked."

"That's what's wrong with you. You're suffering from Chevy deprivation."

"Maybe," Claire said.

"See you at Emilio's."

Claire had two glasses of wine at dinner and laughed at all of John's jokes. After dinner he walked her to her car, hesitated, poked the pavement with the toe of his shoe, then said, "Listen, I can follow you home if you want."

"I only had two glasses of wine," Claire said. "I'm sober."

"That's not what I'm worrying about. I don't want someone to try to run you off Tramway."

"I'll be all right," Claire said.

"You sure?"

"Yeah. Someone may have cared about my going by Isabel Santos's house, but I don't think anyone cares what I do on Tramway."

She got home safe, parked the rental car in the garage, and let herself into the house. Ignoring Nemesis's pleas for attention, she went right to bed and fell into a deep sleep.

After a decent night's sleep, Celia's bracelets made a pleasant tinkling sound. Or was she wearing fewer of them? Claire wondered when her friend appeared in her office.

"I haven't found Peter Beck's article yet," Celia said.

"I'm not surprised. I doubt it had a very wide distribution."

"But I talked to my friend at Berkeley. She told me that Richard Joslin's wife, Renee, cares for him at home in Oakland. The brilliant, independent scholar has become a helpless, absentminded professor. Can you imagine what it must be like to care for a husband with Alzheimer's? When the mind goes, so goes the heart. Love is based on memory and shared moments. How can it continue without memory? Richard still has moments of lucidity, my friend said. I got his number if you want to call."

"What good would it do to call a man with Alzheimer's?"

"I'm sure Renee answers the phone. She worked in the department, too, and may remember the Peter Beck incident. My friend told me that Joslin was Beck's mentor, so I'm sure it hurt to be rebuked by him."

She handed Claire a piece of paper with the number on it. "Go for it," she said.

Claire couldn't convince herself to make the call while she was at work, but when she got home she wrote down all the reasons she should, skipped all the reasons she shouldn't, prepared what she would say to Renee Joslin, and dialed the number. She heard the phone being removed from the hook but no one spoke.

"Hello?" she said into the void.

"Hello?" a man's voice echoed.

"I have a question for Richard Joslin. Is he there?"

"Is Richard Joslin here? Yes." The man answered his own question. "He's here. Would you like to speak to him?"

He seemed borderline lucid. Not knowing how long the moment would last, she spoke fast, trying to keep her question simple but not so simple as to imply he was dumb. "My name is Claire Reynier. I'm a librarian at the Center for Southwest Research at the University of New Mexico. I'm doing some research into the Jewish mystic Joaquín Rodriguez and I'm looking for an article Peter Beck wrote about the identity of a man at his Inquisition. The article was supplemental reading for one of your courses." First she'd see if he remembered the article; then she'd ask why he disagreed with it.

"Peter Beck," was all he said.

She had no idea what to say next. Not wanting to challenge him, she resorted to "He's a brilliant scholar."

"Peter Beck," he said again with a deep sadness in his voice. For the Peter Beck he remembered or the Peter Beck he did not? He paused and Claire had an image of him trying to pull facts out of an empty hat. "The father and the son," he said. If the father was the first fact, Claire thought as she waited for Richard Joslin to continue, the son would be the second. Joslin seemed to catch his breath and then his voice turned stubborn and angry. "Not so brilliant. He said the Jew became the son. But there's no proof. Sloppy scholarship. Pure speculation."

"Richard," Claire heard a woman say in the tired voice of a scold. "What are you doing? Whom are you talking to?"

"I don't know," Richard replied.

It was tempting for Claire to pretend she was an automated call and hang up, but that seemed dishonorable.

"Hello?" the woman's voice said into the phone.

"Is this Mrs. Joslin?"

"Yes?" the woman said, changing her tone to the annoyed voice reserved for credit card solicitors.

Claire suspected that if she said she was calling on behalf of Visa or MasterCard, Renee Joslin would hang up and that would be the end of it, but she took a chance and identified herself. "My name is Claire Reynier. I'm a librarian at the University of New Mexico."

"Oh?"

"I'm doing research into the Mexican Inquisition and I'm looking for an article written by Peter Beck," she said, although she feared her query might make its way back to Peter Beck.

"Did you ask my husband about *that*?"

"Yes."

"You've upset him. Please don't call here ever again."

Claire's ear rang as Renee banged down the phone. Alzheimer's wasn't a physically contagious illness, but the mental frustration it caused spread like ink seeping into a blotter. She went outside, listened to the cicadas strumming in the trees, and watched night fall behind the West Mesa. The lights in the Rio Grande Valley twinkled on. The sky near the horizon was the blue-green twilight color that follows a sunset. A bright light appeared in the west that might have been an approaching plane but hovered in place long enough for Claire to determine it was the planet Venus. She had read that Venus was always visible in the sky and people could train themselves to see it even in the daytime.

As she watched the other planets and stars come out, pieces of the Rodriguez/Santos puzzle began to fall into place. "The father and the son" could be Richard Joslin and Peter Beck. She didn't know whether Joslin had his own son, but the mentor might have thought of the student as a son. "The Jew became the son." She sent that phrase into the night and waited to see what came back.

She saw a sprinkling of what-ifs that mirrored the lights on the ground and the stars in the sky. What if the Catholic family that adopted the orphan Daniel Rodriguez happened to be the family of Manuel Santos, the Inquisitor? It had to have been a family with good standing in the church. What if Daniel became Manuel's adopted son and took his name? What if he was the young man who approached Joaquín Rodriguez on his way to the *quemadero* then persuaded Manuel Santos to give his brother a less painful death? What if Daniel Rodriguez was the ancestor of the current Santos family, and he was the one buried with Joaquín's last words under the house on Calle Luna?

What if this was the information contained in Peter Beck's article and he lied when he said he believed Joaquín Rodriguez's conversion was sincere? After his book came out, he might have come across long-hidden records in the archives in Mexico City stating that Daniel Rodriguez was given to Manuel Santos to raise. But there might have been no written evidence that Daniel Rodriguez took Manuel Santos's name and found his way to New Mexico until Joaquín's last words showed up inside a cross with specks of green paint.

For Peter Beck it would be the solution to an intellectual puzzle, proof of his hypothesis. He'd be unlikely to feel any emotional connection to the people involved. But for Claire, thinking that Daniel Rodriguez had made his way to New Mexico and brought his brother's last words with him, that the beliefs of Joaquín were honored by Tey Santos four hundred years later, was a discovery as magical as the night sky. She wanted to gift wrap the discovery, put a bow on it, and deliver it to Tey, but first she needed to be sure and that meant finding Peter's article.

She looked up again before she went inside. The sky was black velvet and thousands of stars were visible. They all seemed to be in place, but stars and planets had no fixed place in the sky. Their location changed with the days and the seasons. Tomorrow Venus wouldn't be exactly where it was today, and next month it would be somewhere else.

She went inside and called May Brennan again. After she heard May's recorded voice mail message she said, "May, this is Claire. I need to talk to you. Please call me back." It was getting close to ten o'clock. She believed May was home and screening her calls. She couldn't make May answer her phone, so she gave up and went to bed.

Chapter Twenty-six

It would take time to track down Peter's article. The response from interlibrary loan had not been encouraging; several copies of the journal were reported missing. Waiting was frustrating but Claire trusted the people who were searching on her behalf—August, Harold, John, and Celia. She didn't want to be a nudge and bother them every day, so she kept quiet and waited. On Thursday Mauricio Casados, the mechanic in Bernalillo, called to say her truck was ready.

"Yea!" she said.

She returned her rental car after work and got a ride to Bernalillo with a coworker who lived in Placitas.

The mechanic's hands were covered with grease. His smile was missing a tooth. But to Claire he was beautiful.

"Good as new," he said, handing over the keys.

The truck looked almost new, better than it had before the wreck. Mauricio had taken out all the small old dings along with all the large new ones, but vehicles that were in major accidents often didn't achieve the alignment they had before. Her expres-

sion must have shown doubt because Mauricio asked
if she would like to take the truck for a ride to make
sure it was all right.

She agreed and took it for a drive around Bernalillo before she paid him.

"Rides good, no?" he asked.

"Yes," she agreed.

On her drive she had seen that Silva's Saloon on
Camino del Pueblo was having one of its occasional
poetry readings. After she paid Mauricio she stopped
in. Silva's walls were a collage of photographs and
magazine clippings featuring decades of women,
dogs, and motorcycles. The poet reading in the back
room was a Lakota Sioux from South Dakota. Claire
sat on a stool at the bar, ordered a glass of white
wine, and listened to him read. He had an easy style
and a subtle sense of humor. He was followed by
another poet in a pair of dirty overalls who looked
like a Jemez hippie. Next came an Albuquerque poet
who wore an elegant pair of hand-tooled cowboy
boots but whose poetry lacked finesse. She paid for
her drink, asked for directions to May Brennan's
house, and left.

It was nearly eight o'clock. May was sure to be
home from work by now. Although she had known
May for years, Claire had never been to her house.
Considering her interest in history, she expected to
find a restored adobe, but May lived in a frame
stucco ranch, bland enough for suburbia but lacking
a suburban lawn. Her yard had a few sad weeds
and some thorny Russian thistle that would turn into
tumbleweed and move on at the end of summer. The
car parked in the driveway was a Subaru Outback.
Beneath layers of dust it was black, but too small to
be the vehicle that ran Claire off the road unless her

imagination had blown that event way out of proportion.

She parked in front of the house, straightened her back, walked up the path to the front door, and pushed the bell. She saw TV light flickering behind a lace curtain.

"Coming," May called. She yanked the door open and said, "Oh . . ."

Expectation segued into disappointment in her distracted eyes. Claire wondered just whom May had been expecting.

"What are you doing in Bernalillo?" she asked.

"I was having some work done on my truck. I came to pick it up."

"You came all the way to Bernalillo to have work done on your truck?"

"It was in a wreck here. If you'd answered my calls, I would have told you about it."

"I've been busy," May said.

She didn't look like she'd been busy. She looked like she barely had the energy to get off the sofa. May's divorce had aged her. Her spine had compressed from lack of calcium or lack of energy. It brought her hips and breasts too close together and gave her the rounded shape of a muffin.

"Can I come in?" Claire asked.

May's expression protested, "Do you have to?" but her words were a lackadaisical, "Sure, why not?"

She led the way into the living room decorated in baby blue recliners with footrests that popped up when the sitter leaned back, the kind of furniture Claire swore she would never put in her own house no matter how long she lived. May picked a stack of newspapers off the sofa and cleared a spot for Claire. She returned to her armchair, leaned back, and the footrest snapped into place with military precision. She picked the remote off the coffee table and dropped it in her lap but didn't bother to turn off the television set or even to lower the volume. She didn't offer Claire anything to drink. The house felt damp and had a musty smell as if she had been running her swamp cooler 24-7.

A woman with a normal sense of curiosity would have asked Claire about her wreck. May kept silent so Claire answered her own question. "I was on my way to Tey Santos's house by way of the ditch road last Friday and someone ran me off the road into a cottonwood."

May lifted herself out of her lethargy long enough to inquire, "Were you hurt?"

"Not really, but there was a lot of damage to my truck. Mauricio Casados fixed it."

"He's a good mechanic. Why were you going to Tey's house?"

"To talk to her about Isabel's death."

"I hear she believes Tony Atencio is responsible." May's voice had more hope in it than belief.

"Not anymore. Something else was stolen from the house Friday. Tony Atencio is still in jail." Claire moved to the edge of the sofa. "Do you know anything about Isabel Santos you're not telling me?"

"No, of course not. Why do you think that?"

"Because of the way you've been acting. You've never tried to avoid me before."

"I said I've been busy."

"So busy that you're willing to let a murderer get away?"

May sat up. The footrest fell forward and collapsed beneath the chair. "What's your problem, Claire? As far as I know, Tony Atencio was responsible. Why are you bugging me about it? This has been a hard time and now Rex has a girlfriend. Look at this." May picked up a newspaper clipping lying on the end table and handed it to Claire. "She's young; she's beautiful; she's skinny. She's everything I'm not."

It was a photograph of Rex and another woman arm in arm at a charity event. Rex looked paunchier and balder than Claire remembered. The woman *was* thinner than May, but in Claire's eyes she wasn't beautiful and she wasn't all that young. She had the skinny, undeveloped body of an adolescent, but her thinness emphasized the wrinkles in her face. Her hair was blonde and bouffant and she wore a lot of Indian jewelry. It made Claire think that sooner or later you have to grow up and develop a woman's style, but that didn't have to mean getting sloppy and matronly like May. She wouldn't tell May that, but she thought some firmness was in order.

"I know how much it hurts, May, but you've got to move on and make a new life. You're letting your breakup with Rex interfere with your work and obscure your judgment."

"Easy enough for you to say," May snapped.

"It's not easy for me to say, but I know you can't sit around wallowing in self-pity."

"At least you were able to get out of town."

"It helped. It sounds trite, I know, but fixing yourself up, losing weight, getting your hair done, taking a trip, buying new clothes—all those things will make you feel better."

"I'll never be glamorous no matter how many spas I go to or how much money I spend."

"Maybe not, but you're smart; you're interesting. You have a job you love. You're respected in this town. Keep putting one foot in front of the other, doing your best day by day. Get out of your recliner. You'll get through this. You'll get your self-respect back." Claire balanced on the edge of the sofa and lowered her voice to a conspiratorial whisper. "Tell me what you know about Isabel's death, May. It's important."

May sighed and leaned into her recliner. Claire was afraid the chair would tip back, the footrest would pop up, and May would sink further into her depression. Since they seemed to have fallen into some kind of push-pull dynamic, she slid back into the sofa and spoke in a conciliatory voice. "It can't be that bad, can it?"

"I don't know how bad it is, Claire. I told some people about the document Isabel found. Maybe I shouldn't have."

"Why not?"

"She asked me not to."

"Then why did you tell people?"

"Honestly? I did it because I wanted to impress them. In our world, finding the last words of Joaquín Rodriguez will get you more respect than being young and beautiful."

"You knew those were his last words?"

"Who else would say 'the fire or the garrote.' The way she described the document I knew it was authentic, too." Her eyes burned with the fire of discovery as she turned into the May Claire used to know.

"But you never actually saw it?"

"No. I wanted to put it in the Historical Society safe, but Isabel wouldn't let me. She said she was going to take it home and decide what to do. I gave her your name first and then Peter Beck's and Warren Isles's. After she left, I called them and her brother Manuel. Isabel was known to have problems with drugs. I was afraid she might sell it for drug money. I thought Manuel should know."

"How did those men react when you told them?"

"Peter and Warren got greedy. They wanted to see it. Manuel asked me what it meant and what it was worth. I said I didn't know exactly what it was worth, but I knew it was valuable."

"Did you give him Peter and Warren's names, too?"

"Yes, and I regretted it, considering what happened."

"Why didn't you tell the police?"

"I felt guilty. Then I felt scared. Thoughts that used to be field mice when I was married have become grizzly bears now that I live alone. The police had a good suspect. They seemed to think Tony Atencio was guilty. Why not leave it at that?"

"Was Manuel curious about how the words of a Jew ended up under the floor of his family's house?"

"Somewhat. Manuel's a politician and a lawyer. He keeps his cards close to his vest."

"Are people in this town afraid of him?"

"I think they're more proud than afraid. The people in Bernalillo identify with him and want him to succeed."

"I've been looking for an article Peter Beck published in the *Historical Journal of the Americas*. Would the Historical Society have a copy?"

"We might if it had to do with New Mexico history, although Peter Beck's scholarship tends to stop at the border."

"It has to do with the Inquisition of Joaquín Rodriguez, but it might reveal how his last words got to Bernalillo."

"I'll look for it tomorrow. It would be thrilling if

the skeleton under the floor turns out to be Manuel Santos the settler."

"How would he have gotten a hold of Joaquín Rodriguez's last words?" Claire had her own theory now, but she was interested in May's opinion.

"He was related to Manuel Santos the Inquisitor, and that Manuel Santos wanted those words to be far away from Mexico City. He wouldn't want it known that he had been unable to convert Joaquín."

"Why not just destroy the document?"

"The Spanish were too compulsive to destroy documents."

"Have you ever heard of a crypto Jew taking the name of an Inquisitor?"

"They were known to take the names of prominent citizens. An Inquisitor would seem like the last name a Jew would want, but it would provide good cover. No one in New Mexico would reveal that fact to me, even if they knew. The crypto Jews have been covering up for so long, they don't even know their own truth. If I don't find Peter's article, I could ask him for a copy."

"I'd rather you didn't."

May didn't question Claire's reticence and Claire was grateful she didn't have to explain. Maybe May was working on the same intuitive level as Claire. Maybe she didn't trust Peter either. Claire gave May a hug when she left, feeling that if she had accomplished nothing else on this visit she'd at least pulled her out of the depths of her recliner.

In the morning May called to say she couldn't find the *Historical Journal of the Americas* that contained Peter Beck's article. Claire broke her own rule and called John Harlan and August Stevenson.

"Hey," John said. "I've been lookin' for that ephemera, but I can't find the damn thing anywhere. Every time I feel like I'm gettin' close it seems like somebody gets there just ahead of me. You want me to keep trying?"

"Please." After she hung up she called August.

"I've been searching, Claire," he said in his slow as a tortoise voice. "But I haven't found it. I ran into Warren Isles at the Palace Restaurant the other day and I mentioned I was interested. He said he'd let me know if he came across one."

"Did you tell him you were looking for me?"

"No, of course not. I told him I'd been working for UC Berkeley."

Claire wondered how hard it would be to link August's inquiry to her. Since they were in the same line of work, it was reasonable for Warren to assume they knew each other.

Chapter Twenty-seven

When she got to her office on Monday morning Claire found a message on her voice mail, apparently left by Warren Isles on Sunday night.

"Ms. Reynier," he said. "I have a document that will interest you. I'll be at Tamaya tomorrow and can meet you there at six-thirty. If you are available please leave a message for me at the front desk."

Claire called his brokerage office in Santa Fe and learned that Mr. Isles would be out all day. She tried his home number and got a recorded message. Since she was unable to connect with the man who preferred to meet face-to-face, she played his message several times, listening for nuance and innuendo. He had said "document" and not "article." He'd said you "will" be interested rather than "may" or "might." Was it possible that he had Joaquín's last words or was that just wishful thinking on her part? It was like him to control the time and place of the meeting and to choose Tamaya as the setting. She hated to be manipulated, but she needed to see what he had. She called Tamaya and left a message at the front desk saying she would meet him at six-thirty.

She spent the rest of the day calculating what time

she should leave and whether she should bring her own checkbook or the one she used to buy collectibles for the center. It took forty minutes to get to Tamaya. She could leave at five-forty, arrive in plenty of time, and be left cooling her heels in the lobby or on the deck. Both were beautiful places to wait, but how long would she have to wait? How long had she and John waited the last time? A half hour? Some chronically late people were so predictable you could almost set your watch by them, which would seem to defeat their purpose. Could she count on Warren Isles to be half an hour late again? The master manipulators were unpredictable. Sometimes it was half an hour, sometimes an hour; sometimes they didn't show up at all; occasionally they even arrived on time. If Warren's goal was to keep her off balance and persuade her to pay too much for whatever document he produced, he'd keep her waiting a long time, so long that she would end up feeling angry and defeated, while he'd be elated by the power he had over her. She hated to be kept waiting, and he may have observed that on their previous meeting. The benefit of arriving late on her part was that she might be less angry when he finally showed. He might actually end up waiting for her. If she had any spine, she thought, she would leave at six and arrive at six-forty, but she was as compulsively on time as Warren Isles was late. When it got down to it, she wasn't capable of even leaving at five-forty-five. At five-thirty she got in her truck and drove to Tamaya.

She made excellent time and arrived at six-ten. She parked in the first space she came to on the south side of the building away from the main entrance. Since she had time to kill, she refused a ride in the jitney cruising the lot and walked. The sun was low enough in the sky now for her to cast a long-legged shadow, but it still had the searing, burning heat that gave mystics their vision, the heat in which nothing mattered but truth or shelter.

She still had a few minutes left when she entered the hotel, and spent them in the shop looking at the Southwestern clothing and jewelry—the broomstick-pleated skirts, the patterned vests and jackets, the elaborate concha belts that no one from Albuquerque would buy and wear. She considered them costumes rather than clothing.

It was a small victory to arrive at the front desk at exactly six-thirty, better at least than getting there early. The desk clerk was busy checking someone in so she walked across the lobby to look at the David Michael Kennedy photos of Indian ceremonial dancers. They were beautifully framed and had the soft edges of old photographs. Her favorite was the hoop dancer. His foot was lifted, his arms extended; one hoop was raised to the sky and the other lowered toward the ground. The dancer seemed trapped in suspension somewhere between anticipation and animation.

"May I help you?" the clerk asked in a courteous, respectful manner.

Claire returned to the desk. "I have an appointment with Warren Isles."

He checked his computer. "Mr. Isles left a message that he has been unavoidably detained. He will be here at eight."

"Thank you," Claire said, making an effort to be as polite as the clerk. She turned and walked across the lobby, glancing at the hoop dancer again. She had the illusion that he'd moved his foot a fraction while she'd looked away.

She went into the living room and sat on a sofa facing a fireplace with an Edward Curtis print above the mantel. She'd seen that particular print numerous times and felt no need to study it again. She stared at the fake logs in the fireplace. Tamaya burned gas here, not wood, better for the environment but lacking the crackle, heat, and wildness of a wood fire always in danger of getting out of control. She wished she could strike a match and start a real fire instead of seething within. It might be considered thoughtful of Warren Isles to leave her a message instead of letting her wait and wait and wait. Now she knew how long she had to wait if he showed up at eight, but he might not. At eight there might be another message saying he'd be later or wasn't coming, or there would be no message at all and she'd be put on hold again. What was he doing? Showing his document to someone else and trying to get a better price? Eating dinner? Having a massage? Playing golf? Stuck in nonexistent traffic somewhere between Tamaya and Santa Fe?

She got up and went into the bar, wondering if she might see Warren or anyone else she knew. She didn't. She could have one of Tamaya's oversized margaritas, which would either calm her down or make her angrier. For some people, provoking anger was a sign of power, which to them had to be better than not getting any reaction at all. As a person Warren was lacking in looks, talent, charm, and intellect. It was the things he owned that gave him his power. Since she wanted something he owned, she had to find a productive way to pass the time.

She decided to walk in the bosque, where the wandering branches of the cottonwoods offered cool, green shelter. She thought about taking her purse

back to her truck, but it was a long walk from here.
Tamaya was a place that would look after its guests.
As she crossed the field the trees shimmered like a
green mirage. The temperature dropped ten degrees
once she stepped under the branches. She followed
the trail that curved and wandered through the
woods, seeing no one else. Eventually the path led
to the open banks of the Rio Grande, where the cottonwoods had been destroyed by flood or by fire.
New trees had been planted but they were still small
and the banks of the river were bare except for the
occasional red twigs of salt cedar. The river was shallow here but the current ran strong. From above, the
water was a muddy brown, but from an angle it was
even bluer than the sky. A flock of small, dark, unidentifiable birds cawed and flew over. Claire sat
down on a solitary bench beside the river, stared at
the Sandias, and waited for the sun to set off an
afterglow. It seemed to hover just before dropping
behind the horizon, as if preparing to release its
power. A hawk flew in and circled lazily over the
river, causing the flock of small birds to squawk and
scatter. As it turned in its gyre, the sun caught its
white underbelly and burnished it gold.

The only sound Claire could hear was the lapping
of the river. In the silence and the beauty, she tried
to put human greed aside and focus on the golden
hawk. A branch snapped behind her. She turned and
saw nothing but the shadows in the woods. She
glanced at her watch. Seven-twenty. She could head
back now or wait until the sunset ended. She waited,
watching the rosy afterglow climb the mountains as
the western sky turned orange. The sun dropped behind the horizon; the glow lifted off the peaks; the
hawk flew north. A vulture dropped into a tree. A

coyote on the east side of the river began to yip. She got up and headed back to the hotel without checking her watch, thinking the best way to deal with Warren Isles was not to focus on time. The meeting would happen when it was supposed to happen or it wouldn't.

Shadows filled the bosque. The leaves rustled in a breeze that picked up as soon as the sun went down. The gravel path crunched beneath her feet. The coyote began a lonesome howl. Claire was glad she'd encountered no one at the river, but in the growing darkness she would have liked to see a runner or a friendly face. She did what she usually did when threatened by darkness and isolation, took her key ring from her purse and inserted the keys between her fingers. Up ahead she saw lights in the crotches of the cottonwoods and beyond that the yellow lights of Tamaya. She walked faster, drawn like a moth to the artificial light. As she neared the edge of the bosque, the tree lights illuminated the curving branches and the shifting shapes of the leaves. The path opened to a panoramic view of the hotel, which resembled a spacious country home hosting a private party. People sat in the lights on the deck laughing and drinking, giving Claire the feeling that they were golden, privileged, and much farther away from her than the width of the field.

A branch snapped in the woods. As she swiveled sideways to see, she heard the crunch of gravel behind her. She turned in that direction and saw a swirling shadow or a person hiding under the hood of a cape.

"What do you want?" she cried.

The figure raised its arm holding something in its hand. A bat? A branch? She watched it with a strange sense of detachment. This can't be happening to me, Claire Reynier, a voice inside her brain said. Then the weapon came down hard on the place where her shoulder met her neck. The blow knocked her to the ground. As she fell, her purse was yanked from her arm, and her keys dropped out of her fingers. She saw the golden glow of Tamaya flickering through the trees and then it went out.

Chapter Twenty-eight

She came to in the dirt with a branch beside her head and the feeling she'd been dragged into a place with oversized trees toppled upside down and illuminated by lights. From where she lay, the twisting shapes looked more like roots than branches. She had no idea how long she had been out. She tried lifting her head from the ground and felt a sharp pain in her shoulder and a dull pain in her head. She rolled over onto her stomach, hoping to get to her knees and raise herself from that position. She heard distant laughter, saw the lights from the deck, and thought there must be a party somewhere. Then she remembered she had come to Tamaya to talk to Warren Isles. Someone had attacked her on the gravel path, but there was no gravel beneath her now, just soft dirt created by millennia of floods. She got to her knees. The pain in her right shoulder was intense. She pushed with her left hand and sat up. There was enough light from the trees to see that her purse was not in the dirt beside her.

Was it possible someone had attacked her just to steal her purse? She tried to remember what she had heard or seen of the thief, but all she could recall was the sense of a shadow in motion. What had happened to her keys? They'd been useless for defense, but she needed them to get into her truck. She crawled along the ground using her left arm and her knees like a three-legged animal, heading for the direction where the path should be, stopping periodically to run her hand across the dirt and feel for the keys. It was slow and uncomfortable going and she didn't know whether her assailant would return. She heard footsteps crunching the gravel up ahead, the sound of someone running. She saw the shape of the runner just beyond the trees. She thought of calling to him but feared he could be her assailant.

At least she'd learned where the path was. She crawled to it, feeling for her keys, making her way around fallen twigs and branches. The path became visible with scuff marks in the gravel from boots and shoes. She remembered she'd fallen near the edge of the woods and headed in that direction. Crawling on the path made her too visible and the gravel scraped her hand and knees so she crawled beside it in the dirt. She came to a spot where the gravel had been brushed aside, reminding her of the sliding marks of children making angels in the snow. This was where she'd fallen, but she hadn't really fallen. She'd been surprised and knocked down just like Isabel Santos had been. This attack may have had more to do with Isabel Santos than with anything in her purse.

She felt around the edges of the scuff marks, reaching onto the path and into the woods until her hand landed on the jagged edges of her keys. "Yes," she whispered. She picked them up, crawled back into the woods, and considered what to do next. There was a tiny flashlight at the edge of her key chain, but she hesitated to use it and call attention to herself. She had to ignore the part of her that wanted to curl up in a ball and hide here like a wounded animal. She could scream for help, but that might attract the wrong person. She needed to get to the cell phone in her car and call Jimmy Romero; she trusted him more than anybody inside Tamaya.

She pressed her back against the rough bark of a cottonwood and worked her way up until she reached a standing position. Getting there was painful but once she was standing she reached a sort of equilibrium. She straightened her spine and neck, and her shoulder and head didn't hurt so much. She took a step forward. Her head spun and she leaned back against the tree. When her head cleared she took a second step and then another. There were plenty of trees to lean on when she got dizzy. With this thought in mind she worked her way through the bosque along the edge of the field, stepping from one tree to the next, aiming for the parking lot and the shelter of her truck.

Ahead of her something flapped in the wind. A solid shadow took shape among the sinuous bosque branches. Had her assailant returned in the cape? She pressed herself against a tree. The shadow moved, caught a breeze, became a bad memory. Claire tried to blend into her cottonwood. The wind lifted the edge of the shadow and beneath it she saw the limbs of a tree, not the limbs of a person. Someone had disposed of the cape by tossing it over a branch. She went to the branch, picked up the cape, and found her purse lying on the ground beneath it. She took the cape and the purse with her, planning to wait until she was inside her truck before examining them.

Where had her assailant gone? she wondered. Back

to the hotel, to a vehicle in the parking lot, or was that person still in the woods? She remembered the cavalier coyote trotting across the field totally oblivious to its audience. Her neck hurt but she felt less woozy now, less in need of a tree to lean on. She had to cross the field to get to her truck and she stepped into the open space. She was outside the circle of the light and the people on the deck were within it. They couldn't see her but she could see them. She was close enough that if she screamed they might hear. In the field she could see if anyone was coming.

She walked across the open space, glad now that she had parked at this end of the lot. She approached with her keys between her fingers, since the shape of a vehicle could be concealing her assailant. The keys hadn't worked earlier, but it was the only protection she had. When she reached her truck, she inserted the keys in the lock, pulled the handle, and let herself in. She didn't want to call attention to herself by turning on the overhead light. Using the light on the end of her key chain, she looked through her purse. Her checkbook was there and so was her wallet. Her credit cards and driver's license were all in place. Only the fifty dollars she'd been carrying in cash was missing. Had cash been the motive or had the thief been looking for something else?

Claire took an aspirin from her purse and washed it down with the bottled water she kept in the truck. She beamed the light over her clothes, then on the reflection of her face in the rearview mirror. Her forehead was scratched and bruised. There was dirt on her hands and knees, twigs and leaves in her hair, the alarm of the hunted in her eyes. She couldn't go inside Tamaya looking like prey.

Her watch said it was close to nine, an hour more

or less since she'd been attacked. How much of that time had she been unconscious? Long enough for her assailant to drag her off the path and into the woods. Long enough to cause a rupture in the artery of awareness. She wondered what the thief had done during the past hour. Driven away, gone deeper into the woods, returned to Tamaya?

She picked up her cell phone and held it in her hand, knowing she should call Detective Romero but not wanting to reveal she'd been attacked once again with no proof. She didn't want to be seen as a person who couldn't get out of harm's way, or even worse as a woman capable of imagining she was in harm's way. She wanted to give Romero something other than shadows to go on. A description of the assailant or the assailant's vehicle would help. A license plate number would be even better. It was possible the assailant's vehicle was still in the lot. No one would have walked all the way to Tamaya to attack her.

She started her truck, turned on the headlights, stepped on the gas, and drove at a snail's pace to the end of her row in the parking lot. The leg on the gas pedal had a tremor. Her shoulder hurt when she turned her head. Negotiating a parking lot could be almost as difficult as driving in heavy traffic. You never knew when another driver would do something unpredictable or back out of a space without warning. The rows were narrow and dangerous. But Claire drove so slowly that if anything happened it would be a bump and not a crash. She saw safety in the number of vehicles in the lot. Most were empty but any one might contain a witness.

When she reached the end of her row, Claire turned and drove down the next one; then she turned again, making a series of hairpin turns while she

searched the lot. Her eyes were drawn to black SUVs.
There were almost as many here as there were white
rental cars at the airport, too many for any one to
stand out. They came in many brands: Isuzu, GMC,
Chevy, Ford, Subaru, Honda, BMW. She saw New
Mexico plates, Colorado plates, Arizona plates, Texas
plates, California plates. She saw no way to identify
the SUV that had run her off the road if it was
even here.

She was ready to give up and dial Detective Romero's number when she thought she saw someone she
recognized step out of the jitney transporting guests
from the hotel to their vehicles. It was a row away
so it was hard to be sure. The person clicked a remote
and turned on the lights of a vehicle, but it wasn't a
black SUV. It was a medium-sized white car similar
to the one Claire had rented. The driver got into it
and began to back out of the parking space.

Not wishing to be seen, Claire turned off her lights.
The car headed for the exit road. She pulled out, too.
When the car turned left at the road, she followed.
As soon as she turned onto the narrow road, she
flipped on her high beams, making it harder for the
other driver to see and identify her truck. She forgot
about the tremor in her leg and the pain in her shoulder as she negotiated the road that was barely wider
than her Chevy. Her thoughts were on getting the
license plate number and how fast she could go without spinning off the road into the desert. When she
reached the 17 mph sign she was doing 25 and not
getting any closer to the car. When she picked up
speed, it did, too, making it difficult to narrow the
gap between them and get close enough to read the
plate. Claire slowed down and let the gap grow, hop-

ing the car might go slower if the driver didn't feel pursued, hoping to catch up at the stop sign.

By the 27 mph sign she was three or four car lengths behind. She negotiated the last curve and stepped on the gas, planning to read the plate when the car stopped. But the other driver ignored the stop sign, swinging wide and turning onto the two-lane road. Holding her breath, Claire clutched the steering wheel and swung wide, too. One wheel teetered on the place where the desert met the road but she held tight and straightened out again. The white car picked up speed—50, 55, 60. This road was wider and straighter than the other one. Claire could go faster here but not this fast. She looked down at her speedometer—65 and not gaining an inch. Feeling connected to this car by a tether, she tried slowing down again, lifting her foot from the pedal, falling behind, remembering that there was a traffic light ahead at Route 44 that was impossible to ignore.

For the first time ever she was pleased to see a red light. The white car had stopped and there was no one between them. She was almost close enough to read the numbers when the light turned green. The car sped through and turned left onto 44. Claire followed. Cars were feeding into Route 44 from 528 and the traffic became her ally. She blended into the flow and closed in on the white car, which could only go as fast as the traffic allowed. When she thought she was close enough to read the plate, she swung into the white car's lane, got behind it, and read the critical numbers. She repeated them out loud a few times and then over and over silently until they were etched in her brain. She dropped back and let other vehicles fill the space between her and the white car.

There was no need to be bumper-to-bumper now, only to be close enough to see where the car turned off.

She watched it head south at I-25; then she turned onto the road that led to the cemetery, parked, and dialed Detective Romero's cell phone number.

"This is Claire Reynier," she said when he answered the call.

"Hey. Are you all right?"

She relayed what had happened and gave him the license plate number. It was a relief to get it out of her mind and into his. "The car turned south on I-25," she said. "It looked like a rental car. It could be headed for the airport."

"We'll stop it and question the driver. Wait for me there."

"I'm too exposed here," Claire said. "Do you have permission to operate on the Santa Ana Pueblo?"

"Yeah. They're too small to have their own force."

"Then I'll meet you at Tamaya." Claire hung up before Romero tried to change her mind.

Chapter Twenty-nine

When she got back to the hotel, she parked as close to the door as she could and accepted the ride offered by the jitney driver. The well-dressed couple on board looked at her with the distaste reserved for bag ladies and rodents. Her trump card for respectability had always been that she was a middle-aged woman but it wasn't working with them. They were middle-aged, too, and infinitely more respectable right now than she was. The couple squeezed into the corner, getting as far away from her as possible. The driver passed the bronze fountain and parked in front of Tamaya's entrance. A fire burned in the outdoor fireplace. Claire wanted to stand in front of it and absorb its warmth, but she went to the shop instead.

The clerk gave her a wary welcome. Guests might come here after a round of golf but not after crawling through the bosque. Golf wasn't a contact sport.

Claire improvised. "I was in a minor car accident," she said. "I'm meeting someone for dinner and I can't show up looking like this. Could I buy some clothes, wash up, and change?" Her purse dangled from her shoulder. She took it off and rested it on the counter in front of the clerk.

"Okay," the clerk replied.

Claire picked some dresses off the rack, tried them on, and bought the first one that fit. It was denim with a broomstick-pleated skirt, silver buttons on the bodice, and lots of Santa Fe style, more of a disguise than a dress. She thought this might be a good time to step out of character.

"That's an improvement," the clerk said as she rang up the sale.

The dress was too expensive but Claire paid the price, went to the ladies' room, washed up, massaged her sore shoulder, dressed, combed her hair, and put on some makeup. She put her own dress in the bag the store provided and walked out to the lobby to wait for Detective Romero. She was surprised to see him already there, standing by the entrance wearing the Sheriff's Department uniform that made him hard to ignore.

"Ms. Reynier?" he asked.

"You got here fast," she replied.

"I was in Placitas when I got your call. You look different. I almost didn't recognize you."

"I was a mess. I had to buy some new clothes." Just in case he had any doubts, she opened the bag to show him the dirty dress she'd been wearing when she was attacked.

"Warren Isles is registered," Romero said. "He took a room for the night, but he's not there. I need your help to find him. I don't know what the guy looks like."

"He looks plump and prosperous," Claire said.

"Everybody here looks like that."

"Let's try the bar," Claire suggested.

As they walked through the living room and into the bar, the hotel guests pulled back when they saw a police uniform. Romero didn't seem to notice, but Claire did. She supposed he'd gotten used to being treated like an unwelcome intruder. Fires burned in the fireplaces on the deck. People sat in the light drinking and laughing. They were the golden, privileged people who seemed so remote when Claire was in the bosque. Now that she'd joined them they appeared more human.

Warren Isles wasn't in the bar and she didn't see anyone else she knew.

"Let's try the restaurants," she said.

They walked down the stairs to the medium-priced restaurant, which was framed by layers of stone that reminded Claire of the ruins of Chaco Canyon.

"This is a beautiful place," Romero said.

There weren't many diners left at this hour. Claire and Romero circled the room but didn't see Warren Isles. They went outside and followed the path to Corn Maiden, the more expensive restaurant, which was still half full. Did people who paid more eat later or linger longer? Claire wondered.

She picked out Warren as soon as they stepped into the restaurant. He sat alone at his table in a chair that faced the door. There was no one left at the adjacent tables. The ceiling light was overhead. His skin had a ruddy tone as if he'd played golf that afternoon or taken a sauna. His hair seemed slick, maybe even damp. It was possible he'd attacked her, taken a shower, dressed, and come here for dinner. He'd had time. When he saw her approach he looked at his watch.

"That's him," Claire said.

There was a sleek attaché case at Warren's feet, an

expensive and nearly empty bottle of wine on the table, a clean plate. He had a full and self-satisfied glow. He smiled his half-moon smile as they approached.

"Claire," he said. "Didn't we have an appointment for six-thirty?"

"I was here at six-thirty," Claire replied, "and was told you were unavailable and would meet me at eight."

"Really? I didn't leave that message. I was in the lobby then waiting for you. Nice dress. The color becomes you. I'm Warren Isles," he said.

"Detective Romero," the detective replied.

"Have a seat. Please." He waved his hand at the empty chairs around the table. "The salmon is superb. I recommend it."

Claire wanted to sit down but Detective Romero remained standing, hovering over the table, and she followed his lead.

"I brought a document here that I thought would interest you," Warren said to Claire. "I heard talk in Santa Fe that you were looking for a *Historical Journal of the Americas*."

Her proximity to the food, the wine, and Peter's article made Claire feel weak and famished. "May I see it?"

Warren flipped his half-moon smile into a fake frown. "I don't have the journal anymore. You didn't show up and I had another customer."

Warren Isles would never come to Tamaya to see one customer if two would get him a better price. Romero stood still, letting Claire and Warren dance this dance. She was grateful to him for that.

"I received such a good offer that I had no choice

but to part with it. After all it was only a scholarly article with a limited market."

"Who made the offer?"

"Peter Beck. The author of the article."

Claire longed to sit down now but remained standing, trying not to show anger, weak knees, or any other feeling while Detective Romero took charge.

"When exactly did this transaction take place?" he asked.

"Forty-five minutes ago more or less," Warren said. "I asked him to join me for dinner but he was in a rush."

"And where is this Peter Beck now?" Romero asked.

"Catching a late flight back to California, I suspect."

"He came all the way from California to buy this journal from you?"

"He wanted it very badly. It's an article he wrote several years ago. I gather he had very few copies left."

Romero stared at the attaché case beside Warren's foot. "Do you always bring your briefcase to dinner?"

"Only when I'm conducting business."

"Do you care to show me what else is in it?"

The emotions played across Warren's face as he calculated what was good for Warren and what was best for Warren.

"Do you have a warrant?" he asked.

"No, but someone attacked Ms. Reynier in the bosque while she was waiting for you. I could bring you in for questioning and hold you until I get a warrant."

"You were attacked?" Warren asked. "I'm shocked. No damage was done, I hope. You look well."

"I changed my clothes and cleaned up," Claire said.

Warren took a deep sip of his wine. "I had no idea you were attacked. I didn't even know you were here. Of course I will show you what is in my briefcase." He picked it up, placed it on the table, keyed in the combination, and snapped open the brass latch.

A small document encased in plastic lay on top of a pile of papers. The paper inside the document was crinkled and had rough edges. The words written in ink in an elegant script were faded but legible. They had survived for more than four hundred years in New Mexico's dry climate. To Claire it was a voice from the grave. She leaned close and read, " *'Todo sta de arriva abasho. El fuego o el garrote. Dame el fuego. Adonay es mi dio. Joaquín.'* "

The tremor in her knee got out of control and she had to sit down. "Where did this come from?" she asked.

"Peter Beck. In exchange for his article and a considerable amount of my money, he gave it to me. Here." Warren Isles slid his plump fingers inside the protective cover and touched the precious paper that held Joaquín Rodriguez's last words.

"Leave it alone," Romero said, while Claire thought of the wine, the butter, the salmon Warren had eaten for dinner, the greasy fingerprints he was putting on a priceless document.

Warren removed his fingers.

"You are aware, aren't you, that this is evidence in a murder investigation?" Romero asked.

"Lieutenant Kearns told me that when he interviewed me. I intended to bring it to the Sheriff's Department just as soon as I finished dinner."

"How did Peter Beck explain having the document in his possession?" Romero asked.

"He says Isabel sold it to him. He claims he had nothing to do with her death and that she was fine when he saw her last. He feared the document would be lost or damaged if he turned it over to the police as evidence."

"Did you read his article before you sold it to him?" Claire asked.

"Yes. In fact I made a Xerox copy. You might find it useful. Do you mind?" he asked Romero as he reached for the case again.

"Are there any other valuable documents in there?" Detective Romero asked Warren while he looked at Claire.

She couldn't think of anything. Besides, everything in the briefcase already had Warren's fingerprints on it.

"Just the usual ephemera," Warren said. He flipped through the papers until he found the one he was looking for and handed it to Claire.

He and Romero parried while Claire read the Xerox of the article, learning, just as she had expected, that an archivist in Mexico City presented Peter with long-lost documentation that the orphan Daniel Rodriguez was given to Manuel Santos to raise, that he took his adopted father's name, that he left Mexico City and came north with Oñate's expedition in 1598. It was Peter's theory that Daniel stepped out of the crowd and spoke to his brother as he was led to the burning ground. That Daniel convinced the Inquisitor Manuel Santos not to burn his brother

alive. Peter admitted it was quite possible there had
been no conversion, which would mean the words
now in Detective Romero's possession represented
Joaquín Rodriguez's last feelings.

This was the theory the scholar and mentor Richard Joslin questioned. It remained unproved until the
cross and the document turned up under Isabel Santos's floor and tied the Santos family to the Rodriguezes. Peter Beck was the one person who knew
exactly what Isabel's find meant. Had Isabel refused
to sell it to him? Claire wondered. Had Peter Beck
lost his temper and killed her accidentally or with
intent? He'd ended up with the document that
proved his theory, but what good had it done him?
It resembled having a stolen Van Gogh in the closet,
a guilty pleasure to admire but impossible to share
with anyone else; to do so would implicate him in
Isabel's death. Claire had seen Beck drive away in
the white car. He could well have been the one who
attacked her in the bosque wrapped in the black cape
and armed with the viciousness of an Inquisitor. But
what about the person who ran her off the road and
stole the mezuzah from Isabel's house? The mezuzah
was evidence that the Santoses had a crypto Jewish
connection. Peter might wish to have it in his possession and hide that evidence, but where was the
black SUV?

Warren Isles was also a skillful liar, and they only
had his word for how the document ended up in
his briefcase.

"Have you and Peter ever met before?" she
asked Warren.

"As a matter of fact we met the same day I first
met you. I was curious about the document. He

wasn't willing to admit he had it at that point, but he did ask me to find copies of his article."

"What kind of a car do you drive?" Romero asked.

"A Jaguar. It's in the parking lot. Would you like to see it?"

"Yes," Romero said. His cell phone rang. He listened for a few minutes, then said, "We're in the Corn Maiden Restaurant."

"Backup has arrived," he said to Claire. "And Peter Beck was apprehended on I-25." He turned to Warren. "He claims that you were in possession of Joaquín Rodriguez's last words and tried to sell them to him."

"Well, that's a lie. When you examine the document I'm sure you will find Peter's fingerprints all over it."

And he'd covered himself by putting his own fingerprints on it, thought Claire. What else would the physical evidence show? Anything Peter or Warren said could be dismissed as self-serving.

"We're bringing both of you in for questioning," Detective Romero said.

"You're arresting me here in the Corn Maiden?" Warren asked.

"Only if you don't come in voluntarily."

"Well then, of course, I'd be happy to help," Warren said.

Chapter Thirty

Romero's backup was the deputies Claire had met earlier—Anna Ortiz and Michael Daniels. Deputy Ortiz was assigned to take Claire's statement. Romero and Daniels took Warren out to the parking lot to examine his Jaguar and then to the detention facility.

By now the last few diners had left the Corn Maiden. Only the staff remained, and they were busy shutting down for the night. Claire opened her purse to demonstrate to Deputy Ortiz that nothing but cash had been taken.

"I need to take your purse and wallet to test for prints," Ortiz said, "but you can keep your credit cards, driver's license, and ID. Show me where you were attacked. I'll take your statement there."

"All right," Claire said, although she had no desire to return to the bosque.

Anna Ortiz's Sheriff's Department vehicle earned her a parking space right in front of the hotel entrance. They drove to Claire's truck.

Claire handed her the black cape, which became a hooded poncho once the lights were turned on.

"The assailant wore this when he attacked you?" Ortiz asked.

"Yes. I found it later in the woods with my purse."

"We'll check it for evidence."

The emblem on Ortiz's car also gave her permission to drive across the field and they were back at the bosque all too soon. They found the spot where Claire had been knocked down. To her the dirt looked like it had been disturbed by wings. They walked through the woods to the tree where she had found the poncho and her purse. The bosque that had seemed so gray and spooky earlier became black and white under the beam of Ortiz's flashlight.

They returned to the car, where Ortiz called for someone to guard the crime scene. Then she took Claire's statement.

Once the statement was finished and more deputies had arrived, she drove Claire to her truck. "Are you all right to drive home?" she asked. "Can I follow you?"

"I'll be all right." Claire felt better as time went by.

"Take care," Deputy Ortiz said. "We'll be in touch."

Claire took the interstate back to Albuquerque, wondering if she might see a white car beside the road or any sign of Peter Beck's arrest. She didn't. Lightning flashed, splitting open the darkness above the West Mesa. When she got home she gave Nemesis his dinner, worked the stiffness out of her shoulder with a shower massage, took a painkiller, and climbed into bed.

Hours later the sound of thunder woke her. The clap was so loud and close she expected the smell of ozone to fill her house. She calculated lightning had struck ground somewhere in the nearby Sandias. The reverberating sound of thunder brought back the pain in her shoulder and the fear of the day. Next came the sound of rain, a rushing, purging, cleansing rain that turned the drainage arroyos to white-water rapids. Any animals on the prowl would be scurrying for cover. As she lay awake listening, Claire remembered she'd been in the middle of a dream when the thunder clapped. She'd been chasing a white rabbit down a narrow, winding road. The rabbit came to a hole and hopped in. She followed, tumbling through emptiness until she landed in a hall of mirrors with gigantic images of the duplicitous faces of Peter Beck and Warren Isles facing each other. Whatever statements they gave were smoke and mirrors. In this case physical evidence was everything.

The thunder clapped again, but it didn't shake her house this time. It sounded as if it had moved to the far side of the Sandias, a sign the storm was heading east. The rush of the rain was over. Now it had the gentle, pinging sounds of the strings of a guitar. It soothed her pain and lulled her to sleep.

When the pain woke her in the morning, she took some aspirin and went to work. Later in the day Romero called and confirmed that Peter Beck's and Warren Isles's statements were self-serving and contradictory. Each claimed the other had tried to sell him the document. Both of their prints were on it. They released Warren but were holding Peter until his house in California could be searched. A *Historical Journal of the Americas* was found in his car along with considerable cash, far more cash than Warren Isles carried. Claire was convinced Peter had attacked her, but she would have felt safer if Warren had been incarcerated, too.

"Have you released Tony Atencio?" she asked.

"Not yet."

When they got off the phone she called Harold Marcus and told him the Sheriff's Department was holding Peter Beck in custody as a suspect in the death of Isabel Santos.

"You think he killed her over the document?" Harold asked. "There's a man who takes his work far too seriously."

"He found evidence in the archives in Mexico City that Manuel Santos adopted Daniel Rodriguez, Joaquín's brother, and that Daniel took Manuel Santos's name. It would be wonderful if we could prove that Daniel brought his brother's last words with him to Bernalillo."

"The staff here is working on the DNA analysis and testing the tooth enamel. We should have the results soon," Harold said.

"Thanks," Claire replied.

It was a long week. Every morning Celia poked her head into Claire's office and asked, "Heard anything yet?"

And every morning Claire had to answer, "No."

Romero called on Friday to ask if he could stop by her office.

"Of course," Claire said.

"What time would be good for you?"

"After three," she said. That was when Harrison left for the weekend.

"I'll be there," Romero said. He didn't bother to stop at the information desk this time and surprised Claire by knocking on her office door a few minutes after three.

He sat down in the visitor's chair and said, "We released Tony Atencio on bail. He'll be tried for theft, but Beck's our suspect in Isabel's death. He's a college professor. Atencio's a gangbanger. But you know there really isn't a lot of difference between 'em. They're both the kind of guys who will do anything to make their names come out and feel important. Atencio didn't lie to us anyway. Beck did."

Claire saw disappointment in his face that the academic world he had admired at a distance turned out to be no better than the petty criminal world he dealt with every day. She didn't know his world, but she'd lost any illusions she had about academia once she took her first job at the U of A.

"We established that Beck flew to Albuquerque four times this summer," Romero continued. "Once on the day Isabel Santos died, once to talk to us, once on the day you met Warren at Tamaya and were attacked at the Santos house, and once more on the day we arrested him. On every trip he used a different airline and rental car company. Hertz rented him the SUV. Did he think he was concealing his actions by spreading his business around? The guy may be a brilliant scholar, but some of his other actions weren't too smart."

"Scholars are better at work than they are at life," Claire said. "People who can write a brilliant book can't fix a leaking faucet."

"Beck likes silk shirts," Romero said. "The fiber we found, which was on Isabel's clothes, matched a shirt in his closet. We never did make a fiber match with Tony Atencio. We located the SUV Beck rented, took paint samples, and matched the paint found on your bumper. Tey Santos identified the mezuzah that was in Beck's safe deposit box. He must have gone back to the house looking for anything that could tie him to Isabel's death."

"The mezuzah proves that the Santos family had a Jewish connection and Peter Beck was probably the only person outside the family who knew that."

"We also found twenty copies of the *Journal* with his article in it. Some of them were library copies. It would have been better for him if he had destroyed the stuff."

"Historians are pack rats," Claire said. "It's impossible for them to destroy anything."

Romero's eyes circled the crowded bookshelves in her office, and Claire wondered if he thought she was a pack rat, too.

"The article proves Beck knew the Santoses were descended from Daniel Rodriguez. He must have known that a smart person like you . . ." Romero smiled at Claire.

She smiled back.

". . . would track the article down and come to the conclusion that once Beck heard a document from the Inquisition was found in the house of a family named Santos, he would want it badly."

"It proved his hypothesis. My thought was that once I had the article in hand I could persuade you to investigate Beck further, to get a warrant and search his house."

"When we confronted him with the evidence we had, he admitted he'd been to Isabel's but he claimed she was alive when he left. He says Isabel sold the document to him, but there is no record he took any money out of his accounts to pay her. We believe Isabel refused to sell. There was an argument that became a physical struggle. Isabel fell on top of her purse with the cross inside, or else Beck would have grabbed that, too. He panicked, took the document, and left the house. In our opinion Isabel was dead at that point. If he'd left her alive, she would have been able to ID him."

"I suppose he justified taking the document by convincing himself that something could have happened to it if he left it there."

"Something might have. Tony Atencio or even Manuel Santos could have destroyed it. But if Beck had called us, we would have taken care of the document. If Isabel was still alive, we would have taken care of her."

"But then Peter would have had to admit what he'd done."

"Better to have admitted it right away. The longer he denies it, the tougher the prosecutor's gonna be. If he'd come clean immediately, we wouldn't have any more crimes to charge him with. What do you think? Was he trying to kill you or just stop you from connecting with Warren?" Romero moved forward in his chair and Claire saw curiosity and concern in his eyes.

"I don't know," she answered. It wasn't a subject she enjoyed thinking about. "Runners use the trail. Peter was in plain sight and he didn't have much time. A murder in the bosque would have been investigated a lot more thoroughly than a mugging. A murder investigation might have led to Peter. I also think he's a coward who runs away when he's in trouble. By selling the document to Warren, he preserved it. Possession would have made Warren a suspect in Isabel's death if you hadn't accumulated all the other evidence."

"Most of the evidence we have is circumstantial,

but we have a lot of it. It's just a question of what
he'll be charged with."

"Did anyone else in the family receive money from
him?" Claire asked.

"There's no evidence of that."

"Who paid off Chuy's gambling debts?"

"Manuel. It was bad for his image to have a
brother way deep in debt. We couldn't get any prints
from the poncho or your purse, but we traced a call
from Beck's cell phone to the front desk at Tamaya
around the time the message was left that Warren
would be late. There's no evidence Warren ever
made that call himself. Beck will be arraigned on
Monday morning. I thought you might like to be
there."

"I would."

Romero stood up. "We've set up a meeting with
the family after the arraignment to talk about the
document and the mezuzah. The OMI says they
should have the results of the DNA comparison by
then. Can you come?"

"Yes," Claire said. She stood up, too.

"See you at the meeting," Romero said.

He knew the way so Claire didn't walk him out
to the exit. She stood in her doorway and watched
until he turned the corner.

Chapter Thirty-one

She arrived early for the arraignment, took a seat, and watched the courthouse fill up. Chuy, wearing clean jeans and a T-shirt, escorted his grandmother down the aisle. Tey's hand resembled the talons of a hawk as she gripped his arm. Manuel was smooth and handsome in a dark suit. He brought his blonde wife, who also wore an expensive suit. They sat apart from Tey and Chuy. Lieutenant Kearns and Detective Romero were present, too.

Peter Beck had only been in custody a short time, but Claire saw a pronounced change in his appearance. He wore a prison uniform. He was pale. His gray ponytail was limp and pencil thin. He had hired a prominent lawyer from Albuquerque.

The prosecutor, Joe Burgess, was a stocky, athletic-looking man who clapped his hands for emphasis. He seemed confident. And why wouldn't he be? Claire thought. Premeditation and first-degree murder would be difficult to prove, but he was only charging Peter Beck with grand larceny, assault and battery, and murder in the second degree.

When asked how he wished to plead, Peter replied "not guilty" to all the charges. Claire didn't hear confidence in his voice. She heard contempt for the charge, for the process, for the court that tried him. He didn't sound like he ever intended to plea-bargain, but she thought he might be better off if he did. The case against him seemed solid. She was sure he would do time, but not as much as he deserved.

Before he left the courtroom, Peter raised his head high, which made his nose seem even more promi-nent. He turned and scanned the crowd. It would be his last look at his accusers before the trial began. He acted like he wanted to fix them in his brain, take the image back to his cell, examine it, and probe for weaknesses. He skipped over Manuel, lingered on Tey and Chuy. Then his gray eyes landed on Claire. He took a deep breath and his nostrils widened. His lips turned into a sneer. She saw no remorse in his expression, only anger that he had been caught. She felt that if she were a student and this were a lecture hall, he would eviscerate her with words, humiliate her and cut her work to ribbons before the class. She hoped Peter Beck would never lecture again. She hoped he would stay in prison for the rest of his life and if there were any further victims of his anger, they would be fellow inmates.

When the arraignment was over, the family, the investigators, and Claire met in Joe Burgess's office. Lieutenant Kearns thanked Claire for her help. If he had any doubts about her involvement, he seemed to have pushed them far back in his mind.

Claire sat down beside Tey and took her hand. "I know you're glad this is all over."

"It won't be over until that dude is locked up for good," Chuy said.

"Almost over," Claire corrected herself.

"Thank you very much," Tey said, squeezing

Claire's hand, "for helping us find my Isabelita's killer. When I saw that man's eyes I knew he was the one. That man does not deserve to be a teacher."

"He deserves to be a prisoner," Chuy said.

Manuel Santos came alone to the meeting. He thanked Claire and shook her hand, but his eyes never met hers. She felt he wished she had had nothing to do with this. He would have preferred that Tony Atencio had been charged with the crime and he didn't have to deal with the weight of his family's past, that he would be known as Manuel Santos the Catholic, rather than Manuel Santos the crypto Jew whose sister was killed over an historic family document. It was a conflict known to split families in two.

When everyone else was seated, Lieutenant Kearns stood, opened the file he held, and said, "I have received the report on the skeleton from the Office of the Medical Investigator. I know you're all very interested to hear what it says. The Smithsonian and OMI couldn't establish for sure if he is Daniel Rodriguez or Manuel Santos, whatever name you want to use, but there is a DNA match to Tey. He is definitely your ancestor."

"*A la,*" Chuy said.

Manuel looked out the window and said nothing.

"By strontium testing of the tooth enamel the Smithsonian established that your ancestor spent his youth in Portugal in the late sixteenth century," Kearns said.

"Does that coincide with what you know about the Rodriguez family history?" Joe Burgess asked Claire.

"Yes. According to Peter Beck's book, Daniel Rodriguez spent his childhood in Portugal before the family emigrated to Mexico. Peter's scholarship in the book has never been questioned."

"I'd like to have a copy," Burgess said. "Can you get me one?"

"Yes."

"Would you be willing to testify as an expert at the trial?" Burgess asked.

"I'd be glad to help, but I'm not an expert, just an interested party. I can refer you to some experts." May Brennan came to mind.

"I'll get in touch with you later about it," Joe Burgess said. He clapped his hands and Kearns picked up the beat.

"The cross was also dated to the late sixteenth century," Kearns said. "I'm the first to admit that I don't know much about history, but it looks like the skeleton is Daniel Rodriguez and he brought his brother's last words to Bernalillo with him hidden inside the cross."

"It's obvious those are Joaquín Rodriguez's words, but it's impossible to establish they were his last words," Manuel, the lawyer, said, already beginning his defense of the family's Catholicism. "Joaquín's conversion to Catholicism could have been sincere, and Daniel could have converted to Catholicism, too."

It was possible, but Claire didn't believe it. Tey had too many connections to Judaism. She knew that Catholicism and Judaism were issues that would never be resolved in some families. As the centuries went by and the number of descendents increased, some became devout Catholics, some remained fervent Jews, and some were neither. When it came to religious beliefs, there was no proof.

"A mezuzah is a box with a Hebrew prayer inside, right?" Joe Burgess asked anyone willing to provide an answer.

"It's a prayer to keep the house safe," Tey said.

Lieutenant Kearns showed them the mezuzah tucked inside an evidence bag.

"This is the one we found in Peter Beck's safe deposit box. We need to keep it as evidence, but we should be able to give it back to you after the trial is over," Joe Burgess said.

Then Lieutenant Kearns displayed Joaquín's faded and elegant last words, also in an evidence bag. Claire caught her breath; the document was so significant, so old, so valuable. It was incredible it had endured for four hundred years and could still speak.

"Isabel showed this document to you, is that correct?" Joe Burgess asked Manuel.

"Yes," he admitted.

It was the first Claire had heard of this. She reviewed her conversation with Manuel at the duck pond, wishing she had recorded it on tape. As she recalled, he implied there had never been a document, but had he actually said so? She suspected if she replayed the conversation she'd find it was all innuendo, that Manuel was too careful a lawyer to lie to her.

"It's the document she showed me, but I knew nothing about Joaquín then. I asked her not to say anything until I could find out more, but May Brennan called Peter Beck and he went to the house. I thought when Tony Atencio robbed the house, the document got destroyed in the robbery."

Not telling anyone this earlier bordered on criminal activity in Claire's mind but she supposed that prosecuting Manuel Santos for concealing the truth wouldn't help the case against Peter Beck.

"We will need to keep this until the trial is over, too," Lieutenant Kearns said, displaying the cross, also in an evidence bag. It was the cross Isabel had protected when she fell. All together the cross, the mezuzah, and the document were potent symbols of the family's complicated past and present.

"As a family, you need to start thinking about what to do with these objects when you get them back," Burgess said. "My only suggestion is that you put them in a very safe place."

"We will do that," Tey said.

"We'll be talking to all of you again before we go to trial. Does anyone have any questions for now?" the prosecutor asked.

No one did.

"Okay then." He gave one final clap. "We're done here."

Detective Romero had sat in the back of the room and kept quiet during this meeting. Lieutenant Kearns hadn't taken all the credit for solving the crime, but he hadn't given any to Romero either. Claire caught up to him at the door and walked him down the hall.

"I hope you get credit for the work you did," she said. "Your open-mindedness and your availability made it possible to catch Peter Beck. If it weren't for you, Tony Atencio would still be in jail."

"Thanks," Romero said. "You did a pretty good job yourself."

They stood in the hallway, smiling and congratulating each other until Tey came along and tapped Claire on the arm. "Chuy and I are going to visit Isabelita's grave now," she said. "Can you come with us?"

"Yes," Claire said.

"We will meet you there."

Claire took her time as she walked out to her car

in the parking lot. One remaining question she had
was the kind of vehicle Manuel Santos drove. She
knew it wasn't the SUV that ran her off the road, but
she wanted to know if Chuy had been telling her the
truth when he told her it was gray. She was relieved
to see him step into a gray SUV and drive away. It
was one less lie to ponder.

When Claire got to the cemetery, Chuy was helping his grandmother step down from his truck. She
heard the traffic whiz by on the interstate and the
sign at the trailer lot flap in the breeze. They walked
to Isabel's grave at Tey's leisurely pace. It took disci-
pline to slow down and walk as slowly as Tey did,
but once Claire made the transition she felt the benefits. She no longer heard or saw the interstate. She
had time to focus on what was close up, time to
remember and look back at the past. Getting the cemetery to reveal its secrets was like turning the pages
of a book. She saw the red cloth flowers on Isabel's
grave. Claire knew now they hadn't been put there
by Tey. They stood in front of the tombstone for a
few minutes while Chuy remembered the past.

"Isabel, Manuel, and I saw that mezuzah in the
closet when we were little," he said. "We wondered
what it was, but it seemed like a secret of the house
so we put it back. We saw you lighting the candles
and blowing the smoke around, Grandma. We remembered you and our father and uncles chanting
in a language we didn't understand. Sometimes we
wondered if we were Marranos. That was before
Manuel became so Catholic."

"Did you tell your father this?" Tey asked.

"No. It was like it was your secret."

"I wish I had told Isabelita before she died. It's

something the women pass on." Tey touched the tombstone. "My precious, why didn't you come to me when you found that paper?"

"I'm sure Manuel told her not to," Chuy said. "He didn't want anybody else to know."

"That's the way the Catholics are," Tey said. "They only know one truth. It's too bad we have to bury our people here with them. I'm telling you this now, Chuy, because who knows if I will be alive when we get that paper back. I want you to give it to Claire. I want UNM to keep it. I don't care who knows about us now."

"Okay, Grandma," Chuy said.

"We'll take good care of it," Claire said. "I promise."

"I know you will. Now I want you to show me what you discovered at the other Isabel Santos grave."

They walked across the graveyard keeping to Tey's measured beat. They passed the graves of the soldiers who died in Vietnam, Korea, World War II, and World War I, the children who died too young, and the couples who were *juntos para siempre*. They passed the section where the nuns were buried and approached the place where the jackrabbit lived and the grave sites were marked by wooden crosses lying on the ground. At the edge of this section they found the grave of Isabel and Moises Suazo.

Claire pointed out the six-petaled flower. "It could be interpreted as the symbol of the Star of David," she said. "And the faint carving of a candelabra— that could be a menorah. I sketched the flower and the symbol in the middle and I faxed it to Harold Marcus at the Smithsonian. It could be a stamen in the flower but he interpreted it as a shin. That's the twenty-second letter of the Hebrew alphabet and the first letter of Shema, the prayer Jews say." Claire hoped she was getting the essence of what Harold told her if not the literal meaning. "It means 'Hear O Israel, the Lord is our God, the Lord is One.'"

"*Adonay es mi dio,*" Tey said. "He is with me when I walk along the way. I love him with all my heart." She'd been holding a pebble in her hand and she placed it on Isabel Santos de Suazo's tombstone.

The sound the stone made resonated. Claire thought of the millions of years it took to turn sand and water into stone, how ancient the Hebrew prayers were, how timeless Adonay.

They walked slowly back to Isabel's grave. Tey picked up another pebble and placed it on top of her tombstone.

"*Descanse en paz, mi nieta,*" she said.

Claire heard the flapping sound. It was only the breeze lifting and dropping the edge of a sign, but to her it had the echo of the beating wings of time.